EVA CHASE

GANG OF GHOULS

THE COMPLETE SERIES

Gang of Ghouls: The Complete Series

First Digital Edition, 2023

Cover design: JoY Author Design Studio

Ebook ISBN: 978-1-998752-38-6

Hardcover ISBN: 978-1-998752-39-3

The Stalking Dead

GANG OF GHOULS #1

Chapter One

Lily

NEAR-DEATH EXPERIENCES HAVE this funny way of putting everything else in perspective. I almost kicked the bucket in five feet of murky marsh water when I was six, and compared to that, nothing at Lovell Rise College could be all that horrifying. Even if this was my first full day back in town after seven years in a mental hospital.

Even if the question of what I'd done to be committed was still a huge, ominous blank in the back of my mind. Even if the only family I had in town had basically disowned me. Even if… there was a pair of frogs getting busy on the steps outside the main administrative building.

I stopped in my tracks before I stomped on the amphibious lovers, doing a bit of a double-take. I'd always come across frogs regularly in Lovell Rise, probably because the marshlands ran the whole length of town. But I couldn't say I'd ever seen two of them going at it quite so blatantly before. The male had melded himself to the female's back with no sign of ever intending to let go.

Welp, more power to them. *Get them tadpoles*, I thought at them instead of saying it out loud, like I might have if I wasn't starkly aware of the other students meandering around the courtyard and lawns around me. I gave the frogs a wide berth as I continued my way up the steps.

Now that I was back home, it was more important than ever that I looked, talked, and acted normal in every possible way. I'd only get one chance at a fresh start. Just one chance to prove who I really was—and that it wasn't a girl who should be sent back to a loony bin halfway across the state.

I paused at the end of the smaller courtyard at the top of the steps, taking a moment to gather myself. The tapping and thudding of dozens of feet around me condensed into a weird sort of melody in my head. I could almost put lyrics to it, a trudging back-to-class anthem. *Here we go, like it or not, to stuff our brains full of facts and—*

Shaking myself, I pushed the impulse aside. I wouldn't *actually* turn footsteps into a song. That would be the opposite of normal.

I checked the campus map and veered left toward one of the smaller white buildings that held the first class on my schedule: Juvenile Delinquency taught by Mr. Leon Grimes. My first real step toward a degree in sociology. I'd already done a year's groundwork of general education classes at the community college near the hospital before the doctors had decided I was sane enough to completely fly the coop.

Here was hoping it turned out that I'd gotten enough distance from my own mess to help clean up other people's messiness.

The cool September breeze licked over my face and flicked my wavy, flax-blond hair. I restrained a shiver, wishing I'd brought a jacket or a cardigan to wear over my thin blouse. Laughter rippled across the courtyard, but I ignored it other than as a minor accompaniment to the rhythm of marching feet, until it was followed by a brash voice.

"Hey, it's psycho girl!"

I should have kept walking. But the words were so jarring and unexpected—and so almost definitely aimed at *me*—that my legs locked up and my head jerked around to see who'd said it.

The guy sauntering toward me with a gaggle of friends in tow was unfortunately familiar. The local elementary and middle schools were small enough that there'd only been one class per grade, and so I'd been stuck in the same room as Ansel Hunter from age four through thirteen.

Seven years later, his shoulders had filled out and the angles of his face had taken on harder edges, but he had the same smooth golden hair, unshakeable ego, and supposedly charming grin that'd had most of the girls swooning over him the instant they hit puberty. Five seconds into our re-introduction, I could already tell his ego had only gotten bigger since I'd known him as a middle-schooler.

I'd realized that a number of the kids from town opted to go to Lovell Rise College if they met the entrance requirements so that they could stay on their home turf. It was a small campus, only eight hundred undergrads according to the new student orientation guide, but with several well-ranked programs and high admission standards. I'd busted my ass making the grades to transfer for my second year.

Somehow I hadn't pictured running into anyone who'd recognize me. It wasn't as if I'd been Miss Popular as a kid or, you know, had any friends at all. Real ones, anyway. I'd let myself assume no one would have even noticed I was missing, let alone figured out what had happened to me.

I guessed I hadn't given small-town gossip enough credit.

I didn't recognize any of the guys and girls who made up Ansel's current pack. He'd probably ditched his old hangers-on for shiny new models when he'd had a wider range to pick from. Otherwise he wouldn't have felt the need to "introduce" me to all of them.

"She went batshit right before high school and had to be shipped off to the insane asylum," he said to his entourage with a toss of his hand toward me, still grinning away, and turned his gaze with its malicious gleam on me. "What was your name again? Tulip? Daffodil?"

The girls in the pack tittered. I focused my gaze slightly above Ansel's eyes, where I pictured a tiny crocodile perched on his sun-bleached hair. One of my fellow patients in the psychiatric ward had insisted that everyone she met had an animal of some kind riding around on their heads. She'd told me I had a frog, which figured. She'd also used to talk to those invisible animals—more than to their hosts, most of the time.

I didn't actually see any animals like that—and I sure as hell wasn't crazy enough to talk to them—but I'd found that pretending I did made stressful situations somehow easier to get through. It was hard to get very worked up about the opinions of a guy who didn't even know he had a crocodile camped out on his cranium.

The imagined crocodile started gnawing on Ansel's pretty hair. I smiled evenly back at my former classmate, molding myself into the perfect picture of a totally sane and stable human being. "It's Lily, actually. Well, I'd better get to class."

I turned away, but Ansel shifted into my path, the gleam in his eyes getting fiercer. I started to wish the crocodile was real so it could chomp his nose right off.

"Oh, come on," he said. "How'd you get the head shrinkers to let you go after all this time? I think we've got a right to know how worried we should be. How can we be sure you're not going to show up one day and mow us all down in a hail of bullets?"

Well, for starters, I've never held a gun in my life, so I wouldn't even know how to get the safety off, answered the snarky voice in the back of my head, which I kept tightly under wraps. I'd realized a long time before I even ended up in the loony bin that people didn't like it when I let that voice out. I'd missed out on a lot of recesses before I'd learned that lesson.

"They decided I'm cured," I said evenly. "No threat to anyone. Nothing exciting here." *Except that crocodile that's chowing down on your artful fringe now.*

Ansel snorted. "Or maybe you've got them all fooled. Isn't that what psychopaths *do*?"

The girl standing closest to him, willowy with thick chestnut hair, an arched nose, and a cup of coffee clutched in one hand, gave him an awestruck look and then narrowed her eyes at me. "Yeah, I don't really think they should let psychos just enroll in classes here."

Hey, serial killers have a right to an education too, said the snark. A little of its edge crept into my voice, despite my best efforts. "Lucky for you, I've never been diagnosed as a psychopath. Just a regular girl who had an unfortunate episode a long time ago. Now if you'll excuse me—"

I tried to dodge around the crowd, and at the same moment, Ansel's arm shot out. He might have been trying to grab my elbow—or he might have purposefully knocked his hand into the wrist of that willowy girl next to him, sending her cup flying. Streams of coffee soared through the air and splattered all over the front of my blouse.

I yelped and jumped back a step, but it was too late. Hot liquid plastered the thin, baby-blue fabric to my chest with a brown splotch that was clearly going to stain. I swallowed a string of curses and held on to my cool as tightly as I could.

"My coffee," the girl muttered, her face falling, as if the biggest problem here was the loss of her beverage.

Ansel chuckled. "Let's see if the crazy comes out now."

As I tugged my shirt away from the outline of my bra, I imagined his mini-croc gnawing on his ear. "I'd better get this washed off," I said, stiffly now, and hustled away with determined strides.

This time, his fun apparently finished for the moment, Ansel let me go. More laughter followed me.

And that, according to some expert, was "normal." Standing around mocking a former classmate about something he didn't know anything about.

Of course, the fact that he didn't know might have made the comments harder to take. Because the truth was, *I* didn't know anything about it either. I had no idea what the "episode" that'd sent me to the hospital was. It'd short-circuited my brain, wiping all memory of what'd happened between walking up to my house one day and waking up in the ward the next.

Whatever had happened, it hadn't been *good*—that much was obvious. I was pretty sure doctors didn't keep you under supervision for seven years and refuse to talk to you about the specifics of your case unless you'd done something very bad.

Bad enough that my mom hadn't reached out once in all those years. Bad enough that my little sister…

I shoved those thoughts aside and sped up to a jog. Inside the building I'd been headed toward, I found a restroom halfway down the hall to my class. I ducked inside and splashed water on my blouse until I'd rinsed out the stain enough to take it from dark brown to medium tan. I still had a light blue shirt with a big brown stain all over the front, only now it was even more wet. Wonderful.

I held the fabric out under the blow dryer for as long as I could while keeping an eye on the time. When I had exactly one minute left before class started, I gave the shirt one last blast, grimaced at it, and hurried to the door.

Unfortunately, a gaggle of other girls burst in right then, so I had to dodge around them getting back to the hall. By the time I made it all the way to the lecture room at the far end, the clock inside was just ticking over to one minute past the hour.

I wouldn't have thought one minute would be that big a deal. The lecturers at the community college usually took at least five minutes just to rev up to anything resembling teaching. But the man by the projector screen at the front of the room—looking young-ish for a professor, maybe in his early 30s—was already in mid-sentence, tapping a pointer stick against the class syllabus displayed on the screen.

At my entrance, his body snapped toward the door, his eyes narrowing over high, sharp cheekbones. He shook his head disapprovingly, forcefully enough that a few tufts of his close-cropped brown hair stirred along his forehead. I darted toward the nearest seat at the end of the first tiered row, but he wasn't content to leave it at that.

"Who would you be, Miss…?"

I stopped a few feet from the desks and looked back at him. "Strom. Lily Strom."

His gaze flicked to a folder on his lectern and then back to me. Somehow his eyes managed to narrow even more. It was a wonder I could even make out the irises still. "Miss Strom. I did note your name in my enrollment list. Thank you for making it so easy to identify you."

Mr. Grimes turned to the rest of the students, some two dozen of them. "Class, it seems we have an exemplar of the subject of our course right here among us, and not just the delinquency of tardiness. In her juvenile years, this young lady was involved in an incident that required her to be removed from her home by the police followed by several years of rehabilitation."

Was he seriously going to make a production out of my past in front of all my peers? Well, yes—the answer was obviously yes.

My cheeks flamed, and my body burned with the conflicting urges to flee for the door and throw the textbook I'd already started getting out of my bag at his head.

But either of those behaviors would pretty much prove his point. I forced myself to breathe steadily, picturing a parakeet hopping around on the dickwad's head and pecking at those neatly combed strands. "I'm sorry I was late. It won't happen again. I just—"

"And perhaps next time you can manage to show up in more study-appropriate attire as well," Mr. Grimes interrupted in an icy tone, lifting his chin toward my wet blouse.

I crossed my arms in front of my chest instinctively, hugging the textbook to me. Did he think I'd *wanted* to get splattered in coffee? But from his sneer, he'd already made up his mind about me.

Think about what you're doing this for, Lily. Who *you're doing this for. This asshat doesn't matter. If you do the work, he'll have to give you the grades you deserve. You'll prove him wrong too.*

The little pep talk gave me the resolve to walk the rest of the way to my seat without a word. I got out my notebook and spent the rest of the class dutifully jotting down everything Mr. Grimes mentioned, no matter how unimportant-sounding. If I was going to be an exemp-anything, it was an exemplary student.

That didn't stop the professor from singling me out a few more times with pointed asides like, "Have you made note of that, Miss Strom?" I tuned out those remarks and kept my grip loose on my pen. And visualized the parakeet making explosive diarrhea all down the back of Mr. Grimes's head.

When class finished, I gathered up my things as quickly as I could and hustled to the door. Whispers followed me. "That girl..." "I heard about..."

There weren't *that* many locals here, but anyone in the room who hadn't already known the basics of my history did now. Mr. Grimes must have already been teaching at the college and living in Lovell Rise way back then, so he'd heard about it when it happened. Shit.

How many other professors were going to look at me the same way? With both a professor and Mr. Popular harassing me, how long would it take before the murmurs spread across the whole campus?

I couldn't think about that. I literally couldn't think about anything other than getting off the campus so I could breathe. Someone had turned the air into soup, which really wasn't very considerate of them, because you could drown in that stuff.

I strode right out to the far end of the parking lot where I'd had to park my junker of a car, the cheapest thing that still drove that I'd been able to track down. As soon as I reached it, I dropped into the driver's seat, jammed the key into the ignition, and gunned it out of there.

The engine coughed several times as if it wanted to remind me how lucky I was that it was still running. "Keep it together, Fred," I told it. "If I can get through this catastrophe of a day, so can you."

My grandfather had always named his cars, but he'd given them women's names, with a gag-worthy comment about women's duty to carry the load. I'd vowed to always name mine as men, because if I was going to ride anything, it'd be a dude.

And yeah, I talked to inanimate objects. It's the sort of habit you'd get into too if your main friends during your formative years were imaginary. At least the car actually existed.

Fred hung in there as I drove around town and took a turn toward the marshlands. Toward the place that'd been my home for the first thirteen years of my life. My hands tightened on the wheel, but I took the far lane that wouldn't bring me in view of Mom and Wade's house.

Even without seeing the building, my last conversation with Mom —through the screen door, with her hand braced against the frame as if she thought I'd try to ram it down—rose up in my head.

I just want to say "Happy birthday!" It's her sweet sixteen. She's my sister. Please.

How are we supposed to be sure that you're really well now? They kept you in treatment for so long. I don't think it's worth the risk, Lily.

They'd see. I'd show them. I hadn't hurt anyone, hadn't done anything wrong…

Except whatever I'd done seven years ago that'd sent me to St. Elspeth's Psychiatric Center in the first place.

When I reached the end of the lane near the marsh, I got out and told Fred, "Thank you," because it never hurt to be polite, even to a car. Then I walked down to where the ground got squishy under my feet.

The cattails rattled against each other in the damp breeze. This end of the lake was choked with vegetation for almost a mile out before you got to the open water, which was exactly how a six-year-old girl could end up wandering out into the middle of the marsh from clump to clump before suddenly setting a foot wrong and going under. I shied away from the distant memory of the cold, dark wetness closing over me.

I didn't know what I was looking for out here. I'd spent so much time by the marsh over the years when I'd hardly felt welcome in my own house with Wade lurking around scowling at me and Marisol. I'd played down here by myself and with my sister when she was old enough that I wasn't scared of her tumbling in. I'd make up songs for her to go with the warbling of the wind in the reeds.

A dull ache came into my throat. There wasn't anyone to sing for now.

The rasp of the jostling leaves formed a sound almost like someone else's voice. For a second, staring out at them, I could have sworn I heard my name. Something almost like a plea to listen.

But that—that was *really* crazy.

No wonder I'd been able to imagine up four invisible protectors out of the marsh, though. All it took was a little moving air to make the place sound haunted.

For a long time, I'd believed I wasn't really by myself even when I came down here alone. I'd imagined I heard voices in the breeze and that I could see the barest outlines of figures standing around me. That I'd felt the faint impression of their hands when we'd played tag or they'd caught me at hide and seek—that when I'd sung for *them*, they'd swayed along and applauded. In my head, they'd given me their own private nicknames like "Waterlily" and "Minnow," "Lil" and plain old "kid." When Wade would drive up, they'd make rude gestures in his direction, because obviously my imagination was more comfortable expressing how I felt about him than I was out loud.

Every time I'd come down here, I'd known I'd find them waiting. Watching over me. That certainty had made everything else bearable.

But they weren't really here. Of course they weren't.

An itch tickled my inner arm just below the pit. I scratched the spot without looking, not needing to look to know it was where I'd discovered the nickel-sized blotch of a new birthmark days after I'd come back to my senses in the hospital. As if whatever had happened that day, it'd marked me inside and out.

Some things would always be true. Marisol needed me, and I wasn't going to let her down. I'd make things right for her and with her however I could.

That meant I had to get through whatever life threw at me from here forward—no matter how many assholes came with it.

The sense of my name being called swept over me with the wind again, distant and wavering: *Lily!* I shook off the impression and the pang that followed it, and turned to face the cold reality I actually had to work with.

Chapter Two

Nox

I'd say I shouted Lily's name until my throat was hoarse, but I didn't really have a throat. Or a neck or a mouth, come to think of it.

Just one of the many ways that being dead was deeply fucked up.

"Lily!" I hollered again, standing right next to her, as much as I could stand when I also didn't currently have legs or feet or—you get the picture.

Her gaze twitched a little, those pale blue-green eyes like the sky reflecting off the marsh water turning pensive, but I could tell she still hadn't really heard anything. Not enough to realize that someone was actually speaking to her, let alone who.

It was still hard to wrap my head around the fact that she was right here in front of me. Even after all this time, I'd recognized her instantly. I wasn't sure how exactly long it had been since she'd vanished from our afterlives, but even though she'd grown from a gawky barely-teenager to a fully-fledged woman, so much of her had stayed the same.

Those eyes. The hair that gleamed like goddamned sunbeams as it spilled over her slim shoulders. The rosy lips that were set at an angle that looked both determined and sad.

I hadn't seen her smile since she'd turned up back at the house a few days ago, but it wasn't hard to figure out why with the way her dishtowel of a mother had sent her off—and then those pricks at school had started tearing into her. That was a fucking travesty right there. How could the idiots at that stupid college not see this was a girl—a *woman*—who needed to be held up and cherished, not ground into the dirt?

We'd see who got ground into what next… if I only had some real way of accomplishing that.

I swiped the vague impression of where I should have had a hand over Lily's hair, and the wavy strands fluttered, but little enough that she could dismiss the motion as the breeze. With the same stoutly defiant poise she'd sported since she was a little kid, she turned and walked back to the clunker she'd been driving.

At least no one had managed to beat the spirit out of her yet.

I spun around. I couldn't exactly *see* my friends, what with them being also dead and bodiless, but they gave off their own vague impressions, concrete enough to me that I had a sense of where the three of them hovered around me and even what gestures they were making. Or maybe the second part was only because I'd spent so much time around them when we'd been alive.

"What the hell is wrong?" I demanded to the landscape at large. "Why can't she hear us anymore?"

Kai was probably pushing glasses that no longer existed up his nose that also no longer existed. "She's grown up. Her mind has matured—it must have become too closed off to accept the possibility of people she can't really see."

Ruin hummed to himself in his typically carefree way, ever the optimist. "She could always hear us before. She's got to get used to it again, right? We haven't had much time to get through to her."

"She was pretty young when we first started talking to her," Kai said. "And she kept getting practice on a regular basis. It's been… a long time since she probably thought we were real. I don't know if we'd be able to establish that kind of connection again."

Ruin chuckled. "She's Lily. Of course all we need to do is make the connection."

The guy had the habit of not hearing so well—he tended to take whatever you said and spin it in the most upbeat way possible. Sometimes it was kind of cute. Frequently it was fucking annoying. It was a good thing I liked plenty of other things about him.

Jett, who'd stayed silent so far like he often did, let out an inarticulate grumble before saying, "What now? Those fuckers… We've got to do *something*."

None of us needed to ask which fuckers he meant. The same ones that had rage searing all through my irritatingly ephemeral presence. From the moment Lily had made her first appearance in Lovell Rise since we'd last seen her however many years ago, we'd kept a close eye on her, following her to the apartment she'd rented and the school where a bunch of dorks with high degrees thought they could teach her something useful.

I'd stopped going to classes partway through eleventh grade, and I'd turned out just fine.

Okay, I'd turned out dead, but that'd been almost ten years later, and getting gunned down hadn't had anything to do with my lack of algebra skills.

It wasn't the *dorks* at the college I had a real problem with, obviously. It was the asshole bullies who thought they could tear a strip out of our Lily. As if her prick of a stepdad and pathetic mom hadn't been bad enough. As if she deserved anyone harassing her after… after whatever she'd been through while she'd been gone.

I had no idea what that even was.

Kai spoke up again, picking up on my train of thought without me saying anything at all, which was *his* special unnerving habit. "The professor mentioned the police. The dick who splashed her with coffee talked about an 'insane asylum.' Whatever took her away from here, it must have been awful. And they *enjoyed* belittling her over it." His voice got sharper rather than louder when he was pissed off, and right now it could have cut through a Range Rover.

"We'll take care of them," Ruin announced. "A stab here, a bullet there." He was probably gleefully cracking his knuckles at the thought.

"How the hell are we supposed to do that when we're all fucked up like this?" Jett burst out, with what was possibly the longest sentence he'd uttered in at least two decades.

My non-existent teeth gritted with my own frustration. Every particle of my soul was screaming with the need to charge across campus and rip through all the jerks who'd so much as looked sideways at Lily... but I couldn't do more than mimic a bit of breeze. A growl escaped me.

We'd never really been able to protect her from her shitty so-called parents either, only given her an escape and a sense that she had someone on her side. Which was something, but clearly not fucking enough, given how much shit had gone down next.

Those long stretches of numbing ghostly nothingness brought what really mattered into sharp relief. Lily shone like a star, and everyone else in this podunk town was sewage.

I had the blurry impression that maybe life had seemed slightly more complicated before, but I didn't have a life anymore, so what the hell did that matter?

"If I could raise my fucking skeleton out of the marsh for even five minutes, I'd gut them all with a rusty butcher knife," I muttered.

"Choke them with their own eyeballs," Jett added.

Ruin's grin shone through in his voice. "Cut off their feet and shove them up their asses."

Kai was unusually quiet for a moment. Usually it was hard to shut the guy up, he had so many ideas and observations just spilling out of his brain. I whirled toward him. "Don't you think we've got to take the bastards down?"

"Of course," he said, and I could picture the glitter of inspiration sparking into being behind the panes of his glasses. "There was something I was looking into, before Lily vanished. I'd almost forgotten. I shouldn't have."

I wasn't going to get on his case about that. I wasn't sure what'd happened to any of us during the years of her absence. The day she'd crashed into the marsh, she'd stirred our water-logged spirits back to some kind of life. Being with her had kept us going for years after that. But without her presence, we must have drifted back off into a muddled, monotonous limbo. That state wasn't really a great environment for brilliant brainstorms.

"Well, what is it?" I prodded Kai.

"I'm not sure about this yet. I still need to do some experiments to make sure it'll all come together. But the theory is sound."

"The theory for *what*?" Jett said impatiently.

Kai's intellectual delight came through in his voice. "We might be able to get bodies again. Permanently."

I felt the attention of all three of my men shift to me. They *were* my men—I'd been the leader of the Skullbreakers, and they'd been my closest colleagues as we built the gang together. We were in all of this together, in life and death… but ultimately, I called the shots.

This one wasn't remotely hard to call, though.

My theoretical eyebrows had shot up as if propelled by the rush of exhilaration that'd surged through me at the thought. "Seriously? Hell, yes. Experiment your fucking heart out and let's get this done."

Ruin let out a little whoop. His soul was probably doing a shimmy of a happy-dance that I was glad I didn't have to see.

Kai must have been rubbing his non-existent hands together like the maniac genius he often was. "No problem. I'm looking forward to it. Just to be clear, we can't create forms out of nothing or grow flesh back on our old bones. For the final plan, we're going to need to commit a few murders so we have bodies to take over."

A grin stretched across the face I no longer had, and a dark laugh spilled out of me. "Perfect. I know at least a couple of people who'll totally deserve it."

Chapter Three

Lily

As far as I knew, Lovell Rise College didn't have much of a sports program, but its one claim to fame in that area was its football team. According to the student handbook, anyway. I hadn't given athletics much thought until I was skirting the main practice field during what looked like a casual scrimmage, and the ball came spiraling through the air to thump on the ground outside the foul line just a few feet ahead of me.

A bunch of the jocks came barreling over, hassling the guy who'd apparently made the "lame" throw. When they caught sight of me, they drew up short.

My skin prickled with trepidation. After a few more days on campus, I could recognize in a matter of seconds what was about to go down.

Word about my psycho status had spread faster than the speed of light. Scientists should come study the bending of natural laws. I was seriously considering cutting my hair off and dyeing what remained black so I looked like a different person, but that'd probably help me for all of a millisecond before the asswipes caught on. And then I'd just be a pariah with really bad hair.

"Oooh," one of the guys said in a ghostly tone. "It's the loony girl. Are you going to put a curse on the ball for almost hitting you?"

It took a massive feat of strength not to roll my eyes. "I think you're confusing 'psychopath' with 'psychic,'" I said evenly, and kept walking by.

"She's going to come with a butcher knife and kill us all in our sleep," one of the other guys said.

"Better start double-checking the locks."

"I wonder what it'd take for her to drop the normal act and let the freak flag fly?"

"Let's find out," yet another of the guys said, far enough away now that I didn't even glance backward. Then a hurtling force slammed into the middle of my back.

I stumbled forward as the football that'd smacked me bounced on the ground. "Nice one, Zach!" someone crowed.

Spinning around, I saw the bunch of guys snickering with each other while also watching me with avid curiosity, probably hoping I'd snap. As my pulse thumped hard, I narrowed my attention to the guy in the middle of the bunch who was grinning most broadly while others slapped him on the back.

He must have been the one who'd thrown the football. Like a typical football player, he was beefy, though not especially tall, with his light brown hair slicked back and grazing the tops of his ears. A tattoo so amateurish I couldn't tell whether it was a skull or a soap dish marked one of his bulging biceps.

Oh, what a tough guy, Zach—hurling projectiles at unarmed women, my inner voice said. *Tom Brady would be so proud of you.* I willed myself calm while picturing a rhino prancing around on the jerkwad's head, kicking up those gelled strands.

"I think you misplaced this," I said, and gave the football a light punt toward them. Then I hurried away from the field even faster, tuning out the chuckles that followed me. For a second—just a second—I wished I really was a murderous psychopath who wouldn't hesitate to carve them up. We'd see how long they kept laughing then.

But so far, no matter what I *had* done, as far as I knew I hadn't murdered anyone, and getting a lethal rap sheet was not going to help my case in convincing Mom to let me see Marisol. Lucky for those dickheads.

I just wanted to get away from campus with the whispers and the speculative glances, but the student affairs office had called me in for an appointment they hadn't really explained. I strode into the admin building and managed to reach the office on time despite getting lost in the maze of hallways twice on the way there. I was starting to think they'd set the building up that way specifically to challenge students' commitment to their schooling.

I came into the office to find a woman built like an ostrich—big hips, tiny shoulders, long neck, big eyes—talking to a tall, skinny guy with dirty blond hair that was carefully tucked behind his prominent ears.

"Of course, Ms. Baxter," he was saying in an emphatically eager voice. "Whatever I can do to help the school run smoothly. It's my pleasure to help."

"Well, here she is now," Ms. Baxter said with a harried-looking smile. She waved me over. "Miss Strom, I'm so sorry I didn't manage to get this support set up until a few days into your time here. So many new students each year." Her head bobbed a bit from side to side, adding to the ostrich impression. "This is Vincent Barnes. He'll be your peer advisor during the next month, ready to assist you with anything you need when it comes to transitioning into life at Lovell Rise College. He's one of our top performing students, so I'm sure he'll be a great help. Any questions you have, you can reach out to him."

Well, that was a lot better than the interrogation or expulsion I'd been half expecting after the rest of the reception I'd gotten here. I glanced at Vincent as he turned around.

He was smiling brightly when his focus shifted from the staff person to me. The second his gaze landed on my face, his own face started to fall. He caught it with a flick of his eyes toward Ms. Baxter as if worried she might have noticed, but it'd gotten noticeably stiffer.

Okay, maybe this wasn't much better after all.

Ms. Baxter didn't appear to have picked up on his reaction. Her hands fluttered in the air, all flightless bird. "We've found the peer advisor program is very helpful for both the new students and the established peers who get to take on a leadership role. It's one of the things that make Lovell Rise College so special and welcoming."

I almost choked on my spit. As words to describe this place went, I'd put "welcoming" down at the bottom of the list. And that included the guy currently attempting to incinerate me with his eyes.

"I try to pitch in around the college every way I can," Vincent said, with a more brittle-sounding enthusiasm than he'd shown before. "Why don't we get started?"

"Perfect!" Still oblivious, Ms. Baxter clapped her hands together and shooed us off.

I curled my fingers around the strap of my shoulder bag as I walked with Vincent into the narrow hallway. One of the florescent lights was sputtering with a tinny noise, like it had a mouse inside it drumming on the glass.

Vincent marched around a bend in the hall that took us out of hearing of the student affairs office and then stopped with his posture drawn up rigidly straight. He shoved a slip of paper at me.

"That's my email and the number where you can text me," he spat out. "If you have any *legitimate* concerns, it's my duty to answer them. You can forget about trying to copy my work or getting you out of whatever trouble you get yourself into. You won't be leaching off my GPA."

I stared at him. "Um, this wasn't my idea. I didn't ask for a peer advisor. And I can do my own work just fine, thanks." Clearly *he* hadn't volunteered for the peer advisor role out of any desire to be welcoming, only for extra credit or to look good for his favorite professors.

He let out a huff as if he didn't believe that I could possibly have had any plans other than to take advantage of him. "I know who you are. *Everyone* knows who you are. I don't know why they'd have let you enroll in the first place—" He cut himself off with a brisk shake of his head. "Let's leave it at this: You'd better not screw anything up for me. I've worked too hard to earn the grades and the respect that comes with them around here."

My teeth set on edge. Which might have been a good thing, because in the few seconds it took me to unclamp them, I had time to swallow the several heated responses I'd have liked to make.

Who the hell did this twerp think he was? I'd never even seen him before, let alone spoken to him, and he was already treating me like some kind of demonic force. With all his supposed smarts, you'd think he'd have picked up on the fact that no one could actually say what I'd done—and that whatever it'd been, it'd happened years ago.

"You don't need to worry," I said tightly, crumpling the slip of paper in my hand. "I won't be bothering you at all." *Let's just hope that whatever prime job you're hoping to score right out of college, it doesn't require treating the people around you like human beings, since you'd obviously flunk any course on that subject.*

Vincent apparently needed to work on his hearing too. He continued as if I hadn't spoken. "Don't come up to me on campus either. You need anything, we hash it out digitally. I don't need people associating me with you."

He stalked off with an offended air as if I'd orchestrated this situation specifically to piss him off. My fingers curled into my palms, acting out the intense desire to strangle the douche-canoe.

Well, he was gone now, and his contact info was going in the garbage. I had exactly zero interest in finding out what kind of "assistance" Vincent Barnes could offer.

Thankfully, his departure meant I was free to get the hell away from this school for the day. I wove through the halls and made it to the front door after only getting lost once this time. From there it was only a short trot across the lawn and the parking lot to the desolate spot at the far end that I'd picked to avoid notice.

It appeared my strategy hadn't worked out so well. As I came up on my junkpile of a car, my stomach clenched.

It looked even more junky than usual—because one of the back tires had sagged totally flat.

Swearing under my breath, I sped up to a jog. As soon as I knelt by the tire, it was obvious the flat was no accident. Someone had jabbed a hole into the rubber.

I stood up again and glanced around as if the offender might have stuck around to watch my reaction to his—or her—work. The lot around me was empty other than a few students just ambling over to cars closer to the buildings. No sign of the pissbrain responsible.

A surge of hopelessness washed over me. I'd been here almost a week, I hadn't lifted a finger against anyone, and still people were taking their emotional issues out on me. I had to get to my job—this was going to make me late for my shift. If I lost the job, I'd lose my apartment…

I dragged in one breath and another, shoving those despairing thoughts away. I was stronger than this. I was stronger than *them*.

They'd made one very major miscalculation: they'd only stabbed *one* tire.

Gathering my resolve, I opened up the trunk and tugged out my kit of car tools and the spare I'd made sure to have on hand specifically because I hadn't been sure how much life any of Fred's tires still had in them.

Thank God for the life skills course that'd been offered as part of St. Elspeth's rehabilitation program. Shove the jack in here, crank the lever. The faint, rhythmic squeaking formed a defiant melody in my head.

"I'm sorry you took the beating for my crimes," I informed the old tire in a whisper of a voice. "I promise to get justice for you if I can manage it without looking even more psycho than everyone already thinks I am."

Which meant I should probably stop talking to random hunks of rubber too.

I loosened the nuts, unable to stop myself from thinking about a whole lot of *other* kinds of nuts I wouldn't have minded detaching from the slimeballs around this school. Then I pumped the crank some more. I hoped the asshat who'd done this *was* watching so they could see that they hadn't fucked me over half as much as they'd intended to.

I might be a psycho, but I was a psycho who knew her way around a tire.

"There we go," I couldn't help murmuring to the new tire as I slid it into place and finished attaching it. "Good hunk of rubber. Make Fred proud."

The tire didn't say anything back, but I liked to think the ridges formed a bit of a smile.

I tossed the punctured tire in the trunk just in case I needed it as evidence… of the fact that this was a school full of massive scumbuckets? There wasn't anywhere to throw it out anyway. Then I wiped the grease off my hands as well as I could with a tissue and checked the time. If the car held in there for me otherwise, I might be able to hoof it to the grocery store *just* in time to start shoving cans onto shelves by the assigned schedule.

"All right, Fred," I muttered as I dropped into the driver's seat. "Let's do this thing."

I grabbed the door to yank it shut, and my gaze veered across the dashboard at the same moment. My fingers froze around the handle.

I'd grabbed fast food from a drive-through for a hasty lunch before my afternoon classes. The salt packets I'd carelessly tossed up on the dash had ruptured, spilling little white grains all over the dark plastic. But that wasn't what made me pause.

The grains had spilled in a very precise pattern. Into wavery lines that I'd swear spelled out *words*. It looked like they said… *We re coming.*

We're coming?

The next second, a gust of wind blew past the open door, and all the salt scattered. Now it was just tiny white polka dots all over the dash, the passenger seat, and the floor, spelling out nothing at all.

I slammed the door closed and sat there with my pulse thudding hard enough to drown out the chatter of a couple sauntering by arm-in-arm outside. My mouth had gone dry.

I'd just imagined that, right? With the way I kept getting harassed, maybe it wasn't surprising that I'd see ominous messages in random condiments.

I definitely wasn't hallucinating or anything. Because then I really would be crazy.

Nausea wrapped around my gut. I stared at the dash for a minute longer, trying to make sense of what I'd seen. Then I shook my head and turned the key to spark the ignition.

Crazy or not, I still had a job to do. Those grocery store shelves weren't going to stock themselves.

Chapter Four

Kai

THE ROOM *HAD* to be perfect. We were only going to get one shot at this.

And I'd told the guys my strategy would work—I didn't plan on getting heckled by them for the rest of our eternal afterlives for getting their hopes up.

"Yes," I said before Ruin even needed to ask the question from where he'd glanced my way. He'd just finished nudging the jug of bleach Nox had painstakingly opened to the edge of the shelf. "Get it all the way to where you can feel it *just* about to tip. We need to have it ready to spill the second they're all inside."

"Fucking tiring," Jett muttered, as if he'd been doing anything other than lurking in a corner of the janitor's storage room and being his usual brooding self for the past half an hour. I guessed I'd give him a little credit for managing to spread the chemicals we'd dragged together in a narrow puddle along the concrete floor just below the shelf with the bleach.

I could only pick up scents vaguely in my current state, but I felt pretty confident in saying that this place smelled… unusual. I waved into being some semblance of an air current to try to keep the odor to the far side of the room.

"Not going to do us much good if they turn around the second they get a whiff of this place," Nox pointed out. I sensed his grin. "We'll have to give them a good shove."

"If we have the energy left," Jett grumbled.

"We're going to have *so* much energy and everything else," Ruin pipped up in typical chipper fashion. "We're going to have *bodies* again! All the pricks in this town had better watch out." He whirled around us so fast I had the impression of my hair rippling.

"We'll need to take things slow at first," I reminded him. "We don't know what effect the possession is going to have on our connection to the bodies. It might take a while for us to be fully coordinated." A grin of my own sprang to my ghostly lips. "But it's only a matter of time until we make all those assholes regret every jab they made at our girl."

"It shouldn't have taken us this long," Jett muttered.

"She'll know we're coming," Nox said. "We left that message in her car."

Ruin spun again. "Right. Help is on the way! And we deal with four of the worst assholes at the same time." He cackled to himself. "She's going to be so happy when she realizes we're back with her."

Yes. As much as I reveled in the thought of taking a whole lot of jerks around this place down several pegs, I enjoyed my vision of how Lily's face would light up even more. I'd never been the most popular guy around, alive or dead. People tended to be put off by the fact that, frankly, I knew a hell of a lot more than the vast majority of them did. They could have benefitted from my smarts, but instead they'd rather sneer at or shun me.

Well, their loss. Sometimes quite literally, considering all the objects and body parts I'd removed from their owners in my time.

But Lily… even when she'd only been a little kid without much sense of social graces, she'd never shied away from me. She'd laughed with delight when I could predict what she was thinking, ask me all kinds of questions to ferret out the knowledge I'd accumulated about one thing or another, as well as I could convey those facts through our ghostly channels of communication. Even my closest associates around me now had never been *that* enthusiastic.

I mentally rubbed my hands together in anticipation and took a final circuit of the room. Everything was in place. Nox had practiced turning the deadbolt in the door several times to make sure he could do it quickly. Our toxic cocktail was ready to tango. And I'd chosen the brief messages we'd imposed into ink on notepaper insightfully tailored to our targets' horrible personalities.

Nox turned with a hint of a huff he probably didn't even realize betrayed his impatience. He was going to ask me how much longer we had to wait, so I answered him before he had to speak the words.

"Ten more minutes. I wanted to leave us plenty of time in case we had trouble with the set-up."

He shook his head. "It's still creepy the way you do that."

"Don't be so easy to read and I won't be able to read you," I retorted lightly, and a sudden thought struck me like a bolt of lightning. How could I have left that one variable unconsidered? Death had clearly muddled my mind.

"We need to be clear on who's taking which body," I said quickly. "We want to dive in fast, and we can't have two of us colliding in the same one." That'd be a recipe for disaster… or else multiple personality disorder, but I wasn't keen on testing out the possibilities.

Even as I said the words, the gears in my head were already spinning through what I knew about my friends and our soon-to-be puppets. I could make a solid guess about who'd want who, but they did *occasionally* surprise me.

Nox spoke up first, which was fair since he was the man in charge. "The teacher's mine. Let's see how the idiots around here like it when they've got a real authority figure." He chuckled.

"I'll take the one with all the friends who follow him around listening to what he says," Ruin announced. "Lots of people to 'play' with. And I've got tons of better things to tell them about Lily."

"I can go with the grades-obsessed guy who just wanted to be left alone," Jett said. "Works for me." He turned his attention my way. "Or were you hoping to take the nerd, Kai?"

I snorted. "It wouldn't work in my favor very well if I picked the one with the same strengths I already have. I'm happy to take the football player. My brains and his brawn should be an unstoppable combination."

A ghostly sort-of adrenaline thrummed through me at the thought. I hadn't been a weakling before by any means—you didn't survive in our kind of life if you couldn't throw a punch and slash a knife when you needed to—but I'd admit physical combat hadn't been my strongest skillset. Death was giving me the opportunity for an upgrade.

At the sound of voices in the distance, my senses went on the alert. No one came down into this dim hallway of the college unless they had to—or they'd been given a very good reason to think it'd be worth their while.

I snapped my fingers at Ruin. "Get ready by the bleach. The second you hear the lock slam into place behind them, give it a shove."

"On it!" Ruin flew to the high shelf, practically vibrating with excitement. I wouldn't have entrusted that part of the assignment to him if I hadn't thought all that energy would help give his push the heft it needed. Besides, I needed to oversee all the other variables, and Nox packed the most punch of the power we needed to lock the door.

Jett, well... There was always a risk with him that he'd get distracted ruminating about the paint he wanted to smear all over something and miss his cue. He didn't even bother to stir from his corner, not caring about the details of the plan until he got his chance to nab a body.

Nox followed me through the wall into the hallway, where three of our unlucky four were walking toward us.

"...some kind of special assignment," the golden boy said, not looking so special now that he didn't have an army of minions in tow. "He said it was important that he get exactly the right people for the job." He glanced at the others as if he was having trouble imagining how either of *them* could have qualified as "special."

"I just know he said the team would get new equipment if I pitched in," the jock replied. "And they'll all know it's thanks to me. Sweet."

The geeky guy had folded his arms over his chest as if to reduce the chances that he might brush against one of the other two and catch slacker cooties. "He mentioned extra credit," he said stiffly. "I wouldn't have bothered otherwise."

The golden boy smiled the same way he had when he'd been tearing down Lily. "There's something in it for all of us then."

Oh, there'd be something in him, all right. Unfortunately for him, there'd be something coming *out* too—specifically his soul.

They peered at the doors they passed, the nerd's nose wrinkling and the jock's forehead furrowing. "Are we sure this is the right place?" the beefy guy asked.

Golden Boy checked the plates over the doors and a piece of paper he dug out of his pocket. "It should be just down here… I don't know why he picked this spot, but I guess this project is something *really* off the radar."

My hearing caught footsteps farther in the distance, and apprehension prickled over me. If the professor caught up with this bunch before they disappeared into the room, they might consult each other before they entered, and then they'd never go in at all.

"Wait there!" I ordered Nox, hoping he wouldn't decapitate me as soon as I had a head to remove for bossing him around, and dashed toward the bend in the hall.

The professor who'd berated Lily on her first day—and who hadn't let up on her since—was striding toward me from the stairwell. I'd told him to come five minutes later than the others, but apparently he had a hard-on for over-punctuality. Shit.

I darted past him into a room he'd already passed where the door was slightly ajar. A shove was a lot easier than manipulating a lock with our ghostly energies. I could manage that much even with the power I'd already expended setting this plan in motion.

I hurled myself at the door from inside, picturing my ghostly shoulder solidifying against it, the energy propelling it forward. In my mind's eye, it slammed into the frame with a thunderous *thwack*.

In actuality, it clicked into place with a light thud and the faintest crackle of the supernatural electricity our energy condensed into. I tumbled the rest of the way through the door, back into the hall.

The noise was still enough for the professor to pause and glance behind him. He frowned and rubbed his jaw. Any second he was going to keep walking.

I darted inside and rammed myself with another imperceptible sizzle into the nearest free-standing object, which happened to be a mop. It tumbled over with a clatter.

Thankfully, this stickler also had a hard-on for telling off delinquent students. He marched over to the room and flung open the door with a triumphant expression.

His delight faltered when he took in the room currently uninhabited by anyone living. Taking a few steps inside, he scanned the shelves and even the bucket by the door, as if a freshman might be hiding in there. Then, with a sigh, he strode back out.

As he left, I caught the click of the other door closing around the bend. I'd bought us enough time. Now to see the final part of this plan through.

Back in the janitor's room, Ruin was jittering behind the bleach bottle like a kitten that'd bit a live wire. Our first three doofuses were inspecting the room around them with growing confusion.

"Why would Mr. Grimes want to meet us *here*?" the nerd said.

"With professors, you've really just got to go along with what they say," the jock said with an air of pathetic certainty. "That's what makes them happy."

"Fuck, it smells weird in here," the golden boy said, waving his hand under his nose. He took a step toward the puddle of chemicals on the floor. "Maybe this is some kind of test. He wants to see if we're really up to the challenge of the assignment."

That's right, I thought at him. *It's a big elaborate test designed to give you every opportunity to prove what a spectacular human being you are—oh, sorry, I mean what a pretentious prick you are. Congratulations, you're a winner!*

"I don't know about this," the nerd said, edging back toward the door, and I thought I might have to pull out a few more stops. But right then, the professor barged into the room.

He stopped just inside, the door swinging shut behind him, and stared at the collection of imbeciles we'd brought together. I'd bet he didn't recognize that he was the biggest one of all. His eyebrows drew together as he tried to figure out how this could possibly be the result of the note I'd sent supposedly from a female student hoping to get a little "extra help" away from prying eyes.

"What are—?" he started.

In the same instant, I called out to Nox. "Lock it!"

Our fearless leader slammed the full force of his energy into the deadbolt. It rasped over with an audible *thunk*. Ruin sucked in a giddy breath and hurled himself at the bleach bottle.

The dolts had whipped around at the sound of the lock. They whipped back when the bleach bottle careened off the shelf with a splatter of noxious liquid spilling from its mouth as it fell. The stuff hissed into the chemicals we'd sloshed on the floor, and the waft of stink shifted from weird to deadly.

Our dupes gagged and sputtered. I'd kind of wanted to watch them staggering around in agony for a little while, but we must have dosed them hard enough that the toxic gasses didn't take long overwhelming them. One and then another toppled to the floor like dominos. The professor, closest to the door, rattled the knob like his life depended on it—which, to be fair, it did—and then keeled over flat on his face.

I whisked from one to the next, grazing my spirit over them just long enough to confirm that their hearts had stopped beating. Their deathly silence was the most beautiful sound I'd ever heard. Anticipation hummed through me.

We were so close. Was this really going to work? Had I pulled off the ultimate gambit?

Only one way to find out.

"Open the door!" I hollered. "Get the fan going!" It wouldn't do us any good to resurrect ourselves only to die all over again.

Nox smacked the lock open and threw wide the door. Jett got off his ephemeral ass long enough to light a spark in the circuitry of the industrial fan next to his corner. A blast of air washed the worst of the poisonous perfume out of the room.

"Now?" Ruin asked, hopping up and down as much as a being without legs could.

"Now!" I declared, and dove into the jock.

I'd told the others to go straight for the heart. Pummel right into it like one giant shock paddle, as if our entire spirits would fit in that four-chambered organ. Let our supernatural energies jumpstart the currents that would set it pumping again. Rev it like a Harley and settle in for the ride. And that's exactly what I did.

A shrieking darkness closed around me. An electric jolt reverberated through my being into the space around me. Then something shuddered, and a pulse echoed through my spirit. It sounded erratic at first before settling into a steady thumping.

My sense of myself stretched as if I were being smeared through the body like peanut butter on toast, tingling with the awakening nerves, heaving with the air rushing into the lungs, blinking…

Blinking eyes that now belonged to me.

I pushed myself to my feet and swayed. I *had* feet. Halle-fucking-lujah. And legs and arms and a big brawny chest—more body than I'd had to begin with.

A laugh spilled from my mouth. *My* mouth, that could now make noises people who weren't dead could properly hear.

Fuck Christmas. We should christen a new holiday right now. Un-undead Day. All right, that didn't have the best ring to it, but I'd figure out something better when I was done losing my shit with joy.

Around me, the other bodies were heaving themselves upright. "Fuck, yeah!" Nox said through the professor's mouth, the voice lighter than his previous baritone but the attitude all Lennox Savage.

Jett just stared at his hands, turning them back to front, like they were a fucking miracle. Which they kind of were.

Ruin bounded right at me, throwing his almost-as-brawny arms around me. Right. I'd forgotten that when he *had* arms, he was a hugger.

"You did it! It's fucking fantastic," he crowed, and launched himself at Nox next. "We're back!"

"Hell yes, we are," Nox said, shooting me a wicked grin that no one could have believed belonged to his host. "Now let's get out there and teach these assholes the lessons they've been begging for."

Chapter Five

Lily

I COULD TELL something was up the second I reached the edge of campus. Gods be praised, this time it didn't appear to have anything to do with me.

A horde of students was swarming the field to the left of the admin building, chattering to each other with a buzz of anticipation. I'd swear there were more bodies on the lawn than were enrolled in the entire school. Resisting the urge to start accusing people that they didn't even go here, I eased closer to the crowd with my ears pricked. Maybe I could find out what the hell was going on without turning into a target.

"I wonder how many people they're actually looking to hire," one girl was saying to another. "Seems like a lot of competition."

Her friend bobbed eagerly on the balls of her feet, craning her neck as if searching for something amid the other students. "I heard they've been expanding a lot in the last decade, so they always need fresh blood. It'd be pretty amazing to get in with them right out of college. Sometimes they even take people on before they've graduated, starting them parttime until they're done with classes."

A third girl glanced back at them. "Aren't you majoring in biology? Would they even have positions for that?"

The second girl shrugged. "They're into all kinds of areas these days. It couldn't hurt to try. Everyone says they're one of the best companies to work for in the country."

I ventured farther along the fringes of the crowd, trying to figure out who this mysterious "they" was and why people seemed to think they'd be tossing out jobs like tees shot from a shirt cannon. I got a few wary looks as I brushed past my fellow students, but no one said anything, which made this a good day. They all appeared to be too distracted to worry about me going psycho on their butts.

I'd made it about halfway around the field when I spotted the billboard-like sign set up near a small temporary platform with a podium. *Thrivewell Enterprises Recruitment Event*, it said in big crimson letters, and lower down, in darker, more subdued type, *Established in Mayfield in 1912. You've got a hometown advantage!*

A shiver I couldn't explain ran over my skin as I took in the words. Mayfield was the nearest city to Lovell Rise, close enough that its suburbs rubbed up against the edges of town. I hesitated to call it *big*, since it wasn't exactly Manhattan, but it had about a hundred times our population. When urbanites drove out here to enjoy the apple orchards and corn fields or to take a paddle in the lake, a lot of them seemed to forget that this wasn't just an extension of their city.

But I guessed sometimes that worked in our favor, like when some hotshot business that'd been founded in Mayfield wanted to round up new employees. Recruitment campaigns and corporate expansion hadn't exactly been on my radar in middle school, so I wasn't super familiar with Thrivewell, but the name sent a jab of recognition through me, a certainty that I'd heard it before. And the jab came with another shiver, one that sent my skin outright crawling.

What had Thrivewell Enterprises ever done to me? I had no memory of being bitten as a child by a dog sporting the Thrivewell logo, having my Halloween candy stolen by a jerk shouting, "Long live Thrivewell!", or anything else that could have resulted in deep, unresolved trauma. Maybe there wasn't anything all that deep about it, and it was just that I found the name pompously repetitive—was it possible to thrive *badly*?—to the point that even my body rejected it.

Several company reps in red-and-gray uniforms were handing out flyers and forms. A couple of them ushered students selected by uncertain criteria into little tent-like cubicles, I assumed to conduct impromptu interviews with the chosen few. As far as I could tell, everyone at Lovell Rise College was looking to get hired by these people.

Well, everyone except me. For now, I'd happily stick to my grocery-store stock-girl career where no one scrutinized my past all that closely, thank you.

I swiveled to head to class, wondering if I'd be the only one there —I thought I'd spotted a few professors in the crowd too, so even the teacher wasn't a guarantee—and a joyful-sounding *whoop* pealed out behind me. It was so unlike any sound I'd heard directed at me since I'd returned to town that I had no idea it was meant for me until the same voice called out, "Lily! There you are!"

The voice was… unnervingly familiar, and not least because wherever I was familiar with it from, I'd never heard it take on that cheerful tone before. And who the heck around here would be *happy* to see me?

With my nerves prickling on high alert, braced for whatever fresh hell the student body intended to rain down on me for simply existing, I turned around. Even if I couldn't avoid that hell, it was better to know what was coming so I could at least prepare.

When my gaze latched on to the figure pushing through the horde to reach me, my jaw dropped. It took me a second before I recovered enough to reel it back in.

Ansel Hunter was jostling past his peers to reach me. His eyes had lit up with an almost manically delighted gleam, and he was beaming from ear to ear. Not his typical broad but polished grin. This expression was so wildly gleeful I'd have believed he was genuinely ecstatic to see me… if he hadn't been *him*.

My first instinct was to turn tail and run like a rabbit in the sights of a fox. My dignity went halfsies with my sense of self-preservation, and I hurried away at a brisk walk.

Unfortunately, Ansel walked brisker. Actually, he ran me down like he'd been waiting his whole life just to have this conversation.

"Lily!" he exclaimed again, grabbing my arm as he caught up with me. He waved a half-eaten croissant with his other. "Have you had one of these here? They're fucking amazing. I swear I've never eaten anything this good in my life. Of course, it has been a while… You want a bite?"

He hadn't squeezed my arm hard, but my pulse lurched before he'd gotten through his second sentence. I wrenched myself away automatically, whirling around. "What? No. What do you want?" I asked, my voice firm but as even as I could keep it. What the hell had gotten into the guy?

Ansel blinked at me, still smiling away, no hint of animosity in his expression. Without his usual perpetual haughtiness and the cruel glint in his hazel eyes, which were shining now like autumn sunlight, he almost looked like a different person. I found myself studying him to confirm that it really was my former classmate and not just his evil twin… or, well, I guessed his *good* twin in this particular case.

"We've been looking for you," he said, with no indication of who 'we' was or why they'd have wanted to see me. He gulped down the rest of the croissant and spread his arms with a gesture toward himself. "Isn't this amazing? It'll be even better than old times."

Had Ansel taken a hard blow to the head? Or been snorting something he really shouldn't have? Because the only "old times" I had any memory of involved him smirking with his middle-school friends after calling me a weirdo. I'd agree that his current attitude was better than that, but it was a pretty low bar. I'd rather have chewed on nail clippings than go back to eighth grade.

"I don't know what you're talking about," I said. "Anyway, I have to get to class."

"But wait!" He sprang after me again, giving a very solid impression of an overgrown—and overenthusiastic—puppy. I had the impression he would have wrapped those well-muscled arms right around me if I hadn't dodged at the last second, leaving him simply holding them out beseechingly. "You don't understand. It's *me*. From the marsh. From before. I know you have to remember."

I definitely didn't remember ever seeing Ansel down by the marsh. He and his crowd had used to make fun of me for supposedly smelling like "swamp water."

"Look," I said, an edge I couldn't suppress creeping into my voice, "I don't know what kind of bizarro game you're playing here, but right now *you're* acting way more psycho than I ever have. Like I said, I'm going to class."

And maybe you should consider getting *a little class*, my inner snark added, just barely stifled.

I whirled away from him again, too bewildered to be paying full attention to where I was going, and my elbow smacked a guy who'd been walking past me with his gaze on the recruitment tables.

"Sorry," I said quickly, meaning to continue my getaway, but the second the guy laid eyes on me, those eyes narrowed.

"Eight years in a mental hospital, and they still didn't manage to teach you to keep your hands to yourself, you crazy cunt?" he snapped, patting himself down as if checking to see if I'd somehow picked his pockets with my elbow. Which would have made me some kind of genius thief more than a psychopath, but whatever, not worth mentioning.

I also restrained myself from correcting him that it was *seven* years, opening my mouth to instead repeat my hollow apology, but I didn't get the chance to do even that.

"What the fuck did you call her?" Ansel snarled, switching from exuberant puppy to rabid pitbull in an instant. He slammed his hand into the guy's throat and somehow lifted him right off his feet so the guy's sneakers dangled inches off the ground.

The guy gurgled and flailed, unable to answer the question, not that I expected he wanted to admit to what he'd said right now. People in the crowd near us turned to see what the commotion was, with a chorus of gasps and squeals of horror—and, let's be real, maybe a little excitement. I'd lost my breath and my voice entirely, my jaw hanging open so far you could have stuffed a bowling ball in there.

"That's what I thought," Ansel said, still in that feral tone, and tossed the guy aside like he was an inflatable dummy rather than an actual human being. The crowd parted, none of them wanting to face a collision, and he thumped to the ground in their midst, right on his sorry ass. And oh boy, did he look sorry.

A couple of bystanders, now that they were no longer in danger of being battered by his careening body, knelt by the groaning guy with murmurs of concern. Ansel's fingers had left angry red marks all across the guy's neck.

Ansel considered him with a huff and turned back to me, his smile springing back into place as if it and his fierce expression were opposite ends of a yoyo. "No one's ever going to talk to you like that again while we're around," he promised.

Again with this "we." Again with the acting like he had some kind of commitment to me instead of being a stuck-up bully. I couldn't wrap my head around any of this. It took all the effort I had in me just to collect my jaw again.

"I—I—" I stammered, and then I spotted two of the professors from the crowd weaving our way. Panic spiked through my veins.

If they saw me here in the middle of this, if people started talking —dollars to donuts, it'd be spun into being all my fault, even though all I'd done was try to walk away. For fuck's sake, even Ansel being "nice" to me was getting me into trouble I didn't want.

"I'm sorry," I said quickly to the onlookers. "I had no idea he'd do that." Then I whirled on Ansel. "I don't know what's gotten into you or why you hurt that guy, but I never asked you to. All I want is for you to leave me alone."

"Yes," he said as if he hadn't heard me at all. "We should go off alone, away from these assholes."

What was it going to take to drive the point home?

I shook my head vehemently. "I want *you* to leave me alone. Stop talking to me, stop following me. Just… stop!"

The beaming grin faltered. Ansel started at me with such bewilderment that a twinge of guilt ran through my stomach despite myself. But I couldn't stay and find out what this craziness was all about. Not while I was trying so hard to convince everyone else that I *wasn't* crazy.

"But, Lily…" he said.

"No," I interrupted before he could figure out what else he was going to say. "Stay away from me." Then I marched off as quickly as my feet could carry me, wondering if there was any pill in the world that could take away the headache of confusion that'd started to pound in my temples.

Chapter Six

Lily

My Sociology of the Family class went by totally normally, other than only half of the seats being filled. It was *so* normal that I almost convinced myself that the incident with Ansel had been a hallucination that I'd hopefully never repeat.

By the time I'd finished my second class of the day, my nerves had settled completely. I walked along the paved paths toward the main parking lot, the rasp of my shoes over the asphalt blending with the rattling of nearby tree branches in the wind into a subtle melody. I'd have been tempted to let myself sing with it if there hadn't been other people around.

I was just beginning to think I'd make it through the rest of the day unscathed when I glanced across the parking lot and spotted Ansel staked out next to my car.

And not just Ansel. Like the worst kind of bad dream, standing next to him were the three other men who'd been competing for a top spot in my Worst Dickbrains at Lovell Rise College list: Mr. Grimes, my Juvenile Delinquency professor; Vincent Barnes, my peer advisor so reluctant you could have called him a peer adversary; and Zach something-or-other, who'd decided to step up the harassment from throwing words at me to hurling footballs.

I stopped in my tracks halfway across the lot with a good hundred feet still between me and them. Unfortunately, they'd already noticed me. All their heads turned my way from where they'd been clustered together as if in intense conversation. Although what this odd combination of people would have had to talk about for long, I couldn't imagine.

No, that wasn't true. Clearly they'd been talking about *me*—and whatever horrible plan they'd somehow decided to collaborate on to continue my massive unwelcoming party.

I blinked a few times as if I might have somehow been seeing things wrong. The four men were still standing there by my car, watching me. Ansel waved me over with the same apparent eagerness he'd shown at the recruitment rally. Zach cocked his head at a contemplative angle that didn't fit what I'd seen of the musclehead before at all.

There was no way this situation wasn't bad news. The trouble was, I didn't have any good options. They were standing between me and my one way off of campus. Lovell Rise didn't have any public bus service. I guessed I could have walked the ten miles from the sprawling campus grounds to the other end of town, but I was hardly going to make it to my shift at the grocery store in less than an hour that way. Unless I grew wings on my feet, I'd get there just as I was supposed to be clocking out.

And that was assuming this bunch didn't come after me if I tried to make a hasty escape.

I wavered on my feet for several seconds longer, taking stock of my surroundings. There were a few other students drifting in and out of the parking lot. I was within screaming distance of the admin building. Surely if these asswipes decided to try to outright *murder* me, someone would step in on my behalf?

It was a little sad that I couldn't answer that question with any certainty, but I would put more faith in my fellow human beings than they'd shown me. Besides, that car might be a piece of junk, but it was *my* junker, and no bullies were going to take it away from me.

As I walked closer, my gaze flicked between the four men and the car behind them, scanning Fred for any signs of damage. As far as I could tell, all the tires were intact today. No cracks marked the windows or scratches marred the patchy finish—at least, no scratches big enough to stand out amid the marks and rust already dappling the frame.

They were cutting me off from my car, but they hadn't disabled it.

I halted again when I was about ten feet away, which felt like a safe-ish distance. By that point, Ansel was grinning his head off. Mr. Grimes was smiling too, in a self-assured way that felt weirdly warmer than his usual expressions—but then, I didn't think I'd ever seen him really smile before. Zach still had an unexpectedly incisive look on his face, as if he were a mad scientist eagerly analyzing me for some unknown purpose.

Vincent was the only one who didn't give off any enthusiasm at all, but even that felt out of character. He stood with his previously rigid posture a bit slouched, his hands slung carelessly in the pockets of his pressed slacks.

Every inch of my skin prickled with the sense that something was *very* wrong here. I mean, I'd pretty much figured that out when Ansel had gone into his buddy-buddy routine before, but I hadn't realized whatever disease he'd come down with was contagious.

Mr. Grimes stepped forward first, his gaze sweeping over me, avid and almost… heated? In a way that instantly made me twice as uncomfortable. "Fuck, it's good to be able to actually see you like this," he said in a cocky voice that didn't sound like the professor at all. "Properly, I mean—with *eyes*."

Who with the what now? I was starting to think Ansel really had caught and spread some kind of deadly illness, maybe of the brain-eating parasite variety. Even my inner voice couldn't come up with an appropriate snarky remark. It just gaped like I was holding myself back from doing on the outside.

"Of course this is confusing," Zach spoke up in a calmly matter-of-fact tone that would have fit the professor a lot better than the jock. "I promise you'll get used to it. It was the only way we could come back—it's pretty much a miracle we managed even this." He looked down at his body with a sharp little smile, as if awed by himself.

Picturing animals on their heads or throwing snark at them in *my* head wasn't going to make this scenario any more tolerable. "I have no idea what either of you are talking about," I said. "I don't know if this is a very convoluted joke or if you've actually gone off the deep end, but I'd rather not be a part of it either way. I just want to get to my car and go to work."

Ansel let out a huff that managed to sound cheerful and turned to the others. "We can't let her keep working at that drudge of a job. She deserves better. We've all got some money, don't we? I mean, *they* did, and now it's ours." His grin widened. "Which means it should be Lily's too."

"Definitely," Mr. Grimes said without a hint of irony. He swiveled around to consider Fred. "And a new car. We can do *way* better than this. Some of these new models… I'd like to give this baby a ride." He ambled a little farther to skim his fingers over the hood of a Mazda that was nice enough but didn't look all that special to me. Then his gaze settled on a motorcycle parked in the next aisle. "And I'm going to get the best bike they've dreamed up while we were gone."

I opened my mouth and closed it again, grappling for the right words to respond. Now they were planning out my life, even offering to buy me a car if I was understanding properly? My head was spinning so hard it was a wonder it didn't fly right off my neck.

"I'm fine with both my car and my job," I said firmly. "They let me get done what I need to get done. And I sure as hell wouldn't come to any of you asking for handouts."

Mr. Grimes turned back toward me. "You don't have to ask. This is why we're here. All the jackasses around here are pissing on you, so you'd better believe we're going to do whatever we can to make up for that… and make them pay." His smirk after that statement was downright evil.

My inner voice finally woke from its stunned stupor enough to sputter, *But… you all were some of the biggest jackasses of them all! Maybe deal with yourselves first?*

"Please," I said out loud, holding up my hands. "Don't go after anyone on my behalf. Like I said, I don't want anything to do with this. Why can't you leave me alone so I can just live my life?"

"Don't you see?" Ansel said, bounding over to me like he had on the field. He swung his arms as if to grab me in a hug but dropped them when I jerked out of the way. Instead, he motioned to the other guys. "It's *us*. We came to take care of you."

Vincent finally spoke up, in a flat but unshakeable voice. "It took longer than it should have. We wanted to be here sooner."

"I don't know what went down when you left town," Mr. Grimes put in, "but all these assholes trying to tear you down can go eat shit. Literally, if I have anything to say about it. You're our Lily, and no one's going to get away with beating up on you."

"I'm not 'your' fucking *anything*!" I burst out, unable to contain my frustration.

Mr. Grimes raised his eyebrows. Ansel looked so startled I wanted to smack the surprise off his normally smug face.

Zach cleared his throat and raised his hands. "Guys, guys," he said in that same authoritative, almost condescending tone. "We've hardly even explained. We can't expect her to understand right off the bat."

He met my eyes, his bright gray-green irises strangely penetrating. "We're not who we look like. We dispatched the pricks who used to own these bodies and took them over for ourselves. I don't know if we ever managed to get across our names to you, but I'm Malachi—stick with Kai, thanks. Mr. Happy over here is Ruin, the sullen silent one is Jett, and of course this is our fearless leader, Lennox."

"Nox," Mr. Grimes corrected with a brief glower. He nodded to me. "Maybe you couldn't hear us anymore, but you've got to remember. We dragged you out of the marsh. We hung out with you for *years* until you went away. Did a hell of a lot better job of looking after you than that shithead stepdad of yours and your weakling mom just going along with whatever he said."

I hadn't thought my mind could whirl any more than it already was, but suddenly I was so dizzy I thought I might puke. How the hell did my professor know anything about my family life? And what did he mean about dragging me out of the marsh? This all sounded insane.

I pressed my hands over my ears as if I could block out everything they were saying. It wasn't the most dignified move ever, but it was either that or scream hysterically, so at least this route would draw fewer onlookers.

"Stop it," I said, my own words oddly muffled inside my skull. "I don't want to hear any more. This is crazy, and I'm not crazy. Please, just stop and let me go to my shift at the grocery store. I never did anything to any of you."

By the end of that little speech, my voice had gone ragged. Tears burned in the backs of my eyes.

The men looked at each other with expressions of utter bewilderment—and what I'd have sworn was concern. Ansel backed away, a hopeful light managing to shine through the misery on his face even now. "It'll be okay," he said. "We'll get it all sorted out, and it'll be just like before, only better."

"We're here for you, Lily," Vincent said, like it wasn't the total opposite of what he'd been telling me the last time I'd seen him.

Zach waved the others to the side. "I think she needs some time to absorb it all. *We* could use some time to really get settled in and figure out what we've got to work with."

"But—" Mr. Grimes let out a sound like a growl of frustration and gave me an insistent look, as if he could make me react the way he wanted if he stared hard enough. When I didn't budge, he eased to the side with the others. "We aren't leaving you alone again. You'll see that."

The words should have sounded ominous, but something in his expression took away any trace of a threat. And they'd cleared the way to my car.

I hustled past them, fumbling for my keys. Naturally, a frog had chosen this moment to perch on the roof right by the windshield. I shooed it off as quickly as I could so it wouldn't get flying lessons when I drove off and threw myself into the driver's seat.

I half-expected the men to change their minds and move to stop me. Instead, they hung off to the side, just watching me go. I didn't give them any more chance to rethink their stance. Hitting the gas, I steered Fred toward the exit as fast as the stuttering engine would take me.

"What the fuck do you make of that, old boy?" I asked the car, disbelief and confusion still tangled up inside me.

Fred answered with only a gargling sound.

"No kidding," I muttered, and tried to breathe evenly through the rapid thudding of my heart.

I'd left them behind. I was okay. Whatever wacko stuff they'd been saying, it didn't matter now.

Other than the fact that they'd all but promised that this reprieve was only temporary. And I had no idea when or how I'd find myself dealing with them next.

Chapter Seven

Ruin

I WOULDN'T HAVE THOUGHT anything could get me down now that Lily was back with us. I hadn't counted on how awful it'd be to have her more than ever before but not really have her at all.

"She was right here," I said, making a grabby motion in the space where she'd been standing in the parking lot. "Right in front of us. But she still didn't know us."

I felt as if I'd have known her anywhere, no matter what face she'd had on. But I guessed she'd never seen us wearing any face at all.

I spun toward the others with a rush of hope. "It'll just take a little while, right? When she understands who we are, she'll be ecstatic."

Kai rubbed his eyes. It was weird seeing him without his glasses, even though the guy he was currently inhabiting hadn't worn them. Glasses just went with Kai the same way paint went with Jett. He squinted for a second before focusing on me, as if the lack of glass panes bothered him too.

"I may have miscalculated slightly about how easily she'd recognize us in our new forms," he said. "She was obviously incredibly confused. I'm not sure… It's not as if we ever told her anything about who we were before. We just went along with her games and whatever she needed."

Nox's mouth tensed. "She's never seen us before. It's been years since she even heard us—and then it wasn't even clearly. What if she *has* forgotten all about us? Fuck!" He kicked at the tire of the Mazda he'd been admiring earlier.

"She couldn't have forgotten," I said with total certainty. "We just have to figure out a way to convince her that we're us."

Jett let out a low cough. "Not just that. She might not even believe we're *real*."

I furrowed my forehead. I was about to ask him what that was supposed to mean when Kai jumped in, always quick with the answers.

"As far as she knows, we were just whispers in the breeze, vague impressions of friends…" he said. "It *is* possible she never knew we were really there. She might think she made us up. Holy shit." He blinked and squeezed the bridge of his nose.

The thought of Lily not even knowing I existed—never having known it—made my stomach ache in a way I didn't like at all. I groped in my pockets and found the beef jerky someone had been handing out samples of. The first piece had been so satisfying I'd gone back for more.

I bit into it now, my senses sparking at the flood of spicy flavor. A lot of the students I'd seen chomping on the samples had started coughing and chugging whatever drinks they had within reach, but I grinned through the burn on my tongue. Anything that got my nerves singing was awesome in my book.

And I'd been extra hungry ever since I'd gotten into this dude's body, which maybe made sense since technically I hadn't eaten anything in about twenty years.

Nox scowled. The teacher he'd taken over didn't look all that much like his former self, but I could already see bits and pieces of the real him showing through. That squaring of his shoulders like he was about to go into battle, and the way his eyes flared with brutal determination. I'd follow our captain to the ends of the earth, because he got things done.

"We'll make her see. Whatever it is she needs to see, we'll get it straight for her." He shook his head. "It isn't her fault she's freaking out over this. After the way the pricks around here have been treating her because we didn't get here fast enough to stop them…" His lips pulled back from his clenched teeth with a growl.

"We're not letting any of *that* happen ever again," I said, and grinned wider at the memory of the asshole I'd tossed out of her way on the field this afternoon. "That part is going to be fun."

Jett rolled his eyes, a gesture that made the narrow face he'd taken on look a little more like him. "They'll regret messing with her—that's for sure," he muttered, and glanced at the piece of jerky I was just popping into my mouth. "You got any more of that stuff? I'm starving."

"Sure!" I fished another piece out of my pocket and handed it over. I might have cleared out the rest of the sample container when the woman handing them out had been distracted. It'd seemed only fair when I'd gone without for two decades.

Kai chuckled. "You'd better be careful with that. Knowing Ruin's tastes, it'll ruin your tongue."

Jett wrinkled his nose. "I know what he's like. Some things don't change." He took a bit of the jerky and shuddered but kept chewing.

As usual, Kai answered the question we hadn't asked yet before it'd even totally formed in my head. "It's to be expected that our metabolism will be all over the place for at least the first little while. Ghostly energies mingling with the systems of a living body… The transition must take a certain amount of fuel… We should be prepared for unpredictable fluctuations in all bodily functions."

"Fucking fantastic," Jett grumbled, popping the rest of the strip into his mouth.

Nox stalked back and forth in the parking space where Lily's car had been. "How long will we be dealing with that effect?"

Kai shrugged. "I don't know. It isn't as if *anyone* has ever done this before and written up a report about it. I'm just giving you my best speculation. Our physical manifestation might become more even-keel over time as we adjust to the new situation, or we might have minor oddities crop up for the rest of our, well, lives." A thin smile curved his lips.

Nox grunted. His gaze skimmed over the parking lot, occasionally resting covetously on the motorcycle he'd noticed. I had the feeling that if the owner turned up while we were here, they weren't going to own that bike for much longer. Nox was very good at making things his.

If he thought we could get through to Lily, then I'd assume he was right. He'd always led us well before. We weren't going to let her down ever again.

The idea that we'd let her down already by fading out of her life and taking too long to get back into it brought back my stomachache. I started gnawing on another piece of jerky to douse the discomfort.

Kai's head swiveled around. "Looks like we have company. Those are some of the idiots who were hanging around your boy, weren't they, Ruin?"

I followed his gaze, my spirits rising at the thought of more company. There was a certain energy in a crowd of people that I hadn't gotten to experience to full effect in as long as it'd been since I last had a square meal. Even when the people in that crowd were mostly jackasses, I was all for it.

Three guys and a couple of girls were sauntering toward us. They did look familiar, although I'd seen so many new faces in the past week—and I hadn't really been focusing on any of them except Lily's and the biggest jerks'—that I couldn't have said for sure who these ones were. They definitely appeared to know *me*, or at least the guy who'd used to inhabit this body. They looked from me to the company I was keeping with puzzled frowns, and one of the guys motioned me over to them.

"Hey, Ansel," another called out.

Right, that was who they saw. What were they up to?

I ambled over to find out. Ansel's friends kept eyeing the guys behind me as if they were trying to read something on their foreheads that they couldn't quite make out. What was so fascinating about them?

"Hey," I said, smiling at them the way you do with friends. Ansel's buddies weren't necessarily all bad. He'd set an awfully bad example, which wasn't their fault.

"Ansel," one of the girls said in a simpering voice, and tilted her head coyly to one side so her thick brown hair swished over her shoulder. "We've been looking all over for you."

"Why are you hanging out with *them*?" one of the guys asked, peering at my bros again like I'd been consorting with green Martians or something.

"Nothing wrong with making new friends, right?" I said, flashing a brighter grin as I laughed inwardly. I'd been friends with the guys behind me before this bunch were even born.

"Right..." another guy said in a skeptical tone. "I've been trying to text you for the last couple of hours. Peyton was too." He motioned to the girl with the swishy brown hair.

Oh! I touched my pocket where I could feel the sleek rectangle that was apparently Ansel's phone. It didn't look anything like the clunky plastic devices we'd used to shoot quick messages to each other in our lives before. I'd jabbed at it a little and then forgotten about it.

"Sorry," I said. "Didn't realize. What's going on?"

"We were just going to grab some burgers at Philmore's. You said this morning that you were dying for one."

That'd been another man who wasn't me, but I had the feeling it wouldn't go over well to tell them that. I was supposed to be covert and undercover here, using my new identity to my—and Lily's—advantage. I nodded as if I remembered, my mouth watering and my stomach grumbling at the thought of a thick, juicy burger.

I wouldn't *die* for one—been there, done that, not interested in repeating—but I'd happily live through that meal.

Of course, I had other responsibilities. But we could make a larger group outing of it, right? Maybe Kai could do some kind of research on these students that'd help us somehow.

"Right," I said. "Absolutely. I'll just see if the other guys want to come along—"

I started to motion to my bros, and all the faces in front of me stiffened. "What are you talking about?" the third guy said. "I mean, Zach's kind of okay, I guess, for a freshman, but that dweeb what's his name? And why the hell would you invite a professor along? Have you gone mental?"

"I think he must have," the second girl piped up. "I saw him talking with psycho girl at the recruitment rally. He seemed like he was trying to get cozy with her."

The brunette—Peyton—went even more rigid. The first guy sputtered a laugh. "Hey, don't have fun with her on your own. I bet she's got plenty of wildness to go around, if you know what I mean."

"Oh, yeah," the second guy said with a leering grin, and made a pumping gesture with his arms and hips. "They say don't put your dick in crazy, but I bet it's a real thrill while it lasts. You just don't stick around too long. Gotta use trash like that for the little bit she's worth—"

My vision hazed red. Every shred of jauntiness I'd been feeling seared away beneath a surge of rage.

It was Lily they were talking about. Our Lily—*my* Lily.

I didn't think, but that wasn't my strong point anyway. I just moved. My hand shot out like it had when the guy had cursed her out at the rally, but this time it closed into a fist and socked the last guy who'd spoken in the nose. Bone crunched; blood gushed over his chin and shirt like one of Jett's warped paintings.

The guy yelped and staggered backward, but I was already closing in on him. The whip of my other fist threw his head to the side. I stomped on his foot, kicked the other leg out from under him when he wobbled, and caught him in the gut with the toe of my sneakers as he tumbled to the ground. Then I slammed my heel down on one of the arms that'd formed his crude demonstration of what he wanted to do to my woman hard enough that another bone snapped.

He wasn't going to be pumping into anyone for a while.

I stood over him as he moaned and made a mess of the pavement, my lips pulled back in a fierce grin.

"What the *fuck*?" sputtered the other guy who'd joined in the taunting.

I swung around to face him, the rush of getting to put this new body to use washing through me like the best kind of high. Oh, I'd missed this. Stretching my muscles—and other people's—to their limits. Destroying anyone who fucked around where they shouldn't have fucking tried it.

"You want a taste too?" I jeered, my grin widening, daring him to try me.

The guy blanched. They were all staring at me like *I* was the alien now. Then they helped the bleeding guy onto his feet and scuttled away with him in a flurry of nervous murmurs.

I swiped the back of my hand across my mouth, triumph thumping through my veins. One step closer to crushing every one of Lily's enemies.

When I walked back to the others, Nox tipped his head to me approvingly. "They're all going to get what's coming to them. But we need to sort out ourselves and Lily first."

Yes, it didn't do Lily much good for us to fight for her if she thought we were still trying to mess with her. I shook out my limbs, adrenaline jangling through me followed by a roar of hunger. "I'm starving again."

"I could eat a fucking moose," Nox agreed. "Okay. You've all got at least a little money on you, right? Let's go out into town, get what we need to feel more like ourselves again, and chow down on some fuel. We meet up outside the hardware store at eight." He pulled his own phone, which looked like a slightly older version of mine, out of his back pocket and turned it around. "These things still show the time along with the million ways they're hardly phones anymore, don't they?"

"I think they can send messages too," Jett said. "If you can turn it all the way on." He shook his and jabbed at the screen, scowling at it.

I peered at mine, turning it upside down and then waving it back and forth. It felt way too light to hold half the things I'd heard people saying they were doing with theirs. Then I tapped the round button with my left thumb. The screen just jittered.

Kai let out a cry of victory and gestured to me. "Try your other thumb."

Ansel must have been right-handed, because pressing the button with that thumb did the trick. I found myself staring at a screen of a gazillion little icons laid over a bikini babe with duck lips shoving her tits toward my face. If that was the kind of girl Ansel was into, no wonder he couldn't appreciate Lily.

"Let's all get each other's phone numbers," Nox ordered. "We need a way to stay in touch. If… If you can figure out what your number even is. Who the hell thought these were an improvement over our old phones anyway? And they think Lily's the crazy one."

He blew out his breath. "We're going to get these working, and we're going to get Lily to see who we are. That's all there is to it."

Chapter Eight

Lily

My car might have been a junker, but at least I'd coordinated it with the rest of my life. If there'd been such a thing as junker apartments, the one I was living in definitely qualified.

It was in a basement set so low in the ground that the few windows were more like peepholes. In September, it was already chilly down there, so I could just imagine how many blankets I needed to stock up on for the winter.

The "kitchen" consisted of a fridge that'd probably worked well in the '80s, a sink with a thick ring of rust around the drain, and a hot plate. I'd tried adding a microwave to the mix, but it'd blown a fuse every time I ran it for more than five seconds, which didn't let me heat up anything. So now I also had a way-too-expensive paperweight sitting on the floor next to the fridge.

I hadn't had the money to buy much in the way of furnishings yet, so other than the kitchen area, the only things in the boxy room that played a triple threat of living room and dining room as well were a wobbly glass dining table with a crack running down the middle that'd come with the place, a couple of splintery crates I was using as end tables, and a futon couch that sagged so bad in the middle you could feel the bumps in the cement floor through the cushions.

I did have the luxury of a separate bedroom, although it was only just big enough for a twin bed and the narrowest, tallest dresser I'd been able to find, which I'd swear was going to topple over and kill me in my sleep someday.

It was a place that was all *mine*, though, which I'd never had before, and that made it pretty special no matter how awful it was. It worked just fine for me, and I didn't plan on inviting company over.

Unfortunately, company decided to invite themselves.

I'd just finished a gourmet dinner of canned stew heated on the hot plate and eaten right out of the can when someone rapped on the door. It could have been my landlord stopping by, but after the day I'd had, my nerves jumped. I tramped over, wishing the door had an actual peephole on it.

"Who's there?" I asked, feeling like I'd entered a knock-knock joke and hoping it turned out to be one that was actually funny.

"That's what we'd like to explain," said a voice it was hard to identify after it'd traveled through the door. "I promise you, we're only here to help."

That sounded an awful lot like the kinds of things four guys I definitely didn't want to talk to anymore had been saying just a few hours ago. "If it's the same bunch of you who swarmed me in the parking lot, I think you've said everything you could say."

"No, we haven't," a firmer voice replied. "You need to listen to this, Lily. It's a matter of life and death."

Not even that claim budged me, but then a third voice said, "It's a pretty pathetic lock. I could pick it in a few seconds."

"Are you serious?" I demanded.

"Give us a chance, and it'll make a lot more sense once you've heard the whole thing," the second guy, who I thought was Mr. Grimes, said.

How had they even found my address? I guessed in a town this small it wouldn't have been too hard to find someone who'd seen me heading home. I gritted my teeth, but under my trepidation, a tiny part of me itched with curiosity.

What the hell *was* going on with them? They hadn't tried to hurt me at all before—they hadn't even insulted me. What was the worst that could happen if I let them talk a little more? It might be more interesting than anything on TV.

"Okay, but you'd better explain fast," I said. I eased open the door, planning on making them stand where they were while they told their story.

I hadn't counted on the momentum of four eager male bodies. The second the door swung aside, all four of them—Mr. Grimes, Ansel, Vincent, and Zach—barged right past me into the apartment.

I didn't protest, because I was too busy staring at them to form words.

It *was* the same four as this afternoon in the parking lot, but they'd all gotten makeovers. Mr. Grimes had styled his short hair up in little spikes, dyed black with crimson at the tips. Somehow his presence felt bigger, bulkier, than it had just a few hours ago.

The others had dyed their hair too. Ansel had gone for a vibrant fox-red. Vincent had turned his blond locks a deep plum and cut them so they flopped across his dark eyes instead of tucking behind his ears. Zach had only darkened his brown hair to a richer shade, but he was also sporting a pair of rectangular glasses that looked unexpectedly natural on his face. Maybe because that face seemed somehow leaner than before, just like Mr. Grimes had expanded.

Mr. Grimes was prowling around the room, frowning at everything he set eyes on. "*This* is how you're having to live? Hell, no."

I'd have said that he was welcome to offer me someplace better if I hadn't been afraid he'd take me up on that suggestion after the way they'd talked about my car and my job earlier.

"It's the best I could manage," I said stiffly. "I couldn't go home."

"Of course not. That fucking prick."

Wade, I guessed he meant after his comment about my stepdad before.

My attention was diverted by Vincent in his new weird combination of geek and goth. He was chugging from a can of cola in one hand and using the other to re-arrange the random assortment of objects on my tiny kitchen counter: saltshaker, pen, rubber band, scraps of paper, a bill I hadn't opened yet. When the elastic was dangling over the side of the shaker and the scraps were arranged in a triangle around the pen, he stepped back with a satisfied hum, as if he'd created a grand piece of art.

Oh-kay, then.

"I think it's kind of cozy," Ansel declared in his new role as The Most Optimistic Guy Alive. I was starting to think if I offered him a glass with only a dribble of water in the bottom, he'd still say it was half full. "And it's great that you have your own space."

That much was true, but it wasn't what I wanted to be discussing with these dudes anyway. I opened my mouth, and Zach jumped in with that new disturbing way he had of knowing what was running through my head.

"You want us to get on with explaining, obviously," he said.

I guessed that wasn't so hard to figure out. "Yeah," I said. "And not in here. I didn't say you could come in, in case you didn't notice. How about you start by getting out of my apartment?"

Mr. Grimes gave me an incredulous look, which I returned automatically, because it was so bizarre seeing my professor with this new punk hairdo. "We're not going anywhere. This isn't stuff for anyone else's ears anyway."

In a show of bravado, I pulled out my phone and waved it at them. "You can get out *now*, or I'll call the police. Trespassing is against the law, you know."

I wasn't sure if I really would have followed through on that threat. I had no idea if the police would arrest these guys or assume I was delusional in thinking I hadn't invited them in, since the local cops probably knew who I was too. Apparently some of the officers had been part of that horrible blank in my past. But I wanted the men to know that I wasn't going to just sit here and accept them stomping all over my boundaries.

In theory. In practice, Mr. Grimes snatched the phone out of my hand without missing a beat and shoved it into his own pocket. "No need to be calling anyone, least of all those idiots. Why don't you sit down?"

I set my hands on my hips. "Now you're stealing my property?"

He folded his arms over his chest. "I'll give it back when we're done here. You *need* to hear this, for your own good. So, are you going to sit on your own, or am I going to have to pick you up and put you on your ass myself?"

"Nox," Ansel said in a breezily chiding voice, and hustled over to slip his arm around me as if to guide me over more gently. I slipped his grasp with a flinch, but I sank onto one end of the futon.

Mr. Grimes had sounded like he'd meant his sort-of threat. I'd rather not test it out.

"Talk already," I said.

The guys gathered in a semi-circle in front of me. "Let's get one thing straight from the start," Mr. Grimes said. "We're *not* the guys who treated you like shit. They're gone. We kicked them to Kingdom Come and confiscated their bodies to put to better use." He grinned.

Yeah, this didn't sound any saner than the things they'd said before had. "What does that even mean? You're not making any sense."

Zach let out a breath with a rasp of frustration and pushed his new glasses up his nose. "We should start at the beginning. I assume you remember falling into the marsh at the end of your yard and nearly drowning when you were a little kid?"

I glowered at him, willing myself not to shudder as the memory rolled over me like the water had, shutting out the light and the warmth. "That's the kind of thing it'd be hard to forget. How exactly do *you* know about it?"

I'd never told anyone—hadn't even mentioned it to Mom when I'd gone in later that day. I hadn't figured she'd care. Marisol had only been two, so she would hardly have understood why I'd been shaken by the incident.

No, wait, it wasn't totally true that I'd never told anyone. It'd come up in therapy a few times at St. Elspeth's.

As I worked that out in my head, Zach nodded. "We know about it because we were there too. You *almost* drowned, but you didn't. Because you got a push toward shore. We encouraged you, told you to cough up the water, reassured you afterward."

Ansel dropped onto the futon on the other side of the dip, his face lit with hope. "You remember *that*, right?"

I did… but not the way they were talking about it. I eyed each of them one after the other. "I pulled myself out of the marsh—I made up voices in my head talking me through it." I hesitated, a hint of a blush coloring my cheeks at the fact that I was going to admit it, but clearly they already knew about my childhood pretend play. "I created imaginary friends who'd protect me. It's not that strange for a six-year-old."

It was a heck of a lot more strange that I'd still talked to those imaginary friends when I was thirteen, but my circumstances hadn't exactly been normal.

Ansel laughed. "You didn't create us. We were *there*. We heard you splashing and it woke us up, and after we helped you we wanted to stick around. Because you're special." He shot me a bright little smile that made my stomach wobble in an unexpected way.

I rubbed my forehead. "You're not making any sense. No one was there. No one else ever saw those 'friends.'"

"Because we weren't properly visible. That's why we needed bodies." Mr. Grimes gestured to himself. "How else would we know about all this?"

I fixed my gaze on him. "Maybe you got into my files from the hospital somehow? Or someone overheard me talking with my imaginary friends when I was a kid and spread that info around now that I'm back in town with a target painted on my back? There are ways. Ways that make a lot more sense than *you* having been some invisible being."

"We were ghosts," Zach said matter-of-factly. "In some ways, we still are, just possessing new bodies."

"Ghosts," I repeated. My head was starting to ache again.

"We were dead," Vincent said shortly. "Some fuckers shot us down."

"And dumped us in the marsh," Mr. Grimes said, picking up the story. "A few years before you took your tumble. I guess we would have faded away completely if it wasn't for that. We wanted payback, but there hadn't been any coming. Kai hadn't come up with this fantastic strategy yet." He tapped his chest.

I leaned back on the futon. "Let me get this straight. You're telling me that you're ghosts. Someone killed you, and then you haunted me for most of my childhood. And now you've decided to take over new bodies so you can… hang out with me again?" Did they seriously expect me to believe that load of bull?

Apparently so. "Exactly!" Ansel said brightly, oblivious to the skepticism in my tone. He beamed at me. "Now you understand."

"Except we didn't come back just to 'hang out,'" Mr. Grimes said. "You *needed* us. All the shitheads around here were beating up on you, and we weren't going to stand back and let them get away with it."

Zach—who was also Kai?—clapped his hands together. "Exactly. We'll be protecting you from now on. Helping you however you need it."

They sounded earnest. I couldn't deny that. Whatever the hell was going on, I couldn't shake the sense that *they* bought into this shared delusion. But it was impossible, wasn't it?

No matter what was really going on with these guys, their approach to "helping" me had nearly screwed me over at least once already. The last thing I needed if I was going to prove I was on the straight and narrow was four crazy dudes following me around laying down their own violent kind of justice.

"Attacking people who are being assholes isn't going to help me," I said in the steeliest voice I could summon. "I came back because my sister needs *me*. My mom and stepdad won't let me see her. I have to prove that I've gotten better from… from what happened before, and that means I can't get into even a tiny shred of trouble. Why do you think I've been putting up with the crap everyone's been putting me through instead of snapping back at them?"

A puzzled hush fell over the group. Ansel cocked his head. "But they shouldn't be able to get away with it."

"I don't care! All I care about is getting to be a sister again, and that's not going to happen if you get me into trouble because everyone thinks I'm asking you to beat people up for me. The best thing you can do is back off and let me handle this my way."

Mr. Grimes's eyes had narrowed. "What *did* happen 'before'? Where have you been? What made them send you away?"

My pulse stuttered. I was weirdly both grateful and disappointed that they didn't know either. Admitting that I had no clue felt like a risky move. Even thinking about that fact made my gut twist.

"It doesn't matter," I said, standing up. "Shit went down, and now I have to deal with it. Now will you give me my phone back and leave? I heard you out. I got your story. It doesn't change anything. I still need you to leave me alone."

"Lily," Ansel said pleadingly.

I pointed to the door. "Out. Now. I'm tired, and this has been the craziest day in my entire life. And you still look a hell of a lot like four jerks who were pretty awful to me, whoever you really are. You wanted to help. I'm telling you how. Give me a break and let me show that I'm *not* some crazy, dangerous girl who hangs out with crazy, dangerous people."

The four of them exchanged a glance. Vincent threw back the rest of his cola and crushed the can in his fist. Mr. Grimes grimaced, but he nodded to me.

"We're going to do right by you," he said. "If that's what you want right now, then that's what we'll give you. But we *are* going to be here when you need more than that, and I don't think it's going to be very long before you do."

He handed my phone back to me and motioned to the others. They stalked out as quickly as they'd barreled in.

I shut the door behind them and shoved the deadbolt over, exhaling in a rush. They were gone, and they'd taken their delusions with them. I could pretend everything was normal again.

The apartment definitely didn't suddenly feel twice as lonely as it ever had before.

Chapter Nine

Jett

IT TOOK a few tries before I found myself at the room that went with the key I'd found in the nerd's bag. The two small residence buildings looked like identical dreary blocks of brick, and each of their floors showed the same puke-green walls with a line of smog-gray doors. The only difference was how many steps I had to walk up. And for some reason they'd started with 0 on the first floor, so 2-14 was actually on the third floor, not the second.

I was going to guess that whoever had built this place wasn't great with design *or* math.

The room itself was even more depressing than Lily's apartment, which was saying a lot. The smog-gray extended over the interior walls, like I'd stepped into an exhaust pipe, and a faint whiff of BO hung in the air. The room was laid out with a twin bed and narrow desk crammed next to each other on either side with the sliding door to a closet just beyond the headboard. It only gave about five feet of space between the two sides. You could have been lying on one bed and given a high five to a guy on the other without getting off.

It suited me just fine that there *was* no other guy in the room at the moment. I shoved the neatly stacked piles of binders and textbooks off the desk I could tell was the nerd's with one sweep of my arm, not caring how they tumbled onto the bed for now, and grabbed one of the pieces of blank paper he had sitting in a tiered tray toward the back. One tier for lined, one for unlined, another for various writing instruments.

I'd have laughed at him for being such a dork if I hadn't appreciated his organization skills in this particular way. Making art on lined paper was like cutting cheese with a chainsaw.

Of course the doofus didn't have any paint—or pastels, or markers other than highlighters, or anything remotely decent for getting color and texture on the page. I grimaced at the offerings, wishing I'd tracked down an art store after I'd fixed my hair as well as I could and lifted a shirt that didn't make me feel like a total dweeb. But the itch to create jabbed at my gut too insistently for me to put it off.

Putting forms to paper had always been how I worked through the mess of ideas and emotions that so often cluttered my head. And I had a hell of a mess now, after our conversation with Lily.

Talking wasn't my thing, but Nox could usually make any order he gave stick, no matter who he was giving it to. Kai could talk circles around anyone arguing with him, and Ruin's perpetual good mood might be irritating, but it also tended to disarm people… sometimes with perfect timing for him to hit them where it hurt. But somehow none of them had been able to get through to her—to make her want us around the way she always had before.

Maybe there were other answers. Maybe there was something I just wasn't seeing. The best way to find it was to spill my guts and my brains onto the paper and take a look at what I ended up with.

I cracked open another can of cola and took a long chug, wishing I had some actual coke to lace it with. The sugar and caffeine combo sent a hum through my nerves, but I craved a stronger buzz. After so long without any real bodily sensations, I wanted to soak in every bit of sensation I could get. Even the pinch of hunger that kept rising up to gnaw at my stomach no matter how much I ate was a fucking miracle.

Then I got to work.

I snapped the nibs off three of the nerd's—now my—pens: one blue, one black, one red. Let me never again mock a brownnoser for his thoroughness. There were plenty of other things to mock anyway.

Dribbling ink from each on the paper, I smeared it with my other hand, letting instinct and the thrum of emotion whirling through me guide my fingers. I never *thought* about what I was making or how it'd look to anyone else. Art was pure feeling, and anyone who didn't get that could suck my balls.

Just as I started rubbing some of the blue and red together in a purplish haze, another key clicked in the dorm room door. A guy I assumed was the nerd's—now my, *shit*—roommate strolled in. From the corner of my eye, I saw him do a doubletake as he took in me, the paper I was working over, and the jumble of books on the bed.

"Vince?" he said in an incredulous tone. "What the hell are you *doing*? What's going on?"

I debated not answering since my name wasn't Vince anymore, but it was going to be hard to keep that up with this idiot standing two feet away from me spewing peanut breath all over me. I didn't know what he'd been eating, but he could have sent someone allergic to the hospital just by exhaling in their general vicinity.

I finished the last line of color that'd called to me and glanced up at the guy. He was a collection of shapes and colors: a tan circle topped with cinnamon brown hair, skinny blue body—okay, the blue was his shirt and jeans, not his skin—with brown lumps of loafers at the bottom.

My mind had always been in the habit of breaking people down into an impressionistic version of themselves, like they were walking Monet paintings, but since my death, I'd been veering all the way from impressionist to abstract. Roomie here looked more like a Picasso. If my brain kept heading in the same direction, it was only a matter of time before the whole world was a blur of Rothko rectangles.

Except my crew and Lily. I saw them, even the guys in their not-quite-right bodies, exactly as they were. They were the only ones who mattered.

"I'm painting," I said, since the dimwit apparently couldn't figure that out for himself.

The guy's eyes bugged out even more. You'd have thought he'd have heard of the concept back in kindergarten. "Painting?" he said in disbelief, and then shook his head. "And you dyed your hair? What's gotten into you, man? Don't tell me the stress is cracking you up."

"No stress," I said. Other than the effort it was taking not to jam one of these broken pens into his eyeball so he'd shut up. Actually, he'd probably get louder then, unless I shoved it in far enough that I'd then need to figure out hiding a body. I didn't have time for that right now. "Just wanted a change."

My roomie flopped onto his bed, still staring at me. "Well, whatever. Stop 'painting' so we can get to work on that proposal. We need to get it turned in by tomorrow."

"Proposal?" I asked, not that I cared. This prick was dampening my buzz. I brought the can of cola to my lips, but only a dribble seeped out. Maybe if I shoved it down his throat, he'd shut up?

Very soon, the dolt's eyes were going to pop right out of their sockets. "The proposal!" he shouted. "For Thrivewell. Don't jerk me around like this. I know you want it just as bad as I do. If we get it right, the Gauntts might even look at it. They run the whole show—if we impress them, we have it made."

Most of that went in one of my ears and out the other, jumbling into little more than a bunch of hysterical jabbering. I shrugged and turned back to my painting. "I don't care about that anymore. Do whatever you want with it."

"*What?*" For a few seconds, the guy only sputtered incoherently. "We were in this together. I need your accounting expertise to get the numbers all lined up. You're joking, right?"

"Nope."

I narrowed my eyes at the picture. It wasn't speaking to me yet. The smears and smudges needed something more to bring them together.

Or maybe the chaos in me was just too much to ever make anything quite right.

I shoved that flicker of panic down and reached for one of the broken pens. There was one surefire way to spill enough on the page to bring it to life—and that was literally spilling some of my life there. Or what had been Vince's life, but he wasn't around to care about that now.

The broken plastic edge sliced through my skin with a stabbing pain. I closed my eyes, taking in the sensation and the flares of red and violet that shot with it through my nerves.

A fucking miracle, all right.

Then I brought my bleeding thumb to the paper. A streak here, a dabble there…

As the deeper scarlet brought the other colors into sharper relief, I was so fixated on the image in front of me that I didn't register my roommate's reaction. The next thing I knew, he'd sprung off the bed and grabbed my shoulder.

"What the fuck is up with you? Have you gone totally insane? Snap out of it, man!"

I swatted him off me, my teeth gritting at the interruption. "Who the hell asked you?"

"We've been working on this proposal all week! And now you're slicing up your hand and making freaky pictures and— You're having some kind of breakdown. You can't do this to me!"

"Write your own fucking proposal," I snapped at him, and brought my thumb back to the picture.

"You promised we were going in on it together, as a team. Look, I've got all the texts. You can't deny that. It's in writing—that's practically a contract."

He fished out his phone and tapped at the screen, which somehow activated the circuitry within those bizarre devices. What ever happened to buttons?

Then he thrust the shiny thing at me, its screen showing a bunch of blue and gray blobs, as if that was going to mean anything to me. "Look. Right here. Those are your words. You can't fucking—"

I'd show him what I could fucking or not fucking do. My blood-smeared hand shot out. I snatched the phone out of his waving hand and rammed it into the edge of my desk. Once, twice, three times.

The screen sputtered black. The glass had splintered into a spiderweb of shards. I admired the erratic pattern for a moment before tossing the thing back at the idiot. "Now it doesn't show anything."

"What the hell!? Vince, you totally broke it. I can't believe—"

"Believe it," I interrupted, losing my last bit of patience. "And also believe that if you don't shut up and leave me alone, it isn't the only thing that'll get broken."

I shot a glance over my shoulder, fixing my gaze on the blobs of vague color that were the nitwit's eyes. His jaw swung up and down for a few iterations without any sound coming out. The color drained from his face, taking it from tan to an ashy beige. A noise like a strangled groan finally worked its way out of him. Then he fled out into the hall.

Mission accomplished. Maybe next time he'd get the message faster. I licked my thumb to start the blood seeping again and added a few more streaks to the image on the paper before me.

A tingling of satisfaction crept up over me. Crossing my arms on the desk and leaning on my elbows, I peered down at the warped jumble of colors.

Yes. I could see it now. There was Lily, a fragile form in the middle of a swirling storm. She'd said she wanted to stay out of trouble, but there was so much of it blustering around her, trying to suck her down into it. How could she avoid getting pulled under?

She didn't want us with her right now? Fine. We could keep our distance *and* make sure everyone else who wanted a piece of her did too. And once she'd gotten the peace she needed, maybe she'd welcome us back with open arms.

The only question was, which of the assholes circling around her did we dispose of first?

Chapter Ten

Lily

"SHOULD they even let her in this class?" a girl seated behind me faux-whispered to her friend. "I mean, 'Deviance in the Modern World'? What if it sets her off on the crazy train again or something?"

"Maybe next time we shouldn't sit so close," her friend muttered back. "I heard she murdered half her family."

"*I* heard she ate someone's brains for breakfast."

I grimaced to myself and tuned out their voices as well as I could. Even if I had no idea what I'd actually done that'd gotten me shipped off to St. Elspeth's, I was one hundred percent sure it was neither of those things. For one, I had visual confirmation that all of my existing family members were fully in the world of the living. And I'd never had the slightest urge to chow on anyone's brain.

But the gossip mill ran best on the juiciest—and bloodiest—material it could get, so it was no surprise that those were the sorts of stories making the rounds. I doubted my classmates believed them either, or they wouldn't have sat within stabbing range to begin with.

I couldn't see them, but that didn't stop me from imagining a possum hopping from one of their heads to the other, making their hair increasingly messy as it went. One more crappy day, a few more idiotic comments. Eventually they had to get bored when I didn't fly into a psychotic rage, and then they'd find something else to blather about, right?

Unfortunately, some of my fellow students weren't content to stick to talking. I seemed to have gathered a small but adamant group of "fans" who were dedicated to making me crack whatever way they could… either because they were convinced I was going to go batshit sometime and they'd rather it was on their terms, or because they thought it'd be funny to see. Maybe it was a little of both. It was hard to tell.

But that was probably why I walked out of the lecture hall at the end of the class into a sudden deluge. A plastic fast-food cup bonked me in the head; chilly liquid laced with ice cubes splashed my face and trickled down my shirt. The culprits snickered somewhere to my left.

I swiped my hand across my eyes and mouth, getting an unwilling taste—Mountain Dew, *ugh*—and didn't even glance backward. Why give them the satisfaction?

Good job putting that beverage out of its misery, my inner voice snarked as I strode onward. It was my last class of the day, so I could go right home and change. Whatever.

I'd just turned a corner in the path to veer around the admin building when my ears caught a distant yelp. It shouldn't have meant anything to me. The more social students were hollering or cackling or whooping about one thing or another all the time. But there was a distinct edge of pain to this sound even hearing it so faintly, and my experiences from the past few days had me immediately on red alert.

Reluctantly, I swiveled on my heel and marched back the way I'd come. I didn't see anything unusual near the doorway, but another noise of protest, this one mostly muffled, carried from around the side of the building. Crossing my arms over my damp shirt, I stalked around it—and found Vincent and Zach in the middle of some kind of bizarre game.

Zach was holding a guy I didn't recognize upside down by his ankles, swinging him back and forth. Vincent was whacking him from his hips down to his head with a large stick, like the guy was some kind of living pinata. From the force of his strikes, he might literally have been hoping to burst him right open.

The thumping of the smacks and the grunts emanating from the guy fused together in a bizarre harmony that made me start to sway instinctively. Then I caught myself and stiffened my posture, because I *wasn't* some kind of maniac.

The guy's cries were muffled because of the fast-food wrapper stuffed in his mouth. A fast-food wrapper with a logo I could just barely make out, the same one that'd been on the cup hurled at my head. Suddenly I didn't need any other explanation.

Zach chuckled and said, "Come on, you should be able to break a rib or two. Then we can work on his skull."

Vincent made a grumbling sound. "Can't I just stab him right through?"

My heart had sunk, but I forced myself to quickly clear my throat. "Let him go."

The two guys—the ones on their feet, not dangling in mid-air—jerked their heads around with vaguely guilty expressions. Although not guilty like they thought they shouldn't have been doing what they were doing, only like they'd screwed up by getting caught at it.

Zach raised his eyebrows at me, his glasses having slid down his nose during their game. "We're just dealing out some justice. You asked us to stay away from you, and we did."

Obeying the fucking letter of the law but not much else. And breaking who knew how many other laws in the process.

I waved at them haphazardly. "I don't want this either. No justice on my behalf. Nothing for me at all. I thought I was pretty clear about that."

Vincent shrugged and looked down at his stick. "What if we just think it's fun?"

I glowered at him. "Then pick on someone who has nothing to do with me, please."

"Fine, fine," Zach muttered, and tossed their victim feet over head against the wall. As the guy lay there groaning, the—former?—jock shoved his glasses back up. "It's a good outlet for us too," he informed me in his matter-of-fact tone. "Our transition has left us with a lot of erratic energies."

Oh, right, their supposed transition from being dead to uninvited bodily hitchhikers. I shot him a skeptical look and gave my inner voice free rein. "Tell me you didn't just try to justify attempted murder on the basis that you needed a good workout."

Vincent had been pretty dour most of the time I'd seen him, but now a hint of a smile touched his lips. "If it's accurate…"

I let out my breath in a huff. My hair was still dripping Mountain Dew, and my shirt was getting sticky against my skin. I didn't have the bandwidth to deal with this extra brand of craziness on top of everything else.

"Whatever," I said. "Just find a new hobby that doesn't involve me in any way."

I hurried back toward the parking lot before I had to hear any more of their insanity. And before anyone else could stumble on the scene and think I'd had something to do with it instead of doing my best to prevent it.

When I reached my car, I flopped into the driver's seat and tipped over to rest my forehead against the steering wheel. My insides felt as if they'd bunched into one big knot.

This was all so ridiculous. Everything—the guys claiming to be who they said they were, the way half the student body was harassing me and the other half avoiding me like I really did eat brains for breakfast, me trying to keep a calm front in the face of all that…

Was it even worth it? Why didn't I just drive the fuck out of here and start a new life somewhere I'd never even been to before, like Timbuktu or Finland?

But even as I asked the question, my whole body resonated with the answer: Marisol. My little sister was the reason I'd come back, and so far I hadn't even gotten a glimpse of her except briefly from afar as she'd gotten into Wade's car. And even stealing that peek had been risky—I'd just needed to be sure she was really here and okay.

Of course, I wasn't actually sure about the second part of that statement yet. Just because she could walk around didn't mean she was *okay*.

Maybe I'd been playing it too safe, following Wade's rules when he was nothing to Marisol and me except the jerk Mom had married, letting my fears of what I didn't know I'd done stop me from reaching out to her directly.

I'd looked after Marisol her whole life—while I'd been around. Until she was nine. What kind of sister was I if I couldn't look her in the face and ask her what I'd done wrong… and how I could make up for it?

Resolve congealed in my chest. It was time to try, if for no other reason than because I wasn't sure how much longer I could keep going the way things were without at least letting her know I was fighting for her.

Showing up drenched in sticky soda wasn't going to make the right impression, so I took a detour for a quick shower and change before I drove out to the high school that served the teens of Lovell Rise as well as a couple of neighboring small towns.

I had a half hour before classes got out, so I sat in Fred a few blocks away and rehearsed what I wanted to say in my head. The practice didn't help much, because I had no idea how Marisol was going to react to seeing me. She might fling herself at me in one of those epic hugs I'd used to savor. Or she might run in the other direction screaming. And there were a whole lot of other possibilities on the broad range in between those extremes.

By the time the final bell rang, my palms were sweaty. I got out of my car and nearly tripped over a frog that was hopping its slow and steady way along the sidewalk in the opposite direction.

"Where are you going?" I asked it. "Hot date?"

I'd swear it let out a faint croak in answer before hopping on.

I approached the high school on the opposite side of the street, both to be a little stealthy and so I could scan the kids emerging from the wide front doors more easily. I'd barely seen my sister in seven years, but I recognized her the instant she stepped outside.

The sun caught on her wavy blond hair, which had always been a richer golden shade than my pale flax. She had sections of it woven into narrow braids that swung amid the loose strands. She hustled down the front walk amid her peers with her head low and her hands gripped around the straps of her backpack, not making eye contact with anyone. No waving good-bye to friends, no shooting flirty glances at a crush.

My stomach knotted. She didn't look all that okay right now. She looked… a lot like I'd probably looked back in middle school. Except I'd at least had a few casual acquaintances I might have nodded to on my way out.

Marisol had always been more mellow and affable than I'd been, even when she was little. What had changed?

Had *I* done this to her?

That question stalled me in my tracks for long enough that I almost lost her. Rather than heading in my general direction to make the two-mile trek home, she veered left and then around the corner out of sight. I gave myself a shove forward and hurried after her.

I'd been counting on approaching her on one of the quiet residential streets between the school and our house. Instead, she was heading toward the small shopping strip a couple of blocks away. Hanging half a block back and still on the opposite side of the road, I debated my best course of action.

Maybe somewhere more public would be better? She could feel safer knowing that there were more people around if she felt like she needed to call for help… to save her from me.

The thought twisted me up even more inside, but I put on a fresh burst of speed to pull ahead of my sister. Then I crossed the street and doubled back, slowing my pace so that I didn't barge right into her.

Marisol still had her head low, but that didn't mean she wasn't taking in her surroundings. When she was a couple of storefronts away from me, her chin jerked up and her gaze caught mine. She froze in place, her eyes widening.

"Mare," I said. My voice came out in a croak like one of those damned frogs had taken up residence in my throat. I cleared it and tried again. "Hey. I just—I wanted to see you. I didn't know if Mom and Wade even told you I was back in town."

I tried to keep my posture as non-threatening as possible, although it was hard to decide how to do that when I'd never felt particularly threatening in the first place. Marisol didn't move an inch. I couldn't tell if she was even breathing.

"Lily?" she whispered.

I guessed I must have looked at least a little different than I had the last time she'd seen me. And it'd been a long time.

I nodded slowly, pushing my mouth into a careful smile. "I'm home. I mean, kind of. Mom won't let me stay at the house." *Not that I'd have wanted to shack up with her and the dipshit again anyway*, my inner voice added. "She and Wade didn't want me to see you, but… you're my sister. You're the whole reason I came back here. I came as soon as the hospital would let me."

The mention of where I'd been for the last seven years made my chest clench up. I added quickly, "I don't—I can't remember what happened when they took me away. People have made it sound like you were there—like maybe I did something that hurt you. I know I'd never have meant to do that. I hope you know that too. Whatever happened, you can tell me, and I'll do whatever I can to prove it's never going to happen again."

A tiny crease had formed in Marisol's forehead, more like she was confused than nervous. But then her gaze darted from side to side, her shoulders tensing as she took in the pedestrians ambling by and the figures behind the store windows. She took a step back, still watching them rather than me.

My own forehead furrowed. She did seem scared, but… not of me. More like she was scared about who else might see her. See us?

Had Mom or Wade threatened her because she'd wanted to see me and they didn't agree? My hands clenched at my sides, and I forced them to relax before she could notice. The birthmark-like blotch on my arm started itching, as if it had secrets to spill. Too bad it couldn't speak.

"Please, just talk to me, Mare," I said quietly. "You know you could always count on me."

My sister drew in a shaky breath and yanked her gaze back to me. "You're all right? You're not, like, sick or something?"

Was that what they'd told her? I frowned. "No, I was never sick. The doctors just took a long time deciding that I had my head on straight. I've been totally cleared. One hundred percent sane." Although they might have revised that decision if they'd heard about the strange company I'd been inadvertently keeping lately.

"Oh." Marisol seemed to draw in on herself a little more with another flick of her eyes along the street.

"Who are you looking for?" I asked.

A little shudder ran through her. "I—no one. I just—I should go." She started to turn.

A bolt of panic shot through me. "No!" I forced my voice to soften. "Marisol, I just need to know what happened so I can make it right. *Were* you there? What did I do?"

She paused just long enough to catch my eye once more. The words tumbled out so fast they bled into each other. "You didn't hurt me. You didn't—I'm sorry."

She darted across the street and around another bend. My legs ached to run after her, but at the same moment, a police car cruised by along the street. My stance went rigid until it'd passed.

Marisol had said I hadn't hurt her. But I'd done something back then, something awful enough to get me locked away. If I chased her down, tried to force her to talk to me, that wouldn't make me look like any kind of model of stability.

I hadn't hurt her. But I couldn't help thinking after seeing her reaction that someone sure as hell had. Why had everyone talked as if I'd traumatized her somehow?

Suddenly I was sure of two things. The stories I'd been told weren't totally right… and my sister needed me in her life even more than I'd imagined. She needed my help.

I just had no idea with what or how to give it.

Chapter Eleven

Lily

Ultimately, talking with Marisol didn't really change anything about what I needed to do. It only made me ten times as determined to actually do it.

I had to be the most stable, sane, upstanding citizen Lovell Rise had ever seen, and when people stopped seeing me as a psycho, I could get some real answers. I could force Mom and Wade to let me have a proper conversation with my sister.

I just had to be sure they wouldn't have the slightest excuse to call the cops or the loony doctors to pick me up again.

I thought I'd get a break at work from the craziness that'd been following me around. Mart's Supermarket was the one big grocery store in Lovell Rise, off on the outskirts of town where people ventured when the mom'n'pop corner stores wouldn't quite do the trick. The place felt as big as a football stadium and as sterile as a doctor's office, all off-white walls and polished steel shelving. The air was always a bit too chilly, people always talked in hushed voices because the high ceiling tended to echo, and everything that happened there was utterly mundane.

At least, that's how it'd used to be. When I arrived for my late afternoon shift an hour after I'd seen Marisol, Burt Bower—the manager—was waiting near the row of cash registers.

He beckoned to me with one of his fat fingers. "Lily, a quick word?"

Even as I followed him over to the cramped office next to the stock rooms at the back, I assumed he wanted to talk to me about some normal job consideration. He needed me to work an extra shift next week or to cut my hours a little. I was packing the cereal boxes too tightly or stacking the cans too high. Something like that.

Instead, the second we stepped into the office, he turned and said, "What's this I'm hearing about some trouble between you and the police?"

A finger of ice traced down my back. Who'd he been hearing about that *from*? It wouldn't look good if I asked that instead of answering his question, though.

"That was a long time ago," I said quickly, deciding it was better not to mention that I didn't actually remember what the cops had done or why they'd been called in the first place. "I was only a kid—I had a bit of a breakdown. I didn't get in any legal trouble. I don't have a record." The job application hadn't required that I disclose mental health treatments or hospitalizations. I'd been able to put down the online high school degree I'd gotten while I was at St. Elspeth's, as well as my year in community college and summer internship, so I guessed my history had looked pretty normal.

The hospital hadn't *wanted* to give people an excuse to shun me when I'd returned to regular society. The only reason I'd run into problems at school was because of former classmates like Ansel spreading rumors. It hadn't seemed like anyone else in town cared all that much—if they even recalled—what'd happened seven years ago to some random teenager barely any of them had interacted with anyway.

But then, I didn't remember Burt being around back then. Maybe I just hadn't noticed him with typical teenage myopia, or maybe he was new to the area, so he couldn't have remembered anyway.

He was frowning, his doughy face dour. "I know there's no record. I called the police department to confirm. But it does raise some concerns. I hope I don't have to worry about you finding yourself in a questionable situation again."

I'd be able to guarantee that more easily if I had any fucking clue what the first "questionable situation" was, I muttered inwardly. Outside, I gave him my best placating smile. "I'm sure it won't be a problem. If there are any ways I can improve my work, just let me know."

Burt still looked uneasy, but he had to admit, "So far you've been doing just fine. Well, get on with your shift. It started five minutes ago."

Like it was my fault he'd dragged me over here for this conversation before I could get started. I managed not to roll my eyes at him and tried to lift my spirits by picturing a cat washing its ass on the rounded dome of his head. But as I hustled over to the stock room to pick up my first load, my stomach stayed knotted.

Who would have bothered to mention my past to the manager of the grocery store? I guessed it could have been anyone who'd found out at school and then noticed me working here. Trying to get me in trouble at my job was a huge step above harassing me at the college, though. Who had it in for me so much that they'd want to totally screw me over?

I'd have suspected Ansel, but he'd been the opposite of hostile since his sudden personality transplant. Unless that transplant had included a dose of multiple personality disorder? How the hell should I know what to think when he and his buddies were claiming to literally be ghosts possessing some of the biggest jerks at school?

It didn't matter. As long as I kept doing my job and keeping my nose clean, Burt and everyone else would have nothing real to complain about.

"That's right," I murmured to the jars of pickles I was adding to the shelf. "All in a nice row, pretty and shiny." Then I snapped my mouth shut. Getting caught talking to the merchandise wasn't going to win me any sanity points, even if it was a satisfying way of staving off boredom.

I focused on the clink and thunk of the bottles, cans, and boxes sliding into place. There was a beat to it when I got a rhythm going, something that could have gone well with a twang of country lyrics.

Those lyrics had started composing themselves in the back of my head when the last voice I wanted to hear, no matter how cheerful it was, rang out from the other end of the aisle.

"Lily! You can help me with my shopping."

My head jerked up, my heart already sinking. Ansel was standing by the canned vegetables—if it was still Ansel behind that pretty boy face with his hair dyed red and his features somehow softer-looking every time I saw him.

I couldn't exactly run away from him now without abandoning my shift. Gritting my teeth, I shuffled closer to shove cans of diced tomatoes onto the shelf near him.

"What are you doing here?" I muttered under my breath. "I told you guys to stay away from me."

As usual, the new Ansel seemed totally oblivious to my trepidation. "I had no idea you'd be here," he said, as if my presence was the best surprise he'd ever gotten across all his birthdays and Christmases. "I'm just looking to stock up. Got quite the appetite these days. What've you got around here that's really spicy? Or sour, that might work too. Mmm." He licked his lips. Which were annoyingly delectable lips, now that he'd drawn my attention to them.

It didn't look like there'd be any budging him before he'd gotten what he was looking for, so I figured my best bet was fulfilling his demands ASAP. I glanced at the shelf of veggies. "I don't think you're going to find much here… unless you want to chug pickled jalapenos."

I'd meant that as a clear non-starter, but Ansel brightened up like a kid who'd been offered a trip to the ice cream store and snatched several jars off the shelf, chucking them into the plastic basket he'd slung over his arm. The last one, he popped open and took a swig of chopped peppers and pickle juice right there in the aisle.

My jaw went slack. At this rate, it was going to fall off its hinges permanently around these weirdos.

I half-expected smoke to start billowing out of Ansel's ears like in an old cartoon, but he just grinned even wider as he screwed the lid back on. "Perfect. What else have you got in here like that?"

"You know, you're supposed to *pay* for things before you start eating them," I grumbled, motioning him farther down the aisle.

"We make a point of paying for as little as possible," he replied in the same cheery voice. "The Man's already got enough money."

I stopped in my tracks. "If you shop and dash on me, *I'm* the one who's going to get the blame, you know."

Ansel froze, his upbeat demeanor vanishing for just an instant. "I won't let that happen. I can cover these. Of course I wouldn't get you in trouble." His expression flashed back to a brilliant smile an instant later. "You never have to worry at all when we're around."

Past experience would indicate otherwise, my inner voice retorted.

I pointed him to the salsa jars, where he grabbed the ones labeled *Extra Hot*, and then the rows of various barbeque sauces. He popped open one with a ghost pepper warning and threw back a third of the bottle in one go. His eyes went briefly wide, and I'd swear a hint of a flame sputtered from his mouth along with his gleeful laugh. He did at least put the lid back on and stick it in his basket with the rest of his intended purchases.

"Why do you need my help finding stuff?" I asked quietly as I ushered him to the candy aisle. "How long ago did you supposedly die anyway? Didn't they have groceries back then?"

Ansel chuckled again. "It's only been about twenty years. Not that we could tell while we were in limbo, but now that we've been able to check the date, we know. A lot of the brands are different—there's tons of new products they didn't use to sell. I figure you can get me to the good stuff faster than I'll find it on my own. And so far that was right on the money." He beamed at me.

I sighed. "So glad to be of service."

My sarcasm went right over his head. "Then we're both happy," he said, and strode ahead of me with a bounce in his step to consider the rows of chip bags.

I still wasn't buying this whole undead thing, but it was possible that packaging and flavors had changed a fair bit in the past twenty years. It wasn't like I remembered what'd been on offer the year I was born. I motioned to the spicy nacho-flavored corn chips and salt-and-vinegar flavor potato chips, since he'd mentioned sour too. Ansel tossed in several bags of sour gummies, apparently unfazed by how heavy his basket must have been getting. Then I glanced over at the produce section.

"I mean, there's lemons," I said doubtfully.

"Right!" Ansel gave me a thumbs up and dashed over to scoop up a few handfuls of those.

Was he going to eat them on their own, like they were oranges or something? A shudder ran through me at the thought, but I guessed he could put whatever the hell he wanted in his mouth.

Feeling I'd completed my mission, I went back to the stock room to grab another cart. I'd just emerged when Ansel popped up seemingly out of nowhere, springing in front of me so abruptly a squeak slipped from my lips before I clamped them shut.

My glower had no effect on his good cheer. "I just wanted to say that I'm really happy we could spend a little time together like this," he said with that unshakeable smile. "You're getting used to us being back —that's fantastic."

I wouldn't have put it that way, but somehow I couldn't bring myself to go any farther to dampen his mood. "Well, go pay for that stuff," I said. "I've got to get back to my real job."

"Of course, of course." He gave me a joyful little wave and ambled off. To my relief, I saw him approach one of the cash registers. I wasn't going to get written up for aiding and abetting a shoplifter, at least.

And maybe Ansel's presence hadn't been so bad this once. He'd distracted me from my unsettling conversation with Burt. It might even have been comforting—just slightly—to have someone around for a little while who acted happy to be with me instead of like I was a loose cannon one spark away from exploding.

So I ended the shift in a little better mood than I started it off in. As I crossed the parking lot to my car in the far corner, where it was less likely to be noticed by the kinds of idiots who liked to write *Garbage bin* and *Tow this!* on it, I swung the frozen lasagna I'd bought for my dinner at my side and might even have smiled a tiny bit myself.

Then a convertible sped by on the street next to the parking lot, and the prick I barely had a chance to glance at in the passenger seat hollered, "Go back to the psycho ward, crazy cunt!" A mostly eaten carton of fries flew from his hand to smack into my chest, splattering my shirt—which I actually *liked*—with ketchup and grease.

Something in my mind went icily blank. I looked down at myself, not quite processing the mess plastered all over me.

The carton thumped to the ground. The convertible roared off. Footsteps pounded across the asphalt behind me.

"That fucker," Ansel snarled in a voice so different from the buoyant one he'd given me earlier that I did a double-take to make sure I hadn't mistaken someone else for him. But no, there was no mixing up that stark red hair and well-built body. Those didn't come in value packs.

He was glaring after the convertible, his hands clenched at his sides. He moved forward as if he was going to try to chase the damn thing down, but then his gaze darted to me, and his stance tensed even more. He looked me over.

"Did that asshole hurt you?" he demanded, his pale eyes flashing with searing fury.

A giggle that sounded hysterical even to my own ears tumbled out of me. "No. Not really. I'm just starting to wonder if I've somehow become a magnet that specifically attracts fast food, since I can't seem to go a day without getting some flung at me."

My chest was clenching up. As the humorless laugh died in my throat, the burn of tears abruptly seared in my eyes. I turned around and braced my hands against the side of the car, holding myself together as hard as I could.

I wasn't going to cry. It was just one more asshat being an asshat, someone who didn't know me at all. That jerkwad's opinion mattered less than a flea's fart. I wasn't going to let him or anyone else in this stupid town break me.

But it felt as if a crack were opening up inside me right now.

"Lily." I'd never heard my name said so tenderly. The next instant, Ansel was there beside me. He wrapped his muscular arms around me like he'd been trying to do since our encounter at the recruitment rally, and this time I didn't have the wherewithal to dodge. He hugged me gently but steadily, not minding that I didn't budge from the spot where I'd been standing.

"We're not going to let *anyone* hurt you," he said in a fierce whisper. "Not in any way. If I see that prick again—"

"No," I said through the lump in my throat. "I don't want *you* hurting anyone either."

"He fucking deserves it. First all those jackasses at the college, and now here where you work—they won't get away with this."

His words sunk in, and I realized that was the problem. Before, the harassment had all been at the college. Ansel—the old Ansel—and maybe a few of his friends had spread the word around about my supposed psychotic tendencies, but I'd been able to escape the jeers whenever I'd left campus.

What had just happened, both the convertible driver and Burt pulling me aside, meant the plague was spreading. People were starting to talk about me all through Lovell Rise.

No matter where I went, they'd be watching me, judging me. Evaluating whether every word I said and every move I made showed that I was on the edge of fracturing into insanity again.

And none of them had any more clue what I'd actually done than I did. The one person who definitely knew wouldn't talk to me about it. I was fucked to the moon and back.

A wave of despair rolled over me, threatening to pull me down into its hopeless undertow, and I clung to the one solid thing I had: Ansel. Or whoever he claimed to be. He was *here*, holding me close, murmuring reassurances by my ear that I'd stopped really listening to.

I turned toward him, pressing my face into his chest, and his arms tightened around me. He stroked one hand over my hair.

"We've got you," he said. "We would have been there for you all along if we'd known where you were. Now that we're here with you properly, we're never letting anyone beat you down again."

My body gradually relaxed into his. As the wrenching emotions that'd threatened to overwhelm me dwindled in the warmth of his embrace, I became increasingly aware of the solid planes of muscle beneath the thin fabric of the shirt I was clutching. Of the way his bright, emphatic tenor hummed through my ears into my nerves, settling them.

And had Ansel always smelled this good? I didn't know if I'd ever gotten close enough to him to tell before. He was all sunny amber with a whiff of musk.

Something stirred inside me with a hitch of my pulse and a spike of heat that shot through my belly. When Ansel ran his fingers over my hair again, a tingle spread through my skin in their wake. My heart thumped a little harder, with a weird mix of anticipation and fear.

What was I thinking? What was I *feeling*? How could any part of me—?

I knew sexual attraction when it came over me. After all, I'd spent my teen years in a hospital, not a nunnery. I'd gotten away with makeout sessions and a brief hookup with a guy who'd done a quick stint at St. Elspeth's a couple of years ago, and had a short relationship with a classmate in the community college that'd been more friends-with-benefits than anything else… and not so much with the friends part.

I just hadn't expected to feel it now—with this guy—like this…

Another flare of longing rippled through me, hotter than I could ever remember experiencing before, at least not with someone who'd barely done more than hug me. Some part of me wanted to meld right into Ansel's body this very second.

And it seemed like it wasn't just me. Ansel swallowed audibly and eased back just a few inches so he could meet my gaze. A hungry light danced in his hazel eyes, tempered by a hint of confusion. His hand slipped over my hair to my cheek and rested there, his thumb teasing over my cheekbone in a way that made my pulse skip another beat. Then a new smile stretched his lips, this one softer and so sweet it made me ache to see it.

Deep down, I knew it was just for me. I wanted to fall right into the look on his face. I'd never thought he was so amazingly good-looking before, but like this…

"I forgot," he murmured in a tone full of awed exhilaration. "I forgot what it's like to have a woman in my arms. And you *are* a woman now, aren't you, Lily? I can't forget *that*."

I didn't want him to forget it—and at the same time, his words terrified me.

What the hell was I doing? This maniac had been going around thrashing anyone who said a harsh word to me and talking about coming back from the dead, and I was an inch away from mashing lips with him.

Now who was the insane one?

A flood of cold washed away the heat that had kindled in me. I jerked away from Ansel, a tremor running through my body that was desire and panic colliding.

"I have—I have to go home," I babbled, and scrambled for my keys.

Ansel didn't try to stop me as I dove into the driver's seat. He just stood there and watched, close enough that I had to veer to the side to avoid running him over as I pulled out of the parking spot. I'd swear I felt his gaze on me even after I'd rounded the bend and left him and the lot behind.

I squirmed in my seat, trying and failing not to notice how damp my panties had gotten. These guys might be dangerous in ways I'd never even considered.

Chapter Twelve

Nox

The worst part of being an official authority figure was that people expected you to actually go and be officially authoritative about things. To other people. On subjects you probably didn't care about, because you weren't really the guy they thought you were anyway.

It was a heavy burden, and I wasn't enjoying bearing it.

I'd shown up for today's lecture that Mr. Grimes was supposed to be giving because a secretary of something or other had called me specifically to remind me, and I'd been in such a low mood that I'd thought bossing around some dorks might improve my spirits. I was in a low mood because I'd just gotten back from visiting Gram's grave.

I hadn't even known she was in a grave until this morning.

Gram had been both mom and dad to me when my actual Mom and Dad had flaked out on us to run around getting stoned and funding their habit with petty crimes. She'd *always* been there, even though she barely had enough for herself. I'd sworn that I was going to set her up with a better life as soon as I really built a name for myself with the Skullbreakers: a new, nicer house, a fancy car like she'd always admired, takeout every day of the week…

But before I'd gotten a chance to do much of that, those fuckers who'd stormed our clubhouse had pumped me full of bullets and dumped me in the marsh. And while I'd been gone, Gram had passed on without me.

I hadn't been there for her, and now I wasn't being there for Lily either. I couldn't even get her to *let* me look after her.

This whole rising from the dead thing wasn't opening anywhere near as many doors as I'd been counting on. I'd have to chew Kai out about that the next time I saw him.

But for now, I was lecturing the dorks who were taking Mr. Grimes's class. Fine. If they wanted to learn something, I'd teach them a thing or ten. I'd bet I knew a billion times more about actual juvenile delinquency than the nitwit I'd possessed had anyway.

When the forty or so students had filtered into the room and taken their seats, I clambered onto the chair and then onto the desk, where I had the best vantage point of the entire room. Several eyebrows shot up, but everyone fell totally silent.

Ha. I was already better at commanding their attention than their former professor.

Lily wasn't here. I had the vague memory that it'd been a morning class when she'd had to deal with Mr. Grimes. This must be another section of the same course. Maybe another year? It could even have been another subject—I hadn't exactly committed the prof's schedule to memory. I didn't see how it really mattered.

I was nursing a ginger beer in one hand and chowing down on an apple fritter from the campus bakery with the other. If I didn't keep fueling myself every hour or so, it felt like little lightning bolts were going off inside my stomach. Before I'd experienced it, I might have thought that eating lightning would be cool, but I could now say it was very definitely not.

I popped the rest of the fritter into my mouth, chewed hard, chased the swallow with a swig of ginger beer, and peered over the rows of seats. "So. Juvenile delinquency. Why don't we switch things up? I've associated with all kinds of juvenile delinquents. I was a pretty awesome one myself. Ask me what you want to know, and I can tell you all kinds of shit that doorstop of a textbook won't cover."

A girl in the second row raised her hand tentatively. She was going to need to learn to buck up if she didn't want to get trampled in this world. I waved at her, and she said, even more timidly, "Sir… are you all right?"

I narrowed my eyes at her. "I'm completely fine. Better than ever. Do you have a problem with creative teaching strategies?"

She paled. "Um, no, not at all, I just wanted to make sure."

I glowered around the room. "Anyone else have a problem with me teaching this class however the hell I want to teach it? Speak up, and I'll demonstrate some juvenile delinquency on your asses right now."

Everyone stayed totally silent and rigid in their seats. Another score for me.

I paced from one side of the desk to the other, shoving back the taunting image of Gram's plain gravestone when it rose up in the back of my mind. "Doesn't anyone have anything to ask about the actual topic of the course? This is a rare opportunity for you to learn something real around here. But I guess you all prefer the neat and pretty version on paper, huh?"

A guy in the front row cleared his throat. "Well… what did you mean when you said you *were* a juvenile delinquent?"

I chuckled darkly. "I wouldn't have called myself that. But the cops sure would have. It's a dog-eat-dog world, right? And you've got to be the top dog if you want things to turn out in your favor. I took what I wanted when I wanted it, crushed anyone who got in my way, raised up the guys who'd have my back, and we had it made. Just about."

My mood abruptly soured even more. Those fucking pricks who'd blasted up our clubhouse and screwed up all our plans… I wasn't even sure which rival gang they'd belonged to. They hadn't bothered with introductions before they'd opened fire.

A girl at the back raised her hand and started talking before I'd even called on her. "Like… what kind of crimes are we talking about?"

I let out a snort. "Whatever did the trick. Robbery, extortion, gambling, blah, blah, blah. You want a list?"

"Is this some kind of joke?" a guy off to the side demanded.

I fixed my gaze on him. "Do I look like I'm joking?"

I hopped off the desk and strode right over to him. This body had felt too small when I'd first inhabited it, but with every passing hour, my spirit expanded its limits. Mr. Grimes had never packed this much muscle, that was for sure.

The idiot who'd shot off his mouth cowered in his seat. I swatted him across the head anyway. "Does that *feel* like a joke?"

"N-no, sir," he mumbled. I hoped he'd brought a change of pants, because he looked ready to wet the ones he had on.

"You can't go pushing us around!" another guy protested.

I spun around and stalked over to the twerp. Grabbed him by the front of his shirt and yanked him right out of his desk. Oh, yes, just a few workouts in my soul's new home, and all my old brawn was coming back.

I cocked my head and aimed a jagged smile at the guy. "Funny, it seems like I can." Then I shoved him back into his seat. He landed there with his mouth agape, looking like a total goon.

All at once, I was fed up. What was the point in trying to teach these idiots anything when they cared more about keeping their existence all nice and peaceful than finding out how the world really worked?

I marched back to the desk and swung my arm toward the door. "Okay, we're done for the day. I hope the next time I see you, you're ready to stop whining like a bunch of asslickers."

A few *very* hushed murmurs passed between the students as they hustled out, but no one dared to even look at me after my demonstration of who was boss. I set my hands on my hips, wishing I could feel happier about my success, and waited until the last of them had filed out. You didn't want to turn your back on anyone who might have it in for you, even if they were asslickers.

When I strode out of the lecture hall a minute later, two very stern and stodgy men were standing just outside. They both took a small step back in the wake of my exit, their postures stiffening as if they thought I might take a swing at them. Good. I would if they gave me a hard time.

"Leon," one of them said in a hesitant voice a lot like the girl who'd first spoken up in class. More twerps. "We've had some... concerning reports about your recent behavior in class."

Had one of the dorks gone running off to the dean that quickly? Or maybe during class someone had been twitting or tick-tocking or whatever the hell it was kids did now on those tiny computer-cameras they still called "phones" for some ungodly reason. I hadn't seen anyone actually talking into one my entire time on campus.

Either way, my response was the same. I shrugged. "I'm trying out some new teaching methods. More of a hands-on approach. If they can't handle it, they probably shouldn't be gearing up to work with criminals, huh?"

The second man grimaced. His gaze lingered on my hair. The hairdresser I'd gone to had matched my old style almost perfectly, but this dude didn't look suitably impressed.

"Well, I suppose you might have a bit of a point there," he said. "But we do have policies about student and staff behavior, which include expectations of language and physical aggression… I'm sure you can understand that there are lines we need to draw, or the legal ramifications could be immense."

I felt like he could have said all that in half as many smaller words and he'd have sounded a lot less pompous. But from the looks of him, pompous was probably what he was going for.

I spread my arms. "You hired me to teach because of my expertise or whatever. I'm teaching. Or at least trying to, if the kids get their heads out of their asses."

The first man coughed. "See that right there—throwing around that sort of inflammatory language—"

I rolled my eyes. "Are you serious? *Asses*? We've all got them, and a shitload of people around here *are* them, so I'm going to say it."

They both winced, possibly at "shitload." I'd better not pull out "motherfucker" or "cuntbugger," or they might have a joint heart attack.

Actually, maybe we'd all be better off if they did.

Before I could test that theory, the second man rubbed his mouth and said, "Yes, I see the problem is as severe as reported. I'm going to recommend that you take a leave of absence and talk to your doctor, perhaps about a referral to a psychologist?"

"Are you calling me fucking nuts?" I demanded, fixing him with a glare and stepping forward to loom on him.

"Uh, no, not exactly—only you seem like you could use a break from the stresses of your course load," he babbled. "We could discuss the details later. It'd be paid leave at least to start, I'm sure—"

The full meaning of what he was offering sank in. A grin spread across my face. "You're saying I'd get paid to *not* teach classes."

"Well, er, yes. Essentially. While you get some help."

I wasn't here to get help but to give it, but it'd be a heck a lot easier to look after Lily if I didn't have these academic twits breathing down my neck. I slapped the man on the shoulder. "You should have said so from the start. I'm in. Or out, I guess. Looking forward to not seeing you around!"

I set off down the hall with a bit more of a spring in my step, glad to have at least that one problem off my plate. It wasn't as if I could have kept on being Mr. Grimes the professor forever anyway. As soon as we got all the assholes off Lily's back, the Skullbreakers were going to have a grand reunion. I looked forward to seeing the whole town piss themselves then.

I'd just come outside when furtive voices caught my attention. A small cluster of students was standing off to the side, gesturing to each other like they'd been electrocuted with excitement.

"…stuffed her right in the trunk," one of them was saying.

I drew up short and sidled a little closer without glancing at them openly. My senses were already jangling, and for good reason, because the next thing I heard was, "She's *really* going to go psycho on them now."

"I think that's the idea. They're saying she's screwed with their friend's head, and maybe some other people too. Gotten them wrapped around her finger somehow. The one guy broke someone's *arm.* So they're going to prove how loony she really is."

My jaw clenched so hard I practically cracked my teeth. I barged over to the cluster and grabbed the guy who'd said the last bit by the shoulder. With one sharp heave, I sent him stumbling into the side of the building, barreling after him so I could pin him there the second his back hit the bricks.

"You're talking about Lily?" I growled.

The guy stared at me, his mouth gaping. "I—the girl they're saying is psycho. I don't remember her name."

"What the hell are you doing?" one of his friends barked, and I swung around just long enough to clock that guy in the face. He doubled over, clutching his bruised cheek. I didn't bother to tell him he'd look better with some color in it.

"Where did they take her?" I said, turning back to the guy at the wall. "*Who* took her?"

"I—I'm not sure—I—"

Fuck that stammering. I snatched one of his hands and squeezed his little finger between my forefinger and thumb. Some guys like to go for the big pain all the time, but if you have half a brain, you figure out that a whole bunch of little pains often gets the job done better. There's time to anticipate in between. Time to realize it's only getting worse and worse. And it saved me having to work any harder than a quick twist of my hand…

Snap. The bones in the guy's finger fractured. He yelped, all the color draining from his face. When he tried to jerk away from me, I slammed him back into the wall with my other hand on his chest. "You're staying right there until you tell me who has Lily and where they took her. Get talking!"

"I think—it was that guy named Adam or Aaron or something—his friends are the ones who got pissed off. They didn't tell me anything about it."

Ansel. The fucking king of campus who'd started this whole mess. As if Ruin's revision to his personality hadn't been a stunning improvement.

I grasped the guy's ring finger and broke it with another swift flick. He hissed through his teeth, his eyes squeezing shut.

"They didn't tell you, but you heard anyway," I said. "Where. Did. They. Go?"

"They mentioned something about the docks," he spat out in a strangled voice. "That's all I know. I swear."

I believed him, but he'd also pissed me off taking so long to get to the point. So I broke his middle finger for good measure before I pushed away from him. I glared at him and the friends standing dumbstruck around him.

"No one touches or insults or even *thinks* anything about Lily Strom again," I informed them. "Or I can break a whole lot more than that. Any questions?"

Like good little students, they quickly shook their heads. My mouth pulled into a grim smirk. "Class dismissed."

As they dashed off, converging around their injured friend, I strode toward the staff parking lot where I'd left Mr. Grimes's car. I fished his phone out of my pocket at the same time, but it took almost the whole journey there before I found the right icon out of the million or so on the screen to get into the address book and find my crew's numbers.

"Kai," I snapped, getting ahold of him first. "Get the others. We're going out to the docks. Someone's got Lily."

"How the fuck— On it," Kai replied without hesitation.

In a just world, I'd have had a sweet bike to hop onto and roar down the street on. Instead, I was stuck with the professor's decade-old Nissan, which looked like a box on wheels, and not even a pretty box. I scowled at it as I unlocked it, swearing to myself that I'd trade it in for a proper ride the first chance I got. Then I was gunning the engine, nothing on my mind except for getting to the docks ASAP.

And oh boy, were the fuckers out there *not* going to be happy to see me.

Chapter Thirteen

Lily

THE CAR JERKED TO A HALT, throwing me against the back of the trunk. I winced, grateful that I'd wrapped my arm around my head to cushion it. I'd tried banging and yelling for the first five minutes of the drive, but all I'd gotten was sore hands and an aching throat. Since then, I'd gone into defensive mode.

It wasn't the car's fault I'd been shoved in here anyway. I had nothing against it. If anyone was going to end up sore, I'd rather it was the dipshits who'd tossed me in here.

Assault. Abduction. Hopefully not too many more a-words to come. And they called *me* crazy?

A tiny bit of air filtered into the dark space of the trunk, with enough of a marshy scent to tip me off that we were near the lake even before the lead dipshit swung the top open.

He glowered down at me with a hard-edged grin, two of his companions flanking him. I recognized them from Ansel's usual gaggle of friends. Or maybe it was more like a cult, given the lengths they were going to on his behalf.

At least, I assumed this had to do with Mr. Popular and his sudden personality transplant. I couldn't see them acting without his guidance otherwise.

Does your mother know you're offering up human sacrifices? my inner voice snarked, but my mouth stayed tightly shut. I didn't know how to play this situation yet—and as much as I was trying not to let it show, I was pretty freaked out. My heart was thudding double-time, and a cold sweat had broken out down my back. I couldn't even bring myself to imagine bizarre beasts frolicking on their heads.

These goons had literally tossed me in the trunk of their car and driven me to the outskirts of town with evil intentions in mind. I had no idea what to expect from them next. They were worried about me going on some kind of manic rampage while they were already in the middle of one.

The hypocrisy was intense around here.

"Out you come," the leader announced, and yanked me up by the arm so hard my shoulder banged the rim of the trunk. I stumbled out onto the gravel road, my legs wobbly after being cramped in that tight space for so long. His friends, including the fourth who'd just gotten out of the car, spun me around and pushed me toward the scene waiting up ahead.

They'd brought me to the docks. The sagging wooden structures arced along the shoreline and jutted over the murky water at the spot where the marshy coastline gave way to stony beach and open water.

Apparently, several decades ago, some mayor had built up this spot figuring it'd make for lovely family picnics and fishing excursions. But then acid rain had killed all the decent-sized fish and it'd turned out docks were easier to build than to maintain, so the whole project had turned into a decrepit mess that no one bothered with except bored teenagers and asshats like the guys around me.

And maybe the smell had something to do with it too. I kind of like the marshland scents in the marsh proper, all wild and seaweedy. Out here, I got the less pleasant notes of rotten fish—from the old fisherman's shack at the base of the dock area—and gasoline—from the boats that occasionally cruised by from farther down the lake. No watercraft hung around here except an old rowboat that had taken on so much water only an inch of the bow still protruded above the waterline like one last, plaintive cry for help.

There was no one *I* could call out to for help. The lake was still, no boats out on the water on this hazy fall day, no teenagers doing cannonballs into depths that really weren't deep enough for it or jumping across the gaps where boards had outright splintered away. Just me and the four stooges who'd dragged me here.

"You know, this is technically kidnapping," I found myself babbling as they prodded me toward the longest dock. "I'm not sure you've totally thought this through. If you figure I'm so dangerous, shouldn't you be staying away from me, not forcing me to hang out with you? I'm sure there are lots of other people who'd volunteer to keep you company if you're so lonely."

"Shut up," the leader snapped, and got out his phone. So did one of his friends. They held them up in a way that told me they'd started recording me. "You've already fucked up Ansel. We're staying here until you admit what you did to him or let loose all the crazy you've been pretending you're over. We know *something's* rotten in that head of yours."

Um, no, that would be the ancient fish guts over there, I thought but managed not to say out loud. Provoking them was seeming like less and less a good idea by the second.

I looked for a way to dash past them, but they kept in a close semicircle, herding me up the dock. They all had at least fifty pounds and a several inches on me. Even if I managed to dodge around one of them, they'd tackle me in two seconds flat.

Could I make up some story about Ansel? Tell them he'd been bullying me so intently he'd tripped over his shoelaces and hit his head, so it was brain damage and really not my fault after all?

Somehow I didn't think they were going to buy that.

The boards creaked under my feet. I had to tear my eyes away from my harassers to make sure I didn't step through one of the gaps or a crumbling plank on the verge of becoming one. Our march was starting to turn into a demented game of hopscotch.

One of the guys scooped a rusted can off the ground and hurled it at me. It glanced off my shoulder. Another snatched up a long stick and jabbed me with it.

I bit my tongue to keep the acidic remark I wanted to make inside. *You know what they say about guys who carry around big sticks. Overcompensating much?*

The guys kept herding me on until I was just a couple of steps from the end of the dock. The water lapped gently at the aged supports. It might have been a peaceful setting if not for the douche-nozzles penning me in.

"Come on," the leader said, waving his phone as his friend swung the stick at me again. "Are you going to dance for us, psycho girl? You're really just going to stand there and take it? We can dunk you right in the lake if that's what it takes to set you off."

I stared firmly at the cameras. "There's nothing to set off. There's nothing wrong with me, and I had nothing to do with whatever's going on with Ansel."

"Oh, yeah?" another guy said. "He's sure been hanging around you a lot lately. Talking about you. Attacking people over you. Breaking the *bones* of people who used to be his friends over you. Doesn't sound like that has nothing to do with you."

"Peyton says she saw you hanging all over him, getting him riled up," the third guy added.

I didn't have any idea who "Peyton" even was or why she was making up lies about me, but I was sure of one thing.

"I don't have any control over what he says or does," I retorted. "I thought you were all saying I'm crazy, not that I'm some kind of voodoo sorceress."

"But somehow this all started when you came into town, and now he's totally fixated on you," the leader shot back. "You've done *something*. Everything started going crazy the moment you got back into Lovell Rise. You don't belong at the college, and we want you out of here."

You're not really giving me much opportunity to leave, my inner voice said. I glanced down at the greenish water.

At the same moment, a frog leapt right out of it onto the edge of the dock. I looked at it, and it looked at me as if to say, *Where do we go from here?*

As if I knew.

An itch prickled from the mark on the underside of my arm. My chest started to constrict around an uncomfortable hum that spread up through my lungs. I dragged in a breath, trying to steady myself. I couldn't let these asswipes break me down.

What if I simply jumped into the water and swam away from them? I could paddle off into the reeds where they wouldn't be able to see me, wait them out until they got tired and went home. Of course, that could mean hours crouching in the muck and the wet in the autumn chill, probably getting hypothermia, and then walking all the way home as an ice cube in the dark.

Understandably, I hesitated.

Staying on the dock was seeming like a worse option by the second. The guy with the stick rammed it at my thigh. The other one who wasn't recording spat at me. He missed, the glob of his spit dropping to the boards by the toe of my sneakers, but I couldn't call that much of a win. The hum inside me expanded, my hands shaking.

Then a rumble sounded in the distance and quickly rose into a roar. Three cars came tearing up the gravel road, spewing pebbles and grit everywhere.

My tormenters' heads whipped around. The cars slammed to a halt around theirs, and four figures sprang out.

Mr. Grimes. Vincent. Zach. And my kidnappers' good buddy Ansel.

Relief and horror smacked into me together, choking me up. I couldn't tell whether I was happy to see them or twice as terrified as before. But I didn't have much time to debate the issue with myself.

My four self-proclaimed protectors didn't waste time hashing things out with words. They lunged at Ansel's friends with a whoop of a battle cry and a feral snarl. And then things really went crazy.

Vincent—scrawny, nerdy Vincent, who'd somehow gotten significantly less scrawny in the past few days—slammed into the guy who'd spat at me with a one-two-three flurry of punches that left the guy's lip split and his eye swollen shut like he'd just gone through a four-hour torture session.

The guy wheeled around like he was thinking of escaping by jumping into the lake like I'd been considering a moment ago, and Vincent helped him along with a kick in the ass. He hit the water in a clumsy belly flop.

As that guy thrashed around in the water like a half-beached fish, groaning and muttering, Mr. Grimes let out a roar and slashed at the leader of the bunch with a handful of little barbed whips—old fishing lines he must have grabbed from near the fishing shack, I realized. The tiny rusty hooks caught on the guy's nose, forehead, and chin, and he shrieked like a little kid.

"Look what I caught," Mr. Grimes said with a broad grin. He took the opportunity to snatch the guy's phone, crack it over his knee, and shove it into its owner's mouth so far the guy gagged. Then he pushed him into the lake after his friend.

Beefy Zach had slimmed down since the football incident, but he still barreled into the other amateur documentarian without breaking a sweat. He heaved the guy right over his shoulder and snickered as he swung his opponent around so his head smacked into one of the dock posts. Grabbing the back of the stooge's jeans, he yanked them up so high the guy hissed through his teeth and folded them over the pointed top of the post to hang him there in an endless wedgie.

And Ansel, dear ol' Ansel who my kidnappers had been supposedly defending, let out a sound somewhere between a cackle and a growl as he bounded into the fray. He yanked the stick from the last guy's hands to ram it against the guy's throat. While the prick sputtered, Ansel kneed him in the back so hard his knees buckled. With a triumphant whoop, he brought the stick down on the guy's head hard enough to split it in half. Then he held the pieces as if considering stabbing them into his opponent's temples to turn him into some kind of grotesque reindeer.

I'd stood frozen at the end of the dock during that entire barrage of action. Abruptly, my voice broke from my throat. "No! Don't—don't *kill* them." I found I couldn't quite bring myself to care about anything that fell short of literal murder. But somewhere in the back of my mind, images of cop cars and the guys in handcuffs were flashing like a siren, and I… didn't want that.

Ansel glanced at me and hesitated.

"It'll just make everything worse," I added. "For *you*, not just for them."

Next to him, Zach sighed and sneered at the guy squirming on the post. He picked up the phone the dipshit had dropped, snapped a picture, and tapped the screen until there was the sound of the image soaring off. "I hope everyone on your Contacts list enjoys that," he said, tossing the device beneath the guy's feet.

Ansel settled for rapping the sticks on the guy's head like he was performing a drum solo, only stopping when his former friend groaned.

"Got a headache?" he asked, smiling fiercely as he tossed the sticks aside. "You only have a *head* still because she asked. You'd better remember to show her nothing but gratitude for that from now on."

Mr. Grimes whistled and whirled a few more hooked lines in a circle by his hand, watching the asshats in the lake. "Should I see if I can hook some bully fish and hang them out to dry? We don't have to kill them ourselves. We can leave them on the verge and let nature take its course."

I didn't have any sympathy for my tormentors, but my stomach turned at the thought of ordering their deaths. "No. Just tell them to get out of here. You've hurt them plenty already."

One of the guys whimpered as if in agreement. Mr. Grimes gave a huff and glowered down at them. "If you're gone from my sight in ten seconds, I won't decide I'd rather listen to my gut than hers."

They splashed and staggered out of the water, bleeding and swaying. As they dashed for their car, the one sprawled on the dock lurched to his wedgied-companion. He hauled the guy down so abruptly they tumbled over together in a tangle of limbs that flailed like an overturned spider before they managed to scramble for dry land. Vincent gave one a boot to the butt to hurry him on his way.

The stooges were in such a hurry they collided with each other and tumbled over each other trying to dive into their vehicle like clowns into a car that shouldn't hold them. Then they were racing away with a cough of the exhaust.

A smile sprang across Ansel's face. He bobbed on his feet with a whoop of victory. "That felt *good.* Laying down the real law with those fuckers." He made a few hasty punches at the air.

Mr. Grimes's smile was grimmer but still satisfied. "They shouldn't have gotten their hands on Lily in the first place." He caught my gaze. "We're not leaving you alone like that again. I don't care what you have to say about it."

My legs trembled under me. I swiped my hand over my face, my throat so tight it took a moment for me to speak. "Is this really better? You think they're going to be *nicer* to me after you went to town on their asses?"

His eyebrows shot up. "You'd rather we let them keep thrashing you?"

My hand dropped to the spot where the stick had jabbed me the hardest. I was going to have a bruise. But all the same…

"They were looking for an excuse to say I'm trouble. Now they have one, don't they? They were upset in the first place because Ansel's been acting so weird. I… I'm glad they're gone, but when word gets around tomorrow…"

Oh, God, what was I going to be dealing with then? Would anyone believe me that I hadn't put these guys up to this fight somehow?

Mr. Grimes shook his head. "We're not backing down. No way, no how. If they come at you again, then we make them pay even more. That's how it goes from now on."

"But—"

"No arguments. We tried your way, and they made you walk the fucking plank. Not one of those pricks is getting his hands on you ever again."

I inhaled, and the trembling spread through my whole body. I wanted to just get out of here, but the four of them were standing between me and the foot of the dock.

Mr. Grimes stepped up to me, and I was struck by how he'd changed too. He seemed taller now, and broader, and his chin seemed to have filled out into more of a square than a point. Between that and the spiky crimson-tipped hair, he barely passed for my professor at all.

He rested his hand on my shoulder, renewed fury burning in his dark blue eyes as he looked me over. "They did a number on you, but you're okay now. We're going to make sure you're okay. We're here for real, and no one's getting through us. I'm going to keep telling you that until you believe me."

I hugged myself. "I just want—I just wanted things to be normal."

He chuckled dryly and rubbed his hand up and down my arm. "You've never been normal. Normal's for losers. You're with us, Minnow, just like you're meant to be, and we can show you ten times better than any fucking *normal*."

Minnow. The nickname sank into my brain with a spike of adrenaline.

I stared at him. My voice came out in a whisper. "What did you just call me?"

Mr. Grimes—or the man who wasn't really Mr. Grimes anymore—grinned. "Minnow. Like old times, when you were a little thing splashing around in the marsh like you were going to learn to breathe water. Are you going to complain about *that* now? I guess I can come up with a more fitting one since you're not so little anymore."

No. It couldn't be.

I gaped at him. He… He knew. In therapy, I'd talked a little about the imaginary friends who'd occupied so much of my free time, but I'd never gotten into that much detail. I'd never told anyone—and it'd always been him talking to me when he called me that name, not the other way around, so no one could have overheard—*no one* could have known about that…

Except the guy who'd coined the nickname in the first place.

Swallowing hard, I studied every plane of his face, every angle of his body, as if I'd be able to recognize the hazy impressions of those ephemeral presences in this new manifestation. "It's… *How* did you know that?"

He squeezed my shoulder. "How could I forget? Technically we rose from the dead last week with Kai's little trick, but really *you* brought us back to life ages before that. If it wasn't for you, we'd have faded away into that numb nothingness. Fuck that."

"We all remember, Waterlily," Ansel said, taking a step closer. At the second familiar nickname, my heart stuttered.

Zach shrugged. "We've been trying to tell you all along, kid."

Vincent shot him a look. "She's not a kid anymore. But that doesn't mean she doesn't need us. She's our Lily." He shot me a hesitant smile. "Or maybe Lil when the mood is right."

My head was spinning. How could their crazy story be true? How could they be the formless figures who'd romped through my childhood games? How could my imaginary friends actually be the ghosts of a bunch of murdered guys? How could those ghosts have stolen totally new lives?

But either I'd hallucinated most of the past week… or any other explanation I could come up with was just as impossible.

They were here. My protectors, my friends, my voices in the dark. And however that'd happened, they'd made it more than clear that I wasn't getting rid of them. I wasn't even sure I'd want to anymore.

I couldn't run away from this insanity anymore.

I drew my spine up straighter and looked each of them in the face. "I think you'd better come back to my apartment, and I'll let you really explain this time."

What was the worst that could happen?

No, wait, after the day I'd just had, I didn't really want the answer to that.

Chapter Fourteen

Lily

If I'd thought having the guys around would somehow feel less weird now that I'd started to believe they were who they said they were —and not who they continued to kind of look like—I'd been wrong. It was still absolutely fucking bizarre.

They burst into the apartment like a storm of clashing air currents. Ansel bounded through the space, back to his now-typical cheerful energy, and stopped with a smile in front of the old boombox that I'd found in the apartment when I moved in. He flicked through the radio stations, evaluating one after another and shaking his head.

Vincent moved in his more languid way toward the futon. He sank into it on one side of the deadly dip and leaned forward to nudge the items I'd left on the crate that served as an end table next to him. For whatever reason, he seemed to think the novel I'd been reading belonged on top of my empty juice glass, and that the sociology textbook next to them should be tilted at a forty-five degree angle.

Mr. Grimes barreled through the kitchen-living-dining room like a human-shaped tank, his gaze sweeping this way and that as if he thought there might be more tormentors lurking under the table or behind the fridge. He even checked inside the microwave. I guessed I should be grateful he didn't comment on the bits of food splattered on the inside.

I was going to clean it, really! In all the free time I'd have approximately never from now.

Zach only took a few steps inside before stopping with a contemplative air that was starting to seem almost normal behind those new glasses. He narrowed his eyes, making a similar if less active scan of the room to what Mr. Grimes had.

"You haven't had anyone over since we were here," he said—an observation, not a question.

I gave him a baleful glance. "I don't exactly have a thrilling social life, in case you haven't noticed. I didn't even mean to have *you* guys over the first time."

"Fair," he said with a vaguely approving nod, as if I'd passed a test I hadn't known I was taking.

Ansel settled on a hard rock station spewing screeching guitars and thunderous drums into the room. At a hard look from Mr. Grimes, who I was gathering was the boss of the bunch just like he would have been if the other guys had been his students, he nudged the volume down. Then he wandered over to my fridge. He swung the door wide and peered in, his tongue coming out to flick over his lips.

The gesture brought back the image of his face so close to mine yesterday, his arms around me, his warmth and scent enveloping me. An equally uninvited flare of heat tingled through my belly.

He straightened up abruptly with an abashed look. "We shouldn't eat any of Lily's food. It's for her."

Vincent waved toward the door. "There's all that stuff in your car."

"Right!"

Ansel all but skipped out of the apartment and returned in a flash with his arms laden with bags of the spicy chips I'd pointed out to him yesterday. He handed one to each of the guys and then produced a lemon he'd also grabbed. Before my horrified eyes, he dug into it with his teeth to break the peel and then squeezed sour juice all over the contents of his chip bag.

That right there was the scariest thing I'd seen all day.

I managed not to grimace as he popped the first few chips into his mouth and chewed with a blissful expression, but I almost sprained my face with the effort. To divert myself, I sank down onto the futon opposite Vincent and swiped my hands back over my hair.

"Okay," I said. "This is all still really confusing to me. And impossible-sounding. So can you start from the beginning and explain to me—slowly—who you are and what you're doing here?"

Maybe I shouldn't have been surprised that Zach took the lead when it came to giving explanations rather than orders. He spun one of the chairs at the table to face me and dropped into it.

"We were dead," he said. "Someone mowed us down in our clubhouse and dumped our bodies in the marsh—weighted down so they wouldn't float and be found."

"Your clubhouse," I repeated. "What kind of club? Why would anyone want to murder you?"

"We had a gang," Mr. Grimes put in. "*My* gang. The Skullbreakers. It must have been rivals who wanted our territory."

A gang. These were gangsters.

Somehow that realization didn't surprise me. The extreme violence I'd already seen them commit might have had something to do with that.

I did remember, from the muddled blur our past conversations had become in my memory—"You have names. I mean, obviously you do. But you're not really… the guys you took over or however exactly that worked."

Zach gave me a pleased little smile that warmed me more than was optimal. "That's right. Zach Oberly kicked the bucket when I claimed this body. I'm Malachi Quinto. But everyone calls me Kai, so it's probably better if you do too."

"Kai." I studied him for a long moment, as if I could mold the name to this face in my memory. It wasn't just his dyed hair that was a darker brown than before but his skin too, deepened from peachy pink to a more tan shade even though he couldn't have spent all that much time in the sun in the past few days.

Then I turned to Vincent, who was plowing through his bag of chips with a pensive expression. "And you're not really Vincent."

The guy who looked like Vincent shook his head. "Jett," he said tersely. "Jett Vandamme."

"Doesn't pack quite as much of a punch as that name would make you believe," Kai said, his smile turning a bit teasing.

Jett glowered at him and popped another chip into his mouth. I thought that name would stick in my head easily enough. With his new goth appearance, he looked more like a "Jett" anyway.

"I'm Ruin," not-really-Ansel said with a little wave and another cheery smile. "Ruin Wolfrum. My parents had strange taste in names."

Mr. Grimes cuffed him on the shoulder. "The dire, foreboding vibe fits him so well, doesn't it?" he said with sarcastic amusement, and fixed his dark gaze on me. "My name's Lennox, but that sounds like a dork, so we'll stick with Nox. Nox Savage. It's good to finally—*properly*—meet you after all this time."

Kai, Jett, Ruin, and Nox. The names sank in slowly, but they were only one small piece of the puzzle. "So, you were murdered and dumped in the marsh," I prompted. "About twenty years ago?"

Kai picked up the thread again. "Twenty-one, to be exact. We hung in there as spirits… I'm not sure how far gone we'd gotten when you came along. Time turns pretty hazy. The whole situation messes with your mental state."

Yeah, I could imagine death would have a way of doing that. From what I'd seen, un-dying hadn't exactly restored their mental states to anything resembling normal. But then, who knew what they'd been like in their original lives? Maybe they'd always been this bonkers.

Ruin grinned. "It was all a big fog. But then you crashed in and woke us up."

"We sensed another life slipping away nearby," Nox said. "I don't know if all spirits are sensitive or what. But you were drowning, and you were just an innocent little kid—and we all just knew we had to try to stop you from ending up like we were."

My throat constricted, thinking back to the pressure of the water closing in around me and the darkness that'd started to consume my mind as I'd run out of air. It'd been *their* voices back then—these four men. Like a faint echo in the back of my mind. *You can do it. Kick those feet, they're coming free. Just reach—reach!* Tiny nudges against my limbs, prodding me forward.

"We could manipulate the physical world a little with a lot of effort in that state," Kai went on. "We managed to untangle your ankles from the weeds that'd wrapped around them, gave you a push toward solid ground."

Ruin nodded. "You did the rest. We couldn't have dragged you out on our own. You were so strong—you *are* so strong."

I didn't feel it. Even my bones wobbled reliving that moment, understanding it in a totally different, unnerving way.

Unnerving, but their story rang utterly true, right down to my soul.

"And then you stuck around," I said, my voice coming out in a rasp.

Nox made a careless gesture with his hand. "Like Ruin said, you woke us up. You were the first thing that really brought us to life in years. It was a good feeling. We liked it, and we liked being around you. All your games kept us entertained, and of course we had to make sure you steered clear of any other dangerous situations."

"You talked to us like we were really there," Jett added.

"Looking out for you gave us mental and emotional stimulation, as well as a sense of purpose," Kai said in his matter-of-fact tone. "You grounded us in this world, and we wanted to be here."

"And you needed us like we needed you." Ruin's smile softened. "So strong but with so many people trying to pick away at that strength."

I couldn't argue with that assessment. They'd been a bigger part of my life than I'd ever wanted to admit to anyone when I hadn't known they were actual people. When I'd thought I was just clinging on to figments of my imagination to keep myself sane. As if that wasn't kind of insane on its own.

But the only truly insane part of this was the fact that they were real.

Nox frowned. "Then you disappeared. One day you just never came out to any of the usual spots, and we couldn't find you around the house… Are you going to tell us what happened, Lily?"

Shame washed over me, leaving my skin tight and hot. I felt like a hotdog left too long on a barbeque. "I—I don't actually know."

Kai's eyebrows leapt up. "What?"

My gaze dropped to my hands on my lap. "Yeah. I went back to the house one day, and something happened… Mom and Wade have made it sound like I traumatized my sister, but they've refused to give any details, like they can't bear to talk about it… and they—and she—were the only ones there. I think. It's just a big blank in my memory. I can see myself walking up to the house, and the next thing is waking up in the hospital."

I raised my head. "I was in a psych ward for most of the last seven years. I never did anything crazy there, so whatever I was going through when I was admitted, it *must* have been bad, or how could they have held on to me for so long? When I turned eighteen, they only just started letting me transition out of in-patient care, but it was a long time before they agreed I was stable enough to live completely on my own. As soon as that happened, I came right back here. I have to— You know what my mom and stepdad were like. Marisol's still stuck with them."

Nothing I'd done to her could be as bad as living with them on her own. If I'd even done anything at all.

"Those fuckers," Nox growled. "We can go right over there and knock some sense into that stepdad of yours. It'll have been a long time coming."

Panic flashed through me. "No. You can't just go beating up whoever you're pissed off at. They'll stick *you* in the psych ward—or in jail."

Kai shrugged. "We managed to avoid getting arrested for years in our lives before."

I gave him a skeptical look. "Somehow I have to believe that back then you were *slightly* more discreet than playing pinata with students in broad daylight on campus."

He cocked his head. "Our inhibitions may have dwindled with death. But we can still keep ahead of the cops. If you don't care about the law, it can rarely touch you."

"And our way works." Nox folded his arms over his chest in an authoritarian pose that brought back dissonant echoes of the man he'd possessed. "We're putting the fear into people, and they're figuring out not to mess with you. It's only been a slow start because you kept telling us to back off."

"And you listened so well," I muttered, but part of me unraveled with a sense of resignation. What was the point in continuing to argue with them about it? Was I *really* bothered by what they'd done to the jerks who'd hauled me across town in their trunk?

As long as I didn't do anything crazy myself, it didn't matter what stunts the guys pulled, did it? If people got scared and backed off, then there'd be less chance of me slipping up because of their pranks and harassment.

I wasn't sure if that line of thinking really made sense or I only wanted to believe it, but I was going to go with it either way.

"Okay," I said. "But no attacking Wade—no one in my family. I need to be the one who tackles them. You don't know them like I do."

Nox's frown deepened, but after a moment, he dipped his head. "All right. For now. If they come at you, though—"

"It's not going to happen," I said wearily. "They want to keep as far away from me as they can."

"We'll get your answers," Kai promised, his gray-green eyes sparking even brighter. "Unravel the mystery. You've got all of us working with you now."

I exhaled in a rush and sagged back against the futon's lumpy cushions. Was it possible it really would be easier with these guys around? Would they find some way to help me figure out what'd gone down seven years ago?

A pretty big part of me suspected my life was only getting more complicated, not less, but it was nice to dream.

As if he'd picked up on that thought, Jett reached across the futon and twirled a lock of my hair between his fingers before letting it go. "You don't sing anymore," he said abruptly. "You used to—every day. Making up songs, singing your favorites. Why'd you stop?"

All of the guys waited for my answer intently. My throat closed up all over again.

"I just... it was something I mostly did for Marisol," I said quietly.

"I mean, I'd sing on my own—or with you—too, but it was always the best when I could use it to get her smiling or even singing along. When I can't be around her… when I maybe even hurt her… it's felt wrong somehow."

None of the guys told me that my reasoning sounded stupid or that I was making too big a deal of it. Jett simply nodded.

Ruin came over behind the futon and brushed his fingers over the top of my head in a reassuring gesture. "We'll fix that too," he said, firm but eager.

I didn't share his optimistic outlook, but I wasn't going to put a damper on it right now, not when he was being so hopeful on my behalf.

I looked around the room. "So… what now? How did you see this working after you got me to believe who you are?"

The guys exchanged a glance. Nox focused on me. "We're going to stick close by. Make sure no one gets in your face or takes any jabs at you. Deal with anyone who tries. I don't think it'll take very long—most of the kids at that college have never had to deal with a *real* threat in their lives." His face split with a vicious grin that shouldn't have thrilled me… but did.

Please tell me my panties didn't just get wet, I begged myself. Myself pleaded the fifth.

He was my professor—but he wasn't. He was a gang leader—but he wasn't. He was a guy who'd flung rusty fishhooks into another guy's face—yeah, that one was definitely true.

He was also, with his new imposing presence and dark demeanor, undeniably hot.

And damn it, he wasn't the only one. They were actually all pretty easy on the eyes now that they'd mostly obliterated my associations with the men they'd used to be. In ways I definitely hadn't noticed or even been thinking about when I'd been a kid and they'd barely been real.

"If there's anything else you need from us, you just let us know," Ruin said, his gentle touch stirring up more little sparks of heat.

Kai tapped his lips. "It would be easiest if we could stay nearby at night as well as during the day. Our current accommodations aren't exactly ideal. I've got a roommate who seems to think that talking is an Olympic sport he's training for, but somehow never has anything remotely interesting to say."

"Oh, Lord, don't get me started on roommates," Jett grumbled.

"I'm not totally sure where this guy used to stay," Ruin announced. "I've been parking out past the college and sleeping in his car."

He said it without a hint of concern, but the words tugged at my heart all the same. These guys had literally come back from the dead—and for *me*.

I opened my mouth, closed it again, and decided I owed them. If not for that, since I'd never asked them to resurrect themselves, then for making sure *I* had hung on to any life at all fourteen years ago.

"You can crash here as long as you want," I said quickly, before I could regret the offer. "It's not super comfy—I'm keeping the bed, just to be clear—but there's the futon. It folds down into a big enough bed for two, if you can stand sharing. And I guess if you got sleeping bags or something, or air mattresses…" I eyed the floor, trying to figure out how they'd all fit.

Nox clapped his hands together. "We'll figure it out. And we'll bring our own food. We're not going to have you starving either." He motioned to Ruin. "Come on, you bottomless pit. Let's go out for supplies."

Jett got up too. "I'm going to grab a few things from Vincent's room before that doofus of a roommate messes with them."

Kai stole Jett's spot on the sofa and picked up my textbook. "I'm perfectly happy staying right here, thank you. Bring me back something comfy and something tasty. But not both in the same item."

Nox snorted and headed out with the others. Kai started flipping through the textbook so fast he couldn't have spent more than a couple of seconds on each page. I watched him for a minute before venturing, "What are you doing?"

"This is how fast I read," he replied. "Speedreading is a very useful skill for absorbing as much information as possible. The more I know, the more I can get done."

I wasn't sure I wanted to ask what kinds of things he'd generally gotten done in this gang of theirs. *The Skullbreakers.* After today's performance, I could see how they could have come up with that name.

A trickle of dread ran through my gut. What if I'd just made the worst decision of my life?

But it had to be better keeping these guys mostly contained in my apartment than having them running around interacting with all kinds of other people, right? Maybe I couldn't cage the chaos, but I could rein it in a little.

I looked at the coffee table and then the still-screeching radio, both of which I might have made a few wry remarks to on any other day. But I didn't have to talk to random objects now. If I wanted to start a conversation, I had actual people—the people I'd always been talking to before, without fully realizing it—right here with me.

A feather of a smile touched my lips, dulling the edges of my apprehension. I'd never really been alone when I was in Lovell Rise, and I still wasn't.

Now I just had to make it so Marisol could say the same.

Chapter Fifteen

Ruin

THE THIN BEAM of sunlight that came through the tiny basement window managed to hit right on my closed eyelids. It poked right through into my brain and jabbed me out of sleep.

But I didn't mind. Waking up early gave me even more time to revel in the fact that I was waking up *here*, in Lily's home. Just a few feet from her bedroom door. I could even make out the hushed rasp of her sleeping breath through the gap where that door had drifted ajar. The latch didn't appear to work right.

Her smell permeated the whole space, lightly sweet with an aquatic tang, like wildflowers that'd been drifting down a river. I wanted to roll around in it and slather it all over me like a cologne.

We were here. Really here with her, in every possible way, not just as the phantoms we'd been before.

Well, not quite in *every* way. There was still a wall between me and her right now.

I peeled off the sleeping bag and got up, careful not to disturb my friends. Kai and Jett had grudgingly agreed to share the futon, where they were currently stretched out at opposite ends with at least two feet of empty space in between them. Nox had insisted on taking the other air mattress, which he'd laid out right by the front door as if he thought he might need to defend Lily from middle-of-the-night intruders.

Of course, who knew if we might after all? The pricks around here had gone way too far already. We couldn't be too prepared.

But for now, all was peaceful in the apartment. It might have been cramped and dingy, but it was Lily's, and that made the whole space brighter all on its own.

I eased the bedroom door wider open and slipped inside. That room was even more cramped. My knees brushed the side of her bed. Lily sprawled on her side facing the wall, her face angelic in sleep, her pale hair fanned across the pillow.

A swell of affection filled my chest. She'd been through so much, but she'd hung in there. She'd grown up from that quirky, lonely kid into a woman who was maybe still quirky but also tough as steel and fiercely determined beneath the "normal" front she was trying to keep up.

And she didn't have to be lonely anymore.

I couldn't just stand there looking at her, not with all those joyful emotions whirling inside me. I sank down onto the edge of the mattress and tucked myself against her with the blanket between us, looping my arm loosely around her waist and nestling my face against her hair. Even through the covers, her figure was soft and warm against mine. Her smell flooded my lungs.

Maybe the four of us lost souls had never gotten there the usual way, but I'd finally made it to heaven right now.

Lily adjusted her position in her sleep. Her muscles twitched as she must have registered my presence. Her body went rigid with a sharp inhalation.

"It's just me," I murmured, and loosened my embrace even more, ready to roll away if she pushed. As much as she'd accepted my hug outside the grocery store two days ago, before that she'd shied away from physical affection. I wanted her to feel how much I adored her, but only if she was enjoying the demonstration.

She stayed tensed for several seconds, but she didn't pull away from me. Gradually, her body relaxed, sinking into the bed and my arms. "Are you always this cuddly first thing in the morning?" she muttered in her softly husky voice.

"Only with people I like!" I declared, and nuzzled the back of her neck—gently, still careful not to overstep my welcome.

Lily snorted. "Somehow I don't think you spoon the other guys in bed. And I assume you like them."

I cocked my head, considering. "I *would* if they wouldn't punch me in the face. The guys aren't much for PDAs. But they're like brothers to me. I'd die for them. Of course I'd *hug* them. If they wanted." Every now and then, they did give in. First thing in the morning was definitely not the best time to try it, though.

Lily grumbled something inarticulate and doubtful before burrowing her head back into the pillow. The tiny movements of her body against mine stirred another sensation, one that was more than affection. One I hadn't felt in decades, because spirits didn't have skin that heated or dicks that hardened at the feel of a pretty woman's curves.

A flicker of the same desire had teased through me when I'd held Lily in the parking lot, but it was nothing compared to the fire that licked over me now. I'd forgotten how overwhelming this kind of hunger could be. How torturous it was but thrilling at the same time.

I couldn't remember exactly what lust had felt like all those years ago, but I wasn't sure it'd ever hit me quite as hard as this back when I'd had my original physical form to get all hot and bothered.

But then, no one had ever affected me like Lily in any way. She was woven right into my soul. And she was so much more now than she'd already become when I'd last been around her. She *was* a woman now…

She must have hungers like this too.

If we'd already had that kind of relationship, I might have tugged her ass against my rising cock and dipped my hand right between her legs to wake her up in a very different way. But I wasn't going to assume that she'd be hungry for *me* that way.

Words lodged in the base of my throat—*I love you. I want you.—*

but I swallowed them down. Not now. I might be overflowing with happiness at being around her, but I wasn't so dizzy with it that I couldn't tell she was still getting used to the situation.

I couldn't resist pressing the softest of kisses to the crook of her neck. Lily's breath caught, and something in her scent changed just slightly in a way I didn't think I'd ever have been able to notice before. Maybe it was another one of those strange effects Kai talked about, from our spirits mingling with these new forms.

I liked it. It made my dick even harder. I kissed her an inch higher on her neck, stroking my thumb over her belly through the blanket.

"What are you doing?" she asked, her voice gone a bit rough.

"Making you feel good," I said, watching my breath stir the wisps of hair behind her ear. "I hope."

"And do you do *that* with everyone you like?"

My entire body stiffened up. I'd fooled around with plenty of girls when I'd been alive before—if they were up for it and so was I, why not?—but the idea of so much as *thinking* of touching any other woman like I was Lily right now made every nerve in me pang in refusal.

I hadn't had Lily back then, and I did now. I couldn't imagine getting friendly with anyone other than my own hand if she didn't want me. There wasn't room for any other woman in the life I had now. I wouldn't have this life at all if it wasn't for her.

"No," I said with absolute certainty. "No one but you. There never will be anyone else from now on. And I don't mean just for enjoying ourselves. You've got my whole heart."

Lily shifted away from me, but only so that she could roll over toward me. She peered into my eyes, her face so close now that it took my breath away. Her pale blue-green irises shimmered like the water in the lake at dawn, as if she'd always been a part of the marsh, as if she'd been meant to crash into it and our afterlives from the moment she was born.

"Am I really that special?" she asked.

I had to scoff at the question. "Of course. Even when we knew you before, you were all kinds of special."

At the slight lift of her eyebrows, I felt the need to convince her. I reached back in my mind to all the things that'd made our existence alongside her wonderful.

"You could find things to celebrate everywhere you went—in the trees, in the grass," I said. "Everything was an adventure with you. You could make me laugh—the things you'd notice, the way you'd talk about them… And you came back. Even after everything that happened here, how awful your parents were, you came back because you care so much. There aren't many people like that, you know."

Lily swallowed audibly, still holding my gaze. Her tongue darted out to wet her lips. "This is totally insane. You know that, right?"

I grinned at her. "But it's pretty fucking amazing too, isn't it?"

"Yeah, maybe it kind of is." And then she nudged forward and brushed her lips to mine.

Oh, hell, if that'd been heaven before, then I didn't have the words to know what to call this bliss.

I kissed her back, stroking my fingers over her scalp and into her hair, and she let out a little gasp that fanned the fire inside me into a full-out blaze. Still kissing her, because you couldn't have dragged me away from this delight with a bullet train, I tugged down the blanket with my other hand to reveal the thin T-shirt she'd slept in.

At first I only trailed my fingers up and down her bare arm while I got familiar with the taste and texture of her lips. But as she scooted closer to me, melding her mouth even hotter against mine, I couldn't resist tracing them across her chest over the subtle swell of her breasts.

Lily kissed me harder, her fingers curling into the shaggy strands of my hair. When I flicked my thumb over the nub of one nipple, she tugged hard enough to kindle sparks in my scalp. Her chest hitched with a whimper, and I knew I had to work even more of those perfect sounds out of her.

"My waterlily," I murmured against her skin, nibbling her jaw, kissing my way down her neck. "My angelfish."

A giggle tumbled out of Lily at the old nicknames, cut off with another gasp when I rolled her nipple between my fingers. "Ruin," she said, her voice thick as honey now. I wished I could engrave that tone into my name.

"That's right, precious," I said, sliding up her shirt to bare her chest. "I'm gonna take care of you. You just keep telling me how much you're liking it."

I slicked my tongue over the nipple I'd been playing with, lapping up her watery wildflower scent. A soft moan escaped her.

My dick was hard as granite now. Maybe I'd get the chance to show her where I could take her on *that.* I sucked the peak of her breast right into my mouth, nipping the sensitive nub between my teeth—

And the door creaked wider open, with the growl of my boss's unmistakable voice. "Ruin," Nox said. "Get your ass out here."

Lily flinched. I pulled back quickly, tugging her shirt back down to cover her and giving her one last quick kiss on the mouth to show her nothing was wrong before turning to face Nox. He *was* my boss, and my friend and practically my brother, but a faintly defiant air came over me. I wasn't going to apologize for this.

Nox simply glared at me without saying anything. His gaze softened as it shifted to Lily. "Everything okay?"

When I glanced back, she was blushing so hard her pale skin had gone nearly as red as my hair. Her lips looked delectably tender from all our kissing.

"Yes," she said, with a hint of her own defiance. "And it might have gotten even better if you hadn't interrupted."

Nox huffed and ushered me out of the room, yanking the door shut behind him. Kai and Jett were just stretching into alertness on the futon. The boss walked me right over to the other end of the apartment.

"What the fuck was that about?" he demanded, keeping his voice low.

I gazed steadily back at him, the pleasure of my interlude with Lily thrumming through my veins, and smiled. "We were enjoying ourselves. I didn't see why I couldn't look after her *that* way too."

Nox's jaw worked. "Our first priority is keeping her safe. And making sure those assholes don't pull any more crap on her."

"I'm not going to get distracted from that mission."

"You'd better not," he grumbled, and sighed. "It seems like she wanted it too. So fine. But that's not— You shouldn't— We have to be careful with her. She's been through too much crap already."

My heart lurched. "Of course I wouldn't do anything she didn't want. She's our girl. Our woman." My lips curved back into a smile at my self-correction. And then another reason Nox might have been upset occurred to me. "I'm not trying to make her all mine. We're all with her. However she wants any of us."

The thought of her kissing any of the other guys sent a twinge of jealousy through me that quickly faded. I'd messed around with however many girls had made me happy back before. Why shouldn't Lily have as many guys as made *her* happy, if she decided to?

As long as they were the right guys and not some random assholes who wouldn't understand how precious she was.

Nox gave me a glower. "Good. You'd better remember that. Now why don't you make yourself useful and grab us some breakfast. Something extra nice for Lily too. All she's got right now is one sad box of cereal."

I offered him a salute and gave myself a quick onceover to make sure sleep and the make-out session hadn't wrinkled my jeans and tee too horribly. Then I popped in the earphones I'd gotten during my last shoplifting spree and set the phone that was now mine blaring a raucous metal tune as I headed out.

The constant assault of auditory sensation kept my stomach's grumbling at bay. I found a bakery I'd visited before, bought enough muffins and cinnamon rolls to feed an army—or four very hungry, recently resurrected ghosts and their gal—and didn't even mind running the card that said *Ansel Hunter* on it through the machine. You burned bridges if you dashed without paying on little stores where people would actually recognize you if you came in again, and anyway, it wasn't even my money.

I was just ambling back down the street when a silver SUV pulled up to the curb just ahead of me and idled there. I just strode on by, rocking on my feet with the roar of the music.

Apparently I'd missed some cue I wasn't aware of. Suddenly a guy was leaping out of the SUV's passenger side and striding over to cut me off.

The sun shone off his bald head, and his eyes got all squinty while he said something I couldn't hear over the music with very emphatic motions of his mouth. Total dork.

I laughed and popped out one of the earbuds. "What?"

The man scowled. He didn't look old enough to be bald from hair loss, his eyebrows still bushy and brown. "I said, where have you been? You haven't reported in at the expected times. What, did you have one long hair appointment?"

He eyed my newly dyed hair with obvious disdain. I'd only been returning it to its proper color. Not that I gave a flying fuck what this idiot thought of me anyway.

I blinked at him. Whatever he wanted, it must have had something to do with the prick I'd ousted from this body and not me at all.

"I'm done with all that," I said breezily, which was the same excuse I'd given when a couple of teachers had asked why I hadn't shown up in class and when Ansel's old friends had badgered him about hanging out with them. It was an excellent catch-all explanation. "Sorry."

The man coughed and blocked me again when I tried to walk around him. "That's not how this works, kid. You made a commitment."

I raised my hands innocently. "I'm not very good at keeping those. You'll have to find someone else. Have a nice life!"

This time when I made to brush past him, he grabbed my elbow. Bad idea.

I whirled, careful of my load of baked goods, and yanked my arm away from him only to swing it right back and wallop him in the throat.

Baldie doubled over, sputtering, and I strode off at twice the pace I'd used before. The sun was still shining brightly, I still had a bulging bag of breakfast delicacies, and Lily was waiting for me back at her apartment. But a shadow had slipped over my mood.

What the fuck had Ansel Hunter gotten himself mixed up in anyway? And how many bones was I going to have to break before I got *myself* out of it?

Oh, well. Breaking bones was kind of fun, really. They'd just better not bring their grievances around my woman.

Chapter Sixteen

Lily

I DIDN'T KNOW when Kai had managed to go to a library, but somehow he'd borrowed a stack of news magazines as tall as my supposed end tables—magazines he was now flipping through so fast the pages made a whirring sound.

I flopped down on the other end of the re-folded futon with one of the few leftover cinnamon rolls from breakfast clutched in my hand. If it looked like I was afraid someone might try to snatch it from me, I kind of was. The guys had plowed through the spread Ruin had brought back like they hadn't eaten in years.

Which, okay, was sort of true. I guessed they had a lot of meals to make up for. But it'd been hard not to watch them for signs of impending explosion.

"When you're Pope Somebody the 16th, you've really got to wonder if they should put more names in circulation," Kai muttered to himself, dropping one magazine and reaching for the next.

"You know, everything in those you can find on the internet," I told the former gangster with glasses, who still kind of looked like Zach.

He made a scoffing sound. "The world wide web is a *mess* these days. Everything is trying to sell you something, or else trying to sell you on selling things. This is a much more straightforward way to catch up on what we've missed in the last two decades. I'll deal with the internet when I'm up to current events."

He said all that while flipping away. Apparently Kai could talk and speed-read at the same time.

He might have had a point about the internet. If I could have inhaled a book in five minutes flat, maybe I'd have spent more time at the library than on my clunky secondhand laptop. And Google mustn't have been much of a thing back when these guys had last been in the realm of the living. I took my ability to filter out the bullshit for granted.

"Seems like those weapons of mass destruction were as AWOL as we were," Kai murmured, and read on without missing a beat.

He definitely had some catching up to do on recent history. I stretched out my legs on the nearest box and nestled myself into the futon's cushions while I savored the iced pastry with its cinnamon zing. It was my one rare day with only one class late in the afternoon and no shift at the grocery store. I'd finished all my reading, and I didn't have any assignments due for the next few days. I could chill out for a few hours.

Chill out, and observe my new roommates in their new habitat. As Kai whipped through magazines, Jett had stationed himself at my rickety table. He'd brought back a paint set after he'd gone out with the others yesterday, and he was smearing some of the colors across a broad sheet of thick paper with his hands. Somehow he made it look a lot more elegant than a toddler fingerpainting, even though the motions were technically the same. I wasn't about to question his technique.

Nox and Ruin had gone out a couple of hours ago after a muttered conversation with each other. Well, Nox had been muttering and Ruin had been responding in typical bright whispers, like he even spoke sunshine. They'd been cagey when I'd asked where they were going, which made me suspect I didn't really want to know. If I wasn't there and I had no idea what they intended, then nothing they got up to could be blamed on me, right?

Thinking of Ruin—his pale eyes and the sweep of his blazing hair, the brush of his hands and mouth over me this morning—sent a quiver of heat through my belly. It was hard to even imagine him having been Ansel before. He owned that body now, and he'd owned mine pretty damn skillfully too.

I hadn't meant to start anything with him, but he'd been right there, talking to me like I'd hung the moon, and he'd made it clear *he* was game… Maybe it was crazy, but I deserved a little craziness after how hard I'd been working at being a picture of perfect sanity.

I just hoped I could keep that craziness contained. Living in the same small space as the guy who gave out hugs as freely as he did smiles could be a lot of temptation. And that was without getting into the other guys who'd staked out my apartment.

The more they settled into the forms they'd taken over, the more the traces of the men they'd used to be faded away. All I could see when I looked at Kai now was the analytical set of his jaw and the intensity in his eyes beneath the fall of his dark brown hair, nothing that said *Zach*. Unless I really searched for it, no Vincent showed through Jett's deep purple tufts and the ropey muscle that was filling out his arms.

I didn't know exactly what the guys had looked like before they'd died, but their spirits were clearly shifting their new physical presences to match their most essential qualities.

Then there was Nox. Lennox Savage. Something about the name sent another quiver through me that was both giddy and unsettled. Every time I saw him, the professor guise had fallen away more, brawn taking over the formerly mediocre build, his square jaw getting stronger.

He ruled this crew like he had when they'd been the Skullbreakers, and I suspected he had twice as much brutality in him as the rest of them. So why wasn't I outright scared of him?

Because he looked at me like the world began and ended with me, and I didn't have the slightest concern that he'd ever aim his brutality my way. If I was going to be scared for anyone, it was the people who came near me… and I was having more and more trouble summoning much worry for those dicksicles.

It was still kind of hard to believe these guys were for real at all. Four fearsome spirits who'd saved my life and stuck around for years just to watch over me? Considering that even my own mother hadn't cared how many marshes I fell in, I wouldn't exactly have expected to inspire that level of devotion.

As if summoned by my thoughts, my phone rang. Mom's number appeared on the screen.

I stared at the phone for a few seconds, my heart thudding. Mom hadn't reached out to me since I was back in town—hell, since I'd been admitted to St. Elspeth's, really. This could either be really good or really bad. It was possible she'd decided Marisol should have her big sister back in her life after all my being on my best behavior, right?

Kai and Jett had paused in their respective work to focus on me. I raised the phone tentatively to my ear. "Hello?"

"Lily! I can't believe—after everything we've said—you tracked down Marisol at her school?"

She had that tone I hated, all wispy and yet scathing at the same time, like she didn't know whether to bawl or snarl. My shoulders came up instinctively. "It wasn't exactly *tracking down*. There's only one high school. Everyone knows where it is."

"We told you clearly that you need to leave her alone. You've already put her through enough!"

With the guys' gazes on me, a sudden spurt of defiance seared through me. I'd been playing by my parents' rules as well as I could, and where had that gotten me? I wasn't going to sit here and be berated.

"*She* didn't seem to mind seeing me," I retorted. "You've never told me what it is I supposedly did to her. What horrible crime did I commit that no one's ever been able to explain anyway?"

Mom let out a sound somewhere between a cough and an indignant sputter. She'd learned the second part from Wade. "You're in no position to question our judgment. What Wade saw—the way you acted—we can't trust you around here and certainly not around Marisol ever again."

"Maybe if you'd tell me what exactly I did, I could accept that," I protested.

"I don't want to have an argument about how bad or not it was," she replied. "Stay away from your sister. Stay away from us. If I find out you've been harassing her again, we'll notify the police."

She hung up, leaving the dead air in my ear. I lowered the phone, my stomach twisting.

I hadn't been *harassing* Marisol… but Mom and Wade could definitely spin it that way.

The way she'd talked, it'd sounded like nothing I did was going to be good enough. I could graduate at the top of Lovell Rise College with commendations from my manager under my belt, and she'd still talk to me like a psychotic mental patient.

My hands balled on my lap. I'd been angry at Ansel for spreading the story and the other students—and professors—for running with it, but the worst betrayal by far was my own mother. The words she'd just thrown at me stung ten times more than anything hurled at me before. I'd rather have been stabbed by a stick and shoved off the docks.

"What was that?" Jett demanded, shoving back the chair. Blue and purple paint mottled his hands like the deepest of bruises.

"My mom," I said quickly. "She found out I talked to Marisol—just for a couple of minutes… She and Wade are pissed. They said they'd call the cops on me if I go near her again."

Kai took in my clenched hands, and something in his gray-green eyes hardened. "Are you sure we can't simply get rid of them?" he asked in his usual even tone that nevertheless left no doubt about what he meant by *get rid of.* Especially after he added, "We can make sure the bodies aren't found."

He spoke with so much certainty I shivered. I still didn't want to order anyone's death, although I didn't think that was an excuse that'd hold much weight with these guys. But besides that— "Wouldn't that just make things worse? Child services would probably take Marisol away, and I'd lose her completely."

Jett sucked a breath through his teeth. "If it wasn't for that, I'd go take care of them right fucking now."

I held up my hands. "No. No taking care of or getting rid of. I'll—

I'll deal with them somehow. I haven't had much time to make a case for myself yet."

Kai made a skeptical sound but turned back to his magazines. A moment later, he was shaking his head incredulously. "They gave *Ant-Man* a movie before the freaking Black Panther?"

Jett sank into his chair and glowered at his painting as if it'd offended him. I swallowed the last of my cinnamon roll, but the sugar tasted like dust in my mouth.

The gloom of my conversation with Mom trailed after me all the way to class. There were no snappy remarks I could imagine or goofy images I could conjure that'd erase what she'd said. Or how forcefully she'd said it.

What if I was still delusional—delusional to think she'd ever give me a second chance?

Jett had insisted on coming along to campus with me, but he stayed on the lawn outside after I persuaded him that it'd raise more questions than would be helpful if he kept hanging around near lecture halls he wasn't meant to be at. I didn't think anything too horrible could happen while I was in the building. So I headed down the hall alone.

I was so lost in my thoughts about Mom—and trying to avoid thinking them—that I didn't pay attention to the footsteps around me. I didn't realize how closely I was being followed until I stumbled backward to dodge a frog that'd hopped into the middle of the hall of all places. My unsteady feet sent me bumping into a body right behind me.

"Watch where you're going. Walk much, klutz?"

I spun around and found myself faced with three girls. They all looked vaguely familiar, but the only one I was sure of was the slim girl in the middle with the cascade of chestnut-brown hair. As she peered down her arched nose at me, a flash of memory rose up—her hanging so close by Ansel he'd splashed her coffee onto me. I'd seen her with him before too, hadn't I?

She was carrying a bottle of water today rather than a coffee cup. Both of the other girls were too, like they'd decided to go for matching accessories.

The other two gave me looks of bored hostility while Ansel's fan drew her lips back in a sneer. "Oh, it's psycho girl. I guess we can't expect her to know where to put her feet when she's barely got her head on straight."

The girl on the left snickered. "Good one, Peyton."

Ah, so *this* was the Peyton who'd been making up new rumors about me, as if the shit already being talked hadn't been smelly enough. I couldn't summon even a flicker of surprise.

The girls were acting like they hadn't known who I was until I'd turned around. I couldn't help thinking it was an awfully big coincidence that they'd been sauntering along so close behind me if they *hadn't* been hoping for an opportunity like this.

"Sorry," I said briskly. I didn't have much patience left to put up with their crap, and I didn't think telling them that messing with me might put them on a bunch of undead gangsters' shit list would do anything but reinforce their ideas about my sanity or lack thereof. "I'll stay out of your way." I swept my arm in a motion for them to go ahead of me.

Instead, they stepped a little closer, backing me up toward the wall. My pulse hiccupped. I could have hollered for Jett, and I'd bet he'd stayed close enough to hear me and come running. But then I'd be making even more of a scene over a few girls who were just looking to flash their claws around. I could fight some kinds of battles on my own.

Peyton waved her bottle at me aggressively enough that a little water spurted from the mouth and splashed my shirt. "You'd better stay away from Ansel from now on."

I should have said, *I haven't been anywhere near him*, which was sort of true, even if the guy wearing his body had been all over me this morning. Instead, the snappy response I'd usually have kept in slipped out. "Why, does he belong to you or something?"

Something flickered in the girl's eyes, a hint of pain followed by a hardening of determination, and that was enough of an answer. He didn't, but she wanted him to. "He doesn't belong to anybody," she announced, "even if you're trying to warp his mind with your craziness."

My teeth set on edge. "I'm pretty sure he makes his own decisions. Why don't you go tell *him* to stay away from me? I'm sure that'll go really well."

"Bitch," Peyton snapped, and my last nerve frayed. The unsettling hum that'd risen up inside me yesterday on the docks reverberated through my chest again, potent enough that my ears started to ring. My breath snagged in my throat.

And the entire contents of Peyton's water bottle leapt from its opening and splatted into her face.

"What the— You—" she spluttered, swiping the drips from her cheeks and eyes. Her mascara was already running down her cheeks, her lipstick smudging, like she was a watercolor painting someone had hung up before the colors were dry.

A giggle bubbled up inside me. "I didn't do anything!" I said, suppressing it. "I didn't touch it."

"You did something," she snarled, and hustled off toward the nearest washroom with her lackeys in tow.

Any sense of amusement drained away with her last words. The hum had quieted, but now my nerves were jangling in a totally different way.

I hadn't done anything on purpose. Maybe I really hadn't done anything at all. But water didn't fling itself out of its container on a whim. Something must have propelled it out.

And I had no idea what.

Fear prickled over my skin. There were too many things I didn't know, too much I didn't understand. I didn't need more to add to the list.

Hugging myself, I hurried the rest of the way to class.

Chapter Seventeen

Lily

I WOKE up tucked against planes of taut muscle and knew from the warm, musky scent filling my nose that it was Ruin's sinewy arms wrapped around me. He was really making a habit of this sneaking into bed with me thing, even though I'd gotten the impression that Nox had told him off the last time.

From the slow rhythm of his breaths, he'd slipped in here long enough ago that he'd fallen back asleep himself. This time he'd eased under the blanket, though not the sheet, and the heat of his body engulfed me as much as his arms did.

It was kind of like having a very large cat suddenly take up residence in my home—the persistent kind that'd squirm into bed next to you and purr like a chainsaw in your ear.

I should be glad he didn't bat at my nose to wake me up or yowl about how hungry he was. Because he probably was hungry. The guys all seemed to be at any given moment unless they were already in the middle of the meal, and Ruin's appetite topped them all. Somehow he'd only seemed to get leaner since taking over Ansel's broad-shouldered frame, though.

The mysteries of ghostly resurrection.

I didn't let myself think too hard about that. Why shouldn't I be able to simply enjoy the exuberant affection he offered so easily without worrying about how it was possible or who he'd been before?

The truth was… no one had ever *wanted* to be this close to me, to watch over me like this, before the guys I'd thought were imaginary had crashed back into my life. Marisol had loved me, but I was the one who'd watched over her. It'd always been me acting as her shield against the rest of the big, bad world.

Now I had four shields of my own. Somewhat unhinged shields with no apparent moral compass, but who was I to complain?

Ruin stirred and stretched with a brief yawn. He gazed at me with eyes still heavy-lidded from sleep. "Good morning, Angelfish."

My lips twitched upward at the silly nickname. I guessed I'd earned all the water references after swimming my way out of my childhood near-drowning. "Good morning."

He gave a pleased hum that amplified the feline impression and nuzzled my temple. My heart skipped a beat, and parts of me lower down woke up twice as much in anticipation of a repeat of yesterday.

Ruin only pressed a quick kiss to my forehead and drew back. His stomach grumbled loud enough for me to hear. He grinned. "How about some breakfast? What do you want me to bring you today?"

He made it sound like he could have scrounged up a banquet if I'd asked for it. I decided not to aim quite that high and test the limits of his admittedly supernatural abilities. "I wouldn't mind something with eggs."

He snapped his fingers. "Eggs it is. Lots and lots of eggs. The chickens will be all out."

As I snorted with laughter, he loped out of the room.

A minute into my shower, the pipes started groaning, as if protesting the quadrupled work load they were now getting. I wondered exactly how in violation of my lease I was by moving in four additional tenants. Was it possible to double-plus evict someone? I doubted my landlord would buy, "But they aren't even technically alive!" as an excuse.

By the time I emerged, the apartment was full of the smell of buttery fried eggs. Based on the takeout boxes cluttering the table, there really might not be a single egg left in all of Lovell Rise.

I found scrambled eggs and poached eggs, deviled eggs and hard-boiled eggs. Thankfully Ruin hadn't gone totally egg-crazy, so there was also an entire loaf of bread in toasted slices dripping with butter and a big serving of bacon and sausages too.

My stomach just about burst from looking at it. The guys had all already grabbed plates and started digging in. I grabbed a little of everything and savored it bite by bite.

This part of the whole undead gangster invasion thing I could totally get used to.

It didn't take long before the guys were hassling each other in their usual companionable way.

"It's breakfast, not a work of art," Kai told Jett, who was rearranging the bits of food on his plate with a studied eye.

The other guy raised an eyebrow. "It can be both."

Nox was staring at the copious amounts of hot sauce Ruin was splattering on his meal. "You're going to burn right through your gut like that."

"As long as it tastes good," Ruin replied cheerfully, and started forking the stuff into his mouth without even sitting down.

I sat on one of the rickety chairs by the table and soaked up both the breakfast deliciousness and the comradery that thrummed between my new roommates. It felt like being surrounded by a family. A real family, not my old fractured one with Wade's judgmental gloominess and Mom's pathetic attempts to mollify him, while me and Marisol were shunted off to the side as an afterthought.

And I was part of this family too. Even though I didn't add much to the conversation, the guys all glanced my way regularly, as if checking that I had everything I needed.

Just for the moment, I kind of did.

Nox watched me the most, his usual cocky attitude somewhat subdued this morning. There was a fierce grimness in his dark gaze, like he was prepared to take on a whole world of trouble. Hopefully there wasn't a whole lot more than I was already aware of.

When all of the food had somehow vanished between the five of us

—and mostly not me—the former Skullbreakers boss set down his plate with a thump. "We need to get Lily back with her sister. And that means we've got to find out what happened when they sent her away."

I gave him a crooked smile. "I want to know as much as anyone, but it's not that easy. I've tried all kinds of things to remember, and the only people who could tell me anything are keeping their mouths shut."

"You didn't have us helping you before," he insisted, which was both reassuring and ominous in one.

"I appreciate that," I said, "but I'm not sure how much you can help at unlocking something in my own head."

He was silent for a moment and then jerked his hand toward the front door. "Come on. I think we need to take a road trip."

We all marched out to where he'd parked Mr. Grimes's old car. Nox didn't disguise the wrinkling of his nose as he opened the driver's side door, but he tossed the keys into the air with a satisfied jangle. "Lily rides shotgun."

I wouldn't have cared either way, and all of the guys could have used the extra space more than I did, but the other three immediately piled into the back without complaint. I plopped down in the seat next to Nox, studying him as he revved the engine.

What was he up to? And how did he think this trip was going to unravel any of the uncertainties that loomed over my life?

Ruin squeezed between the front seats to fiddle with the radio until Nox swatted his hand. "Not this time. No distractions."

"Distractions from what?" Kai asked.

"With all your brilliance, you haven't deduced it yet?" Nox teased.

Kai grunted and poked at his glasses. "I'll take that challenge." He gazed out the window, the mid-morning sunlight glinting off the panes over his eyes.

Nox took one turn and another. Kai's lips slowly pulled into a smile. "Ah."

"*Ah* what?" I demanded.

"Practice your patience, Minnow," Nox said, giving my knee a quick, playful squeeze that shouldn't have sent a bolt of heat up my inner thigh. But it did. I swallowed hard and yanked my gaze away from the brawny hand that'd delivered it.

It was wrong to find all four of these guys attractive, right? But Nox had somehow transformed my bitter professor into a stud. I mean, Mr. Grimes had been a hardass, but not in the literal sense.

Nox veered onto the country highway that ran along the outskirts of town perpendicular with the marshlands. About halfway down it, he pulled off onto the shoulder. A hush had fallen over all of the guys. *They* clearly recognized the significance of the moment.

All I saw in front of us was a discount housewares store called Dishes for Dollars. Maybe they were very special dishes?

"Is this a hint that you're not happy with my selection of dinnerware?" I asked.

Nox gave me a baleful look. Then he lifted his chin toward the building. "That used to be the Skullbreakers' clubhouse."

I blinked and stared at the store again. "You ran your gang out of Dishes for Dollars?"

He snorted. "No. It was there, and after those other pricks wiped us out, someone took over the land, bulldozed the old place, and built this pathetic thing. But the clubhouse is still there underneath in every way that matters."

"I can feel it," Ruin said softly.

"Like we never left," Jett agreed in his low voice.

"How many fucking dishes can they be selling all the way out here anyway?" Kai muttered. "Stupid place for a low-rent shop."

Nox's gaze stayed fixed on the building. His voice came out all heated determination. "It won't be theirs for long. Now that we've returned, we're going to take our property back. Make them an offer they can't refuse. Raze that place to the ground and rebuild what's meant to be there, even better than before."

I really hoped that by "an offer they can't refuse" he meant because it'd be so much money, not because the current owners would fear for their lives. It could go either way with these guys. But a tingle ran over my skin at the same time that was much more excitement than apprehension.

In that moment, I could almost see the old clubhouse too, a vague, boxy shape where the guys had planned their dark deeds… and where Ruin had bounded around to blaring music, Jett had smeared vivid paint on the walls, and Kai had whizzed through reading material like he was trying to set a record.

I could picture Nox there too, the presiding king, calling out orders and grinning fiercely as he laid out their next moves with all the same passion I'd just heard ringing through his words. Another, deeper tingle raced through me, setting off a fresh flare of heat between my legs.

I kind of wanted to know what it'd be like to have him ordering me around. To find out what he'd like to order me to do. There was obviously something very wrong with me after all.

To avoid dwelling on that possibility, I started talking. "Why did you want to show me this?"

Nox turned to me. The fervent intensity in his eyes stirred up the emotions I'd been trying to stifle twice as hot as before.

"You've been through a lot, but the truth about what happened that day is in you somewhere," he said. "It hasn't gone away—it's only buried. We'll unearth everything that matters in your past just like we brought ourselves back, just like we'll resurrect the clubhouse. And your mystery we can get started on right now."

He shifted his gaze to the windshield. The air rushed out of me as he released me from the pressure of his gaze. "You'd say we should start at the beginning, wouldn't you, Kai?"

"That generally makes the most sense," the other guy said from the back. "What's the last thing you remember before it all goes blank, Lily?"

I didn't even have to strain my mind to answer. I'd gone over those shreds of memory so many times in the past, searching for answers in them. "I'd just been down by the marsh—wandering around… with you guys… making up some random song, braiding flowers. I was bringing one of the chains back for Marisol. It was the middle of the afternoon, but it was pretty dark—it was going to rain soon, lots of clouds. I looked up at the house and noticed the light was on in Mare's bedroom." I stopped. "That's it. There's nothing between that and the hospital."

Nox had started driving again without my noticing. He was taking the route toward the house. "You don't even remember going inside?"

"No. For all I know, I didn't."

Kai hummed thoughtfully. Nox gunned the engine, and we roared through the lonely streets until we passed by the lane that stretched all the way to the desolate property that'd once been my home.

To my relief, he stopped several feet down from the lane in a spot where we could only see the house with its weathered white siding and gray shingles at a distance. "You were here," he said. "When you look around, does that jog anything else loose?"

I peered across the scruffy grass and patches of weeds for a minute, but nothing else emerged, so I shook my head. "No. It didn't when I went right up to the house the one time either—and I don't think it'd be a good idea to try that again." Mom's threat to call the police was fresh in my mind. Trespassing was a criminal offense, no matter how much of a dick the accuser was being.

Ruin's voice went uncharacteristically somber. "I don't understand how they can treat you like it's not even your home."

"That's just... how it always was." I guessed I'd never really explained it to the guys when I'd thought they were imaginary—I'd assumed they knew everything I did, since theoretically they'd come out of my head. They'd figured out the gist of it, but the details wouldn't have been obvious.

I sucked in a breath and went on. "When my mom was pregnant with Marisol—I was four—our dad took off. After that, once every couple of years he'd send a postcard from wherever, but nothing else. Having him ditch us felt like shit, and it hit Mom even harder than me. She met Wade like a year later and fell head over heels, so she did whatever she could to make him happy... I think she was always afraid she'd piss him off and he'd leave like Dad did."

"Not exactly relationship goals," Jett remarked.

"No. She wasn't necessarily wrong about him, though—that he had one foot out the door. Wade wasn't all that keen on the fact that she already had kids. I always got the impression he only tolerated us because she buttered him up and doted on him so much. And then after trying and never managing to have kids of their own... He went more and more from tolerating to full-out resentment. So that was fun."

I'd kept my tone dry, but it was hard to squeeze all the emotion out of it. These days that emotion was more anger than anything else. I'd given up on being sad about my family situation ages ago.

The guys were silent for a long moment. Then Nox said, in more a growl than anything else, "We will take care of him. One way or another." When I opened my mouth, he added, "I know. Not yet. Not until you're sure your sister is safe. But he's going down."

I couldn't bring myself to argue with him. Instead, I rubbed my hand over my face. "What now?"

"If you were picked up by the cops on your property, then they'd have driven along this route away from there," Kai piped up. "I think the typical procedure would be to take you into custody at the nearest station and then arrange transport to the hospital. We could try following that route."

"Sure. Might as well."

Nox put his foot to the gas again. We cruised more slowly down the country road and onto the larger thoroughfare that I knew would eventually take us to the county police station halfway between Lovell Rise and the next town over. I'd come this way for other reasons before, but not the slightest flicker of what I might have seen from the back of a cop car came to me.

When we'd passed the station and Nox pulled over again, I shifted in my seat with a wordless grumble of frustration. "There's nothing." The mark on my arm prickled with a sudden itch. I scratched at it, frowning. "I don't understand. I've never forgotten anything else like this before."

"Trauma," Kai said. "Intense mental or emotional overload. It happens."

Nox reached over and grasped my knee again, letting his hand linger there this time as he caught my gaze. Heat coursed through my leg from where his palm rested, but what called to my heart were the words he said.

"We'll get there. No matter how deep it's buried or how much has been built over top, we'll dig it up. I fucking swear it."

Right then, with part of me wanting to melt into his touch, I believed he'd fulfill everything he promised—and more.

Chapter Eighteen

Kai

It seemed somehow fitting that Lily's stepdad Wade owned and managed a sporting goods store. He was a dingbat with a stick up his ass, after all. Maybe I'd get the opportunity to stick a real bat up his actual ass before my mission here was over.

I pushed my glasses up my nose and sauntered in, keeping a casual air but scanning every inch of my surroundings. You never knew what minor details might fill in the blanks when trying to figure out a person.

Not that I cared about finding any kind of sympathetic harmony with the prick. I just wanted to know what *he* knew about the incident that'd sent Lily away to the psych ward.

The place held no obvious surprises at a glance. He'd arranged the aisles by sport, including some that a lot of people with too much time on their hands would have debated calling a sport at all but that were necessities in this kind of town, like fishing and hiking. A faintly sweaty odor hung in the air as if some of the merchandise had already been used for its intended purpose.

A tinny announcer's voice carried from a little TV mounted over the front counter where a football game was playing. Its wiring ran along the wall to a junction box mounted near the ceiling that'd clearly seen better days. I'd read a few books on electrical work, and despite being nothing close to an expert, I could spot a couple of irregularities at a glance.

But I wasn't here to search for code violations. The man who was the focus of my visit stood behind that counter in a self-satisfied stance, ringing up a customer who'd bought an armload of pool noodles. Even *I* was pretty sure there weren't any sports you played with those, but I didn't think either of them wanted to hear my opinion on the subject. I ambled closer, running my fingers over a rack of ski poles, and eyed my target surreptitiously.

Wade Locust was the kind of guy who gave dweebs a bad name. His taffy-brown hair had thinned to the point that you could see slivers of pale skull through his combover, and both his chin and his nose jabbed out at sharp points. He wore a baseball jersey that was a little too tight on his stocky frame but maybe had fit years ago when he'd bought it. One glance at his hand told me he still regularly chewed on his fingernails.

One glance at his smile as he waved the customer off told me he'd never said anything he wasn't willing to take back.

I already hadn't liked him before I'd properly met him, and he'd somehow dropped from the bottom of my esteem to unplumbed depths I doubted he'd ever return from. Had he been more of a catch when Lily's mom had gone gaga for him, or did she just have really crappy taste in men?

I was going to assume it was a heaping portion of both.

Now that he wasn't occupied anymore, I meandered over to the counter and nodded at the TV. "Quite a game."

I had no idea whether it was at all remarkable or not, but Wade happily agreed. "Sure is. Can I help you with anything?"

"I need to get a new rod," I said, motioning to the fishing aisle. "Not sure what'd suit me best. Can you make any recommendations?"

"Happy to help."

He hustled from behind the counter with more enthusiasm than he'd offered either of his step-daughters in their entire existence. "What kind of fish are you looking to catch?" he asked.

"Pike," I said, picking the first fish name that came to mind that I was reasonably sure lived in the waters around here. I'd actually gone fishing approximately zero times in my life.

Wade gave me a bit of an odd look, but I was used to people finding me strange, even if it usually wasn't because of my preferences in aquatic animals. I barreled right on to the real conversation I wanted to start.

I patted the beige shelving unit as if it was somehow impressive. "So this is your place?"

Wade puffed up his chest a bit, which only emphasized the straining of the jersey. "Yep. Started this baby twenty-five years ago and grew it from the ground up."

I nodded to his left hand with its thin band around the ring finger. "And you're a family man. Living the dream."

A shadow crossed Wade's face. "In some ways. We do all right."

He'd sounded ten times prouder talking about the store than the human babies he'd had a hand in raising. Although maybe "raising" wasn't the right word for it when he'd spent more time wishing Lily and her sister would die than teaching them how to live.

"Kids?" I asked conversationally, contemplating the array of rods.

Wade frowned. "A daughter," he said grudgingly.

Singular, not plural. The fucker. I let myself look straight at him then, widening my eyes as if I'd just remembered something. "Oh, yeah, weren't you— I heard some of the guys at the college talking about it— There was some kind of incident with a girl named Lily…?"

The man's face shuttered in an instant. If he thought that'd stop me from picking up on his cues, he was shit out of luck. His hands twitched with obvious anxiety. Something about the subject made him *nervous*. Because he didn't want that reputation associated with his store, or was there more to it?

"She's gotten the help she needs," he said brusquely. "I married into the family—she probably got it from her birth father. Now, for a fish the size of a pike, I'd normally recommend something in this range." He motioned to several of the poles.

"Isn't she back in town, though?" I said as I picked one up. "I thought she was at the college. I guess you'll be supporting her transition from the hospital."

Wade's entire face twitched that time. He looked like he'd swallowed a lemon—whole. Abruptly, he leaned his hand against one of the shelves and narrowed his eyes at me. "Are you here to check up on me? Because he should know that nothing's changed—there's no reason to worry."

Now *this* was interesting. I folded my arms over my chest. I'd get more by playing along than revealing I had no idea what he was talking about. "And what if he did send me, and he's not satisfied with that answer?"

"If he runs into any problems, he can take them up with me. Himself, not any go-between." He motioned to the door, his mouth twisted between disgust and what I'd swear was panic. "If you're not here to buy, I think you'd better go."

"Not open to browsers, huh?" I couldn't help remarking. "I'd say that's bad for business."

"You know that's not what this is about," he hissed, and came as close to shoving me down the aisle as he could get without actually assaulting me.

"Maybe he'd be more satisfied if you explained right now how you're so sure that everything's under control," I suggested, fishing in the way I was much more comfortable with.

Unfortunately, the prick had decided to shut his mouth to me as well as his store. "Just go. We had an agreement."

Frustration flickered up inside me. I'd gotten something, but it didn't feel like anywhere near enough. And everything about this idiot made me want to end him. How did he deserve to keep breathing after the way he'd treated Lily and then kicked her aside?

My hands clenched, and an odd energy crackled through my veins. Suddenly I was sure that if I'd wanted to, I could have short-circuited his heart on the spot. My spirit wasn't fully fused with this body yet—maybe it never would be. I had at least a little of my ephemeral energies at my disposal.

But Lily hadn't wanted him dead—and he did know more than I'd been able to find out this time.

I bit back the worst of my rage, and my gaze snagged on the junction box again. I kept my expression impassive, but inside I started smirking.

I knew exactly how to deliver maximum agony without touching a hair on his body.

I kept walking, squeezing the doorframe just for a second as I stepped outside. My fingers shot a surge of energy through the wall straight to that bundle of wires.

The first sparks hissed as the door swung shut behind me. I was nowhere near it, so Wade definitely couldn't accuse me of setting it off. I'd made it halfway down the block when his smoke detector started wailing loud enough to reach my ears. Then I let out my smirk.

Wade burst out of the store a moment later, hollering, "Help! Does anyone have a fire extinguisher? It's—it's catching all over." Then he shouted into his phone, "Can't you get here any faster?"

I was absolutely certain the rinky dink small-town fire department wouldn't get here in time to save even half his merchandise. Poor Wade.

Resisting the urge to watch the destruction play out, I turned the corner to head toward Lily's apartment. She should know what I'd found out as soon as I could tell her. But I'd only made it a couple of blocks when a car pulled up alongside me.

A guy poked his head out of the window. "Hey, Zach, where've you been? What the hell's been up with you, man?"

Lord deliver me from this dimwit jock's idiotic friends. "What's up is I'm making some life changes," I informed him. "I'm done with football, remember?"

"You can't be fucking serious. The coach is going to kick you off the team if you don't show up to practice soon."

"That'll be hard when I've already quit." I stopped for just long enough to fix them with a hard stare. "I've got better things to do than hang around you dumbasses anymore. So fuck off and leave me alone. How much clearer can I say it?"

They hurled a bunch of curses back at me, but they did drive off. I shrugged and walked on. Plenty of people hadn't liked me in my time. It didn't particularly sting when it was those bozos. It was time they got used to the new Zach who wasn't Zach at all.

Really I was doing him and his reputation a favor.

At the apartment, I opened the door with one of the spare keys we'd had cut and walked in to find Lily cuddled up with Ruin on the futon. Or, well, cuddling might not have been quite the right word, but she was sitting with her legs stretched toward him while she took notes from one of her textbooks, and he'd taken it upon himself to pull off her sock and give her a foot massage. Because naturally Ruin could never keep his hands off anything.

The unexpected bolt of jealousy that shot through me came with a hormonal flush that raced through my body straight to my groin. Over seeing her naked foot, for fuck's sake. I closed my eyes for a second to get a hold of myself.

Why the hell had I gone and picked the youngest of our possible hosts? This dude had only been nineteen, and he had idiotic hormones flooding his body at all the wrong times like he was a freaking baboon. My twenty-five-year-old soul and its much more self-controlled influence hadn't calmed down *that* part of his physiology anywhere near enough yet.

We were here to help and protect Lily, not fuck her. I'd never *needed* to fuck anyone, even if I had from time to time because it'd been a change of pace and burned off some steam. I wasn't becoming a slave to teenage horniness.

"Are you okay?" Lily asked as I opened my eyes again. She'd twisted around on the futon at my entrance and now was looking at me with eyes way too wide with concern.

I switched gears to a much more acceptable topic. "Yes. Better than okay. I just had a little chat with your stepdad."

"What?" Lily's forehead furrowed. "I told you guys that *I'd* deal with him."

I held up my hands. I'd kind of figured she'd be pissed. The trick was turning her initial judgment around.

"I didn't do anything to him." His store was another matter. "I just wanted to see how much I could get a read on him." My smirk came back. "And I did find out one interesting tidbit."

Lily's expression wavered between annoyance and hope. Ruin sat up straighter, already bringing out his grin. "That's awesome!" he said.

"Maybe." Lily nodded to me. "Fine. What did he say?"

I could respect a woman who didn't retract her first reaction right away. I settled into one of the wobbly chairs by the kitchen table. "I couldn't get a lot of specifics out of him, not during this first run. But he did give us a clear sense of direction. After I mentioned you, he got thinking that someone might have sent me. A mysterious 'he.' Whatever happened that day, it must have involved more than just your family, unless you have a secret brother or uncle you've never mentioned."

Lily shook her head slowly. Her gaze turned distant and pensive. "I don't remember anyone—but I don't remember any-fucking-thing." She sucked in a breath with a frustrated hiss. "Marisol acted like she was worried about someone other than me too. I figured it was probably Wade or my mom, but maybe that's all connected somehow."

"It must be." Ruin glanced from one of us to the other, his eyes alight with eagerness. "What do we do now?"

I let my smile grow. Mission accomplished. "Lily can keep focusing on getting all the crap she's taken on done and being a good influence over little sisters everywhere. The rest of us are going to look into everyone who's ever had any dealings with Wade Locust."

Chapter Nineteen

Lily

I SHOULD HAVE KNOWN that Peyton wouldn't let the water bottle incident slide forever, even if it'd have to take plenty of mental gymnastics to blame me for it. When I walked into a class I shared with one of her friends the next morning and felt the girl's gaze jabbing into me, maybe I should have been more on guard.

But there wasn't much I could have done to avert disaster anyway.

My mind was too taken up with questions about Wade and the unknown "he" my stepdad had mentioned to Kai to bother worrying about Peyton's friend much. I simply sat at the opposite end of the room and pretended she didn't exist.

Too bad for me, she didn't extend me a similar favor. Just as the professor walked in, she got up and snagged an empty seat behind me.

I dutifully got out my notebook and pen, planning to do nothing but take notes on the lecture. For the first several minutes, it seemed like I might get away with that. Maybe she was hoping she could literally shoot daggers into my back with her eyes, and that was as far as she intended to go.

No such luck. About quarter of the way through the lecture, a faint tap radiated through my chair. After the third iteration, I realized she was kicking the back of it. Lightly enough that it didn't make a sound, but firmly enough to be deeply annoying.

The Skullbreakers guys were clearly a bad influence, because the first response I imagined was whirling around and snapping her ankle in two. Not that I knew how to break bones with my bare hands anyway. Not that I *wanted* to.

I gritted my teeth and kept writing, tuning out the erratic rhythm of her swinging foot as well as I could. I only had forty-five minutes to get through. She wasn't going to fray my nerves that easily.

But of course she didn't stop there. Something pattered against my back—she was tossing little bits of… tissue? Pencil shavings? Had she brought popcorn to class? Flicking whatever it was subtly enough that the professor still didn't clue in.

I could picture my antagonist's reaction if I spun around and accused her. She'd play all innocent, and I'd look like a lunatic having delusions. No, thank you.

There was about a half hour left when something jabbed into my tailbone so hard and unexpectedly I shot out of my seat with a yelp. Instinctively, I jerked around to see what Peyton's friend had done to me—and just as I swiveled to face her, her desk toppled over, clanging into the back of my chair.

She must have flipped it purposefully. But she stepped back with her hands held up and her eyes wide with a shocked expression, as if she had no idea how it'd been upended. Her act was so convincing that even I felt a flicker of doubt. Had something happened like with the water leaping from Peyton's bottle?

The girl's voice pealed out with words that sounded so rehearsed any doubt I'd felt vanished. "Sir, she knocked my whole *desk* over. I don't know why she's bothering me, but I can't work like this."

The professor was already frowning at both of us. His gaze zeroed in on me. "Miss Strom—"

"I didn't do anything," I protested. "She—"

But how crazy would it sound to say that the girl had tossed her own desk over just to make me look bad? He'd probably see the excuse as proof that I had it in for her.

As I scrambled for the right response, he pointed to the door. "Disruptions like this are unacceptable. Take a walk and cool down. If we have any more incidents in the future, I'll have to talk to Student Services."

Embarrassment prickled over me, but I didn't know how to argue his decision without looking like an even bigger problem. Resisting the urge to glare over my shoulder at Peyton's friend, I stuffed my notebook into my shoulder bag and hustled out of the room.

My biggest mistake was thinking getting me kicked out of class was the ultimate goal. I was so peeved I barely paid attention to what was waiting out in the hall—or rather, who.

The door thumped shut behind me, I veered out of the alcove into the wider hall, and two pairs of hands clamped around my arms.

I twisted automatically to try to break their hold and caught a glimpse of Peyton's cold eyes and haughty nose as she kicked my legs out from under me. While I stumbled, another girl yanked open a door across the hall.

"This'll give you lots of time to think about why you should never mess with me or Ansel again," Peyton hissed at me. Then she and her other friend hurled me through the doorway.

It opened to a flight of concrete steps. My hands flailed out, snatching at the railing, but the girls had shoved me too hard for me to catch myself. I tumbled over and slid most of the way down on my side, flinging my arms up to protect my head.

I hit the floor at the bottom and jostled to the side, and my elbow smacked into a pipe so hot I'd swear I heard my skin sizzle. Searing pain shot through my arm.

I rolled in the opposite direction, a cry crackling up my throat. From above, an ominous scraping sound reached my ears, followed by a heavy click. A sadistic snicker filtered through the door. Then there was only silence.

Well, not exactly silence. The dark room I'd fallen into hummed, whirred, and clinked in a cacophony of mechanical sounds. I might have enjoyed the orchestra if my arm hadn't still been throbbing and the rest of me aching in all the places I'd have bruises tomorrow.

At least I didn't appear to have broken anything. I sat up

tentatively, testing my limbs. My right shoulder twinged when I rotated it, and my probing fingers found a scrape on my shin, but otherwise I was uninjured.

Even though I was on the basement level, the air that closed around me was thick and hot. That and the noises tipped me off—this must be the utility room.

And I was pretty sure Peyton and her friends had trapped me in here.

I pushed myself to my feet, confirmed that my legs could hold me just fine, and stomped back up the stairs that'd battered me. As I'd expected, when I jerked at the door handle, it refused to budge. Probably this room was locked most of the time. One of the girls must have pilfered a key from the maintenance staff so they could toss me in here… and then seal me away.

I felt all along the door for anything that'd let me unlock it from the inside, but I came up with nothing. Shit. Squeezing my hand into a fist, I banged on the door. "Hey! Can someone get me out of here? Hello?"

No sound reached me from the other side. Classes let out on the hour—there'd be a flood of students in the hall in twenty minutes or so. I just had to wait for that.

If any of them bothered to answer my call for help. If they even could. Hopefully someone would at least notify the staff so someone could come by with a key. I didn't think Peyton was such a criminal mastermind that she'd have stolen all the means to unlock this room or melted the keyhole or some ultra nefarious move like that.

All the same, I didn't love the idea of being rescued in front of a sizeable portion of the student body. Grimacing, I pounded on the door again. If I could get someone's attention before there was a whole crowd of witnesses, that'd be ten times better.

As my hand fell to my side, it occurred to me that I had another option. My phone was still in my pocket. Nox had come with me onto campus today, glowering at anyone who so much as glanced at me. He'd meant to prowl around the college while he waited for my class to be over, but he'd be nearby.

Calling on him like I was a kitten stuck up a tree made me wince, but it was the best of my bad options. Not that he'd have a key either. But anything my classmates could figure out, he could too.

Or something completely different. Less than five minutes after my hasty text, the door handle jiggled. There was a metallic groan and a faint screech, and then a clanking sound as if the whole mechanism had fractured into pieces. Which for all I knew, it had. From what I'd seen, the guys had never met anything they wouldn't happily bash given the excuse to.

Nox yanked open the door, all fuming menace. When I squeezed out into the cooler air of the hall, he loomed over me, checking me over for any fatal injuries I might have forgotten to tell him about.

"Who did this?" he snarled. "When I get my hands on them—"

His gaze caught on the burn—a strip of mottled pink skin from my elbow to halfway down my forearm—and he bared his teeth like he was ready to chomp someone's head right off. "Who did this to you?" he repeated in an even more ominous voice.

The fury radiating off him sent a shiver through me—not an entirely unpleasant one, I had to admit, but with enough apprehension that my answer stuck in my throat. I was pissed off at Peyton, but that didn't mean I wanted to see her eviscerated. And from the looks of things, that was exactly what I'd be sentencing her to if I let her name slip.

"It doesn't matter," I said. "It's over now. They let out their anger, and now they'll leave me alone."

I didn't totally believe that, so I couldn't blame Nox for his scoffing laugh. "They'll do something worse next time. I'm not giving them the chance."

"I'm *fine*," I insisted.

"You're not," he growled. "They hurt you, and they're going to pay. *Tell* me who it was."

His voice was getting louder. The squeak of moving chairs carried from a nearby room, and my pulse hiccupped. "Everyone's going to be leaving class in a moment," I said. "This really isn't a good place—"

With another growl, Nox swept me right off my feet into his arms. I wasn't the tiniest girl ever, but he hefted me like I was made of air. Air and glass. I might have protested harder if he hadn't tucked me against him so gingerly before he marched off down the hall.

"What the fuck are you doing?" I grumbled.

"Taking you someplace else where I expect you to give me some answers," he retorted, and hurtled on up the stairs to the second floor.

"You could put me down and let me walk there."

"This is faster."

I couldn't deny that. Or the fact that the well-muscled planes of his chest felt awfully good against me. My heart was still thumping hard, but it wasn't all nerves now.

A metallic, smoky scent rose off his skin, as if his brawny body had been forged out of fire and steel. Some strange part of me wanted to know how it'd taste.

Nox fished a key out of his pocket while balancing my weight with one arm seemingly effortlessly and barged into a room I immediately realized was Mr. Grimes's office. The space wasn't much bigger than a walk-in closet, with an overladen bookshelf along one wall, a narrow window with crooked blinds, and a large metal desk scattered with papers and books.

Nox shoved the mess onto the floor with one swipe of his arm and set me on the edge of the desk, my legs dangling. Then he leaned in, his nose nearly touching mine. "Who locked you up in that room? Who hurt you? We're staying right here until you tell me."

In that moment, with the heat of his body wafting over me and his smell flooding my lungs, I couldn't say that sounded like much of a threat.

"I'm not telling you," I said, staring right back at him as my heart thumped on. "You're too worked up. You're going to do something crazy."

"It's not *crazy* to look after you. It's crazy that you don't think you deserve it. Anyone who touches you is fucking *dead*."

He wasn't exactly making a case in his favor, but another quiver ran through me at his words. A hunger woke up inside me as if I'd been craving this vicious devotion my entire life and never known until now.

Of its own accord, my hand rose up, my fingers curling into the fabric of his shirt and brushing the muscles flexed underneath. A voice that hardly sounded like my own spilled from my lips as if the words were being pulled out of me by a magnetic force.

"Instead of making them feel worse, why don't you make *me* feel better?"

Desire flared in Nox's eyes. He looked down at me, his jaw working, and slowly raised his hand to my chin. His thumb grazed the seam of my lips, torturously light.

Somehow that delicate touch set off so many sparks in me I had to swallow a whimper. All at once, the office felt hotter than the utility room had.

"You aren't a minnow anymore, are you, Lily?" Nox said, his baritone dipping even lower. "You're a goddamned siren." He brushed his thumb over my mouth again. "You liked having Ruin all over you."

A pulse of heat between my thighs agreed with that assessment. It only fueled the wildness that'd come over me. "Maybe I'd like you too. Is that a problem?"

He sucked in a breath. "Hell, no," he muttered, and then his mouth crashed into mine.

If Ruin's kiss was all bright exuberance, then Nox's was total darkness. A pure, intoxicating darkness like the headiest of liquors, drenching me from head to toes in an instant. Just like that, I soaked my panties.

He nudged my knees apart so my legs splayed around him, pushing in on me where I was perched on the desk. The feel of his solid thighs between mine only drove me wilder. My hand stayed clamped around his shirt. The other wrapped around his shoulders as if I could pull him right into me.

He claimed my mouth so thoroughly that all I was aware of was the brutally blissful pressure and his body aligning with mine. One hand cupped my jaw, his thumb stroking my cheek, while the other squeezed my ass and tugged me even closer against him. The bulge behind the fly of his jeans collided with my sex, and a moan tumbled out of me.

Nox drank in the sound and pressed another scorching kiss to the crook of my neck. "You're a good girl, aren't you, Lily?" he murmured, every word like a flame. "No one's treating you fucking right. But I've got you. I'm going to make you sing again."

I was too dazed to wonder what he meant until his fingers slipped over my hip to delve between us. They rubbed over my clit through my jeans, and I trembled against him with the flurry of pleasure the one small gesture provoked.

Nox growled, but there was nothing angry in the sound now. "That's right. I can't wait to see you unravel for me. I'm going to take you so high, baby."

He captured my mouth again, devouring me with searing lips and a flick of his tongue while his hand worked over me below. Each press of his fingers brought a more potent surge of bliss.

I couldn't stop myself from squirming, rocking into him as if I needed to urge him on, while I kissed him back just as hard. My breath slipped out of me in little hitches and gasps between the melding of our mouths.

I *had* needed this. I hadn't known it, but I'd been starving for it, and now the flood of giddy satisfaction was sweeping me away.

When my body started to shake with the pulsing of Nox's touch, he drew back enough to watch my expression. My muscles were turning to jelly, wave after wave of delight washing through them. A smile curved the former gang boss's lips, so heated it sent me spiraling faster toward my release.

"You're fucking gorgeous like this," he said. "So fucking beautiful when you're moaning for me."

He hooked his fingers at just the right spot against me, and I shattered with the moan he'd been asking for. A whirlwind of pleasure whipped through me, thrumming through every nerve and leaving me breathless. I clung to Nox as I came down from the high.

But with the release, some of the wildness that'd brought me here washed away too. My ears picked up the chatter of voices filtering in from the hall outside—students and professors in conversation. All at once, the objective reality of my situation sank in.

To anyone else's eyes, I'd just been all but finger-fucked on a desk by one of my professors. What if someone had heard those moans—what if they saw us coming out together—

And even if no one had, I'd just hooked up with a guy who'd been swearing to commit murder on my behalf a few minutes ago. What the hell had I been thinking?

I hadn't been thinking, that much was clear. And it got harder to think again when Nox teased his hand up just high enough to finger the button on my fly.

"That was just an appetizer. Wait until you get the main course."

A whole lot of me screamed *hell, yes!* but my momentary panic overwhelmed my hormones. I jerked away from him.

"No," I said in a voice that was way too breathy. "No, I think we'd better stop there. I—I need to get some air."

"Lily?" Nox said as I slid off the desk. Then a hint of a growl came back into his voice. "You still haven't told me—"

"Just—just leave me alone for five fucking minutes!" I said, the words tasting sour and unfair even as I spat them out. But they worked, at least for long enough that I could make my getaway. I hurried out of the office and down the hall, and no footsteps thundered after me. In the stairwell, I paused for a second and pressed my palm to my forehead.

I wasn't crazy. I *wasn't.*

But right now I felt like I was teetering way too close to the edge.

Chapter Twenty

Lily

I DIDN'T GO BACK to my apartment that night. I couldn't have said whether I was more embarrassed by how I'd stormed off on Nox or scared of how I'd feel when I saw the guys, but either way, I wasn't ready to face the way-too-literal ghosts of my past.

My phone had been blowing up with calls and texts since about ten minutes after I'd left Nox in the professor's office. I'd ignored all of those, texted Ruin—who seemed the least likely to totally blow his top—to say I needed a little space to get my head on straight and they should let me have that. Then I turned off my phone altogether.

After my closing shift at the grocery store, I curled up on the armchair in the corner of the stock room that doubled as the employee lounge and managed a stretch of broken sleep. A couple of times, I heard the rumble of a car engine outside, but no one banged on the door. It might not have been the guys at all.

I ducked out the next morning before the first shift started, feeling not a whole lot saner than I had the night before. Squirming in front of Fred's rearview mirror, I combed my fingers through my hair, smoothed the wrinkles out of my shirt with some strategic dabs of water, and applied a quick swipe of lip gloss so I didn't look like a total disaster.

Still, I was enough out of sorts that I drove right down Main Street on my way to my morning class instead of avoiding the strip that held Wade's store like I normally did.

I remembered awfully fast when I saw it didn't hold Triumphant Sporting Goods anymore. At least, not the building I remembered. Instead, there was only a blackened frame with fragments of charred wall here and there. I stared at it as I cruised past, my mouth going dry.

Kai's smirk from when he'd told me about his conversation with my stepdad floated up through my memory. I was going to guess he'd done a little more than just talk after all. My stomach twisted, but my horror was as much at the sense of approval that'd rushed through me as at the destruction itself.

Maybe I wasn't teetering on the edge after all. Maybe I'd already gone so far off the deep end that the pool drain I was getting sucked down into simply looked like an edge.

I arrived at the college an hour before my first class and immediately determined that move had been a mistake. As I left the car behind to cross the parking lot, as I popped into the campus café to grab a cherry danish for breakfast, as I meandered across the lawns nibbling at it, every glance shot my way felt even warier than before.

Was I imagining it, or had those freshmen veered to the far edge of the field to avoid me? Was that bunch of girls peeking my way between their furtive whispers?

If people here had found out about my stepdad's store, word had probably spread that I'd done it. It'd fit the picture they'd drawn of me, right? The police obviously didn't think I was responsible, or they'd have been knocking at my door two nights ago, but facts had never gotten in the way of juicy campus gossip before.

Or maybe I'd been spotted rushing out of Mr. Grimes's office all flushed and recently ravished, and they were gossiping about that. Hell, it could even be both. Whatever the case, I had the feeling my reputation had gone from in the toilet to sewer level.

The best way to keep it from sinking any lower seemed to be

keeping my head low. I slunk in and out of class without saying a word, and no one got in my way. I did my reading under a tree out in the lonely reaches beyond the greenhouse that belonged to the Environmental Studies department. After my last class of the day, I meandered back toward the parking lot feeling adrift.

It was only mid-afternoon. The guys were probably still hanging out at my apartment—or prowling around town looking for other ways to avenge me. The one time I'd turned my phone on, the massive number of notifications had horrified me enough that I'd shut it right back down. I was lucky I hadn't run into any of them on campus. And at the same time, some stupid part of me was *disappointed* that they'd followed my request for space.

I'd had great plans when I came back to town. I'd done everything right, or as right as I could. So why did it seem like every step forward I took, I slid five more backward?

I walked over to my car because I didn't want to stick around campus any longer than I needed to, taking a small bit of comfort from the rhythm of my sneakers smacking the pavement. Then my gaze caught on the unnatural glints of reflected sunlight sparking on the asphalt around the junker's tires.

As I hurried over, my chest clenched up. Whoever had it in for Fred—and me—had really gone to town this time. Holes had been punched in all of the windows, including the windshield, leaving glass shards scattered on both the seats and the pavement. The window frames were full of jagged chunks, fracturing any view through them into a kaleidoscope of shapes.

Something inside me cracked apart as if echoing the scene in front of me. All at once, I couldn't bring myself to give a fuck.

This was what I was working with. Screw everyone who thought they could pull shit like this and I'd roll over. Underneath all the crap, I had one mission here, and it didn't even have anything to do with this school or the asswipes who went here.

I grabbed the emergency blanket from the trunk and wrapped it thickly around my arm before smacking away the remaining knives of glass lodged in the window frames. It wasn't like the windows were doing me any good the way they were, and I'd see better without the broken bits in the way. Then I brushed off the driver's seat, since the situation was enough of a pain in my ass without me having literal shards poking my behind.

As I sank into the driver's seat, a sense of certainty settled over me. I'd been avoiding the thing most likely to get me answers because I'd been afraid of the consequences. But consequences kept raining down on me no matter how carefully I played the game. So, fuck the rules. It was my life. I deserved to know how it'd been ruined.

That didn't mean I was going to be an idiot about my quest, of course. I drove slowly out within view of my old house but far off the lane that led right up to it and peered across the scruffy fields. The breeze passing through the open windshield frame rushed over me with an aquatic tang from the marsh.

Neither Mom's car nor Wade's was parked next to the house. That was a promising sign. I couldn't imagine either of them letting Marisol borrow their vehicle, so it meant they were both probably gone too.

Marisol would still be in school. Mom should be at work in the dental office where she was a receptionist. I didn't know what Wade was doing now that his store was in cinders, but I'd guess he had all kinds of insurance claims and who knew what else to sort through.

That meant I had no way of predicting when he'd be home, but I'd take that chance. This had been my house for years before it'd been his. I knew the ins and outs. I'd just keep my ears pricked for the sound of the engine.

I crossed the field on foot, the overgrown grass hissing against my calves. Nothing stirred in the windows or around the house. When I was close, I circled to the left so that I could approach it on the trampled path that led toward the marsh—the way I'd have been coming the day everything had gone wrong.

I stopped there for a moment, looking up at the house and superimposing my remembered image of it from that day in my mind's eye. Then I walked slowly up to the side door I'd usually entered through, all my senses alert for any twinges of recognition.

Nothing came. The side door was locked, which it'd rarely been back then, but Mom and Wade hadn't changed their usual tricks much. I checked a few stones along the edge of the flowerbed nearby and found the key under the third.

As I eased the door open, a frog hopped up beside me with a faint croak. I raised my eyebrow at it. "You stay out here."

I shut the door behind me but didn't lock it in case I needed to make a hasty escape. The smell of the place washed over me, familiar and yet not.

My mom still used the potpourri that was mostly cloves. A sour note of lemon cleaner trickled through it. She'd fried bacon this morning—a little of the greasy odor laced the air alongside the rest.

I hadn't breathed in that concoction of scents in seven years. It no longer gave me the immediate pang of *home.*

It didn't jostle loose any stray recollections either. I walked through the kitchen, where the table was clear and dishes were drying in the rack—Mom always kept everything as tidy as possible so Wade had nothing to complain about, not that it stopped him complaining. Then on into the dining room and down the hall past the living room. I'd never spent any more time on the first floor than I could help. After Wade had moved in, the only part of the house that'd really been mine was my bedroom upstairs.

When I reached the staircase, a frog jumped out of nowhere to land on the steps ahead of me. As I cocked my head at it, another sprang after. They literally leapfrogged after each other all the way up to the second floor. I watched them go, wondering what crevice they'd slipped in through—and why they'd bothered.

"You do you!" I called after them. "Just stay out of Wade's closet, or he might turn you into frog-leg soup."

They'd made the trip more eloquently than I could. The stairs creaked under my feet loud enough that I winced. But it wasn't as if anyone could hear me from all the way out in town.

At the top, I took a left—and discovered that even my room wasn't really mine.

It wasn't a surprise. I'd been gone all those years, and Wade had wanted me gone for way longer than that. But somehow it still hit me like a jab to the gut, seeing the sunny yellow walls hidden away behind piles of storage boxes.

I mean, I'd never been a sunny girl, but the room had always given me the sense that maybe I could be, even as the paint faded. Wade had turned the space into a combination junk yard and pawn-shop depot.

I spotted one of those stupid singing fish poking from the top of one haphazardly stacked box, and a wooden goblet that looked like it should have belonged to a Viking, not my weaselly stepdad, protruding from another. There was a jumble of pipes in one corner that could have been a modern art installation, half of them old and rust-blotched, half shiny and new.

It was like they'd stuck everything they didn't want anymore but couldn't be bothered to actually get rid of into my old room. If that wasn't an appropriate metaphor for my life here, I didn't know what would be.

I couldn't even tell if my bed or any of my other furniture was still stashed away amid the heaps. I didn't have time for a full-on excavation, and anyway, there was no guarantee those fossils of my childhood existence would provide any insight. Nothing about this house had made a lightbulb go off in my brain so far.

I toyed fleetingly with the thought of dumping a bunch of this junk on Mom and Wade's bed and seeing how they liked being relegated to trash, but common sense won out. It was way better for everyone if they never realized I was here.

Backing away from the doorway, I found myself eyeing the room at the end of the hall. Marisol's bedroom door was closed. Even though I knew she wasn't behind it, even though I'd already seen her in her sixteen-year-old state, part of me stared at it with a tickle of conviction that if I yanked it open, I'd find her nine-year-old self sprawled on the floor on the other side. She'd glance up from where she was doodling farting unicorns and dimpled dragons with her markers and grin at me. *What're we doing today, Lily?*

As that image receded, a strange flash of emotion came over me. There was something—I had to—She *needed* me.

I'd taken three steps down the hall before I caught myself. She wasn't *here*. Yeah, she needed me, but walking into her empty room wasn't going to accomplish that.

But for some reason, a deep trepidation gripped me as I grasped the doorknob, as if I were going to swing open the door and find a monster on the other side—and not one of the shaggy, cuddly ones with fanged smiles that'd been in her drawing repertoire.

I shoved the door wide and peered into the space, braced for the worst.

But there was nothing. Nothing except the same old bed and dresser she'd had before, more flakes of the white paint worn off to show the pale wood underneath. The walls were bare now, none of her drawings tacked up. *Did* she even draw still?

I thought of how I'd stopped singing, and my stomach clenched up.

The two frogs hopped past my feet, seemed to consider the room, and hopped back out again. "It was nicer before," I informed them. Back when I'd been here with Mare.

The mark on my arm itched, and I scratched it as I gave the room a long, careful look. No further emotions stirred. The anxiety I'd felt moments ago dwindled. Had it just been a trick of my head, or did it mean something?

It'd sure be nice if my internal states came with a secret decoder ring.

My gaze settled on a lump of bundled fabric nestled beside Marisol's pillow. There was something oddly familiar about it. I took a couple of steps closer and then realized why.

It was my old hoodie—the purple one with the raincloud pattern that I'd adored so much I'd worn it even when I was frying in the summer heat, back when I was thirteen. I hadn't had it on the day I'd been taken away because Marisol had asked to borrow it the night before to help her sleep, and she hadn't been up yet when I'd left the house in the morning. I had a vivid memory of tucking her into bed with it enveloping her skinny nine-year-old frame.

Seven years later, she was still keeping it close. A lump filled my throat. I couldn't have asked for better proof that she still needed *me.* All she'd had was this scrap of fabric instead of her actual big sister.

Swallowing hard, I shut the door again and turned toward Mom and Wade's room. As little as I wanted to go sticking my nose quite that far up their asses, it was my last chance at finding some clue about what else had gotten up Wade's ass—and why he'd thought Kai had been sent by someone to hassle him. I couldn't help Marisol if I didn't have the answers I needed.

But I'd only crossed the hallway as far as the top of the stairs when the thrum of a car engine penetrated the walls, way too close outside to be heading anywhere but here.

My heart flipped over. I dashed down the stairs and to the side door—and then crouched there behind the counters, listening. I couldn't make a run for it now without whoever was driving up seeing me.

If I'd been anyone else, maybe I'd have felt like a super spy. Instead I had the impression of myself as a naughty child shirking the punishment to come, like I'd left muddy fingerprints all over the walls or something.

I didn't stick around to find out what my punishment would be. The second I heard the front door click open and footsteps creak inside, I slipped out into the yard. Then I took off for the span of trees that stood between our official property and the area near the marsh as fast as my feet could carry me.

As soon as I was in the shelter of the trees with no accusing shouts lobbed after me, I followed the line of trunks until I was parallel with my car and headed back to Fred. There, I flopped into the driver's seat and exhaled.

I'd done it. I'd done it… and I didn't have any more answers than I'd had before.

I wet my lips, tasting the marsh on the air that flowed through all the glassless windows around me. A pang that was almost like homesickness formed in my abdomen, which didn't make a whole lot of sense, considering I'd just been closer to my theoretical home than I'd gotten in seven years before.

But it wasn't that house I was missing. Or my dreary apartment. No… I was aching for company.

I looked off toward the town where the four guys who'd risen from the dead for me were waiting. The sensation around my heart tugged harder.

I *missed* them. I missed having them around, with all their banter and laughter, their proclamations and their growls for vengeance. Even their craziness.

What was the point in denying myself that, really? Either *I* was crazy, or I wasn't. Being around them wasn't going to change that. Look what I'd done all on my own.

I wet my lips and pulled out my phone. This might be the most idiotic decision of my life, but it was *mine*.

Chapter Twenty-One

Jett

THE BAR WAS LOUD, smelly, and totally lacking in artistic stimulation. Flat dun-brown paint coated the walls, and smooth, pitch-black tiles covered the floor. The most interesting thing was the formica tabletop, also black but with a mottling of scratches and dents, but the other guys kept grabbing their drinks every time I moved them into an appealing visual composition.

Someday I was going to teach them that you could get buzzed on art just as much as alcohol.

I guessed I couldn't blame them though, because I knew what they were like—and this was our first real night out with Lily. She sat kitty-corner to me at the cramped rectangular table, nursing a dark ale and somehow looking radiant even in the dim bar lighting. Maybe it was just that her pale hair and skin stood out against the dark furnishings to the point that she practically glowed in comparison.

It was almost like she was the ghost among the bunch of us.

That thought would have amused me more if it hadn't come with a weird twinge of guilt. I'd had a cramp in my stomach since Nox had driven us out to look at the indignity our old clubhouse site had been subjected to. I was trying not to examine that cramp too closely. My left hand ached from the little cuts where I'd drawn blood for an epic painting this morning, trying to work all the lingering uneasiness out of me.

It hadn't worked, but the result hadn't been bad. Almost inspired. If I could just find that one missing element…

Ruin clapped his arm around my shoulder and leaned in. "Don't look so gloomy, Jett! Do you want some of my wings?" He grabbed another off the heaping plate he'd ordered.

The cramp in my stomach hadn't stopped me from getting fucking hungry all the time, but I eyed Ruin's order skeptically. He'd always gone for intensity, and based on how he'd been acting in our new lives, that habit had only gotten stronger. The sauce slicked across the wings made my eyes burn just looking at it. Lord only knew what it'd do to my tongue.

It might make an interesting medium, though. I unfolded my napkin to its full size and took a wing to set it at one corner. The neon orange sauce stung my skin in the process. Better keep that away from the bandaids on my other hand.

Kai sensed my hesitation. "We could order some nachos," he suggested from the other side of the table, where he was leafing through yet another book. With all the speed-reading he'd been doing the past few days, you'd think he'd be all caught up already and well into the future of mankind by now. "That's the most recommended item in the reviews for this place."

Of course he'd read those too. I shrugged and downed a gulp of my Jack and Coke. "Doesn't matter. I ate before we left."

Kai peered at me over his glasses in that irritatingly knowing way of his. "But you're hungry again, and you value your tongue enough not to sear it off with those wings."

"I'm fine," I grumbled, and started dabbing the spicy sauce onto the rest of the napkin. The blotches looked like the figures all around us, at least how they appeared to my eyes—so many jumbles of color and motion. Nothing artistically appealing about any of *them* in here.

Which was fine, since it made it easier not to pay attention to them. No one really mattered except our little group… and Lily.

"You're a little hungry too," Kai said to her—still a know-it-all, but a little gentler in tone with her, I'd noticed. "Nachos? Or we could get the stuffed jalapenos. Maybe those would have almost enough kick for our spice-demon here." He shot Ruin a baleful look.

Ruin huffed and moved from me to peck a kiss to Lily's temple. "Lily can share my wings too."

Lily laughed. "I tried one little taste and I'm not sure my mouth will ever recover. Nachos sounds fine, as long as you guys are eating too." She paused. "You're okay for money, right?"

Nox stretched out his legs where he was sitting at my other side. "Don't worry about that. We've got it covered."

The truth was we'd burned through all the cash we'd originally had in our wallets, but Kai's host had been dim enough to write his bank PIN code down on a sticky note, and Ruin could get into his account using the fingerprint recognition on his phone. He'd sent himself a bank draft that we'd immediately cashed. From the size of that posh dude's savings, that should keep us going for a while. But I suspected Nox was a little annoyed that he hadn't been able to contribute from the professor's stash so far.

Of course, he found his own ways. His gaze settled on a pinball machine at the other end of the bar, and his eyes lit up. "Tonight is on me," he announced, shooting Lily a cocky grin, and got up to saunter over to it. From the gestures he made at the figures standing around it, he was arranging bets.

Kai flagged down the waitress and then watched our boss's progress. "He'll bring in enough for tonight and another couple besides, it looks like," he said.

Lily cocked an eyebrow. "He's that good?"

"Nox is the *best*," Ruin declared. "He once kept the ball going for five hours straight."

"The guys he bet against had already paid up and left for closing," Kai added. "We had to hold the owner at gunpoint to stop him from shutting Nox down." When Lily's eyebrows jumped even higher, he raised his hands. "It was either that or let Nox shoot him for throwing off his game."

"He takes his pinball *very* seriously," I muttered, and added another streak of sauce to my composition.

"I see," Lily said, blinking, but she didn't look as disturbed as the average woman might. But then, I'd already known she wasn't an average woman.

She scooted her chair over to take a closer look at my napkin. Her elbow grazed my arm, and my nerve endings flickered into sharper awareness of her presence.

"That's amazing," she said with an awed little laugh.

"You think so?" I studied the image that'd come together with the smudges of sauce. It was a tree sprouting from a haze, the orange hue making it look as if it were made out of fire.

"I'd hang it on my wall, if my wall was worthy of it," she said. "What you're doing always looks so simple, but then it comes together into this image that just hits me." She brought her hand to her chest and then shook her head. "And you managed that with hot sauce on a napkin!"

"I've seen him use weirder materials," Ruin said with a chuckle, and Kai grunted in agreement.

The picture still felt like it wasn't quite *there*, but with Lily's praise beaming over me like sunlight, I didn't totally care. The guys had never said anything about my art like that. It just didn't really register for them. They were more interested in the scenes I could create with a gun and a knife. Which, okay, I did enjoy too.

But Lily's smile made me want to paint every surface in the world just for her. I *should* be able to create something epic with a muse like this. Having her next to me, I had to believe she could fill those empty spaces inside me that I'd never been able to satisfy on my own.

I managed to smile back at her, a gesture my mouth didn't form without conscious effort. Then my senses prickled with a twinge of apprehension.

My gaze slid away from her and settled on a lanky collection of shapes crammed into a booth halfway down the bar. When I focused in on him, his features gradually came into sharper focus: a knob of a nose, puffy lips, and beady eyes that were fixed right on our woman.

My hackles rose automatically. The man's posture oozed slimy and his expression screamed predator. I'd like to stuff a few of Ruin's wings down *his* throat.

A second later, the guy caught me glaring at him. His head twitched to the side, the leer that'd twisted his mouth snapping away. It appeared I could spare Ruin's food from the dire fate I'd pictured.

The nachos arrived, and we all dug in—including Nox, who returned flush with cash that he tossed on the tabletop. Ruin got Lily up to dance, even though no one else was boogeying, but she followed him anyway and giggled as he spun her around in the strip of clear floor between the bar and the tables.

The bartender rolled his eyes, and I contemplated removing them from his head.

The slimy creep stalked over to a woman sitting on her own at the smallest table. He bought her a drink and another, his hand lingering on her wrist even when her shoulders tensed up a little. Every now and then, he glanced over at Lily, so I kept glancing at him.

When Lily started yawning, Nox took one look at her and declared that it was time to get home. I tossed my napkin painting on the nachos platter with the rest of the garbage—I'd do better next time, and in a medium that wouldn't start to stink—and considered the creep once more.

"I've got to take care of a couple things," I told the others. "I'll meet you there."

"Is everything okay?" Lily asked with a furrow of concern on her forehead, as if *she* needed to be worrying about me.

"No big deal," I told her.

"Jett *always* looks like the world's about to end," Nox informed her, tucking his arm around her waist as the four of them headed out. "You'll get used to it."

I didn't have to wait long. It couldn't have been more than five minutes of lurking outside the bar when the creep came sauntering out with his hand locked around the woman's wrist. She was wobbling on her feet, obviously drunk. He led her down a couple of blocks, around a corner, and then hauled her into a narrow alley there. She was only aware enough to let out a confused mumble of protest.

I didn't know her. She had no bearing on my life. But I knew pricks like him—and I knew he was about to do to her what he'd *wanted* to do to Lily. I was just taking care of a little trash.

They disappeared into the shadows farther down the alley. There was a gasp and a little squeal quickly muffled by the clap of a hand over a mouth. I pulled out the knife I'd outfitted myself with using the last of the nerd's cash.

I hadn't done the job all the way to the end the one time it'd mattered most, but I wasn't going to make that mistake again.

The man was too busy wrenching at the woman's panties to notice me stalking over behind him. I plunged the knife right into his jugular and shoved him toward the end of the alley. The woman gasped and staggered away. Her uneven footsteps pattered into the distance. No shouts of alarm. She was just glad to get out of here.

The creep gurgled and sprayed the grungy walls with his blood. I traced the lines with my eyes, tempted to direct him a little further but holding myself back. I needed him dead, not pretty.

He slumped right over on the ground. After a few minutes, he stopped twitching. I checked his pulse to be completely sure he was a goner. Then I swiped his wallet, because a little extra cash wouldn't hurt, and that way it'd look like a mugging. We could dodge the police, but it was easier if they weren't looking for us in the first place.

The creep had created a sort of bloody snow angel on the pavement. I committed the image to memory as I wiped the knife on his pants and stuffed it back in my pocket. It could make a nice painting someday.

But there was too much threatening Lily in this town, and I'd only dealt with a little of the danger. We were going to have to step up our game.

Chapter Twenty-Two

Lily

"Of all the crap we missed in the last twenty-one years, this Bennifer thing has got to be the weirdest," Kai remarked as I drove toward Mart's Supermarket, twisting his phone in his hand as if looking at it upside down would make the news easier to swallow. "The two of them don't make any sense together, so how are they a couple *again*? Wasn't the first time enough?"

My lips twitched with amusement. "I thought you were getting caught up on actual news, not celebrity gossip."

"All news is 'actual.' You can learn tons of things about how people think from the superficial stuff."

I glanced over at him as I slowed for a red light. By their own special methods, the guys had found someone to replace all Fred's windows overnight, so we weren't taking a blast of wind in the face like we might have yesterday.

"Is that what you want—to figure out how people think?" I asked.

He shrugged, still eyeing his phone. "The better grasp I have on the psyche of the average human being, the better I can manipulate them. I got a lot done for the Skullbreakers that way."

I guessed that explanation made a sort of sense. I didn't have much chance to ponder it, because as I cruised around the next bend and the grocery store came into view, the scene in the parking lot seared every other thought from my mind with a shock of panic.

Two cop cars were parked outside the store entrance. It must have been a slow day for the county's tiny police force, because that might have been all the cars they had in the whole department. A few men in uniform were standing in a semi-circle around Burt Bower, who was motioning to the front of the store—

"Oh, fuck," I said under my breath as my gaze traveled that far. Kai's head jerked up.

The entire face of Mart's Supermarket, from the bold-lettered sign up top to the tall windows that stretched out on either side of the glass doors, had been marked with broad slashes of red spray paint. Mostly they cut across the panes and pale siding seemingly at random, like cuts gouged into the store by giant claws. But here and there they formed more coherent patterns… like the words *FUCK YOU* blazoned right across the door right next to a jutting illustrated dick.

For just a second, I thought of Jett and his affinity for paint, but this crude mess looked way too rough and amateurish to be his work. And I couldn't see any reason he would have attacked my workplace this way. Burt had been a bit of a jerk, but Jett didn't know that, and the guys were all aware of how much I needed this job.

Why would *anyone* have messed with the grocery store like this? Had my manager made unexpected enemies among an underground punk gang?

I drew into the lot tentatively and parked several spots away from the police cars. The lot was mostly empty—the store didn't open for another half an hour—but a few other vehicles had pulled in on the far side, people watching the scene through the windows. In Lovell Rise, this incident definitely counted as major news. It'd keep the gossip channels going for weeks.

As I stepped out of the car with Kai following, Burt waved toward me. The cops turned to inspect my approach. I tamped down on the prickle of nerves that rippled through me.

It was possible one or more of these officers had been involved when I'd been hauled away seven years ago, but I didn't remember any of them. No reason to assume they'd recognize me. They should have bigger things on their minds right now than a thirteen-year-old's mental breakdown nearly a decade ago.

"What happened?" I asked, focusing on Burt. Where we even still opening today? I had a feeling he'd want to get the paint cleaned off rather than have people walking through the doors with a giant erect dick pointing at them.

One of the cops puffed out his chest as he looked me up and down and said, "We were hoping you could tell us about that."

I blinked at him. "I'm sorry?"

"Yes, you should be," Burt snapped, in a tone so seething I was surprised smoke wasn't billowing out of his ears.

Neither of them were making any sense. I turned to the puffed-up cop. "I really don't understand what you mean. I only just got here."

One of the other cops let out a disbelieving grunt and jabbed his thumb toward a few figures I hadn't noticed who'd gotten out of their car. "We've received a report from witnesses who saw a woman fitting your description leaving the scene with a paint can in your hand."

As I took in my accusers, my blood went cold. Peyton shot me a tightly triumphant smile, her skinny arms folded over her chest. The guy next to her was another of Ansel's friends, the one my guys had hung from the dock post a few days ago. He glared more at Kai than at me. And beside him was some dude I'd never talked to before but who I thought I remembered from the football field when Zach and his teammates had harassed me.

"Yeah, that's her all right," he said. "She did it." The others nodded.

My jaw dropped. "I—You've got to be kidding me." I glanced from one cop to another. "I swear I had nothing to do with this. I haven't been at the store since my closing shift two days ago." Well, technically I'd been here the next morning after sleeping in the lounge, but that wasn't relevant. "I don't even know where I'd *buy* spray paint."

The first cop scoffed. "I'm going to have to go with the eyewitness report on this one. You'd better—"

Kai cleared his throat to interrupt, tucking his phone into his pocket and stepping forward so he was right beside me. He pushed up his glasses and gave the police officers an incisive look through the panes. "Even when the eyewitnesses are heavily biased?"

The lead cop's brow furrowed. "What are you talking about?"

Kai raised his chin toward my trio of accusers. "A bunch of Lily's fellow students have been harassing her for several days now, including those three. I'd bet they defaced the store so that they could pin the blame on her. I know *she* didn't do it, because I was out with her and then at her apartment all night."

"This guy and his… friends have been harassing *us* because of her," Ansel's friend retorted.

The cops looked between us and the other group with increasingly put-upon expressions. They must have been starting to think they'd been caught up in a petty college-student squabble, but there'd still been an actual crime committed here. They still needed to find the perpetrator.

Kai ignored the other guy's statement and motioned to a security camera mounted by the front door. "Your camera must have caught the person who did this. Have you even looked at the footage?"

Burt raised his chin. "Of course. There was only one person in view, and she was wearing a hoodie. She never turned her face toward the camera, so she can't be IDed from that alone, but it definitely could have been Lily."

Or it could have been Peyton, or even a slim guy, with all the shadows obscuring the image.

Kai wasn't deterred. "What time did this all happen?"

"Just after midnight."

A hint of a smile curled the former gangster's lips. "No problem, then. We left The Deep Dive around twelve-thirty last night. I'm pretty sure the bar has security footage too. One quick check, and you'll see Lily couldn't have been here making this wonderful art, unless you're going to claim she can clone herself."

His know-it-all tone clearly raised Burt's hackles, but facts were facts. The cops stepped aside to mutter with one another, and Peyton's crew tried to murder us with their eyes. I wondered if it was possible to charge someone with attempted assault by death glare.

One of the cops got on his phone, I guessed with the bar. After he nodded to his colleagues, the lead officer turned toward me. "We're going to check out your alibi. If your friend here is telling the truth, there shouldn't be any trouble. But I don't want you leaving town in the meantime."

"I wasn't planning on it," I said, doing my best to sound agreeable and not snarky.

From his expression, I only half succeeded, but that was enough for them to leave. Peyton and co drew back to their car to hash out the situation among themselves, and Burt swiveled to face me. His peevish expression made me tense up all over again.

"Are we opening the store?" I ventured.

His scowl deepened. "Not for the moment. And you won't be opening it at any point. I'm going to have to let you go."

I stared at him. "But—I didn't *do* this. I didn't do anything wrong. As soon as the cops check with the bar—"

He was already shaking his head. "It doesn't matter either way. This incident clearly had something to do with you, one way or another. You're bringing too much trouble to this store—after just a couple of weeks on the job. You can pick up your paycheck for the hours you did work on Friday."

With that, he stalked across the parking lot to his own car, leaving me standing there with my heart plummeting to my feet. The other spectators were driving away too, the excitement having dwindled with the cops' departure. In a minute, it was just Kai and me near the doors and Peyton's group by their car.

Kai gave my shoulder a quick squeeze. "We'll figure something else out."

I swallowed hard. "It's going to be all of ten seconds before every employer in town hears about this—and half of them will probably only get the part of the story where I was spraying dicks on my workplace's door. Damn it."

As I stood there, momentarily adrift, a jeep pulled into the parking lot. It rumbled over to stop next to Peyton and the others, and five more guys got out—a couple of them people I'd seen hanging out with Ansel, others who might have been footballers, at least one I had no clue about whatsoever. Apparently the sport of ganging up on Lily had become a free-for-all.

The pack of them marched over to us together, Peyton staying off to the side but looking as fiercely eager as the others. I backed up a step instinctively, but Kai held his ground, his shoulders squaring.

"Not so confident when it's just you on your own, I bet," one of the guys sneered at him. "You think you're so tough. Time we taught you a lesson."

Kai chuckled, not sounding remotely fazed. "The lesson that it takes seven of you to come at one of me? I already knew you were wimps."

The guy who'd spoken let out a growl and stomped forward. But at the same moment, two more engines roared into hearing behind us.

First came the car that'd once been Ansel's, with Ruin behind the wheel and Jett braced in the passenger seat. As it jolted to a halt next to us, a motorcycle whipped into the lot with Nox poised on its seat. His teeth were bared in something half grin, half snarl.

He'd finally gotten the bike he'd wanted so much, some distant part of my mind registered. Kai must have texted for them to come before he'd started debating with the cops.

The guys leapt out of the car, and Nox hurtled off the motorcycle. Even though they still had nearly twice the numbers, our opponents fell back, their threatening expressions turning comically uncertain.

One of them broke and ran for the cars. Kai whipped a switchblade from his pocket and flung it across the pavement so fast it was a blur—until it slammed into one of the tires. The air groaned out. Jett hurled a knife of his own at the second vehicle.

"You're not going anywhere until we're good and done with you," Nox said. "And probably not even then."

"We shouldn't kill them," Kai piped up. "The three of them have been connected to Lily just now in front of law enforcement. Adding murder to the mix might be dicey for her."

Nox let out a huff of disappointment, but his eyes flared. "Fine. We'll just make them very, very sorry."

He stalked toward the bullies with murder radiating from every pore.

Chapter Twenty-Three

Lily

My bullies weren't stupid. They could obviously tell they were about to be dead meat, or at least the closest thing to that without actually meeting their ends.

The group broke apart, the assholes scattering in every direction, Peyton dashing around the side of the store. But my guys were faster.

Nox caught one of Ansel's friends and hurled him right through the spray-painted windows. The guy crashed to the floor with a cacophony of breaking glass. Ruin wrapped his arms around another in a deadly bear hug and whipped him after his companion. Kai tripped one and sent him rolling. Jett flipped another over his shoulder and flung him through the broken window. The two of them grabbed their knives from the sunken tires.

Peyton had vanished, but there was no escape for the others. At the brandishing of Kai's and Jett's knives in between them and the other end of the parking lot, the remainders fled into the store after their friends, maybe hoping they could find a back entrance to flee out of. Of course, that door would be locked.

The Skullbreakers charged after their foes. Yelps and squelches emanated from within the grocery store. My whole body had gone numb, but I managed to move my feet to step through the window and witness the fate my accusers were meeting.

The grocery store had transformed into a whirlwind of violence. Over in the produce aisle, Jett was pelting two of the guys with potatoes, hard enough for each strike to land with a meaty thunk and a pained gasp from his targets.

Kai had toppled another dude. He swept a heap of grapes off the display onto the guy's back and then leapt onto him to mash the fruit in with his stomping feet. At the guy's whimper, he smirked. "That's right, we're making a little whine."

Down the other aisles, Ruin had grabbed two bottles of his favorite hot sauce. He squirted it at the faces of three guys who tried to hurtle past him, and they stumbled into the shelves, groping at their eyes. As he cackled, Nox cracked a frozen pizza over the last bully's head. Pepperoni rained down, sticking to the dipshit's cheeks like clown make-up.

Ruin snatched a jug of apple juice and heaved it right into one guy's groin. The lid popped open on impact. The dickhead doubled over, juice sloshing down his khakis as if he'd wet himself. From the look on his face, he might have done that too.

Jett had rushed in on one of his targets. He scooped him up and rammed him headfirst into a pre-packaged meat display. The guy rolled off the shelves, bleeding from his head and smeared with ground beef and bits of porkchop as if his innards had popped right through his skin without breaking it. Jett gave him another kick to the head for good measure.

At a choking sound, I spun around to see Kai ramming a handful of hotdogs into the other potato-pelted dude's mouth. They poked from the guy's swollen lips like a meme about chowing down on dicks. Kai straightened up and pushed them deeper with his heel.

A hysterical laugh bubbled in my throat. I couldn't decide whether I was more horrified or amused. One thing was for sure—these fucknuts were never going to forget *this* beating.

Over by the cash registers, Nox had now knocked down two guys. He had them both pinned with a knee on each gut, stabbing them with spikes of dry spaghetti so they were gradually turning into human porcupines. At their groans and hisses of pain, he glowered at them. "If there has to be a next time, I'll be stabbing these right through your intestines. Keep that in mind."

Ruin dashed by, shoving a guy into a tower of canned veggies and then smacking the rest to rain down on him, bashing the douche-nozzle's head and chest. "Best possible use for lima beans!" he crowed.

Jett leapt back into view, his knife in one hand and a Pop Tart in the other. He slashed out at the last guy still on his feet, cutting sliver-thin cuts with the knife and broader gouges with the corner of the breakfast pastry. When the jerkwad slipped and sprawled face-first in a puddle of sour juice from a pickle jar someone had smashed on the floor, Jett leaned over to carve the words *PICKLE PRICK* across his shoulder blades. He let out a dark laugh. "Your dates deserve fair warning."

The sounds of the mayhem swirled around me, grunts and gasps, sloshes and crackles. It filled my head with a weird, wavering melody that begged for words. Crazed as it was, there was something so brilliantly orchestral about the maelstrom of violence…

The hum I'd felt before expanded through my chest as if to match that strange harmony. My nerves quivered, and my stomach lurched. I'd felt that sensation right when Peyton's water had started jumping around—

Kai glanced over at me, and a gleam lit in his eyes. He grinned at me as if I'd done something fantastic, even though I hadn't done anything except stand here staring for the last several minutes. Then he noticed one of the guys half crawling, half sliding through the mess on the floor toward the stock room. He bared his teeth. "Oh, no, you don't. You don't know *half* of what we're capable of."

Neither did I, it seemed. Kai slammed his hand down at the edge of the wet streak, and sparks shot across the mess of liquid. The guy's body seized and spasmed as if he'd been struck by lightning.

Ruin, watching, let out a whoop. "Can we *all* do that?" he asked, and spun on a guy sitting in a puddle of hot sauce before Kai even answered. At the smack of his fingers, his foe jolted on his ass, teeth rattling.

Holy shit. They hadn't lost all their supernatural powers when they'd dived into their new bodies. What were my bullies going to make of that?

Nox cocked his head with curiosity and sent a zap through a pool of juice toward the two guys who were slumped in it. At the twitch of their bodies, a satisfied smile curled his lips.

"You stay away from us, and you stay away from Lily," he bellowed to the store at large. "This was us playing nice. You don't want to find out what mean looks like." Then, apparently determining that their work here was done, he motioned for the others to tramp with him over to the broken window where I was still standing frozen.

The rising hum inside me had faded. The bottom of my stomach had fallen out, leaving me uncomfortably empty and more than a little dazed. I wobbled out of the store, images and sounds still whirling in my head, and my gaze caught on the camera that had factored so much into the accusations against me. My heart stopped.

"The security system!" I said. "The owner hasn't bothered with alarms"—because things like this didn't happen around here, not in Lovell Rise—"but we'll be on camera." It didn't matter if Nox had scared the scumbags out of tattling on him and his men if the video footage told the story for them.

Kai made a dismissive sound and clapped his hand to the doorframe below the camera. With a sizzling noise, the camera gave off a few sparks and sagged slightly. Kai wiped his hands together with a triumphant air. "I fried it all the way to the hard drive that's storing the footage. There won't be anything to look at except our redecorating efforts." He glanced at the wrecked store with an arch of his eyebrows.

I looked at it too, and my chest constricted. My daze was washed away by a flood of panic.

The guys had gotten revenge on my bullies, sure, but how much did that really change? They'd given away so much about what they were and what they could do, while leaving a trail of wreckage in their wake.

How much of my life was about to get so much worse?

I swept my fingers back into my hair, my breath coming short. "I lost my job. I don't have any way to make more money. People are going to be talking about me all around town as it is. If anyone realizes I was at all connected to what just happened here—"

"They won't," Kai said calmly. "The police will clear you of the graffiti, which'll make it obvious that your accusers were the real criminals. Who knows what else they might be mixed up in to end up like this?" He waved toward the store. "Things that have nothing to do with you or us."

He sounded utterly confident, but I couldn't quite wrap my head around it being that easy. *Nothing* had been easy since I'd gotten back here.

"There could be something we haven't thought of," I said, the words tumbling out of me. "I can't come back from this. Everything's—everything's gotten turned upside down. How'm I supposed to get back to Marisol when I'm mixed up in this mess?"

Nox set his hand on my back. "Let's get you back home," he said firmly. "We don't want to hang around here now that we've taken care of those dolts. Then we'll have a real conversation. It's all going to be fine. We've got you now, no matter what comes."

He hopped onto his new motorcycle with a nod to the other guys. Ruin escorted me over to my car. He nudged me into the passenger seat and got in behind the wheel. I let him take the keys, sinking into the lumpy padding and closing my eyes.

Had I made a mistake letting these guys into my life? Had they always been this wild, or had death left them even more unhinged than in their original existence?

Who was going to protect me from *them* if they got too crazy? They might only want to protect me, but that didn't mean it'd work out that way.

Ruin switched the radio to a station that was more noise than melody and turned it up loud enough that conversation would have been impossible anyway. He tore through the streets so fast that it only took the length of one song to make it back to the apartment. After he parked, he came around to my door, and I got the impression that he'd have carried me inside like Nox had hauled me into his office the other day if I didn't show I could manage it on my own.

I pushed myself to my feet, willing my legs to stay steady, and trudged down the steps to the apartment door. Inside, I flopped onto the futon and immediately slid into the dip in the middle. I couldn't summon the resolve to clamber back out.

The guys gathered around me as they followed us in, Nox sitting on one side of me and Ruin on the other, Jett and Kai dragging over chairs from the table.

"What's bothering you?" Nox asked, with an edge to a tone that suggested he hoped it was something he could shoot or stab.

I bent over, pressing my hands against my face. "I was trying to build a normal life so that Mom and Wade wouldn't have any excuse to keep me away from Marisol. But that's all gone to hell, hasn't it? Everything's just a mess."

"You couldn't let those pricks keep treating you like a punching bag. They weren't stopping just because you weren't fighting back."

Ruin rubbed my arm. "*They're* the ones who screwed things up. You deserve to have someone defending you."

"You should let us wipe them out completely," Jett muttered.

I tensed. "People *dying* isn't going to make the situation better."

Kai leaned forward. "If you won't let us crush the bullies completely, then *you* need to put them in their place. Show them you won't be a target anymore. There'll be others like the pricks we dealt with today. Rolling over for them wasn't working, so it's time to stand up."

I raised my head to stare at him. "How am I supposed to do that? Go around punching and knifing anyone who makes a nasty comment at me?"

He smiled, his eyes glinting behind his glasses. "I think you can do something better than that. You just need to let loose that power inside you. I could feel it back at the grocery store. You could have all these assholes shaking in their designer sneakers if you let yourself."

"Power?" I repeated, but my hand rose to my chest at the same moment, thinking of the hum that'd resonated there. Of Kai looking at me as the vibration had filled my torso.

Ruin sucked in a breath. "I noticed it too! You've got some kind of energy in you—kind of like ours." He looked down at his free hand. "But *you* were never a ghost."

"She almost was," Nox said into the sudden silence. "We don't know how close she got to crossing over—close enough that her spirit called out to us." He caught my gaze. "Maybe you came out of the marsh with more than you went in with."

"It's hardly typical science, but that possibility seems plausible to me," Kai said. "There's definitely *something* more to you than you're letting out."

A shiver ran over my skin at the thought of some unknown power inside me. "I don't even know what it is. If there's some special magic inside me, how'm I supposed to control it? How can I bring it out when I actually want it?" I dropped my head back into my hands and shook it. "Fuck. This is too insane."

Maybe Mom and Wade hadn't been wrong to shut me away with the psychos after all.

Chapter Twenty-Four

Nox

Lily's pose, so hopeless and terrified, made me want to burn the world down. Although I had the feeling that would make her more upset, not less.

Why couldn't she see that the strangeness that shone in her made her something *more* than any regular human being, not less? That she could rise above all the assholes who wanted to crush her under their heels and put them in their places instead?

I'd lost my crew once and gotten them back, but now I felt like I was losing her too, after all the lengths I'd gone to so I could be here for her. What was the point of any of this if the pricks like those college bullies and her stepdad won in the end?

A growl formed in the back of my throat, but I held it in. She'd spent too long having all those living voices around her telling her she was worthless, nothing but an inconvenience. Our ghostly chorus hadn't been enough to drown them out. And now, with the four of us braced around her, maybe we were suffocating with our own expectations.

I stood up abruptly. "Out!" I barked at my friends. "All of you, find something else useful to do with yourselves. I'm going to talk Lily through this alone. She doesn't need all four of us breathing down her neck at the same time."

Ruin's arm tightened around her with a possessiveness that rankled me. "But—"

"*Out*," I repeated, and he didn't rebel any further. He pressed a quick kiss to Lily's forehead and got to his feet. Kai caught my gaze with a questioning glance, but when I jerked my head toward the door, he went. Jett followed the two of them with his usual brooding silence.

When the door clicked shut and it was just me and Lily, she stayed sitting there with her face in her hands. Her long, pale hair fell forward like a veil. She looked *small* somehow, and that wasn't right at all.

It occurred to me that I had no idea what to do next. I ruled the Skullbreakers, so I should be the one to tackle this problem too… but it wasn't anything I could threaten or batter into going my way. Lily's greatest enemy was something *inside* her that was freaking her out, and I wasn't going to let myself break her trying to get at it. Not when all I wanted to do was put her together into the stunning woman she should have already known she was.

Maybe I should have let Ruin handle this. What the hell did I know about being gentle? I flexed my hands at my sides, groping for the right thing to say, the right thing to do.

"Come here," I said finally. Without waiting to see if she'd listen, I scooped her off the couch and carried her into her bedroom.

Setting her on the edge of the bed, I knelt in front of her. The frame was so low that position brought us eye-to-eye.

It should have felt awkward being on my knees in front of anyone. But with Lily, the pose didn't feel like any kind of humiliation. I was showing her we were on the same level. Could be that was the best place to start.

I brushed my fingers over her cheek and into her hair, unable to resist giving it a playful tug. "You didn't let the marsh swallow you, and you're not letting whatever this is beat you either," I informed her. "What's really the problem here? Why do you give a single shit what any of those people think of you?"

Lily drew in a wobbly breath. "A few of those people are standing between me and my sister. A lot of the others could get me in trouble with the first people if they complain about me enough… or even with the cops. I can't get sent back to St. Elspeth's. I don't know if the doctors would ever let me back out."

"*We'd* break you out of there if it came to that," I said, my jaw tensing at the thought. "But it won't. You've got us now, and you've got *you*. You don't have to let any of them get between you and your sister."

"But—"

"You've got the strength to shove them aside and take what you know you're owed," I went on before she could dismiss my words. "That's how we live. Fuck the rules. Fuck catering to assholes' judgements. If you let yourself stop caring what the people who don't matter want, *nothing* can get in your way. Can't you feel that power Kai was talking about in here?" I tapped her chest.

Lily shivered. "It doesn't feel like power. It feels like… like I'm going to lose control, and I don't know what'll happen then. I don't know who I might hurt. And what if I *want* a life that's at least kind of normal? I've got to follow the rules then."

I raised my eyebrows at her. "Do you actually want something normal, or are you just scared that you'll be punished if you carve your own path?" I guessed me and my bros weren't the best example of that. *Our* paths had been cut short by other pricks who hadn't liked the rules we made for ourselves. But we were back, and we weren't going to let anyone get in our way now.

And I'd rather live free for a short while than be tied up in some straitjacket of politeness for an eternity.

"I don't know," Lily whispered. "Marisol needs me. I don't want to let her down."

I pushed myself straighter and leaned in so my face was just inches from hers, teasing my fingers into her hair again. Her intoxicating scent swept into my lungs, wild and sweet, and suddenly the correct path for me right now stretched out in my mind, perfectly clear.

"I think the reason you feel out of control is that you're not used to using your power," I said. "You didn't even know you had it. But you've got all kinds of power, Minnow. Do you have any idea how much power you hold over *me*? You're my siren. You're the reason I'm here at all. The things you do to me, just having you so close…"

Just saying the words, desire flickered through me like a flame over kerosene. It'd been too fucking long since I'd gotten to indulge these bodily urges, since I'd had a body to indulge them with, and my nerves screamed for more. I held myself back with a fraying thread of self-control.

What I wanted wasn't the important part. Lily needed to be the one who crossed the line this time. She needed to *take* instead of being taken.

She reached up, her soft fingers tracing along my jaw and lighting more flames in their wake. "I really mean that much to you?"

"To all of us," I said, reluctantly but honestly. I owed that much to the guys who'd stood by me. "I'm going to rebuild the Skullbreakers and remake our name—but I came back for *you*. I already had one life that was all about me. In this one, you come first."

She inhaled with a little hitch of her chest that sounded more awed than anxious. I grazed my fingers over her scalp and pressed my advantage while my hardening cock pressed against the seam of my jeans in tandem.

"Why don't you find out what it's like working some of that power on me? Get a little practice in. See just how much you can rule even when you're letting go."

Lily hesitated just for a second. Then, thank the Devil, she tugged me toward her to capture my mouth with hers.

It wasn't the epic collision of our first kiss, but the tender eagerness of her lips sliding against mine sent a rush of satisfaction through me that was just as heady. I let her take her fill of me, kissing her back but not taking over, running my fingertips up and down the side of her neck as I did. She let out a pleased murmur and kissed me harder with a passion that had me rigid as rock down below.

She'd spent a lifetime being told she wasn't good enough for anyone. I had to show her with every gesture and word I could offer how fucking cherished she was now. How much she was really worth.

Until I convinced her. And then I'd keep reminding her so she never forgot.

I eased my other hand under her shirt, tracing her smooth skin up to the curve of her chest. Her bra was thin enough that her nipple poked through the fabric when I swiped my thumb over it.

Lily made another sound that was more of a growl, scooting even closer, and a smile curved my lips against hers.

"Every part of you drives me crazy," I murmured, trailing my mouth along her jaw. "Your mouth. Your cheeks. Your fucking *ears*." I nipped her earlobe, and she gave a tiny gasp. "This neck is goddamned delicious." I teased my teeth down the slope of it, bringing out a perfect whimper of need.

It was a miracle being able to touch *any* woman like this again. My veins were on fire. But the fact that it was Lily made it ten times sweeter. I hadn't known we'd careen toward each other like this—had never looked at her this way in the times before when she'd only been a kid—but now it was nothing short of perfect.

No other woman had ever held a candle to the inferno she'd set off in me.

"I want to see you," Lily said abruptly, her hands fisting in my shirt.

I was more than happy to oblige. I peeled off the Henley and pulled her tee over her head in turn. She sat there on the bed without the slightest hint of self-consciousness about being bared to her bra in front of me, her attention fixed on my torso.

I'd grown into this body that hadn't been shaped quite right to fit me when I'd first possessed it. The muscles that'd filled out my chest and shoulders were almost on par with what I'd sported back in the day. I might still be a few inches shorter than my former glory of height, but I'd just have to make up for that with an even more massive presence.

Lily trailed her fingers over my pecs, and I had to clench my hands to stop myself from yanking her right to me. "Is this how you looked before?" she asked tentatively.

"I'm getting there," I said. "No professor bod is going to get in my way for long." I glanced down at myself, taking a measure of the terrain. "My tattoos haven't reemerged. I guess they weren't inked right on my spirit. I'll have to get them done when I don't have more important things occupying me."

She swiveled her thumb over one of my nipples, watching my face to catch how my eyes blazed at the quiver of pleasure. A growl crept into my voice, but it wasn't remotely angry. "I love having you touch me almost as much as I love touching you."

And because I was a man of action, I followed that statement up by reaching around her to unclasp her bra. I ducked my head to lap the peak of one breast into my mouth and worked it over with my tongue and teeth until Lily was moaning and clutching my hair.

"That's right, baby," I said as I moved to worship her other breast. "I've got so much more for you. You taste so good."

I'd bet she tasted even better farther down. As I sucked on her nipple, bringing another gasp to her lips, I flicked open the fly of her jeans and tugged them down her legs.

Her panties were soaked. Approval thrummed through my chest as I stroked her through them.

"Good girl. So fucking wet for me. Do you have any idea how hard I am for you? You make me want to explode. But I'm going to look after you first."

I wrenched her panties down too and buried my face between her thighs.

Lily gave a shriek that was all pleasure. I devoured her, flicking my tongue over her clit and delving it right into her pussy, drinking up those sharply sweet juices that flooded out of her at my call. Hell, this was the best meal I'd had since I'd gotten back my mouth.

It was a fucking crime that no one had ever worshiped her the way she deserved until now.

As I suckled her harder, her breath broke into stuttered pants. She tipped back on the bed, her head resting against the wall, her hips rocking to meet the thrusts of my tongue. I focused my mouth over her clit and brought two fingers up to hook inside her. With a few testing strokes, I found the special spot inside her that made her shudder.

It only took a few pulses of my fingertips against that place alongside the pressure of my mouth to bring her to a quaking release. Her pussy clamped around my fingers and her back arched up as the sweetest moan in existence reverberated out of her. I'd taken her even higher than I had the other day on the professor's desk.

Part of me wished I'd drawn out her gratification even longer, but a bigger part was desperate to fuse my body to hers in the most primal possible way. I gave her pussy one last lingering kiss and loomed up over her, fumbling in my pocket for the condom I'd thankfully had the foresight to carry. I had no idea if possessed swimmers swam well, but after all the weirdness of our ghostly union with these bodies, I didn't think knocking our woman up with ghostly jizz was a smart idea.

Lily undid my fly for me, freeing my cock into her waiting hand and then gazing up at me with heavy-lidded eyes. I practically came just looking at her. As she swiveled her fingers around my straining shaft, a groan tumbled out of me.

"God, I want you so fucking badly. You're my universe, Lily. You defied death and dragged me back to life. There isn't anyone in their right mind who should mess with you."

A glow lit in her face that hadn't been there before. Maybe I was getting through to her.

I kicked off my jeans, pausing every now and then to hiss a breath and pump into her stroking hand. As she tugged my boxers down, biting her lower lip as she did, I knew just how to take this final step.

I slicked the condom over my rigid cock and sank down onto the mattress on my back. When my own hand worked up and down my shaft, making my balls ache, Lily's gaze followed the movement. She licked her lips, and my dick twitched.

"You want this?" I asked in a low voice.

Lily lifted her head to meet my eyes. Her cheeks were flushed from her first orgasm, all of her absolutely radiant. "Yeah," she said, soft but certain. "I do."

I grinned. "Then come and get it, baby."

And fuck me if she didn't clamber right onto me, straddling my hips. I pushed myself up on my elbow, and she bent down to claim my mouth. Her tongue cautiously slipped between my lips and then tangled with mine. I hummed encouragingly, massaging her ass with my free hand.

She lined herself up over me and sank onto my cock, impaling herself with that jutting length. Her slick cunt closed tight around me, and sparks went off behind my eyes. I couldn't hold back another groan—but why should I? I wanted her to know how much she affected me.

"Your pussy feels so good around me," I muttered. "So fucking good. Take me all the way—I know you can."

She eased lower with a rock of her hips, and I gripped her ass to steady her. Giddy heat flooded my entire body, with the tightest knot of need at the base of my groin. "Oh, yeah. Just like that. I can't wait to make you scream."

She let out a mewling sound, and I took that as my cue to move. As her hands braced against my chest, I bucked up to meet her, thrusting even deeper inside her.

Lily swayed with the rhythm, arching her back and pumping up and down over me at the same time. Her eyelids fluttered shut. Her lips parted to form a gorgeous O. I'd take her to an even better one.

"Keep doing that, baby," I said, massaging her thigh. "You feel fucking incredible. You ride me so good."

A whimper spilled out of her, and then a sound that wasn't the scream I'd been searching for but something so much better.

She was singing. In a pale, whispery voice that rose and fell with the colliding of our bodies, but it was the first melody I'd heard from her lips since she'd come back into our lives.

"So high… soaring all the way to the sky… Never felt, never knew… that it could be so bright…"

She made up a song just for me. For us and this sweaty, blissful moment. Somehow or other, I'd managed to heal that one part of her that'd been broken. I'd done something really fucking right.

My heart swelled nearly as much as my cock. I was right on the verge.

Squeezing her ass, I plunged up into her with a swivel of my hips, seeking that perfect spot she needed. On the second try, a shudder wracked her body.

Her head dropped back, her whole body tightening against me with the spasm of her pussy, and my cock erupted. My vision sizzled with the force of my coming.

Lily bowed over me with a hitch of breath and a small, sly smile. As she nestled her head against my shoulder, I wrapped my arms around her and smirked at the thought of all the bastards who were going to pay when she showed them just what she was made of.

Chapter Twenty-Five

Lily

SOMETHING HAD SHIFTED in the air. When the rest of the guys came back to the apartment with Chinese takeout, when Nox ran a possessive hand down my back and Ruin slung a companionable arm around my shoulders, when I snuggled in the bed that still smelled like heavenly sex while the sound of their sleeping breaths filtered through the wall, every motion I made and every sound that stirred around me blended together into a giddy sort of harmony.

It sang through my nerves and tingled over my skin every place Nox had touched me. With his adoring words in my ears and bliss rushing through my body, I'd felt as if I really was as powerful as he said. A goddess who could bend the world to her will.

The thought seemed a little silly now, but the sense of weightlessness remained. No one was going to hold me down. I could make the world I wanted to live in… Insist on a life where Mom and Wade couldn't keep me from Marisol… Ward off anyone who tried to trip me up or insult me. Even the music that wove from the world into me felt right, like it would be okay for me to put a voice to it again.

Like I deserved a chance to let out the songs that tickled up through my mind.

But that sense only stayed solid while I was in the bubble of my apartment with the guys. Outside under the mid-morning sun with the crisp fall breeze in my nose, reality came crashing back in on me.

I paused on the sidewalk outside the side lane that led to my apartment steps, inhaling and exhaling, wondering what the police were saying about me now after the mess they'd have found in Mart's Supermarket yesterday. What the whole town was saying about me. A shiver of uncertainty rippled through my previous confidence.

Ruin slipped his arm around my waist with his usual warm affection and nuzzled my temple. I was pretty sure all the guys had been able to tell what Nox and I had gotten up to, but if it put off the cheerful former gangster, he hadn't shown it.

"We can all go with you," he suggested. "Walk you right to class. Make anyone who even looks at you funny sorry."

A despairing chuckle fell from my mouth. Imagine what my classmates and professors would think of me having that devoted an entourage—and one composed of a guy they still recognized as a professor and students who'd never had anything to do with each other before.

But that wasn't really the point, was it? If I'd wanted the guys with me, then I shouldn't care what anyone else thought about it. These men could handle any backlash that came their way.

What mattered was that they'd been right about one thing: I needed to stand on my own two feet. As long as they were doing all the defending, the people who wanted to push me around would just keep doing it when they felt they could get away with it.

I had to show them it wasn't worth it even when they were only dealing with me.

I still wasn't totally sure how I was going to accomplish that or that the attempt wouldn't go horribly wrong, but enough resolve condensed inside me that I raised my chin. "No. You can come with me to campus, but I'll go on my own from there. If anyone comes at me, I'll figure out my own way of changing their tune."

"That's my girl," Nox said, and I wondered if the new baritone quality to his voice had gotten even deeper overnight. It sent a pleasant shiver through me, which amplified when he glanced around at the others and corrected himself. "*Our* girl."

"Our *woman*," Ruin said with a grin, and sought out my lips for a kiss so brilliant that all of a sudden I was much more concerned about when I could drag *him* into bed for more than just a cuddle than what challenges waited for me on campus.

I glanced back at the apartment. "I'm still going to need rent money and the rest. I have a little savings from the work placements I got through St. Elspeth's, but that won't last long."

Kai's eyes glinted behind his glasses. "Don't worry about it. If you can find a job with a boss who's not a prick, go for it, but we have our own ways of getting the bills paid in the meantime."

I wasn't sure I wanted to ask what those ways were.

I insisted on driving out to the school in my own car while the guys followed behind with Nox on his motorcycle and the other three in Ansel's old sports car like a bizarro presidential motorcade. Fred's engine grumbled and sputtered a few times, but it got me to the college parking lot just fine. I found a spot closer to the campus buildings than was usually free and decided that was a good omen.

"If you need us, you know how to call on us," Nox reminded me, with a flare of heat in his eyes that suggested he'd have liked to take a page out of Ruin's book and steal a kiss for himself. But I wasn't throwing caution to the wind so much that making out with a supposed professor in broad daylight seemed like a good idea, no matter how much the former gangsters' covers were already blown at this point.

I strode across the lawns and into the building for my first class of the day braced for the worst, but I didn't even hear a whisper of derision. I took my notes and managed not to nod off when the professor got particularly drone-y about Organized Criminal Behavior, which I was starting to realize he knew shit-all about. No one kicked my chair or tossed any beverages in my face. It was shaping up to be a pretty okay day.

At first. Between classes, I ducked into the restroom. When I came out of the stall, Peyton was standing by the sinks, looking no worse for wear after yesterday's confrontation but still just as pissed off with me.

I froze in my tracks, glancing around. We were alone in the bathroom. I willed someone to walk in to act as a witness, but no one came. I could have made a run for the door with my germy hands—ew—but she probably wouldn't have let me get that far anyway.

I settled for walking to the farthest sink from her and lathering up as if I didn't give a shit that she was glaring daggers at me. My nonchalance must have pissed her off even more, because I'd swear she sharpened those daggers in mid-stare.

"You're a menace," she spat out. "Everyone knows it, even if those guys you've roped into fighting your battles for you are beating them into silence. Funny how you're never so tough on your own."

I turned toward her, crossing my arms. My nerves jittered, but I kept my voice steady. "Maybe that's going to change."

"Oh, yeah? What are you going to do when I smash your head into one of those toilets? Seems like fair payback for what you brought down on all those guys yesterday. For what you're making Ansel do." She sucked in a harsh breath. "There are no cameras in the bathrooms. I could shove your head underwater until you drown, and no one would be able to prove a thing. I'd just be cleaning up the college and setting those men free."

I raised my eyebrows even though my pulse was thumping so hard I was surprised she couldn't see it vibrating through my stance. That deep, dark hum that was becoming familiar started to resonate through me, swelling in my chest. "It's funny hearing that coming from a girl who's tossed me down a flight of stairs, falsely accused me of a crime, and gotten me fired. From where I'm standing, the only menace here is you."

"I've only been protecting this school and the people in it from *your* nasty influence," Peyton shot back, and came at me with her hands raised.

The hum inside me blared louder, with a whooshing sound in my ears like I was plunging through a waterfall. A flicker of panic shot through my veins—what was going to happen if I gave it free rein?—

but I squared my shoulders and stepped back into a defensive pose. "You don't want to do that."

"Why not?" Peyton taunted, squeezing her hands into fists. "Are you going to pout and cry out for your boys at me?"

My jaw clenched. "I can do something way worse than that." I just… wasn't totally sure what that was. But we were both about to find out.

I focused on the thrumming within, and for the first time I urged it farther, higher, louder. It spread through my whole being, reverberating along my cells as if I were a church organ being played to grand effect.

I'd expected the energy to go surging out of me, but instead it only condensed with a growing, silent peal, like every note was a war horn being sounded, calling… something… to battle.

And something was coming. I could feel it in every inch of my skin. Peyton swung a balled hand at me and snatched at my wrist, I jerked out of the way—and the small window behind me rattled.

Peyton froze for just a second, and in the same moment, the pane burst open. A flurry of green flashes cascaded through it. More were rushing in under the door. It took a second for my mind to wrap around what I was seeing.

Frogs. A flood of frogs, flinging themselves toward Peyton from both sides.

I'd summoned an army of fucking *frogs*.

Maybe it wasn't actually normal for people to run into the croaking creatures all over town. Maybe they just liked me. Huh.

The sleek green bodies hurtled at Peyton with a cacophony of croaks. They leapt off the floor at her legs and bounded off the sinks to land on her chest and shoulders, a few even clinging onto her hair.

I couldn't imagine they were doing a whole lot more than sticking themselves to her, because it wasn't like they had claws or teeth or anything that would have been remotely painful. But Peyton reacted as if she was being swarmed by stinging hornets or chomping mice.

She screamed, whirling around with her legs and arms flailing in a frantic dance. But for every frog she shook off, two more jumped up in its place. They swarmed across the floor now, ribbiting merrily and bouncing about as if they were having the time of their lives.

A laugh burst out of me. Peyton howled and pawed at her head. I felt a little sorry for the frogs she swatted, but they didn't seem bothered by her hysteria.

"What the fuck did you do?" she shrieked at me. "Get them off me! This is insane!"

My heartbeat had slowed to a steady, even rhythm. I smiled at her and took a step toward the door through the narrow clear path the frogs had left for me. "What else do you expect from a psycho? Trust me, you don't want to find out what else I can do."

I wasn't sure I even wanted to find out, but I didn't have to mention that.

Peyton wailed and continued her desperate dance of frog-revulsion. "You can't just… just do things like this to people. I'm going to tell security—the dean—"

I snorted, cutting her off. "Tell them what? That I sicced a horde of frogs on you? Who are they going to think is insane then? It's not like there are any witnesses. After all, there are no cameras in here, just like you wanted."

I spun on my heel and walked out without looking back, leaving her to her new amphibious friends.

Chapter Twenty-Six

Lily

WHEN I MET up with the guys after my last class, I found a very different array of escort vehicles around my car in the parking lot. It appeared they'd all taken a page out of Nox's book. Each of them stood beside a shiny new motorcycle.

Jett's was bulky and muscular-looking like Nox's. Kai had gone for one sleek and compact as a greyhound. Ruin's had flashes of neon trim, because of course it did. It probably also had a hot sauce dispenser.

"We figured it was time to get back into the Skullbreaker groove," Ruin said with a grin as I checked them out. The bikes, not the guys. Although I might have ogled the guys a little too. I had to admit they looked pretty hot sitting astride those beasts.

I patted Fred, even if my growing affection for the heap of junk was kind of ridiculous. "There are some benefits to car ownership. More storage space, for instance."

Nox looked me over, appreciation gleaming in his eyes as he must have taken in my lingering sense of victory. "You've been busy."

I couldn't stop a smile from curling my lips. The hum of power inside me had died down, but the exhilaration of the moment when I'd shown Peyton just who she was trying to mess with still tickled through my veins.

It'd been crazy—what I'd done, the fact that I could do it at all. I was a little scared to think too hard about it. But at the same time… maybe crazy was the real way out of this. Maybe it simply wasn't possible to be sane enough to make all the assholes around me satisfied anyway.

"I don't think I'll be having any more trouble with my classmates," I said. The Skullbreakers had already put fear into the worst of the guys, and Peyton had been the ringleader among the girls. And if anyone else decided to get mouthy or handsy, I knew now that I could set them straight.

Kai's eyes glinted too. "Excellent. Did you zap a few souls?"

I laughed, thinking of the supernatural power their spirits had brought into their new bodies. "No. It seems like whatever energies I can draw on, they're more… marshy."

He made a thoughtful sound. "Fascinating. I suppose you took a little of the marsh with you when it didn't manage to take you. I look forward to seeing you in action."

"What now?" Ruin asked eagerly.

I ran my hand over the car's hood, and a jab of certainty I couldn't deny lanced through my gut. "I need answers. I need to know what really happened seven years ago and if there's anything I need to do to make amends with Marisol."

And there were only two people I was sure knew the full story—the two people who'd sent me off to the loony bin to begin with.

I considered confronting Mom, but something in me balked. She'd been a crappy mother, and I'd rather have eaten worms than make nice with her, but she'd been in a crappy situation. Dad's abandonment had screwed with her head and wrung her out until there was barely any of herself left.

It was Wade who'd let her get so small and meek. Wade who'd encouraged her simpering and berated her if she ever disappointed him by not catering to his every whim. I had no doubt it'd been his idea to threaten to call the police on me.

And he was the one who'd been talking about some mysterious other person who might somehow be involved.

As so often, Kai picked up on my thoughts before I said them out loud. "We're going after your stepdad."

Jett let out an approving grunt. "Let's crush that motherfucker."

I sucked my lower lip under my teeth to worry at it. "I guess he won't be at work, since he doesn't have much of a workplace anymore..." I gave Kai a pointed look, and he just smirked. "I might as well start with the house and then expand the search from there. Marisol won't be home from school yet." I didn't know exactly what was going to go down between me and Wade, but I suspected I'd rather she didn't witness it as her first introduction to the stranger parts of me.

The mark on the inside of my arm itched. I scratched at it idly and considered the guys. "I have to do this by myself too. I want him to know he can't intimidate me even when I'm on my own." And if I could help it, I didn't want him making more trouble for the guys than they'd already gotten into, not that I thought they'd accept that reasoning. They seemed to think the protecting could only go one way around here.

Nox nodded. "We'll follow you out there. Make sure you don't run into any problems along the way—and be ready as backup if anything goes wrong."

"Fair." I dragged in a breath and went around to Fred's driver's side door. "Here goes nothing."

It didn't feel like nothing, though. It felt like... well, *everything*. Like the whole world and all the hopes I'd had for my life in that world were weighing down on my shoulders as I drove toward the house where I'd lived for the first thirteen years of my life. I guessed you could say I came with a lot of baggage.

But Wade was the one who'd put most of it there, and I was about to unload.

The guys roared around me on their bikes, zipping ahead and then falling back behind as the whim took them. Every now and then Ruin gunned his engine as hard as he could and soared into the distance like he'd taken off on a jumbo jet. I suspected he enjoyed the extremes of speed just as much as all the other extremes he'd been indulging in, from flavors to sound.

He drew up beside me as we reached the lane that led to the old house. Wade's not-particularly-posh sedan sat in the driveway. A quiver of anticipation ran through me.

I might finally unlock the mystery that'd been haunting me for seven years—more than a third of my life. Suddenly it seemed so simple. But I wouldn't have had the courage to confront him like this —I wouldn't have believed it wouldn't ruin my chances even more and get me nowhere at the same time—until the friends who weren't so imaginary after all had barged back into my life.

Friends who weren't exactly just friends, either. After I'd gotten out of the car, Nox tucked a few stray strands of my hair behind my ear with fingers that left a trail of heat in their wake. Ruin grasped my hand and squeezed. This wasn't the place for a PDA, but a palpable ripple of devotion passed from them into me even with those small gestures.

"We're right here if you need us," Nox said.

"I know." I drew up my chin and marched to the front door of the house.

It was hard to believe I'd been here just a couple of days ago in much stealthier fashion. The house looked somehow bigger approaching it from the front, but also shabbier, as if it'd gotten more run-down in that time.

There wasn't anything so imposing about it, even if I'd been banned from the premises. In ways Wade could never erase, it was mine, tied to my history and my childhood.

I rang the doorbell and held myself still and straight while I waited. It took a while before I heard footsteps creak toward the front hall. There was no peephole, so my stepfather had no idea who was waiting for him on the other side until he swung the door wide.

Wade's posture went rigid, his gaze snagging on me and sticking there. Then he started to sputter. "What the hell are you doing here? Your mother said she warned you—you're not welcome on this property—"

"It's my house too, Wade," I interrupted, sharp and firm. "And I say I am. We need to talk. Why don't you step inside so we can do it like civilized people?"

"I'll have the cops here in a minute—"

He pulled his cell phone out of his pocket. I snatched it out of his hands and hurled it over my shoulder.

Wade stared at me, his eyes going even wider and a little of the color draining from his face. He wasn't that much taller than me, really, even if he had at least fifty pounds more pudge. In the past seven years, more crow's feet had formed at the corners of his eyes, and frown lines had dug in at the corners of his mouth.

Looking at him with an adult's eyes rather than a kid's, it was hard to believe I'd ever found him intimidating. He was pathetic. A miserable weaselly man who'd made himself feel bigger by bullying literal children. Who probably continued to do that when it came to my sister.

That last thought set my teeth on edge and brought the first hint of the unnatural hum into my chest.

Wade moved as if to push past me, and I shoved him backward instead. He hadn't been expecting that, and he stumbled a few feet before catching himself. His face went from pale to ruddy with a furious flush. "Who the hell do you think you—"

"I think I'm Lily Strom, and this house was mine before it was ever yours, and you're going to tell me what the hell happened here seven years ago that you used as an excuse to ship me off to the psych ward."

Wade's mouth tightened, but his eyes darted back and forth with an anxious twitch. He wasn't much of a physical fighter. I'd never challenged him this openly before. He might even have heard some of the stories about what'd been happening to people who messed with me lately.

His gaze slid past me to the guys on their motorcycles parked outside and then focused on me again. He wet his lips. "Fine. You're not going to like it, but fine. Come to the kitchen and we'll talk."

I had the feeling he'd picked the kitchen because that was where the phone with the landline was located. I followed him there at his heels and grabbed the cable before he could so much as reach for it, tugging it out of the outlet. "We wouldn't want any interruptions."

Wade pursed his lips. He leaned against one of the laminate counters and narrowed his eyes at me. "It's a short story. You should have heard it already. You had a total mental breakdown. You went wild, throwing things around, attacking us. Your sister was terrified. We put you away for your own good. Lord only knows why they let you out. You're obviously not much more stable than you were back then." A trace of nervousness crept into his tone.

I *had* heard that story before. It was the one everyone had been telling me in bits and pieces since it'd become obvious that I couldn't tell *them* what'd gone down. But the doctors had heard it from Mom and Wade. They didn't know any better. There had to be more to it.

The hum expanded through my veins. I restrained a shiver. Resting my hand on the counter beside the phone, I started to drum my fingers. The sound fell into rhythm with the subtle but familiar creaks of the old walls and the warble of the rising breeze outside the windows.

The steady tempo formed by that unexpected symphony smoothed out my nerves. It didn't diminish the growing swell of energy within me, only seemed to hone it, as if it were more a weapon I could wield than a surge of random power.

"That can't be the whole story," I replied, focusing on my stepdad more intently. "*Why* did I go 'wild'? What made me upset?"

Wade's jaw wobbled, so minutely I might not have noticed if I hadn't been watching him closely. He didn't want to tell me that part. "None of us did anything," he insisted. "And nothing could have justified—the fit you had—"

A flare of the anger I'd been suppressing so long under shame and doubt spiked to the surface. He was dicking around with my fucking *life* here. He'd stolen seven years of that life from me, and he couldn't even bring himself to tell me why?

I smacked both my hands on the counter. "*I'd* like to be the one who decides what was justified. What the hell happened?"

Wade jumped, but his mouth clamped tighter shut. The hum inside me rose to a roar, but the melody I'd latched onto wove through it, keeping me steady.

I didn't want frogs this time. I wanted—

My mind leapt to the marsh, to the sensation of sinking down into the sluggish current with slimy weeds tangling around my six-years-old legs—and the sink faucet gurgled to life. Water sprayed from the tap hard enough to splash Wade where he stood a few feet away.

As he jerked away from it, it gushed even harder. The pipes in the walls groaned. My mouth set in a grim smile, and I let the power thundering through me sweep from my body like a tsunami.

And a tsunami it was. The pipes burst, bits of plaster flying with torrents of water careening out in their wake. The blasts whipped up and around rather than falling straight to earth.

One slapped Wade across the face with a wet wallop. Another pummeled him in the gut, sending him toppling onto his ass. Smaller jets smacked him back and forth like a boxer's fists toying with an opponent.

He cringed there on the floor, a thin whine creeping from his throat. His arms swung this way and that in an attempt to fend off the assault, as if it was something more horrifying than the same water he drank and flushed down the toilet every day.

"They didn't fix you," he babbled. "They didn't fix you at all. You're *crazy*. This is crazy!"

The truth clicked in my head with a wave of shock. This wasn't *his* first introduction to the stranger parts of me. What I was doing right now, or something like it, was what he'd meant by going wild.

I'd brought out my powers once before, all those years ago… and somehow I'd forgotten.

How could I have forgotten? I wasn't an elephant, but sudden marshy magical abilities seemed like the kind of thing that'd stick in your mind.

And I still didn't know what'd stirred me up enough for me to let them out.

The water kept pouring across the floor in an erratic waterfall, but the more punishing streams eased off. I sloshed over and bent down in front of Wade, grabbing his soaking shirt collar in my hand.

"It is crazy," I said in a menacing voice. "But whatever set me off must have been even crazier. What. Fucking. Happened? Or do you need me to drown you a few times before you'll think about answering?"

I didn't have enough faith in my ability to inspire dudes to rise from the dead that I actually meant that threat, but Wade started to blubber like a toddler. Maybe the sight of my crazy powers had sent his mind into meltdown mode.

"I don't know," he wailed between hitches of sobs. "You came down and you started yelling at me and your mother, and I told Eleanor to leave so she didn't have to hear, and then… and then all of this…" He gestured toward the broken pipes weakly. But there was still something hesitant in the twisting of his mouth.

"Don't hold back on me," I snapped. Behind me, a swell of water arched up like a wave captured in mid-tumble. "I came down from where? What was going on with Marisol during all this? Why don't I *remember*?"

"I really don't know. He—he just wanted—I was only trying—I can't—"

"Who?" I shouted, shaking him. A faint mist rained down on us as the wave loomed higher.

A shudder ran through Wade's body, and his answer tumbled out in a gasp. "Talk to the Gauntts. They handled everything. They— He wanted to see your sister. I didn't badger him about why. I didn't— Ask *them*, and keep me out of it."

The Gauntts? I frowned, groping for why that name was familiar.

Thrivewell Enterprises. They were the family that owned the company, weren't they? The company with a name that'd chilled me for no obvious reason when I'd heard it last week.

How the hell were *they* connected to my life?

"Which one?" I demanded. "Who's 'he'?"

Wade shook his head, but the name tumbled out in a trembling whisper. "Nolan. I told you everything I know. Please."

I let go of him with a shove and stepped aside. The wave released, crashing over him but without any additional force than gravity. All it did was dislodge his comb-over so it splayed over his forehead and drench him even more than he'd already been.

The Gauntts. Nolan Gauntt. They had something to do with

Marisol—something that'd sent me into a supernatural rage at thirteen years of age. I didn't think Wade had absolutely *no* idea what that might have been, but when it came to men and little girls, I could put all the horrible pieces together well enough on my own.

The rest I was better off getting straight from the source.

"No more threats about calling the police on me," I said to the sopping man who was cowering at my feet. "And if I want to see Marisol and she wants to see me, you're not going to stop me. You're going to tell my mom not to get in the way either. Understood?"

"Yes," Wade mumbled with a cringe.

"Good. Looks like you'd better invest in a good plumber." I turned on my heel and walked out of the house dripping but with twice as much resolve as before.

Chapter Twenty-Seven

Lily

As I TRAMPED into my apartment with the guys half an hour later, still damp but not uncomfortably so, Nox looked around and let out a gruff sigh. "We are *definitely* getting you better digs than this. No arguments."

I wrinkled my nose at him. "That might be a little difficult considering I have no idea how I'm going to afford even these digs going forward."

"We told you not to worry about that."

"Fine." I flopped onto the futon. "I'm a lot more worried about these Gauntt people."

"Well, for starters, they should probably eat more," Ruin suggested.

The other guys all rolled their eyes at him, and he held up his hands with a grin. "Hey, with a name like that, they're just asking for it."

"You should stick something in your mouth and chew instead of talking," Jett muttered.

"Excellent idea. I was getting kind of hungry." Ruin bounded over to the fridge.

Nox's gaze followed him with an expression that seemed to say, *When is he not?* But then the boss tossed out, "Throw me some leftover dumplings or something, will you?"

They'd better come up with some kind of income source, or they'd eat through their hosts' savings in another few days.

"You could talk to your sister again now that you put Wade in his place," Jett pointed out.

I hesitated. Marisol's obvious anxiety when I'd come near her was still clear in my memory. "I want to, but I think I need to have a better idea what we're dealing with first. If these dickheads have been threatening her, I have to be sure they can't actually hurt her." The underside of my arm itched, and I scratched at it absently as I pondered our options.

Kai had whipped out his phone the second he'd gotten off his bike. His thumbs pattered away on the screen. "Let's see, then. The Gauntts... Thrivewell Enterprises... Hmm."

I'd filled them in on what Wade had told me when I'd returned to my car outside the house, but then, other than the name, Wade hadn't told me much at all. All I knew about them was what I'd picked up at the rally—and that the name Thrivewell made my skin shiver in ways that weren't at all promising.

I leaned forward on the cushions. "What did you find? Who's this Nolan guy? I mean, other than probably a creepy pedophile."

Ruin coughed from over by the fridge. "Um, it looks like I already ate all the leftovers. Well, maybe not just me, but—probably a lot of it me." He shot us a sheepish smile. "I'll go out and grab some more. It's almost dinner time anyway."

"Fine, fine," Nox said with a dismissive wave. "Just make sure you don't eat it all on the way back. And ask for the hot sauce *on the side*!" he added in a holler as Ruin vanished into the stairwell.

"Nolan Gauntt is the current patriarch of the Thrivewell Enterprises empire," Kai said without missing a beat, as if the conversation had never veered off course. "He shares joint responsibilities with his wife, Marie. No specific age given, but from the looks of them, they're in their 60s. There haven't been any scandals big enough to make the news, but who knows what's been covered up."

"Do they still live in Mayfield?" I asked. "Can we—"

My question was cut off by a thump and a loud clatter from above —the kind of thunderous clatter you'd expect if an entire motorcycle toppled over on its side. The hairs on the back of my neck stood on end.

"Ruin!" Jett rasped, and all three guys launched themselves out of their seats and toward the stairs as one being.

I ran after them, close enough behind them that I burst out the door on their heels. In the lane at the top of the stairs, a man was poised, so burly and bearded that if he'd been wearing plaid instead of polka dots, he'd have passed for a lumberjack.

He had Ruin shoved face-first against the side wall of the building, arms yanked behind his back and a pistol pressed to his forehead.

"Ansel Hunter," he was rumbling, "you've got a lot to fucking answer for."

Criminal Spirits

GANG OF GHOULS #2

Chapter One

Lily

As shocking developments go, seeing a childhood-friend-turned-sort-of-lover shoved up against a wall with a gun to his head was one I could have skipped. 0/10, would not recommend.

The man with the gun—a burly, lumberjack-looking guy—had Ruin pinned against the building in the lane over my basement apartment. He jabbed his pistol more firmly against Ruin's forehead and whipped his head around at the thump of the apartment door. Ruin's three friends and former gang colleagues were already hurtling up the stairs with murder emanating from their every movement.

A yelp caught in my throat as I scrambled after them. I had the urge to shout at them to be careful, which struck me as totally ridiculous at the same time. Both because these guys were never exactly careful, and because how the hell could anyone be *careful* when the life of one of our own was on the line?

That might have been the first time I'd really thought of myself as part of their group. An honorary Skullbreaker of sorts. But I was a little too frantic to contemplate the significance of my shift in mindset.

"Don't get any—" the lumberjack with the gun started to growl, but he didn't have the chance to finish his threat, because Nox barreled right into him.

The massive leader of the Skullbreakers slammed the gunman away from Ruin, his fists already flying to smack the pistol from the dickhead's hand and send the guy's jaw soaring upward with a pained grunt. Jett was there an instant later, bringing a knee to the asshat's gut and an elbow to his nose, setting loose an impressive flow of blood.

Freed from his attacker's grasp, Ruin spun around and added his own limbs to the mix. Despite the deadly situation he'd been in just seconds ago, he laughed as he slammed his heel into the guy's ribs, sending the douche-nozzle reeling into the opposite wall. The rhythm of fleshy thuds, vengeful growls, and agonized breaths created a strange sort of melody. Part of me wanted to put words to it, a fierce song of retribution.

The pseudo-lumberjack rebounded off the wall, his face swollen and legs wobbling. He looked as though he might have been regretting a few of his life choices. He glanced toward the street at the mouth of the alley as if he was considering turning tail and running.

The guys didn't give him the option. Jett snatched up his helmet from where he'd left it on his parked motorcycle and bashed the jerkwad across the side of his head with it. Kai, who'd hung back a little from the fray while waiting for an opening, held up a rope he'd found somewhere or other. "We're going to need some answers," he said. "Get him immobile and we'll interrogate him."

Nox had just been snatching up a bent fork someone had tossed aside in the alley. He jabbed it into the douchebag's side with a crackling hiss that made the man's body spasm like a marionette that'd been shaken on its strings. Between the sound, the motion, and the faint whiff of burnt meat, I knew the former gang boss had sent a jolt of his ghostly electrical energy into his opponent.

Jett let out a sound that was half whoop, half snarl, and swung his helmet into the guy's face so forcefully the slimeball's head whipped back on his neck. The lumberjack gunman rammed into the wall with a crunch of shattering skull. Several shards of that skull remained mashed into the bricks as he crumpled in a heap on the ground.

Jett looked at the mangled mess on the back of the guy's head and then at Kai, swiping his messy purple-dyed hair back from his face with a slightly apologetic grimace. "Oops. Sorry. I didn't realize I was going to hit him quite that hard."

"He was trying to kill Ruin," Nox growled, his broad shoulders flexing. "He deserves what he got."

Ruin bobbed up and down on his feet with his fists raised as if he was hoping another attacker would come lunging out of the shadows for a second round. His hazel eyes gleamed with excitement. "That was a workout, all right."

Somehow the guy always managed to look on the bright side of things.

Kai dropped the rope with an exasperated sigh and nudged his rectangular glasses up his nose. "It would have been nice if we could have found out *why* he gave us that workout. I don't suppose he mentioned anything about what he wanted with you before he put that gun to your head?"

"He wasn't after Ruin," I said first, the memory coming back to me of the few words I'd heard the attacker speak before the guys had charged at him. "He thought he was threatening Ansel."

The four guys fell into a momentary silence to consider that fact. The truth was that none of them were exactly the men they appeared to be. A couple of weeks ago, the bunch of them had been among the worst of the tormenters who'd insulted and attacked me at Lovell Rise College. But then those jackasses had been possessed by the former gangsters they were now: my childhood not-so-imaginary-after-all friends who'd decided they needed to show up and protect me.

It was all a little complicated. I hadn't quite finished wrapping my head around the situation.

But it was getting easier to think of these four as the men they claimed to be now rather than the sneering popular guy, the bullying jock, the judgmental brownnoser, and the hostile professor they'd been before. For one thing, their personalities couldn't be more different. For another, their ghostly energies and their own efforts had been gradually transforming their bodies in ways that matched their former selves better.

Zach the jock had never worn glasses like Kai did. Professor

Grimes hadn't been anywhere near as buff as Nox was quickly becoming, and he definitely hadn't gelled up his hair into little black spikes tipped with red. Vincent the brownnoser's body had also filled out significantly with Jett in possession of it, and he'd probably have shrieked in horror at the sight of his new purple hair. Golden boy Ansel's hard-edged good looks had softened with Ruin's influence, and his once golden locks were now bright scarlet.

But that hadn't stopped Mr. Lumberjack from coming after him for who he'd once been.

Ruin's eyes had turned briefly distant with thought. He waved his hand as if he needed to catch our attention. "There was some dude who bugged me before! A different guy—he stopped me from a car when I was out grabbing some food and wanted to know…" He knit his forehead as he reached for the memory. "Where I'd been. He said I hadn't reported in when I was supposed to, or something like that."

Nox blinked at him. "Why the fuck didn't you mention that earlier?"

Ruin shrugged, smiling contentedly. "It obviously didn't have to do with *me* me. I told him to take a hike and figured that was it—and that if it wasn't, we'd just take care of things. And we did. So it's all good."

"It's not all good." Kai motioned to the dead man. "You said the guy who harassed you before was someone different. So *that* guy is still out there, and thanks to *some* people taking the Skullbreaker name a little too literally, we have no idea who they are or what they want."

"I said I was sorry," Jett muttered.

I rubbed my forehead. "The guy didn't say anything at all about what he wanted—neither of them did? What you were supposed to be reporting about? Who you were reporting to?"

Ruin shook his head. "They mostly just seemed angry and like they wanted to push me around. They had no idea who they were dealing with now." His smile stretched into a grin.

Nox turned to me. "You knew this Ansel guy from before, right? Was he mixed up in anything when you were younger?"

I spread my hands. "I have no clue. It wasn't like we talked about our hobbies and the secret clubs we were members of. The only time he spoke to me when we were kids was to make fun of me for being a loser and smelling like marsh water."

Ruin bristled as quickly as he'd smiled before. "You're not a loser, and you smell much nicer than the marsh. We should know, after all the time we spent in it."

I gave him a baleful look. "I appreciate the vote of confidence. Although I probably did smell kind of marshy back then because of all the time I spent hanging out down there with the bunch of you."

"Time well spent," Nox said.

"No argument here," I replied. "But anyway, all I know about Ansel is that almost everyone liked him and wanted to be his friend, and his parents have quite a bit of money. His dad owns the marina down the lake and a few other properties in town, and he's friends with the mayor too. But the last time I was around Ansel for any length of time, we were both thirteen. I have no idea what he might have gotten into while I was off in the looney bin."

I had been gone for seven years, after all. And Ansel had grown from a pompous just-past-preteen to a fully-fledged adult prick in that time. The possibilities were pretty much endless.

"Well, let's look this asshole over," Jett said, like he was impatient to get past any conversation that might circle back around to how unfortunate it was that he'd killed the guy, and crouched down next to the pseudo-lumberjack. The others went over to join him.

They patted him down with unusual efficiency. After a moment, Ruin seemed to get bored and went over to straighten up his motorcycle, which had toppled over during the assault.

Kai dug a few slips of paper out of the guy's shirt pocket which he appeared to dismiss as useless and flicked away. Nox pulled a phone out of the back of the man's jeans. He jabbed his thumbs at it with the typical impatience the guys seemed to have for technology that was two decades ahead of what they'd been used to before their murders.

"I can't get it to open up," he grumbled. "This is where the good stuff would be, right?"

"Let me see." Kai held out his hand, and his boss handed it over. But while Kai was incisive enough to frequently give the impression that he read people's minds and to have absorbed two decades of recent events by speed-reading news magazines at a hundred pages a minute, he apparently didn't have the same skills when it came to electronic devices. He tapped at the screen and the buttons, tried pressing the dead man's phone to the same spots, and finally gave it a little zap of supernatural energy which only made the screen jitter briefly.

"Don't break it," Jett said.

Kai shot him a narrow sideways glance. "What, like you broke *him*?" He grimaced at the phone. "I don't know how to unlock it. It needs a passcode. If I still had my old network of contacts… We haven't had a chance to build that up again. I have no idea who could handle something like this."

"It's not that urgent, right?" Ruin said. "So far these people have been no big deal. We can look into what Ansel was up to in other ways."

"And if the phone gets any calls, those should come through without needing the passcode," I said. "Someone will check up on him eventually, right? We could try to find out what's going on from them."

Kai nodded, aiming an approving smile my way that sent a warm if slightly unnerving tingle through my body. I'd only had any kind of intimate relations with Nox and Ruin, but I'd be lying if I said I wasn't finding all four of these men increasingly appealing in their own ways. Which was probably insane, because they were criminally homicidal and also, y'know, technically *dead*, but I'd decided yesterday that sanity was overrated. So here we were.

At least so far all of the Skullbreakers' homicidal-ness had been in defense of themselves or me.

My gaze slid back to the dead man. "What are we going to do with him? We can't just… leave him here in the alley by my apartment, right?" He really wasn't an attractive addition to the décor, even when that décor was a grungy alley. And I'd also had the police breathing down my neck just a few days ago.

Nox hummed and then nodded to himself. "We'll take care of it. Ruin, you should finish taking care of getting us all some food. *I'm* starving now."

He paused and touched my cheek with a gentleness so off-kilter with the rest of his cocky, aggressive demeanor that it woke up a heck of a lot more than a tingle inside me. "You go down and wait in the apartment, Lily. We wouldn't want you being seen around the body, and I don't want you off with Ruin when he could be a target."

I wanted to argue, but there wasn't really any good argument to offer. He'd made good points. Gritting my teeth, I dipped my head in acknowledgment.

"Be careful," I said, the caution I'd wanted to give them before seeming only slightly less absurd now. Then I walked down the stairs to the dingy apartment with my stomach sinking even faster than my feet.

I didn't like this. I didn't like it at all. We'd already figured out that my sister was under some kind of threat, probably from a scarily powerful businessman, and now it turned out Ansel had been wrapped up in something dangerous too?

I had to protect Marisol, and I had to protect the men who'd risen from the dead to defend me, as much as they'd let me defend them. And it looked like I was going to need to tackle both problems at the same time if I wanted to be sure that everyone I cared about—the only people who'd ever cared about *me* too—made it through the next few days alive.

Chapter Two

Lily

RUIN CAME BACK LOADED with so many bags of Indian takeout that he looked like one of those peddlers in fairy tale illustrations carrying their entire inventory on their backs. My rickety table almost toppled over as he laid out the spread, which involved multiple tiers by necessity. The rest of the guys had returned to the apartment by then, and they all fell on the containers of curry, roti, and biryani rice like they'd been starving for half a century.

I wasn't sure I was ever going to get used to their constant need for fuel. Was that going to taper off as their spirits got more acclimatized to their bodies—and to the fact that they hadn't gotten to eat at all during the twenty-one years they'd been deceased—or were they always going to have the appetite of great white sharks?

My stomach was still knotted up from the most recent conundrum we'd gotten into, but it was almost dinner time now, and I'd been so keyed up from my personal confrontations earlier today that I hadn't eaten much before. I squeezed in to snag a piece of garlic-stuffed naan here and a dollop of butter chicken there. Then Nox let out a gruff sound, and suddenly all four of the guys were assembling a plate for me that held more food than I was likely to eat in a week.

I sank onto my futon to the left of its saggy middle and took my first few bites gingerly. Ruin had a particular liking for extreme levels of spice. Extreme levels of everything, really. But the guys had clearly avoided loading my plate from any dishes he'd ordered for his specific tastes, because my tongue didn't go up in flames. It was actually pretty freaking delicious.

I decided not to worry about corpses or guns or shady old businessmen for a half hour or so while I got a decent meal into me. They'd still be waiting when I finished, after all.

Even though the guys were eating about a hundred times more than me, they finished before I was full. Jett set to work either tidying or artistically arranging the remnants on the table—possibly both—and paused to smear a little vindaloo sauce on one of the thick pages of paper he'd picked up with his other painting supplies. He cocked his head at it and then crumpled it and tossed it in the trash with a wrinkle of his nose.

Ruin dropped onto the broad wooden arm of the futon right next to me so he could sling his arm across my shoulders and stroke my hair. I let my head tip toward him, enjoying the affectionate but undemanding touch. We'd made out once, and he gave out hugs and kisses like there was a fire sale, but I never felt like he was unhappy with how far we'd gone—or hadn't gone. There was something kind of miraculous about the sense that he adored me exactly as I was.

Nox sat at the other end of the futon, and Kai pulled a chair over to what was becoming his usual spot across from us. He swiped his hand over his face, where his skin had darkened to a golden tan from Zach's previous peachy pale, and studied the rest of us.

"We can't just sit around and wait for that phone to ring. We need to come up with a plan of action."

"For figuring out who's after Ruin—Ansel—and for protecting Marisol," I filled in.

He nodded, and Ruin perked up. "We can add it to the list!"

I raised my eyebrows. "The list?"

Nox motioned at Kai, who retrieved a folded piece of paper from the pocket of his jeans. "That night you stayed out," the Skullbreakers' leader said, "we came up with a list of our next steps toward reestablishing ourselves with the respect we deserve."

Of course they had. Why wouldn't they? It was probably full of items like, "Smash all their heads in," and "Hang them in a tree by their toenails."

Kai tapped his lips with a pen he'd also produced. "Find out who has it in for Ruin's host. That should get pretty high priority, don't you think?"

Nox made a noncommittal sound. "We did put that idiot in his place pretty fast, and it isn't *really* anything to do with us. I think figuring out who offed *us* way back when is more important. Better to deal with them before we make an official return and they realize we'll be gunning for them."

I reached up to curl my fingers around Ruin's. "We can't ignore the problem with Ansel. What if someone comes at Ruin someplace he can't count on you guys for help?"

Ruin leaned over to nuzzle my hair. "I could have handled him on my own. I was just giving him a chance to get confident before I taught him a thing or two."

Kai's gray-green eyes glinted menacingly behind his glasses. "And there are a lot of other people who need their lessons delivered." He sighed. "Well, we've got no other responsibilities at the moment, and both might take some time. I think we can follow two threads simultaneously."

"Good." I ran my thumb over the back of Ruin's hand. The image of him squashed against the bricks with the pistol jammed to his temple rose up in my mind, making my pulse lurch. I weirdly felt as if I'd known him forever and also only a couple of weeks. Maybe both of those things were true, but however weird it was, the thought of losing him after all that time or so little sent a stab of panic through my chest.

I tucked myself closer against his side, and Ruin let out a pleased hum. Without warning, he adjusted his position so he could scoop me up and hop off the futon arm simultaneously, landing on the cushion with me tucked onto his lap.

"You don't need to worry about me, Angelfish," he told me, tipping his face close to mine. "I'm not going anywhere, not when I can be here with you."

My heart skipped a beat in a totally different way, and then he was kissing me, tenderly but eagerly, drawing it out until every nerve started to thrum with building heat.

More heat pooled between my thighs. Ruin's hand stroked down my side, and the urge to grind against him gripped me. I tensed up to hold myself back, thinking of the other guys sitting all around us.

Ruin drew back from the kiss and studied me with obvious concern. "Too much?"

"No, I— I mean, it was fine—it was good—I just—" I clamped my mouth shut for a second while I got my thoughts in some kind of coherent order. Then I dragged in a breath and peeked around at the rest of the resurrected gangsters.

"Maybe we should talk about this. About… about what exactly this is. I don't know what you all were expecting. *I* definitely didn't have any ideas of getting involved with you like this back when I was younger. I mean, I didn't even think of you as being actual people…" I trailed off again and bit my lip.

Nox looked vaguely horrified. I had another momentary panic that he was offended I'd even brought up the subject before he said, "*We* weren't thinking like that either back then. For fuck's sake, you were a kid." He paused, his dark blue eyes holding a tumultuous mix of envy and desire as he took in the sight of me on Ruin's lap. "You're not a kid now. I look at you and see the woman you are, not the girl you used to be. And now that we *are* 'actual' people again—you know how I feel about you."

Yes, I did. The memory of his worshipful words and equally ardent hands and mouth set a lick of fire over my skin.

"But we don't want anything to happen that doesn't make you happy too," Ruin said emphatically. "We're here for *you*, not the other way around."

"And we're *all* here for you, or not, however you like it," Nox added, with a flick of a glance toward the two men who hadn't spoken yet. "None of us is going to be staking any separate claim on you, including me. You mean the world to all of us. No one can say you're more theirs than the others."

Jett had gone a bit rigid where he was still standing near the table. He held up his hands, his jaw flexing. "Lily's my muse," he said, his voice a little stiff too. "I'm not going to ask for more than that from her. I'll share a hell of a lot with you guys, but orgies aren't really my thing." He tipped his head to me, his expression softening. "It's a lot harder to find the right muse. You're something fucking special, Lil."

If I'd felt any unexpected twinge of disappointment at his dismissal of orgies, those last words swept it away. I smiled back at him and glanced at Kai.

The brainiac of the former gang shifted on his chair awkwardly. "I'll admit I'm not *unaware* of your appeal," he said in his usual matter-of-fact tone. "This body… Fucking teenage hormones. I should have picked an older host." He let out a huff. "But I wouldn't expect you to return that sort of interest, and I think at this point it's really more of a distraction than anything else." His gaze flicked to Nox. "For me. By all means, you two give Lily whatever you'd like to. She sure as hell deserves better after the shit she's had to go through before now."

Nox caught Ruin's gaze. "Just the two of us then. I think we can manage to keep our woman's needs satisfied."

A blush flared in my cheeks. Ruin gave a pleased chuckle and kissed my cheek. "I'm sure we can," he murmured happily, but for now he only gave me another hug. "But we have gotten distracted. You need to help your little sister too."

"Yes," I said, latching on to that change of subject with relief, even though I was the one who'd brought up the previous topic. Now that the air had been cleared and everyone knew where everyone stood when it came to getting handsy with me, I'd rather not dissect my exact "needs" in any more detail in a group setting.

"We know the Gauntts are involved," Kai said, looking equally eager to get onto a new topic. "Or at least Nolan Gauntt, the patriarch of Thrivewell Enterprises."

"Yes, he's the one my stepfather mentioned." Under extreme duress. I rubbed my mouth. Kai had done some preliminary research into the business mogul whose company seemed to employ half of

Lovell Rise as well as the surrounding towns, his home city of Mayfield, and who knew where else. None of it had explained why he would have been at all involved in my or my sister's life. Other than that Wade had undoubtedly found it very hard to say no to whatever Nolan had asked for. My stepdad liked to lord his authority over people he knew he could beat up on, but he cowered before anyone who was a real big dog.

"It'd be hard to go at this guy head-on," I said. "We can't just find him on the street and intimidate him into talking. He probably has, like, a gazillion bodyguards. And whatever happened with him—as much as I plan to make sure he pays for it—it was seven years ago. Marisol seemed nervous *now*. Before we do anything else, I'd like to check whether she has a good reason to worry or if it's just leftover nerves. I don't want to do anything that could put her in danger."

"How are you thinking you'd check?" Nox asked.

I worried at my lower lip, considering. "I can keep an eye on her from a distance when she's going to and from school—and wherever else she goes between there and the house. Or, not so much keep an eye on her but check whether I can see anyone *else* monitoring her. I should be able to cover a lot of that time in between my classes, now that I'm out of a job."

I winced inwardly at the thought of my manager's last words to me outside the grocery store. It hadn't been a pleasant firing, and it didn't bode well for future job prospects. Basically, I'd made too much trouble for him simply by existing—and by other people having a problem with me existing.

"We can help too," Ruin volunteered. "Watch for any shady characters lurking around."

I immediately pictured the former gangsters barging up to random strangers on the street who happened to look at Marisol sideways for a split-second and pummeling them as punishment. "Um. Sure. But you have to let me take the lead with this one, all right? We'll talk about how you can keep watch, but I don't want you going near Marisol or taking any other kind of action until we've talked about it first."

Jett grunted in a way that suggested he felt being reined in was unnecessary, but Nox was already nodding. "Your arena, you call the shots. Unless she's under attack. Anyone lays a finger on her, we aren't going to stand by."

I gave him a skeptical look. "More than a finger. Tapping her on the shoulder to get her attention doesn't deserve a beatdown."

"It depends on the tap," he said, and waved off my glower. "All right, all right. We'll work it out." He rubbed his hands together. "It sounds like it's time to get busy."

Chapter Three

Ruin

In some ways, Lily's bed was less comfortable than the air mattress and sleeping bag that were technically mine in the living room. For one, her mattress was kind of lumpy. For another, it was only twin-sized, which was barely big enough for *one* person to stretch out, let alone two.

But it had Lily in it, and as long as that was the case, it was my favorite place in the world.

I hadn't been able to resist slipping in here a little earlier than usual and squeezing myself between her and the wall with my arm looped around her waist, spooning her. She was used to my presence enough by now that she'd simply given a sleepy murmur, scooted a little closer, and gone right back to sleep. I'd drifted back off too with her watery wildflower scent in my nose.

When I woke up again, she was still sleeping, her breaths soft and even. I trailed my fingertips up and down her bare arm that'd tucked over the blankets, delighting in the smoothness of her pale skin.

She rolled toward me onto her back, her eyes still half-closed. I let my fingers glide across her shoulder and over her collarbone just above the neckline of her baggy sleepshirt. Lily squirmed a little and opened her eyes wider. "Tease," she muttered.

Who was teasing who was really debatable after the way my dick had jerked to attention at the brush of her thigh, but I had no interest in arguing. I leaned closer and nuzzled the side of her face, letting my lips brush her cheek as I spoke. "If you want more than what I'm doing, I'm perfectly happy to keep going."

She tipped her face toward mine, and I caught her mouth for a perfect kiss, waking from drowsy tenderness to heated alertness as our mouths moved together. My hand drifted lower, displacing the blanket in its wake, and traced the curve of her breast through the thin cotton of her shirt.

Lily let out an impatient sound that made me even harder and pressed into my hand. I smiled against her mouth, joy lighting me from the inside like someone had set a flame to a fuse.

Nox had told me before that we needed to be careful with Lily. We didn't want to hurt her more than she'd already been hurt, to take anything she didn't want to give when she'd already lost so much. But she'd made it very clear since then—and especially last night—that she was fully on board with receiving all the affection we were dying to offer.

Still, it couldn't hurt to make sure. I nudged my nose against hers and skimmed my fingers over her breast again, grinning as her nipple pebbled at my touch. "Would you like more of this, precious?"

"Fuck, yes," she grumbled, and tugged my mouth back to hers.

I rolled her nipple until it was taut and straining against the fabric and she was whimpering against my lips. Then I eased my hand to the other side with a glimmer of mischief. "And how about here?"

Lily gave a little growl that electrified me and pressed into my touch. I slipped my tongue between her lips as I flicked my thumb over the peak of her breast, mimicking the same movement. Her hands came up to grip my hair, her fingernails striking sparks across my scalp. I restrained a groan, my cock aching, and slid down to nibble her neck.

"Are you enjoying this, Angelfish?" I murmured.

She sputtered a laugh. "What do you think?"

"I want to hear you say it. Just to be sure."

She swatted me lightly and then dug her fingers into my hair again. When I swiped my tongue along the column of her throat, her voice turned breathless. "Yes, I'm enjoying it a lot. Please don't stop. Full speed ahead."

I hummed my approval and moved even lower, tugging up her shirt at the same time to bare her perfect pert breasts. When I flicked my tongue over one of her stiffened nipples, she gasped and clutched me tighter.

"That's right," I mumbled as I nuzzled closer. "I love hearing all the ways you let me know what you like. And I'm going to make sure you get all the goodness you deserve."

I closed my mouth around her breast with a swivel of my tongue, and a full moan tumbled out of her. Her thighs were rubbing together, the scent of her arousal lacing the air. I dipped my hand lower and almost moaned myself at the dampness of her panties.

"So happy already," I said, and licked her other nipple. "Should I do something about this, do you think?"

I curled my fingers against the dampness as I asked, and Lily arched up to meet me, her breath stuttering. "Ruin," she muttered impatiently.

I beamed at her. "I'll take that as a yes."

As I delved my hand beneath her panties, I returned the attentions of my mouth to her neck. I wanted to leave her mouth unoccupied so I could hear all the delicious sounds she made as I worked her over in her most sensitive places.

My fingers slipped easily into her slick channel. She rocked with my movements as I pulsed them deeper and deeper. Her pussy quivered around me. If she was aching even half as much as my cock was, I shouldn't leave her hanging much longer. We could have plenty more fun after she'd gotten her first release from the torment.

I massaged the heel of my hand against her clit while I plunged a third finger into her. Lily yanked my head up and kissed me so hard her teeth nicked my lip. I savored the brief sting, leaning into the kiss, thrusting my hand faster. And then she came, with a choked little cry and a shudder that ran through her whole body against mine, making her pussy clamp around my fingers.

As she sagged into the mattress, panting, I brought my hand to my mouth and licked her tangy juices off my fingers. A renewed hunger flared in Lily's eyes as she watched. She reached to pull her panties right off—

And just then Nox walked in, as usual not bothering to knock.

He took us in and simply sighed, heat flickering through his own eyes at the same time. "I'm glad someone's having a good morning," he said. "But we were going to get over to that prick Ansel's house before Lily has to get to her morning class. So put *your* prick away and let's get going."

Lily gave a huff, but he was already leaving, not offering a chance for debate. I dipped my face close to hers.

"Soon," I said. "You have no idea how much I want you too. But I can wait until we don't have anyone breathing down our necks."

A wicked little smile crossed Lily's lips. "Maybe it'd be even more fun if we made him watch."

I didn't know if it was that this new body of mine was high on all the sensations I hadn't gotten to enjoy in decades or if this woman's appeal was just that potent, but I nearly came in my boxers simply hearing her say those words. I swallowed another groan and stole one last, quick kiss before pushing myself off the bed. "Soon."

Even though I'd been left wanting, energy thrummed through my body with the knowledge of the pleasure I'd given Lily. I bounded into the living room, tossed on some clothes, took those off and pulled on some different clothes when Kai pointed out that I needed to look as Ansel-ish as possible, and gulped down about five pounds of bacon drenched in hot sauce until at least one kind of hunger was totally quiet. For the moment.

Kai was already dressed in fairly posh clothes—a collared button-up and dark jeans that didn't have any wrinkles—which was typical for him. He was coming along with us so that he could observe the situation the way only he knew how. I was totally aware that some subtleties would go straight over my head.

Especially since Lily was joining us as well. She'd pointed out that since she'd known Ansel at least a little and she was more familiar with the recent state of the town than we were, she might be able to pick up on clues the rest of us wouldn't realize were relevant. Her presence was definitely going to make the trip much more enjoyable. Unlike Kai's.

"If we run into anyone from his family, don't talk too much," he ordered me as we got into Ansel's car. Unfortunately, Kai had also insisted that showing up on our motorcycles would raise too many questions. "And try not to be so happy about everything while you're there. We don't want them suspecting anything."

"I've got to be totally Ansel," I said with a bob of my head. "No problem!"

"Yes, problem," he grumbled. "You don't sound like some arrogant golden boy at all."

"They're going to notice *something's* different," Lily pointed out, reaching forward from the back seat to ruffle my hair. "He has had a bit of a makeover."

Kai sighed. "Tell them it was a dare," he instructed. "A hazing ritual for a club at school. Maybe we should splash a little alcohol on your clothes so you'll smell like you're drunk. That could explain a personality shift."

I patted the polo shirt that'd been left over from Ansel's wardrobe, pre-makeover. "I thought you wanted my clothes to look *nice*. Or are we going to make this a game? What crazy things can we trick them into believing! Ha."

As I started the engine, Kai rolled his eyes skyward. "That wasn't exactly what I had in mind."

Technically I had Ansel's home address from the driver's license in his wallet, but Lily knew exactly where that section of street was. She gave a few directions and sat perched in her seat, peering out the windows. It occurred to me that she might be nervous about running into other people—the kind of people who'd been hurling insults and garbage at her since she'd come back home. I flexed my hands against the steering wheel and made secret plans for running *over* anyone who attempted to harass her.

We didn't pass any bystanders who seemed to notice her, though. When we got to the house, I fished the keys that had also come with

Ansel's packaging out of my pocket and then contemplated them as we ambled up to the front porch.

There were several different keys on the ring, and I had no idea which one fit the front door. Kai would probably nag me that it looked weird to go through different tries to find the right one, but I wasn't going to suddenly become psychic. Maybe I should exclaim loudly about how very drunk I was.

But it turned out I didn't need to try any of the keys. I was just playing a silent game of eenie meenie miney moe to decide which to lead with when the front door swung open. A woman with feathery blond hair, smile lines etched around her mouth, and a pearl choker at her throat peered out at us. At the sight of me, she blinked and did a double-take. The smile she gave me looked awfully stiff.

"Ansel!" she said. "I— Well. This is an interesting look. You haven't been home in a while. At least not while I've been here." She gave an awkward twittering sort of laugh.

I beamed back at her and then, remembering what Kai had said about being too happy, reined it in to what I thought was a reserved smile. Ansel obviously knew this woman. She was too old to be his sister, right? Probably mother?

It seemed risky to open by calling her "Mom," just in case he had some atypical family situation going on, so I gave her a quick nod and said, "The hair was a dare. Hazing for a club. I kind of like it, though! Just needed to pick something up from my room. Oh, and hang out with a couple of my friends."

Kai made a quietly strangled noise like he was considering dying on the spot, but I didn't see how anything I'd said was all that bad. A guy like Ansel must have been reasonably upbeat about coming home, right? It was a nice house, all high ceilings and polished floors, if you went for that kind of thing. I had a brief image of myself sliding along that front hall in my socked feet and caught the goofy grin that wanted to spring across my face just in time.

The woman's gaze slid past me to the "friends" I'd mentioned. Kai didn't seem to have any effect on her, but her eyes narrowed slightly when they focused on Lily.

"You're the Strom girl," she said in a clipped tone full of disdain.

I bristled automatically, my shoulders coming up. Kai snagged my wrist, which might have been a good thing as annoying as it was, because I was already tempted to take a swing at her. I guessed that definitely wasn't how Ansel would have responded to his mother. Even if she was being incredibly judgmental and bitchy.

Lily's jaw tightened, but she gazed straight back at the woman. "I am. Ansel and I go way back."

I knew from what she'd said before that they hadn't been at all *close*, but I realized she was just needling the woman for the exact reaction she got. Ansel's mom—or whoever she was—widened her eyes and then let out a dry little chuckle. "Well." She turned back to me. "Whatever you need, be quick about it. The cleaners will be here in a few minutes. And don't bring any of your hazing or what-have-you into the house."

"Absolutely," I said, and gave her a brisk salute that made Kai's grip on my other wrist clench. Then I remembered the other thing we'd talked about that I should check. "Has anyone come by or called asking for me?"

The woman knit her brow. "Not that I can think of. I'm sure they'd reach out to you on your own phone—you haven't broken it, have you?"

"Oh, no, it works just great," I said, patting my pocket. "Well, thank you!"

Her smile turned even stiffer, but she gave us a little wave and walked onward.

"Charming," Lily muttered under her breath.

"Maybe you just have to get to know her," I said. Or maybe she actually did deserve a fist to the face. Or, even better, we'd find what we needed today and not have to worry about which it was.

"I suppose we know where Ansel got his stunning personality from," Kai said, striding up the stairs. "If he was into anything questionable, it'll be in his own room, not in the common areas. It wouldn't make any sense for him to stash things where the family could find them."

I hadn't drawn that conclusion yet myself, but as usual, what Kai said made sense. I nodded and bounded up the stairs two at a time.

It wasn't hard to figure out which room was Ansel's. The big bedroom at the front of the house with a bay window and a wedding photo on the wall was obviously his parents'. Next to it we came to a guest room without a single personal touch, like a blank canvas before Jett had his way with it. Then there was a doorknob that jiggled but wouldn't open.

"He's locked it," Lily said, her eyebrows rising. "From his own family. I guess that's a good sign for there being secrets inside."

I got it to open with the third key on Ansel's ring, and we stepped inside. The space was about three times bigger than Lily's cramped bedroom in her apartment, with a queen-sized bed, a sleek wooden desk, and a TV with a massive stereo system set up by a narrow sofa. My eyes bugged out at the sight of his game system. "Why haven't I been here before? These are all mine now!"

As I dove down to check out the titles, some of which were weirdly sequels to games I'd played way back when I was alive before, Kai clucked his tongue chidingly. "We're not here to play around. And you can't bring that stuff with you. The family will probably assume it's been stolen—and the mom saw Lily with you. It'd be a bad scene all around."

"But it's *mine*," I protested, at least, as much as I was Ansel, which I did have to admit wasn't very much, thank God.

"Hey, you still have access to the asshole's bank account," Kai reminded me with a pat to my arm. "You can buy yourself a new one."

My smile came back at full force. "Right. Of course." I rubbed my hands together. "Now where would a popular jerk keep his secrets?"

Lily was already poking around under the bed. She dragged out a suitcase, opened it up, and made a gagging expression. "Okay, that was one secret I didn't need to see."

I peered over her should and caught a glimpse of stacks of creased magazine covers all featuring naked women… wearing diapers? One had a pacifier in her mouth. I snorted a laugh. "I'm definitely not him when it comes to my tastes in that department."

"Praise the heavens for that." Lily shoved the suitcase back under the bed. "Nothing else under here but some dirty clothes and a bottle of cheap rum." She looked it over. "I don't think having bad taste in alcohol is a murder-worthy crime."

I went back to the video games, because even if I couldn't play them, there might be something interesting tucked away in there. Kai looked over the bookcase. By the time I'd determined that nothing was hidden away among the game cases—but that they really did keep making new editions of *Street Fighter*—he'd moved to the desk.

I poked around the speakers and patted the walls, because sometimes people in movies turned up secret compartments and shit that way, right? Then Kai tugged a scrap of paper from between the pages of a novel from one of the desk drawers.

"Ah ha!" he said as he looked it over.

"What?" I dashed to his side. Lily dropped the mattress she'd been peering under to come join us.

Kai waved the paper like a pennant. "He was keeping very close track of Lily's schedule. Look at this."

She snatched the paper out of his hand and stared at it. "Those are my class times and the buildings they're in. What the hell? Was he stalking me or something? I don't remember seeing him around *that* much."

"His friends could have all contributed," Kai pointed out.

I frowned. "What does it mean? Was that guy with the beard trying to kill him for following Lily?"

Kai knuckled me in the chest. "No, you dork. I haven't found anything that explains the whole murderous stalkers thing." He grimaced and lifted his chin toward the paper. "It just means Ansel was a lot more invested in bullying Lily than we realized. Tracking her movements instead of just targeting her when he happened to cross paths with her."

"But that doesn't matter now, does it?" I said hopefully. "I mean… he's not around anymore. And Lily doesn't mind *me* following her around." I shot her a grin.

She elbowed me in response. "Most of the time." But her expression stayed pensive.

"We'll have to keep a close eye on his friends," Kai said. "We cracked down on them hard, but we need to be sure it was hard enough." He glanced around at the room. "I think the rest of this place is a bust. If he kept any evidence of what he'd gotten into, it wasn't here."

As I followed his gaze, my mood dimmed. Not only was I in the body of a jerk who'd been trying to make Lily's life even more hell than we'd realized, I hadn't turned up anything useful myself.

What was the point in being here for her if I couldn't come through when she needed it the most?

Chapter Four

Lily

SITTING in the second-story café looking out over the street, I felt like a character in a spy flick. I had a felt hat pulled low on my head to shadow my face, with most of my hair tucked up under it so the pale blond strands wouldn't catch anyone's notice. I'd even put on makeup when I hadn't usually bothered since I got back in town, so my face wouldn't look exactly like me at a glance.

There was only so much I could do to disguise myself, but I didn't want anyone catching a glimpse of me and immediately thinking, *There's Lily Strom.*

The café gave an angled view toward the high school my little sister currently attended. The students were due to get out in five minutes. I sipped my caramel latte, rolling the bittersweet liquid across my tongue, and willed myself not to fidget with nerves.

Besides, I had to concentrate before Marisol even left the building. If someone *else* was spying on her, monitoring her movements and making her feel she couldn't trust her surroundings, they were the ones I wanted to catch. I needed to know whether I could go over and talk to her again without bringing a heap more trouble down on her head.

I'd been carefully watching what I could see of the street for almost half an hour now, since I'd gotten out of my last class at the college. I hadn't seen anyone lingering by the school looking suspicious, but I assumed a creep keeping tabs on her wouldn't walk around wearing a neon sign saying *Stalker.*

I had to consider everyone, no matter how innocuous-looking. The elderly man shuffling over to the bingo hall across the road. The perky woman in a pastel jumpsuit who emerged from a house farther down the street. The toddler jumping along as he clutched her hand—okay, maybe not him.

My phone vibrated with an incoming text. *No one's been sticking around by this end of the school,* Jett reported. *Anything over there?*

Not so far, I wrote back. *Hold your post and keep watching.* I'd given all four of the guys *very* specific locations to stay in, with strict orders not to budge one step from those places unless I explicitly said so. Short of someone coming at Marisol with a gun or dragging her into a car, I didn't want them to do much more than breathe and keep their eyes open.

Not that they couldn't have helped in other ways. The problem was that once they started helping, they sometimes got caught up in the momentum and ended up solving problems I really hadn't thought needed tackling… at least not by literally tackling anyone.

One by one, the others texted to report the same thing. Then I made out the peal of the final bell distantly through the windowpane. I shifted a smidge forward in my seat. Any second now…

Teenagers started pouring out onto the sidewalk, some stopping there in clusters, others walking off toward home or afterschool jobs or whatever else they got up to. One couple were so glued at the lips they nearly walked into a telephone pole. I alternated between scanning all of them for Marisol's golden hair and checking the streets nearby for any sign that some lurker had emerged with similar interests.

I didn't spot anyone other than typical pedestrians, and my phone didn't chime with notifications from the guys of threatening figures they'd spotted. They had much more of a hair trigger than I did, so if *they* weren't worried—

There she was. I caught sight of her bright, wavy hair amid the crowd. My heart skipped a beat with a painful pang. I wanted to be down there hooking my arm around hers and telling her I'd make everything all right, not way up here separated by glass and a whole lot of distance.

She wove through the mass of her peers like she had the first time I'd come out to the school, when I'd tried to talk to her: shoulders hunched, head low. She didn't wave at or speak to anyone. Just tramped through their midst and drifted on down the street.

It looked like she was heading in the same direction as before. That made my job easier. I didn't have to follow as closely to still know where she was going.

I stayed braced by the window as she came almost to the storefront beneath me and then turned the corner. A few other students rambled along a similar route, but none of them appeared to be paying any attention to her. A couple headed up to the coffee shop without a glance her way. A few shoppers walked by from another direction, but no one who'd tailed her from the area of the school.

It didn't seem like she was being followed. Quite possibly she was just worried that it *could* be happening.

I sucked my lower lip under my teeth and then left behind my half-full mug to hustle down the stairs so I didn't lose her completely. As I stepped out onto the sidewalk into the brisk September breeze, a small green form sprang past my feet. I glanced down.

A frog—what else could I have expected? It took another few hops forward and then peered back at me as if wondering what the holdup was.

I'd come to realize that Lovell Rise wasn't simply a town infested with frogs. They had a particular affinity for me, something to do with the weird powers I'd apparently picked up during my near-death experience half-drowning in the marsh as a kid. The guys had said I must have brought some of the marsh back with me when I'd reclaimed my life, and the evidence did support that conclusion.

Frogs and water—my superpowers. Get me tights and a cape and call me Swamp Woman.

Actually, no, definitely don't do that.

I trotted down the street with the frog keeping pace next to me as if we were out for a casual jog. When I caught a glimpse of Marisol a few blocks ahead, I slowed and pretended I was deeply fascinated by the shop windows next to me. Really, I was studying their reflections for any covert moves people nearby might make when they thought no one was watching.

Nobody twigged my concerns, as much as I was trying to stay alert to the slightest hint of suspicious behavior. Nothing unsettled me at all until my phone buzzed in my purse.

I jumped, startled, and then pulled it out. It was a text from Nox.

Saw a guy walking across the schoolyard who didn't have a good reason for being there. Following him now.

Oh, fuck. *Was he anywhere near Marisol?* I asked, jabbing my keys across the phone frantically.

No, but he's heading your way. I don't like the look of him. Followed by a scowling emoji. Of course he'd already figured out those after just a couple of weeks' exposure to modern phones.

My heart started thumping twice as fast for reasons that had nothing to do with my sister. I darted across the street, still keeping an eye out for hazardous strangers but mostly heading to intercept Nox. *I told you to stay in position unless someone actually went after her.*

He COULD be going after her. I won't know if I don't keep an eye on him, will I?

I made a face at the phone. *Where are you now?*

Coming up on Hyacinth St.

I dashed down a side-street so Marisol wouldn't notice me charging over from behind her and then loped up to Hyacinth. I reached it just as a man in a slightly oversized suit with sweaty armpits strode past me—and immediately ducked into a dentist's office on the opposite corner. Through the window, I saw him greet the receptionist, who was clearly expecting him.

I spun around to glower at Nox, who was just slowing down where he'd been storming down the street after the guy. He looked from me to the dentist's office and back and raked his hand through his spiky hair.

"He was weird," he said as he reached me, before I could criticize him. "In a suit but kind of shabby-looking, walking through the yard outside the school."

"He was probably just taking a short cut," I said. "It's public property, you know. I'm going to bet you've taken plenty of short cuts in your life, probably a bunch of them through places you weren't really allowed to be at all."

Nox grinned as if this were a point of pride rather than a reminder of his wrongdoings and pushed on down the street, bumping his shoulder companionably against mine. "Where's the kid now? You didn't lose her, did you?"

"If I did, it's because I had to go make sure you didn't hoist anyone up a flagpole or drop them down a manhole," I muttered as I hurried along beside him.

"Hey, what are they called 'manholes' for if you're not supposed to drop a man down them when you need to?"

We made it back to the street my sister had been ambling along and spotted her a couple of blocks farther down, standing by a street display of cartoonish sketches. A guy with a limp ponytail was sitting on a stool with an easel, nodding as she asked him a question.

Nox bristled immediately. "What does *he* want?"

I put my hand on his shoulder and gave him a firm nudge in the opposite direction. "Um, he's trying to get paid to draw pictures of people, obviously. It's not his fault she stopped to look."

Nox's eyebrows drew together. "Is that what he calls art? Jett would figure those doodles are criminal right there. Definitely sketchy."

He didn't appear to notice the inadvertent pun, pushing against my hand until I shoved him back. Marisol was already wandering onward, and the guy didn't even glance after her, focusing instead on a middle-aged couple who must have looked like they'd have deeper money pockets.

The woman in the couple abruptly bent down and then ran after Marisol. My pulse skittered only for a second, but Nox leapt forward with a growl as if he was going to go all medieval on the lady's ass right now.

"Nox!" I hissed, and flung my arms around him. My heels skidded on the sidewalk before he jerked to a halt. He wasn't willing to fight me, but he frowned down at me. Thankfully, he came along when I hauled him back into the relative shelter by the building on the corner before anyone noticed the human volcano in their midst.

"We're trying not to get noticed," I hissed at him, and waved toward the woman.

She was just holding out something that glinted to Marisol. "I think you dropped this, hun."

"Oh!" Marisol grabbed the cheap bangle and slipped it back over her hand onto her wrist. "Thank you so much."

The woman walked back to her partner, who appeared to be haggling with the sketch artist over exactly how much a cartoon version of himself was worth.

"There was no way I could have known she was only handing that over," Nox said.

I gave him a pointed look. "Yes, there was. The way we just found out."

"She could have been about to kidnap her. Or knife her. She still could be. Just gaining the mark's trust." He nodded sagely.

I resisted the urge to punch him in his massively muscular chest. It probably would have hurt my hand more than him anyway. "I don't think so. Anyway, we're supposed to be watching for anyone who's *observing* her, watching what she's up to. If someone was trying to hurt her, they'd have done it in the seven years before I got back in town, don't you think?"

Nox paused and rubbed his chin. "I guess you might have a point there. Have you seen anyone like that?"

"No," I admitted. "Have you? Or should I assume if you had, their intestines would be strewn all over Main Street already?"

He looked down at me with an amused but affectionate gleam in his eyes. "You know me so well, Minnow." Then he cocked his head, gazing up the street again. "Where's she going now?"

Marisol was just slipping into a store toward the end of the street. I decided it was safe to venture a little closer, squinting at the sign.

"Oh, it's the bookshop," I said, coming to a stop. Not a place she'd ever been interested in going into when we were kids. Did she prefer looking at other people's pictures to drawing her own now?

We eased closer, me keeping a tight grip on Nox's arm in case he made any sudden moves. I peered through the window.

Marisol didn't appear to have any official reason for coming to the store. There was already a woman stationed behind the counter by the cash register. It took me a few moments to spot my sister way at the back of the store, her shoulders still hunched and head low as if she was trying to be as invisible as possible, turning the page of a book she'd picked up.

My stomach knotted. "She must hang out in there, reading or whatever, until closing," I murmured to Nox. "So she doesn't have to be around Mom and Wade any more than necessary." She didn't feel all that safe out here on the streets, but she felt better than in her own home. That just wasn't right.

Nox jerked his chin toward the window. "Why don't you go over there and get her? Bring her home with you. You said you didn't see anyone watching her, right? None of the other guys have called in any problems, have they?"

They hadn't. Hopefully that meant they'd kept their cool and not that they were now busy stashing bodies. I nibbled at my lower lip again. "I mean, we can't be absolutely sure…"

The former gang boss folded his arms over his chest. "What's going on, Lily? You know you want her away from those deadbeats. You know you can take on anyone who comes at you or her. You've got nothing to be scared of anymore."

As he said those words, the breeze rippled past me, bringing a faint whine into the air as it whipped across a nearby metal awning. A car rumbled past, and a doorbell jingled, and the thumping of my pulse combined with all those sounds into a patchwork of a musical harmony. It rang through my limbs and brought back the image of the water I'd summoned gushing from the walls in my old kitchen to terrorize Wade into answering my questions.

It was true. I was queen of frogs and commander of H2O, it seemed, and that should get us pretty far. What did I really think anyone could do to Marisol that I couldn't defend her from with those new tricks up my sleeve?

I dragged in a breath, and the answer tumbled out of me. "I've just

—I've been worried that I hurt her, that I could hurt her again, for so long. I don't want to mess anything up. I don't want to be the reason she ends up in danger."

Nox considered me for a long moment. "It sounds like she's already been through plenty when you *weren't* around to take care of her. I don't think there's a single chance you'll make her life worse."

"You can't know that for sure," I said, but at the same time, I raised my chin, holding on to the harmony humming through me. "But maybe I should trust me and her more. I'll make sure I've really got a handle on my powers, and then I'll have another talk with her."

If I was going to put myself forward as her protector, I'd better make sure I knew what the hell I was doing with myself.

Chapter Five

Nox

"Do things usually change this much in twenty years?" Ruin asked, shooting a puzzled glance at the antique shop that'd once been the headquarters of another local gang, the Wolverines.

The crystal chandeliers, ornate china plates, and brass candlesticks displayed in the store window definitely didn't fit that ragtag bunch of miscreants. Five minutes in that place, and there'd have been nothing left but chunks of glass and ceramics mixed in with some melted metal. Even without further investigation, I felt comfortable concluding that the guys we'd once squabbled with were no longer operating out of this place.

Maybe they'd completely disbanded. You couldn't expect much consistency out of a bunch of dudes who named themselves after a comic book hero.

"Twenty-one years," Kai corrected automatically. "And you have *no* idea how much has happened in that time." He shook his head as if jostling all the pieces of information he'd consumed in the past couple of weeks into order. He'd stuffed so much into his brain I was kind of surprised he could even hold the damn thing up.

"The guys we knew would all be old now," I said. "Like—as old as our parents were when we got started." A smile tugged at my lips. "Bald spots and crow's feet."

Jett's mouth twisted into a rare smirk. "Dad bods and beer guts."

Ruin snickered and bounced on his feet with eager energy. "Then we'll have no problem taking them down if they're the ones who did us in. How are we going to find them?"

I rubbed my mouth, considering. The towns like Lovell Rise and those around it weren't big enough for more than one gang to stake a claim for long, so we'd owned the Rise, and various other operations had lorded it over its neighbors, like this shabby collection of buildings.

Our killers must have come from one of those other towns. I was tempted to simply barge from main street to main street, smashing windows and battering doors until someone coughed up the information we needed, but that might only give the pricks a chance to make a run for it.

It was better if they didn't know we were back and looking for vengeance until we had them in our grasp. All it'd take was a little restraint. We could pretend we had a more… academic interest in the murderous history of this area. In Kai's case, that wasn't even totally untrue.

"We know all the gang signs," I said. "And we know what looks like one even if it isn't a logo we recognize from before. Let's just cruise around until we find an indication of who's still pretending to be in charge around here and where they're hanging out these days."

The other guys nodded, and we all revved our bikes' engines. I adjusted my position in my seat, soaking in the reverberation that ran through the powerful machine I was riding. My old Hog hadn't boasted anywhere near this much horsepower. Thank the Devil for modern innovations and a professor's bank account.

It didn't take much cruising before we spotted a hastily spray-painted tag on the wall of a tattoo club, which was currently closed up, probably because it'd take about a week to tattoo the entire population of this area who actually wanted to get inked and then you'd just sit around twiddling your thumbs until the next generation came of age.

I'd been wanting to replace some of my ink, but I wasn't turning to a place that had any affiliation with dorks who used a jagged claw symbol that a three-year-old could have drawn as their calling card. Jett was the artist around here, but I did have *some* standards.

There was a dingy curtain hanging over the window on the second-floor apartment, but it only covered half the pane, letting through the faint yellow glow of an electric light behind it. I parked my bike and motioned to the others to follow me.

We marched around back, noting even more of the Wolverines' tags in the lane and one sprayed right across the rear door. It didn't look like just a drive-by tagging. And if I was wrong and we burst in on some startled family, well, we'd say sorry and leave again. No real harm done.

Anyone living around here could probably use a little more excitement in their lives anyway.

I tested the lock with my hand, judged it wanting, and slammed my heel into it hard enough to snap the latch. It swung open on squeaking hinges, and we hurtled up the stairs to the apartment.

"What the—" some young guy said as we charged into the main room, and then Ruin was crashing into him, knocking him to the ground on his stomach. As he planted himself on the guy's back, grinning as he mashed his victim's face against the ground so the guy couldn't speak any more, two more men, a little older, barreled out of another room. Jett toppled one with a punch and a smack of a chair he snatched up, and I rammed the other right into the wall with my hand around his throat.

"Stay right there," I told him, not like he could go much of anywhere when I pinned his arms over his chest and tightened my grip on his neck at his first feeble kick. Then I took a proper look around the place.

It sure didn't look like the home of any kind of family—other than the halfwit gang type. A ratty sofa stood in one corner, a card table with four dented chairs in the other, playing cards and a few chips still scattered across it. The air stunk of cheap alcohol and weed. Someone had tacked a couple of Playboy centerfolds to the wall next to the oven, I guessed in case you wanted to jack off while you were making a pot roast.

"You're the bunch that calls yourself the Wolverines?" I asked in a growl, turning my attention back to my captive. This guy looked like the oldest of the bunch, but he still couldn't have been much over thirty. At best, he'd have been a teenager when we'd kicked the bucket. That didn't mean he wouldn't know anything, though.

He let out only a faint gurgling noise, which suggested I should loosen my hold a little. I allowed his feet to touch the ground but kept my fingers firmly in place. "Try again."

"Yeah," he rasped. "We're the Wolverines. Who the fuck wants to know?"

"None of your goddamn business." I gave him a vicious smile. "We're here to tie up some loose ends. What do you know about an attack on a gang hangout over in Lovell Rise twenty-one years ago?"

"Twenty-one years ago?" the guy replied. "Fuck, I was in middle school then. What the hell are you talking about?"

But the guy Jett was currently using as a chair cushion made a sound. Jett prodded him. "What's that?"

The guy wheezed and then said, "I heard about that. Dirk mentioned it a couple of times."

Dirk—that'd been one of the dicks who'd run with the Wolverines when we'd known them. I glared at the guy over my shoulder. "And what did Dirk say about it?"

"Just that—that we should watch our backs around the Silver Scythes out in Rushford. I guess they had something to do with getting that whole gang wiped off the map."

My lips pulled back from my teeth in a silent snarl. "The fucking *Silver Scythes*?"

My men looked as disgusted as I felt. It was one thing to name yourself after a comic book, and another level way lower to go for a wimpy-sounding title like Silver Scythes. Like they wanted to be *pretty* about their life of crime or some shit. Maybe they figured people would write poetry about them.

But the name resonated with me with even more horror than just that. The thing was, I'd known the Scythes had it out for us. They'd made a stab at robbing the site where we stashed our stolen goods for fencing, but *because* they'd seemed like such wimps, not much more than a bunch of snot-nosed kids with visions of grandeur they'd never live up to, I hadn't put bullets in their brains. I'd let them off with a few bruises and a firm threat about what they'd face if they messed with us again.

And instead of shaping up, they'd stewed on the situation for six months and then come at us with guns blazing? The fucking bastards. I didn't know who I wanted to rip to shreds more—them or myself for giving them a second chance.

If I hadn't, we might never have died. If I'd laid down the law as hard as they'd obviously deserved, I'd have been there for Gram, I'd have watched the Skullbreakers grow in prestige and power…

Anger and guilt wrapped around my gut like barbed wire. I hurled the guy I'd pinned toward the window, where he cracked his head against the glass. Then I spun around, my hands clenched.

We would build ourselves up again. And we had Lily now. We never would have had her if we hadn't been through all this.

But I still should have fucking known better.

"Move out," I snapped at the other guys. Jett and Ruin got off their human seating. We all stomped down the stairs to our bikes.

"Over to Rushfield?" Kai asked as we mounted. "It sounds like the Silver Scythes are still active." Disbelief laced through his tone. He found the idea that they'd gotten the better of us even more ridiculous than I did.

Jett was frowning. "It *couldn't* have been them," he said.

"They've sure been spreading the story that it was." I gunned my engine. "Let's see what they've got to say for themselves now."

Rushford lay on the opposite side of Lovell Rise, a little bigger but also a little more rundown. It was like someone had cloned our town but ended up with an expanded, grainy copy. They didn't have the lake right there to draw tourists out to the marina, and they weren't quite as close to Mayfield for the city pricks to come looking to get some "country air." As far as I could tell, they didn't have much of anything. Maybe that was why they were such dickheads about everything.

The Scythes hadn't been on my radar enough for me to have

memorized the location of their headquarters, if they'd even had one back then, but it wasn't any harder to find them than it had been with the Wolverines. We roared into town and tore up and down a few streets, observing a tag in silvery metallic paint that might have been supposed to look like a curved blade but really bore more resemblance to a limp dick, which fit better anyway.

There were more tags around a dumpy-looking board game shop than anywhere else. We marched in, strode right past the counter into the back room, and found a couple of idiots lounging on sofas with cartoons on the TV and Cheeto dust smeared on their jeans.

"Are you the fuckers currently calling yourselves the Silver Scythes?" I demanded, wrenching the nearest guy out of his seat and into the wall in the middle of the question.

As he sputtered, I noted the crummy tattoo peeking from beneath the collar of his shirt and the scar across his forehead. I was pretty sure this prick had been part of the Scythes back in my day, as one of the runty high school seniors that made up most of their numbers.

Jett and Ruin had shoved the other guy to the floor. Kai picked his way through the empty junk food bags and opened a cookie tin on a shelf. "They're dealing coke," he reported. "Either that or using so much their noses should be falling off any day now."

"What the fuck—" the guy I was holding spat out. "You can't just—"

"I can do whatever the hell I want," I interrupted. "And I'll take that as a yes, you are the shitty Silver Scythes. You're going to explain to me what went down between you asses and the Skullbreakers twenty years ago, and you're going to explain it to me fast, or I will personally break your skull. Slowly, into many very small pieces."

I might do it anyway, but there was no point in mentioning that upfront. I sure as hell wasn't going to be generous with these imbeciles again.

The guys were clearly still wimps, whatever else they'd done. The one I had pinned shuddered in my grasp. His voice took on more of a whimpering tone. "We didn't really— It wasn't us. We only— They were so full of themselves, and they acted like they owned everything around. But we barely had anything to do with it."

"That's not what you've been saying around town," Kai said in his usual nonchalant tone.

"What exactly *did* you have to do with it?" I asked, yanking him back for just long enough to slam him against the wall again.

"We just—it wasn't even *me*, it was Tony's idea, and he's dead now, so—"

"What the fuck did *Tony* do?" I growled.

"He put out word to one of the big dogs in Mayfield that the Skullbreakers were talking shit about them and making moves to steal ground in the city," the idiot said with a hitch of breath. "I guess he convinced them really well, 'cause they acted on it. *I* had nothing to do with it. I said it was a bad idea getting mixed up in—"

I didn't want to hear his lame-ass excuses. I tossed him on the ground and kicked him in the side hard enough to fracture a rib or two. As he lay there groaning, I exchanged a glance with my comrades.

I had fucked up. My leniency with the Silver Scythes two decades ago had set us up for our fall. But if we wanted to deal with the villains who'd actually mowed us down and dumped us like week-old trash, it sounded like we needed to head to Mayfield.

Before I could say so out loud, a guy came bursting through the back door, gun in hand. The new arrival was pointing it straight at me.

My body reacted instinctively, whipping out a punch even though he was at least a couple of feet beyond my reach. But as I moved, the electric sensation I'd felt when we'd kicked the asses of Lily's bullies in the grocery store crackled through my limbs—and seemingly out of my hand. *Something* walloped the guy across the jaw, sending him careening to the side.

Kai was there a second later, ramming his knee into the prick's wrist and retrieving the gun. He shot the guy in the side of the head without so much as a blink and glanced at my fist as our attacker crumpled. "That's never happened before, has it?"

I looked down at my hand, flexing my fingers. "No. Looks like there's a little more to our superpowers than you'd already figured out."

Chapter Six

Lily

"Do it again!" Ruin crowed, applauding his heart out.

Nox chuckled and swung his fist toward another low branch on the hunched sapling he'd been battering. His knuckles didn't even come close to hitting it—he smacked the empty space about a foot from the bark. But the air shimmered faintly, and the branch split in half as if it'd been struck. The former gang leader raised his hand triumphantly, grinning.

A cool wind swept off the lake and licked over the back of my skin. I wasn't sure how much it was the chill and how much the supernatural energy in the air that raised the hairs on the back of my neck.

After a broken plate, a shattered glass, and a dent in the front door, I'd finally convinced the former Skullbreakers that if they were going to insist on an experimentation session, we really should do it someplace where I didn't have a security deposit hanging over my head. We'd driven out here to a particularly secluded section of the marsh, Ruin opting to ride in my car with me and the others zipping along on their new motorcycles. They made quite the entourage.

And they'd make even more of one if they all developed fancier powers like this one of Nox's. Playing around some more, he reached up and twisted his fingers—and a nearby twig snapped from its branch.

Jett took a few swings at another tree, but he didn't seem to be able to manipulate his lingering ghostly energies in the same way. Ruin and Kai hadn't managed it either, although Ruin seemed content to simply watch Nox work his powers anyway. Right now, Kai was rubbing his chin with a pensive expression.

"It obviously isn't a general effect of our previously free-souled state," he said. "Then we'd all be able to do it. Physical violence has always been one of your primary ways of getting things done, so the energies may be adapting to your specific skill set or focus. We might find that different effects emerge for each of us."

"Let me guess," Jett muttered. "You'd get the power of being a total know-it-all. No, wait, you've already got that."

"Jett, you'd have to get something to do with art," Ruin said gleefully. "And Kai will have to have something smart." He paused, tilting his head to one side. "I'm not sure what would make sense for me."

Nox cuffed him in the arm. "Maybe you'll start literally beaming sunshine out your ass like you already do metaphorically."

Ruin laughed. "I guess that'd be handy in the dark."

Kai had ignored Jett's remark. He nudged at his glasses and contemplated his friends. "We'll have to stay alert to shifts in the energy moving through us and new manifestations of it. It's important that we're aware of our capabilities so we can work to our full potential."

Nox cuffed him next. "Now you sound like a self-help guru." He turned to me. "What about you, Siren? Didn't you say you wanted to play around with your powers some more, see what *you're* capable of?"

I had, and I'd been thinking about that ever since we'd come out here. But somehow, now that I was faced with a stretch of the reed-choked water that'd almost swallowed me up fourteen years ago, an immense sense of hesitation gripped my mind. Some part of me would rather dunk my head in that cold marsh water than try to manipulate it again.

I'd used my powers two times so far—well, two times on purpose. There was also the time when I'd splashed the girl who'd been one of the ringleaders of my bullies, Peyton, with water that'd jumped right out of its bottle in her hands. And the time when I'd frightened my stepdad and possibly my mom too by throwing water around the house after I'd discovered Nolan Gauntt with my sister… doing something. That incident was still a total blank in my mind.

That fact unsettled me too. I had to take Wade's word for what had happened. His babbled, terrified words, which suggested he'd been scared into honesty. But who knew how accurately he even remembered what'd gone down seven years ago?

The underside of my arm itched in the spot where I had a birthmark-like splotch, one I'd only discovered after I'd started my stay at the looney bin, like the stress had caused even my skin to freak out. I scratched at it as I gathered my resolve.

"I do need to experiment—and get better control over what I can do," I said. "I'm just not sure where to start. I don't want to destroy anything out here."

Ruin shrugged with a smile. "You've got marsh magic, and we're at the marsh. I don't think you can mess it up by making it marshier."

He might have had a point there. I dragged in a breath and tried to tap into the feelings that'd surged through me when I'd used my unexpected powers before.

A humming sensation had risen up in my chest and expanded through my whole body. And—listening to the sounds around me, forming a rhythm with them, had helped me focus the power. I squared my shoulders and willed something to happen… but no hum rushed up inside me. No tingling spread to my fingertips.

I wiggled my fingers, but that didn't summon anything. Frowning at my hands didn't help either.

"I don't know how to get it started," I admitted. "Before it always just… happened."

"Something provoked you," Kai suggested. "What were the circumstances when you tapped into it before?"

That question was easy to answer. "I was angry. Or upset, at least. And feeling under threat, some of the time." I had no idea how I'd been feeling when my strange power had first emerged at age thirteen, but I obviously hadn't been *happy*.

"Hmm," Nox said with a teasing lilt to his tone. "So we need to piss you off to let you get some practice in."

I glowered at him. "I'd really rather you didn't volunteer. Maybe if I just *think* about situations that would bother me…"

I tried imagining scenarios from the past, like a bunch of the guys from school showing up at my work to frame me and then trying to beat up Kai. Or Peyton and her friends shoving me into the school's basement utility room. Or Wade complaining that the mental hospital hadn't "fixed" me.

Little whiffs of anger flickered through me, but they didn't provoke the hum I was looking for. Maybe it wouldn't get riled up when I already knew how those situations had been resolved. I rolled my neck, stretching the tension out of my muscles, and imagined up new encounters that hadn't actually happened but could.

What if Wade went back on his word and tried to move Mom and Marisol away from Lovell Rise? I could show up at the house and find them and all their stuff gone…

Picturing walking up to the empty shell of a home brought out the first strains of the hum reverberating up from my gut. I imagined seeing the car driving off, Marisol screaming my name from the back window, and my blood quivered in my veins.

I held on to those taut emotions and drummed my fingers against my thigh, feeling the beat all through my body. Lacing it through the hiss of the wind through the cattails and the chirping of a nearby bird into a minor orchestration. Any other time, my throat would have tickled with the urge to put words to the melody. Now, I was reaching for something else.

The first time I'd used my power on purpose, I'd called in an army of frogs on Peyton. My lips twitched with the memory. Could I do that again, just by wanting it?

Thinking back to that moment, I did my best to send out a call to those jumpy creatures who seemed to follow me around so often of their own accord already. *Come on, slimy green friends,* I thought into the void. *Nothing so urgent today. Just want to see whether you can hear me.*

It wasn't like the other day with Peyton. The reeds rustled, and there was a pattering of soft thumps as one and another squat body leapt from the marsh water onto the grass to join me. They came. But when I opened my eyes and looked down, only a couple dozen were clustered around my feet.

I'd brought at least a hundred down on Peyton, and I'd been miles from the marsh when I'd accomplished that.

"Hey," I said to the ones who'd answered my call. "Good to see you. I guess you're the overachievers, huh?"

Ruin crouched down and let one hop onto his hand. He stroked its sleek back and grinned up at me. "They're cute!"

"Not exactly going to put the fear of, well, me into anyone, though," I grumbled. "Two dozen frogs—just enough to be very weird, not enough to send anyone running."

"That's not what you unleashed on your stepdad," Nox reminded me.

"It's not." I eyed the span of tangled reeds that stretched at least a quarter of a mile out before thinning into open water. I'd called to the water running through the pipes in my childhood home. Conducting the marsh water to my will, if it was where I'd gotten these powers in the first place, should be a piece of cake. But I already felt tired. Why was this so hard?

"You're worried," Kai said, evenly but quietly, answering the question I hadn't voiced out loud. "Your powers make you nervous. You're still afraid you'll hurt someone."

My hands balled at my sides. "Yeah."

"You *can't* really hurt us," Ruin pointed out, straightening up. "I mean, we've already been dead. I guess if something happens to these bodies, we'd just… find new ones?" He cocked his head at Kai.

The other guy lifted his hands. "I'm not sure, but that'd be my best guess."

I *really* didn't want to think about that. When the guys had first barged into my life, without me really understanding who and what they were, I'd wanted nothing more than to get away from them. But now, just weeks later, the thought of losing them might as well have ripped me down the middle. An ache swelled around my heart.

They'd been the first people who'd really supported me and been there for me when I was a kid, and they were the only people I'd been able to turn to since I'd gotten back into town. They'd recognized the strength I had in me, both supernatural and otherwise, and helped me bring it out. I didn't know what I'd do if they vanished and I was left to deal with this insanity on my own all over again.

The pain of that possibility sent the hum roaring through me with twice as much force as before. A shiver ran down my back, and I gulped the damp air. Then I fixed my attention on the lake and beckoned.

A warbling sound filled the air and rang through my nerves. A taste like algae crept into the back of my mouth. Then a surge of water swept up over the bank and rippled across the grass to kiss my feet.

More, I thought, leaning into that warbled harmony. Twisting the melody in my mind into a shape I wanted to see.

The water slipped back toward the marsh—and then shot upward in a thin but towering wave.

My control wasn't perfect. Little droplets rained down on us as the wave held its rigid loom. Jett looked up at it and gave a low whistle, lifting his hands as if he were framing the image with them for a future painting.

This time, Nox was the one who applauded, with an emphatic slow clap. Ruin let out a joyful little whoop. I inhaled shakily, a smile crossing my lips, and shooed the water back toward the marsh.

The wave flipped over and crashed down into the reeds, splattering the tree trunks along the shore.

"What do you think?" Nox asked me, his eyes smoldering with appreciation. "Ready to take on the world?"

An unsteady giggle tumbled out of me. "Maybe not the entire world quite yet. But I think it's time I talked to my sister and found out exactly what she's scared of. Because whatever it is—whoever it is—they're going down."

Chapter Seven

Lily

When I'd parked a couple of blocks down from the bookstore and gotten out, the guys converged on the car.

"Are you sure it's still safe to drive this thing?" Jett said in a doubtful tone, tapping the rust-speckled hood. "The engine was making more noise than a woodchipper."

"We're getting her a new ride," Nox said before I had a chance to answer. "We already decided that."

"*I* didn't decide it," I protested. I'd fully admit that the car—which I'd affectionately named Fred—was a junker, but it was *my* junker. Bought with hard-earned cash I'd scraped together during the work placements that St. Elspeth's Hospital had let me take on in the past year as I'd proved my mental stability.

Okay, so maybe the melodies Fred's engine produced were more in the vein of heavy metal screeching than I'd generally prefer. And the front passenger door was a thread from falling off its hinges. And an occasional plume of smoke emanated from beneath the hood. But only occasionally! I could live with that.

Ruin slung his arm around me. "You don't need to decide," he said with his usual buoyant optimism. "We'll take care of everything for you. We're taking care of *you.*"

Jett made a rough coughing sound and muttered something under his breath that might have been, "Some of us more than others." But then he nodded in agreement with the overall statement.

"It would be better if you were driving a vehicle that wasn't quite so… on the verge of breaking down," Kai said.

Nox fixed me with a firm gaze. "It isn't an argument. You can keep *this* car if you really want it, but we're getting you another one." A slow, cocky smile curved his lips. "I mean, we do owe you, right? It's kind of our fault that you lost your job. What kind of men would we be if we didn't make it up to you?"

I could have pointed out that the men who were more responsible for me losing that job had done shit-all and still seemed to consider themselves manly enough, but I didn't really want my ghostly avengers thinking I saw my bullies as a suitable model of behavior. Instead, I let out a huff of a sigh. "I don't want you stealing Fred away in the middle of the night. He's doing his best." I patted the hood. "If he actually breaks down, then you'll have a point."

Nox let out a noncommittal grumble.

"Are we going to get to meet your sister too?" Ruin asked, beaming in the general direction of the store. "I don't really remember her that well from back before."

The guys had never really joined in with the games Marisol and I had played together back when I'd thought they were my imaginary friends. I'd assumed it was because it hadn't made sense in my mind for them to interfere when I already had company. I guessed that'd been essentially true, except it'd been them deciding it of their own accord.

I eyed the four of them with a twist of my mouth. "Um… Maybe it's better if we hold off on those introductions until she's totally comfortable with *me* being around again. I mean, your situation is a whole nother level of crazy." I waved my hands in their general vicinity.

That statement was so undeniable that none of them bothered to argue. "Next time!" Ruin said cheerfully, like everything was going to be sorted out that fast.

"We can keep an eye on things out here while you're talking with her," Nox said. "I haven't seen those pricks who had it in for you making any moves lately, but we've got to make sure it stays that way. How long until she should show up?"

I was pretty sure the beating the guys had given my tormenters up and down the aisles of the grocery store had driven the message home pretty solidly. People at school were looking at me like they were afraid I'd randomly decide to stab them, but they'd already been doing that. At least they weren't also making snarky comments and tossing garbage at me anymore.

I checked the time on my phone. "About ten minutes. I'll go into the store in a moment so I'm already in there. Hopefully she'll feel safer talking to me where there'll be less chance of prying eyes."

As I finished speaking, an alert sounded from Kai's pocket. He got out his own phone and peered at the screen.

"I've been tracking any new mentions on the internet about Thrivewell Enterprises and the Gauntts," he informed us, answering the question before it'd been asked as usual.

My heart skipped a beat. "Anything interesting?"

He shook his head. "Unless you consider the fact that they're looking for a new mailroom clerk damning evidence of anything other than high employee turnover at the grunt level, nope. I'll let you know as soon as anything comes up."

"Okay." I rolled my shoulders and bounced on my feet to loosen myself up, like I was about to go into a boxing ring rather than a bookstore. "I'll see you all in a bit. Wish me luck."

Ruin gave me one last squeeze before letting me go. "It'll be fine. She loves you."

His words sent a little pang through me. Marisol had *used* to love me. She was practically a different person now than she'd been back then. Sixteen was leagues away from nine. And she hadn't seen me or spoken to me in those seven years except for our brief conversation last week.

I walked over to the bookstore and pushed inside. A waft of crisp, vaguely lemon-scented air washed over me.

It wasn't one of those cozy bookshops full of old wooden bookcases and tables, ancient volumes bound in fabric and leather, and the smell of dust and old paper. The shelving units shone so starkly white I could make out a glimmer of my reflection, and they were lined with brightly colored spines of what were obviously mostly new releases.

But there was nothing wrong with that. I could imagine taking a kind of comfort in the shiny freshness of the place, especially if other parts of your life felt awfully murky.

As I walked down an aisle of travel guides and biographies to the back of the store, I trailed my fingers over the smooth spines—until I noticed the woman behind the counter narrowing her eyes in my direction. Jerking my hand back to my side, I ended up in the back corner in between the picture books and children's novels. I pretended to be fascinated by a neon-hued cover for a story about an octopus that was sad because it didn't get to wear shoes.

Actually, I kind of did want to know what the moral of that story could possibly be.

I debated flipping through it, wondering if browsing that avidly without buying might bring the wrath of the counter lady down on me. Then the door squeaked open again, and Marisol walked in.

"Hello, again," the woman said in a dry voice that wasn't exactly friendly. I guessed Marisol hadn't usually been buying whatever books she'd been looking through in here either. I'd give the woman credit for having a *little* patience with her.

Marisol slunk to the opposite end of the back and sank down on a stool in between Science Fiction & Fantasy and General Fiction. She contemplated the titles but didn't pick anything up, just hugging her backpack on her lap.

Did she usually not even let herself steal a chapter or two of reading while she holed up in here? It looked like no. After a moment, she pulled a book out of her backpack instead, one that I assumed had been assigned in class based on the dreary cover, and opened it up.

I could think of all kinds of reasons why she wouldn't want to hang out at home. But why here? I guessed it was getting chilly to hang out in the park, and the nearest library was a twenty-minute walk farther from the high school, so there might not have been any other options. But still, something about the image before me was so pitiful it made my heart ache.

My sister shouldn't have needed to resort to hiding away in some random store to feel any kind of security.

She'd turned her back mostly to me, not even noticing I was there in her attempt to make herself as unnoticeable as possible. I eased over and spoke quietly. "Marisol."

Despite my efforts, she startled and jerked around. When she saw me, her gaze immediately darted around the store, giving me the same impression I'd gotten before that she was worried about someone seeing us together.

"Hey," I said quickly, crouching down so we were at the same eye level and setting a careful hand on her arm. "No one's in here who'd hurt you. And I talked to Wade a few days ago—I made sure he isn't going to get in the way of us seeing each other anymore. Talking to me won't get either of us in trouble with him or Mom."

Marisol dragged in a shaky breath. "Okay." She stared at me, her eyes nearly round.

I had to ask, as much as the possible answers scared me— "Do *you* not want to talk to me? Because the last thing I want is to be harassing you."

"No!" she said hastily. "No, it's—it's really good to see you." Her tone was still nervous, but after she'd spoken, a smile touched her face, soft but bright enough to convince me she meant it. "It's been such a long time," she added.

A lump filled my throat. "I know. I'm so sorry. I *wanted* to call you or send you letters, but Mom and Wade put a ban on that. It was never because I didn't want to be here for you. And now that I'm back, I'm going to do whatever I can to have your *back*, like always."

Marisol's shoulders came down, but her gaze flicked to the store around us again. I had to ask the next tough question.

"Mare, is there someone else you're worried about? Has anyone been giving you a hard time or following you around?"

She hugged her backpack, her mouth twisting. "I—I don't totally know."

"Wade mentioned something about Nolan Gauntt," I prodded gently.

Marisol blinked at me, her expression vaguely puzzled, not horrified the way I'd have expected at the mention of her probable abuser. Had I been wrong in my assumptions?

"Him?" she said. "There's nothing… I mean, I'm not sure…" She rubbed her forehead. "I just—a long time ago, after you got taken away, I thought I saw people hanging around who seemed to be watching me. I got it in my head that they might take *me* away too. But then… nothing ever happened. So maybe I just imagined it." She frowned. "But every now and then I still get the feeling like someone's watching me. And it's not a good feeling."

I wasn't sure if that was a good or a bad thing. It sounded like her current meekness was more a result of living under Wade and Mom's roof with no one to stand up for her than any other villain's involvement. But on the other hand, her instincts could be right.

"Has anything at all happened that would prove someone's keeping an eye on you?" I asked. "Or has anyone mentioned anything about me?"

"Only Mom and Wade," Marisol said. "And no. I couldn't prove it. I never even mentioned it to them because I knew what they'd say. But because it happened right after you left… And I always had this feeling it was somehow connected, like they had it out for me *and* you… That doesn't really make sense." She looked at me beseechingly. "I'm sorry for taking off on you the other day. I *wanted* to talk to you."

I risked leaning forward and giving her a quick hug. To my relief, Marisol leaned into my embrace with a ragged little sigh that broke my heart. When I pulled back, she'd relaxed even more.

I hated to ask this last thing, but I had to. "I know things got pretty crazy the day I got taken away. I don't remember exactly what happened, but I know I saw something that made me upset. Maybe something to do with you. Mr. Gauntt was there at the house, wasn't he? Did he or someone else… do something to you?"

The puzzled look came back. Marisol's gaze went distant as if she was trying to remember. Her jaw tightened. "I don't— He just wanted to talk to me. They do some kind of special placements for kids. He thought maybe..." She knit her brow. "I didn't want to anyway. I think that was all. Then he left. And you got mad at him. It's kind of jumbled up in my head. I thought you were upset because you figured he was going to make me go with him or something?"

It sounded like the craziness of the situation and my emerging powers had rattled her so much she'd detached herself from those memories over the years. I didn't buy that I hadn't seen anything other than Nolan Gauntt suggesting Marisol take some extra classes. I hadn't been an aggressive person—I still wasn't one—and I couldn't picture myself flying off the handle over that. The bullies on campus had done way worse before I'd finally unleashed my powers on them.

No, what made the most sense was that something worse had happened, and the Gauntts were spying on Marisol while also keeping tabs on me to make sure neither of us spoke up about it.

But that meant that Marisol might not be really safe talking to me. At least not until I sorted everything else out. I squeezed her shoulder and held her gaze.

"I'm going to make sure that no one's taking you or me anywhere, all right? We don't know yet whether that was just your imagination or something real, and it's better to be careful. And then I'm going to set things up so you can stay with me instead of Mom and Wade, for as long as you'd like. If you'd want that."

A wider smile stretched across Marisol's face. "That would be amazing."

The sense prickled over my skin that I might have already put her at risk by talking with her for so long. I straightened up. "I'll get everything figured out as quickly as possible and keep you in the loop. Have you got a phone so I don't have to keep going all stalker on you?"

Marisol managed a quick laugh. "I don't mind when it's you. But I do."

As we exchanged numbers, my mind whirled with the challenge ahead of me. Somehow I had to figure out if the Gauntts were keeping tabs on my sister—if they were still invested in her situation at all. Wade had certainly seemed to think so.

An idea sprang to the front of my mind like a frog out of the marsh. That… that might be crazy, but so far crazy had been working pretty well for me.

I left Marisol to her reading and went out to regroup with the guys by their motorcycles.

"Everything went according to plan?" Nox asked.

"Yep," I said. "And now I've got a new plan." I turned to Kai. "I need to get that mailroom job at Thrivewell. It's time to take our mission straight to the source."

Chapter Eight

Lily

I NEVER REALLY THOUGHT ABOUT how small Lovell Rise was until I went someplace else. Standing on the busy street in downtown Mayfield with glossy high-rises looming all around me, my chest constricted. It wasn't like I stood taller than the houses or stodgy college buildings in town either, but for some reason this place in particular made me feel very small.

Kai took in my expression and slipped his hand around mine to give it a quick squeeze. The brief gesture felt like something bigger coming from the detached, analytical guy, the equivalent of a hug from Ruin. He could probably read my nervousness just looking at me.

He confirmed that a moment later with his next remarks. "You'll be fine. Everything's set up to work in your favor. The interview is only a formality so they can show they checked off all the boxes."

I focused on the one particular glossy high-rise up ahead, the shiniest and highest of them all: the headquarters of Thrivewell Enterprises. Nolan Gauntt's main workplace.

"I'm the goddaughter of Harmon Kitteridge," I said, going over the story Kai had coached me on one last time to shore up my courage. "He told me *all* about what a great place Thrivewell is to get started at. I know he's looking forward to doing more business with them and knowing he's got family there now."

"Exactly." Kai smiled, his gray-green eyes gleaming behind his glasses. "Thrivewell has a bunch of contracts with Kitteridge, some of them coming up for renewal soon. They won't want to risk pissing him off. I've already laid the groundwork with a few phone calls and well-placed documents. You just have to show up and be your sweet self, and they'll be glad to get the position filled that easily."

I dragged in a breath. "And if someone mentions Harmon's goddaughter to him?"

Kai's smile grew into a smirk. "Oh, I've laid the groundwork with him too. He knows that he'd better continue having a goddaughter named Lily Strom, or his business partner might receive certain files that show Harmon's been screwing the guy's wife for several years now."

"The Gauntts would probably suspect something. They know at least a little about my family."

"They're not likely to be paying much attention to new hires at the mailroom level. And if they do, it's unlikely Kitteridge ever mentioned to them that he specifically *didn't* have a goddaughter. If any problems come up, we'll deal with them as they do."

The confidence in his words steadied my nerves. Kai had managed to arrange all this—what *couldn't* he do?

"Who are you a secret relative of to get your job?" I asked. Kai had decided he was going to interview for another open position—something a little higher up in the offices doing market research. He'd pointed out that it'd be easier for us to find out what we needed to with both of us there coordinating our efforts.

Kai rocked on his heels with an eager energy I wasn't sure I'd ever witnessed in him before. "Oh, I'm not going to need that. I've done my diligence on the hiring staff. All I've got to do is walk in there, read the room, and I'll have them eating out of my hand in a matter of minutes."

I'd never seen him fully in his element before, I realized. Nox came totally to life in a fight, Jett did when he was immersed in his art, and

Ruin found joy everywhere he looked. Kai was lit up by working his machinations on the world around him. His body, though it still held some of Zack's footballer muscle, didn't exude physical might the same way the others' did, but right now, the air around him hummed with his own kind of power.

There was something magnetic about it. I had the urge to grab him by that collared shirt and find out what it'd feel like to kiss him in this state. But I held myself back, because I'd never kissed Kai in any state. When we'd had that group discussion about my relationship with the guys, he'd seemed reluctant to pursue anything like that. He'd said it'd be too much of a distraction.

It wasn't like I was getting a shortage of action from his friends, anyway.

He peered down at me, and for a second I thought I might have caught a flicker of interest in his gaze too. Then it vanished, leaving only measured concern. "Are you completely sure you're okay with this? I mean, giving up your studies and everything?"

There was no way I could hold down a fulltime job at Thrivewell while also attending classes at the college. But as soon as I'd realized that, it'd been relief that'd hit me, not regret.

"All I've got from campus is a bunch of bad memories," I said. "I still think I might want to go into sociology, but that can wait. A few of my courses let me transfer to the online option, so I'll still be working toward it anyway." And Kai had worked his persuasive magic there too, convincing the admin office that they really needed to refund me for the courses I couldn't continue on the basis of the hostile environment their school had provided.

Marisol needed me. That was more important than any of the bullshit I'd put up with from those asshats.

"Good," Kai said. "Ready to head in there?"

"Absolutely," I said, raising my chin. "Let's do this."

As we set off down the sidewalk toward the Thrivewell headquarters, my phone chimed. A text from Ruin had popped up. *You're going to knock them dead, Waterlily! Not the way I knock people dead, but that wouldn't work out so well for getting a job anyway. Anyone with eyes will be able to see how amazing you are.*

The corners of my lips quirked upward at his overboard enthusiasm. *About to head in now*, I texted back. *Thank you for the cheerleading.*

Kai caught my eye and nodded to me with another small smile of encouragement. Then he strode ahead of me so we didn't come in together, which might look odd if anyone noticed and thought about it later. His host had only been nineteen, and I'd gotten the impression that the Skullbreakers had all been in their early 20s when they'd died, but in the business casual suit with his dark brown hair carefully styled, self-assurance radiating off his stance, he could easily have passed for ten years older.

So, yeah, I might have checked him out as he ambled into the building half a block ahead of me. Sue me.

I tugged my blouse straight and zoned out for a second into the rumble of the passing cars and the clacking of my heels against the pavement. A battle chant of a song rose up in my chest. *Here I go to take my stand. Defend my sister and stick it to the man.*

By the time I reached the building's immense lobby, Kai had already passed through. A skeletal man behind a huge marble reception desk studied me as I approached.

"Hi," I said, willing my voice to stay steady even though he looked like he might be sizing me up for his stew pot. "I have an interview with Ms. Fuller at ten o'clock."

He consulted his computer, which apparently contained all the things, because a moment later, he said, "Miss Strom?"

"Yes, that's me."

He pointed to the elevator alcove just past the desk. "Third floor and to your left."

The short elevator trip took me to an open-concept office area full of cubicles and fronted by another polished reception desk half the size of the one downstairs. When I introduced myself to the woman there, she motioned me to a row of chairs outside one of the smaller office rooms that actually had doors.

Ms. Fuller's office had a window, but the blinds were drawn. I was the only person sitting outside. I clasped my hands on my lap, and then dropped them to my sides, and then folded my arms over my chest, and started worrying I'd look too fidgety for a job in this place.

Would she know about my past—about my stay at St. Elspeth's? I couldn't see how, but word had certainly gotten around Lovell Rise at lightning speed.

I only had a few seconds to worry about that possibility, my pulse kicking up another notch, before the office door swung open.

A petite woman in a beige dress suit bobbed her head to me. "Miss Strom? Please come in."

With her curly, white-blond hair swept into a fuzzy ball on top of her head, her big dark eyes, and her bulging nose, she could have passed for a sheep without needing a costume. It was hard to be all that scared of a farm animal in human form. I managed a smile that didn't feel totally stiff and followed her into the office.

"Well, now," she said, sitting down at her desk and shuffling some papers there. "You come with glowing recommendations. I understand your godfather, Mr. Kitteridge, is particularly approving of you joining our team."

Getting right to the nepotistic point, were we? "Yes," I said, smiling brighter. "He says Thrivewell is a great place to work."

"Oh, we are. We certainly are." She gave a soft little laugh with a faint *baa* to it and looked at her papers again. "You don't have any previous mailroom experience?"

"No," I said quickly. "But I've done a bunch of retail work, which I think has pretty similar skills. Making sure everything goes in the right place, getting things to people who need them."

I'd rehearsed that pitch for my skills beforehand. Ms. Fuller didn't look particularly impressed, but she didn't look concerned either, so I guessed that was a win.

"It is an entry level position," she said. "And I'd imagine fairly easy to pick up the details as you go. You'd have a senior assistant there to advise—oh!"

Her eyes widened, and she jerked back in her chair. The frog that had just leapt onto her desk let out an inquisitive *ribbit?* and hopped over to her pencil holder.

"Er." I panicked for a moment before it occurred to me that my interviewer wasn't going to assume the frog had anything to do with me. How ridiculous would that be? People didn't go walking around with frogs trailing after them. Ha ha ha.

I let out a little of that laughter, hopefully more convincingly than it'd sounded in my head, and acted like I was surprised too. "Would you look at that. Where did it come from?"

"I have no idea!" Ms. Fuller exclaimed. She waved her hands vaguely at the frog until it hopped off the side of her desk and then scrambled to grab her phone. "I'll have… the maintenance staff see about it. They must have some idea what to do."

Yeah, I'm sure they deal with invading frogs all the time, the snarky voice in my head remarked.

As we waited for a janitor to come scoop up the frog, I sat straighter in my chair, feeling the need to demonstrate in every way possible that I was an upstanding citizen who definitely wouldn't bring random amphibious creatures into the workplace. "You were saying about the job being entry level. I'm a fast learner—I'm sure I can get up to speed quickly."

"Yes, yes, excellent." Ms. Fuller shuffled her papers again, clearly flustered. I found myself picturing a kitten curled up in the fluff of her hair. The absurdity of the image calmed me down just a little.

A man hustled in, muttered at the frog as he retrieved it, and hustled back out again. I resisted the impulse to call after him to be gentle with the poor thing. Were there any ponds in the city where he could deposit it?

Maybe it was better not to think too hard about that.

"And you're living in Lovell Rise at the moment," my interviewer said, seeming to relax once our unexpected visitor was gone. "You won't find the commute too long?"

I shook my head. "To get a chance to work here, it's worth the drive. And I'm planning on looking for an apartment in the city too."

I hadn't exactly been planning that until the moment the words came out of my mouth, but as soon as they did, it sounded like a brilliant idea. There was no room for Marisol in my current place, and it'd be hard to find a better apartment in town, where there wasn't a ton of selection. And everyone saw me as the psycho girl there now.

Maybe I could find a place at the end of the city that was closest to Lovell Rise and drive her out to school and back… or she could even transfer to a high school here in Mayfield. A fresh start might be just what she needed too.

Ms. Fuller cleared her throat and broke me out of that daydream. "Excellent. Well, I'm sure you realize that an entry-level position comes with a corresponding level of pay and benefits. But there will be opportunities to work your way up if you apply yourself."

"Of course," I said, putting my smile back on. "I hope to do just that."

It seemed like a perfect note to end the interview on, except just then another note pealed out—from my phone. I'd gotten another text. And another, and another, in quick succession. I peeked at my phone just long enough to turn it off—why hadn't I done that to begin with?—seeing that Ruin had just sent me a bunch more cheerleading plus questions of whether I was done yet.

I shoved the phone back into my pocket, my cheeks flushing. "Sorry, I should have shut it off before."

Ms. Fuller's eyebrows had arched slightly. "Is there a problem?"

"No, not at all." Then a brainstorm hit me, and for a second, I felt like I was channeling Kai. "It was just Uncle Harmon. That's what I always call him. He wanted to know how the interview went—I told him I was coming in this morning."

"Oh!" My interviewer flushed in turn. "I suppose you can give him good news, then. You're the best candidate we've had, and we'd be happy to have you start on Monday. If that sounds good to you."

I beamed at her, my fluster falling away. One step closer to finding out what was up with the Gauntts. "Yes. Thank you. I'm looking forward to it."

I texted Ruin back on my way out of the building. By the time I reached Fred where I'd parked him, the guys had already roared up on their bikes. Kai joined us a moment later with a satisfied smile that said he'd landed his job as easily as he'd expected.

"Hurray to being gainfully employed!" I said, and Ruin wrapped me in a hug. "Did you guys find out anything?" They'd taken the opportunity to prowl around the city searching for information on which of the urban gangs had decided to come after them decades ago.

Nox frowned. "Nothing solid. But we'll get there. They can't hide for long." He looked me over in my business clothes and gave me a smile just short of a leer. "We don't have to worry about that right now. You deserve a celebration."

He patted the back of his motorcycle. I hesitated for a second and then clambered on, deciding not to think about the way my skirt rode up my thighs, just tucking my arms around his well-built frame.

I was on my way to tackling the most powerful man in the city, and just for the moment, victory felt like it was already within my grasp.

Chapter Nine

Kai

"IF YOU COULD HAVE those leads sorted out by the end of the day?" my supervisor said as he paused by my desk.

"Not a problem," I replied with an ingratiating smile, not bothering to mention that I'd already worked through all my assignments for the day. I would put the files on his desk before I clocked out, and in the meantime, he could think I was hard at work making his life easier while instead I looked into making the Gauntts' lives harder.

Most of those efforts were going to need to be centered on the woman with the largest desk at the far end of the room. Her fortress guarded the private elevator that was the only one to ascend to the top floors where the high executives—including, of course, Nolan and Marie Gauntt—had their offices. They all had their own personal admin assistants… and Ms. Townsend played gatekeeper to those PAs.

I guessed you knew a business was at the top of the food chain when even the secretaries had secretaries.

Ms. Townsend didn't look all that impressive. She was slight with a head a bit too big for her slim frame, like a living bobblehead, and her voice was so soft you had to be standing within five feet of her to make it out. In the few days I'd been here, I'd noticed she touched up the pearly polish on her fingernails regularly—to hide a bad habit of nibbling on them, most likely.

But despite all that, she seemed to have no problem sending people off with that soft voice, refusing appointments and other attempts to reach the bigwigs on the top floors. She did get her job done.

One of the most important things I'd figured out in my old life was that people's biggest weakness was usually other people. So I'd spent most of my investigative time so far observing how the secretaries' secretary interacted with her various colleagues. A couple of interesting facts had become clear.

Ms. Townsend had a thing for a woman in the accounting section, who she called "Alice" rather than by her last name and blushed a little about—not while they were talking but as Alice walked away. Possibly Alice would have been receptive to that interest. She seemed awfully smiley during a simple conversation about whether the budget could accept a third brand of coffee added to the breakroom.

This was all bad news for Mike Philmore, one of my colleagues in market research, who found some excuse to talk to Ms. Townsend about three times a day, always looking like he was just barely holding back his drool. She didn't appear to have noticed that he wanted anything out of her other than small talk, but then, I'd also figured out early on that I picked up on a lot of things others didn't.

That was why I was here and the rest of the Skullbreakers weren't. *I* could help Lily in ways none of the others were even capable of. That knowledge left me with a weird ache in my stomach that was probably partly the ever-returning hunger but with at least a little guilt and irritation mixed in.

If they'd *all* been able to work at my level, we might have solved her problems by now, not to mention our own.

This wasn't the time to dwell on that thought, though. I had a gambit to work here, and Lily was waiting to do her part.

I got a text ready to send and slipped my phone into my pocket.

Then I ambled over to Ms. Townsend's desk, having confirmed that she wasn't occupied by anyone else at the moment.

Although she had a computer on her desk, she seemed to do most of the scheduling part of her work using five immense agendas that lay across her broad desk, one for each of the executive assistants. I'd already determined that the one at the farthest right was for Nolan Gauntt's assistant. That was my goal.

But first, I might as well dig up what I could out of the woman herself. I stopped at the distance from the desk I'd noticed she appeared most comfortable with and shot her a smile. "I hear you're the woman with all the power around here."

I'd also observed that she enjoyed having her status acknowledged, even if she acted humble about it. She let out a little laugh and swiped her hand across her mouth, though her eyes stayed professionally focused.

"You're the new one in market research," she said, tapping her pen on the cover of one of the agendas. "What can I do for you?"

I ducked my head as if I were feeling awkward about the subject, still smiling. "This might sound a little strange, but I have a cousin, a lot younger than me—she's ten this year—who was really impressed when she heard I was starting at Thrivewell. I know the company's been involved in a lot of different initiatives. I don't suppose they do any outreach involving kids?"

I hadn't found any clear evidence of that in my own research—a few workshops at schools here and there, but nothing ongoing. Nothing that would confirm what Lily's sister currently believed Nolan had been visiting her about. But it couldn't hurt to check right at the source.

Ms. Townsend tilted her head in thought and brought up something on her computer. "We do have a few initiatives that involve school visits," she said. "But those are only on an occasional basis, not anything longer-running."

"Fair enough," I said. "Is that something Thrivewell has done at all in the past—a more involved program—or should I let her know she'll just have to wait until she's employable age?" I added a little chuckle to show I wasn't overly invested.

"I can't think of when we've done anything intensive on the educational side, but I've only been here nine years, so it's possible farther back, that was a thing. I can't say I'm aware of any upcoming plans, though. It's sweet that she's interested." The secretary smiled back at me.

I had her eating out of my hand now, but I needed to land the second part of my gambit before her work interrupted us. "Oh, well, she's old enough to understand that she can't always get everything she wants. If the company decided to launch something like that, they'd obviously need to get you involved. Alice from accounting was saying to me how impressed she is by the way you go above and beyond to help the rest of us."

I didn't hammer the point home, just gave Ms. Townsend a brief lift of my hand in farewell as I took my leave and walked away leaving that last statement wriggling through her brain. While her attention shifted to her crush and the joys of the second-hand compliment, I sidled over to Philmore by the water cooler.

"Heard you were having some trouble with the new photocopier," I said, which was completely true, although only because I'd been eavesdropping like a champ for the past day.

The other guy sighed. "Yeah. Programming that thing to do what you want is a nightmare. I swear it's possessed."

I had to restrain a chortle at the idea of a spirit taking over that hulking machine. Where would you even fit? What would be the point? But of course, Philmore had no direct experience with possessions to inform his perspective.

I made a vague motion toward the secretary's desk. "Townsend was just telling me how much she appreciates the new features." Actually, she'd been telling Alice that yesterday, but it amounted to the same thing. "You should ask her to give you a tutorial. She seems like she'd be happy to help anyone who needs it."

Philmore brightened like I'd lit a candle up his ass and headed right over to the secretary's desk without so much as a thank you. That was fine. His acting on my advice was thanks enough.

He said something to Ms. Townsend, and she got up immediately and ushered him over to the photocopier room, shooting a glance toward the accounting department and walking slower as she passed it to make sure Alice noticed her being her helpful self.

I restrained a smile. It was almost too fucking easy. Like most people, I just gave them a little nudge, and they hopped to my command like a bunch of puppets.

That left Ms. Townsend's desk—and her precious agendas—unguarded for at least a few minutes. I surreptitiously sent off my prepared text without taking my phone from my pocket and ambled back over.

Before I'd quite made it there, Lily came bustling into the office area with a cart of envelopes and packages. Conveniently, she had actually gotten a package for one of the employees who had a view of the secretary's desk from theirs, which she'd simply held on to until it could be put to optimal use. We'd arranged some surprise mail for the other main potential witness. She went to that woman's desk first.

"Mail for you," she said cheerfully, not even glancing my way.

The woman cocked her head at the padded envelope, ripped it open, and immediately hustled off to the bathroom where she could examine the… provocative contents more carefully in the privacy of a stall. Lily pretended not to notice her reaction as she headed over to the man who'd gotten a proper package. She placed herself right where she was in between him and Ms. Townsend's desk and made a production of offering it up.

"It seems pretty important," she said, lifting it slowly. "I wanted to make sure it got to you safely. Do you need help getting the tape off? There is an awful lot."

Because she'd added two extra layers.

The man struggled with the packing tape and ultimately accepted Lily's offer to cut through it with a utility knife that she then spent a minute searching her cart for. In the meantime, I darted behind the secretary's desk and flipped open the agenda for Nolan Gauntt's assistant. My gaze whipped over the pages, absorbing the dates and notations so quickly the data might as well have been uploaded into my brain. By the time the guy finally had his package open, I'd taken in the entire year's schedule and set the bookmark ribbon back in its correct place.

At the same moment, Ms. Townsend's voice reached my ears, much closer than I'd anticipated. She'd obviously sped through her little photocopier tutoring session with Philmore. I hustled from behind the desk, needing to get well clear of it without drawing attention. No doubt she'd wonder why I was over there at all. My throat tightened with the thought that I might have jeopardized my standing in the company this early on—

And then Lily collided with me as if she'd backed up her cart without seeing I was there.

She didn't hit me hard, but I caught the concerned gleam in her eyes and knew what she was trying to do. So I let my feet slip from under me as if she'd knocked me right over, grabbing her as if for balance and tugging her with me for extra effect. I landed on the linoleum floor on my ass with Lily in my lap.

For just a few seconds, I had her entire, softly toned body pressed up against me. A startling heat swept through my veins as all my nineteen-year-old host's hormones sprang to attention.

"Oh my God, I'm so sorry," Lily started babbling, scrambling up. Ms. Townsend was hurrying over, and I realized I had something different to cover up now: the bulge of my overeager dick, aching at the loss of contact. I shoved myself onto my feet at a crouch, bringing to mind the best cold shower of an image I could summon—Lily's asshole of a stepfather dancing around in the shower to the tune of the Macarena—and willing down my sudden erection.

By the time I could safely stand, Ms. Townsend had reached my side. "Is everything all right here?" she asked, and I could tell from the fret lines on her forehead that it was. Lily's trick had made the secretary worried about me rather than suspicious about my location in the office.

"Yes, totally fine," I said, brushing myself off and smiling at both Ms. Townsend and Lily. "No harm done. Those things are pretty tricky to maneuver. Glad it's not my job!" I nodded to the mail cart.

Lily poured out several more apologies and then hightailed it out of there, and I went back to my desk to contemplate the months of data I'd taken in… and definitely not the feel of Lily's ass against my groin.

We'd planned to meet up with the rest of the gang at a bar several blocks from the office after the end of the workday. I stayed a few minutes late to put on the appearance of a dedicated worker and then walked fast enough to catch up with Lily halfway to the bar. She grinned at me, and even without any part of our bodies in contact, that smile and the sight of her windblown hair sent another flare of lust through me. Damn it if I didn't want to pin her up against the side of the bank we were walking past and kiss her brains out.

More than just kiss, if I was being totally honest with myself, which I did attempt to be.

I mentally shook myself, as if that would calm the teenage hormones I'd technically outgrown six—or twenty-seven, if you counted my body-less time—years ago. Would it be so horrible if I just acted on them? I knew I didn't have to worry about Lily demanding more from me than I could give her. She'd always accepted me exactly as I was, even when she'd thought I was a figment invented by her imagination.

"Did you find out anything?" Lily asked, and I yanked my attention back to more important matters.

"First steps," I said. "I know when Nolan's executive assistant is regularly away from her desk. Now I just need to get up to her office and take a look at *his* schedule when she's not around to stop me."

Lily knit her brow. "That sounds risky."

I shrugged. "I'll figure it out. I managed just fine today, didn't I?" I shot her a smile more genuine than anything I'd aimed at my coworkers today. "You were brilliant with that last-second save. Thanks for that quick thinking."

She laughed. "It was the only thing I *could* think of to do in the moment. Hopefully they don't all figure I'm a horrible klutz now."

"Hey, getting that kind of reputation can be useful in unexpected ways."

We walked into the warm, boozy-smelling air of the bar to find the other three guys clustered in a booth in the front corner, looking vaguely panicked as they stared at a phone in the middle of the table. A phone that let out a peal of a ringtone a second later.

"What's going on?" I demanded, dashing over.

Ruin waved toward the phone, his body bobbing with an erratic mixture of excitement and uncertainty. "The guy's phone! The one who attacked me. It's finally ringing."

"So answer it!"

"I don't know what to say," Ruin said, wide-eyed.

"Just ask whoever it is what the fuck they want with you," Nox growled.

"No." I held up my hands before this turned into a total disaster. "That'll be too obvious. Play it cool. Talk vaguely, use the same kind of phrasing these people did when they came after you before. The guy… he had kind of a gruff voice, right? So try to talk like him. And hurry on and pick it up before it goes to voicemail!"

Ruin snatched up the phone and jerked it to his ear as he hit the answer button. "Hello," he said in a voice so gravelly you'd have thought he was auditioning to play the new Batman.

I winced, but whoever was on the other end must have had a bad enough connection that it didn't sound too weird to them. Ruin nodded. "Yes, I was just taking a bit of a break."

Oh, sure, that'd sound just wonderful. I tugged the phone from his grasp and set it on speaker so I could hear what the other party was saying too.

"—the hell are you taking breaks for? That's not why you get paid. Did you set the Hunter kid straight or not?"

Ruin gave me another pleading look. I nodded sharply. "Uh, yeah," he said. "He knows what's good for him now. Won't be giving any more trouble."

"What's the latest report on the target's movements, then?" snapped the man on the other end.

"Well, he's been going to class and hanging out with his friends—"

"Not *Hunter's* movements. The girl he's supposed to be keeping an eye on."

Ruin's eyebrows leapt up. He gestured wildly toward Lily, as if we all couldn't figure out instantly who the speaker had meant, and seemed to forget about the fact that he was still in the middle of a conversation.

I jabbed my finger toward the phone and mouthed the words, *What do they want?*

Ruin frowned at me, which I didn't understand until he repeated what he must have thought I'd been prompting. "What a cunt."

"Excuse me?" the voice on the other end said, and I pressed the heel of my hand to my forehead.

"That's what he said," Ruin improvised. "I mean, he's kind of an asshole himself. Anyway, she hasn't done anything all that interesting either."

I restrained a groan. Before I could coach the other guy any further, the caller made a disgruntled sound. "Fine." And he hung up without so much as a good-bye.

Ruin beamed at us. "That didn't go so badly." A shadow crossed his expression a second later. "But why did these people want Ansel to follow Lily around?"

"That's what I was trying to get you to ask them," I said, keeping my voice low despite my frustration.

There'd always been a place for me in the Skullbreakers. The guys had appreciated the talents and knowledge I'd brought to the table, and I'd appreciated having the three of them around to enforce certain types of plans way better than I could on my own. But sometimes… sometimes I wondered why I bothered working with anyone at all.

"It doesn't matter," Nox said firmly, shoving the phone back toward Ruin. "They'll call again. Ruin knows what to ask about next time. Are we going to go do some ass-kicking now or what?"

Ruin slipped his arm around Lily and gave her a peck on the temple. "Shouldn't we spend a little time with Lily before we go charging off? She's had to put up with those office people all day."

"Hold on." Lily managed to put her hands on her hips without displacing her admirer. "If you guys are going off to find out more about who attacked you, I want to come along. I'm mixed up in this now too. I should have some idea what we're up against."

Nox and Jett both looked doubtful, but admiration flickered up through my chest. The guys might be on the dim side sometimes, but I couldn't complain about Lily. She was right there with us, ready to face anything, despite everything she'd already been through.

I set my hand on her shoulder—the one Ruin wasn't hanging all over. "Sounds good to me. You're stronger than all those pricks anyway."

And I wasn't sure I really wanted to let her out of my sight for any longer than I absolutely had to.

Chapter Ten

Lily

The helmet Nox had gotten me so I could ride with him on his motorcycle rather than dragging Fred's sorry fender all over town muffled the roar of traffic around us. The cacophony blended into a wavering melody that seemed to match the steady thump of my heart. I kept my arms wrapped tight around Nox's torso, as much terrified that I'd topple off as enjoying the heat that seeped through his new leather jacket into my chest.

These guys would never hurt me on purpose, but they hadn't shown the soundest judgment when it came to risk assessment.

I wasn't sure where we were going—and maybe neither were the former Skullbreakers. All at once, Nox raised his hand and pointed, and the four guys swerved their motorcycles down a side-street.

We'd come into a grungier part of town where the buildings were covered in grubby brick and concrete rather than glossy glass. Litter tumbled down the street in the breeze. The streets were narrower, the smell of car exhaust thicker, and someone a couple of blocks away was yelling at someone else loud enough to wake the dead.

And now I had to wonder if that was a real method of resurrection, seeing as it turned out the dead could actually be woken.

A few guys were hanging out on the more secluded side-street, slouching in hoodies and baggy jeans, one of them taking a drag from a cigarette. As we roared toward them, a couple of girls in garish makeup approached and started gesturing like they were talking as much with their hands as their mouths.

Nox jerked to a halt with a screech of the tires. He and the others leapt off their bikes so fast the girls took one look at them and paled.

"Beat it," Nox snapped, and they took off with a clatter of tapping heels.

"What the fuck, man," one of the hoodie guys protested as the Skullbreakers converged on them. "We were trying to move some product there."

"What makes you think we give a shit about your product?" Jett asked, and punched the guy who'd spoken in the stomach hard enough that he smacked into the wall behind him ass-first.

Obviously my guys were still subscribing to the hit first, ask questions later school of thinking.

I stayed perched on the motorcycle as the four of them batted their prey around a little, more like cats playing with mice than tigers going in for the kill. They didn't have any specific vendetta against this bunch, at least not yet. They were just… loosening them up, as Nox would probably have put it.

The thump of fists against flesh made me a little queasy, but I didn't let myself look away. This was what I'd signed up for when I'd thrown my lot in with these guys. And I had no doubt the guys they were beating down would have happily done the same to anyone weaker they thought they'd get something out of.

When the three drug dealers were all slumped against the wall, groaning and grumbling, Nox loomed over them with his hands still fisted. "What do you know about a hit that went down a couple decades ago?" he asked. "Some pricks from Mayfield took out the entire leadership of the Skullbreakers out in Lovell Rise. You ever hear about that?"

"Who the fuck wants to know?" one of the drug dealers muttered.

"The king of Constantinople," Kai said sarcastically. "So you'd better cough up what you've heard, or the royal guard will chop you up."

When the dealers just stared at him in bewilderment, Nox rolled his eyes. "*We* want to know, you idiots. We can keep going if you need more help jogging your memory." He waggled a fist.

"Twenty years ago, I was two," the second guy whined. "How the hell should I know?"

Nox glowered at him. "People talk on the street. People brag."

"No one in our crew," the first dealer said. "I've never heard of the Skullbreakers. You—" He cut himself off abruptly, his mouth pressing flat.

"We what?" Kai demanded, his eyes narrowing.

"You should suck my dick," the guy shot back in a brief show of bravado.

Ruin twirled a knife he'd snatched off one of them and grinned. "It'd be more fun to cut it off."

Bravado vanished. All three guys staggered to their feet and dashed down the street as fast as they could go.

Nox glanced at Kai. "You believe them?"

Kai nodded. "I didn't see any sign that they recognized our name. Whatever the guy was going to say that he stopped himself from, it didn't have to do with us."

"It had to do with *something*," Jett muttered.

Ruin bobbed on his feet, grinning away as usual. "Let's go find out what! So many outfits in this city; so many heads to crack." He let out a laugh that was as close to a maniacal cackle as I'd heard any real person produce. Somehow, on him, it was cute.

It was getting late, the sun nearly sunk, the shadows stretching long. We tore through the city for another several minutes until Nox spotted a building marked up with gang tags that he wanted to check out.

We stepped inside to amber lighting that might have been purposefully dim to disguise the worn patches on the velvet-cushioned chairs and benches. A crooning jazz orchestration wove through the room from a band up on the little stage at the far end of the space. It was some kind of dining club, with little black tables placed between the seats. Apparently, the kind of crowd this atmosphere appealed to dined late, because only a few of the tables were occupied this early in the evening.

My body started to sway with the music automatically. Nox ran his fingers lightly down my back. "We'll need to get you to compose a battle song for us," he said, playful but not entirely teasing, and directed us all toward the back of the room, where a narrow door stood next to the stage area.

As we reached it, a woman stepped out on stage. She might have been middle-aged under the foundation caked on her face, but in the hazy light, she looked ageless, almost ethereal in her gauzy white dress. She leaned toward a microphone on a stand in the midst of the musicians and started to sing.

It was another language—Spanish, I thought, or maybe Portuguese—and I didn't understand the words. But the emotion that rippled through them grabbed me by the heart in an instant. The woman used her voice as just as much of an instrument as the men with their guitars and keyboard and saxophone. Any chatter in the room fell silent. The hairs tickled along the backs of my arms.

We ducked through the door into the back rooms, but the song followed us, filtering faintly through the walls. The sensation around my heart solidified into an ache.

If I was being totally true to myself, I knew that my ideal future didn't involve year after year going over case files in an office or trying to mediate couples and families into making a better life for themselves. I wanted to help people, sure, but more than anything, I wanted to touch them the way that woman out there could with the simple lilt of her voice. My throat tingled with the urge to join her right now with my own.

Was that even possible? Since I'd gotten dragged off to the psych ward, I hadn't let myself sing other than briefly, while Nox and I were having sex. It hadn't felt like I deserved to take joy in music. But he'd reminded me that other people's judgments didn't have to weigh me down. I knew now that I hadn't really hurt Marisol—that I'd at least believed I was defending her. Why should I punish myself?

Why shouldn't I chase the dream I really wanted?

This obviously wasn't a good time to start making career plans, though.

The guys barged ahead of me into a large room that stunk of nicotine. An old steel desk stood in the back corner and a long wooden table ran down most of the rest of the space, with a bench on either side. Five men were sitting around it, a few of them with bottles of beer, a couple with their phones out. From the tone of their voices, they were haggling over some decision when we burst in, but the second they saw us, they leapt to their feet.

"Who the hell are you?" one of the men snarled.

"Your worst nightmare," Nox retorted, springing at him. "Up to you how soon you wake up."

I hung back by the door, my pulse thudding faster as all four of the guys sprang into action. They were outnumbered this time, and the men they were up against were clearly more experienced than the drug dealers they'd taken down before. The men dodged as many fists as hit the mark, and one of them whipped into a maneuver that sent Kai stumbling backward, clutching his glasses to keep them from falling.

A few of the others yanked out guns. Nox whacked one pistol aside with one of his ghostly punches that didn't quite make contact with the guy's hand, leaving the dude startled and blinking for a second before the former gang leader flipped him heels over head and stomped on his neck. Jett managed to send a little jolt of electrical energy through another guy's arm as he tackled him, making his opponent's fingers spasm and drop the weapon. But the one who aimed at Ruin didn't have anyone close enough to stop him.

The now-familiar hum rang out inside me, swelling through my whole body in the space of a breath. "Ruin!" I shouted, and in the same moment, a gush of beer sprang out of the nearest bottle on the table.

The dollop of sour liquid smacked the guy right in the eyes. As his lips parted in surprise, another splash socked him right in the mouth. He choked and sputtered, swiping frantically at his eyes, and Kai dashed in there to wrench the weapon from his hand.

Ruin didn't seem to care that there were still a few men not yet incapacitated. He flung his arms around me in a bear hug with a victory cheer. "That's our woman. You can't find anyone better." He let go of me to swing around and slam his fist into the jaw of a guy who'd just lunged at him. "And no one's going to convince me otherwise," he added.

A weirdly delirious smile spread over the guy's face as he swayed on his feet with the punch. "You're right," he said. "She's pretty amazing. All of you are something to watch."

Ruin gave him an amused but puzzled look. "Thank you for agreeing." He looked down at his fist, and then pummeled another of the men who were still standing. This time, I heard a faint hiss of electricity with the impact. "You should all bow down before us," Ruin declared at the same time. "Anyone who messes with us will end up shitting their pants in terror."

He didn't even appear to hit the guy that hard, but his opponent immediately crumpled on the floor, hugging himself and shivering. "Please, just leave us alone. We'll do whatever you want. Just don't hurt us anymore."

A radiant grin stretched across Ruin's face. He let out a whoop and spun around. "I think I've found my special power!"

"He hits them with his happiness," Jett muttered. "Or whatever else. Oh, joy."

But whatever the others might have said about Ruin's newfound ability to impose his feelings on others, it did help turn the tide. Ruin seemed to have used up all his current emotion-warping ability on his first two targets—his next few punches didn't have the same impact—but the colleagues of those two were distracted enough by the weird effects and their friends' bizarre reactions that they faltered.

In a minute or two, the former Skullbreakers had tossed the rest of their opponents into a heap next to the desk. Ruin declared himself the king of the mountain and perched on it, jabbing and kicking anyone who started to stir. He watched with avid interest as the other three closed in on the two he'd infected, one of whom kept smiling giddily and the other cowering in fear.

"All we want to know is what you've heard about an attack on the

Skullbreakers twenty years ago," Nox said, glaring at them. "From the looks of you, you were all well out of diapers by then."

"Skullbreakers, Skullbreakers," the happy guy murmured to himself. "What a great name. Never heard it before."

"I'd tell you if I knew anything," the frightened dude whimpered. "Please, I've never heard anything about that."

"Do you know anyone else who might have an idea?" Kai asked, stepping forward with his arms folded over his chest.

The guy shuddered. "I—I mean—there's the Skeleton Corps. They've got a hand in almost everything. But even they aren't as scary as you."

Someone in the heap under Ruin let out a hiss as if he thought his colleague had made a mistake. Nox glanced at Kai. "Why hasn't anyone mentioned the Skeleton Corps to us before if they're so important?"

Kai shrugged. "We didn't ask about that."

"Where can we find them?" I asked, wanting to get to the point before any more guns came flying out. I didn't think the sole remaining beer bottle would be enough for me to save anyone.

"Around… all different places." The scared guy cringed. "They move their headquarters all the time."

"You want to hang with them, just put word out on the street," the happy guy said cheerfully.

"Great." Jett wrinkled his nose at them. "I wonder how long these two are going to be stuck like this."

"Their problem, not ours." Nox spun on his heel. "We got what we need out of these dorks."

Ruin scrambled down his human mountain to join us. As we walked out through the club, Nox grasped my hand.

"You *were* amazing in there," he said. "I didn't know you could throw beer around like you can with water."

A giggle tumbled out of me. "Neither did I. I guess it's *mostly* water."

"Let's get some more beers!" Ruin declared. "Lily deserves a toast."

A quiver of triumph ran through my chest. I'd helped Kai with his plan to get at Nolan Gauntt today, and tonight I'd saved one of my guy's lives. I was Lily fucking Strom, and I wasn't letting anyone mess with me and mine anymore.

That fact felt like it deserved more than a toast.

My gaze caught on a pharmacy down the street. A spark of inspiration lit inside me. "There's something I want to pick up first."

Chapter Eleven

Lily

I STARED into my apartment's chipped mirror, combing my fingers through the waves of my hair. Some of them looked like actual ocean waves now. I'd streaked in blue dye last night that'd turned out even more vibrant than I'd expected against my usual flaxen blond. I looked like… some kind of mermaid. Like I really could have emerged from the marsh with watery magic inside me.

Like a siren, as Nox called me.

The memory of the first time he'd said it, of the hungry huskiness in his voice, sent a pulse of heat low in my belly. I hadn't been thinking of that when I'd bought the dye, only of finding a visible way of manifesting the strength that now hummed through me. Turning myself more into the woman I could be, just like the guys had recovered some of their former looks. And every time I caught a glimpse of my reflection, it'd remind *me* what I was really capable of.

I swept my hair behind my ears, shot a quick smile at myself, and went back out into the cramped living room.

It was less cramped at the moment because only two of my four new roommates were present. Kai and Jett had gone out to pick up "supplies," which from them could mean anything from news magazines to art supplies to a mountain of food. Nox and Ruin were lounging on the sofa, Nox currently squinting at something on his phone's screen. He'd gotten more comfortable with the modern device over time, but he still seemed to consider its multitude of features an annoyance rather than a bonus.

"There's a place we should check out," he announced to Ruin. "Fast, before anyone else nabs it." He shifted his attention to me. "Now that we're getting ready to deal out some vengeance, it'll be better if we have a temporary clubhouse to operate out of. I don't want to have any pissed off thugs coming around here."

"I thought you were going to get your old place back," I said, remembering the Dishes for Dollars store he'd pointed out to me, which had been built on the spot where the Skullbreakers' original clubhouse used to stand. The guys had seemed to take the existence of the discount shop as a personal affront.

Nox nodded. "We'll get our real home turf back. But that's going to take a little more time, and we need to settle the score with the pricks who offed us before they know we're back in town." He cracked his knuckles and smirked with a fierceness that provoked another heady tingling inside me.

"We'll find Lily a better place than this too," Ruin piped up, beaming at me. "Something much nicer. You were thinking you could move into Mayfield, right?"

"For now," I said. "It seems like that would be easier than trying to get Lovell Rise to like me again."

Nox scoffed. "They should be worried about *you* liking them."

I gave him a baleful look. "It's still not fun being the resident 'psycho girl,' even if I don't care as much anymore. And it'd be a fresh start for me and Marisol." And if I did want to pursue some kind of musical career… that would be easier in a larger city too, wouldn't it?

I hadn't mentioned that part to the guys yet. The idea felt too fragile to say it out loud.

"We can definitely get a place that's fresh," Ruin said, bounding onto his feet.

"Not this place tonight," Nox said. "It's definitely clubhouse, not house-house, material. But I'll find an apartment too. I think Kai's already been scanning the listings." He got up and motioned to Ruin. "Come on. The guy said we can take a look now as long as we're out by ten." Then he extended his gesture toward me as well, with a warmer smile. "And you should join us, if you want. After you pitched in with the tussle last night, you're basically part of the gang."

A sense of mingled relief and pride washed through me, more than I'd expected. I'd been dreading the thought of being left on my own in the dingy apartment, even though I hadn't intended to ever share this place with anyone, let alone four kind-of dead gangsters. They did grow on a person.

And it could be that I'd been craving friendly company for longer than I'd let myself acknowledge.

I also still wasn't sure about my part in the gang battle last night, but it had felt pretty awesome being able to protect my men like they'd protected me so many times, if not always in ways I'd wanted in the moment. I didn't want to be just some pathetic creature they had to defend at every turn. The new Lily, the Lily who didn't care about being sane or polite to people who crapped on her, could hold her own with the former Skullbreakers.

Maybe I'd end up breaking a skull or two myself if the people deserved it.

I'd swapped my office-appropriate blouse for a more relaxed sweater and stripped off my tights, but I'd left my skirt on. As I followed the guys up to the alley, the evening breeze tickled over my bare legs. Nox glanced at me, his gaze lingering for a moment on my naked calves, and then motioned to Fred. "We'll take your car. Better if the owner doesn't realize exactly what types he'd be renting to." He winked at me.

So I ended up driving, cruising along the highway into Mayfield and then weaving through the streets following Nox's somewhat haphazard directions. He kept turning his phone around as he looked at the map in a way that wasn't particularly reassuring. I think we circled the spot we were trying to reach five times, like a dog getting settled to sleep, before we actually came to a stop outside the building.

The building itself was a narrow restaurant with the front window shuttered, squeezed between a sushi place and a brunch spot. I didn't pay much mind to the crown symbol painted onto the faded sign until Nox had tapped in the code on the key box and we walked into the main space.

The former tenants had gone all-out with their Medieval theme. The dusty wooden chairs and tables had fake coats of arms printed on them. Suits of costume armor, axes, pikes, and surprisingly sharp-looking broadswords decorated the walls. And at the far end, one larger table that I guessed was for special events stretched most of the width of the room, with the central chair behind it a full-out throne, gleaming with gold-tinted paint.

"This is fantastic!" Ruin enthused, roaming through the space. He grabbed a sword off the wall and swung it experimentally, laughing. "No one better try to take us down in here. It comes with all this stuff?"

"Yep." Nox strode toward the banquet table at the back. "The old tenants couldn't be bothered to take their shit with them, so we inherit it if we want it." He stopped across from the throne. "Fit for a fucking king."

I wandered over to join him, taking in the space and noticing all the extra details that added to the vibe, like the fortune teller's orb on a velvet-draped stand in one corner and a rearing brass horse statue next to the entrance to the kitchens. My brain couldn't quite decide whether this was all horribly cheesy or impressively horrible.

"I know you want to rule the city," I said, "but don't you think it's a little on the nose?"

Nox snorted. "No such thing. We didn't call ourselves the Skullbreakers because we like to gently nudge our enemies."

Okay, fair enough.

He ambled off to the side, where a King Arthur themed pinball machine stood. He rubbed his hands together in anticipation, but when he pulled at the levers, nothing lit up or made any sound. Nox gave the machine a smack, but that didn't wake it up.

"Maybe you need to unplug it and plug it back in?" I suggested, since that seemed to be the standard tech support advice for all electronic equipment.

He muttered to himself and crouched down by the base.

Ruin grabbed my hand and tugged me over to the throne. He set his sword on the table before whisking me up and onto the seat. The wood was actually comfortably worn and smooth, high enough that my feet dangled off the ground.

Ruin let his hand linger on my knee, grinning at me. "If we're the kings of the city, then Lily is our queen." A sly glint lit in his hazel eyes. "And we should worship her the way she deserves."

He knelt before me and slipped his hands around one calf, raising it so he could press a kiss to my shin. Heat rippled up my leg and flushed my cheeks. "Um, are you sure this is a good idea?" I asked.

Ruin just kissed the inside of my knee, in a sensitive spot that made my core clench with need and went a long way to convincing me all on its own. Nox abandoned the pinball machine at the sound of this new game, which apparently appealed to him even more.

He came around to the other side of the throne, his gaze heated. "I think it's a good start, but I can think of plenty of ideas that are even better."

"That wasn't exactly what I meant," I protested half-heartedly, and then he'd captured my mouth with his, and I didn't really want to protest in any way after all.

I wasn't exactly a master of sexuality. I'd only had two partners before these guys, and not at the same time. Feeling both of the guys' mouths on me in unison set off a flare of hunger that blazed in my chest and pooled between my legs.

I was embracing the insanity of our situation, wasn't I? Why shouldn't I enjoy every bit of the craziness?

Nox eased back to trail his scorching lips along my jaw to the crook of my neck. "We didn't thank you properly for stepping up last night, Siren. If this is going to be the Skullbreakers' new hangout, then we definitely need to break it in with the woman who kept our spirits alive and brought us back."

Ruin hummed against my leg where he'd switched to kissing the side of my other knee. His hands slid up under my skirt, his fingertips teasing across my thighs. "We have lots of time, don't we?" he asked

Nox. "No interruptions? I want to make my first time with our Angelfish something to remember."

Nox chuckled. "The owner said it was ours to look around until ten. We've got a couple of hours. And I locked the door." He nibbled his way down my neck, with one slightly sharper nip that made me gasp with a spark of painful pleasure. "Such a good girl. We can show her just what a queen she is."

A very un-queenly whimper of need crept from my throat. Ruin responded to it by dragging me closer, yanking down my panties with the same motion. He shoved up my skirt and buried his face between my legs.

The first swipe of his tongue across my sex brought a jolt so thrilling I gasped. Nox swallowed the sound with the crash of his lips against mine. He devoured my mouth as Ruin savored my clit.

I dug my fingers into their hair, one hand fisted in Nox's short spikes, the other in Ruin's tousled locks. All sense of the room faded away. My awareness narrowed down to the heat of their bodies next to mine and the bliss surging through my nerves.

If this was what being queen of the Skullbreakers meant, then engrave my name over the fucking door.

I rocked with the deft movements of Ruin's mouth. He sucked on my clit so hard I moaned and flicked his tongue right into my opening.

Nox kissed me again and eased back with a feral grin. "I love watching you go wild as you're coming undone. You can take even more, can't you, Siren?"

When he stroked his hands across my chest to fondle my breasts, all I could do was gasp my agreement. I gripped his shirt, tugging him closer for another kiss, and his chest thrummed with his approval. "That's right. You manhandle me all you want. Everywhere you touch me, you set me on fucking fire, baby."

"So fucking precious," Ruin mumbled against me, and teased his teeth over my clit. I cried out against Nox's mouth, my body quaking. Nox's demanding kiss, his thumb sweeping over my taut nipple, and Ruin's fingers delving in to join his tongue against my sex all swelled together into a maelstrom of pleasure that burst inside me.

I felt myself gush with my release and Ruin lapping it up. Nox kissed my cheek and my jaw, murmuring more praise, and then glanced down at Ruin with hooded eyes. "I think we should give her something even more special. Make full use of the wonders of our new headquarters."

I was too dazed from my orgasm to totally follow the silent exchange that followed. The next thing I knew, Ruin was stepping back and Nox was lifting me onto one of the throne's broad wooden arms. My legs splayed over the edge.

Ruin grabbed the sword he'd left on the table by the guard and waggled the hilt. He glanced from it to me and then cocked his head with a momentary flicker of concern. "We don't know who else was touching this before."

Nox tossed a couple of foil packets at him. "Good thing I have extra. Suit it up."

"What—?" I started to ask in bewilderment, and Nox's palms swiveled over my breasts as he leaned against me from behind. The friction and the giddy rush that came with his touch knocked the words from my mind.

"Feels good, doesn't it?" he murmured, kissing my neck again and then across my shoulder. "We're going to make you feel even better. Like no one ever made you feel before. Just trust us, and we'll take care of you."

I did trust them, I realized with a little flash of shock. Sometime over the past few weeks, I'd gone from wary to welcoming to utterly committed, without even totally realizing it.

I was safe in their hands. More than safe. I was ecstatic putty, and I didn't see any reason to get off the ride before it'd reached its final destination.

Ruin had opened one of the condom packets and stretched its contents over the hilt of the sword. The grip wasn't particularly larger than the average dick, as far as I knew from the few examples I'd encountered, but it was tapered toward the guard where he was holding it and rounded at the pommel, a little wider there than anything I'd taken inside me before.

My lungs gave a nervous hitch as he brought the sword closer, but he didn't try to thrust the hilt right into me. He rubbed the rounded end over my slick sex, dampening it with my arousal, twisting it against my clit. As little quivers of pleasure built up between my legs, the cool surface warmed. Ruin watched my responses avidly.

Nox kept stroking my chest and marking my neck with his mouth. "Are you ready, baby?" he asked, and my hips canted toward the sword of their own volition. Nox let out a low laugh. "That's right. I can't wait to see you ride it." He tipped his head toward Ruin. "Nice and slow."

Ruin grinned and dipped the pommel to my slit. My channel stretched to admit it with a heady burn that made my breath shudder in a way that was all delight. A whine tumbled out of me as he slid it deeper, his free hand massaging my thigh in tandem.

I was fucking a sword. I was Lily Strom, getting off on a deadly weapon, and it felt absolutely amazing.

I groaned and clutched at Nox, arcing toward Ruin at the same time. He leaned in to claim my mouth as he started to pulse the hilt in and out of me. The heat of his mouth burned into mine and the swell of the pommel brushed against the most eager place deep inside me, and the wave of bliss started to sweep me higher all over again.

My groping hand slipped down Ruin's muscled chest. My fingers brushed the substantial bulge behind his jeans, and his breath stuttered where our mouths were still melded together. My sex ached for release, but suddenly the metal shaft between my legs wasn't enough.

I tore my lips from his. "I want *you*," I said firmly, squeezing his groin for emphasis. From the first morning when he'd snuck into my bed and we'd ended up making out, I'd been dying to know what the full experience would be like. Ruin seemed like the kind of guy who could, well, ruin a woman. I didn't know how anyone could ever top his blend of enthusiasm and devotion.

Ruin let out a choked sound that somehow also sounded cheerful and tossed the sword aside, condom and all. As I fumbled with the fly of his jeans, he spun me on the throne arm so I was facing forward instead of sideways. When my hand delved into his boxers, he bucked into my hand.

"That's right," Nox said with only a tiny edge of envy. "You look after him too. Look at how hard he is for you already."

Ruin's eyelids had drifted to half-mast. Now he opened them all the way to shoot a determined look at his boss. "You keep taking care of Lily," he said, apparently deciding he got to give orders now too. "She should get everything we can both give her."

"No arguments there," Nox murmured, and nipped my earlobe as he teased his hands down my torso. He dipped one between my thighs, inhaled sharply at the feel of my wetness, and spread my legs even wider for his friend.

I leaned into his embrace, tilting my head to kiss him where he knelt beside me while yanking Ruin closer. My fingers wrapped around the redhead's erection and gave it a few encouraging pumps.

Ruin groaned and gripped my hips to tug me right to the end of the wooden arm. He wrenched open another packet, readied himself, and plunged into me in one smooth movement.

"Fuck," he murmured breathlessly when he was fully embedded in me. My channel throbbed around him, hungry for more. I tucked one arm around him and tore my mouth from Nox to kiss Ruin instead.

Our mouths collided, all harsh breath and dueling tongues. Ruin withdrew halfway and then thrust in even deeper. A soft keening emanated from my chest at the giddy sensation spreading through me from my core.

"This is paradise," he mumbled between eager kisses, drinking in every sound I made. "You're all the heaven I need, Angelfish."

When he plunged even deeper, I gasped. I kept clutching Ruin as I turned back to Nox, not wanting to leave my other lover neglected. The Skullbreakers' boss pinched my nipples to ignite electric shocks of pleasure and kissed me so hard my head spun.

This didn't feel like enough either. I wanted *both* of them, as fully as I could have them. I wanted to feel how much we were all in this together.

I managed to focus enough through the tingling pulses of bliss that came with Ruin's quickening thrusts to reach for Nox's jeans. He was hard too, his cock straining against his fly. When my knuckles grazed him, he growled.

"Oh, baby, just keep doing that," he muttered.

"I could do even better," I said raggedly.

He caught my gaze, passion blazing in his eyes, and eased up onto his feet on the seat of the throne beside me. "You want this, Siren?" He ran his hand over his groin and licked his lips. "I bet you can handle it. You're bold enough to take both of us, aren't you?"

I yanked at his jeans in answer. He unzipped his fly and freed himself. When he brushed the head of his erection across my lips with a shaky breath, I flicked out my tongue to lick it.

"Oh, *fuck*, yes," Nox said with a groan. "That's so good. You're fucking perfect."

I responded by parting my lips and drawing him right into my mouth. He rested his hand on my hair, his fingers tangling with the strands but not forcing me faster or closer than I was ready for.

Ruin let out a pleased sound and bucked into me faster. The ecstatic burn of our connection sizzled through my veins. I bucked with him and tightened my lips around Nox, swirling my tongue at the same time. Nox pumped into me, matching the rhythm of my mouth.

In that moment, it didn't even seem crazy. It only felt like a culmination of all the affection and passion they'd been showering me with from the beginning.

I was one of them now, and we could make a beautiful symphony of bodily bliss together. Every grunt and gasp and hum twined together into a buoyant melody. I was careening higher and higher on the thrill of it all—

My second orgasm exploded through me, whiting out my mind with a hail of shooting stars. I sucked hard on Nox instinctively, and he swore as he emptied himself into my mouth.

"So precious," Ruin mumbled, pounding his last few joyful strokes into me. "Our Waterlily. Oh, Lily." With a half-swallowed cry, he stiffened as he found his own release.

Nox sank down beside me, kissing me before I'd even finished swallowing his cum. He didn't seem to care about his taste on my lips—maybe that made the kiss even hotter for him. He pressed another to the side of my head and tucked his arm around my shoulders in an iron embrace. "Our queen. Couldn't have earned the title more thoroughly."

A giggle spilled out of me. Ruin leaned in as he softened inside me and hugged me too, and right then it was hard to imagine why anyone *wouldn't* want their very own gang of semi-ghostly lovers.

"So this is the place, then?" I said.

Nox let out a laugh. "I think it'd better be after all that. Now all we need is to find *you* a real home."

Chapter Twelve

Lily

THE MOMENT I spotted the envelope marked *CONFIDENTIAL* with Nolan Gauntt's name on it, I ever-so-carefully tucked it into a spot I'd already scouted out between two of the mailroom shelves. If my supervisor noticed it, he'd tell me to take it up right away. But unfortunately for him, doing my job efficiently was a lower priority to me than getting a better scoop on the man in charge.

Kai had found out when Nolan's admin assistant would be away from his desk for half an hour today. I had no idea what the big boss himself would be doing during that time, but at least I'd have an excuse to go up to his floor and hang around the assistant's desk for a minute. I didn't have Kai's manipulative skills or speed-reading ability, but an ordinary gal could figure out a thing or two.

I hoped.

I was queen of the Skullbreakers, I reminded myself as I sorted a bunch of other envelopes that'd arrived and slapped labels on a stack of packages that were supposed to go out this afternoon. I'd held two powerful gangsters in my sway last night. I had the power of the marsh inside me and marked into my hair.

I was a force to be reckoned with, and the Gauntts and whoever else would regret the day they'd messed with my sister.

My supervisor, a pasty-faced man named Rupert, marched through the room and let out a faint huff when he glanced my way. He'd been doing that ever since I'd turned up yesterday morning with the blue streaks in my hair. *His* hair was the faded, yellow-brown hue of dying marsh grass, so I didn't think he was in much of a position to criticize. I satisfied my annoyance by picturing a miniature heron stalking around the combed strands, pecking at imaginary bugs.

"Make sure you line up the labels totally straight," he sniped at me a minute later. "We have an image to maintain, you know."

I stared down at the package I'd just applied the mailing address to, unable to see how it could get any straighter. Did he have a ruler stuck up his ass to make him so anal?

"I'll be more careful," I said, resisting the urge to grit my teeth.

When he picked up his cup of coffee, a small hum tickled through my chest. I let just a little of it loose, flicking a tiny splash that he could believe was a slip of his hand onto his shirt collar.

A giddy shiver ran down my spine when it worked. Rupert grumbled and dashed off to dampen a tissue to wipe at the stain.

It seemed like anything liquid—at least, liquid that was mostly water—I could command. Although water on its own was pretty handy. Every modern building had plumbing. There were sewers and water mains under every street in the city and back in town.

And the frogs appeared to have no problem with long distance travel. A faint croaking caught my ears, and I ducked down by the table to find another green friend perched on a plastic crate.

"You should go home," I whispered to him. "No good flies here." I didn't figure I was going to come at anyone in Thrivewell with a frog army. Somehow I didn't think the head honchos here would be quite as easily intimidated as Peyton had been.

Lucky for me, Rupert stepped out for his break a few minutes before Nolan Gauntt's assistant was due to take a hike. I retrieved the prized envelope from its hiding place, tossed a few other recently arrived pieces of mail into a satchel so it wouldn't look like I was making the trip up there just for him, even though I really was, and headed to the elevator.

I had to go past the woman on Kai's floor who guarded the more exclusive elevator first. But I'd already texted Kai about my plans, and he was over by her desk exchanging some quick remarks with her when I breezed up.

I flashed the envelope at her. "Confidential mail for Mr. Gauntt."

The secretaries' secretary was distracted enough that she didn't scrutinize me super closely, not that I thought I'd given her any reason to deny me regardless. *No point in making it harder for ourselves than it has to be,* Kai had said. She waved me on to the elevator and tapped in a code that opened the door for me.

The mirrored doors boxed me in. Then I was soaring upwards in the metal box, closer than ever to the man who'd started the catastrophe my life had become seven years ago.

There were actually four Gauntts in the building. Nolan and Marie had offices on either side of the top floor, and their son and his wife had offices below them, in whatever roles nepotism had bought them. When I stepped out into the vast, high-ceilinged hall on the penthouse level, I realized that was a bit of a problem.

Nolan's admin assistant had abandoned her post, but Marie's was still staked out at his desk at the opposite end. Granted, with the hall being as palatial as it was, that meant he was still thirty feet away from where I stood as I came to a stop outside Nolan's office, but he wasn't blind. If I started poking around on the other assistant's desk, he'd notice.

I tapped the envelope against the desk and glanced around as if searching for the desk's expected occupant, my nerves prickling in anticipation of the other assistant telling me he'd handle the letter. Could I reasonably insist that I needed to deliver it to Nolan or his representative directly?

But it seemed that Marie's assistant didn't give a shit about his boss's husband's business. I stood there for about a minute without the man saying a word, and then his phone pinged. He ducked into Marie's office, and all at once I was on my own.

My pulse stuttered. I dashed around the assistant's desk, my gaze darting over the objects I'd already noted there. No paper agenda for this dude, only a computer, the monitor currently asleep. Otherwise there were just a few pens and a box of tissues, which weren't likely to offer up much intel.

"Wake up, wake up," I sang under my breath in a reverse lullaby to the computer, tapping the space bar. Thankfully, the monitor blinked on. Less helpfully, a password box appeared.

I glowered at it as if I could intimidate it into filling in the correct combination of characters myself. "I could drench your circuitry," I muttered at it, but the computer remained impervious to my threat. I decided I was better off checking out other avenues rather than continuing to try to bully the machine into compliance.

I spotted a postcard tucked partway under the tissue box and tugged it out to check it. The glossy announcement was for some special benefit dinner—at a restaurant full of crystal chandeliers and copious wine, based on the imagery on one side. Some spiffy business association that went by the acronym BLEC. Maybe it was better that they didn't spell out what that stood for.

In any case, the benefit dinner was happening in two weeks on a Wednesday, and tidy scrawl at the bottom of the card said, *Looking forward to seeing Nolan and Marie there!* I didn't know for sure that they were going, but the sender seemed pretty confident, and the assistant had set it aside. I snapped a quick picture of the card with my phone to be sure I remembered the date and tucked it back into place.

The only thing left was the half-full trash can tucked mostly behind one end of the desk. I squatted down next to that, grimaced, and started pawing through it. Desperate times called for desperate measures and all that.

"What've you got for me?" I murmured to the metal bin and its crumpled papers and cellophane wrappers. "Cut me a break here, won't you?"

For all Nolan's admin assistant's high standing in this posh office building, he definitely had tastes that were a little low brow. Toward the bottom of the bin, I found a ticket stub from a theater with three Xs in the name and a wrapper from a pack of… Pokémon cards? Gotta catch 'em all, I guess. Where possibly 'em referred to STDs.

I was just reaching for another postcard that looked like an invitation when the handle of the office door clicked over. My heart lurched to the top of my throat.

I sprang away from the trash can, swiping my hand across my skirt as if I might have X-rated cooties on it now, and jerked to attention with the envelope that was *my* ticket—to being here—clutched in my hands.

The man who was just stepping out looked me over. He wasn't Nolan Gauntt, unless the man had gotten extreme plastic surgery since the photos Kai had pulled up for me to check, but he was obviously someone important enough to have a personal meeting with the big boss.

I waved the envelope and did my best to channel my panic into the appearance of starstruck nerves. "I just—I'm new in the mailroom. There was a letter for Mr. Gauntt. I think it's important. But his secretary isn't here. I wasn't sure if I should knock…"

My cheeks were burning, but at least that fit my intimidated ditz act. As did the fact that I accidentally let the envelope slip from my fingers and had to fumble to snatch it up again. If I kept this up, they'd fire me for having the approximate coordination of a toddler.

"Is Mr. Gauntt still busy?" I added, my pulse thumping with a heady mix of hope and terror. "Can I bring it in to him?"

Would I get to stare my theoretical enemy straight in the face? Did I *want* to? All of a sudden I was scared Nolan would see right through my act to my true intentions.

Well, so what if he did? *He* was the one in the wrong in this scenario, when you cut down to the root of it.

I drew my shoulders back with that surge of defiant confidence, but the man was shaking his head. "I don't think that's a wise idea. Here, I'll hand it over to him. We shouldn't leave it any longer if it's important."

Before I could put my plans of arguing for chain of custody or whatever the right term would be in an office setting, the stranger had already plucked the envelope from my hands. I managed to get out an, "Oh!" and then he'd slipped back into the office, shutting the door firmly behind him. All I caught was a brief glimpse of thick, crimson carpeting and gleaming gold filigree worked into the wallpaper.

So, Nolan Gauntt was an opulent ass. Not exactly a surprise, seeing his place of work. With no further excuse to hang around, I slunk back to the elevator. But I wasn't leaving empty-handed.

In a couple of weeks, that office and the one down the hall would be vacant while the Gauntts attended the benefit dinner. With Kai's help, maybe I could penetrate the inner sanctum of the villain.

Chapter Thirteen

Jett

As I TOOK in the three-story building, where the beige doorframe clashed with the maroon bricks, my heart sank.

"Kai said this was your best bet," I said to Lily, unable to suppress a frown. The guy knew plenty about a lot of things, but aesthetic analysis wasn't exactly his strong suit. "But if it's bad, I'm sure he can dig up some others."

"Well, let's go up and see the apartment," Lily said, nudging my arm with her elbow.

I did my best not to show any reaction, but inside, I stiffened up against the rush of heat that came with her closeness. I *had* to tense a little, or my arm might have gone slipping around her to tug her even closer of its own accord. As if that was what I wanted to be to her—yet another one of us aiming to get into her pants.

Not that I thought Nox and Ruin had any bad intentions. She had needs, they had needs, and there was no reason they shouldn't satisfy those together. Actually, that was a hell of a lot better than imagining her getting it on with some creep we knew nothing about. But she did have the two of them—and maybe Kai too if he stopped conducting data comparisons for long enough to make a move—so it wasn't like I could offer her something she didn't already have in that area.

I could be totally happy with her just sparking inspiration in me while I ignored the lust that sometimes came along with it.

The rental agent who was a collection of brown, black, and navy blue shapes, many of them long and angular, shifted on her feet where she'd been standing by the door. "Yes. You really should take a look at the space." So we headed in.

There was no elevator, of course. We tramped up the stairwell, which might have been Victorian once upon a time but had been transformed over the ages into a hodgepodge of art deco detailing and modernist fixtures. I managed not to wince when we got to the hallway with its olive-green carpet and lemon-yellow walls. As the rental agent fit the key into the lock of a door at the end of the hall, I braced myself.

The door swung wide—and I froze for a second, blinking and taking in the bright, airy space that was the complete opposite of what I'd been expecting.

Lily strode right inside, her pale hair gleaming in the sunlight that streamed through the main room's two broad windows. The hardwood floor creaked faintly under her feet, but it was *real* hardwood, not modern over-polished stuff. You could see the history of the trees in the knots and whirls of the grain—and the history of past inhabitants in the scuffs and scratches laid over top.

The apartments hadn't been updated with the same regularity as the building's common areas. Art deco had touched this space in the geometric flare to the baseboards and the moldings along the ceiling, but only subtly. The walls had been left white, a total blank slate. My fingers itched with the urge to splash some color over them and see just how stunning we could make the room.

It wasn't huge. Lily wandered from the living room area to where she could set up a small dining table with just a few paces, and the kitchen was walk-in closet sized, with just a half-wall separating it from the rest of the room. But the place was still twice the size of her stuffy basement without even getting into the other rooms yet.

"Since it's one of the corner apartments, there are three bedrooms," the rental agent was saying in her brisk, slightly desperate-sounding voice. "Each of them nice and cozy. And on the top floor, you don't have to worry about noise from neighbors overhead."

One of the reasons Kai had picked out this place was its price. We'd afford whatever Lily needed, but she'd already insisted that she wanted to pay her own way as much as possible, and there was no good in stressing her out with a massive rent bill. The neighborhood was halfway through a surge of gentrification, getting too posh and stuffy and just a little out of reach for the low-income families who might have snatched this place up before. But this particular building must be having trouble competing with the sleek modern apartments going up around it.

No doubt in another few years the owners would want to gut it and start from scratch, if they could come up with the dough. By then we'd just have to be ready to buy the whole building out from under them—if Lily still wanted to live here.

From the looks of things, she did. She drifted from one bedroom to another with a shimmer in her eyes and a quiet smile playing with her lips. I wanted to paint her like that. But then, I wanted to paint her every which way. She'd have set off something in me even standing on her head with her tongue stuck out.

In real estate terms, I knew enough to realize that "cozy" meant "tiny." But each of the bedrooms was big enough to fit a double bed and a dresser, maybe even a small armchair or vanity, without leaving you crushed against the wall. The third had a built-in Murphy bed that swung down from the wall at the push of a button.

"We'd take that one," I told Lily. "You and Marisol should get proper beds."

Lily raised an eyebrow at me. "All four of you on that thing? You'd be getting awfully up close and personal."

A smile twitched at my lips despite myself. "We can set up cots too," I said. "I definitely don't want Ruin flailing around in my face. And we won't all be here all the time. We'll have a couple of pullout couches set up in the new hangout too."

I also figured that when we *were* staying here, one of the other guys would be sharing Lily's bed at least some of the time. Ruin was already making a partial habit of that.

An image flashed through my mind of lying on that mattress with her tucked against *me*, and this time it was my dick that twitched. I turned away, looking across the main room from the doorway.

The rental agent had gone over to the door to give us some space to settle into the place. Lily came up beside me, still absorbing it all.

"It's nice," she said softly. "I mean, it'd be perfect. But I don't know how long I'll have this job at Thrivewell—I don't know what kind of work I'll be able to get after."

"It's cheap for what it is," I said. "Everyone else wants the fancy fixtures, so skipping this place is their loss and your gain. We'll have plenty of cash soon to tide you over if you need it."

"I know. But you shouldn't have to. It should be *me* looking after Marisol—she's my sister."

The determination in her voice sparked a different sort of sensation in me. Memories wavered up of the kind of treatment I'd gotten from *my* family: my parents' harsh words and harder fists. Family ties had been something to survive and overcome, not anything you could count on for support.

Lily could have learned the same lesson from her own asshole parents. But she'd never lost the sweetness she'd had even as a little kid.

"We're looking out for *you*," I said with a sudden determination of my own. We were her family more than the jerks who'd claimed the official titles. We'd been there for her more than her mom and stepdad ever had. "Whatever you need help with, you can count on us."

"I know. I just…" She bit her lip. I knew how strong Lily was, but in certain moments an inner fragility showed through, and I wanted nothing more than to charge with fists swinging at anyone who brought it out in her.

"What?" I demanded, unable to stop my voice from getting gruffer.

She looked down, her fingers drifting along the doorframe. "I've been thinking… I'd like to do more with music. I always loved singing. If there's a way I could make some kind of career out of that

—but I know anything in the arts is a tough road. Maybe I'm being ridiculous."

My heart swelled, and even though I'd been making a point of avoiding physical contact, I gripped her arm. "You have to go for that. Your voice—" I hadn't heard her sing in years, but the delicate strains of the melodies she'd produced had stuck in my memory. I'd bet they wove through my own art even now. She'd always been able to transform the sounds around her into something beautiful, tying it all together with the harmony she created as it spilled from her lips.

The general public should consider themselves fucking *blessed* if she offered that talent up to the rest of them.

"When you've got something like that inside you, you have to let it out," I went on. "I'd be miserable if I wasn't making my paintings and the rest." Okay, I was miserable plenty of the time regardless, but I'd have been more so without the outlet. "You let it out, and you see where it can take you. You can always take on other jobs while you give it a shot."

At my emphatic insistence, Lily's smile came back, if shier than before. But her next words came with a teasing note. "Like you do."

I shrugged. "Hey, I see skull-breaking as more of a hobby than a career, but it does pay the bills too." As long as I didn't let my artistic inclinations take over *too* much…

A spurt of guilt seared up from my gut at the thought of the time I had let too much go. I clamped down on it, willing my expression to stay calm. Lily hadn't been any part of that, and I wasn't going to lay it on her.

She shook her head in amusement and stepped back into the main room. At the same moment, my phone jangled with the stupidly dramatic classical song my nerd host had programmed it with, like getting a call was an epic event. Making a face, I drew back into the bedroom and shut the door for privacy.

The screen just said *Dad*, so I guessed I was hearing from another family today. This one I wanted even less to do with than my own. But it'd been inevitable that we'd have to deal with parents eventually, even with the guys who'd been living on campus rather than at home. I had to give the relatives something so they didn't file a missing person report and create even more of a hassle for me.

From what I'd found out so far about the guy whose body I'd taken over, I wouldn't be surprised if he'd previously been in the habit of sending weekly reports to his family, complete with a spreadsheet breaking down recent fluctuations to his GPA and number of professors' asses he'd kissed. They could forget about that from here on. Their boy Vince had flown the coop.

"Hello," I answered in the most even voice I could produce.

"Vincent!" the man on the other end said, with that stiff kind of enthusiasm people use when they're trying to pretend they're happy but are actually pissed off. "You missed our usual family video chat. Your mother's been getting worried about you."

But the man talking to me hadn't been? I swallowed that sarcastic remark and said, "Classes have gotten me really busy. Term papers, extra credit, group presentations, band practice, you know." Were there any other school terms I could throw in there for good measure? I'd only just graduated high school by the skin of my teeth.

"Band practice?" Vince's dad said, and then seemed to shake himself. "You do have a responsibility to the family as well. I hope you won't get distracted from that. We had an agreement—"

His superior tone was already rankling me. "Look," I interrupted, "I'm 21. Officially an adult in every possible way. I get to make my own decisions about what my responsibilities are now. I'm sure you'll be very proud of what I accomplish."

The man started to sputter. "Now wait a minute here. You can't talk to me like—"

"Funny, I just did. I'll call or video chatter or whatever when I feel like it. In the meantime, let me do my thing."

Then I hung up.

It might not have been the most graceful exit, but if I'd stayed on the line much longer, I might have started describing in detail how he should shove his head up his ass, and that would have gone over even worse.

The phone started ringing again. I jabbed at it until it shut up and smacked my hand against the wall with a growl of frustration.

The electric energy that still tingled lightly through my veins, leftover from my previous ghostly state, zapped through my arm with the impact. The wall beneath my hand flickered… and suddenly I was staring at a fog-blue surface instead of the previous white.

I yanked my hand back, staring. The entire wall had changed color, just like that. I glanced around to make sure the other walls were still white and it wasn't just that my vision had fogged, but nope, my gloom hadn't gotten quite that literal. Motherfucker.

Was that my special angle on our supernatural energies? Nox could beat people down from a distance, Ruin could infect them with his feels, and I could give a room a makeover?

Actually, maybe I was okay with that.

I flexed my fingers, wanting to see what else I might be able to alter, and heard footsteps coming toward the room. The rental agent's footsteps, from the tapping of sharp heels. Shit. I didn't think she'd appreciate my new paint job on a place we hadn't even signed a contract for yet.

My nerves jumped, and I slapped my hand against the wall again. It blinked white an instant later, just as the agent opened the door. If maybe there was a tiny blue tint to that surface still, she was too busy glaring at me to notice.

"I'm not sure what you're doing, but I'd appreciate it if you didn't damage the plaster."

I held up my hands apologetically. "Sorry! Just testing the walls to make sure they're good and solid."

She kept eyeing me as I strode back out to rejoin Lily. The agent cleared her throat. "We do expect certain standards of behavior: there are noise regulations, and the unit should be left in a similar condition to as it started."

"Of course," Lily said, gazing around her again. I knew just looking at her that she was taking the place. She arched an eyebrow at me. "I can keep my friends in line."

I was definitely having my way with these walls as soon as they were in our possession, though. And maybe this newfound talent could be useful when it came to a certain other project the other guys and I had been discussing…

Lily got a contract to sign from the rental agent, promised to return by the end of the day with the deposit, and headed back to the street with more of a spring in her step than I could remember seeing since she was a kid. "This could be good," she said. "It could be *really* good. I hope Marisol likes it."

"She will," I told her. "A hole in the ground would be better than staying with your parental units any longer, if you're there with her."

She smiled at me, and my heart gave that weird little hitch it'd never done for anyone else in my life. Either of my lives. Then we turned the corner outside and were swarmed by the rest of the crew, who must have just finished up the other business they'd been seeing to.

"Did you like it?" Ruin asked, grabbing Lily in one of his usual bear hugs. Kai didn't say anything, but his eyes gleamed with intense alertness. He was the one who'd picked out the apartment, after all.

"It's great," Lily said. "I'm going to go for it. It sounds like as long as I put down the deposit today, it's mine."

"We've got that covered," Nox announced, and before she could protest, added, "It's our payback for losing you your other job. No arguments. We owe you. We'll cover any charges from breaking your lease on the basement too. How soon can you move in?"

"Two weeks," Kai said. "I specifically looked for places that would be available quickly."

A smile that was outright luminescent crossed Lily's face. We all basked in it for a few seconds before I turned to Nox. "You got the other stuff sorted out?"

"Yep." He tossed me a pistol, which I shoved into the back of my jeans. A twist of tension I hadn't registered before loosened in my chest with the weapon in my grasp.

I'd always preferred working with my hands directly, but a bullet was an excellent equalizer. Strength and speed barely came into it. After the last gang we'd hit up for info had come at us with firearms to our fists, we'd realized it was time to make some new connections in the black market.

"And we found out more about these Skeleton Corps guys," Ruin said cheerfully.

Kai rolled his eyes at him. "Nothing good. While we asked around, putting out feelers, it got obvious very quickly that no one wants to mess with these people. They were practically pissing their pants just hearing the name. These guys have a lot of sway in the city."

"And they were scared of *us* enough to come after us," Ruin added, still spinning this in a positive light the way only he could.

"The guy who told us about them didn't say they offed us," Nox reminded him. "Just that they were the most likely people to know who did. But if it was them, we have a few different tricks up our sleeves this time." His mouth curved into a cocky grin, and he glanced around at all of us. "Are we ready to pay back the pricks who killed us, no matter what they're going to throw at us?"

My stomach had twisted up again, but I spoke without a second's hesitation. "Hell, yes."

Maybe this city gang was big enough to crush us all over again, ghostly powers or not. But I'd already gotten one life, and I'd fucked up both it and three others with my stupidity. So if any of us ended up going down, it could be me.

At least I'd die the second time knowing my friends were shooting the smirks off the rest of those pricks' faces.

Chapter Fourteen

Lily

RUPERT STORMED into the mailroom with a severe case of the Mondays. He stomped this way and that, slapped labels onto the outgoing packages like they'd kicked his puppy, and nearly bit the head off the office worker who came down to deliver a verbal message.

"Are you kidding me?" he said, his eyes bulging, and then drew himself up straighter as if good posture would make up for his unprofessional tone. His gaze cut across the room to me where I was sorting mail into the carts for the different floors. His voice lowered, but not so much that I couldn't make out the words. "Why would they want to speak with her? There must be a mistake."

The guy he was talking to shook his head and murmured something that was actually discreet. Rupert let out one of his trademark huffs, and I gleefully pictured the mini heron on his head taking a massive crap. Then my supervisor turned toward me.

"Miss Strom, you've been instructed to go up to Nolan Gauntt's office. Apparently Mr. Gauntt has something he needs to speak to you about."

I froze, the envelope I'd been lifting slipping from my fingers and bouncing off the assorted mail already in the cart in front of me. Okay, maybe I couldn't blame him for his skepticism when I was totally bewildered myself.

"Me?" I said, like there might be another Miss Strom in the room that I simply hadn't noticed before. "Why?"

"A very good question," Rupert muttered. The messenger had already fled. My supervisor eyed me as if I'd set this whole thing up to undermine his authority, and I decided I was best off getting the heck out of there ASAP.

"I'm supposed to go now?" I clarified.

He gave a sharp nod. "Get a move on. He keeps this entire company running. I'm sure he doesn't have time to wait on a dawdling mail clerk."

I had no idea why Nolan Gauntt would want to talk to a mail clerk at all. As I hurried into the hall toward the elevators, my pulse started pounding.

Had Nolan or his admin assistant realized I'd been snooping? Maybe there'd been hidden security cameras in the hall, or the visitor I'd passed the envelope to had seen more than I realized? Was he calling me in to chew me out?

Or maybe Harmon Kitteridge had spilled the beans and they've realized I'd gotten the job under false pretenses. Kai's blackmail material might not have been enough of a threat.

Either way, did that mean Nolan had also put the pieces together about who *I* was? Would he think of me as simply the sister of a girl he'd done something untoward with years ago, or had he taken a more recent role in my family's lives? Wade had seemed to think Nolan loomed large, but he hadn't actually given any proof of that, and it hadn't sounded like Marisol had seen the man since the incident that'd set me off seven years ago.

My fingers brushed over the outline of my phone in my purse's outer pocket. I had the urge to text Kai and tell him what was happening, like a hiker setting off into uncharted wilderness wanting a record in case they didn't return, but I wasn't totally sure that the former gangster would be content sitting on his butt while I walked into the lion's den. He might insist on barging in or making some kind of commotion in the hopes of getting me out of this meeting, and I wasn't sure that was what I needed.

I'd been wanting to figure out what Nolan Gauntt was up to since the moment I'd heard his name from my stepfather's lips. It was the whole reason I'd applied for this job. Now the man himself had called me in for a chat. How could I pass up the opportunity, even if it might end with me getting booted out the front door?

If he was pissed off at me, nothing Kai could do was going to change that anyway. The brilliant gangster might be able to read and manipulate people based on what they thought and felt, but he couldn't make them think something totally different. If we could get Ruin in here to work a little of his magic of feels, maybe…

No, that would wear off, and then I'd be back where I'd started. The only thing to do was to meet this confrontation head-on.

The elevator took about a century to reach the basement floor that held the mailroom, and then another century to rise up to the fifteenth floor where I had to switch over. I smoothed my skirt straight and checked that my blouse and cardigan hadn't picked up any crumbs or stains, but the assistant to the executive assistants still looked me over with a pinched frown before motioning me on toward the exclusive elevator to the upper floors.

When I reached the top floor and stepped out of the elevator, the man whose desk I'd been accosting a few days ago got up and walked to the door to Nolan's office. "Miss Strom is here," he said, and motioned for me to walk past him into the room.

I slipped inside onto that thick crimson carpet. The gold filigree I'd noticed on the wallpaper gleamed against its midnight-blue background. It should have made the space feel dark, but the ceiling was so high and lit with beaming crystal fixtures, with more light streaming through the windows along the far end of the immense office, that it gave me the impression of a vast, stately expanse instead.

Not just one but two figures were standing just in front of the antique mahogany desk near the far windows. I walked toward them warily, recognizing them both from the pictures Kai had dug up during his research.

To the left stood the man I'd been expecting, although even more imposing in the flesh. Nolan Gauntt must have stood nearly as tall as Nox's massive form. Even in his advancing age, he had the build of a linebacker, broad-shouldered and barrel-chested. His smooth, silvery hair still held a few streaks of blond; his jaw was clean-shaven. He watched me approach with a gaze that felt both flat and penetrating at the same time.

To the right waited the woman I knew was his wife. Marie Gauntt stood almost a full head shorter than her husband, but her hair made up for a lot of that difference, rising in a neat, colorless cone the texture of cotton candy. Her thin lips were pursed. Despite her shorter stature, her presence was no less intimidating. The soft grays of her business suit contrasted with the hard angles to her face and body.

It was easy to tell that both of them had been quite the stunners in their younger days. They were still incredibly striking, although there was a detached sheen to their eyes that made my nerves jitter. It was like they were studying my every move while not really giving a shit what I actually did.

"Miss Strom," Nolan said in a cool baritone, just before I got close enough that I felt *I* had to break the ice. I stopped in my tracks as he went on. "I'm glad you could join us. I'm Nolan Gauntt, and this is my wife, Marie. We run Thrivewell together."

"We're making a point of touching base with the new hires here," Marie added, her own voice quiet but dry.

"Oh," I said, groping for the appropriate words. "That's very nice of you."

I might have felt less unsettled if I could have pictured some bizarre animal tromping around on each of their heads, but somehow my mind jarred when I tried to conjure so much as a trunk or a hoof. It was as if the Gauntts' presence was so potent even my imagination couldn't challenge it.

Did they make all the new hires walk a mile across this office while staring them down like prey they were picking the best caliber of shotgun for? Kai hadn't mentioned any meetings like this, and I'd have thought they'd call in someone at his level before a random mailroom clerk.

They'd gone silent again, just contemplating me. Were they looking for some specific reaction?

They did know who I was. I had no doubt about that now. Why else this whole production? But of course they weren't going to admit it or that they'd had anything to do with my sister. What would they get out of showing so many of their cards?

I shifted my weight from one foot to the other. "Was there anything in particular you wanted to know?" I ventured. "I think I've been getting the hang of things in the mailroom, and I like working here."

"Ah, well, you've only just gotten started, haven't you?" Marie said, her tone light but the words undeniably ominous.

"Yes," I said hesitantly. "This is my second week."

Nolan gave a somber nod and an odd flick of his hand, as if he were brushing a bug off his suit lapel. "We did have some concerns. We understand you don't have any prior office experience. The atmosphere here in the head office can get rather… intense."

"Oh." I was so articulate today. I sucked in a breath and reminded myself that the man in front of me might look like important stuff, but he also apparently needed to mess with little kids to make himself feel big. No matter what front he put on, he was a creep underneath.

"I'm sure I can handle that," I continued, raising my chin. I wasn't in a position to challenge him right now, but I didn't want them to think I was some kind of wimp either.

It'd have been handy if either of them had given away something about their association with my family, but they hadn't even used my first name. Marie tapped her fingernails against the top of the desk with a crisp rattling sound. "I'm not sure you can reasonably assume that's true when you haven't experienced it. That's why we felt we should offer you the opportunity to settle in somewhere that might be more your speed."

My stomach knotted. "What do you mean?" Were they kicking me out after all? So far neither of them had mentioned my investigative activities or my supposed godfather—but could I hope they really didn't know?

Nolan swept his arm toward the world beyond the wall. "We have another, smaller office set up in Bedard. That would be a shorter commute for you, coming all the way from Lovell Rise, and it's slower paced there. Less urgency to the communications passing through. They could use a new mailroom clerk there as well. The pay would remain the same, of course, in accordance with your hiring conditions."

"Oh," I said again, resisting the urge to hug myself. They were trying to get rid of me, but in the kindest-looking way possible.

They didn't want me under the same roof as them. This offer would get me out of the way without giving me any reason for complaint. Who could argue about the same pay for an easier job, after all?

But there was a threat implicit in the talk about how "intense" the company could be too. Nolan drove it home, folding his arms over his chest and fixing his flat blue eyes even more intently on me. "I wouldn't want to see an employee burn out by remaining here when it's more of a trial than they can handle. We have your best interests at heart."

I swallowed hard. Yeah right, they did.

But how would they destroy me if I defied them? I wasn't so worried about me, but if Marisol ended up paying for my refusal… How could I put *her* at risk over a plan I might not have thought through as well as I should have?

Maybe I could investigate the Gauntts from this other office? Kai would still be here checking up on things… I didn't think they could have connected him to me.

The idea started to feel so tempting that my lips parted to accept. I caught myself, my fingers curling into my palms. A sudden jolt of anger rushed through my chest—anger mostly at myself.

I'd tried running away before. I'd done everything I could to dodge my bullies at the college, and they'd just kept coming down on me harder and harder. It hadn't been until I pushed back that they'd finally eased off.

Something Ruin had said yesterday tickled up from my memory. It'd been his usual turning-an-empty-glass-full style optimism, but at the same time, he hadn't been wrong.

And they were scared of us *enough to come after us.*

He'd been talking about this Skeleton Corps gang, but it applied to this situation just as well. If the Gauntts hadn't been worried about what I might accomplish while working here, they wouldn't have bothered to try to send me elsewhere. The very fact that they'd gone on the attack meant that they had something to defend.

Resolve solidified inside me. I'd come here to uncover the mysteries around my sister and me, and I wasn't turning tail just because a couple of much bigger bullies had decided they should call the shots in my life instead.

"Actually," I said, willing my voice to stay steady despite my quaking nerves, "I just put down a deposit on an apartment here in Mayfield. And I've been through plenty of high-pressure scenarios in the past, even if not in an office environment." They didn't know the half of it. "I'd really love to stay on here and prove myself. If you find any problems with my work, I'd understand the transfer, but for now, I hope you'll give me a real chance."

I smiled at them tightly, almost a dare. Were they going to try to force the issue and show how much it mattered to them?

They eyed me for a few seconds longer while my heart thudded in my ears. Nolan tilted his head to one side. Marie tugged her elbow back in an odd gesture I didn't understand. Then they sighed nearly in unison.

"I suppose that's fair," Marie said.

"We will keep a close eye on how well you're keeping up here," Nolan said. "There's no shame in working your way up gradually."

I forced Ruin-level brightness into my voice. "I know. But I really think I'm up to it. I won't let you down."

Maybe that was laying it on a bit thick, but Nolan nodded. "I appreciate your dedication," he said in a tone that suggested he really didn't at all. "We won't keep you from your work any longer."

At that dismissal, I turned and hurried back across the expanse of the room. My chest had constricted around my lungs.

I'd won whatever small battle this had been. Now I'd better hope it'd definitely been one worth fighting.

Chapter Fifteen

Lily

AT FIRST, everything was simply dark. Darkness everywhere I turned, and the unnerving sensation crept over me that I wasn't standing but floating.

The darkness rippled around me. The currents rushed faster and stronger, tugging at my limbs. They were dragging me down, down into the even thicker blackness that would swallow me up completely.

I opened my mouth to scream, and more liquid darkness gushed down my throat, choking me. My lungs seized up. I couldn't breathe, couldn't speak, and I was sinking, falling, sucked down and down while the last glimmers of light blinked out overhead—

I jerked out of the nightmare with a gasped cry, my lungs still straining for breath. Ruin's arms wrapped around me.

"Hey," he said, low and sweet. "Hey, it's all right, Waterlily. I'm right here with you."

Before I'd quite recovered from my panicked daze, three more forms burst into the dimness of my bedroom.

"Is she okay?" Nox demanded.

"What's happening?" Kai asked, fumbling his glasses onto his nose.

"If someone's managed to hurt her here…" Jett said darkly with a smack of his fist against his other hand.

Now I was drowning in concern.

"I'm all right," I muttered, swiping my hand across my eyes. "It was just a bad dream. There's no one to beat up, unless you have some ghostly way of punching my subconscious."

Kai cocked his head as if he was working out the logistics of that maneuver.

Nox frowned, his jaw flexing. "Are you sure? It wasn't a bad dream *about* something shitty someone's done to you?"

I glowered at him. "I'm absolutely sure there's no one whose skull you need to crack to avenge my interrupted sleep. Speaking of which, I'd kind of like to get back to sleep if that's at all possible."

"We should all get some more sleep," Ruin put in cheerfully. "With better dreams."

The other guys wavered on their feet for a moment indecisively, no doubt still searching for a way they could defend me from the products of my inner mind. Then they all tramped back out again.

Ruin stayed, cuddled against me on the narrow bed. I let my head come to rest on his shoulder, inhaling his warm, musky scent. "How long have you been in here?"

He'd been slipping into my room earlier and earlier over the past few days, though always managing to tuck himself against me without waking me up. I hadn't yet definitively determined that he wasn't just a giant housecat in human form.

The impression was only amplified by the purr-like hum he let out as he nuzzled my hair. "Just a half hour ago. It's hard sleeping alone when I know you're in here. But I don't want to crowd you." He let out a happy sigh. "It'll be perfect when you have a proper-sized bed."

"I suppose I'll never get rid of you then," I muttered without any actual complaint in the words.

"Nope!" Ruin declared brightly. But he did adjust himself to give me a tiny bit more space on the mattress, with his back pressed against the wall. He stroked his fingers over my hair. "What *were* you dreaming about? I'll talk your subconscious out of making you think about it again."

My lips twitched with a smile I couldn't completely constrain. "I don't know how well that'll work. It was…" I thought back to the smothering, choking darkness, and my pulse hitched all over again. I swallowed thickly. "I was drowning. Like I almost did in the marsh."

Weirdly, I'd never had nightmares about that moment before, even though it was by far the closest I'd ever come to dying, so you'd think it should be my most traumatic memory. But my plunge into the chilly marsh-water had ended with finding four new friends I'd thought were imaginary but who'd still been a hell of a lot more company than the nothing I'd had before. In a warped way, my near-death experience had made my life *better*.

So why was my brain tossing the worst parts of that moment at me all over again, fourteen years later?

A tendril of uneasiness wound through my insides. My ghostly guys had helped me save myself back then. They'd stood by me while Wade and my mom had treated me like table scraps. But now…

The image rose up in my mind of Nolan and Marie Gauntt, looming large in their cold, stately authority. They controlled an entire corporate empire. They had bank accounts bigger than everyone in the whole county combined. Was a little watery magic and four former gangsters who were only just getting back on their feet really enough to tackle them?

My guys had been protecting me every step of the way since they'd come back to me in bodily form, and I might have just dragged them into a war that was a thousand times more dangerous than anything they'd faced before.

I shoved those thoughts away and burrowed into Ruin's embrace. His arms tightened around me. "We'll kick the marsh's ass before we let it take you again," he informed me, but this time I couldn't quite manage a smile.

The Gauntts might be powerful, but they were still just people, I reminded myself. If I could get proof that they'd hurt my sister and maybe other kids too, their corporate ties and bank accounts shouldn't matter. I just had to keep at it, even if I wasn't sure how I was going to get that proof yet.

Maybe it'd help if I was sure that the other parts of my plans were completely solid. I'd told Marisol I was going to look after her from now on, but I hadn't laid down the law with the people who considered themselves her current caretakers. If Nolan and Marie decided to come after us, it was better she was with me than our crappy excuse for parents, wasn't it? Wade would probably kick her out the door before Nolan had even asked him to.

That thought lingered in my head through the rest of my fitful sleep and while I showered in the morning. I emerged from the bathroom with a sense of conviction that was only a little shaky.

"Before I go in to work, I'm going to stop by my old house and make sure everything's ready for Marisol to come with me once I have the new apartment."

Ruin perked up. "We'll come with you in case your mom and that jerk make any trouble."

As the others started to stir with agreement, I shook my head. "No, I still think it's better if I handle my family on my own. For now. If we have to force the issue, I'll let you know I need backup. But I don't think it should have to come to that."

Wade had cowered in the face of my powers, and I hadn't done anything more than splash him a couple of times. As angry as I was with him and Mom, I didn't see any point in breaking bones if we didn't have to.

Nox clapped his hands together. "We do have something else to take care of this morning. But all you have to do is send a text if you need us."

I ate breakfast in the car, with Fred sputtering and rumbling as if he wished he could share the meal. I wanted as much time as possible for this confrontation before I was due at work. It wouldn't look good if the day after my lecture from the big bosses, I showed up tardy.

As I drove along the lane that led to the house, I was relieved to see that Wade's car wasn't parked outside. I'd already dealt with him anyway. He didn't hold much authority over what Marisol did, since he'd never adopted either of us—any say he had was through my mom. She was the one I really needed to tackle.

I didn't have to knock. I'd only just parked and stepped out of the car when the door swung open and Mom came out on the front step.

She looked like an even more faded version of a self that'd already faded when I'd been shipped off to the mental ward, like a photocopy of a photocopy. I'd seen old pictures of her where her hair was as brightly gold as Marisol's—now it had enough gray woven in to look like day-old dishwater. It drifted fine and limp across her shoulders. The lines around her mouth spoke of how often she forced smiles for Wade's benefit, but in my presence her lips slumped into a frown. Even her skin seemed to have grayed, more a washed-out beige than its former peachy tint.

"What are you doing here?" she asked.

She didn't tell me to leave, and there was a nervous defensiveness to her posture. I guessed Wade had filled her in on the basics of my last conversation with him. It occurred to me that I wasn't even sure how much she knew about the specifics. Wade had said something about telling Mom to leave when I'd started yelling at them over the thing with Nolan Gauntt and Marisol. Did she have any idea how I'd cowed her husband in the end?

She might soon enough. Just seeing her sent the hum reverberating through my chest as my own inner defenses came up. I squared my shoulders.

"I want to talk to my sister," I said. "And in a little while, she's going to be moving in with me. I'm going to take care of her from now on."

Mom blinked at me, her mouth opening and closing a few times before she found words. "What are you talking about? You can't just run off with her."

"I can if she agrees," I said. *And I can make you allow it if you try to stop me.* But I didn't think it was going to come to that. I lowered my voice in case Marisol was listening inside. "I know you'd rather she was out of your hair anyway. You *never* wanted us around after you found Wade. So let me fix that 'problem' for all of us."

Mom's thin jaw worked. A soft pattering sounded on the patchy lawn beyond us. We both glanced over to see a squad of frogs hopping over from the marsh toward us.

I say "squad" because it definitely wasn't an army on the level of the one that'd descended on Peyton in the college restroom weeks ago.

There were maybe two or three dozen of the sleek green bodies leaping along in an off-kilter rhythm. They all stopped several feet from where we were standing and squatted there as if waiting to see if they were needed. A few let out quizzical croaks.

I glanced back at my mother. She took in the frogs and then met my gaze again, and the slightly hysterical light that gleamed in her eyes told me she wasn't totally unaware that I might have connections to powers beyond what a regular woman should. I hadn't called up the frogs on purpose, but now that they were here, I didn't mind having the moral support.

We were in this together, apparently: me and the marsh.

And then—maybe because she knew Wade had already backed down and sometime in the past fifteen years, she'd made him her spine—Mom crumpled. Her shoulders sagged, and she drew back into the doorway. "Do what you want. I can't control either of you, obviously. Just don't come to us for help if it doesn't work out the way you wanted."

As if I'd ever imagined she or Wade would help me regardless of the situation. I doubted either of them would piss on me if they saw me on fire.

I stepped past her into the house and headed upstairs. Marisol was rustling around in her bedroom, the door open. As I reached it, she zipped her backpack shut for school and straightened up. Her eyes gleamed with a wild sort of light, anxious but eager.

"It's really happening?" she said. "I'm going to move in with you?"

I grinned at her, the tension clamped around my chest subsiding. "Yep. I've already arranged the apartment—out in Mayfield, where I've got my new job. It'll be mine in less than two weeks. We'll have to decide if I need to arrange a way for you to commute or get you transferred to a closer—"

"Transfer," Marisol said before I could finish that sentence. "There's nothing I like about the high school here anyway. And they hardly have any of the more interesting classes."

She tugged at one of the braided strands of her hair after she said that, looking suddenly awkward. My gaze flicked around the room, remembering the sketches that had once decorated it. "Don't they even have art class?"

My sister shrugged. "Sort of. It's mostly about the history and stuff."

"You haven't been drawing in a while."

"I know. It started to seem kind of… silly."

An ache gripped my gut. I reached out to squeeze her shoulder. "I don't think it is at all. I miss your farting unicorns and goofy dragons and all the rest. If you're making people smile, that's something pretty important."

"I guess."

Marisol's voice was so small that I wanted to hit someone—whoever had belittled her love of putting pencil to paper. Obviously, moving her in with me wasn't going to be enough. She'd gone seven years without me here to offset Mom and Wade's disapproval. It could be a long rebuilding process.

Was I even steady enough myself to get her all the way back on track?

A faint honking carried through the bedroom window. It repeated a few seconds later. I followed Marisol when she went over to peer outside.

On one of the more distant laneways beyond the scruffy fields that covered a lot of the outskirts of town, four figures with motorcycles were standing around a car. They must have spotted us in the window, because one of them waved energetically and another simply gave a small tip of his hand and a beckoning gesture.

"Who are *they*?" Marisol asked, raising her eyebrows.

That… was a complicated question to answer. "Friends of mine," I said. "They're helping look out for us too. You'll get a chance to meet them after you've moved in." And after I'd had a *very* firm talk with the former Skullbreakers about acceptable conversation topics around my little sister.

"I'd better go see what they want—and let you get to school," I said, and gave Marisol a quick hug. "Just remember you're getting out of here soon."

Mom didn't even bother to say goodbye. I didn't force it. I

tramped out to my car and drove Fred around to the lane where the guys were waiting. When I got out to see what the welcoming party was for, my stomach flipped over.

The car they were standing around… looked just like Fred. Except not at all junker-y. The boxy exterior didn't show a hint of rust, and the blue paint shone with a recent polishing. Not a single dent marked the bumper. The rearview mirror on the driver's side didn't sag slightly downward.

"What's this?" I asked, blinking as if it might be a hallucination I could clear out of my eyes like a bit of dust.

Nox smiled broadly and patted the car's hood. "Your new ride. We told you we'd see about getting you one. But since you're so attached to the old beast, we figured we should track you down the same model. If we could manage to take over four dorks totally different from our old selves, I'm sure your junker's soul could transfer over to this one."

My throat constricted with awed gratitude. I couldn't imagine how they'd managed to track the thing down—to find the exact right shade of paint even—and this could be a new Fred, couldn't it? Fred 2.0, same old spirit in a tuned-up body. Like Nox had said, why shouldn't it be possible?

I stepped closer and let my fingertips rest on the smooth hood. The guys all watched me with their varied expressions of eagerness, and I didn't know what to say.

"It's perfect," I managed. "Thank you so much."

It really was. And some part of me couldn't quite believe I deserved the level of dedication that'd gone into this gift.

Chapter Sixteen

Ruin

Lily returned home from work just as I was heading out of her apartment. I saw her before she saw me. She got out of the new car and paused to glide her fingers along the frame, a small, delighted smile curving her lips.

The smile lit a spark of delight in me too. She'd seemed almost downcast underneath her appreciation when we'd first shown her the car this morning, but she really did like it. While I wasn't sure why she'd hesitated to embrace it at first, all that mattered was that she was happy now.

I loped over and grabbed her in a hug, pressing a kiss to the extra soft spot behind her ear at the same time. Lily let out a perfect breathy gasp of pleased surprise and then relaxed into my embrace. "Hello to you too. Are you trying to give me a heart attack?"

"You're irresistible," I informed her, and eased back just enough to clasp her hand and tug her with me. "I've been put in charge of buying takeout for dinner. Come with me."

She tipped her head toward the car. "We could drive."

"Nah, there are lots of good places around, and I like getting my legs moving." Ever since I'd dropped into this body, my nerves had twanged with a constant need for stimulation.

I would have popped in my earphones too and blared some of the pounding rock music I'd figured out how to download until it rattled my eardrums, but since Lily was with me, I wanted to be able to hear her. Even the tap of her shoes against the pavement—the glossy ones with the harder soles that she wore for work instead of her usual sneakers—invigorated me.

Because I was walking right here next to her. I *could* hear every sound she made with perfect clarity instead of the hazy blur of when I'd been without a body and so without proper ears. It really was a miracle.

I swung our hands together. Lily shook her head at me in exasperation, but she didn't stop me, so I figured she didn't mind my enthusiasm too much. She'd used to love my jokes and excited observations when she was younger… but she hadn't been through quite so much back then. I guessed it made sense she'd gotten more serious, more tense.

But the longer she was with us, the more she'd see she didn't need to be. Everything was going to be all right. She'd never have to worry again.

That cheerful thought was running through my head as we turned the corner toward a couple of my favorite restaurants on the main strip in town. Just as my mouth started watering while I debated between Thai and BBQ chicken, two burly men barreled across the street toward the alley we were passing and bumped into me.

Not just me. The one man's shoulder knocked Lily to the side, and protectiveness flared inside me with a sharp jolt that wouldn't have come at all if it'd only been me getting assaulted. I whipped around, defensive energy crackling through me, and that's the only reason I spotted the gleam of the thin blade tucked in the man's hand an instant before he jabbed it at me.

It really *was* an assault. He was aiming it at my chest, probably intending to stab it between my ribs into my heart, but my sudden movement threw him off. My arm flew up, smacking his hand wide. The blade sliced only the air.

A deeper fury blazed through me. I slammed my fist into the guy's head and yanked Lily behind me so I could act as her shield. The man reeled but swung at us again at the same time. Lily let out a squeak, and I snarled. I rammed my foot into my attacker's gut, electric energy crackling through my veins with the surge of feral emotion.

The other man sprang at me too, reaching for my throat. I shoved him to the side and whipped around to see the first man growling through bared teeth, his expression twisted with vicious rage.

Oh. Oops. I'd forgotten about my new talent for pummeling my feelings into people around me. Infecting him with the same fury I felt probably hadn't been a great strategy.

I moved to launch myself at him and end his murderous rage before he fully unleashed it, but he spun toward his friend instead of me. He slashed the knife through the air, cutting the other guy's cheek.

Huh. It seemed like I'd transferred the target of my anger along with the anger itself. Maybe that wasn't such a bad thing after all.

"What the fuck, you maniac?" the second guy spat out under his breath, raising his arms defensively. The other man just charged at him with nothing more than a wordless howl.

The second man yelped like a frightened puppy and took off down the street. The man with the knife raced after him, now letting out battle cries that sounded like something out of a civil war movie. I threw myself after both of them, my vision still glazed red, my pulse thrumming through my body.

Even if the one guy was acting in my favor for now, they both needed to pay for coming at me and Lily like this. We needed to know who the fuck they were. Had those overblown Skeleton dudes come at me? Was this about Ansel's whole deal again?

Kai would want me to batter that information out of these dudes, and I'd be only too happy to deal out that beating.

Down the street, the first guy dove into a car parked by the curb. The second man flung himself at the door, yanking it open even as the first set the engine roaring. The car tore off down the road with the man with the knife still hanging halfway out. Curses and thumps emanated from within. But it was still going too fast for me to catch them. It swerved around a bend, dangling legs and all, and vanished from view.

My heart thumped with the urge to chase them down somehow or other. But a chill flashed through me at the thought of Lily and how I'd left her behind. What if some other prick came at her?

I spun around and dashed back toward the alley where we'd been attacked. Lily had ducked into the mouth of it, mostly hidden in the shadows. She was looking down at her arm. As I reached her, my gaze caught on the streak of red showing through her sweater's sleeve, and rage blared through me all over again.

"He hurt you!" I said, grasping her wrist. The knife had cut right through the fabric and into her flesh. More blood was seeping out as I looked at it.

My teeth clenched. That knife had been meant for me. I hadn't taken the men out quickly enough—I hadn't managed to take them out at all. And Lily was hurt.

For a second, I felt torn down the middle, half of me wanting to rampage after the getaway car and smash the assholes' heads under my heels like busted jack-o-lanterns, the other half desperate to fix the damage done to my woman. She was bleeding right here in front of me.

The second urge won out. I ripped at my own shirt and wrenched the sleeve off from the shoulder seam.

"It's not that bad," Lily said, though I could hear the pain in her voice. "I don't think it cut that deep."

"I'll cut him into a billion fucking pieces," I promised, wrapping my sleeve around her forearm in some kind of bandage.

But how was I going to keep that promise? I didn't even know where those fuckers had come from, let alone where they were now. I wanted to tell Lily it'd all be okay, that all was good in the world again, but I didn't really believe that.

I raked my hand into my hair and stalked from one end of the alley to the other. It was a short walk, but I couldn't seem to stop myself. I smacked the toe of my shoe against one wall, swung around, paced over to kick the other, back and forth, like one of Nox's pinballs. So many emotions churned inside me that I had the sense that if I punched one of those walls right now, I'd send the whole thing tumbling down.

Probably on Lily's head. *That* wouldn't help anything. A groan of frustration reverberated out of me.

"Hey," Lily said. "Ruin, it's all right. It looks like the bleeding's already stopped. And you're okay, aren't you? Those asswipes were trying to *kill* you." Anger rippled through her voice. "I should have summoned a wave of sewer water to knock them over. I was so startled—"

"It's not your fault," I interrupted, still ping-ponging back and forth through the alley. "I should have realized—I should have taken them down faster—I shouldn't have let them *get away*—shit."

"It isn't your fault either," Lily said defiantly, but her eyes had widened with obvious worry. For *me*. When she was the one who'd actually been hurt here.

I had to get control of myself, find the upbeat attitude that'd gotten me through so much in life. But I couldn't seem to get a handle on it, and that only made me more pissed off with myself.

"Just—just stop," Lily said. "Stop and talk to me. People have done crap like this before. A couple weeks ago, a guy had a gun to your head. I almost got pirate-walked off a dock. What's different about this?"

I didn't exactly know, but I slowed and then came to a halt as her appeal sank in. She grasped my arm, and I bowed my head over hers, trying to sort through the thoughts ricocheting around in my head.

"They hurt you," I said, "and I couldn't even make them pay. And I can't make it better. I can't even cheer you up, because I can't cheer myself up, and that's the only thing I'm really good at normally. Being happy. Making people happy. If I can't manage that, then I'm just making things worse."

Even when I could cheer people up, that didn't necessarily stop the world from going to hell. Back when Lily was a kid, I'd brightened her days every way I could, but everything had gone horribly wrong anyway. I'd promised her I was there for her, and the pricks in her life had managed to rip her away from us anyway. All the hope I'd offered her had been a *lie*.

Lily's arms came up to wrap around me. She tucked her head against my shoulder. "You're not making things worse. And you don't have to be happy all the time. No one is."

"It's the only way I can make sure no one can bring me down," I said. "It's how I stop the guys from getting too low—it's how I keep you from getting too sad. But… you don't really like it anymore, do you? So it doesn't even work."

Lily hugged me tighter. "It does," she said fiercely. "I'm sorry if I haven't shown it. I—I don't always know how to react to how positive you are about everything usually, and maybe I get a bit grumbly about it, but it doesn't mean it bothers me. I like you the way you are. I like that you can see the good side of everything and that you make me notice the good sides too. Okay?"

Gradually, the clenching sensation inside me let go. I drank in Lily's watery floral smell and let out a ragged sigh. Then, with a glimmer of lightness inside me, a smile curled my lips. "You like me."

Lily snorted with amusement. "As if *that* hasn't been pretty obvious already. I wouldn't put up with you stealing half my bed otherwise."

"A quarter," I argued. "I leave most of it for you."

"Maybe a third, then," she said in that grumbly voice, but I could hear the thread of affection running through it. "You can't protect me from everything, Ruin. None of you can. I wish I could protect *you* better. But this is all new territory, so we'll just muddle through it the best way we can, right? And it's easier muddling if you're looking on the bright side for the rest of us. At least, I think so."

"Okay." The light inside me brightened into a glow that filled my entire chest. I pulled back to kiss Lily on the lips, reveling in the contented noise she made and the softness of her mouth. Then my stomach growled.

Lily laughed and poked me in the belly. "We'd better go get that dinner." She eyed my torn shirt. "If they're not going to look at us too weird."

I shrugged, barely feeling the chilly air on my bared arm. "It's a new fashion statement," I announced.

"If anyone could make it one, you could," Lily muttered through her smile.

I tucked my arm through hers and leaned close to murmur in her ear as I ushered her back onto the sidewalk. "We'll go get dinner, and when we get back to your apartment, I'm going to devour *you*."

The flush that colored Lily's cheeks made me want to bring her to moaning pleasure this very instant, but I couldn't get that distracted out here. The pricks who'd come after me were still lurking around.

If I got eyes on them again, I'd make them pay until they needed to be scraped off the sidewalk. And then I'd kill them a little more, just because.

Chapter Seventeen

Lily

THE FIRST SIGN that something wasn't quite right at work was the envelope labeled *URGENT* that was sitting in the middle of the packing table when I got back to the mailroom after a trip through the building with my cart. Rupert was standing over it with his arms folded over his chest.

"Why didn't you bring this one with you?" he demanded. "It was supposed to be in Horace Sanders' hands an hour ago!"

I stared at the offending envelope, which was a total stranger to me as far as I could remember. "It wasn't here an hour ago."

Rupert let out one of those huffs I was starting to think he should trademark. "Of course it was here an hour ago. The delivery manifest indicates it was delivered at ten this morning."

"Well, it wasn't *here* in the—"

"Stop making excuses," he barked at me. "You obviously weren't paying enough attention, and it got missed under the other mail. Just get it to Mr. Sanders now!"

I imagined his head heron pecking him hard enough to split his skull as I snatched up the envelope and hustled to the fifth floor to deliver it.

I might have thought it really had been a mistake on my part—that I was still kind of rattled from the attack on Ruin last night and the stinging scratch that was bandaged and hidden under the sleeve of my work blouse, and so had let something slip—except it happened again right after my lunch break. When I returned to the mailroom after my hasty meal, a small box was perched on one of the shelves in plain view, with big letters stamped on it saying, *To be received by noon.*

It was almost one.

Surely I hadn't missed seeing that package too, especially after I'd been on high alert because of my previous oversight? I got the distinct impression it was thumbing its nose at me… somehow, without having a nose or thumbs.

But there wasn't anyone to argue with about it, since Rupert had gone off to eat his own lunch. I just grabbed the package, muttered, "I hope you're happy with yourself" at it, and hightailed it to the eleventh floor as fast as my feet could take me. The woman I handed the box off to glowered at me as she took it.

Today was not going well at all. So much for proving to the Gauntts that I could handle the pace of the head office.

As soon as that thought crossed through my mind, I froze in place.

That was it, wasn't it? They didn't *want* me to be able to handle things here. They'd clearly hoped to push me out. When I hadn't taken the direct bait, they'd decided to force the issue rather than asking nicely.

Someone was messing with the mail to make me look incompetent. Unfortunately, they were succeeding.

I didn't have much time to dig into that problem, or I'd fall behind on the duties I actually could keep up with. The Gauntts hadn't been lying that this was a busy workplace. I spent a few minutes searching the mailroom for any tucked away letters or packages or, hell, secret passageways, but when I didn't turn up anything right away, I had to get back on the everyday mail sorting. There were a whole bunch of glossy laminated envelopes that needed to be out of here within the hour.

Rupert returned while I was doing that, gave me a vaguely disgruntled look as if I were slacking rather than doing the basics of my job, and puttered around for several minutes before heading off with a small cart.

Was he involved in the plot to screw me over? He definitely didn't seem all that happy about me being here, but that'd started before I'd talked to the Gauntts.

I had no idea how to tell whether he was actively sabotaging me on their instructions or just being a sourpuss about the fact that I had a fashion sense he didn't totally approve of.

I was just finishing with the batch of mailings when a slim man with brown hair combed forward so straight you could have used it as a ruler marched into the room. When he spotted me, he kept marching right over to my table.

"I'm admin assistant to Casper Dodds. He was supposed to have an important package delivered this morning, but it hasn't been brought to his desk. The instructions should have been *very* clear."

A chill trickled down my back. I recognized Dodds as one of the bigwigs who had their offices on the upper floors. I'd never met this admin assistant because all his communications went through the woman who was secretary to the secretaries.

I waved vaguely at the shelving units and empty carts around me. "All the incoming mail has already been distributed through the building. This stuff is outgoing. I can't bring up what hasn't arrived."

The assistant drew his chin up higher, as if that would make him taller than me instead of the same height. "We have confirmation from the sender that it was shipped out, and confirmation from the delivery service that it arrived at this building. I hope you aren't suggesting that you *lost* it."

"No, no, of course not," I said quickly. I definitely couldn't accuse the owners of the company of having hidden it away to make a lowly mail clerk look bad.

Gritting my teeth, I crouched down to check if any packages could have fallen to the floor beneath the tables or shelving units. Wouldn't it be nice to get a solution that easy? But there was nothing down there except a few scraps of paper the janitor would sweep up and a worn spot on the linoleum where Rupert liked to pace.

Oh, and a frog. It hopped over to me from the other side of the table, like I'd ducked down here to have a chat. Perfect.

"I'm *waiting*," the admin assistant said in a voice that was freezing over. "A lot of business is riding on Mr. Dodds receiving this package in a timely matter. If you've dropped the ball on it, I'll have to report the matter higher up."

Shit. And that might be enough of an excuse for the big bosses to kick me to the curb. I wet my lips, scrambling for an answer. What the hell could be in this package that was so important anyway? A scroll holding the secrets of eternal life?

The Skullbreakers might have been able to help advise on that one.

The frog hopped closer, but it wasn't carrying any errant packages. It was only hanging out here making me look crazy.

I paused, letting that thought sink in. A sliver of a smile tugged at my lips.

I set down my hand and surreptitiously scooped up the frog and set it on my shoulder—at the opposite side from where the assistant was standing. Then I straightened back up with my arms at my sides, paying no attention to it at all.

"I'm sorry," I said in an even voice. "My supervisor should be back soon—it's possible he took the package with him on his last delivery run. In the meantime—"

The assistant's gaze had zeroed in on my shoulder. Or rather, the friendly amphibian currently perched on my shoulder. His eyes bugged out. "Why are you carrying around a *frog*?"

I blinked at him, knitting my brow as if I didn't understand what he'd said. "Pardon me?"

He flicked his hand toward my shoulder. "There's a frog sitting on your shoulder! Where did that come from? What are you trying to pull here?"

I glanced over at my shoulder and gave my best impression of seeing only the fabric of my sweater. Then I gave the assistant an even more puzzled look. "What are *you* trying to pull? I don't have anything on my shoulder. And how could I have a frog with me?"

I must have been convincing enough in my disbelief, because the man grimaced and rubbed at his eyes. "It's right *there*," he said, and motioned at me even more briskly, as if to poke my slimy companion.

I couldn't let him touch it and feel that it was really there. I flinched as if I thought he was going to smack me, and the frog went leaping away to who knew where. Hopefully somewhere far out of sight. But the other outcome of my reaction was that the assistant's fingers swiped over my chest instead of my shoulder.

He jerked his hand back as if he'd been burned, but I'd already urged my eyebrows to shoot up as far as they could go. "Whoa!" I said, summoning all the offense I could. "You come down here threatening my job and then try to grope me?"

His face stiffened in an expression of horror. "It was an accident—the frog—" His gaze darted around searching out the little green animal and clearly didn't find it.

I set my hands on my hips with all the bravado I could muster. "That's a pretty crazy excuse for feeling me up. What is it with you and this frog?"

"Crazy," he murmured to himself, and shook his head as if trying to clear it. "It was *there…*"

"Sure," I scoffed. "Like I wouldn't be able to tell if I had a freaking *frog* sitting on me. I think I should be the one putting in a complaint to HR."

The man blanched. He held up his hands and backed away from me, all his previous haughtiness vanished. "No. There's no need for that. I've just—it's been a tense day—I promise you I didn't mean to touch you at all."

He spun around and hustled out of the mailroom without another word about this super special package. Probably more worried about what was going on inside his head than inside any cardboard box. I exhaled with only a small sense of triumph. I still had to *find* that package before someone else came around demanding it.

I stuck my current batch of envelopes into the spot for outgoing mail and glanced around. The mailroom didn't lead directly outside. Delivery trucks parked by an entrance around the back of the building and unloaded their shipments there, and some worker or another carried the loads of mail into this room, just as they periodically came by and picked up the outgoing bins before one or another truck was due.

Anything coming in could be intercepted along that short route, by the workers themselves or someone coming by under the pretense of overseeing them.

I darted out into the hall and over to the back doors. There was nothing to see outside except a stretch of gloomy asphalt with a currently empty lane and rows of cars parked farther from the building. No precious packages chilling out there.

I pulled back into the building and scanned the hall. There was another room between the door and the mailroom—a supply room I'd had to go into only once in search of a new pen. Most of the mailroom-specific supplies were kept right on hand.

Pulling open that door, I peered into the dim room. My fumbling hand found a light switch. There were shelves stacked with boxes of pens, pencils, and highlighters, reams of printer and photocopier paper, spare keyboards and computer mice… Oh, and there was a cardboard box that didn't look like it really belonged shoved under one of those shelving units with only a bit of the corner in view.

I knelt down and tugged it out. Yep, addressed to Casper Dodds, marked urgent. Someone had stashed it in here, probably to drop it off in the mailroom later as if it'd been there all along, trying to make *me* feel insane.

So much for that, suckers, I thought at my unknown opponents, and pictured waving the package in Nolan Gauntt's face for good measure. Then I dashed off to deliver it to its intended recipient like it was a box of dicks I couldn't wait to get off my hands.

I'd gotten through this attempt at ousting me, but it didn't seem likely that it'd be the last. How far would they go next time?

Chapter Eighteen

Lily

I'd told the guys that I didn't want them experimenting with their superpowers in my apartment, especially now that I'd need to be claiming that damage deposit tout suite. But their supernatural gifts involved frying things, and mine only brought all the frogs in the yard —or got things kind of wet. So I cut myself a little slack when it came to practicing.

And if I did it while they were out doing their gangster things, they couldn't even hassle me about any apparent hypocrisy.

Because I didn't want to explode the pipes in the apartment, and working on subtle effects was better for my control anyway, I'd set up a few water bottles on the table as well as some empty cups. My goal was to practice compelling the water out of the bottles into the cups with minimal spillage. And also to get it jumping between bottles or work my powers on more than one at a time, if I felt ready to get that ambitious.

If I ended up having to go head-to-head with the Gauntts, I'd better be able to wield my marshy magic with all possible skill. I didn't want there to be any chance of screwing up. And the clearer it was that

I was a conscious force to be reckoned with rather than the pipes just happening to burst at the wrong moment, the better.

The hard part, like when I'd been down at the marsh, was getting myself keyed up enough to provoke the hum of power inside me. I still couldn't accomplish anything just by glowering at the table. I dragged in a breath and thought back to the prick who'd barged into the mailroom to berate me—and the Gauntts setting me up so I'd look totally incompetent.

My hands curled into fists at my sides. My jaw tightened. And anger resonated through my chest at just the right harmony.

"No fucking way," I informed the bottle I decided represented Nolan Gauntt, because it looked a little more puffed up than the others. Pretentious prick. "You aren't knocking me down that easily."

I concentrated on the liquid contents, silently calling them to me. But not in a sudden splash—slowly, deliberately.

A wavering stream of water rose up from the mouth of the bottle. A few splatters dropped to dapple the tabletop with tiny puddles. A sudden thin jet shot out and smacked me in the face.

I sputtered, and the rest of the water splashed onto the table, some of it dripping off the sides.

Cursing Nolan—both the real one and his bottle equivalent—and all things aquatic, I sopped up the mess with a dishtowel and squared my shoulders to try again. At least this time I had plenty of irritation coursing through me before I even thought about the jerks I was up against.

After several attempts and a few more watery facials, I finally managed to get all the remaining liquid from one bottle into one of the cups. Then I emptied two simultaneously, switching my focus back and forth as one or the other stream got shaky.

I was about halfway through when a knock thumped on the apartment door.

I flinched, and water spewed everywhere. And I do mean everywhere. It sprayed droplets across the kitchen cabinets, counter, and fridge, rained over the floor, and spurted all over my chest as if several aquatic gods had gotten very enthusiastic with their money shots all at once.

"Lily?" Marisol's voice carried through the door. "Are you home?"

My pulse hiccupped. I grabbed the dish towel, which was unfortunately only slightly less wet than I was, and dabbed at the sopping spots on my shirt as I hustled over to the door. "I'm here. Is everything okay?"

I opened the door maybe a little more frantically than was totally necessary. My little sister peered in at me, her backpack slung casually over one shoulder, and gave me a perfect expression of teenage bemusement. I realized that drips were trickling down my arms from my hair. I basically looked like I'd stepped out of a shower I'd been taking fully clothed.

"Are *you* okay?" Marisol asked.

"Yes, yes," I said, fumbling for an explanation. "I was just... washing dishes, dropped a pot into the sink too fast and splashed myself. No big deal. It'll dry."

Marisol nodded slowly. "Okay. I just—I got your address from some paper at the house. I think the hospital sent it to Mom when you were moving back. I thought since we're going to be living together soon anyway, hopefully it'd be all right if I hung out here for a little while? I can't get away with browsing the bookstore all weekend, and being at home..." She made a face.

A pang of mourning for all the things my sister should have had resonated through me. I motioned her into the apartment past me. "Of course. I—" I followed her path with my gaze, and took in exactly what I was welcoming her into for the first time.

Not that I hadn't known how crappy this apartment was or how chaotic it'd become since the guys had essentially moved in. But I hadn't really *looked* at it, not from the perspective of someone who didn't already have all the backstory, in a while.

A puddle of water was still spreading across the table and dripping into another puddle on the floor. Bottles and glasses stood in its midst like transparent islands. In the living room area, the guys had been cleaning up after their constant snacking, but a couple of chip bags and a few wrappers had been missed, peeking around the shabby furniture. The uninflated mattresses and sleeping bags had been tossed into a haphazard heap like a fabric mountain looming over the back of the futon.

The futon itself was stacked with Kai's latest haul of library news magazines, while the crates that served as end tables had become display stands for Jett's favorite artistic compositions. One of those involved my salt and pepper shakers standing upside down with a tissue box balanced on top of them and an empty Chinese takeout container on top of that. The other was a painted piece of paper folded to stand upright, which wouldn't have been all that concerning if I wasn't abruptly sure that several of the deeper reddish-brown streaks were blood, not paint.

And the place smelled. Not in a horribly offensive way I didn't think, but in a leathery, boozy, vaguely musky way it definitely hadn't before four former gangsters had moved in.

Marisol stopped in her tracks a few steps inside, taking the whole scene in. Her nose wrinkled for a second, and her posture tensed. I got the impression she was considering backing right out again.

"It's been a crazy few weeks," I said quickly. *And I mean that literally.* "I had some unexpected guests come by. But the new apartment I've lined up in Mayfield is way bigger and nicer than this. You'll love it! And we'll get better furniture and stuff as soon as we can." The guys would probably volunteer to fund an entire Pinterest makeover, but I was trying to rely on their generosity—and the questionable methods that funded that generosity—as little as possible.

"Okay," Marisol said again, but she definitely sounded more hesitant now. My chest constricted. She glanced around, her hand tightening around the strap of her backpack. "Can I sit down?"

It was a reasonable question, because the chairs by the kitchen table all held puddles of their own, and Kai's magazines had the prime spots on the futon. I rushed over and hefted them onto the floor, which wouldn't score me points for neatness but at least opened up a seat.

"There you go," I said. "Do you want anything to drink? Or a snack? I'm sure I've got something around." Please, dear Lord, let the guys not have completely cleared out the fridge before they left.

Please let them not come bursting back in here while Marisol was around. I still had to prepare her for meeting *that* craziness up close and personal.

"No, I'm fine," Marisol said in a tone that didn't sound fine at all. She was probably terrified to eat anything that'd been stored in this place.

I groped for the right thing to say to make this better. It wasn't like I could tell her I'd been experimenting with supernatural abilities or that I'd unexpectedly had some childhood friends I'd thought were imaginary show up as houseguests with a kind of skewed sense of propriety. Although maybe she already knew something about my abilities? I wasn't sure how much she'd seen when I'd freaked out all those years ago.

There were still too many things locked away in that blank gap in my memory.

The spot with the birthmark under my arm started to itch. I let myself scratch at it as I sat down on the other side of the futon.

Marisol had started studying Jett's painting. I guessed that wasn't surprising considering her own visual art interests, but I didn't really like her looking at it so close up. Much more chance she'd notice the odd hue to those particular streaks. And had he incorporated some smears of juice from one of Ruin's lemons too?

"This is kind of cool," Marisol said. "Did you make it?"

I couldn't blame her for the skepticism in her voice. When I'd doodled alongside her when we were younger, my attempts at drawing the same sorts of mythical creatures she did had generally resulted in them looking like centaurs or nymphs that'd been run over by a tank. And then pecked at by vultures for good measure.

"Ah, no," I said. "One of my guests. He's quite an artist. You'd probably like him." I hoped that was true. At least she had something in common with one of the guys.

Marisol's gaze flicked to me, and I realized my mistake a moment too late. "*He*?" she repeated, arching her eyebrows. "Was he one of those guys who honked at us the other day at the house? Is this a *boy*friend?"

The funny thing was, out of all four of the guys, Jett was the one who'd been least enthusiastic about anything resembling a dating relationship. But I wasn't going to open that can of worms with my little sister. Instead, I fixed her with my best big sister glower. "Should I start asking you about your love life? All the boys you've been crushing on at school?"

The blush that spread across her cheeks told me I'd won the standoff. She stuck her tongue out at me and then paused as if formulating another question. I wasn't sure whether to be relieved or have another panic attack when a text alert chimed on my phone.

It was from Nox. *We're heading back soon. Figured we'd bring lunch. What do you want? Ruin promises that he'll keep his extreme spice to himself.*

My lips twitched with a smile, and Marisol's eyebrows lifted even higher. Panic attack—panic attack was definitely the correct option here.

No need to bring me anything, I typed hurriedly, and then inspiration struck. *I'm going out to lunch with my sister.*

Perfect! It got Marisol out of the apartment and away from the guys' arrival all in one go, without making her feel unwelcome.

"Hey," I said to her, getting up. "Why don't we get out of this place and grab something to eat? It'll be on me, of course. Do you still like that burger joint over on Washington Avenue?"

"Well..." Marisol said as she stood up too.

I nudged her with my elbow. "It's okay if your tastes have changed since you were nine. I realize you're a sophisticated sixteen-year-old now."

Marisol grinned. "I'd love to go to the Greek place that opened up on Main Street. I had no idea souvlaki was so good! But Wade doesn't like it, so we only went the one time." A shadow crossed her face.

I'd have cracked open my own ribs to stop her from ever having to look like that again. At least I could give her a temporary reprieve. Soon—soon she'd be away from him forever.

"Sounds perfect to me," I said, tugging her along. "And you can tell me all about what kind of school you want me to find for you in Mayfield. I'm sure they've got more choice than we have out here."

My sister's smile came back, just as bright as before, and that felt like a victory—even when I had to stop at the door and rush back to change into a dry shirt, because I'd forgotten my earlier watery accident.

I managed to feel confident through the lunch and after I waved goodbye to Marisol and returned to the apartment to hear about the guys' adventures trying to arrange a confrontation with this Skeleton Corps gang, all the way until I was crawling into bed that night.

But the doubts must have been lingering underneath. It felt like the second I closed my eyes, I was drowning again. The weeds were clutching my ankles and the marsh-water closing over my head. The darkness was choking out the light and suffocating me. Twisting currents turned my skin clammy; chilly liquid flooded my lungs. I kicked and kicked but I just kept sinking down—

I woke up with a jolt and found myself drenched in a cold sweat. Swallowing hard, I swiped my hand across my damp forehead. The darkness of the cramped room around me felt almost as suffocating as my nightmare had.

I'd lost something. Something that was buried way down in the murky depths of my mind, beyond my reach.

For all I knew, it was lurking there ready to pull me under at the moment I least expected it. And if Marisol was with me when that happened, it might drag her down too.

Chapter Nineteen

Nox

"THEY'RE OBVIOUSLY *REALLY* scared of us," Ruin said in his usual breezy way as we got off our bikes outside our new base of Skullbreaker operations. "Why else would the Skeleton Corps be avoiding us so much? They know we'll crush them as soon as we get the chance."

Kai raised his eyebrows at our eternal optimist. "Or they don't think we're worth bothering with. They don't know who we are. We haven't established anything yet. The fact that we're bothering them about murders from more than twenty years ago probably makes them think we've got a screw loose."

"Or they know they're guilty and so they're laying low," Ruin insisted.

"We'll dig them out eventually," I said, stopping at the former restaurant's door to pull out my keys. "And then they'll find out just how many screws got loosened in the last twenty years."

Before I could put the keys to use, a figure got out of a car a little way down the street and ambled over to us with a casual but purposeful air. It was obvious he was aiming for us. I paused, tossing the keys in my hand and studying him.

He looked the equivalent of five in gangster terms, like a kid who's gotten confident on his feet but has no idea how much he doesn't know yet. In actual years, he wasn't much more than a kid either. With that babyface, I didn't figure he'd hit twenty yet. I'd wreaked plenty of havoc before I'd reached official adulthood myself, but he obviously wasn't any sort of high authority figure.

"Gentlemen," he said with a sarcastic lilt to his tone as he came to a stop in front of us. I immediately bristled at the aura of condescension radiating off him, as if he found it *amusing* that he was stooping to speak to us at all. "I heard you've been trying to arrange a meeting with the Skeleton Corps."

At those last two words, I perked up despite my annoyance. Maybe all the busting heads we'd been doing for the past few days had gotten some results.

"We have," I said, stepping in front of the others with a flex of my muscles, which through the magic of ghostly possession and all the workouts I'd been getting while busting those heads were now back to nearly their previous substantial brawn. "Are they ready to talk to us?"

"*I'm* here to talk to you," the kid said, like we should be honored he'd bothered to grace us with his presence. "If you've got anything to say worth passing on, I'll bring it to the rest of them."

I cocked my head, looking him up and down and not finding anything that made me happier in my assessment. The guy clearly hadn't even been born yet when our first lives had ended. He'd know fuck-all about our murders.

I jerked my chin toward him. "We need to speak to someone higher up, someone who's been part of the crew for a while."

"The Skeleton Corps doesn't show up at anyone's beck and call," the kid retorted. "And nothing we've heard has made us think you've got anything to say worth bringing in people who have much better things to spend their time on."

My hands clenched at my sides, and Jett let out a peeved grunt behind me. We'd show them what we were worth, that was for sure.

"We need information about a hostile takedown in Lovell Rise twenty-one years ago," I said. "We were told your boys are the ones most likely to know who was involved. Or maybe your boys are the ones who carried it out."

The kid shrugged. "And why should we dredge up ancient history for a bunch of nobodies who've been going around making a nuisance of themselves?"

Ruin gave a low growl. I suspected we were all quickly getting to the same page that there needed to be a little more head-busting before the day was over.

I moved closer, drawing myself up as straight as I could so I loomed a good six inches over the kid. "Why should we have to explain ourselves to you? There are things you don't know, pipsqueak. Things that are important that you haven't got a clue about. You can get your head out of your ass and arrange a real meet-up, or maybe we'll insert a few more things into that hole for proper motivation."

The guy shook his head with an air like he was five seconds away from tsking his fucking tongue at us. "I'll go with neither. Have a nice life!"

He turned on his heel like he thought we were going to let him just walk away with that send-off. Time to show these pretentious pricks exactly who they were dealing with—and that we wouldn't be ignored.

I made a quick gesture with my hand as I lunged at the guy. My friends followed without a second's hesitation.

He wasn't a total idiot, I'd give him that. He dodged my first punch even though it came from behind and swung around, jerking a gun from the waist of his jeans. But I didn't even give him time to aim it. I was already smashing my elbow into his wrist.

The pistol skittered under a car. The kid sprang backward, and then Ruin and Jett were on him.

Ruin plowed right into the guy, flipping him off his feet. Jett caught him in mid tumble and slammed him downward so his skull smacked against the concrete. As the kid let out a pained grunt, Kai swept in with a few quick strikes that sent him spinning on his head.

Jett chuckled darkly as he whipped the guy around even faster, turning him into a human dreidel. The kid swung out an arm and managed to grab Jett's leg, but Jett simply released him right as I landed a kick to his side that sent him sprawling on his stomach instead.

Before he could scramble upright, I planted one foot between his shoulder blades with just enough weight to strain but not fracture his spine.

"You delivered the Skeleton Corps' message," I said, ignoring the curses he was spitting at us. "Here's one from us: We don't fuck around. It's up to you whether more of you end up bruised and bleeding, but we're getting our answers either way. You know where to find us when you're ready to talk real business."

I finished off with a boot to his butt. He threw himself to his feet and whirled around, but looking at the four of us while he stood unarmed and battered, he made one smart choice. Instead of taking another jab at us, he staggered to his car and dove into the driver's seat.

It only took him a matter of seconds to start the ignition and roar off down the street like a bat out of hell. Or maybe into hell, from the way things were going.

Ruin whooped and pumped his hand in the air. I couldn't share the same exuberance.

"We have to be even more on guard from now on," I told my men. "They might take this as a sign that we deserve serious consideration—but that serious consideration might mean attempting to wipe us off the map all over again. Stay alert, especially around the new headquarters."

I wanted to feel satisfied, but we hadn't gotten any answers at all, only confirmation that these Skeleton Corps assholes knew we existed. If that got us slaughtered all over again because I hadn't made a clear enough impact, I'd come back just to kill *myself* for being such a disaster.

We headed into the former restaurant, but even sitting on the fake throne didn't give me the boost of certainty I wanted. Also, it made me think of Lily and all the fun we'd had there the other night, which I couldn't have without her here. I gave Jett a little while longer to finish rearranging the tables to his indecipherable standards and then announced that we were heading back to her apartment.

Apparently it was a day of interruptions, though. We'd only just come out to our bikes when a white van pulled up on the other side of the street. I wouldn't have thought much of it if three hulking dudes hadn't jumped out of the back, charged straight at Kai, snatched him up, and hauled him away.

"What the fuck!" I shouted, charging after them. But the element of surprise had bought them just enough time that the doors were slamming shut as I reached them. The van roared off down the street so abruptly it nearly tore off my fingers where I'd been grabbing at the handles.

I hurtled back to the bikes and threw myself onto my own. "After them!" I hollered, and the three of us careened after the fleeing vehicle.

Jumbled thoughts whirled through my head as we sped after the van. Had the Skeleton Corps retaliated already? We'd only sent off their kid about a half hour ago. And why would they have wanted specifically Kai? He'd done the least amount of fighting. If they were going to target anyone, it should have been me.

The men who'd grabbed Kai hadn't given me a gangster vibe, now that I looked back on the moment. They'd charged in there so quickly I hadn't had much time to reflect on the details, but they'd been wearing plain tees and slacks, and I didn't remember any tattoos. Tough but more clean-cut than you'd typically get from guys working the street, especially the muscle.

It didn't matter. Whoever they were, they were going to pay. Nobody messed with my men and survived.

The van swerved around a corner up ahead. I motioned to Jett and Ruin and shouted my instructions over the rumble of the engines. "Stay on their tail, as close as you can get. I'm going to try to cut them off."

They both nodded. I shot down the nearest parallel side-street, gunning my engine to even greater speeds. I was probably leaving rubber behind on the asphalt, but that was a small sacrifice to make to the gods of the road.

I wove in between the other vehicles on the street, ignoring the protests and insults yelled after me. The van wouldn't have the same advantage. I needed to get ahead of them. And if there was a space I could squeeze through, who the hell was anyone to tell me I shouldn't take that opening?

After five blocks, I estimated I had enough of a lead. I veered down one of the cross-streets and slowed as I reached the next intersection.

The van was just a block away, rushing toward me. I pulled out my gun and got into position. As I shot at its tires to blow them out, I pulled my bike partly in front of them.

Two of my bullets hit their marks. The van swerved and shuddered as the tires went flat. Jett and Ruin zoomed up on either side.

The guy staring at me through the windshield was about half the size of the hulks who'd kidnapped Kai and looked totally terrified. I shot him through the glass and tore around to the back of the van, not caring about the shrieks that were starting to rise up from bystanders along the street or the traffic we'd stalled. We'd be out of here long before the police could show up.

The back doors flew open as the three of us converged on them. Jett and Ruin had taken out their guns too. In near-perfect unison, we blasted away the three beefy dudes who were making to spring out at us.

They crumpled in a pile by the back tires. It'd been almost too easy. I squinted into the dimness of the van's interior to see what the hell they'd been doing to our guy… and found him tied up and gagged with four dorks who looked like they'd stepped out of a suburban soap opera poised around him.

The middle-aged woman had a fluffy pixie cut and a cardigan tied around her shoulders. The man next to her had slicked his hair back like a business exec and stuffed his broad chest into a polo shirt. They were staring at me with panicked expressions, all the color drained from their faces. The older man and the twenty-something woman with them looked like they were ready to puke.

These were definitely not gangsters.

"Who the hell are you?" I demanded, leaping into the back of the van with my gun still ready. "Get away from him."

"He's our son," the middle-aged woman wailed even as the man I figured was her husband wrapped her arms around her defensively. "I don't know what you've done to our Zach, but he belongs with us."

Oh, fuck. It was Kai's host's family. Unlike Jett's, these folks hadn't been satisfied with phone calls.

Ruin had dashed over to free Kai. As soon as the gag was out of his mouth, our smart-aleck sneered at the suburbanites. "I'm not your son anymore. I don't need any fucking intervention."

"But—" the woman started.

Kai got up as soon as Ruin had untied his legs and glowered down at her. "I'm an adult. That makes this kidnapping, you idiots. Which is illegal, in case you didn't know."

We weren't really in a position to be lecturing them about criminal activities, but his supposed parents cowered a little.

"We're looking after 'Zach' now," I said, folding my arms over my chest. "He's got better things to do than spend time with you all. If you hire any other thugs to arrange some stupid 'intervention,' next time you'll be lying on the pavement with them. Got it?"

At my last words, all four of the family members flinched. No one argued. I nodded to Kai, and we tramped out of the van to return to our bikes, leaving the dimwits inside to figure out where they went from here with a busted van and four murder victims.

Kai tipped his head to me as he got onto Jett's bike behind him. "Thanks. They were babbling all kinds of new age feelings woo woo to try to un-brainwash me or something. And people think *we're* crazy."

The sense of accomplishment I'd been missing earlier trickled up through my torso. I'd done my job as the leader of the Skullbreakers—I'd protected my own. I gave him a grim but genuine smile. "We've got your back, like always."

If only we could have hoped that the Skeleton bozos would be half as easy to terrorize.

Chapter Twenty

Lily

I'd been in worse ladies' rooms, but the restroom on the fourteenth floor of the Thrivewell Enterprises building wasn't exactly a pleasant place to while away the hours. For one, I had to stay in the stall perched on the toilet's tank with my feet on the seat so that anyone who poked their head into the room wouldn't spot my shoes. For another, the sickly-sweet smell of the cleaner they used to make sure the room didn't smell like urine was almost as bad as urine itself.

And then, an hour after my shift ended, the lights went off. Wonderful.

I distracted myself by fiddling around with my phone and hoping that Kai was having at least as bad a time in the men's washroom, since this strategy had been his idea, after all. We'd slipped away right at the time when our shifts usually ended and were now waiting out the last few stragglers in the office. Kai had determined that the security guard did one sweep of all the floors and then settled in on the ground level to watch over the entrance. As soon as he was gone, we could roam freely.

And that meant we should be able to roam right up to Nolan

Gauntt's office. *He* definitely wouldn't be working late, because he and Marie had that benefit dinner tonight. Kai had managed to pick up the code to unlock the private upper-floor elevator from surreptitiously watching the secretary. How he planned to get into Nolan's office itself, I didn't know, but he rarely seemed to act without a strategy in place.

I'd been sitting there another half hour in the dark when the text from Kai finally arrived, with a faint vibration of my phone since I'd turned all the sounds off for this mission. *All clear. Meet me at the stairs.*

On my way, I wrote back, and scrambled out of the stall as fast as my feet could take me.

It was dark in the vast room of cubicles too, only a thin light emanating from the emergency exit sign over the stairwell. The glow gleamed off Kai's glasses as he waited for me to reach him. He motioned for me to follow him into the stairwell.

"I heard the security guy go by twenty minutes ago," he said in a low voice as we headed up to the highest floor we could access by stairs. "Based on his typical schedule, he should have taken the elevator down to the lobby about ten minutes ago. As long as we don't make a racket loud enough to reach down there—and we're careful going out the back way—we should be fine."

I worried at my lower lip. "Are you sure there aren't any security cameras in Nolan's office?"

"There could be," Kai said with no apparent concern. "But it'd only be something he could check on his own after we're long gone. The head honcho wouldn't want any lowly grunt workers getting a glimpse inside his private sanctum." He patted the leather shoulder bag he was carrying. "We'll put on ski masks before we go up that far so that if any of the top brass checks the footage later, if they bother to, they won't be able to tell who we were."

"Okay." I suspected Nolan would be able to guess, but what really mattered was whether he'd have any proof he could give to the police. I suspected I was still on kind of shaky ground with the local law enforcement after the whole being accused of spray-painting dicks on the grocery store incident.

Kai moved with an eager, purposeful energy I didn't often see in him. It reminded me of when we'd gone to interview for these jobs in the first place. Seeing that assured intensity in him again sent a tingle over my skin that I really couldn't indulge right now.

On the fifteenth floor, there was a door to the next level of the stairwell, which was naturally locked. The bigwigs needed an escape route, but they didn't want us plebs having access to them through it. We slipped out into the room where Kai usually worked instead.

He took my hand, the skin-to-skin contact sending a ripple of heat up my arm, and guided me through the dim space toward the exclusive elevator. We'd almost reached that end of the room when the regular elevator, behind us, pinged to signal that the car was about to arrive.

"Shit," Kai hissed, and hauled me through a doorway just ahead of us.

The door clicked shut in our wake. My hip banged into some large rectangular object just inside. Kai steadied me and tugged me farther inside, past the thing.

"Photocopy room," he muttered under his breath. "Security officer must have forgotten something. No reason for him to come in here."

This room was pitch black. I reached out and found the hulking photocopier just inches from where I was standing. My elbow brushed a cabinet on the other side. The space wasn't much bigger than a closet.

We stood there, no sound but the faint rasp of our breaths and the thumping of my heart—until the thud of heavy footsteps reached my ears. It sounded like the security guard was heading right this way.

I froze, knowing we had nowhere to run. Kai's grip on my hand tightened. He held in place for the space of a few more heartbeats and then, when the footsteps came even closer, yanked me deeper into the room.

We stumbled into the gap between the back wall and the cabinet, so narrow I had to round my shoulders so they'd fit. When the door handle squeaked, Kai pushed closer against me to stay completely hidden by the cabinet.

Our bodies aligned from chest to feet. His compact frame was hotter than I'd expected, almost blazing, and it set my own alight as his breath tickled over my face. The scent of his skin filled my nose, a citrusy tang mingled with musky leather. And despite the precarious situation we were in—or maybe partly because of it—a different sort of adrenaline raced through me alongside my fear.

I had the sudden, wild urge to pull him as tight against me as I could, to soak in all his heat and the solid planes of footballer muscle that had gotten leaner but not disappeared since he'd taken over Zach's body. To run my hands down his chest and up into his hair. To find out what noises I could provoke from this intently analytical man's mouth.

He'd said before that he'd noticed my "appeal." That he wasn't going to pursue it only because it'd be a distraction. Of course, what else could it be right now when we were literally in the middle of the riskiest gambit we'd attempted since setting our sights on Nolan Gauntt?

The door swung open. My pulse raced even faster. The beam of a flashlight bounced around the room behind us, and there was a faint tap of something being lifted off a hard surface.

"There you are," the security guard said with a self-deprecating chuckle, and left again with a thump of the door.

Neither Kai nor I moved. There was no way of knowing how close the guard still was, whether he might hear us. Then, slower than before, the heavy footsteps thudded away. The faint chime of the elevator admitting him filtered through the door.

I sagged against the wall. Kai bowed his head over mine, his hands braced by my shoulders. Ever so slowly, he lifted one to trace his fingers along my jaw. It was a whisper of a touch, but it sent a giddy shiver over my skin.

"You smell so fucking good," he muttered.

I held in the giggle that bubbled in my chest. Longing swelled around it, spreading through my limbs and up into my throat. "So do you."

Kai's breath hitched slightly. He shifted his stance, and for one wrenching moment I thought he was going to pull away even though every particle of my body was screaming for… something.

"Fuck," he muttered, with an almost desperate edge to his voice that I'd never heard before. Then his head jerked down, and his mouth crashed into mine.

This. *This* was what my entire being had been screaming for. I kissed him back with everything I had in me.

Kai wrenched off his glasses and shoved them into a pocket before tilting his face at an even more delicious angle. He pressed against me like he had when the security guard had opened the door, but with a very different sense of urgency.

I ran my fingers into his floppy hair like I'd imagined, rumpling it from its previous neatly gelled, business-appropriate state, and couldn't resist tugging on it. A groan reverberated from Kai's throat, even more intoxicating than I'd hoped for.

"Fucking hell," he murmured against my lips. "Fuck it. He's gone now. We have time. We'd fucking well better have time."

With those last words, he caught me by the waist and spun me around, with every appearance on making good on those f-bombs. My ass bumped the photocopier. He shoved the top section back and set me on the edge of the flat, glossy surface underneath. Then he tugged my face down to meet his so he could claim my lips again.

It was a little strange, perched in a spot that made me a few inches taller than him. A weird sense of power washed over me with a thrill I couldn't deny.

I kissed Kai back hard, absorbing the unexpected softness of his lips, the flavor of sugared coffee that slipped from his tongue over mine, the determined sweep of his fingers down the sides of my body to my thighs.

He yanked my skirt all the way to my waist in one swift motion and peeled my panties off an instant later, leaving them to hang from one ankle. The smooth surface of the photocopier pressed into my naked ass. I only had a few seconds to register that before one of our legs jostled a control, and suddenly the machine was humming underneath me.

The vibration rippled through my sex, making me gasp. Light flashed over us. Kai blinked and fished a paper from the output tray, a lewd grin curving his mouth. He waved it in the thin glow of the machine's running lights, showing off the photocopied globes of my butt cheeks. "Now that's fucking art."

A blush burned my other cheeks even as I laughed. Kai folded the paper into a few squares and tucked it into his pocket. His hands returned to my thighs, stroking up and down them as he eased closer between them. His eyes smoldered as he held my gaze.

"I think we're going to need to have a little more fun with that. But first..."

He jerked me forward so I was balanced even more precariously on the edge of the machine. Our mouths collided, my weight leaning into him. He held me firmly, dipping his hands beneath me to squeeze my ass in time with the rhythmic motions of his lips and tongue. I shivered with delight, aching for more.

Still holding on to him for balance, I let my other hand drift down over his chest between us, all the way to the waist of his slacks. When my fingers traced the bulge of his erection, he groaned and ground into me. The tantalizing friction shocked a whimper out of me.

"Naughty girl," Kai said in a voice that sounded just as pleased as Nox's when he called me a "good girl." "You're not a minnow or a siren, I think. You're an absolute barracuda."

Without warning, he tugged me right off the photocopier and whirled me around in front of him so my ass pressed into his groin.

I found myself braced against the machine, bowed at the waist with my elbows leaning against the glass surface. Kai slid up my sweater and scooped my breasts free from my bra. He branded kisses to my spine as he tipped me even farther over so my nipples pebbled against the hard surface. Then he hit the copy button again.

I let out a faint sound of protest as the machine spat out another image of my naked body. Kai chuckled and tucked his hands around me. His fingers swept over the sensitive flesh, fondling the curves and flicking over my nipples. He hummed in approval at their already stiffened state.

"I don't just want a record of you," he said in a scorching whisper. "I want a record of how you were *mine*."

He hit the button with his knee, holding my breasts so the next printout would show his hands cupped around them, marking them as his. The vibration sent a fresh thrill through my chest. So much arousal had pooled between my legs that an embarrassing trickle trailed down my inner thigh.

Kai's breath had roughened, his own need intensifying alongside mine. He didn't leave me hanging for long. He dipped his hand between my legs, stroking my slickness from my clit and along my opening. I let out a needy whine and pushed back against him.

"So impatient," he chided, but the hitch in his voice gave away how close to losing control he was. He kept that hand working over me, curling one finger and then two right inside me, as he fumbled with his fly with the other. "Are you my woman too, Lily? Not just Nox's and Ruin's? Do you want everything I can give you?"

At the pulsing of his fingers, a moan tumbled out of me that was probably an answer all on its own. But I made myself say, in a ragged voice that was the best I could produce, "Yes. Everything. I want all of you."

He kissed my shoulder blade as if in reward and removed his hand for just long enough for the sound of tearing foil to reach my ears. "Good thing I didn't trust my self-control so much I skipped on necessary precautions," he said with a breathless laugh. Then the head of his cock pressed against my slit.

I spread my legs wider instinctively. Kai swiveled his fingers over my clit a few more times, drawing another gasp from my throat, and plunged into me so fast I saw stars.

"Oh, hell, yes," Kai muttered, easing back and ramming into me again. He set a steady, forceful pace, not rushing things but filling me to the brim with every thrust. After just a few, my body was reverberating with pleasure, like I was a fucking gong he was ringing each time he bucked against me.

He didn't neglect the rest of me. His hands traveled all over my body, pinching my nipples, tweaking my clit, finally spreading a little of my slickness into the crack of my ass to tease over my other opening. The unexpected jolt of bliss that came with that touch had me moaning all over again.

"Not too loud," he reminded me, even as he pounded into me with a rhythm that was sending me spiraling more and more out of control with every beat. "I'll have to give you an ink cartridge to bite down on, and that could get messy."

As I sputtered a laugh that turned into a whimper halfway through, he circled my asshole again, lighting up all the nerve-endings there. "So very naughty," he said. "We'll play with this in other ways later, when we have more room to explore. For now, I'll stick to…"

He eased his thumb inside me just as he thrust into me again, and the heady sensations exploded through my body. My sex clenched around his pounding cock, and my head dropped down so my forehead smacked the photocopier, but I barely noticed the momentary prickle of pain with all the ecstasy sweeping through me.

Kai growled low in his throat and bucked into me faster. He pulled me against him as if he could bury himself even deeper than he already had. Then he was letting out a strangled sound of release as he reached his own peak.

A brief worry flashed through me that the normally detached guy would get awkward in the aftermath of our feral fuck. But Kai stayed in a slyly affectionate mood, planting a teasing kiss at the crook of my neck as he sorted out my bra and sweater, shaking his head at himself as he peeled off the condom with its load. "I wonder which of my wonderful coworkers should have this left on their desk."

I paused in the middle of yanking up my panties. "You wouldn't."

He smirked at me. "No, probably not, but only because I don't figure it'd be wise to leave my DNA lying around in hostile territory. Not because they don't deserve the horrified shock."

He swiped the other two photocopies from the tray. "Can't forget these treasures." He folded them to fit his pocket like the first and retrieved his glasses, and just like that, he was his typical pulled-together self, other than his mussed hair. If his face was still a bit flushed like mine, I couldn't tell in the dimness.

But that was Kai for you—straightforward and to-the-point. His even-keel-ness steadied me too. We did still have a job to do here, as diverted as we'd gotten from it.

I inhaled and exhaled slowly, the afterglow of the sex warming me but easing enough that I could concentrate. A renewed flicker of confidence had sparked inside me. "Up to the penthouse?" I suggested.

Kai took my hand like he had before. "No time like the present."

At the exclusive elevator, we tugged on the ski masks and gloves he'd brought along. Then he punched in the code. The door opened before I had a chance to even wonder if he could have made a mistake. We soared up to the building's top floor, Kai's hand lingering on my side with a new possessiveness I couldn't say I minded, and stepped out into that posh executive space.

There was an electronic lock on the door to Nolan's office. I knew Kai wasn't as quick with technology as he was with people, but he fished a device out of his satchel and attached it to the lock.

"I've been making some new contacts while we get settled in here in the city," he explained as the lock started blinking with flickers of codes. "One of them helpfully supplied this ingenious device. Humanity has come up with a few useful inventions in the last two decades."

"Yes," I said dryly, "I'm sure the greatest recent achievement of humankind is the ability to more easily break and enter."

Kai snorted and then inhaled sharply as the device beeped. There was a pause, and then a *thunk* as the lock mechanism slid over.

We nudged open the door and crept into Nolan's office. I stopped breathing for a second, half expecting to find the man in charge standing by his desk as if he hadn't moved since I'd been in here last. But the vast space was empty. The glow of city lights seeped through the huge windows along the far wall.

"Okay," Kai said. "Let's see what the big boss has been keeping hidden away in here."

We peered at Nolan's bookshelves and pawed through his desk drawers, careful to leave everything in the same place we'd found it. It all looked like typical, above-board business stuff to me at first, other than a toy soldier tucked in the corner of one drawer. I studied it in my gloved hand, frowning at the antique styling and faded paint. "I wonder why he keeps this around." It looked older than Nolan was.

Kai shrugged. "Family keepsake? Oh, look at this. I wonder if he's been thinking he needs better security."

He showed me a business card he'd fished out of the back of the drawer—white with dark lettering and a red logo. *Ironguard Security*, the company name said. On the back, Nolan had jotted down a few phone numbers.

"Do you think that's important?" I asked.

"Not for our purposes, but it'd be good to know if he's adding new systems to this building or his home." Kai snapped a picture of both sides, tucked it away where he'd found it, and we both kept digging.

I'd reached the bottom drawer on my side when I lifted a paper and saw something that made me stiffen in place. Kai's head jerked around at my reaction. "What?"

I motioned to the document I'd uncovered, my throat too tight for me to speak.

It was a resume with my name at the top. My address in Lovell Rise was circled.

Nolan Gauntt had been keeping a close eye on me from the moment I'd applied at Thrivewell… and he'd paid particular attention to where I went after work hours, if he wanted to find me.

Chapter Twenty-One

Lily

I KNEW the guys were worried when they all insisted on piling into Fred 2.0 to escort me to work instead of riding alongside me on their motorcycles.

"We have to keep a low profile," Kai had said before he'd set off in his own car, since we didn't want to be seen arriving together.

"Right!" Ruin had nodded and cracked his knuckles with an eager grin. "Better if that psycho doesn't know you have protection. We can take him by surprise for his beat-down."

I might have pointed out that the four of them weren't really in any position to be accusing other people of being psychos, but, well, the knowledge that Nolan Gauntt had been making particular note of my home address… that he might be making plans to launch some attempt at screwing me over outside of work as well as on the job…

Well, let's just say it didn't have me farting rainbows of joy.

Maybe I should have taken comfort in the fact that he hadn't done anything yet, even though he'd had my resume available to him for almost three weeks already. Still, my discovery definitely cast a gloom over my return to work, knowing the guy would be skulking in his office twenty floors over my head.

As the car—which I had to admit ran much more smoothly than the original Fred, bless his vehicular soul—came up on the Thrivewell Enterprises building, I dragged in a breath. "I must have some leverage," I said, as much to reassure myself as the three guys around me. "He's trying to get me out, but he's going out of his way to make it look like a legit firing. He'd only be doing that if he thinks I could get him in trouble if he doesn't have all his bases covered."

"That doesn't mean he won't change his tune." Nox aimed a death glare at the building as I cruised past it and then glanced over at me. "We'll be staked out nearby the whole day. You get any shit at all from him, you text us *immediately*."

Imagining the havoc the former Skullbreakers could wreak on Thrivewell's orderly offices amused and horrified me simultaneously. It'd certainly be quite a show.

"I don't think it's going to come to that," I said as I parked a few blocks away, where no one was likely to notice the company I'd brought with me. At Nox's pointed look, I added, "But yes, if he comes raging at me, I'll give you a heads up before I'm torn limb from limb."

"We'll tear *him* limb from limb," Ruin announced with a pump of his fist.

Jett just eyed the two of them as we all got out and gave a skeptical grunt. "I get to pick where we're hanging out," he said.

Nox clapped him on the shoulders. "Right. We wouldn't want your sensitive artistic sensibilities to be offended."

He was jovial enough about the teasing that Jett's lips twitched with a hint of a smile before he forced his mouth into a grimace. "No, we wouldn't," he replied, and paused. His gaze slid to me. "But what's most important is that we're in easy reach if you need us, of course."

From the guy who rarely said much of anything, let alone anything affectionate, that was practically a declaration of undying loyalty. Not that I had much doubt about his loyalties considering how enthusiastically he'd punished my bullies in the past.

I shot him a smile. "Since it may be a long wait, I'd rather you got to enjoy the scenery in the meantime too."

"I've already gotten to see *my* favorite scenery," Nox said with a smirk, and tugged me to him to kiss my neck so he didn't mess up my lipstick. Ruin took that as his cue to do the same on the other side, and I was lucky I walked away only with giddy heat racing through me and not a pair of matching hickeys.

I headed over to the office building alone and started the new process of my workday. Before I even went into the mailroom, I checked the hall to the back delivery area and the storage room in it. Like the past couple of days, I found a couple of urgent parcels tucked away behind the other supplies. Whoever was trying to screw me over this way hadn't picked up on the fact that I was on to them—or they didn't care.

Maybe they liked knowing that *I* knew someone wanted me gone.

I checked the storage room again on my morning break and during lunch, and found one more envelope the second time. Otherwise, no trouble came my way other than Rupert's chorus of huffs and narrow sideways glances. I still wasn't sure *he* wasn't responsible for the waylaid deliveries.

But nothing required the assistance of my ghostly gangsters. Nothing went really wrong at all… until I returned from a quick pop into the restroom to a bitter smell in the air that hadn't been there before.

Rupert had gone off somewhere or other. I eased warily into the room, taking sniff after sniff, until I stopped at the mail cart I'd been almost finished loading before my bladder had demanded my attention. Then I halted in my tracks and stared.

Dark splotches were splattered across almost every envelope and package in the cart. Dark splotches that still had a faintly wet sheen and that were giving off the bitter scent of black coffee.

It looked like someone had poured an entire freaking pot over the heap.

Oh, fuck. The wheels spun in my head for several seconds before I was capable of conscious thought again. My entire body had gone rigid, my stomach knotted into a solid lump.

No doubt they had a way of blaming this on me. Careless with my morning beverage, ruining a multitude of important documents. The second Rupert walked back in here and saw this—

The memory flashed through my mind of making a spurt of his coffee leap on to his shirt the other day. I paused, inhaling and exhaling slowly as I willed down my panic so I could think clearly.

Coffee was mostly water. I'd manipulated it before. Was it possible I could simply un-drench the cart and pretend this had never happened?

I had no idea, but the thought came with so much vengeful satisfaction that the hum was already resonating in my chest.

I stared at the parcels and envelopes, at the dark liquid staining them, and focused on my frustration with the job. On how pissed off I was with the people who were trying to kick me out and their underhanded methods. On Nolan Gauntt sitting up there in his huge, fancy office probably laughing manically to himself about how he'd gotten the better of me.

No. Fucking. Way.

The hum spread up into my skull and out to the tips of my fingers. I glanced around and grabbed an empty plastic crate so I had somewhere to send the offending liquid to. Then I focused all my searing energy on the cart.

Out. Out. I urged the splatters of coffee with my mind and beckoned to them with my hands. Flickers of warmth washed over my skin as if emanating from the hot beverage. The brown liquid began to rise off the heap of mail in drips and thin rivulets.

I directed them all over to the plastic crate and let them fall there in a dingy rainfall of coffee. Thin liquid snakes wove through the air and fell into the container. I pulled and directed it all, a marshy flavor creeping through my mouth. My body was outright tingling now with the energy flowing through me as I carried out this precise maneuver.

Finally, a faint ache started to creep through my muscles alongside the hum. The rivulets thinned until they were barely visible. I tugged with my powers more and more, determined to pull every driblet I could out of the stack of mail. Then, when nothing more came and it felt like I was yanking at nothing, I let my hands drop to my sides. My breath rushed out of me with a sag of my shoulders.

The bottom of the plastic crate was full of coffee. The packages and envelopes in the cart looked good as new. Maybe there was a slightly darker tint to the paper here and there, but nothing anyone could say was a definite stain. Nothing that could be pinned on me.

Despite the fatigue prickling through me, a smile stretched my mouth. I'd done it. They'd thought they could tear me down, and I'd beat them at their own game.

That sense of triumph faded quickly, though. I carried the crate into the restroom to pour out the coffee and rinse it, since it'd be hard to explain what'd gone on there if anyone else saw it, and by the time I returned, my spirits had dampened.

I'd beaten my enemies *this* time. What were they going to throw at me next? It'd only been luck that their current gambit had involved something I could use my powers on. Next time they might smear packages with cocaine dust or marmalade fingerprints, and there'd be shit-all I could do about that. The longer I waited, the more chance I'd get banned from the building and lose whatever access I had now.

My gaze lifted to the ceiling with the thought of the head honcho in his high office, scheming his schemes. A surge of defiant resolution filled me.

He was trying to push me around, to push me *out*, because he thought he could get away with it. I wasn't sure I could find out much more working here anyway. We'd taken everything we could from his office, which hadn't been a whole lot and nothing we could use to get the upper hand. But I had my own ways of intimidating people.

I could get my full revenge for whatever he'd put Marisol through later. For now, I just needed him to stay the fuck away from me and her. Nolan Gauntt might be full of pompous business authority, but he'd never had to deal with anyone like me. I had to terrorize him enough that he'd decide it was better to steer clear rather than keep coming at me.

My decision solidified in my head as I brought around the cart of newly cleaned mail. The guys wouldn't have liked this plan. They'd have wanted me to call them in so they could carry out the terrorizing.

But they'd already stood up for me so much, and all I'd done in return was get them into more danger. I could handle this myself, like I had with Peyton and Wade.

It was my problem, and I was strong enough to fix it on my own.

Well, mostly on my own. There was still an exclusive executive elevator standing between me and the big boss, and I couldn't waltz right over to it and step on even though I knew the code from watching Kai yesterday. So after I'd dropped off the empty cart in the mailroom, I texted my coworker accomplice a quick message.

I'm coming up to your floor. Need to get on the special elevator. When you see me, can you divert the secretaries' secretary?

The answer came in less than a minute. *Of course. What are you up to? I can join in.*

I'm taking care of this one by myself, I said. *Just get me in.*

Kai didn't argue. When I reached the fifteenth floor, my nerves were already thrumming with a mix of apprehension, anticipation, and righteous anger.

I strode over to the executive elevator as if I did this every day. From the corner of my vision, I saw Kai saunter over to the secretary's desk. He started talking in low, urgent tones that had her springing from her desk and dashing to another part of the room with him.

I didn't glance over to see where they'd gone. I simply drew up in front of the elevator, tapped in the code as quickly as I could, and launched myself through the doors as soon as they opened.

"Hey!" someone said from behind me—maybe not even to me, but I wasn't taking any chances. I jabbed the button for the top floor and didn't breathe again until the doors had closed and the car was gliding upwards.

Naturally, when I reached the top floor, I had another problem that I hadn't fully considered in my sudden rush of determination. Nolan's admin assistant was at his desk, guarding the boss's office door.

Since I didn't have any clever tricks up my sleeve, I decided to see how far bravado would get me. I marched up to him with as commanding an air as I could produce. "I need to see Mr. Gauntt. *Now.*"

The assistant blinked at me, eyeing me as if I had two heads—and both of them were smeared with dog shit. "Who are you, exactly?" he said in a disdainful tone. "*If* you have some business that would concern Mr. Gauntt, his schedule does require a significant amount of advance notice. And I'm afraid—"

I didn't get to find out what patronizing comment he'd make next, because right then, the office door swung open.

I didn't think, just reacted. On a jolt of adrenaline, I sprang past the woman who was just leaving the office and hurtled inside—right past Nolan, who was standing on the other side of the doorway to see his guest out. I spun around to face him, my chin high and my voice firm. "We need to talk."

"I'm so sorry, Mr. Gauntt," the assistant's voice carried from outside as he scrambled to pursue me.

Nolan gave me a measured look, something in his posture making him feel about ten feet taller than me even though it was more like eight inches, and stepped into the doorway. "It's all right," he told his assistant. "I'm sure Miss Strom is only here to follow up on a discussion we had last week. It won't take long."

Oh, he was so sure about that, wasn't he?

His confident air as he shut the door and turned toward me both unnerved me and infuriated me. I held on tightly to the fury, fanning the flames inside me so the hum of supernatural energy rose into a roar.

"This *will* be quick," I said before he could say anything else. "I'm just here to tell you that from now on, you'd better leave me and my sister alone. You don't keep tabs on me or her, and you and anyone working for you had better stay the hell away from my home." Hopefully he couldn't track me to our new apartment, but I wouldn't put it past him.

Nolan continued studying me for a moment without any hint of concern and then ambled deeper into his office. "What makes you think I'd want anything at all to do with you and your sister?"

I stalked after him. "You sure seemed interested in her seven years ago. There won't be any repeats of that."

He rotated on his heel again to fix that penetrating gaze on me. "And what exactly did I do back then? You don't know that I did anything at all, do you? Other than having a simple conversation, and there's no crime in that."

"It was more than a fucking conversation," I snapped, and then reined in my temper. He obviously knew I didn't remember—whether from his observations recently or getting access to my doctors' notes or who knew what. And now he was going to play innocent?

Nolan shrugged like the total douche-canoe he was. His hand twitched where it hung loosely at his side. "That sounds awfully vague to me. Throwing around baseless accusations can get you in a lot of trouble, you know."

Oh, now he was threatening me? My teeth gritted, and I decided we'd done enough talking. He was never going to admit to anything. That wasn't why I'd come up here anyway. I needed to show him how much trouble *he'd* be in if he kept messing with me and mine.

My senses were singing with the awareness of the water running through the building around me. There was a pipe running through the floor and into the wall—a private bathroom just off Nolan's office. I focused on it, on willing a torrent of water to rush up through the pipes. My skin quivered.

"I don't care what excuses you make," I said, low and fierce. "You'll leave us alone from now on, or you'll regret it."

As I said those last three words, I unleashed the pressure I'd forced into the bathroom fixtures. Water exploded from the sink faucet, the shower head, and the toilet tank and slammed into the door so hard it burst open.

The wave crashed into Nolan, tossing him off his feet. He landed on his ass just as a second wave surged out to batter him again. I held off on another, keeping the water at the ready with a heady rhythm flowing through my veins, waiting for his reaction.

Nolan wiped off his face and looked at the carpet around him, which was soaked and covered in puddles where the water hadn't quite absorbed yet. His eyes had widened, and his lips had parted with surprise. Another twitch shook his hand, this one rippling up his arm. But as I watched, his mouth curved into a shape that looked almost… amused?

With a rough chuckle, he pushed himself to his feet, barely

seeming to mind the way his drenched suit clung to his broad body. He slicked his hair back from his face again and met my eyes, still with that sharp smile.

"Well," he said, "that *is* interesting. There must be quite a story there. I assume that's why your stepfather was so overwrought. I thought he was just a hysterical personality. It worked in my favor regardless. No one wondered why you were kept shut away under medical supervision for so long without any clear symptoms."

The bottom of my stomach dropped out. Nolan didn't seem scared or intimidated at all. How could he be so blasé about me hurling water around with the power of my mind? And—

My voice came out taut. "Are you saying that *you* made them keep me in the hospital for all that time?" I'd wondered now and then why my extended stay had been necessary, but the staff had always been quick to assure me they only had my best interests and a smooth recovery in mind…

Had he been paying them off to keep me out of the way?

"I'm not saying anything at all," Nolan said drolly, and squeezed a little water out of his tie. "Did you think that silly stunt would frighten me? I've faced much more difficult issues than getting a little *wet*, you ridiculous girl. Now I'll give you ten seconds to get out of my office and another minute to vacate this building forever, or you can be sure the next time the police haul you away, you won't be coming back."

I didn't know whether he could follow through on that threat or if he was bluffing, but he didn't look the slightest bit worried. And I had no other cards I could play. My thoughts had scattered in bewilderment, my nerves jangling with panic.

If he meant it, if he had that many authorities in his pocket, I'd completely lose any chance I had of helping Marisol. Nothing was worth that risk.

So I fled. I spun and ran for the door, jammed my thumb against the elevator button, and heard nothing but the racing of my pulse as it carried me down to the fifteenth floor. I didn't dare stop to catch Kai's attention. I just kept walking, to the other elevator, pacing back and forth in that car as it carried me to the ground level, and then out onto the sidewalk. There, I exhaled in one long, ragged rush and pressed my hands to my face.

I'd lost. I'd faced the dragon with what I'd thought was an unbeatable enchanted sword, and he'd chomped it in half and sent me scrambling away with my ass on fire.

And now Nolan knew without a doubt why I'd come to Thrivewell. He knew how far I was willing to go. How long would it be before he decided firing me wasn't enough?

Chapter Twenty-Two

Lily

"You shouldn't have gone in there alone," Nox said for approximately the thousandth time as his hands clenched the steering wheel. He'd insisted on driving Fred 2.0 after the guys had seen how shaken I was by my confrontation with Nolan.

"Right," I said. "Because three gangsters storming into the building totally wouldn't have drawn any attention and gotten a heap of security called. You might not even have made it past the first floor."

"We could have tried," Jett grumbled from behind me.

"We'd have shown that asshole a thing or two," Ruin agreed, swinging punches at the back of Nox's seat.

"I don't know." I sank deeper into my own seat, worrying at my lower lip. Would Nolan Gauntt have been afraid even if my guys had come at him with their electrical attacks? I guessed those would have been more painful than the punch of water I'd thrown him. But I could way too easily imagine him sprawled on the floor with his skin singed and his hair smoking while still smiling that same unaffected smirk.

A shiver ran down my spine. "I'm done there now," I said. "I'll have to find *another* new job. At least there are more of those here in the city." I rubbed my hand over my face. "Kai's still at Thrivewell. It's possible the Gauntts will back off now that I'm not nosing around, but if they don't, he'll still have an inside edge."

What exactly we could do with that edge, I wasn't sure. It seemed pretty risky to go in aiming to beat the man to a pulp if we weren't sure that would cow him. A tactic like that could just as easily backfire and end with all of the guys—and maybe me too—behind bars.

Nolan had been too calm about all of it. What could have been going through his head? He obviously hadn't been at my house when I'd unleashed my powers before, because he'd definitely been surprised, just not shocked into a horrified stupor like Wade had been.

But then, maybe it'd been ridiculous of me to think the head of Thrivewell Enterprises would be intimidated as easily as my bully of a stepdad had been.

"That's right," Ruin said, ever chipper. "And we'll use that edge to cut him into little pieces."

Could it be as simple as that? Just eliminate the guy completely? I wasn't exactly an advocate for murder—I'd *stopped* the guys from murdering people on various occasions—but if Nolan was a total menace to society, or at least to Marisol… wouldn't it be better to remove him from the game board?

I just couldn't quite believe it'd be that simple. He'd be even more on guard now than he'd been before. He'd already been looking into that security company. And who knew how many other people in his family or the company were mixed up in the whole thing, who'd come after us even if we succeeded in eliminating Nolan?

I shook myself, closing my eyes. My head was spinning again, my thoughts colliding and fracturing without getting me any answers. I needed to step back and take a breather, and then maybe I could find the right way to come at this problem.

The last of Mayfield's buildings fell away as we passed into the short stretch of countryside between the city and Lovell Rise. Ruin reached over and squeezed my shoulder. As I turned to smile at him, grateful even if the affectionate gesture didn't fix anything, my phone rang.

My heart lurched, though I had no reason to assume the call was about anything bad. I pulled out my phone and raised it to my ear. "Hello?"

"Hello, Miss Strom?" a woman said. It took me a second to place her clipped voice in combination with the company name that'd turned up on my call display. It was the rental agent who'd shown us the new apartment.

"Yes?" I said cautiously. Did she need more paperwork signed? Oh, God, she hadn't already found out that I'd lost my job, had she?

The ripple of tension that carried through the woman's words put me even more on the alert. "There's been an… issue with the apartment on Kastle Street. We're hoping you might be able to shed some light on the situation. Can you come by the building later this afternoon?"

"I can come right now," I said, motioning to Nox so wildly that he gave me a puzzled look. I didn't know how to convey my directions in sign language. "What kind of issue?" My heart was already sinking. Nolan Gauntt must have been pissed off at me for challenging him, even if he hadn't shown it. He'd found out about the apartment somehow—he'd screwed me over in some other way…

"I think you really need to see it," the agent said, which wasn't ominous at all. "How soon can you get here?"

"Um, about twenty minutes? I'll hurry."

I hung up and flailed my arm at Nox again. "We've got to go back to the city. To the new apartment. Something's gone wrong."

"What?" The question came out in a growl. Baring his teeth, the Skullbreakers' leader yanked the car around in a U-turn so abrupt the tires screeched and several honks followed in our wake. But it did get us racing back toward the city in no time flat.

"I have no idea what happened," I said as the engine rumbled with the jam of his foot against the gas pedal. "The rental agent said she wanted me to see it. Let's not get pulled over for speeding before we even make it to the building."

"The cops can eat my exhaust," Nox muttered, but he did slow down enough that my heart stopped trying to jump out of my throat.

I texted Kai, who was still at the office, to let him know about our unexpected detour. I'd only meant to keep him in the loop, but he replied an instant later saying he'd claim he was sick and be right over.

You really don't have to, I wrote back quickly, but he was apparently so busy putting on his show of illness that he didn't even read that message.

As we swerved onto the street the apartment building was on, I didn't expect to see anything all that shocking yet. I assumed it was something to do with only my specific apartment. But when the brick walls came into sight, my gut twisted in on itself. "Oh, fuck."

The windows all along the first floor had been smashed—and they were barred, so someone had gone to a lot of trouble to work around the wrought-iron protections. A few shards of glass still glinted on the sidewalk. The front door had been bashed right off its hinges and now was propped next to the doorway, the steel surface dented like a battering ram had gone at it.

Jett let out a low whistle that was almost as impressed as it was horrified.

"I guess… if they were broken that easily… it's a good thing they'll need to be replaced?" Ruin said, for once in his life struggling to find a cheery way of spinning this particular situation. "Who the hell did this?"

It didn't feel like Gauntt-style work, I had to say. We parked a couple of car-lengths away from the building and got out cautiously.

The rental agent emerged from the entry hall as soon as I'd closed the car door behind me. She glanced from me to the three guys flanking me, and her lips pursed in a way that made my hackles automatically rise.

"What the heck happened here?" I asked, sweeping my arm to encompass the stretch of wreckage.

Somehow, the woman's lips pursed even tighter. She might have been able to turn coal into diamonds with them at this point.

"The building was vandalized and defaced a few hours ago," she said stiffly. "And seeing as the only individual apartment specifically targeted was the one you're due to move into shortly, I have to assume it has something to do with your… associations."

Her gaze flicked to the guys again. They had started looking increasingly gangster-y since they'd taken possession of their bodies, what with the extreme hair colors and their tendency toward hoodies and jeans loose enough to wedge a pistol in them. She'd seen Jett's motorcycle when he'd come with me to check out the apartment the other day. If that was even what she meant.

She didn't think *my* guys had done this, did she? How would that even make sense?

But it couldn't have had anything to do with my conversation with Nolan Gauntt, I realized with a wash of cold. She'd said it'd happened a few hours ago, and it'd been only about one since I'd left his office. He might be an uber-powerful corporate magnate, but I didn't think even he could travel back in time to fuck with my living space.

So who had done this, then? And why would they have gone after my apartment?

It wasn't really mine yet, of course.

"I don't know who could have done this kind of damage," I said, gathering my confidence. "I'm not even living here yet. It probably has something to do with the previous tenants."

The rental agent gave me a withering look. "The previous tenant was a ninety-year-old woman who never left the apartment except to play bingo on Tuesdays."

"You never know," Nox said. "Those bingo halls can get pretty intense."

As the agent glowered at him, I sucked my lower lip under my teeth. As I groped for another alternative suggestion, she motioned for me to follow her into the building. "Why don't you take a look at the message they left behind?"

Message? I stepped into the hallway, my skin creeping with apprehension. Despite the destruction on the outside of the building, it was true that nothing inside appeared to have been touched. Well, not until we got to the third floor, where the chemical smell of spray paint still hung in the air.

It was obvious why before we even went into the corner apartment that was meant to be mine. Someone had sprayed black paint in it in the shape of two bones forming an X, like the bottom of a pirate flag logo. Which I guessed was better than the boner that'd been painted on the grocery store, but not by a large margin.

"Not the same guys," Jett muttered, possibly thinking of the same previous incident that I was. With his artist's eye, he should know. The bones definitely looked more deftly sketched than the crude images before.

The rental agent shot him a sharp look as if he'd admitted guilt. Then she pushed the door open. The lock was broken, and the hinges creaked as if they were a thread from giving way.

The same crossed-bones graphic marked the walls all through the apartment, stark against the white paint and the windowpanes. It'd even been sprayed on the floor—along with puddles that gave off a rank smell that had my stomach turning in an instant.

They'd pissed in here.

In the bathroom, the intruders had marked up the bathtub too. They'd smashed the sink, which now lay in several pieces on the tiles.

My lungs had already constricted when I reached the master bedroom. There was more piss on the floor and bones dancing across the walls… and letters marked in red paint in between the partial pirate graphic.

This was what the rental agent had meant about a message.

Corps crushed the Skullbreakers. We'll crush you too.

For a second, I was confused, thinking the vandals had misspelled "corpse." Nox came up beside me and let out a string of violent curses that made the rental agent cringe. Then understanding clicked into place in my head.

The X of bones—that must be the Skeleton Corps' tag. They'd noticed the guys coming by here with me, or maybe they figured I was part of the gang, which wasn't totally wrong. So they'd decided to send a message.

And now we knew for sure who'd been responsible for the Skullbreakers' first deaths. It didn't feel like good news.

It took a moment for me to realize the rental agent was talking. Her voice came out even brisker than before, almost frantic. "As you can see, it appears you've drawn the attention of some… unsavory characters to our property. There are standards that have to be maintained, and there's the security of the rest of the tenants to consider. I can return your deposit check to you and—"

Panic hit me in an icy splash. I'd lost my job, and now she was trying to take my new home—Marisol's new home—away from us.

"No," I burst out, and fumbled for my composure. "No, I—this won't happen again."

Kai's even voice rang out from the living room. "You and Lily have been the victims of a crime," he said, walking over to where the rental agent was standing. "It seems a little backward to blame her instead of attempting to prosecute the actual perpetrators."

The agent startled, probably wondering where he'd come from. He'd made it here fast. I wondered if he had any treads left on his tires.

In her hesitation, Nox jumped in with a crack of his knuckles. "We'll handle getting this place cleaned and fixed up," he said firmly. "The apartment, and the windows and door downstairs too. You and the management company won't have to lift a finger. As long as you let Lily keep her lease."

Kai nodded. "Let us take care of it. If you approve of the fixes before it's time for Lily to move in, you let her keep the place. That's a fair deal, isn't it? And, I mean, it'll be even harder to rent it to anyone else if word gets out that the building's become a target."

"The people who targeted it won't make that mistake again," Jett said darkly.

Ruin nodded with an eager jerk of his head. "We can take care of that too. Hell, yes."

The rental agent's gaze slid from one of them to the other, somehow hopeful and terrified at the same time. When her eyes reached me, I managed a pained smile. "Please? Give me—give us—a chance."

She let out her breath in a rush. "I—I'll have to check with the office, but I think I can give you a few days to prove you can get things in order—and that there won't be another incident like this. If we have any more issues—"

I held up my hands. "Of course. I totally understand."

With another sigh, she ushered us out of the apartment. Despite her tentative agreement to the deal, my stomach still felt as heavy as if I'd swallowed one of those chunks of sink.

I suspected the only reason she'd agreed was Kai's point about how difficult it'd be to find a new tenant. But that only mattered if my presence wasn't running off the tenants they already had. Could we really clean all this up in just a few days?

And could the guys take down the Skeleton Corps before they came back to make good on their promise?

Chapter Twenty-Three

Jett

Of all the things I'd never wanted to need to know, how to remove piss from hardwood was definitely up there at the top of the list. I wrinkled my nose as I gave the last rag one final scrub over the boards before studying them.

It was lucky they'd already been pretty marked up before the Skeleton Corps had come through here. I couldn't really tell that this spot was any more battered than the rest of the floor. And it didn't stink anymore.

The rag, on the other hand…

I chucked that into the garbage bag sitting open in the middle of the living room and glanced around. Nox was just finishing reinforcing the hinges on the new door he'd picked up for the apartment. From the looks of the thing, it was meant for a maximum-security military base rather than a low-rent apartment building, but I wasn't going to complain if it made it that much harder for the pricks to break in here again.

I'd managed to use my color changing power to erase the gang graffiti in the living room and one of the bedrooms, but then my ghostly juice had run out there. Ruin was swiping a layer of white paint onto the walls in the second bedroom, whistling a happy tune as he did like he was in a fucking Disney movie. I could see Lily doing her own painting, with somewhat less enthusiasm, through the third bedroom's doorway. Kai had gone downstairs to oversee the replacement of the broken first-floor windows.

We'd managed to get through a hell of a lot so far today, but we were hardly done. Even with the windows open, letting a chilly evening breeze wash over us, we wouldn't be able to put down a second layer of paint to cover the last traces of the spray paint until tomorrow. The bathroom sink was still in several pieces. And Kai was working out the best solution for a secure door to the entire building, which also required getting new keys to all the tenants.

But really, the rental company should have been *thanking* us for the renovations we'd had to do on their behalf.

The window replacement people must have finished up, because Kai came striding into the apartment. He scanned the space through his glasses like he was searching it for murder clues.

"As soon as you're done, we should head out," he said to the room at large, nodding at the thickening darkness beyond the windows. "We need to gather all the reinforcements we can as quickly as possible for when we go head-to-head with the Skeleton Corps. And we want to focus their attention on our new headquarters so if they're going to come at us, they do it there, not here."

"Agreed on both." Nox stepped back from the door and wiped his hands together with a satisfied air. Then he glanced toward Lily, who'd just emerged from her room, finished with her painting. "Someone needs to stay with Lily. We can't leave her on her own while they're pulling shit like this."

"They don't seem to know about my apartment in Lovell Rise," Lily said. Nox had ridden out there to confirm it hadn't met the same fate as the new apartment earlier today. "I should be fine there."

Nox let out a dismissive huff. "They tracked us all the way out there in our first lives. If they could connect us to this place, we can't count on them not knowing about where we've been crashing for weeks. And that place has just one crappy door between you and the street." He patted the new one he'd installed. "I think you should stay here with one of us."

It was some kind of crazy world when a place that'd just been broken into and defaced was our safest option, but I had to agree with him. I looked at Ruin, who was just setting aside his paintbrush, expecting him to volunteer for protective duty, but Kai spoke first. "Jett should stay."

My head jerked around. "What? Why?"

The know-it-all glowered at me as if offended that I'd questioned his declaration. "Nox and Ruin have supernatural talents that'll help us show who the new bosses in town are with the other gangs. I don't think giving them a makeover is going to have the same impact."

"*You* haven't figured out what your superpower is at all," I had to point out.

Nox snorted. "Kai knows how to talk people into just about anything and how to get a read on the ones he can't convince. Can't beat that for this job, even with superpowers."

I opened my mouth and closed it again. Lily was watching me, her expression solemn. Maybe she was wondering why I was protesting so much.

To some extent, it was a matter of honor. But also—spending the night with her, alone—there were too many things I wanted that were nagging at the edges of my mind even without me letting myself think about them.

"There's nothing in this place," I said finally. "All our stuff is back at the other apartment."

Nox jabbed his thumb toward the tiny kitchen. "There's the food we picked up. You won't starve. And the one bedroom has that Murphy bed. I'm sure you'll manage." He smirked at me as if *he* knew exactly what urges I was trying to shove way down deep in the basement of my mind.

"I have an emergency blanket in the trunk of my car that I can bring up," Lily said quietly. "For one night—we could make do."

I could tell from her voice that she was already exhausted. And why wouldn't she be? She'd thrown everything she had at that creep Nolan Gauntt and had him laugh in her face, and then spent the rest of the day mopping up piss and painting over deathly graffiti in a panic over losing her new home.

The last thing I wanted was to make this situation any harder for her than it already was.

I shrugged. "Okay. I'm the weakest link. Whatever."

Ruin chuckled and prodded me in the shoulder. "You're not weak. You'll kick the asses of anyone who comes at Lily. And hey, slumber party!" He wagged a finger at Kai. "Next time, it's my turn."

"We'll see how helpful it is to have you literally putting the fear into the bozos around here," Nox said. "Okay, let's move out. I bet the Skeleton Corps aren't sitting around on their asses."

We all headed downstairs, the other guys going to their bikes to take off and me escorting Lily to her car. I peered through the dusk, my nerves jumping at the sight of a figure that turned out to be just a skinny teenager practicing his dance moves to the beat that blared from his headphones. He looked like a scarecrow getting electrocuted, but I decided against offering that critique.

Lily and I didn't talk much as we ate a dinner that consisted of an odd mix of junk food and fresh fruit, which Ruin seemed to think were the only acceptable meal items when there wasn't any microwave for heating things up. Lily just looked tired, and I didn't know what to say to her. My strength was in expressing myself with images, not words.

So maybe Nox and Kai had a fair point about my usefulness in the recruitment campaign.

We were just cleaning up, no interruptions from murderous gangsters so far and a deep weariness sinking into my bones, when Lily spoke up.

"Do you really think it'll be okay? You guys will be able to make sure the Skeleton Corps don't vandalize the apartment building again —you'll be able to make sure they don't *hurt* you?"

I shot her my best confident smile. It felt stiff on my mouth. I didn't do a whole lot of smiling in general, and tonight it felt like an epic task.

"We've beat down everyone who came at us so far, haven't we?" I said.

"I know. But these guys seem a lot more organized than the jerks at the college. And there must be a lot of them." She paused, and a yawn stretched her jaw. "I'm just tired. You all know what you're doing with this gangster stuff way better than I do. Let's get the bed down."

The hinges squeaked as we lowered the Murphy bed. The mattress looked a bit lumpy, but at this point I didn't figure Lily cared. Her eyelids were drooping. As she spread out the wool blanket on it, I turned to leave the bedroom.

"Where are you going?" she asked, stopping me in my tracks. "You need to sleep too, don't you?"

The truth was that I'd assumed I'd hunker down on the floor somewhere and make the best of it. We'd closed up the windows now that the paint smell had mostly aired out. But it was still cold enough to freeze a guy's nuts off in here, and the leather jacket I'd been wearing for warmth—and image—while cruising on my bike only took some of the edge off the chill.

It wasn't going to be a *fun* night, that was for sure.

"I'll be fine," I said brusquely, not wanting to give any impression that I was fishing for an invitation. "I spent twenty-one years lying in the bottom of the marsh. This is luxury."

Lily made a scoffing sound. "Don't be silly. I'm not going to make you sleep on the *floor*. It's a double bed—that means it's meant for two. And the blanket's big. We can share it without having to get at all close to each other, if that's what you're worried about."

It kind of was, but when she'd put it that way, I didn't want to admit it. I looked at the bed and the blanket, focusing on them rather than the woman my gaze wanted to travel to as I weighed my options.

At my hesitation, something in Lily's face fell. My heart plummeted seeing it, and suddenly words were tumbling out of my mouth without consulting my brain. "Yeah. Sure. That'll be better."

Once I'd said it, I couldn't really take my agreement back without making her feel even more rejected. She lay down on one side of the mattress, folding her arm under her head as a sort-of pillow and leaving plenty of blanket on the other side for me. I eased onto the springy surface gingerly, staying as close to the edge as I possibly could, and tucked a bit of the blanket over me.

I kept my back to her, but I was sharply aware of her presence on the other side of the mattress. It trembled when she adjusted her position.

There were three feet between us. I'd stood closer to her than that in the past few days. I could handle sleeping that close without losing my head.

Even if the impulse to roll over and tug her to me was starting to spread through my limbs.

Lily was so quiet for several minutes that I thought she'd fallen asleep. I was still arguing silently with my dick, which had gone half-hard in defiance of my intentions, when her drowsy voice reached my ears.

"It's okay, you know. That you're not into me that way. I'm not—I'm not some nympho who's going to throw herself at any guy in a hundred-foot radius or get all offended that I can't bag every man I meet. I never expected *any* of this to happen this way. You don't have to worry that I'd force anything just because we're alone or whatever."

"I know you wouldn't," I said quickly, my pulse stuttering at the realization that she thought I was worried about *her* self-control. Christ. But how could I tell her she was wrong without opening up a whole can of worms that'd spring free all over the place… or dicks. Yeah, it was more like a can of dicks.

How could I explain how I felt about her? I wanted to paint her, and I wanted to paint my fingers all over her body. But every time I imagined that, I couldn't help picturing the other guys' hands touching every part of her…

It wouldn't be something special to just the two of us. I'd only be one more Skullbreaker looking to get off.

Every part of me balked at that idea. Whatever happened between Lily and me, whatever she became to me, it should be better than that. If I gave in to my baser urges, I might sour everything else amazing between us.

And here she was trying to look out for *me* while I grappled with those urges. She'd always been like that, even when she'd been tough and defiant as well—so soft and gentle when she'd felt someone she cared about needed it.

An unexpected warmth spread through my chest to have that kindness directed at me. *She* was goddamned special, and she deserved to be treated like it.

I wasn't totally sure how to be gentle in return, but I gave it my best shot. "You've never made me feel at all uncomfortable," I added to my initial remark. "I'm always happy having you around. I didn't want to impose on *you*."

"Okay. Well, good. And you didn't."

She gave another yawn and tugged the blanket tighter over her shoulder, and then her breath evened out into the rhythm of sleep.

It took a long time before I drifted off too. I wasn't even aware I had until I jolted awake again to a yank of the blanket and a panicked gasp.

As I sat up, I whirled toward Lily. I found her facing away from me, clutching the blanket with her eyes still shut and her expression taut with tension. Another strained sound escaped her, like she was trying to gulp for air. Her arms twitched, her hands jerking at the blanket.

"Lily?" I said. "Lily!"

My voice didn't wake her. Her head whipped from side to side, and her legs shifted under the covers. A low, anguished moan escaped her lips.

It killed me seeing her like that. I'd stayed here to protect her, and now her own mind was beating up on her.

I didn't let myself debate any longer. I scooted across the mattress and wrapped my arms around her, hugging her to me.

"Lily," I said by her ear. "It's okay. You're all right. Everything's fine, and I'm here with you."

I gave her a little shake, and her muscles jumped. Her eyes popped open. I might have released her right then, but a second later, a shiver ran through her body.

She was cold, I realized. The side of her arm, her hair where my face rested against it…

She'd left herself partly uncovered by the blanket so that I could have more, all the way on the other side of the bed.

Horror and guilt wrenched through me, and I quickly heaved the blanket farther over her so it fully covered both of us. Then I nestled her closer against me. Her body started to relax next to mine.

"I'm sorry," she said. "I—I've been having that dream a lot lately. I don't know why."

I frowned. "What dream?"

"I'm back in the marsh. Drowning. Only this time I can't seem to fight my way back to the surface, no matter what I do."

She shifted her weight, and her ass brushed my groin. With a flare of sensation, I became abruptly aware that my dick was no longer settling for half-hard and had gone all the way to steel post status. Had she noticed? Damn it.

I tried to imperceptibly angle my hips so there was no chance of my erection pressing into her.

Lily swiped her hand over her face. "I'm sorry. I mean, it was just a dream. I shouldn't let it shake me up that much."

Why the hell did she think she had to apologize? "It's fine," I said. "A nightmare can shake anyone up."

"I just… I don't like getting weak."

A pang reverberated through my chest. I had to nudge my face closer to her, tucking my chin over her shoulder from behind. "You're not weak. You're the strongest woman I've ever known. You don't lose that just because things get to you every now and then."

The smell of her was flooding my lungs, sweet with an edge of wildness to it. Her body was so soft and now warming against mine. My cock throbbed, and I lost my grip on my resolve just for a second.

One taste, one tiny little taste couldn't be so bad, could it?

I brushed my lips against the corner of Lily's jaw. She exhaled with a soft little gasp of pleasure that took my desire from smoldering to blazing in an instant. I kissed her again, more firmly this time, letting my tongue flick out across her smooth skin to drink in that delicately delicious flavor.

Before I even knew what was happening, my hands were moving. One slid down to stroke over Lily's stomach. The other rose to caress her cheek and the other side of her jaw as I marked a scorching path down the side of her neck. Lily whimpered, arching back into me. Her ass rubbed against my dick, and a groan broke from my throat.

With a shaky inhalation, Lily flipped over to face me. All at once, her fingers were teasing into my hair and across my scalp, her breasts were pressed against my chest, and my mouth was colliding with hers.

Her lips tasted even better than her neck. I devoured them, grasping one of her legs and slinging it over my hip so our bodies aligned even better. Reveling in the needy noise that escaped her when I rocked my erection against her.

She gripped me tighter, her fingertips digging into my skin in a way I didn't mind at all. Our tongues tangled together, her other hand trailed down my chest, and she pulled just a little away with a stuttered breath—

And suddenly in the back of my head I was on the side of the road again. On the side of the road in the dark listening to the tune of a breath rattling out in perfect harmony with the splattering of blood, and thinking—thinking—

Not thinking at all, not really. Just like now.

A wave of cold washed over me, dousing my lust. I yanked myself away from Lily and stiffened my stance to try to hide how much I was shaking.

"Jett?" she said, her voice full of concern.

I should have been more concerned. I should have been thinking straight. Not—not getting caught up in my impulses and emotions, forgetting all reason…

The last time I'd done that, it hadn't been just me who'd paid the price but everyone around me too. The guys who'd counted on me to have their backs.

Lily was counting on me too. I couldn't fuck things up again by losing sight of what mattered.

I pushed myself off the bed. There wasn't anything I could say to make this better—I might only make it worse if I tried. I kept my voice as calm and even as I could manage.

"I got enough sleep. I'm going to go stand guard in the living room. We can't be too careful with those assholes going on rampages."

Then I left the bedroom without another word, guilt twisting through my gut sharper than ever before.

Chapter Twenty-Four

Lily

The odd assembly of characters the guys had pulled together roamed through the former medieval-themed restaurant like tourists taking in the sights. The Skullbreakers had gotten rid of all of the tables except the long one by the throne and a couple pushed off to the sides, but they'd left the throne in all its gleaming gold-painted glory, as well as the weapons and armor hanging on the walls. Watching from my spot off in the corner, I could tell the visuals had made an impact.

The newcomers looked as intimidated by the guys themselves as by their new clubhouse's décor. When Nox stood up in front of the throne and clapped his hands together for attention, a couple dozen heads swung toward him in an instant. Everyone fell silent.

"You've got your assignments," Nox said, casting his gaze over them with an air I had to admit was pretty regal in that moment. He'd even picked up one of the swords, which he waggled at his audience as he spoke, emphasizing his points with *its* point. "We're not going to let the Skeleton Corps bully us anymore, and the first step in that is making sure our properties stay secure. If you're on guard duty, get to it now! The rest of you, prepare to be called on and keep your ears to the ground in the meantime."

Several of the scruffy-looking gangsters who'd responded to the Skullbreakers' recruitment efforts glanced at the floor as if they thought he might mean that last instruction literally. But I noticed that many of them still paled and tensed up when he mentioned our nemesis by name. They shuffled out of the restaurant quickly, one of them taking up a post right outside the door.

Kai had ambled up beside me. He'd called in sick at Thrivewell so he could stick around to finish getting the new Skullbreaker allies organized.

"Are you sure they'll follow through on their orders?" I asked him. "Are they ready to go up against this gang that's been ruling the city for more than twenty years?"

Kai shrugged. "They're scared of the Skeleton Corps, but they're also scared of us working more of our supernatural voodoo on them. I think that'll work as an excellent motivating factor for most. And they don't *really* have to go up against anyone at this point. The only job we've given them is to keep watch around this place and your apartment building and notify us if they see the Corps coming around so we can intercept before much damage is done."

Nox had sauntered over while the other guy was talking. "Exactly. They'd better be able to handle that much, or they've got no business calling the sketchy organizations they were running 'gangs.' I have four guys scheduled to be around the apartment building at all times, switching off regularly, so even if one or two drop the ball, it's well covered."

My stomach twisted. "Do you really want to focus all your new manpower on defending the building? Don't you want to go after the Skeleton Corps guys for murdering you?"

Not that I particularly wanted him to say yes. I was kind of scared myself—that the men who'd supported me through so much might find themselves murdered all over again. But I had to ask.

Nox teased his fingers over my hair. The gesture and the fact that he still had that damned sword in his hand—it might even be the *same* sword he and Ruin had played with the other night—sparked a flare of heat over my skin. I mentally cracked a whip at my easily-distractable brain and then realized that a whip probably wasn't the best imagery to get my mind out of the gutter. I could picture Kai wielding one as he called me "naughty" way too easily.

Maybe I'd have to bring that imaginary element into reality too.

"We're going to keep you safe," Nox said. "That matters ahead of everything else. The Skullbreakers might as well be dead without you. And I'm including your sister in our mandate too. We have to be sure your home is fully protected before you move her in, and that you get to move her in without any pricks interfering. Once there's nothing left for you to be worried about, we'll get to work on bringing the bastards down."

"It's best that we gather as much intel and as many allies as we can first, anyway," Kai said. "We have our voodoo, but the Skeleton Corps clearly has numbers and influence. Rushing in won't do us any good."

"Kai always knows the smart approach," Ruin announced happily, coming up behind me and giving me one of his trademark bearhugs. "We're going to be so ready when we go after them, they're going to fall like dominos."

I wasn't sure there was any amount of preparation that would make the gang war go *that* smoothly, but who was I to dampen Ruin's enthusiasm?

My mind was still stuck on the other things Nox had said. Particularly the part about there being nothing left for me to worry about. A prickle ran over my skull, and I shivered automatically.

I tried to suppress it, but Kai caught on as quickly as he so often did. Just this once, he didn't figure out what my apprehension was about.

"I'll make sure these hotheads don't go charging into battle before we're sure of victory," he told me.

"It's not that," I said. "I—I don't know how we can be sure that nothing else is going to come up from *my* life that'll get us in trouble when I can't even remember the most important part of my past." I rubbed my forehead. "Even after meeting Nolan face to face, I have no idea what he actually did to Marisol, or what he said that day, or anything else… After the way he reacted when I tried to threaten him, I feel even more like there's something I'm missing."

"Maybe you're missing home," Ruin suggested, nuzzling my temple. "We could go out to the marsh again, walk by your old house—"

"No," I said quickly. A deeper shiver jittered through me at the thought of the marsh. It stirred up too many deep dark images from my nightmares.

I'd gotten a lot of power from the marsh, but my near death experience was haunting me now too. I didn't want to give my subconscious more fuel.

"It didn't work last time," I added. "I don't think just seeing things from back then is going to jog anything loose, or it'd have happened by now."

"I'm inclined to agree," Kai said.

Nox knuckled him. "So what would you suggest then, Mr. Know-it-all?"

Kai cocked his head. "Lily's been under a lot of stress ever since she got back in town. When you're tense, your body and mind go into defensive mode. More might slip out from her unconscious if she was able to really relax."

Ruin straightened up with a wiggle of excitement. "We can make this Lily Day! Do all the things that she'd like, take care of everything for her. I already know where we should go. We just need to—"

"Hold on," Nox said with a laugh. "I don't think you should run the whole show, my very enthusiastic friend. It's a good idea, but if we're going to do that, we should make sure we each get a shot at pampering our woman." He grinned at me. "I've got a few ideas myself."

"We'll take turns then," Kai said in an unconcerned tone, as if he was confident that whatever scheme he came up with was sure to mellow me out enough that all the secrets of my mind would slip free.

My gaze slid to the fourth member of the Skullbreakers, who still hadn't come over to join us. Jett was standing by one of the weapons displays, meticulously rearranging the swords and pikes and other pointy objects into a composition he was more satisfied with. I couldn't have said exactly how he'd changed it, but somehow something about that spot did resonate with me better than the rest.

Since I'd gotten up this morning, Jett had barely spoken to me other than occasional grunts. I didn't know what to make of our hot but very brief collision last night before he'd fled the bedroom. Nothing about his mouth or his hands had *felt* uninterested in me.

But I wasn't sure how to bring it up, especially since he didn't go for talking much on the best of subjects.

"I'll tell Jett," Ruin said, bounding over to retrieve the artist. "But I think I should get first shot, since it was my idea."

"Technically it was mine," Kai muttered, but he was smiling at the same time.

"And technically I'm the boss," Nox reminded him, and shook his head. "We should let him get it over with, or he'll be going on about how great it's going to be through everything else."

"True."

And so it ended up that I found myself being escorted into a neon-colored store that said *Build a Big Bear* on the sign. That name obviously should have tipped me off. Ruin practically bounced off the walls getting everything he wanted from the guy who owned the place, who watched the bunch of us like he wasn't sure whether he should thank us for coming or call the cops, and the next thing I knew, I was shoving armfuls of foamy stuffing into a gigantic shell of faux fur.

"Ram it in there!" Ruin said with fierce enthusiasm. "Imagine you're pummeling around the guts of all the jerks who've hassled you. That's right!"

There was actually something tension-releasing about heaving that stuff around and punching it into place. When I was done, a teddy bear as tall as I was sat in front of me. Ruin laughed with delight.

"Now you put all that toughness into the bear. It's your protector. And you can lean on it for hugs if I don't happen to be around." He paused. "Although if you *really* need a hug, you should just call me."

"I'll keep that in mind," I said dryly.

The bear was kind of horrifying at the moment, because its face was totally blank. The store owner brought out a spread of features that we could choose from to attach. Ruin zoomed in to tweak, twist, and chop them up until he'd assembled an expression that was almost as terrifying as the blankness. The bear's eyes were narrowed, and its mouth pulled back from jagged teeth. It looked ready to chomp someone's head off.

"Ah," the store owner said. "That's not typically the vibe we'd go for—"

Ruin glowered at him. "She needs a bear that's going to defend her. It can be cuddly *and* vicious."

Possibly because he'd just witnessed Ruin switch between those two modes, the store owner swallowed whatever else he'd wanted to say and settled for ringing us up.

I hauled the bear out to the car and managed to squeeze it into the back seat. A little kid walking with his mom glanced over at the windows just as I was getting in and shrieked at the sight of the massive, fearsome teddy bear. Ruin grinned as if he couldn't have asked for a better response.

Nox and Jett had been riding their motorcycles while Ruin and Kai joined me in the car. The Skullbreakers' boss leaned over on his seat, catching my gaze. "Follow me. We can do better than stuffed animals."

He parked outside a bar that was pretty much empty—not surprising considering it was early in the afternoon still—and ushered me inside. In the back, he stopped at a pinball machine to rule all pinball machines.

It had multiple flashing lights. It played a jaunty tune if you hit the innards in just the right way. And there were about five hundred different shiny surfaces to fling the balls at. I'd swear it even had gold leaf on the fucking cabinet.

Nox rubbed his hands together, an eager gleam sparking in his dark blue eyes, but he nudged me in front of him in the player's spot. "There's nothing like getting in the zone," he said. "Nothing else matters when you find it. I'm going to teach you how to get there."

He stood right behind me, his body flush against mine, his fingers sliding over the backs of my hands to guide my grip. With encouraging words murmured in my ear, he had me whacking that ball all over the cabinet. This light flashed and that one did. All the different tunes played. The score on the digital display shot up.

After a little while, Nox withdrew his hands to rest them on my waist. He stayed close, his breath washing over the side of my face. The heat of his body wrapped around me as I played, and I wasn't sure how much I was absorbed in the game vs. absorbed in him.

I mustn't have been the only one having those kinds of thoughts, because it wasn't long before his hands started traveling again, this time to stroke over my belly just above the fly of my jeans. My core tingled, and an ache formed between my legs.

But at the same time, the bar door creaked open to admit a few more patrons. A prickle of self-consciousness ran through my chest.

"Not here," I murmured. "Not with strangers watching."

Nox let out a low growl. "I think *everyone* should see what a good girl you are."

His voice electrified me, but the jab of uneasiness remained. I looked over my shoulder at him. "I wouldn't find it very relaxing. Wasn't that the point of this?"

He grimaced at me, but he returned his hands to my waist.

Without him distracting me, I did get caught up in the flow of the game for a bit. But it was Nox's satisfied hum of approval when I hit my highest score yet that melted my frustrations the most.

Kai slid into the passenger seat next to me when we rejoined the giant teddy bear in Fred 2.0. "*I* know how to pick something that'll fit what matters to *you*, not what I'm interested in," he said, adjusting his glasses, and started giving me directions.

I didn't know if I'd ever gotten to watch Kai fully in action before. We stepped out of the car at what looked like a high school… and turned out to indeed *be* a high school… and he smoothly chatted up a woman in the front office until she was handing a key over to him while smiling at him like he was doing her a favor.

Which maybe he'd convinced her he was. From their conversation, which I couldn't totally follow, he'd already done some buttering up earlier.

He led us through the halls to what turned out to be a sound booth looking onto a large music room. An orchestra of teenagers was practicing on the other side.

"One way glass," he said, motioning to the window at the other end. "And soundproofed." He hit a button, and the song the orchestra was practicing filtered through a speaker mounted on the wall. "We can see and hear them, but they can't see or hear us. So you can do whatever you want with this."

I recognized the tune immediately as something Tchaikovsky. The dramatic strings and woodwinds lilted up and down, alternately urgent and playful. But it wasn't perfect. Here and there, a string twanged out of tune, or a horn didn't quite hit its mark, or a flute's rhythm fell briefly out of pace with the others.

Nox raised his eyebrows. "You brought her to see a crappy high school orchestra?"

"They're not 'crappy,'" Kai said, and glanced at me. "Are they?"

I shook my head, stepping closer to the glass. "No, they're really good. Especially for teenagers. This is a difficult piece."

Kai nodded. "But it hasn't become rote for them yet. They're still feeling their way into the song. It's raw and fresh for them. I think… there's got to be something vital about hearing the music that way rather than honed and polished."

He was right. I wasn't sure how he'd figured that out when he'd never seemed all that interested in music himself—any more than he was interested in any other collections of knowledge he stuffed into his brain—but there was something about hearing the not-quite-perfect rendition that called to me. My heart thumped alongside it. I started to sway with the melody, and words bubbled up my throat in a song of my own.

"New city, new start. So much lost and so much found. Can I hold on to my heart? Can I rise above the ground?"

As I let my voice spill softly out of me, Ruin beamed. "Okay, Kai's was the best. You should always be singing."

"Hey," Jett muttered. "You haven't seen mine yet."

The taciturn guy didn't say anything else until we'd finished watching the rehearsal and driven across the city following his bike. He stopped outside an old warehouse that didn't look like it was in operation on the outside but had at least a few random businesses operating out of it. He spoke to a woman who led us down a broad hallway to a small room and set out several cans of paint in different bright colors.

"Have at it," she said, and left.

Jett motioned to the paints and glanced at me. "You haven't remembered anything yet, have you?"

My mouth twisted with the answer. "No, I haven't." I did feel lighter and looser than before, but nothing had tumbled free.

"Well, this is a way to let out tension and also see what you can create. Maybe when you're slapping paint around, you'll find that something from the back of your mind comes out that way. It works for me."

He was trying to give me a direct gateway to the parts of my past I'd lost. A pang shot through me, and I gave him a fond smile, wishing everything else between us didn't feel so messed up. "Thank you. It's perfect."

He allowed himself a small smile in return and gestured at the room around us, the walls of which were currently blank white. "We're allowed to put paint anywhere we want, as much as we want. It's all water soluble, so it doesn't matter how much of a mess we make—they just hose it down after. Let's get to it."

The woman had left paintbrushes too, but after swiping those around for a bit, I started dipping my hands right into the cans to use my fingers as my instruments the way Jett so often did. As I smeared paint across the vast canvas, the other guys joined in, taking over their own corners. I let my mood direct my motions, not questioning any impulse or letting myself really think about the choices I was making.

The lines and blotches we were creating started to wind together. Then Ruin accidentally brushed his fingers past my jaw while they were damp with paint.

He paused, his expression shifting from apologetic to mischievous in an instant. He reached out again and traced another paint-slick finger down my neck.

My pulse hiccupped, and a fresh heat woke up between my legs.

I swung toward Nox and teased my own colorful fingers across the bare semi-circle of chest above the collar of his tee. His eyes flared.

As he moved to lift my shirt just enough to trail streaks over my stomach, Kai stepped in to flick a finger along the underside of my chin. I grabbed Ruin and drew a sunny yellow smear across his forearm.

The heat in the room was rising—but not in Jett's corner. My eyes snagged on his gloomy form, his back to us, and my hands stilled.

I didn't want to do this in front of him, not when I doubted he'd join in. I had no idea what was going on in his head or his heart—or his pants—when it came to me, but whatever connection we had between us, it felt way too fragile to test it like that.

I pulled away from the other guys and looked down at myself. "I think someone's going to need to hose *me* down."

Ruin laughed. "I can see if they've got any hoses free."

He ran off out of the room, and I was too caught up in the exhilaration of the day to think that he probably shouldn't have been going off on his own in unfamiliar territory—until a gunshot reverberated through the walls.

Chapter Twenty-Five

Kai

ANY DOUBTS I might have had about whether the Skullbreakers were as unified as we'd ever been vanished the second the *boom* of the gun split the air. The four of us in the paint room all bolted for the door like one being.

But maybe I shouldn't have doubted it anyway. We'd come together for Lily today already. *She* united us, just as she'd held our souls in this world with her childhood games.

We burst into the wide hallway down the middle of the repurposed warehouse. Ruin was over near the front doors, grappling with a couple of men and splattered with enough paint that for a second I thought he was bleeding out. But unless he'd become radioactive, I didn't think his heart pumped anything in that vivid shade of scarlet.

As we raced over, the three of us pushing ahead of Lily like a shield, I read the situation as swiftly as I could zoom over a page of text. One of Ruin's attackers was holding a gun, presumably the one that'd gone off—yes, there was the entry mark in the ceiling just to the right of their tussle. Another pistol lay on the floor several feet away, like it'd been kicked there.

These guys weren't messing around. They'd been aiming to kill him this time, like maybe they had with the knife before—it wasn't just threats now.

Ruin was managing to angle the one man's hand away from him to stay out of range of the gun, but he was having to work too hard to deflect the blows of two attackers at once to land any solid strikes of his own. It didn't look as if he'd been able to inflict his weird emotional power on either of them so far.

But they were shit out of luck now.

Nox barreled into the guy with the gun, punching him with an electric sizzle and a fist that didn't even connect with flesh. That didn't matter—the man's head snapped to the side like he'd been pummeled in the jaw by a Mack truck. Jett sprang at the second guy. As he rammed his knee into the man's gut, the attacker's shirt flashed from gray to the dark brownish red of dried blood—the color our artistic friend no doubt wanted to leave in his wake.

I was about to jump in to join the fray when a third attacker leapt out of nowhere—straight at Lily. I didn't know if he meant to hurt her or simply take her hostage, but fury blazed through me in an instant.

"Leave her the fuck alone," I barked, throwing myself in front of her and swinging my fist.

Energy tingled through my limbs. My punch landed on the guy's nose with an electric jolt I felt in my bones. He backed up a step, clutching it and dribbling blood down his chin. I readied myself for him to make another lunge at her, but he glanced at Lily and then… backed away a little farther.

Odd.

The gears in my head started whirring, but a second later Nox tackled the guy to the ground. The other two attackers were already sprawled on the floor, one with a fatal slash across his throat and the other with his neck twisted at an unfortunate angle—well, unfortunate for him, anyway. He stared at his colleague over his shoulder with a dead-eyed expression that seemed regretful that he'd made this grave misjudgment.

"Hold on!" I shouted before Nox could bash the other guy's teeth through to the back of his skull, and dashed over. "We need one alive," I added under my breath, my senses twitching with the awareness of our audience—the frightened faces poking from doors up and down the hall. "We need to ask some questions."

"Right," the boss said gruffly, and motioned Jett and Ruin over as he hauled the guy to his feet.

I stepped closer. "Let me try something?"

Nox gave me a quizzical look, but he nodded—because he trusted me. He and the other guys might tease me about being a know-it-all, but they respected my knowledge, unlike a hell of a lot of the people I'd encountered in my life.

That was why I stuck with them, wasn't it? Because I gave them something they wouldn't have otherwise… and they did the same for me. I'd just lost sight of what that acceptance and respect meant in my exhilaration at being alive at all.

I smiled my thanks and didn't waste any time carrying out my test. The man jerked around like he thought he'd make a run for it, and I aimed another punch at his chest, tossing an order at him as I threw my fist. "Walk with us to the street, and don't make any other moves."

Another pulse of supernatural electricity quivered through my nerves. The man stiffened—and then turned toward the building's entrance. My smile grew into a grin.

When we started walking, the other guys staring at our captive, the man kept pace with us. His mouth had twisted at a horrified angle, and his shoulders twitched as if he was trying to move his arms, but he followed my command to a T.

Halfway down the hall, Ruin whooped and bounced on his feet. "You pulled his strings like he's a puppet!"

Nox glanced back at me, a pleased smirk playing with his lips. "I guess we found out what your ghostly superpower is."

I'd always been able to manipulate people's behavior with my words—and now I could do it with my fists as well. I couldn't think of a more fitting complement to my skillset.

As we reached the doors, sirens sounded in the distance. Someone in our audience had called the police. Nox grunted and muttered, "Fucking cops. Let's move."

Jett frowned. "Are we going to stick this prick in Lily's car?"

"Better than on one of your motorcycles," Lily said from behind us. "Ruin and Kai can keep him under control."

Ruin pumped his fist. "Hell, yes, we can."

I gave the man another punch with the instruction, "Stay with us and follow us to the car." As we stepped out of the building, he turned as if to smack me, so I punched him again. "Follow us *and otherwise leave us alone*."

With a strained grumble, he jerked forward again and walked stiffly with us to where Lily had parked the car.

She looked down at her paint-smeared clothes and skin and sighed. "There are ways to get it out of the upholstery," I said, and shoved the guy toward the back door with another shiver of supernatural energy. "Get in. Sit perfectly still."

He squeezed into the middle next to the giant teddy bear, giving it a nervous glance as if he thought it might turn out to be a living part of our gang too. I sat next to him in case I needed to pummel him into submission a little more. Ruin hopped in up front but stayed twisted in his seat, eyeing the enemy, while Lily started the engine.

"Where should we go?" she asked abruptly as she cruised down the street, ramping up the speed as the sirens wailed closer.

"Take a couple of quick turns so we're out of view of the cops," I said. Nox and Jett were roaring up behind us on their bikes, and I knew they'd follow. "And then…" We wouldn't want to take him back to her apartment. It wouldn't go over well with the rental company to splatter interrogation blood all over those hardwood floors after we'd just gone to so much effort cleaning up the joint. Although with my new talent, maybe there wouldn't need to be any blood involved.

No, still not a good place for holding criminal types. I motioned to the east after Lily had taken her second turn. "Let's head back to the new clubhouse. It's got a good basement. Basements are the best for putting the screws to someone."

Our captive let out a noise of protest where he was sitting rigidly next to us. "You fuckers," he spat out abruptly, as if he'd only just realized he could talk despite my orders about what he did with his body. "I don't know what crazy kind of—"

I socked him in the shoulder. "Shut up and just sit there."

Just like that, he did. Brilliant.

He might have been trying to spew intimidation at us, but he was obviously pretty shaken up. His eyes darted from side to side, the little bit of movement he was capable of after I'd given my commands, and his previously ruddy face had paled. With the dark V of his hairline adding to the effect, he looked like a vampire—a vampire who'd been taken hostage by a bunch of stake-twirling maniacs.

And really, the maniac part of that wasn't untrue.

Lily pulled up outside the clubhouse, and I rapped my knuckles against our reluctant guest's shoulder. "Get out and come into the restaurant with us."

I must have hit him too lightly. No jolt of electricity ran through me, and the guy shifted in his seat as if to take a grab at me.

With a shock of adrenaline, I smacked him again. "Get out and come into the restaurant with us. And that's *all* you're going to do until I say so." I whacked him across the head for good measure to drive that last point home.

The asshole's jaw worked, but he followed my directions this time. Nox and Jett converged on us in the clubhouse's dank basement, and Ruin gleefully brandished a length of rope he'd probably been dying for the chance to use. Since I didn't know whether my ghostly persuasive power might exhaust itself halfway through our little chat, I motioned for him to go ahead and tie the guy to a chair.

The guy's breath was coming in faint wheezes now. I studied him, stalking back and forth in front of him in a way I happened to know unnerved approximately ninety-three percent of all human beings.

"Got a mild case of asthma, do you?" I said. "Only comes out when you're really freaked out. Obviously you haven't had a very challenging job if you've been able to hide it all this time."

"You know fuck all about that," the man snapped, but there was a rasp in his voice. He wasn't shutting up anymore. I took note of the fact that it appeared my orders wore off as soon as I gave a new set. Probably the compulsion would fade given enough time too.

How kind of him to volunteer as a test subject for my trial run.

Since he was tightly bound to the chair now, I didn't have to worry about my previous command staying active. Most important things first—could I compel his vocal cords as well as his other body parts?

I cuffed him across the head. "Tell us who you work for."

"No," he snarled back. Okay, no luck there. I still had plenty of my usual methods to turn to. And I had another experiment to run.

"Wrong answer." I slapped him across the face. "Keep wiggling your fingers until I tell you to stop."

The guy immediately started jiggling his fingers in some very energetic jazz hands where they dangled by the sides of the chair. He couldn't move them any more than that with his arms tied from his shoulders to halfway down his forearms. I checked my phone so I could keep track of how long it took before he stopped and resumed my pacing.

The other guys hung back, watching eagerly but silently. They knew I'd get answers.

And if I needed any help with motivation, *I* knew they'd be only too happy to supply it. Really, it was the perfect symbiosis.

Our captive stared down at his hands, his face outright white now and strained as he must have tried to will his fingers to stop waggling. It didn't work. I strolled over and leaned close so my face was just a foot from his. "If you think that's creepy, wait until you see what else we can do."

His gaze jerked to me, and I grinned. Fear showed in every flicker of his eyes and the bead of perspiration that'd formed at the point of his hairline.

I'd never worked over a guy quite this terrified before. Even if I couldn't supernaturally persuade him into spilling his guts, my ghostly abilities were still giving me a leg up.

"There's a very simple way to get out of this horror show," I went on. "All we want to know is who hired you to go after our friend here and why." I motioned to Ruin.

"Well, you're not getting that," the guy said defiantly. "I don't fucking know."

Nox let out a growl, but I held up my hand to keep him still. I jabbed the man at the base of his throat. "You know who you work for, don't you? Who you take orders from?"

He glowered back at me, keeping his mouth shut. It'd have been a more impressive display if his hands hadn't still been wriggling away at his sides like butterflies on cocaine.

I kept grinning. "Let me put it this way. You've already seen that I can make you act any way I want. You could tell me, and we'll end this cleanly. Or before the end, I could order you to bite off your own dick. If your spine won't stretch that far, you could chew off those wriggling fingers one by one. Maybe we'll stop while you still have your thumbs and you can jam those all the way up your nose."

"Or his ass!" Ruin suggested helpfully.

"Or he could poke out his eyeballs," Jett said.

Nox chuckled. "Why choose? All three sounds good to me."

The bead of sweat had turned into a trickle that was streaming down the guy's face. I saw him make another attempt at controlling his hands… and fail. He'd now gone all the way from white to green. Maybe he'd be reborn as a chameleon.

"You want to do a little self-mutilation first to see how it goes?" I said conversationally when he stayed silent. "Well, I'm sure we'll have fun that way too." I lifted my hand to swing another punch.

"No!" the guy cried, with a pre-emptive wince. "Fine. I—I work for Ironguard Security. It was just a fucking job. We get our assignment; we follow through. That's it."

Lily tensed where she was standing at the edge of the room. My own thoughts had gone abruptly still.

Ironguard Security. We'd found their card in Nolan Gauntt's desk.

"What exactly was your assignment?" I asked.

He jerked his head toward Ruin. "The kid was supposed to be reporting to us on some girl he was monitoring. I don't know why. The orders came from someone high up. The kid stopped delivering, and we were supposed to end him."

"Who gave those orders?" Nox demanded.

"I don't know! I don't deal with the clients. I'm just one of the guys on the ground. I swear."

I cocked my head, raising my hand again. "I really hope you can tell me how your business is connected to the Gauntt family."

The man's eyes widened. "You mean Thrivewell. Sure—sure! I don't think it's supposed to be public knowledge, but I saw a form once—the company's owned by them. Ironguard is run by Thrivewell. Not really surprising, right, when they own half the businesses in the city." He let out a somewhat hysterical laugh.

A chill gripped me. I pulled out my phone, brought up the photo I'd taken of the business card with the numbers Nolan had scrawled on the back, and considered them. The second one was definitely a cell phone. I dialed it.

The phone we'd stolen from Ruin's previous attacker started to peal in his back pocket. Ruin snatched at it, but I ended the call, shaking my head. "Don't bother. That was just me."

The pieces were clicking together into a picture in my head I couldn't deny. Nolan Gauntt had been keeping tabs on Lily. So had Ansel Hunter. Nolan owned the security company Ansel had been reporting to. He'd written down the number of an Ironguard employee who'd gone missing while on Ansel's case. There wasn't a chance in hell this wasn't all part of the same scheme.

I could tell we weren't going to get anything more useful out of this dope. As much as I'd have liked to push the limits of my powers and see how far I could twist his sense of self-preservation, I preferred to stay a man of my word.

My other experiment had delivered results. The man's fingers were slowing in their frantic waggling. I checked my phone.

Fifteen minutes. Fifteen minutes for the effect to start to fade.

I motioned to Nox. "I'm done with him."

I turned my back while the shot rang out and found myself facing Lily. She was hugging herself, her face drawn, but she was looking to the other guys rather than me.

When we'd taken our turns helping her unwind, *I* was the one who'd offered her something that fit who she was. Hadn't that proven I understood her better than anyone?

But maybe I'd underestimated my friends' contributions there too.

I'd given her what she already knew. They'd given her something of themselves. They'd shared part of who *they* were…

What did I have to offer up of myself that wasn't just information I'd gleaned from somewhere or someone else?

I glanced back at the man now slumped in his chair over a pool of blood, and certainty coiled inside me. I was what I was. And even if I couldn't present her with any great gifts that were all my own, I was damn well going to make sure every villain we crossed paths with coughed up everything in them that would help her.

Chapter Twenty-Six

Lily

I DIDN'T KNOW what the Skullbreakers did with the body, and I didn't have any interest in asking. Too many thoughts were whirling around in my brain for me to have much room to worry about it anyway. Even the rush of hot water when I showered off the paint on my hair and skin couldn't sweep the uneasy clamor away.

Ruin and Jett had brought me back to the new apartment while Nox and Kai handled the corpse situation. Technically my lease didn't start until tomorrow, but after the clean-up we'd done and the grudging approval I'd gotten from the rental company—and the fact that I already had the keys to the new doors—I'd unofficially moved in anyway. It'd given us a chance to get a little furniture set up for when I brought Marisol here tomorrow.

I'd wanted the place to look nicer than the old apartment without breaking the bank, especially considering I was out of my second job in a month's time, so everything was basic and modern but sturdy and clean. Mostly I'd given the guys the general specifications, and they'd picked things up here and there…

I hadn't asked much about how that'd happened either. I'd just insisted that no one get hurt in the process, and they hadn't given any indication that they'd broken that rule.

Among the few things I had picked up myself was a small, roll-top secretary desk that I'd already outfitted with pencils and pastels in the drawers and a stack of good drawing paper on the lower shelf. It sat by the window in the bedroom I'd figured would be Marisol's.

I wandered past it now, sweeping my fingertips over the curved top but barely feeling the old wood. The faint rumble of traffic carried through the window. I inhaled, tasting the "clean linen" air freshener I'd sprayed around the place to absorb any lingering odors from our cleaning.

It felt as though I'd traveled in a circuit of the entire apartment over a hundred times. The moment I stopped moving, my thoughts crowded even more heavily into my head, and I started feeling like I was drowning right there in the air.

I'd clearly been on Nolan Gauntt's radar from the moment I'd returned to Lovell Rise. Had he ever *stopped* monitoring me? He'd had Ansel tracking me from the moment I'd returned, so he must have known I was being released from St. Elspeth's.

Was this all because he was worried that I'd spill the beans about what's gone on with my sister seven years ago? But then, why wouldn't he just have *me* offed instead of Ansel?

I had no answers to any of those questions, so they just kept gnawing at my brain.

Finally, Nox and Kai strode in. Ruin perked up where he'd been sitting on the boxy pull-out couch, shooting a hopeful glance my way. Jett turned around, but he never did perky. He'd been flicking his fingers against the wall to adjust the hue of the main room for the last hour, never seeming totally satisfied with what he ended up with. Right now, it was a muted olive green.

I moved to sit on the loveseat kitty-corner with the couch. As if sensing that we were about to have some kind of official debriefing, the rest of the guys assembled in the living area.

Nox took the spot next to me with his usual cocky air but slipping his hand around mine gently. He'd obviously wiped at the paint I'd trailed across his chest, but a smudge of blue remained. Jett dropped down next to Ruin, and Kai spun one of the chairs at the new dining table, which would be able to seat all six of us. If I ever decided to host a dinner party that involved both my sister and the former Skullbreakers, that was.

I should have been happy. I'd won this new home and I was getting Marisol away from Wade, but the interrogation made that victory feel like just one small bubble of okay in a vast sea of pretty-freaking-perilous. How easily would that bubble pop?

"The Gaunts hired this security company to hire Ansel to stalk me and then to kill him when he went AWOL on them," I said, laying out in as brief terms as I could what'd been obvious from the moment Ruin's attacker had mentioned Ironguard Security. "They've been keeping tabs on me since—hell, they must have had him ready to go before I even officially moved in. I guess they found out I'd gotten the old apartment, or heard from the hospital that I was being fully discharged…"

I paused, and a comment Nolan had made came back to me. I'd been so thrown by his blasé attitude about my powers that I hadn't totally wrapped my head around the rest before. "I think he paid off the hospital somehow to keep me under *their* supervision for as long as they did. He said something along those lines… but of course he denied it when I tried to get the real story out of him."

Nox growled, his fingers tightening around mine. "After everything else the bastard's done, I'm not surprised."

"Me neither. But that means…" I lowered my head and ran my free hand into my hair. "I thought all I had to do was find out what he'd done to Marisol seven years ago and make sure he didn't hurt her again. But he's been keeping me down this entire time. He's been trying to have Ruin *murdered*. Who knows what else he might have been doing that we haven't figured out yet?" The enormity of the situation and our enemy on the other side of it threatened to drown me again.

"He hasn't managed to murder me yet," Ruin said cheerfully.

"I know, but he's going to keep trying… and I don't know how to stop him. No wonder he wasn't scared by me hurling around some water when he's got so much regular power he could practically rule the world."

"No one's going to rule this city except for us when we're through," Nox announced.

Kai nodded. "We've learned things. We have a better idea what we're up against now, so we'll come up with better defenses—and offenses, when we're ready. We still have plenty of advantages. Our supernatural voodoo." He wiggled his fingers. "And the fact that we don't care if we break the law and he still has to consider it, even if he circumvents it sometimes."

"All our new friends on the streets, too," Ruin added.

"Friends," Jett scoffed, but he caught my gaze, his deep brown eyes steady. "We're not letting anyone screw you over again."

Their reassurances didn't comfort me the way they must have been hoping, but the worst of my nerves settled. I dragged a breath into my lungs. "Okay. I guess there's nothing to do but keep going forward anyway."

I didn't sleep well that night, though, and my stomach stayed knotted with apprehension for the whole drive out to my old house to pick up Marisol. The guys had insisted on all coming along in case the Gauntts or the Skeleton Corps tried anything, and I'd insisted they stay on their bikes at a reasonable distance so I didn't have to explain about them to my sister just yet. Their forms cruised along behind me in the rearview mirror like they were haunting me, but I'd learned that being haunted wasn't so bad.

As I got closer and closer to the house, the knot balled even tighter. A hint of marshy scent crept into the car, and my chest started to contract too. Flashes of my nightmares flickered through my head, as if some part of me was afraid the lake would reach out and suck me back into it even if I didn't set foot anywhere near the shore.

I wasn't literally drowning, but I was in over my head, wasn't I? Taking Marisol under my protection when I wasn't even sure what I was protecting her from. When I was scared to even let her see the ways I *could* protect her.

How could I be her defender when I was so terrified myself?

The marsh and the shimmer of open water beyond the reeds came into view up ahead. My hands tightened around the steering wheel—and something cracked open inside me. A weird sense of certainty rose up through my chest. The mark on the underside of my arm prickled with a sudden itch, but I ignored it.

Nothing had unlocked my memories so far, but maybe I simply hadn't opened up the doorway wide enough. I'd been afraid to know what'd happened, what I'd done, what I was up against… and I'd let myself become afraid of the source of the power I had.

The marsh didn't want to hurt me. It hadn't dragged me down on purpose. That'd been my six-year-old clumsiness, and when I'd fought through it and clambered my way out, the marsh had let a special piece of itself come with me.

What if it could help me unearth the piece of myself I'd lost?

The itch on my arms sharpened into a jab. That sensation only strengthened my resolve. I turned down the lane before the one that led to my old house, driving all the way out to the parking spot near the edge of the marsh.

The guys followed me. As I got out of the car, they parked their bikes around Fred 2.0. The damp breeze washed over me, and the cattails rattled together. My pulse stuttered with a sudden burst of panic, but I held strong against it.

"What's going on, Siren?" Nox asked, no judgment in his tone, only curiosity. His new nickname for me bolstered my confidence even more.

"A lot of things started here," I said. "And it was near here that everything went wrong. I want to see if the marsh can wash free the memories that I can't seem to get at on my own." I squared my shoulders and looked at the four of them. "No matter what happens or how it looks, I don't want you to come after me. You need to let me figure this out. I think—I think I'll be fine."

I couldn't say I was sure, but then, how many things could you be sure of in life other than taxes and a stomachache after a really greasy pizza?

A couple of frogs had hopped over to greet me. The familiar hum was spreading through my veins, even though I wasn't angry or particularly worked up right now. I was just determined.

I would own my power. I would own everything that'd happened in my life, no matter how horrifying. And that included embracing the moment when I'd nearly lost my life altogether.

I walked over to the water, kicked off my shoes, and stepped down into the mushy bottom. The chilly water lapped around my ankles. Pushing through the reeds and rushes, I waded deeper. The water wavered up to my calves, then my knees, then my thighs. My toes were going numb, but I didn't need them right now anyway.

I was a siren. I was a waterlily, an angelfish, a minnow. I was queen of the marsh, and the water moved to my will. I'd fallen down into it and risen again, and we knew each other now like old friends. Like mother and daughter, better than my birth mother had treated me lately.

My heart was thumping hard, but I kept walking until I was in up to my waist. The damp seeped up through my shirt. I shivered but held firm. Then I closed my eyes and threw myself forward into the water.

The cold liquid closed over me in an instant. Panic blared through my limbs, but I held them rigid, refusing to struggle. Instead, I opened my mouth.

More water streamed down my throat and into my lungs, and weirdly, my body relaxed into it. As if I'd come home. The hum inside me rang out like a note strummed on a heavenly harp, its thrum resonating through my ears and into my mind, and I was abruptly aware of a pain in the mark on my arm and a wall in the back of my mind.

I willed the water's energy through my sinking body. Dug it into the mark to carve out that damned spot. Hurled it at the sense of a barrier within my thoughts.

The power sparked and sizzled, but I drew on more and more.

I was the marsh. The marsh was me. And nothing in me that wasn't part of it belonged.

Something in me that wasn't right at all strained and railed against the onslaught of watery magic. But I willed all the swell and stretch of the marsh into me, battering the strangeness again and again and—

The wall inside me shattered apart with a burst of refreshing cold, and images flooded into my mind.

I was thirteen years old, walking into the house after a wander down by the marsh seven years ago. Mom and Wade were sitting in the living room. Both of their expressions stiffened at the sight of me, but Wade's most of all.

"You're home early," Mom said faintly.

Wade jumped up. "Why don't you go out and play some more? There's nothing for you to do in here."

My senses prickled onto the alert. There was something they didn't want me to know. I glanced toward the stairs, and at the same moment the floor creaked and a gasp filtered through the floor from Marisol's room.

"Lily!" Wade barked, but I was already dashing for the stairs. I leapt up them two at a time, panic blazing through all my senses.

The door to the bedroom was closed. I hurtled to it and flung it open.

A man I hadn't known then but could now recognize as Nolan Gauntt was sitting on my little sister's bed next to Marisol. He was turned toward her, his knee touching hers, one hand stroking over her hair.

His other hand was tucked behind her back, but he withdrew it as I came in. Had he stuck it up her *shirt*?

My earlier panic crackled into rage. "Get the hell away from her!" I snapped, storming into the room. A weird hum tickled up between my ribs. I hadn't known what it meant back then. I'd been too busy wanting to rend him limb from limb to care.

Nolan stood up with a smile so calm it made me even more furious. He patted Marisol, who looked dazed, on the head and said something under his breath that I couldn't make out.

I lunged at him, throwing a punch, but he caught my arm. Holding it firmly, he set one hand on the underside, right by my armpit, and stared down at me with an eerie light dancing in his otherwise flat blue eyes.

"You won't remember this," he said. A thread of energy rippled through his voice and tingled into my flesh. "You won't remember."

"Of course I will," I retorted, and lashed out at him with my other hand.

He batted that one aside too, shoved me onto the bed next to Marisol, and stalked out of the room.

I sprang onto my feet and whirled toward Marisol. She was still sitting there so rigidly. The panic returned, clutching my gut.

"Are you okay, Mare? What did he do to you?"

"Nothing," she said in a distant voice. "It wasn't anything."

My teeth gritted. I dashed after the man who'd been messing with her.

He'd moved fast. By the time I raced to the bottom of the stairs, he was already by the front door. A car engine was revving to life outside. Both Mom and Wade were on their feet.

"I'm so sorry," Wade was saying. "I didn't mean for the interruption—"

"It's fine," Nolan interrupted briskly. "I've taken care of everything. You don't need to worry about her."

Then he swept out of the house.

I stared at Mom and Wade. They'd known. They'd fucking *known* he was up there with Marisol—they'd let him…

The hum that'd been seeping through me rose into a roar. I still hadn't known what it meant, but I did know I wanted to rain down all my fury on the two of them.

"Why did you let him come here?" I yelled, grabbing an empty mug off the coffee table and whipping it at Wade. "How could you do that to her?"

Wade winced as the mug hit his shoulder and held up his hands defensively. "Ellie, I think you'd better let me handle this," he said to Mom, who hesitated for only a split-second before dipping her head and ducking out of the room.

That made me even angrier. "You asshole! You shithead! He *hurt* Marisol, and you let him. I'm going to—"

"Now, Lily," Wade said. "You really have no idea—"

Those words triggered the biggest surge of anger yet. *I* had no idea? I'd been the one who'd gone up there and seen what the weirdo was doing to her.

An inarticulate sound of rage escaped my throat, the hum burst out of me—and a torrent of water exploded through the wall that bordered the kitchen.

The rest was mostly as I'd already pieced it together. Water I hadn't even fully understood I was controlling gushed out of the walls and pummeled Wade and the living room. Wade had shoved at me, and I'd given him a bloody nose and scratched up his cheek while I'd tried to fight him off. Then he'd fled to the kitchen and locked the door.

When the police had arrived, I'd run out of steam. I was standing soggy and screaming in the middle of the living room, with Wade's wounds and the destruction around me as evidence of my crazed meltdown. Someone had stuck a syringe in my arm…

And then I was back in the present day, heaving up out of the water with a groan and a sputter.

Swaying on my feet again, I doubled over and vomited marsh water back to whence it came. It poured out of me, somehow leaving me tingling clean on the inside rather than stinging raw.

"Lily?" Ruin's frantic voice carried from beyond the bullrushes. "Lily, can you hear me?"

I coughed again and found my voice, rough but steady. "I'm here. I'm coming back."

And now I was whole again.

As I strode through the water back to shore, my hand rose to rest on my other arm. I yanked aside the collar of my drenched shirt and peered at the underside.

The random birthmark was gone. It'd been right where Nolan had gripped my arm when he'd said I wouldn't remember, with that unearthly quaver in his voice.

That was how he'd been so sure I didn't remember.

I'd broken it. I'd broken the spell he'd put on me. My magic was stronger than his after all.

Nolan Gauntt had magic.

I hauled myself out of the marsh and went to join the guys, who'd come down to the shore to wait for me. Kai had pulled the spare blanket out of Fred's trunk, where I'd returned it once I had proper bedding in the apartment, and wrapped it around me with uncharacteristic tenderness. And the whole wrenching story spilled out of me.

"The Gauntts have their own voodoo," Nox said when I was done, his expression grim.

"Nolan does, anyway," I said. "But we can beat it. *I* just beat it. And now we know." Of course Nolan wouldn't have been that horrified by my water magic when he knew supernatural powers were possible because of his own. He had no idea how much farther I'd be able to take it.

Kai tipped his head. "Yes, and now that we know, we also know what we need to be watching for. We'll pick apart all his secrets until we figure out exactly how to take him down and make him pay."

For the first time, I completely believed that statement. A smile crossed my lips.

I knew all my own secrets now, and I hadn't done anything horrifying. I hadn't locked them away to protect myself from knowing the truth in the first place. It'd always been Nolan, trying to cover up his own crimes.

I rubbed the corner of the blanket over my hair and turned to look toward my old house. "I'd better go get Marisol." For the first time, that statement didn't come with any apprehension, despite the bizarre act I'd just carried out. My chin lifted higher. "And I think there's something I should show her."

When I pulled up outside the house, the guys staying far back on their bikes, my clothes and hair were still pretty damp. I didn't even have to knock on the door. Marisol had been expecting me. As I stepped out of the car, she came barging out of the house with a purse under one arm and dragging a carry-on sized suitcase by the other hand.

"You came!" she said, as if she hadn't been totally sure, and then took in my appearance. "What happened to you?"

"Nothing I couldn't handle," I said, running my fingers through my hair. "I wanted to make sure I can keep you safe. And I think I can. Definitely better than Wade and Mom have ever done. Do you want to see something crazy?"

Marisol arched her eyebrows, but a curious light flashed in her eyes. "Sure."

A flicker of anxiety still wavered through my chest, but I could ignore it. I drew on my love for my sister and my anger at everyone who'd threatened her, and swiped my hand over the front of my shirt in time with the hum resonating inside me.

A thin stream tugged off the fabric and wove through the air toward my palm as I moved my hand away. I urged it to dance in the air, swinging it higher and twisting it around, like it was a ribbon made out of water. Then I lowered my hand and let it splash to the ground.

Marisol's jaw had dropped. I watched her expression carefully, braced for any hint of fear.

A broad grin stretched across her face. "That's not crazy," she said. "That's fucking amazing! How did you do that?"

"Language," I chided, not that I was anyone to complain about swearing, and ushered her toward the car. "I'll explain everything while I drive."

Chapter Twenty-Seven

Lily

The day after Marisol moved in, Nox texted me while she and I were digging into a late breakfast. I'd made pancakes, which I was proud to say were not at all round but very fluffy, which was obviously what mattered the most. Maximum syrup absorption powers.

Is this a good time to come by and meet her? he asked. *Is she settled in?*

We'd already discussed that the guys should visit so I could introduce them to Marisol before too long. They were going to be a major part of her extended protection squad, so even though the situation was highly bizarre, she needed to at least be aware that they were on her side.

Give us an hour, I wrote back. *I want to prepare her a little more ahead of time.*

What's there to prepare for? We're undeniably amazing. Thankfully he added a winking emoji to show that he hadn't taken on Ruin's overly optimistic personality.

Ha ha. Be on your best behavior. No weapons, no blood.

And what do I get as a reward if I'm good, Siren?

We'll see. I added a tongue stuck-out emoji to emphasize the point and set my phone down. Although he'd probably get all sorts of not-totally-wrong ideas from that tongue.

Marisol had been watching me curiously. "Is everything okay?" she asked, giving her arm an idle scratch.

"Yeah!" I said quickly. "Just talking to some friends. Or, well, I guess more like boyfriends. In some cases."

Marisol's eyebrows jumped to her hairline. "Boyfriend*s*? There's obviously a lot you haven't filled me in on yet."

I let out an embarrassed laugh, wishing my brain had kept up better with my mouth so I hadn't blurted it out quite like that. "It's a long story. But what matters is there are some guys who care a lot about me, and they care about you too because they know how important you are to me. They helped me get to the point where I could look after you. They're going to stop by later today so you can meet them, but first there are a few things I should probably explain about them."

My sister popped another bite of pancake into her mouth and chewed it thoughtfully. "Is this like your crazy water powers? Did they almost drown in the marsh and wake up as superheroes too?"

"I'm not a superhero," I had to protest. "And the guys, well—"

As I spoke, Marisol reached to scratch the underside of her arm again, and her posture went abruptly rigid. She stared at me, dropping her fork onto her plate with a clatter.

I hesitated. "Mare? What's—"

She leapt to her feet. "What are you trying to do to me?" she interrupted. Her eyes had widened. "You're trying to mess with my head, take me away from my family."

My heart started to thud painfully hard. "What are you talking about? *I'm* your family."

"No, you're not. Not after you left, and you've been doing all this crazy stuff—I can't trust you."

I scrambled up to reach for her, but the second I moved toward her, my sister jerked away, her hands flying up defensively. "Don't touch me! Don't come anywhere near me!"

What the hell was going on? It was like *she'd* been possessed—but from what the guys had told me, it couldn't happen in a blink to a person just sitting there eating pancakes.

I held up my own hands in a gesture of peace. "I won't come near you if you don't want me to. But you have to tell me what's going on, Mare. Everything was fine a minute ago. If something's bothering you—"

"Nothing was fine," Marisol shot back. "And I don't have to tell you anything. I'm getting out of here."

She dashed for the door without any further warning—in her short-sleeved pajamas and bare feet, without a single thing she'd brought with her. Like she couldn't bear to be in the same room as me for a second longer.

My gut lurched, but my need to protect her—even if from herself—was stronger than any remaining fear that I would hurt her somehow. I threw myself after her, snatching at her arm.

I caught the sleeve of her pajama top instead. She heaved herself away from me at the same moment, so hard the seam tore. Her arm flew up as she started to smack me away—

And I caught sight of a small, pinkish blotch like a birthmark on the underside of her arm, just a couple of inches from the pit. A blotch that was the same size and color as the one that'd marked my arm until I'd shook off the spell Nolan Gauntt had used to suppress my memory, in almost the exact same spot. Where she'd been scratching just now as if it was niggling at her.

Horror hit me in an icy wave.

Marisol hurtled away from me and flung the door open. "Leave me alone," she shrieked back at me. "Leave me alone!"

No way in hell. I charged after her, but she slammed the door in my face. In my panicked state, it took me too long fumbling with the doorknob and the two thousand automatic locking mechanisms Nox had insisted on. I raced after her, in my own pajamas and slippers, hearing her just a couple of flights below me on the stairs, then the solid thump of the new lobby door when it swung shut in her wake…

I shoved past that door and burst out onto the sidewalk, my head swiveling from side to side. "Marisol!" I cried out.

But she'd already vanished without a trace.

Grave Misconduct

GANG OF GHOULS #3

Chapter One

Lily

It was probably kind of ridiculous to be wandering the streets shouting, "Marisol!" every few seconds, like my sister would come running to me if she heard her name. Like she hadn't purposefully run *away* from me an hour ago, yelling at me to leave her alone. Really, it might have made more sense to shut up so she didn't know I was coming.

But without any idea where she'd run off to, it wasn't as if I could sneak up on her anyway. I couldn't help hoping that whatever magical delusion had come over her to make her think that I was the enemy, it'd fade away, and she'd want to come back.

She'd dashed out of my apartment in nothing but her pajamas, not even slippers on her feet. Even at midday, the fall air was getting nippy, and the city streets in Mayfield weren't exactly meant for barefoot frolicking. I was a little chilled, and that was after Nox had gone back to the apartment to get my housecoat and proper shoes.

"Marisol!" I called again, peering down a dingy alley.

A stray cat hissed at me and raced off between the dumpsters. My panic and frustration thrummed more frantically in my chest. In response, without my intending it, a jet of water shot from a nearby storm drain. It spouted ten feet in the air before splattering back to the ground.

It didn't know how to find my sister either.

I couldn't say that it'd drawn more attention to me than I'd already gotten, though. My apartment was in an up-and-coming neighborhood that was still working on the whole coming part, and I'd ventured into an area that was still pretty down. All the same, there weren't a whole lot of people wandering around in pajamas and a housecoat hollering someone's name, while nearby water sources periodically splashed and splattered like they had a mind of their own.

Oh, and the herd of frogs that'd gathered behind me would have accounted for a lot of the stares I was getting from bystanders too.

I glanced down at my feet. During the hour I'd been searching, more and more desperate energy racing through my body without any real target to direct it at, I'd amassed a small army of about fifty of the eager amphibians. They hopped across the sidewalk, some of them peering up at me as if waiting for my command, others leaping ahead like they thought they might be able to track down my sister on their own. Unfortunately, they didn't seem to be much use as bloodhounds.

"You should go back to the marsh or wherever you came from," I murmured at them from the corner of my mouth. I wasn't so frantic that I couldn't figure out I'd look even more unhinged if it was obvious I was carrying on a conversation with my froggy friends. "You're going to end up roadkill around here." I'd already seen one smashed under a tire during my search.

The frogs kept hopping around, somewhat aimlessly other than their determination to stick with me. I guessed I should appreciate their loyalty even if they were kind of useless. It wasn't like *I* was being of much use to anyone at the moment.

I glanced at the grubby buildings and cracked pavement around me once more and pulled out my phone. For approximately the millionth time, I dialed Marisol's number.

Her cell phone immediately clicked over to voicemail. As her awkward teenage voice announced who I'd reached, I debated leaving a message, but she already had ten or so from me. I didn't really have anything to add at this point.

If I'd known the magic words to bring her back, I'd have said them in the first place.

I wasn't even totally sure she had her phone on her. Most teenagers seemed to be glued to the things, but she might have left it in her bag at my apartment, like she had so much else. I hadn't gone back to check.

As I sighed and shoved the phone into my housecoat's plush pocket, Kai came trotting over from a nearby street. He took in my motion and expression, and his gray-green eyes darkened behind the rectangular panes of his glasses. "Still no answer, huh?"

I shook my head, and he dodged the frogs as he reached to squeeze my shoulder. Kai wasn't really a PDA kind of guy, even though I'd found out just how enthusiastic he could be in private, so that gesture was the equivalent to him sweeping me into a hug.

Speaking of which…

Ruin loped over from a different direction, caught sight of my face, and immediately wrapped his well-muscled arms around me in one of his epic embraces. "We'll find her, Angelfish," he assured me, nuzzling my hair. "With all of us looking, we've got to."

Kai frowned. "I'd imagine if she was somewhere easily locatable in the area, we'd have stumbled on her by now. Maybe it's time to change tactics."

"No sign of her down that way," Jett said, joining us with a jerk of his thumb over his shoulder in the direction he'd come from.

"I couldn't find a trace of her," Nox agreed as he walked over. He cracked his knuckles, looking taller and brawnier than ever in the professor body he'd recently taken over and made his own. "None of the people I *pressed* for information had seen her either."

I wasn't going to ask exactly how he'd "pressed" them. I didn't see any blood on his hands, so he couldn't have done that much damage.

I pinched the bridge of my nose. "We can't leave her running around the city on her own. She doesn't have proper clothes—she doesn't have money—I don't think she's ever even been in Mayfield before!"

Kai cocked his head. "She might not be on her own. You think her outburst was triggered by Nolan Gauntt's magic, right? He might not have only been driving her away from you."

A lump rose in my throat. "You mean he might have been bringing her to him." And what would the uber-powerful business magnate who we'd only recently discovered had unknown amounts of voodoo powers do with her?

Jett raked his fingers through the scruffy hair he'd dyed a deep purple, a far cry from his straightlaced nerd host's previous preppy style. "So we go after him. Easy."

"Not easy," I said, my heart sinking. "We don't know what he's capable of. We're not prepared to go up against him. I threw a bunch of my water magic at him before, and he only laughed."

At the anguish that came with the admission, a sink faucet by a nearby window started sputtering in distress. Several of the frogs croaked in a gloomy chorus. I dragged in a breath and did my best to tamp down on the unsettled energies reverberating through me.

Nox drew himself up to his full, substantial height, the sunlight catching off the red tips of his spiky black hair and making them glow like little flames. "We're not giving up," he said firmly. "We're just regrouping for a more concentrated attack, if that's what we need to do. Let's go back to the apartment, and we can figure out exactly what we've got to work with." He narrowed his eyes, glancing around us. "For all we know, he's got spies out here."

I didn't really want to leave off the search, but I had to admit it'd been hopeless so far. How would it help Marisol to keep roaming around like a crazy woman when maybe we could figure out something better? Gritting my teeth, I nodded.

We trudged toward the apartment, Ruin keeping his arm around me, stroking reassuring fingers up and down my side. Partway there, Kai took out his own phone. "I could try to get in touch with Nolan himself. I haven't been able to get his direct number, but I have his admin assistant's and various other people at Thrivewell."

From the time he'd spent working at the Gauntts' corporate head office. He'd gotten much closer to the upper echelon than I had in my brief mailroom stint. But his proposal brought a flare of panic back into my chest.

"No," I said quickly. "You'll blow your cover. As far as we know, he hasn't found out that there's anyone else connected to me working at Thrivewell. We might need you to go back in on Monday and scope things out from inside the office."

"Good point." He snapped his deft fingers. "I'll give *you* the assistant's number. Nolan obviously called your sister away for a reason. He might want to lord it over you."

I didn't like the idea of hearing my nemesis gloating about how he'd brainwashed Marisol, but I could put up with it if it meant he might spill the beans about more of his plans in typical supervillain style. Unfortunately, when I dialed the number Kai gave me, the phone on the other end didn't even ring. All I got was a digitized female voice informing me, "Sorry, your call could not go through as dialed."

I scowled at the phone and tried again in case I'd tapped the wrong number, but I got the same result. Nox growled under his breath. "The bastard already blocked you. I guess he isn't a gloater."

Maybe that wasn't surprising. We'd found my resume in Nolan's desk—he'd known my main phone number.

"You could get a burner phone and try from a number he won't recognize," Ruin suggested cheerfully. "Sneak past his defenses."

"If he's blocked me, then he isn't going to take any calls from me even if I use the president's phone number," I grumbled. "Not that I can get that."

Kai's gaze went briefly distant. "If I talked to the right people… But it's true. If he doesn't want to talk, he won't talk. Unless we make him." The fierce light that only came into his eyes when he was particularly fired up flashed behind his glasses.

"Oh, we'll make him, all right," Nox muttered. "That pompous prick's ass is toast."

When we came into the apartment, my heart lurched all over again. The plate from Marisol's pancakes was still sitting on the dining table, sticky with syrup. She'd left her hoodie draped over the back of the sofa. I could sense her presence in the space even though she wasn't here now.

In the bathroom, the shower started spewing water in jerky spurts. The frogs who'd followed us upstairs bounded over to have a little bathtub party or something. I sank into the chair next to my own abandoned plate.

Ruin sat next to me, pulling his chair close, and Jett wandered through the room with a pensive expression. It was hard to tell whether the gangster artist was picturing how he'd destroy our enemies or how he'd like to give the room another makeover. Kai stood at my other side, resting his hands on the back of a chair. Nox paced back and forth with a frustrated air that echoed the energy churning inside me.

"What exactly did she say and do?" he asked me. "How did you know it was the Gauntt guy affecting her?"

I squared my shoulders and forced myself to replay the events of this morning in my head. "We were eating pancakes for breakfast right here." I motioned to the plates. "You texted me asking about coming over to meet her. I was about to tell her a little more about the four of you. Then all of a sudden, she jumped up and started accusing me of dragging her away from her family… of acting crazy… She said she couldn't trust me and she didn't want to be around me."

Tears pricked at the backs of my eyes. I'd thought I'd figured that one problem out—I'd gotten my sister away from our mom and stepdad, who'd treated both of us like dirt under their shoes. I'd found this apartment where she had a room of her own, set her up with drawing supplies so she could dig back into her art, and reached out to a nearby high school to work out a transfer.

But the problem wasn't that I hadn't done enough. She'd been happy until that weird spell had gripped her.

I forced myself to keep talking. "She ran for the door. I tried to stop her, because it was obvious something wasn't right. I grabbed her arm, and her pajama top tore—I saw a mark on the underside of her arm." I touched my own arm where I'd had a similar birthmark-like blotch, about the size of a nickel, just beneath my armpit until I'd walked into the marsh yesterday and managed to break Nolan's spell that'd blocked off my memories of finding him with her.

I'd felt so powerful in that moment. Like I could conquer anything he threw at me next. I hadn't had any idea he'd throw this big a pile of shit down on me.

Kai motioned to my arm. "You said you had a mark from when he used his magic on you—that it disappeared after you got back your memories. How similar was the one on your sister's arm?"

"I only saw it for a second." I paused, straining to remember. "It was almost exactly the same size and really close to the same spot, pink, a few shades darker than the rest of her skin. The shape was a little different, but overall fairly round like mine."

"Wait a second!" Ruin groped at his pockets for his phone and started flipping through photos. Then he held up the screen with a triumphant grin. "Look."

At first, all I could see was the fact that it was a naked woman. A naked woman I happened to know. That phone had once belonged to Ruin's host, a jerk named Ansel, and it looked like Peyton, one of my bullies at college who'd had her eyes on Ansel, had been sending him nudes as part of her attempted seduction. This picture showed her from the waist up, totally bare, sprawled out with one arm tucked behind her head and her other hand playing with her lips.

"Ruin," Nox snarled, "I don't think that's the kind of thing you should be showing off around our—"

"No!" I said, my gaze catching on the detail that'd obviously excited Ruin. "He's right. She's got a mark just like mine and Marisol's."

I grabbed the phone and zoomed in the picture, both to get a closer look and so we didn't have perky nipples staring back at us while we studied the image. The details blurred a bit, but the lighting was good enough that the birthmark was still obvious.

"That," I said, pointing at the pink mark with its slightly mottled edges. "That's almost exactly what it looked like." My forehead furrowed. "Why would Peyton have one too?"

Kai had leaned in, studying the picture intently. He turned to Ruin. "Did your boy Ansel get nudes from anyone else?"

"I dunno," Ruin said. "I just flipped by those the other day when I was checking to see if there was anything in here that'd tell us who'd be after him, but I didn't go very far back. Let me check. There could be!"

He started skimming through the photo album in what was now The Great Nudes Search. He hadn't gotten all that far before he gave a little cry of victory. I braced myself for more boobs, but instead he held up a picture of Ansel posing in a Speedo that left nothing to the imagination.

My first thought was that I vastly preferred the slight softness Ruin's possession had brought to all those hard ridges of muscle. My second was that Ansel had an interesting-looking little splotch on the underside of his arm, a little lower down than the others, about halfway between his elbow and armpit.

"Do you still have that?" Jett asked from where he'd come over to join the discussion properly.

Ruin tugged the sleeve of his Henley up to his shoulder and checked. His skin was smooth and unmarked with its fading summer tan. "Nope. I guess the voodoo broke when I took over."

"Let me see." Nox made a grabby gesture at the phone. When Ruin handed it over, he zoomed in, squinting at the image. His square jaw worked. "I think… I think one of those bozos who hauled Lily out to the docks might have had something like that too."

He raised his head to meet my eyes. "Maybe your bullies weren't just jackasses. Maybe they were Nolan Gauntt's puppets."

Chapter Two

Lily

Finding out that Peyton might have had reasons for harassing me beyond being a raging bitch didn't make me all that more eager to talk to her. I mean, the girl had pushed me down a flight of stairs, locked me in a lecture hall's utility room, helped a bunch of other students set me up to get fired from my job and maybe arrested, threatened to drown me in a toilet bowl…

Maybe Nolan had brainwashed her into acting out in particularly extreme ways, but it was hard to believe she'd been all that kindly a soul to begin with.

We started with her anyway, because we also knew enough about her to figure out where she lived. We didn't even know the guy from the dock's first name. Along with the various pictures she'd texted Ansel—which he'd obviously saved even though it didn't seem he'd ever had any intention of using her as more than fapping material, leaving me with even fewer regrets about his death—she'd told him her room number in the college residence building "in case you ever want to stop by."

When we reached the campus, Kai and Jett went off to see what they could find out about the dock guy, and Nox and Ruin joined me in heading over to Peyton's dorm. It was after most classes would have ended but before people would be heading out for evening entertainment, so we figured we had a pretty good chance of catching her there. Ruin was joining in since she still saw him as Ansel, regardless of dyed scarlet hair, softened features, and sunny new disposition. Nox wanted to be sure she didn't throw me down any more stairs.

"I should rearrange her face for everything she did to you already," he muttered as we headed up the stairs.

"Somehow I think that'll make her less likely to talk rather than more," I pointed out, and paused to scoop up one of the few frogs that'd insisted on joining me in the car for the trip over here. "Anyway, I already put the fear of the marsh into her. I don't think she's going to risk another frog attack."

Nox scoffed. "It'll be more than frogs coming at her if she takes a jab at you. I'll hang her out to dry."

Ruin was busy strategizing as he bounded up the stairs. "I could thank her for the pictures—tell her I was looking at them again and noticed her birthmark—maybe she could let us take a look at it in person—"

"Um, no, let's not lead with asking her to get undressed," I said. Even though she might have done it for the guy she thought was Ansel. But I wasn't leaving her alone with Ruin to find out how far she'd try to take her efforts. "I don't think we should talk about the pictures at all. We'll just ask her about the Gauntts and see how she reacts."

"Perfect!" Ruin said cheerfully, never one to be fazed by having his plans shot down.

I tucked the frog I was holding close to my side as we navigated down the busy residence hallway. When we knocked on Peyton's door, no one answered. She and her roommate had a whiteboard tacked to the outside, on which several guys had left propositions directed at one or both of them. These ranged from the very smooth, *DTF? Call me!* to the almost poetic *Bring your P to ride my D, girl.*

And now I was even more glad I'd never attempted to live on campus.

We stood there for a few minutes, getting odd looks from some of the students who passed by, at least a few of whom might have recognized Nox as the former Professor Grimes, even with his makeover. I stroked my thumb over the frog's sleek back and debated leaving a little note of my own. But what was I going to say? *Hey Pey, wanna give it up for me? And by "it" I mean all the dirt about what Nolan Gauntt did to you.*

Yeah, I didn't think that'd go over super well.

I turned to go and spotted the girl we'd been waiting for heading toward us through the hall. Peyton saw me at the exact same moment, her willowy frame tensing. I'd swear even across the several feet between us, her gaze shot straight to the frog in my hand, and she went a little green herself.

Then her eyes landed on Ruin. She slowed, looking torn between running in the opposite direction and throwing herself at him. She settled for coming to a halt just out of arm's reach and hugging herself. She glanced at Ruin. "Hi, Ansel. I wish you'd come on your own."

Ruin beamed at her. "We all had something to talk to you about."

Nox jabbed his thumb toward the door. "Let's get out of the hall so the whole world doesn't know our business."

Peyton eyed me skeptically. "I don't want to go anywhere with *her*."

As if I'd done half the damage to her friends that the guys had. But she'd fled the scene at the grocery store—she'd never seen them fully in action firsthand. And her crush on Ansel had obviously given her rose-tinted glasses so thick it was amazing she wasn't walking into walls.

I tucked the frog into my pocket. "I promise I won't call my friends down on you as long as you keep your hands to yourself."

Peyton let out a little huff, but when Ruin tilted his head to the side and said, "Please?" she gave in and unlocked the door.

It was barely big enough for the four of us to squeeze inside between the two beds. Peyton perched on the edge of her tiny desk and narrowed her eyes at us, letting them soften only briefly when they passed over Ruin. "What's going on? What do you want?"

She couldn't seem to decide whether to sound concerned or hostile. Seeing me and Ruin together was clearly throwing her for a loop, even though she'd known he'd been hanging out with me.

Suddenly I had no idea how to start this conversation. For all intents and purposes, I was about to ask her if a creepy old man had molested her as a child. That was kind of a difficult subject to lead with.

At least, in my mind it was. My guys clearly didn't have the same qualms.

"Has anything happened between you and Nolan Gauntt?" Nox said while I hesitated. "Now or when you were a kid?"

Ruin nodded and clarified, "Weird stuff? Did he touch you?"

Peyton's jaw dropped open in an expression of horror, and I had the urge to bury my face in my hands. Sensitive, the Skullbreakers' approach was not.

"What are you talking about?" she sputtered, recoiling farther back on the desk as if *we'd* been trying to grope her. "I wouldn't—a guy like him wouldn't— You're *sick*."

"Whoa," I said, holding up my hands as I tried to salvage the conversation. "We're not accusing you of anything. We're just… worried." And maybe I needed to bring up her body parts after all. "We found out some… other people he's messed with had these little marks on their arm, and we noticed you have one too. Right here?" I prodded the spot on my own arm. "You do have a birthmark kind of thing there, right? Do you remember how you got it?"

Peyton's face twitched. She grasped her arm, and I could tell from her expression that she knew what mark I meant. But she shook her head vehemently. "Lots of people have birthmarks. It's been there since I was a kid. It doesn't have anything to do with anyone. No one *put* it there. You really are psycho."

My jaw clenched at the familiar insult. It was pretty debatable which of us had actually acted more psycho in the past month.

Nox growled and loomed closer, and I grabbed him before Peyton had to do more than squeak in fear.

"It's fine," I told him. "I'm embracing my crazy." Then I turned back to her. "You're sure you've had that mark since you were a kid?"

"Yeah," Peyton said in an increasingly crabby tone. She hugged herself tighter. "These things don't just appear out of nowhere."

"Sometimes they do," Ruin said, ever so helpfully, but at least he followed it up with a useful question. "Did you have anything to do with the Gauntts when you were a kid?"

"You obviously know who Nolan Gauntt *is*," Nox growled.

Peyton glowered at him. "Of course I do. Everyone does. My mom works for Thrivewell. I'm sure he came to a few dinners at the house, or there were Christmas parties or something. But he didn't put a freaking *birthmark* on my arm."

Not that she remembered. My gut twisted. Nolan had made me forget what I'd seen and Marisol forget that he'd done anything more than talk briefly with her. And he hadn't marked her while I'd been there—he must have seen her again, later. God, how many times had he been alone with my sister after I'd been shipped off to the looney bin?

An icy chill passed through me, but I yanked my mind back to the present. Getting these answers would help me figure out that part—as well as how to find Marisol now.

"There might be things you don't remember," I said. "But maybe I could… jog your memory. If you'd let me try." I reached for her arm, thinking of how I'd shattered the supernatural wall inside my own mind and body with my powers.

Peyton jerked away, her posture going even more rigid. "Get away from me! You're all fucking crazy. Get out of my room." She paused, looking at Ruin for a moment. "I don't know why you're letting them drag you into this, but it's too much. Just get out."

"We only wanted to help," Ruin protested.

Peyton stood up on the chair by the desk. "Get out *now* or I'm going to scream at the top of my lungs. And tell everyone who comes that *you* creeps were 'touching' me."

Nox bared his teeth and moved as if to lunge at her, but I pushed in front of him. "It's not worth it," I said, even though my heart was sinking. "If she won't cooperate, we can't force it. Let's just go."

Nox might have tried to force the issue regardless, but right then his phone pinged with a text. He checked it, and his shoulders relaxed a bit. "Kai came through. We have a plan B."

I opened my mouth, thinking maybe I should clarify in front of Peyton that he didn't mean *that* Plan B, but then I decided trying to tell her more about what was going on here would only make her more likely to scream. She could come up with whatever theories she wanted about what he was talking about. I didn't give a shit.

"Okay," I said. "Where should we meet him and Jett?"

We left Peyton silently behind, closing her dorm-room door behind us. Nox led the way out through the residence building and across campus.

We found Kai, Jett, and the broad-shouldered, snub-nosed guy who'd stuffed me in his trunk a few weeks ago at the edge of the campus parking lot. The guy was sitting on the ground with his back against a tree, his face sallow. When he saw us approaching, he started to whimper.

"Just leave me alone," he said, pulling his knees up to his chest and rocking back and forth. "I'm not going anywhere near her again. You've got to give me a break now."

He looked like he was already on the verge of a mental breakdown. I guessed that was a reasonable response to the Skullbreakers' brand of ghostly gangster justice. The last time he'd seen Nox, Nox had punctured his face with a handful of fishhooks. I could see the little dots on his cheeks where the wounds hadn't quite finished healing.

And it looked like Kai and Jett had been manhandling him already. The sleeve of the guy's shirt was torn as if one of them had wrenched it too hard in a tussle to roll it up.

"He's got that mark thing," Jett reported.

"He claims it's been there since he was 'little,'" Kai added to Jett's typically brusque report. "And that all he knows about Nolan Gauntt is that the guy came by to talk to him about college scholarships back when he was in elementary school." He raised a skeptical eyebrow.

"That *is* all I know," the bully whined. "Please, don't hurt me again."

He was so pathetic I couldn't help pitying him a little. He'd been a shit to me just like Peyton had, but at least he had the sense to realize he'd screwed up and that he should cut out the shit from here on.

"I can try to break any blocks on his memory like I did with my own," I said, and crouched down across from the guy.

He cringed away, folding his arms close to his chest. I didn't like the idea of forcing him either. As I considered my options, Ruin dove down beside me.

"I can help!" he said brightly. "There's nothing to worry about here."

He said that second bit while he was punching the guy in the chest. Which might have contradicted his words, except the punch came with a little crackle of supernatural energy, and suddenly our target was smiling back at us.

"You're right," he said. "I don't know why I was so scared. It's good to see you guys."

Nox snorted and shook his head in bemusement. All of the guys' ghostly energies had been taking on their own unique edge, and Ruin's angle was infecting others with emotions.

It was helpful, though. "What's your name?" I asked the guy, because I wanted to at least know that much about who we were dealing with.

"Fergus," he said easily.

Well, now that the issue had already been forced despite my intentions, it seemed better to do what I could for him rather than leave him in the dark.

"Okay, Fergus," I said like I was talking to a small child. "I'm just going to check out your arm for a minute. I think there might be something a little wrong with it, and I'm going to fix it."

"That's great," Fergus said, smiling away. "Thank you for helping me."

It was even more unnerving seeing him all mellow after his previous terror. I tugged up his sleeve and immediately spotted the birthmark a few inches above his elbow. Readying myself, I wrapped my hands around his bicep.

A hum of tension was still reverberating through me from my distress over Marisol's disappearance. I clicked my tongue against the roof of my mouth, setting a quiet rhythm to go with the thump of my pulse and the rustle of the breeze through the leaves on the branches overhead, and focused my mind.

Nolan Gauntt. This was all about him. He'd cozied up to my sister in totally inappropriate ways—he'd done who knew what to the guy in front of me. The asshat could be putting his hands all over Marisol right now.

I winced inwardly at the image, and my anger and fear roared up inside me, driving the hum to more potency. A tingling sensation spread through my arms to my hands. I closed my eyes.

It was there. Like a storm break, a barrier inside Fergus's flesh that stretched all the way into his mind. I trained all my attention on it, summoning the imaginary waves that I'd used to batter down the wall inside me. Then I threw them at it over and over again like watery punches.

This was for stealing my sister away. *This* was for messing around with who knew how many other kids. *This* was for laughing in my face when I'd challenged him. *This* was for having me shut away in a psych hospital for seven years of my life.

With each punch, I hit harder. Then I threw everything I had at the mark and the barrier emanating from it with one last surge of horror.

The impression of the wall fractured and crumbled away. I let go of Fergus, gasping a breath as I came back to the world around me.

Fergus was staring down at his arm. Then he gaped at all of us. His face had gotten its usual color back after Ruin had calmed him down, but now a sickly hue rolled over it again.

"Nolan Gauntt," he murmured, with a shiver that shook his whole body.

Chapter Three

Ruin

"You remember!" I said eagerly, grinning at the guy Lily had just worked her powers on. It was obvious from the dude's expression that he hadn't remembered anything all that *good*, but really, anything *was* good for our purposes. We just needed to find out what he knew.

As Lily eased back a step, staying crouched in front of the guy, I turned my smile on her. It really was something to watch her put her powers to use. I had no idea how exactly she was breaking Nolan Gauntt's magic, but the energy inside her radiated out into the air when she concentrated like that. It'd sent an unearthly quiver over my skin that reminded me of all the other sensations our woman could stir up in me.

What an amazing woman she was. We'd get her sister back, because I knew there wasn't any chance of her backing down. And the four of us would be right there with her.

The guy—Fergus, that's what he'd said his name was—rubbed his hand over his face. I couldn't tell whether my punch of reassuring emotion had worn off or if his reaction to his uncovered memories was so intense it overwhelmed any comfort I'd given him before.

"What happened with Nolan?" Lily asked in her softly husky voice. Her gentle tone sent another quiver through me right to my groin. She was powerful, yeah, but she could be so sweet as well. The perfect package.

"I—I don't understand." Fergus gulped audibly. "How could all that—I had no idea—"

Kai leaned closer, peering at the dude like he was scientific specimen. "He worked some kind of power on you to block out those memories—it sounds like for good reason. I'm assuming he didn't hide anything pleasant."

"No. No." Another shudder rippled through the guy's body. His mouth clamped tight. He remembered, but he didn't want to talk about it.

Kai could have used his supernatural skills to make the guy move any way he wanted, but we'd already seen that he couldn't force someone to answer questions that way. His usual methods, working them over with manipulation and persuasion, could take a while. And I wasn't sure they'd work at all on a guy this shaken who'd been terrified of *us* just a few minutes ago.

But I could help with that.

I leaned in and gave Fergus a light but purposeful cuff to the side of his head, drawing on all my affection for and trust in Lily and the guys around me as I did. Urging the sense that he could open up to us, that we'd protect and avenge him as much as he needed, through his skull.

The guy's head swayed to the side, and Lily shot a worried look at me, so maybe I tapped him a tad harder than I'd meant to. It was still tricky judging the exact responses of this new body when I hadn't had any physical form at all for more than twenty years. But Fergus's stance relaxed a little at the same time, a hopeful light coming into his eyes.

"You won't let him come near me again?" he said. "You won't let him use me?"

Lily patted his arm a little awkwardly. "We're doing whatever we can to stop him from hurting anyone again."

Fergus's arms tightened where he was hugging his knees. "He didn't exactly hurt me. He just…"

When he trailed off, Nox shifted on his feet with obvious impatience. Before he could demand that the guy get on with his story, Lily aimed a pointed glance at him. She turned back to Fergus. "Why don't you tell us what he did, and then we'll know what we need to stop him from doing again?"

The dude drew in a shaky breath. "It's kind of hazy. I'm not sure how often it happened. I was pretty little. I think… one time was right after my eighth birthday party. The last time I can remember I was maybe ten?"

Lily nodded. From what she'd said, that was around the age her sister had been when she'd caught Nolan with her.

"Some of it was just him sitting with me," Fergus went on. "He'd pat my back or stick his hand right into my hair, and say things I didn't really understand, and this weird feeling would go through me, kind of like getting shocked by static electricity but stretched out longer. I didn't like it, but it was just weird. It was worse when… sometimes he'd start squeezing my legs or touching me under my shirt and put his mouth on my neck, or he'd get me to sit on his lap, and I could tell—"

He paused, looking like he might be about to vomit. His voice came out even rougher afterward. "It was only touching, and he didn't actually— But still. If I tried to get away, he'd hold on to me harder, and he said my parents would be upset that I hadn't 'helped' him. I don't know what to do."

Lily's face had gone hard and fierce. "There's nothing 'only' about any of that. It's horrible. He isn't going to get away with it."

Fergus's gaze had gone distant as he related his memories. Now it snapped to her with sharper focus. "It wasn't just him. Sometimes his wife came with him. Marie. Sometimes she came on her own. They said it was a good thing to share." He winced.

Lily inhaled sharply. "Both of them. Fuck."

So we had two enemies instead of one. It seemed like the Gauntts spent most of their time together. As far as I could see, that wouldn't make anything much harder.

"When did they give you that mark on your arm?" Kai asked.

"Every time before they left—whoever came—they'd squeeze my

arm there and there'd be that electric shock feeling again, all in one spot." Fergus touched his arm where the tiny birthmark had vanished. "Somehow things seemed okay after they did that. Like barely anything had happened."

Kai looked at the rest of us. "And the last time they must have shut off his memories of their visits almost completely."

Lily had knit her brow. "Were they sneaking around your parents all that time? How did they manage to get to you so often?"

A faint, humorless laugh spilled out of Fergus. "My parents knew. They always seemed happy to see the Gauntts. Well, I don't know if they knew what Nolan and Marie were doing exactly, but whatever they told my parents, it made them figure it was a good deal. Mom got a promotion somewhere in there, I think… That's why I believed what the Gauntts said about them wanting me to 'help.' It didn't seem like they'd want to help *me*."

Jett scowled and kicked at the grassy ground. "Of course they knew. Can't count on family to protect you."

Suddenly I was picturing Fergus as a kid, sitting in his bedroom listening to the Gauntts walking up the stairs to "visit" him while his parents chattered away downstairs without a single care. While they got what they wanted without letting themselves care what happened to him. An uncomfortable clenching sensation squeezed around my ribs.

I groped for something happier to say. "But you made it through. You're okay now."

"I don't know, man." Fergus dropped his head into his hands. "I can't wrap my head around all of this. What am I supposed to do now?"

"It wasn't just you," Lily told him. "It seems like it happened to a lot of kids, and it's not your fault at all. Your parents should be ashamed of themselves."

It happened to a lot of kids. I looked down at myself, at my arm. Where I'd seen the mark on Ansel's arm in that photo of him from before I'd taken over.

It'd happened to him. To *me*, sort of. Those memories had fled when we'd shut down his body so it'd be ready for my possession, and none of them had remained when I'd leapt inside, but he'd still experienced the same crap.

His parents, his mother who I'd met briefly when we'd gone to his house—they'd gone along with it just like Fergus's had. Let the Gauntts into their home, looked the other way so they could benefit from the money and prestige…

My jaw clenched. I didn't know how to put a cheerful spin on any of that horribleness. It was shit all the way through. And Lily—there were tears shining in her eyes as she straightened up. What her sister must have gone through, with her mom and stepdad's permission…

The storm of emotion swelled inside me, and right at that moment, my phone—Ansel's old phone—rang.

I froze, my mind blanking momentarily in surprise, and then grabbed it. The call display said it was from *Dad*. My fingers squeezed around the phone as I stared at the word.

"Are you going to answer that?" Nox said, knuckling my arm.

The kind of rage I'd only felt before when seeing assholes attack Lily or my friends surged up inside me. *I* shouldn't have to answer. These people had so much to answer for.

I spun around toward the spot where we'd parked our bikes, jabbing the ignore button on the phone's screen. "I've got something to do."

"What?" Lily said. "Where are you going?"

"To talk to Ansel's parents," I said. "Since he can't speak for himself anymore."

As I marched toward my motorcycle, more fury seared through me. It hazed my mind, drowning out every other sensation. I didn't like it, but I could only think of one way to get it out, to get back to the place where everything had seemed okay: by releasing it on the people who deserved it.

The guys hustled after me, abandoning Fergus. "Hold up," Nox said. "You shouldn't go running off—"

"I need to do this," I repeated, cutting him off. He should have been able to understand. His parents had treated him like crap. But then he'd had his grandmother. At least he'd had her. So maybe he didn't totally see it after all.

I jumped onto the bike and tore out of the parking lot before anyone else could protest. The growl of engines behind me told me I was being pursued, but I didn't care about that.

There was too much awfulness in the world. It'd hurt Fergus and that girl Peyton; it'd hurt Lily so much my heart ached thinking of the look on her face. It'd hurt her sister and who knew how many other people besides. It'd hurt Ansel, even if he was a prick.

And all these parents had stood by and let it happen.

Why the fuck should they get away with that? Why should we let it slide over and over again?

I was barely paying attention to where I was driving, but my body seemed to know the way. I roared up outside the large, bright house where Ansel had used to live, sprang off my bike, and charged to the front door. My stomach gurgled with an inconvenient pang of hunger, but I got those so often these days that I already had supplies at the ready. I shoved a strip of spicy beef jerky into my mouth with one hand as I pounded on the doorbell and then the door itself with the other.

I was just swallowing when the stiff blond woman who'd answered the door before peered out at me. "Ansel?" she said. "We've been trying to reach you. I know you like to have your fun with your friends and all that, but you really need to be accessible to the family every now and—"

"Like you made hi—made *me* accessible to the Gauntts?" I demanded, realizing in mid-sentence that I'd better pretend to be Ansel for the accusation to make any sense. If I started talking like Ansel was some other guy who wasn't standing in front of her, she might pay more attention to evaluating how crazy her supposed son was than evaluating her own awful behavior.

"I—what?" Ansel's mother said, but she paled at the same time, so I knew she was only playing ignorant. "I don't know what on earth you're talking about, dear. If something's upset you, why don't you come in and—"

"You know exactly what I'm talking about," I snarled. I didn't know exactly where all this rage had come from, how there could be so much seemingly out of nowhere, but it was overflowing and I couldn't see any reason to rein it in. "You and my dad were shitty parents, and you're still being shitty—you turned your back on me and let some creepy people use me for their sick games so you could get a leg up somehow or another, and now you're going to pretend like you have no idea why I'm angry?"

I'd thought she'd paled before. Now she went absolutely white. "I—I—" She couldn't seem to get any syllable out other than that one letter.

"You can't even fucking apologize, can you?" I snapped, and shoved her backward into the house. I stormed after her, taking her up on her invitation belatedly and probably not in the way she'd intended. But as I opened my mouth to berate her some more, she raised her hands and started clawing at her face.

"How could I have let them come in here and treat you that way?" she screeched, her voice vibrating with anger. "I *am* shitty. I'm the worst garbage. Your father is too. We should both be torn apart for what we did."

Somehow she managed to throw a punch at herself that clocked her in the forehead. As she reeled, I stared at her, my own voice drying up.

I'd infected her with my fury at her and Ansel's dad, and now she was raging at herself. She whipped around, slapping herself across the cheek, yanking at her hair, gnashing her teeth in frustration. She even stomped on her own foot with one of her high-heeled pumps. It was so ridiculous that a laugh bubbled out of me.

Once I started laughing, I couldn't stop. The sight of her flailing around struck me as so funny the anger washed out of me, as if I'd passed all of it on to her.

What had there been to get so worked up about anyway? It'd all worked out in the end. I'd told her off, she was getting her punishment—exactly how it should be.

"Ruin?" Lily's soft voice reached me with an equally gentle hand around my arm. I hadn't realized anyone had followed me into the house, but as I settled down from my bout of laughter, I saw she and all three of my friends were standing behind me in the front hall of Ansel's house.

Ansel's mother was busy smashing an expensive-looking vase over her head while ranting about all her deficiencies as a parent. I figured I could leave her to it now. My work was done.

I turned toward the door with a spring in my step. "All right. Let's get out of here."

Lily peered at me. "Are you okay?"

I beamed at her. "Of course. I did what I needed to do. Now we can get on with finding your sister. You can break the spell on her just like you did with Fergus. It'll all work out!"

And if there was still a tiny burn of fury lurking under the blanket of good cheer I'd wrapped around myself again, I didn't need to worry about it right now.

Chapter Four

Lily

Marisol's number went to voicemail again. I looked down at the screen with the string of texts I'd also tried sending and bit my lip.

I was pretty sure she had her phone. It wasn't in her things here at the apartment. But one way or another, I'd been blocked there too.

Just in case she might have run back to Mom and Wade, I'd tried calling them too, but Mom's confusion had been obvious even through her cagey remarks. She had no more idea where Marisol was than I did.

So, desperate times called for desperate measures.

I turned back to the laptop I'd placed on the dining room table. It was set to record through the built-in camera, and I frowned at my image on the screen.

"Is this really going to help us find Marisol? So far the people we know who the Gauntts messed with haven't had contact with them in years. It all happened when they were kids."

"We haven't talked to very many victims," Kai pointed out, sitting on the edge of the table with his legs dangling like there wasn't a perfectly good chair right there under his feet. "The more we can find, the more data we can collect. And predators tend to be creatures of habit. It sounds as if he came to that Fergus guy in his own home, but he might have taken others someplace else."

"Someplace where your sister could be now," Ruin said eagerly, picking up the thread.

Nox prowled by behind me. "Exactly. And then we charge in there, get her back, and rip anyone who tries to get in our way to shreds."

I couldn't say I had any issues with that plan, other than the fact that we didn't know where we'd be charging into yet. I dragged in a breath and eyed my image on the screen. "Okay. So we're going to do this viral video thing. Are you sure it should be me on it? A lot of people around here think I'm crazy. And if the Gauntts find out about it—"

Kai made a dismissive sound. "With the filters, we can make sure your face isn't recognizable. But people are more likely to want to watch a hot girl than some random guy. Especially when it comes to removing clothes." He winked at me.

I wrinkled my nose at him, but I could see his point. I stood up, tugging at the sweater I'd put over a fitted tank top.

We wanted to identify who else in Lovell Rise, Mayfield, or anywhere else in the Gauntts' vicinity might have come under their spell, and we couldn't exactly go around asking everyone to take off their shirt so we could inspect their arms for birthmarks. But the magic of social media meant that it was totally acceptable to ask them to take off their shirts on camera and distribute the image to the entire internet.

It didn't totally make sense to me, but then, I was the weirdo crazy girl, so what did I know?

"This feels silly," I said.

Nox paused in his pacing long enough to grin at me. "It is. But from what I've seen, people *love* silly."

"Especially if they think they can prove they're the only ones who can do it without looking silly," Kai said. "Or that they're the silliest of them all. Basically, any excuse to have a competition."

"Hurray for human nature," Jett muttered from over by the sofa, where he was watching this all go down while nursing a can of cola.

"Okay." I rolled my shoulders. "Let me practice a few times."

"Start the camera rolling," Kai said. "You might get a good take during practice—better to capture it than to have to spend hours trying to recreate it."

"Right." I tapped the button on the screen, watching it switch from green to red, and smiled at myself in my best attempt at looking perky. "Hey, everyone! My boyfriend dared me to prove that I can take off my sweater with just one hand. It's harder than it looks. If you think you can manage it, let's see you try—and hashtag it #sweaterchallenge."

I gripped the top of my left sleeve the way we'd worked out after reading numerous online tutorials—the internet giveth as it receiveth—and managed to wrangle the sweater off me with only a little squirming and half of my hair falling into my face. Not quite the graceful execution I was going for, although from the guys' gazes burning into me, they'd been enjoying the view of my cleavage while I flailed.

I pulled the sweater back on and combed my fingers through my hair. "Okay, let's try that again."

"As many times as you like, Siren," Nox said in a voice that practically liquified my panties.

I glowered at him. "This is for finding Marisol, not starting an orgy."

He shrugged with one of his usual cocky smirks. "I think Kai would say there's a lot of benefit in multitasking."

The brainiac himself didn't even bother responding to that. He motioned to me. "Angle your elbow more to the front this time. That should help the sleeve come off more smoothly."

I nodded. "Got it."

It took four more tries before I managed to whip off the sweater with stripper-like skill, which wasn't a quality I'd ever thought I'd be aspiring to. I gave it a little twirl in the air and smiled coyly at the camera again. "Don't forget! It's sweater challenge time." I held up my fingers in a victory sign for good measure.

"Perfect." Kai leapt off the table to come around to the computer keyboard. He started tapping away, flicking through filters and cropping the video down to the right length.

"Do you even know how to do video editing?" I asked him.

He gave a dismissive huff. "The basics are simple enough to pick up reading a few user guides. We'll send this to a social media guru I've connected with who's eager to get into my good graces after our last conversation. He'll do the final polishing and figure out all the hashtags and algorithms and whatever the hell else makes it virulent."

"I think the word is 'viral,' Mr. Know-It-All," Jett remarked.

Kai waved him off and kept flicking through the options that came with the recording software. Jett strode over and leaned in next to him, setting down his cola on the table.

"It's not just all your behavioral patterning bullshit," he said. "The video's got to *look* good. Catch the eye. Hit the visual senses in an appealing way."

Kai elbowed him. "That's just three ways of saying essentially the same thing."

"Which just goes to show that you don't really understand art. Here, let me see." Jett tapped on a few keys and managed to adjust the color of the wall behind me. Then he tweaked the contrast. Suddenly my eyes, set against the startlingly smooth skin the filter had blessed me with, stood out even more starkly with an almost come hither expression.

"Um," I said, "I'm not sure that's the vibe I want to give off."

"Sure it is," Jett said. "You want them to want you. To want to *be* you. Isn't that right?" He raised his eyebrows at Kai.

Kai gazed back at him steadily. "Interesting to hear that point coming from you."

Jett looked as if he'd momentarily swallowed his tongue. It wasn't a secret that *he* didn't want me quite the same way the others did—he'd announced it in front of the whole group a couple of weeks ago. It *was* a secret that despite his announcement, we'd ended up getting very close and personal a few nights ago when we'd ended up sharing a bed together… At least, we had until Jett had become all on-edge about it and stalked out of the room like he hadn't been groping me two seconds ago.

We hadn't talked about that incident since then, and it hadn't seemed right to mention it to any of the other guys. But I still didn't know where the hell I stood with him.

That was hardly important right now while Marisol was missing, though. I gestured broadly at both of them. "Figure out something that works. I spent most of the last seven years not even having a Facebook account—I don't have any more idea what makes something infect social media than you do."

Jett and Kai fell into a discussion about the exact shade they should make my sweater, reaching across to jab the keyboard back and forth like the fairies in Disney's *Sleeping Beauty* adjusting Aurora's dress. I stepped aside and ended up right in Ruin's arms, which really wasn't a bad place to be.

I glanced up over my shoulder at his cheerful face, searching for any sign of the anger he'd shown yesterday. He'd seemed calm enough after he'd inflicted his rage on Ansel's mom, but I'd had no idea that Ruin had that kind of hostility in him to begin with, at least not when we weren't being directly attacked. I guessed it could have simply risen up because he was upset that he couldn't do anything to protect me or Marisol from the Gauntts, but it'd felt like something more.

He'd seemed confused when I'd tried to ask him more about his reaction, though, and I didn't want to badger him.

"One step closer to finding her," he said, pressing a kiss to my temple. "It doesn't seem like the Gauntts outright attacked anyone, right? I'm sure she'll be okay."

"They're just using her as leverage," Nox growled with a flash of his eyes. "How these pricks got away with this crap for so long… I guess that's money for you." He shook his head.

"Money and corporate power and influence," I said, and sighed. "I wonder how many kids he's gone after. Him and Marie too. They probably have others they're going on their 'visits' these days." I shuddered, the warmth of Ruin's body not enough to ward off the chill of that thought. "And all those parents going along with it…"

Kai looked up from where it appeared he and Jett had finally settled on a grudging compromise about the video's color scheme. "The Gauntts could obviously influence Marisol's behavior, presumably through that mark. They quite possibly provoked the bullies against you—at least some of them. Some were probably just following the herd. For all we know, at least a few of the parents were older victims who were affected too."

I hadn't considered that possibility. "But—the Gauntts aren't that much older than most of our parents. They're, what, in their 60s? My mom is forty-eight. Wade is at least fifty. When they were kids, Nolan and Marie wouldn't have been much past their teens. How much social power did they have then to convince *those* kids' parents to let them do their secret business?"

Nox shrugged. "It's all inherited, right? Thrivewell has been around for, like, a century. They had their own parents' influence behind them."

Ruin's head lifted. "Do you think their parents had magic powers too? Is it a family thing? Maybe that's how they got their business to be so big and popular."

Kai nudged his glasses up his nose. "You know, that's not a bad point. We can't be sure what the full extent of their supernatural abilities is, and what we do know about altering people's memories could definitely be useful in some business contexts."

"Fuckers," Nox grumbled, and raised his chin. "Doesn't matter. They could be Superman and Wonder Woman, and we'd still crush them."

The conversation was making me feel depressed rather than optimistic about our chances, regardless of Nox's bravado. I eased away from Ruin and went to join Jett where he'd lingered by the computer, studying the video image. This was the one concrete way I had of trying to take on the Gauntts for now.

"Do you think you've made me pretty enough yet?" I teased.

Jett glanced over at me, and I was abruptly aware that I'd stopped close enough that he'd only have needed to lean over a few inches for his shoulder to brush mine. He paused for a beat too long, our gazes locked together.

"You're always pretty," he said abruptly. Then he yanked his eyes away, followed by the rest of his body as he retreated from the computer. "*I* think it's good to go."

Nox strolled over, giving Jett an assessing look I couldn't quite read before contemplating the screen himself. "Well, you two seem to know what you're doing. Send it off to whoever's going to do the final spiffing up and let's get on to the part where we find out whose heads we need to crack."

At those words, I paused, thinking of the other quest the Skullbreakers had been on before Marisol's disappearance. They'd finally found out which rival gang had been responsible for murdering them all those years ago.

"It's going to take at least a day or two for the video to catch on, if it even does," I said. "Don't you need to go after the Skeleton Corps too?"

Nox folded his arms over his chest. "I've told you before, and I'll keep telling you—you're our first priority. That includes your sister."

"Yeah, but—if we can't do anything for her right now anyway—And it'll be hard for you to help me if they come after you all over again." I tipped my head toward the window. "If you track them down and crack some of *their* heads, maybe some of their people will have heard something about Marisol too. They are supposed to be the most connected gang in the city, right?"

Nox stewed on that for a few moments before a grin stretched across his face. "If you're that eager to get started on the beatdowns, who am I to say no? And we do need to pay back our murderers in kind—with twenty-one years' interest on top of that."

Chapter Five

Lily

I WASN'T sure I'd ever get totally used to riding on the back of a motorcycle. It was thrilling and terrifying all at once, even with the bulky helmet fixed on my head to theoretically prevent *my* skull from getting broken. The Skullbreakers weren't interested in inflicting their brand of havoc on their own.

Small mercies.

Nox had insisted that I ride with him, of course, even though there was less room behind his massive frame than any of the other guys'. But that just meant I had to tuck myself that much closer to him, breathing in the smell of his leather jacket and the musk that was all his own underneath, unable to stop myself from remembering the times I'd had him between my thighs in other ways.

Being around these guys was turning me into a nympho as well as a psycho. But at least I was a well-satisfied nympho.

The four bikes roared through the streets and slammed to a halt outside a dingy-looking mechanic shop. The Skullbreakers all hopped off, Nox gripping my elbow to help me as I slid from the seat. He gave me a brief glance with a tensing of his jaw and a flash of protective concern in his eyes.

One of the hodgepodge of low-level criminal allies the guys had scrounged up in the past few days had given us a tip about where a few men they knew to be part of the Skeleton Corps were working today. We were here to confront them. I suspected Nox would rather I was about a hundred miles away from anything to do with the gang who'd killed him and the others twenty-one years ago, but he also knew there was no way in hell I was hiding anymore.

I was part of the Skullbreakers now. He'd acknowledged it, and so he had to live with it. I'd even helped them out with their past head-cracking and info-searching.

He didn't tell me to stay behind, just marched onward a couple of steps in front of me. Kai came up beside him, and Jett and Ruin formed a shield on either side of me. I was with them, but no one could get at me without going through them first.

I was pretty okay with that.

The hum of my magic tickled through my chest alongside my nerves. Nox tested the front door of the shop's office, found it locked, and proceeded to kick it in with a ram of his heel. The lock snapped, and we all marched inside.

By the time we'd crossed the small office to the expansive mechanic bay it led into, three guys had leapt to their feet among the cars. It looked like they'd been working on a couple of them: a sleek red Jaguar and a posh silver BMW. I'd be willing to bet my entire life savings, as meager as they were, that they weren't fixing up these cars so much as fixing to sell them to the highest bidder after they removed all signs of the legitimate owners they'd stolen them from.

"What the fuck are you doing?" one of the Skeleton Corps guys demanded, smacking a wrench against his open palm.

"We popped by for a little chat," Nox said in a sarcastic tone, but his gaze had veered to the Jag. He stepped closer to skim his fingers over the edge of the roof. "This is a nice find here. How much do you sell these for?"

Kai let out a cough. "*Nox*."

The Skullbreakers leader jerked his attention back to the more important matter at hand. I made a mental note of his car preferences in case I was ever in a position to pick one up—you know, as a Christmas present or something.

"You're with the Skeleton Corps?" he growled, fixing his eyes on each of the guys in turn.

The guy with the wrench narrowed his eyes. "You're those dickhead punks who've been rampaging all over town. Haven't you gotten the message yet? There's no place for you here, and no one cares about your *feelings* about some pricks who died a gazillion years ago."

"Twenty-one," Kai corrected, like he couldn't help being pedantic, which maybe he couldn't.

Jett pushed forward to flank Nox at his other side. "It seems like *you're* the ones who haven't gotten the message."

Ruin chuckled, waving his fists. "And you'd better be worried about your own feelings, because it's not going to feel *good* when we've stomped you into little pieces."

The Corps guy didn't even bother to reply. He made some gesture I barely caught, and the three guys launched themselves at us like one being.

They should have had the advantage. There were only three of them, but they were armed—the one guy with his very large wrench and the other two with guns they whipped out as they came at us. The Skullbreakers had shown up apparently empty-handed, although I knew they had their own pistols tucked away in easy reach. The thing was, these jerks clearly hadn't gotten the news about just how much my men could do with their empty hands.

Nox swung his fists in quick succession, the burst of energy that shot from them extending his reach. He smacked the gun from one guy's grasp and then clocked him in the jaw hard enough to send him reeling into a backflip that would have impressed most Olympic judges before he was even close enough for Nox to touch.

Kai ducked and jabbed the other gunman in the stomach, ordering, "Stop your colleagues from attacking us," as he did.

That guy jerked around toward the wrench-man like he was a

puppet on strings, but before he had to tackle the wrench, Jett and Ruin double-teamed the guy. Jett, his supernatural talent for altering appearances not being particularly helpful in a fight, simply kicked the guy's legs out from under him, sending him staggering right into Ruin's fist. His mouth stretched into a fierce grin, Ruin smacked the guy's hand up to sock him with his own wrench for good measure.

The rhythm of the smacks, thuds, and groans filled my ears, and it occurred to me with a distant sort of uneasiness that I wasn't particularly shocked or horrified by any of the violence anymore. These were my men, dealing out justice the way they knew how, and I was okay with that too. There was almost a music in the sounds of the fighting—an urgent, gritty sort of melody. It resonated through me.

A twinge came into my throat. I could have put words to it, could have sung out a vehement chorus to match our determination to see our mission through, but the impulse dwindled as quickly as it'd risen up. The ache of grief swallowed it up.

How could I sing when I'd lost Marisol, in even direr circumstances than before?

Ruin's victim stumbled backward. I found out what emotion our ever-cheerful guy had inflicted on the leader of this crew when he dropped to his knees in front of us and kowtowed his head to the cement floor. "Have mercy. We're not worthy."

Ruin cackled gleefully and spun toward the first guy, who'd caught his balance against the Jaguar. His gaze shot to his gun, lying on the floor several feet across the bay, but the second he moved, his own friend was on him. The guy Kai had punched tackled the other Skeleton Corps member, and they both tumbled to the floor.

Kai stalked over and gave the guy on the floor a kick to the ribs. "Lie still and don't make a sound."

The guy immediately stiffened, his lips pressing tightly shut, but it turned out that at least today, Kai couldn't impose his will on more than one person at a time. The man who'd tackled his friend leapt up and lunged at Kai.

Nox lashed out with his foot. Even though he was five feet away, his powers neatly tripped the attacker. The guy fell flat on his face, and

Jett knocked both him and the other guy unconscious with a couple of quick blows. Ruin bounded over and tossed one of the now-limp guys on top of the other. He sat on them both. "Everything secure here!" he announced.

Kai stayed where he was, looking ready to aim another commanding strike if need be. Jett prowled through the bay to confirm no one was hiding amid the equipment. Nox loomed over the guy who was still bobbing his head up and down over the floor like one of those drinking-bird toys.

"Oh, please," the guy mumbled. "Take pity on me. I would never have talked back if I'd realized how great you are."

Nox smirked at Ruin. "I like the tune you got this guy playing. Let's use that one again sometime." He turned back to the pleading man. "You deserve to be crushed into dirt, but we'll make an exception if you prove how sorry you are."

"Of course! Anything. Just say the word."

Nox set his hands on his hips. "Tell us who's in charge of the Skeleton Corps, and where we can find them."

The man looked up at him, his face falling in apparent regret. "I can't tell you that. I don't know."

Nox bared his teeth and leaned down with his fist poised. "Do I need to give you even more motivation?"

"No, no, please, I really don't! You have to understand—no one at our level knows. The Corps operates in squads. We only know who's in our squad and one guy higher up who we answer to. But the guy who gives us our marching orders isn't the head honcho."

"Would *he* know who's in charge?" Kai asked.

The guy made a face. "I'm not sure. He might have his own squad leader who isn't the top boss either. I have no idea how many levels there are. We're at the bottom."

"Well, it's a place to start." Nox crouched in front of him, cracking his knuckles. "Where do we find the man you answer to?"

"I—I don't know where he'd be right now. But we meet him once a week around the back of the convenience store at River and Princeton."

Nox made a skeptical sound. "How about you show us this convenience store, just so we can make sure you're not sending us on a wild goose chase?"

The guy scrambled to his feet like he'd been offered a trip to the Bahamas instead of ordered to betray his overlords. He gestured for us to follow him and hustled out of the mechanic shop.

"Keep a close eye on him," Kai muttered to the others under his breath as we left behind the two Skeleton Corps guys who were just starting to come to. "We don't know how long Ruin's emotional voodoo will last."

It turned out the convenience store in question was only a five-minute walk away, and the guy remained his newly deferential self the entire walk over. He swept his arm toward the building like he was presenting us with a prize and then walked around back to show us the alley, planting his feet in the exact spot where he said he normally stood when he met this mid-level boss, whose name he didn't even know.

"We're due to meet with him again next Monday," he said. "Seven sharp."

"At night, I assume," Kai said dryly, and the guy nodded vigorously.

"Listen," Nox said. "You're going to make an excuse to your buddies to keep them from showing up on time so that we can have a word with the dude first. And you're not going to let it slip to anyone that you gave this away. Understood?"

The guy nodded again, his eyes wide, but apprehension twisted my stomach.

"Can we be sure he'll keep to that?" I asked. "Ruin's influence is going to wear off way before then."

Jett cocked his head and stepped in. He looked the guy straight in the eyes from just a foot away and slammed his hand against the guy's chest. "I'll give him something to remember us by. So that he keeps in mind just how hard we can come down on him and how easily we can mess him up if he doesn't do what we say."

He jerked down the collar of the man's shirt to show the blood-red handprint he'd imprinted on the guy's skin like a tattoo. A shudder ran down the man's back. Jett's talents might not be super useful in a battle, but they did have one advantage over the other guys': his were permanent. My apartment walls hadn't lost the color he'd given them days ago.

"I'll remember," the guy said, shaking.

"You'd better," Nox growled. "Because Jett's right. If we hear that you tattled, you'd better believe we can track you down and make you pay in all kinds of ways. You saw how we handled you and your bros back at the shop. We can make you do whatever we want to each other… and to yourself. You'd *kill* yourself if we told you to."

The guy nodded again with a jerk of his head, and his hand shot up to rub at the opposite arm.

Something in me went deathly still. "What are you scratching?" I demanded abruptly.

The guy's gaze darted to me. "I—I just had an itch—"

"Show us your arm," I said, my heart beating faster. A ghost of an itch—the itch that'd niggled at me every so often for years until I'd defeated it—rose up under my own skin.

The guy warily shrugged off his jean jacket and peeled up his sleeve. Just a few inches below his armpit, a small, roundish pink birthmark showed against his tan skin.

I swallowed hard. "The Gauntts messed with him too."

Kai frowned. "We knew they got around."

The guy stared at us. "The Gauntts? You mean the Thrivewell people? I don't have anything to do with them. I mean, I remember they came around for some kind of project that was something to do with school back when I was a kid, but—what are you talking about?"

I glanced at Kai. "Make sure he'll cooperate?"

Kai understood what I meant without any further instruction. He socked the guy in the shoulder. "Stand still while Lily gives you your memories back."

I stepped up to the guy and grasped his arm. He gaped at me even as he followed Kai's command. "I don't get it."

Even though he was one of the enemy, even though he might have been one of the dipshits who'd defaced my apartment and tried to stop me from claiming it, a twinge of sympathy ran through my chest. "You will," I said. "But it isn't going to be fun. I'm sorry."

Then I focused on the mark on his arm, bringing the hum of energy inside me roaring up to the surface.

Chapter Six

Nox

"DID they mess up half the kids in the county?" I growled as we strode back to our bikes. The Skeleton Corps doofus hadn't told us much about his experiences with the Gauntts, but the horror that'd come over his face and the way he'd cringed from talking about it was a story all on its own. He'd mumbled something about "parading around" and "Why would they want my clothes off?" which was enough to draw a very sick picture.

"They obviously didn't discriminate between rich kids and families from the wrong side of the tracks," Kai remarked in his matter-of-fact way. Usually I liked that he didn't get worked up about much of anything. Right now, it kind of made me want to punch him.

"Hurray for equal opportunity," Lily grumbled. Her face was even paler than usual, her expression pained. That made me want to punch several people. Preferably starting with Nolan and Marie Gauntt.

But even as my hands tightened into fists, I knew that barging to the Thrivewell building and starting a fist fight wasn't going to fix this problem. For starters, I wasn't quite so cocky that I figured I could make it up twenty floors of that building including the private elevator

Kai and Lily had described without security catching me. I was a force to be reckoned with and even more powerful with my new ghostly energies, but I wasn't invincible, and pretending I was would only hurt the woman and the guys who were counting on me in the long run.

"What are we going to do?" Ruin asked, his voice taut with both eagerness and tension. We'd seen how pissed off the whole situation made him already. I'd never pried much about what his childhood had been like, but I suspected it hadn't been as sunshine-and-rose-y as his current attitude. He bobbed on his feet with his strides like he couldn't wait to launch himself in whatever direction I pointed him in.

The problem was, I wasn't totally sure what direction that should be. I was the leader of the Skullbreakers—it was my job to get us on the right course and see us through this shitfest. But we had a whole banquet of trouble on our plates, and it was hard to tell what we should dig into first that wouldn't make the rest come crashing down on our heads.

Life had definitely been simpler before I'd died.

That thought brought back the pang of loss and anger from when I'd discovered who else had died while I'd been lingering in limbo. The one guiding light I'd had in my own childhood, who'd maybe saved me from the kind of fate the Gauntts' victims had met. My actual parents probably would have sold me for coke or another round at the slots if they'd been ambitious enough to try.

I couldn't talk to Gram the usual way anymore, but maybe she'd have some insights for me anyway. Hell, it was possible her spirit had stuck around like ours had and just had been off running errands or something the last time I'd stopped by her grave.

"I need to think," I announced as we reached the bikes. "Figure out the big picture and how we rearrange it."

"I vote for starting by bashing in the Gauntts' faces," Jett put in.

"We'll get there." I dragged in a breath, not liking to let Lily out of my sight but knowing she'd be in good hands. "The rest of you take Lily back to the apartment. Hash out what we've learned if you want and see what brilliant ideas you all come up with. I have to take care of a couple of things while I mull this over."

The guys looked reluctant, but they didn't question me. Lily didn't have quite the same respect for my authority, but then, I wouldn't have wanted her to feel she had to shut up and fall in line.

She touched my arm, studying my face. "Are you okay? You're not going to go on some kamikaze mission on your own or something crazy like that, are you?"

I had to grin at her. I didn't think it'd ever stop feeling good having this woman concerned about me. Knowing I'd earned that much affection. "Well, now that you've suggested it…" When she grimaced, I leaned in and gave her a swift but firm kiss. "I'm not planning on going anywhere near our enemies at the moment, Minnow," I assured her. "If they come at me, they'll be sorry. But when we take them down, you're going to be right there with me."

"Good," she said, giving my arm a squeeze and stealing another kiss before she let me go.

I mounted my bike and tore off in the opposite direction from the others. Before I went to pay my respects, I stopped at a couple of stores to procure appropriate offerings. Gram had always believed in bringing hostess gifts, and she expected me to mind my manners at least while I was within her sights.

Unless someone else in her sights was being a total jackass. Then I had free rein to throw politeness out the window. Gram hadn't been any pushover.

The cemetery where she was buried was looking pretty quiet. I parked my motorcycle off by itself and tramped across the grassy slopes between the shiny new stones toward the small plot that was Gram's.

She hadn't had much to her name, but she had insisted on buying the plot well before we'd thought there was any chance of her kicking the bucket. Maybe she'd paid for the headstone in advance too. *I don't want you having to worry about what to do with my decrepit bones when I leave this world,* she'd told me more than once. *It's not like I'll be around to care about any fancy to-dos anyway.* Although maybe she'd been wrong about that last part.

She definitely hadn't gone for anything fancy. Her stone stood out amid the others in its row for just how humble it was. Amid the polished marble and towering granite stood a stumpy chunk of rough limestone, no filigree or hopeful symbols chiseled into it, just her name —*Gloria Louise Savage*—and her dates.

Eighty-three years—not too bad a run. Somehow I'd never realized she was quite as old as she was when I'd been living with her. She must have been in her fifties when she'd taken me in at age seven and her sixties by the time I was in my teens, but she'd had so much energy and attitude I'd never thought of her as a senior citizen.

I stood across from the headstone and brought out my offerings. First came the bottle of strawberry iced tea. If you asked me, the stuff was foul, but Gram had guzzled it like it was the elixir of life. She hadn't drunk much else.

I unscrewed the cap and poured it liberally over the grass. Maybe a little would soak into those old bones of hers and give her one last sip.

Then I placed a copy of the latest bizarro tabloid against her stone, because Gram enjoyed nothing more than finding out who'd recently been kidnapped by snake aliens from outer space or communed with Bigfoot in the Alps. Next to it, I set a snazzy gauze scarf that was all neon pink-and-orange flowers.

Gram used to have a scarf for every type of weather. *No one wants to see this chicken neck of mine*, she'd say. Well, now she could be fashionably insecure in the afterlife too.

No sense of a supernatural presence had touched my awareness while I'd been standing there. Now that I was back in a body, I wasn't sure if I'd be more in tune with a loitering ghost than Lily had been with us pre-possession. Was it possible Gram *was* here, and I just couldn't tell?

That idea was even more awful than her being totally gone, so I'd assume that she was either resting in peace or conducting a very busy spectral social life. Maybe there were ghostly book clubs and craft fairs and who knew what else that no one had bothered to invite me and my crew to.

"Hey, Gram," I said anyway, in case she was looking down on me from some better place, the way people talked about. "I brought you a few things I figure they might not have in large supply Upstairs… or Downstairs, if you decided to chill with the Devil. I wouldn't blame you. I'm sure he's a lot more fun."

The breeze rustled through the nearby trees, but no voice carried on it. No hint of a hug brushed across my shoulders. But I found that I wanted to keep talking. I could see her in my mind's eye, standing over a much younger me while I sat on the hardest of the kitchen chairs, her hands on her hips, asking me what ridiculousness I'd gotten myself into now and whether the other people'd had it coming.

"I'm sorry I didn't make it back in time to see you off," I said. "I hope you had a little company, and that maybe you suspected I wasn't really all gone. You were always pretty sharp like that. Figured out stuff before I even knew. Gave me a lot of practice at keeping the stuff I shouldn't be doing on the down low, which has definitely been useful. So, thank you for that."

I shifted on my feet, rocking back on my heels in silence as a couple walked by on a nearby path. What I said to Gram wasn't any of their business, especially if it might incriminate me in a court of law. I waited until they were way off by a statue of some angel who looked constipated before I spoke up again.

"You always told me I could own the whole world if I was willing to take it on. I'm pretty sure you were exaggerating and just trying to be inspirational, but it kind of feels like I do have to take on the whole world right now. We're going after some big guns, bigger than I ever thought I'd be tangling with, and that's meaning I have to go big too. But it's getting fucking crazy. Like, really crazy, not just what Lily would call crazy. You never got to meet her, but I think the two of you would get along pretty well."

I paused, rummaging through my thoughts. The Gram in my head said, *How crazy are we talking about here?* like I'd imagine she would have if she'd really been here. So naturally, I answered.

"Well, we've all got superpowers. We're whooping people's asses without even touching them, jumbling up their emotions and using mind control and—we'd probably end up in one of your tabloids with the aliens and the Bigfoots. So that's pretty crazy. And we're fighting against one of the biggest corporations in the country, maybe the world, at the same time. But all that is fine. We've got the tools we need to bring the bastards down."

What's the problem then?

I let out a grunt of frustration. "I'm just thinking about all the stuff we're going to have to do to go after them, and it's so much more than I ever figured on when we were just stomping around Lovell Rise… What if I go too far? What if I bite off too much all at once, and the guys and Lily end up choking too? I *want* to tear apart this whole fucking city right now, but if you think about it, that's a hell of a lot of rubble coming down on our heads."

So dodge it, Gram said. *You're fast on your feet still, aren't you? If you're up against big, then you have to go big or go home. If you're up against crazy, sanity's overrated. Hit them where it hurts and don't give them a chance to hit you back, or you might as well not start the fight at all.*

Even though those words were only scraps of things she'd said before, stitched into a sort of patchwork in my imagination, a weird sense of comfort settled over me. Because it wasn't hard at all to picture her actually saying that. And like in most things, she'd have been right.

We had to take on the Gauntts and the Skeleton Corps. There wasn't any "if" about it. And if we were going to smash those fuckers to smithereens, it was going to take everything we had in us, no matter how insane.

I'd had a wild fury bubbling inside me from the moment the bullet one of the Skeleton Corps pricks had fired shattered my skull. Any qualms I'd still had left at that point in my life had gone out the window with my brains.

That wasn't a defect. That was a gift. I could be as fucking savage as I wanted to be without giving a shit what anyone else would think about it.

There was no way the Corps or the Gauntts could be prepared for what I was willing to unleash on them. It was time to lean in and step up.

Chapter Seven

Lily

I'D THOUGHT that I was ready for this new phase in our fight with the Gauntts. But looking up over the stone wall at the posh house—mansion, let's be real—in the Mayfield suburbs, all I wanted to do was make like a gopher and burrow away into the ground.

"Are you sure this is a good idea?" I asked.

Beside me, Nox snorted. "Good isn't a metric we're using these days. It's the right idea if we're going to get a grip on all the shit these pricks are up to. Come on."

He held out his hands to boost me up like he already had the three other guys. I planted my feet on his palms, gripped his broad shoulders for balance, and swiveled to grasp the top of the wall as he lifted me. With a not-particularly-graceful amount of squirming, I swung my legs over the top and dropped down on the other side.

Nox gave a couple of hops and managed between his substantial height and the punch of energy he could produce from his limbs to vault himself high enough to clamber over the wall on his own. The four of us clustered together at the edge of the lawn, partly hidden by a cherry tree, eyeing the big beige-and-blue mansion where the Gauntts lived.

All of them. It turned out that Nolan and Marie lived with the younger generation, Thomas and Olivia. I wasn't even sure which of the second generation was Nolan and Marie's kid and which had married into the family. The house looked big enough to hold about ten different families, so I guessed it wasn't particularly crowded that way, even if staying under the parents' roof was kind of odd these days.

Maybe they just sat around and planned all the next moves of their business over dinner and drinks.

Did the younger Gauntts have special powers too? Were they in on the whole exploit-the-children project Nolan and Marie had going on? None of the victims we'd talked to had mentioned anyone else, but as far as I knew, Thomas and Olivia were in their thirties. They could have been practically kids themselves when Ansel and Peyton and the others had been roped in.

They might be victims too.

A shiver passed through me at the thought. Kai's keen eyes caught the reaction, but he read the wrong reason into it.

"There's definitely no one home," he said. "I confirmed that all four of them left for that business conference before I left the office. And we've had a couple of the sharper new recruits keeping a careful eye on the place all day. No one's driven in."

"They could have housekeeping staff who live on site," Jett pointed out.

Nox hummed in agreement. "They'd practically need an army to keep that place all clean and orderly."

"They must want their privacy too, though," I said. "They get up to a lot of crazy things… They wouldn't want some maid stumbling on them working magic or talking about how great the last molestation went and spreading the word around."

Kai nodded. "There've been no rumors about the Gauntts that've gotten enough traction to warrant even a news article. I've combed the archives of the internet thoroughly." He grimaced, and I remembered his past complaints about wading through the chaos of the world wide web. "I actually identified a woman who does cleaning for them and chatted her up yesterday. She only comes by twice a week—not including today—and she commented that the house is kind of spooky with no one there."

Ruin shuffled his feet, his eyes bright with anticipation. "Let's get on with it, then! Maybe we'll find Lily's sister in there."

I wished I could feel as hopeful as he sounded. "I don't think they'd stash kidnapping victims in their own home. But they might have left some kind of clue about where they *are* holding her."

We pulled up the hoods of the hoodies we'd all donned, extra big so the fabric would shadow our faces. Then we set off across the lawn with our heads low, checking carefully for any signs of life or electronic surveillance. The Gauntts might not have any human beings watching over the property, but it was hard to believe they wouldn't have some kind of security cameras.

"What about the alarm system?" I asked as we approached the house. There was about a snowball's chance in hell they didn't have one of those too.

"Not a problem," Kai said with his usual cool confidence, and waggled his fingers. "We still have electricity on our side. So sad that there'll be a blackout in the neighborhood right when five disreputable types were scoping out the place." He glanced at me and gave me one of his narrow smiles. "Well, four disreputable types and one totally admirable woman who's somehow gotten suckered in by them."

I snorted. "You're doing all this to help me find my sister. Seems like if anyone got suckered, it's you."

"Oh, we're more than adequately compensated," Nox teased, slinging an arm around me and pinching my butt. When I glowered at him, he chuckled and let me go. "That blackout's going to take all of us. Ready?"

The four guys walked right up to the house where the electrical service connected to the building. They raised their hands and without speaking seemed to agree on their timing. Leaping forward, they smacked the wall simultaneously.

A crackling sound burst through the air, followed by a furious sizzling. Then there was a faint *pop* like a cork coming out of a bottle of champagne.

Even late in the afternoon, it wasn't dark enough yet for there to be any lights in view that I could watch blinking off. But the guys seemed totally confident it'd worked. Nox marched up to the front door and slapped his hand against the electronic keypad next. There was another crackle, and the deadbolt in the door slid over. He turned the knob, and we all waltzed inside like we owned the place.

Kai checked the hall light switch and confirmed that it wasn't working. We peered through the shadows at the grand entryway that led to a sweeping mahogany staircase.

Jett let out a low whistle. "It's fucking absurd, but when it comes to absurd levels of pomposity, they do know how to decorate a place."

We treaded farther in over thick, discreetly patterned rugs, past framed landscape paintings and side tables with elegant vases, under unlit brass light fixtures dangling from ornate moldings. There definitely was an eerie hush to the place—I could see why the maid might find it unnerving. But presumably they paid her well enough that she'd gotten over it. It must have taken her the entire day to clean all these rooms.

The Gauntts didn't just keep their home posh. It was also painstakingly neat. I guessed that probably wasn't too difficult to accomplish when they spent most of their lives at work—compared to, say, living in an apartment with four guys who had bottomless pits for stomachs and the frequent urge to test out their budding supernatural powers on everything in their vicinity.

We looked through all the cupboards and drawers in the painfully white kitchen and turned up nothing but standard utensils and dishes, like something out of a home showroom. Several plain round magnets dappled the immense stainless-steel fridge, but none of them actually stuck anything to the surface. No notes, no photos, no delivery menus.

It barely felt like anyone lived here at all.

Wandering through what they might have called living or sitting or family rooms—there were so many of them I had no idea which was which—we found a few signs of life. Someone had left a novel—Stephen King, not the kind of high-brow stuff I'd have expected—on an ebony coffee table. A partly filled out pad of sudoku puzzles lay in an end table's drawer next to a precisely sharpened pencil. I didn't think we could report them to the police on the basis of banal pastimes, though.

The TV room threw me for a bit of a loop. I found myself staring at the rows of movies stashed away behind glossy glass cabinet doors on one side of the huge flatscreen TV. They had an entire set of Disney animated flicks and most of Pixar's oeuvre too, alongside war films and historical dramas and a sizeable collection of horror that fit with the Stephen King book.

Ruin came up beside me and cocked his head. "Young at heart?" he suggested, but even he couldn't quite sell the joke.

Did they bring their victims here sometimes and put on the movies to distract them? Or did the Gauntts just have an unusual appreciation for family features?

It turned out the answer was something else entirely—something I wouldn't have predicted in a million years after seeing the rest of the house. We headed upstairs, stepped into the first bedroom off the broad hallway, and realized they didn't need to bring kids here to visit.

They had kids living right here with them.

The bedroom was painted bright yellow with the furniture done up in a palate of primary colors that made Jett wince. If we'd had any doubt about it being for one specific kid and not occasional visitors, a framed photo on the dresser showed the four Gauntts we'd known about as well as a boy and a girl who looked to be seven or eight, nestled between Thomas and Olivia's arms.

I strode out of that room and into the next one, which looked a lot like the first but all done up in pinks and lilacs. The girl's bedroom, obviously, unless the Gauntts had decided to completely reverse traditional gender expression.

"How did we not know Thomas and Olivia had kids?" I demanded.

Kai was frowning as he poked around the bedroom, which was as painfully neat as the rest of the place. It was hard to believe children actually inhabited this space and not, say, kid-shaped robots. Which would have been an interesting development, but the Gauntts had given every sign of being supernaturally inclined, not mechanical geniuses.

"I don't know," he said. "I haven't seen anything about them in their schedules or heard anyone mention them. The kids must have joined them on this trip or else be staying with other relatives."

Ruin looked unusually downcast. "Who looks after them while their parents are working all the time?"

"They could have a nanny who just doesn't live in the house—she only comes when the kids are out of school and the parents at work," I said, more to reassure Ruin than to justify anything the Gauntts did. I didn't like seeing his good cheer diminish, and they seemed to be having that effect on him a lot these days.

"Or maybe they use their supernatural voodoo on the kids too, so they'll be obedient little dupes," Nox growled. "It'd explain how fucking tidy this place is even with them running around."

It would. And it could be that the Gauntts did other things to those kids, just like they did to those outside their family. I hugged myself, my stomach turning.

Jett had stalked back into the boys' room. I followed him and found him studying the photograph.

"I don't think they're genetically related," he said abruptly. "Their features are too different."

Kai joined us and took the photo from him. He made a thoughtful sound. "I see what you mean. Good eye—of course, that makes sense, coming from you. You know…" His forehead furrowed as he examined the picture even more intently. "I can't tell which of the second generation is related to Nolan and Marie. They both look too different as well."

"There are things like recessive genes and whatever, right?" I said. "Unusual features popping up?"

"Not usually to this extent. The bone structure… set of the eyes… Hmm." Kai snapped a picture of the photo with his phone, presumably to ruminate over more later.

"They might have taken Marisol someplace that their own kids go to, right?" Ruin said, bringing back the optimism.

"Maybe," I agreed. "See if you can find anything about lessons they take or even what school they go to."

We searched through both of the kids' bedrooms and turned up nothing but clothes, books, and evidence that they were at least allowed electronic devices, as there was a charging cable plugged in next to one of the beds. Nothing even indicated what the kids' names were. I stepped back into the hall, my skin creeping.

"I don't like this," I said to Nox. "Everything about these people just seems to get worse and worse. How can we protect their *own* kids from them?"

He rubbed his hand up and down my back. "Rescuing your sister comes first. Then we'll worry about the rest. Hell, if we blow up all the adult Gauntts, someone else will have to adopt the kids."

I raised my eyebrows at him. "Is that the plan now? We're looking to turn them into human dynamite?"

He shrugged with a sly gleam in his dark eyes. "After seeing this place, I don't think I'd trust a simple bullet to do the trick."

He might have had a point there.

Ruin's voice traveled from one of the rooms farther down the hall. "Huh, this is pretty funny."

We all hustled over to join him. He was standing in a bedroom clearly used by adults, with a classy sleigh bed and matching furnishings in dark wood. On the vanity, next to a jewelry box, stood a vase full of dried bullrushes.

Ruin was leaning close. He gave an audible sniff and glanced at the rest of us. "I swear they're from our marsh too!"

Kai gave him a skeptical look. "I'd imagine all marsh vegetation smells pretty similar," he said.

Nox bent in to take a whiff. "I don't know," he said. "We were steeping in that stuff for more than two decades. It does smell awfully familiar."

"What other marshes are around here anyway?" Jett pointed out.

Kai huffed. "They probably bought it from the Pottery Barn or someplace because they thought it was pretty."

"I don't think that's the weird part," I said, and motioned to a portrait hanging on the wall on the other side of the room.

The oil painting showed a couple who appeared to be middle-aged, but they didn't look like Nolan and Marie or the photos I'd seen of Thomas and Olivia. The man had a bulbous nose that would have been unmistakable if I'd seen it on anyone else, and the woman had a bit of a cleft chin.

"Who the heck are *they*?" I asked. "And why do the Gauntts have their portrait hanging in their bedroom?"

"Distant ancestors?" Nox suggested.

"Their clothes aren't that old-fashioned," Kai said. "I'd say those are '40s era. 1940s, that is, not 1840s or something."

"I guess they could be grandparents or great-grandparents," I said, but that explanation didn't sit totally right. Maybe it was just the way the painted figures' eyes seemed to follow me when I walked back out of the room. "There's nothing around that tells us anything about what they've done with Marisol."

"We have a few new leads I can follow up on," Kai said, but optimism didn't sound as natural on him as it did coming from Ruin.

Who was now in another bedroom, calling us over. "We know they really love marshes!"

I stepped in after him and saw what he meant. This was clearly the main master bedroom, presumably where Nolan and Marie slept. There was a faint, crisp scent of cologne lingering in the air that made me think of the imposing man who'd laughed at my magical display. But what drew my attention were the vases on either side of the sprawling California king bed.

They didn't fit with the rest of the décor at all, really. They were too untidy, too wild. Both of them were stuffed full of reeds and bullrushes that did look as if they'd been plucked right out of the marsh where I'd nearly drowned fourteen years ago.

Chapter Eight

Kai

I LEANED against the counter in the school office and formed my best ingratiating smile. "I really am very sorry to bother you about this issue. It's just so important that I make sure I have the correct information so that we don't miss any potential risk factors that could compromise the children's health."

Between the posh formality I'd taken on to fit with the private school atmosphere and my appeal to health concerns, I had the secretary wrapped around my finger. It'd only taken me a matter of seconds after I walked in the door to notice the little signs of hypochondria: the hands slightly chafed from over-washing, the not one but three bottles of hand sanitizer all within easy reach in different directions across her desk area, the faint whiff of tea tree oil that hung around her. It must be awfully hard keeping herself so germ-free while surrounded by elementary school kids.

"Of course, of course," she said with a nervous giggle, and tapped away at her keyboard. The keys were so brightly white I wondered if she bleached them daily. She knit her brow at the screen. "Nolan and Marie Gauntt, you said?"

"Yes." Thanks to a couple of days of ferreting out all the information I could from available sources, I'd managed to determine that the Nolan and Marie we all knew and hated had been honored by their heirs with their grandchildren's renaming. The boy and girl we'd seen in the family photo were Nolan and Marie Junior. How precious. It made me want to puke.

No doubt they were raising the brats in their own image too.

"They were in to see me over the weekend," I added, letting my tone get brisker. "It's a rather urgent matter—just got the test results back."

"I totally understand. I'll do whatever I can to help you. We do normally have that information on file—oh."

"Oh?" I asked, cocking my head and offering a wryer smile.

In spite of her earlier positive reactions to some light teasing, the secretary didn't smile back. Her brow had outright furrowed now. I could see her pulling away from me and the conversation in the tensing of her stance. "I'm afraid I won't be able to help you with this matter," she said.

Frustration prickled through my nerves. Before she could completely dismiss me, I flicked my hand across the counter and gave her a light smack to the shoulder with a quiver of supernatural energy. "Show me the computer screen without making a fuss about it."

My power didn't allow me to order her to say anything in particular, or I'd have simply commanded her to spit out what she knew. But this way worked well enough. With her mouth pressing into a strained line, she swiveled the monitor so I could see it from the other side of the counter.

The file that she'd brought up for Nolan Junior held one piece of information I'd been looking for: his enrollment date. The private school I'd determined that the Gauntt children attended started at kindergarten, but Nolan Junior, currently age ten and in fifth grade, had only started there two years ago. Which dollars to dingoes meant that he'd been adopted around that time, based on the other pieces I'd been able to assemble. There weren't many accessible facts, but those I had were starting to form a picture.

Also forming a picture, one that felt distinctly like a middle finger raised in my direction, was the window that'd popped up covering the rest of the file. *CONFIDENTIAL INFORMATION. Password required for access.*

I swatted the secretary again. "Enter the password, then."

"I can't," she said, staring at my hand as if she thought a swarm of bees might fly from my fingers next. "I don't know what it is. I've never seen this on a file before."

Fuck. It was some special security measure that the Gauntts had put in place. I gritted my teeth and gave her one last smack. "Bring up Marie Gauntt's file."

The granddaughter's profile had the same confidential message, but at least I managed to confirm that she'd also started school two years ago, one grade below her brother. The middle generation of Gauntts had adopted them both around the same time. But I didn't think they were blood siblings. They looked even less like each other than they did like their current parents.

Gritting my teeth in irritation, I dipped my head to the secretary. It wasn't her fault that the Gauntts were such pricks. And a little politeness could grease the wheels for next time… if she somehow forgot that I'd mind-controlled her into jumping to my command. "Thank you for your help."

"My pleasure," she said with a bit of a squeak, sounding surprised at her own politeness even as the words came out on autopilot.

I strode out of the building before she could decide that maybe she should call a security guard or something. For most people, the terror of something unexpected and inexplicable happening to them, something they couldn't prove or explain in any way that'd sound real to someone who hadn't experienced it, would be enough motivation to seal their lips. And if she tried to blab about a young man who'd forced her to reveal private information about students, her higher-ups would be more concerned with disciplining her than following up on her wild story.

I just wished that the effort had gotten me farther. All the time I'd spent chatting people up, conning my way into files, and making swift observations, and I knew little more than the kids' names and approximate arrival date. And none of it had led me any closer to our real goal, which was finding Lily's sister. This trumped-up daycare obviously wouldn't have been hosting brainwashed teenagers.

Thinking of Marisol, I flicked on my phone and checked the video app. New instances of the sweater challenge hashtag were starting to increase exponentially. There were less than a hundred so far, but I could tell from the momentum that it was catching on. In another couple of days, we should have thousands, and then we could hope that at least a few of them were local.

With a small sense of satisfaction, I hopped on my motorcycle and cut across town to deal with a very different sort of business. We were due for another batch of guns and ammo I'd negotiated an order for so that we could make sure our new recruits remained properly equipped. Going up against the Skeleton Corps, I didn't want us to end up with empty chambers in the middle of a shoot-out.

The black-market dealer operated out of the back room in an Irish pub on the shady side of downtown Mayfield. The place was enough of an eyesore to make even me wince, with huge neon four-leaf clovers plastered all over the front and lime-green walls mixed with eggplant-purple tables on the inside. I'd already made a mental note never to bring Jett here or he might have a heart attack. Or a psychotic break that'd have him tearing every person in the place limb from limb.

On the other hand, I didn't always understand his artistic sensibilities. Maybe he'd have found the decor refreshingly unusual. It seemed better not to take the chance, though.

I walked straight through the bar to the back room and strode past the beaded curtain—the beads in the shape of clovers, naturally—without announcing myself. Dirk was expecting me.

Unfortunately, when he turned around from where he'd been sorting through a couple of boxes on a shelving unit behind him, I could immediately tell that he'd expected me with a whole lot of dread. His shoulders slumped, and his fingers flexed like he wished he had an AK-47 in them right now so he could blow me away and not have to deal with me at all.

That was a pretty different response from our first couple of meetings when I'd made the connection and arranged our first batch of weaponry. I hadn't known Dirk would become a dick. Something had happened.

I stepped closer so I was within punching range if need be and crossed my arms over my chest. "Have you got our loot? I have a couple of guys on the way to pick it up."

Dirk's pointed jaw twitched from side to side. "Turns out I can't do business with you lot," he said.

I arched my eyebrows. "Oh, really? And why's that? Was there some problem with the nice stack of cash I handed over last time?"

He coughed. "Your money's fine. But you don't call the shots in Mayfield. I have other… interests to consider."

He didn't have to say anything else. I could put *those* pieces together in an instant.

I had to resist the urge to clock him across the head with the gun he'd already sold me. If I needed to hit him, I could do it in a more productive way than that.

"The Skeleton Corps got to you," I said. "They told you not to sell to us anymore."

Dirk shrugged helplessly, as if he lived at the mercy of whoever jerked his chain the hardest. Which was fine. He hadn't seen how hard *we* could jerk, which was no doubt why he'd cowered at the feet of those boneheaded bozos.

"We can do this the easy way or the hard way," I told him, since it seemed only fair to give him a chance to change his mind. "Either way, you're selling us those guns. But I'd rather we did it peacefully." We had real enemies to fight. Dirk the dork wasn't one of them.

"I'm sorry," he said, splaying his hands.

I sighed. "Fine." Then I punched him in the forehead, maybe a tad harder than I totally needed to.

Supernatural energy zapped along my arm and into his brain. "Shut up and bring the boxes with the guns you were supposed to sell to us out to the car," I said. I'd learned pretty quickly that if I didn't add the first part or something similar to my commands, I had to deal with idiots yelling their heads off while they carried out my orders.

Dirk's mouth clamped shut. Wide-eyed, he turned toward the shelves and pulled down a couple of plastic crates. I grabbed one and motioned for him to take the other. We walked together to the back door, his sneakers dragging across the floor in a futile effort to keep himself from making the trek.

I'd already heard the sound of the engine in the alley out back. At least a few of the bozos on our side were punctual. When I opened the door, the new recruits were standing outside the old Bronco they drove, the doors to the cargo area popped open, bobbing on their feet like they were eager to giddy up.

"Nice!" one guy said as we carried the crates over to the back, like there was anything all that impressive about the containers themselves.

I socked Dirk in the shoulder. "Go back to your office and don't do anything else." As he trudged inside, I turned back to the other guys. "Get these back to the clubhouse immediately, and Nox'll have a bonus for you."

The other guy let out a whoop, and they both dove back into the car. As it roared off, I headed back inside.

Dirk was standing just inside the door to his office, as commanded. I had to push him to the side so I could walk past him. Then I dug the wad of cash that was meant to be our payment out of my pocket and slapped it on the table.

"I don't have to pay you, but I am," I said, holding his frantic gaze. "I hope you'll remember that the next time you're deciding who runs things around here. You'll be able to move again in about ten minutes. Use that time to think carefully about which side you're on. I can always come back and punch you again."

A muscle in his cheek quivered. I thought his brow looked slightly damp. My instincts jangled with the sense that he knew more than what he'd admitted to already.

Thank holy hell for my observational abilities. Because of the extra sense of caution I exited the pub with, I wasn't totally surprised when three jackasses sprang at me.

The problem with trying to attack one guy when there are three of you is that you can't really all swarm him at once or you'll end up punching each other. So I simply drove my fist into the temple of the first guy who reached me and told him, "Kill the other two."

The first guy whirled around, the knife in his hand flashing, and drove it into the neck of the guy who'd been hurtling over right behind him. That guy toppled over onto the sidewalk like a beached fish, his eyes bugging out as if he couldn't believe the blood spurting out in a fountain from his carotid artery.

The third guy dodged his colleague, sputtering in surprise. Word might have gotten around about our unusual fighting techniques, but I'd bet most of the people that word had reached had dismissed it as lies and excuses. Too bad for them—*they* weren't properly prepared.

The third guy tried to lunge at me again, but the first guy charged right at him, getting in his way. They grappled, and the knife went flying. As I pulled out my gun to solve the problem more permanently, the guy I'd instructed to murder his companions spun around and wrenched one of the metal clovers right off the window frame.

He whirled toward his former friend, slashing the clover through the air like some kind of cleaver, as if he'd become a maniacal leprechaun. I stepped back to watch the show, not seeing any reason to end it just as it was getting good.

The two men faced off with a dodge here and a feint there. The first guy raked the edge of the clover across the other guy's arm forcefully enough to cut through his shirt and draw blood. The other guy cursed at him and tried to smack the clover out of his hands like he had the knife, but his opponent wasn't falling for the same trick twice.

"Leo, you numbskull," the other guy shouted in exasperation. Leo just launched himself at him, jabbing the clover at his throat. I guessed his companion had never liked him all that much, because that was the point when the other guy took out his gun and shot Leo in the face.

Leo crumpled over, the other guy whipped toward me, and I finished off the trifecta by lodging a bullet in his skull.

The three gangsters—Skeleton Corps members, I had to assume—lay crumpled on the sidewalk. Sirens sounded in the distance thanks to some concerned citizen putting in a call after the gun shots.

It didn't matter. I'd been about to leave anyway, with as little as I had to show for my trouble. Yet again, the Corps had almost screwed us over, and we'd barely put a dent in their forces. Why couldn't I see their moves farther ahead than this?

As I shoved my pistol back into my jeans, my gaze caught on the blood still spurting from the first corpse's throat like a macabre drinking fountain. Too bad vampires weren't as real as ghosts, or one could have had a nice meal there.

The thought sunk in, and something clicked in my head. I sucked in a breath, a smile stretching across my lips. Then I raced to my bike with more speed than I usually resorted to.

The Gauntts and the Skeleton Corps had been staying ahead of us, outwitting me, far too much. But I might have just stumbled on the key that would turn the tide.

Chapter Nine

Lily

WHEN KAI BROUGHT me over to sit at the dining table with him and produced a deadly-looking paring knife, I knew I probably wasn't going to like whatever he wanted to talk to me about.

"I should have realized it sooner," he said, spinning the knife between his deft fingers like it was a baton. "You've got the power to conquer *anyone*, even the Gauntts."

"Of course she does!" Ruin said cheerfully from where he was perched on the arm of the sofa. "Next time we'll be really ready."

"That's not what I mean," Kai said with a mildly irritated tone.

Nox spun one of the other dining chairs around and sat on it with his arms folded over the top. "Well, why don't you get on with telling us about your new genius idea, then?"

As Jett drifted over from the kitchen and leaned against the wall to watch, Kai rolled up his sleeves to his elbows. The light brown skin beneath was smooth with a dusting of fine hairs.

"I was thinking," he said, looking up at me, "about your trick with the coffee. And your beer attack in the fight the other day. And it occurred to me, way later than it should have, that blood is something like ninety percent water."

A tendril of nausea unfurled in my gut as I caught on to the implications. No, I definitely didn't like the direction this conversation was going in.

"Kai," I started, my instinctive revulsion tickling up through my chest.

"Listen," he insisted. "This could be the answer to everything. Taking on the Gauntts and the Skeleton Corps too if you want to lend us a hand there. Even finding your sister. You and she share the same bloodline, after all. If you can control blood, then you control *life*. But first we need to test my theory out and make sure I'm not blowing hot air."

"Any more than usual," Jett muttered, but he was eyeing us with open curiosity now.

"Fuck," Nox said. "*I* should have thought of that."

Ruin clapped his hands together, his eyes gleaming. "Lily's going to sock it to those rich pricks with their own blood!"

"We don't even know if I can," I protested. "And how can we experiment that won't—"

Kai didn't bother answering with words. He just brought the knife to his arm and cut a shallow line through his skin, about an inch long.

My stomach lurched again. Tiny beads of blood seeped out along the thin cut. He hadn't even winced, so I guessed it hadn't hurt that much. But still. He was carving himself open so I could conduct this experiment. Even if he wanted to see the results as much as anyone, that didn't seem right.

And what if I screwed this up somehow? It wasn't as if I had perfect control even over water. At least if I created an accidental tidal wave, all that would happen was some people getting wet. Blood… Blood was something else entirely.

Like Kai had said, it was life. And now it was his life I'd be playing with.

I swallowed thickly. Kai met my eyes again, his expression showing nothing but confident anticipation. "Give it a shot, Lily. Be the barracuda you know you can be. Make a little art."

The eagerness in his tone and the way he phrased it dampened my disgust just a little. I eyed the droplets of blood that had formed along the cut and dragged in a breath.

Move them around a little. Find out whether I *could* direct them to my will. There wasn't anything so horrible about just testing out that possibility, was there? It wasn't as if I were going to reach out to the rest of the blood inside him. The loss of a few specks obviously hadn't killed him.

Hell, even taking a bullet to his brain hadn't *totally* killed him twenty-one years ago.

My churning emotions had stirred the hum in my chest. I didn't want to rile it up as much as I had in the past. I didn't need to mess around with the blood a *lot* to be sure I could actually affect it. Baby steps seemed like the safest approach.

I set my hand on the tabletop and drummed a soft rhythm with my fingertips, letting that beat and the thump of my heart steady me. Then I focused on the beads of blood and threw a little of that supernatural energy at them, willing them to move toward me.

The second my power touched the ruddy liquid, I felt it resonate with the hum inside me. The drops streaked a couple of inches across Kai's arm toward me, leaving a thin red train in their wake.

A grin split Kai's face. "I was right. You're going to rule them all. You'll be fucking unstoppable."

I let my hand go still, the hum dwindling inside me. My revulsion had faded, but trepidation had taken up residence in my gut in its place. "How? You want me to go around calling people's blood right out of their bodies or something?"

I'd watched the guys commit more than one murder in self-defense… I'd helped them in small ways from the sidelines. But I'd never taken a life myself. The thought of doing it, especially in a way I had to think would be horribly painful—getting the blood wrung out of you while you were alive to feel it?—left me chilled.

"If they deserve it, why the fuck not?" Nox said with a smirk.

Kai shot him a baleful look. "I was thinking of something a little more elegant. No need for you to make a mess if you don't want to. I'd imagine with a little practice you could get to the point where you could send all the blood in a person's body toward their heart and burst it right inside their chest. Neat and contained but gets the job done just fine."

I still felt shivery at the thought, but at the same time, picturing Nolan Gauntt's coolly patronizing face, imagining how his expression would clench with fear as I pummeled his heart with his own blood, gave me a dark sort of thrill.

Could I really do that? And if I could… he really wouldn't be able to stop me, would he?

No matter what powers he had, no one could survive without their heart.

"Give it another try," Kai said, bringing his gaze back to me. His eyes gleamed behind the panes of his glasses. "Draw a little out. I've got plenty to spare. I want to see how much you can do."

I stared at his arm, caught in a weird mix of uneasiness and excitement. The other three guys leaned a little closer in anticipation. I thought of Nolan Gauntt again, of how he'd wrenched my sister away from me just when I'd gotten her out from under Mom's and Wade's thumbs, and the hum reverberated through my chest at a higher pitch.

Wetting my lips, I let my fingers fall back into their steady rhythm against the tabletop. Just a little. Just a little of the blood pulsing through Kai's veins, called out to trickle across his skin. I could do that, couldn't I? I had so much more control over my powers already than I'd had just a few weeks ago.

I tugged at the liquid coursing through his arm with my mind and a quiver of supernatural energy. A speckling of more blood bubbled along the little cut. It formed into a narrow ribbon that dribbled over the curve of his forearm. A metallic taste formed in the back of my mouth, and a heady sense of power rushed through me.

Unfortunately, that rush sent me off balance. As the thrill expanded inside me, I yanked harder than I'd meant to, and a whole spurt of scarlet liquid gushed from the cut to splatter on the dining table.

I yelped, my connection to Kai's pulse shattering. There was a stack of paper napkins left on the table after our last takeout meal. I snatched a handful and pressed them to Kai's arm, even though as far as I could tell the stream of blood had tapered off as soon as I'd withdrawn my control.

Kai curled his fingers around my own arm and gave me a comforting squeeze. No sign of pain showed on his face. "It's okay. It was only a little jolt. I'm perfectly fine."

How could he be so calm?

I grimaced at him. "I don't want to hurt you."

Kai let out a low chuckle that sent a different type of electricity tingling low in my belly. He slid forward on his chair and reached for my other hand. "You don't have to worry about that. Watching you work is having the opposite effect."

I didn't know what he meant until he brought my hand to his groin. My palm came to rest on the unmistakable bulge of an erection. Kai's eyelids dipped, heavy with lust, and all of me flushed, from my cheeks down to my core.

"I'm pretty sure I didn't send any blood flowing *there*," I couldn't help saying. It was impossible not to rub my hand up and down the length of him through his jeans, even more heat racing through me at the concrete evidence of his lustful appreciation.

Kai let out a softly urgent noise and pulled me right onto his lap. He ran his hands up into my hair. "You sent it there just by being your incredible self. You can pull the life right out of me as easily as fucking *breathing*. Do you have any idea what a turn-on that is?"

I wouldn't have thought of it as one, but I couldn't really argue with the bulge of his cock now pressing between my legs or his fingers tracing scorching lines over my scalp—or the kiss he pulled me into.

His lips seared against mine, devouring me. His fingers tangled in my hair and tugged hard enough to bring out pinpricks of pain that sparked pleasure at the same time.

I whimpered, and he smiled against my mouth. Then his tongue swept in to tease over mine, his hands trailing down the sides of my body alongside the kiss. He paused to sweep his fingers over my breasts and then drew them lower to squeeze my ass, pulling me even tighter against him. The feel of him rigidly hard against my sex had me grinding against him, desperate for more.

Kai tipped his head back just far enough to whip off his glasses and toss them onto the table with a clatter, and I became abruptly aware of our audience. The other three Skullbreakers were still in the room, of course.

Nox had gotten up from his chair. His gaze branded my skin, smoldering with an intoxicating combination of hunger and possessiveness. Ruin had sucked his lower lip under his teeth in a way that made me want to go over and kiss him. His eyes sparkled with nothing but enthusiastic desire. And Jett…

Jett remained in his pose leaning against the wall, his shoulders tensed and his expression rigid. But he hadn't torn his attention away from me.

Kai flicked a glance around at the others. "There's plenty of Lily to go around," he said casually. "No need to just stand there." Then he yanked my mouth back to his.

As we kissed, he squeezed my ass again and then dipped one hand between us to stroke my clit through my pants. Bliss shot through me in a crackling bolt, and I outright moaned. Whatever new dimensions to my powers we'd uncovered, they couldn't be all that bad if they made Kai want to do this to me, could they?

And not just him. Nox's massive presence loomed beside me, his mouth seeking out the side of my neck. As his lips marked a blazing trail down the side to the crook of my shoulder, he reached around to cup both my breasts at the same time. I rocked into Kai's hand and arched my back to meet Nox's caresses, delight washing through me in a torrent.

When Kai drew back, his breath was coming rough. "Take her shirt off," he told Nox. I'd noticed he got bossy when he was in makeout mode. But I wasn't complaining.

Neither was Nox. He chuckled and peeled my sweater right off me. Then he unclasped my bra for good measure. As he slid his hands over my breasts skin to skin, tweaking my nipples so I gasped, Ruin stepped up at my other side.

"Our gorgeous, mighty Waterlily," he murmured, and captured my mouth next.

Even being with two guys before had been a novel experience. Three had my thoughts completely spiraling in a whirlwind of shared desire. I ran my hands down Kai's chest and yanked his own shirt up, figuring the nakedness shouldn't go just one way.

As Ruin shifted his kisses to my jaw and then my earlobe with a light nibble, Nox hummed approvingly. "Going to be a good girl for Kai too, aren't you?" he murmured in that voice that instantly turned me to putty.

I circled my hands over Kai's taut nipples and smiled at the genius. "I think Kai likes me better naughty."

Kai let out a heated laugh at the callback to our first hookup and dipped his hand right inside my pants to stroke me more effectively. "Hell yes, I do."

"You can be good at being naughty then," Nox insisted, and lowered his head to claim the other side of my neck while he kept working over my breasts.

I palmed Kai's erection again, and a new hunger spread through my chest, making my mouth water. I knew just how I could be *very* good at naughtiness.

I pushed myself back off his lap and eased to the floor between his splaying knees. As I reached for the button of his fly, Jett let out a curt sound. He shoved off the wall and stalked across the room to the front door, which shut with a thump in his wake.

I hesitated, my stomach twisting, my gaze glued to the door. Nox guided my attention back to the three of them with two fingers under my chin.

"Don't worry about our tortured artist," he said. "He'll sort himself out eventually. What did you have in mind for the rest of us, Siren?"

I glanced up at Kai. A flush had crept up his neck, and he licked his lips. Without prompting, he flicked open the fly of his jeans.

I wanted him. I wanted all of them. That had nothing to do with Jett and whatever the hell *he* wanted. He wasn't into watching or joining in? That was fine. It shouldn't stop me from enjoying myself with the men who were sure of their desires.

I tugged Kai's jeans down his hips and freed his rigid cock from his boxers. Just the pump of my fingers had him groaning.

"Fuck, Lily," he said, his head tipping back in the chair. "Go ahead and eat me alive." He narrowed his eyes at Nox and Ruin. "Make sure she gets off plenty too."

Nox snorted. "Like we'd somehow forget the best part."

As I leaned forward to wrap my lips around the heat of Kai's shaft, Nox took over where his friend had been teasing my clit before. Not content to work around my clothes, he tugged my pants and panties down to my knees. Then he stroked his fingers between my legs with a growl as he felt how wet I was.

I sucked Kai's cock deeper into my mouth, loving the way it twitched at the swirl of my tongue and how his breath hitched at the same time. He was so rarely anything but self-controlled, it felt like some kind of magic to unravel him like this.

As Kai massaged my scalp with encouraging fingers, Ruin slipped beneath me and closed his lips around one of my nipples. He suckled me alongside the pulsing of Nox's hand against my sex until I was moaning my pleasure over Kai.

"I think you're ready for more," Nox said, slipping a finger and then two right inside me. "You can take all of us so good, can't you? Someday we'll fill you to the brim. For now…"

There was a crinkle of foil, and then his cock pressed against my slit. As he pushed into me, filling me with an ecstatic burn, I closed my mouth around Kai's shaft so tightly my teeth grazed the silky skin. Kai's hips jerked up, a curse tumbling from his lips that was all lustful abandon.

Ruin dipped his head lower, nibbling across my belly until he reached the mound of my sex. Without any apparent concern about Nox's cock thrusting in and out of me just a fraction of an inch away, he lapped his tongue across my clit.

A cry I couldn't contain burst out of me. I clamped my mouth around Kai again, but I was lost, swept away on the flood of pleasure coursing through me.

Nox filled me again and again with a slight swivel of his hips that sent me even higher, and Ruin sucked on my clit, and Kai nicked my scalp with his fingernails—and I was coming, breaking apart and melding together and then melting all over again with the heat surging through my nerves.

I sucked hard on Kai's cock, and he erupted into my mouth with a salty gush I didn't mind at all. I swallowed it down through my gasps.

"You milk both of us so sweet," Nox muttered, and then his hips jerked as he groaned. My sex clenched around his final thrusts, which sent me soaring all over again.

Limp with satisfaction, I sagged against the front of Kai's chair, looping one hand around his leg. Ruin nuzzled my temple with a pleased murmur that showed he didn't mind at all that he hadn't gotten any release from this encounter. Nox hunkered down next to me and tucked me onto his lap, letting me keep my hand on Kai's leg.

"Our woman," he said proudly. "No one's but ours. The rest of the world better watch the fuck out."

Chapter Ten

Lily

A COOL FALL breeze teased through my hair as I peered at the tall brick apartment buildings around us. "Why are we starting here?"

When Kai had come hustling out of the bedroom this morning with his latest brilliant brainstorm on his lips, suggesting that maybe I could use my new blood magic to track down Marisol as well, I hadn't wanted to waste any time. Which meant he hadn't had much chance to explain all the particulars before he'd headed off to work. He'd called Nox a couple of times as he'd thought the idea through, and we'd set off shortly afterward.

Now, Nox chuckled. "Mr. Know-It-All had some complex explanation for why he thought this was the best spot. Something about it being halfway between the Thrivewell building and your apartment where your sister went running from, and typical kidnapping patterns and a bunch of other stuff. I bet if you text him, he'll lay it out in full detail."

Jett let out a disgruntled groan from where he was sitting astride his motorcycle. "Can we skip that part?"

When I glanced over at the artist, a wobbly twinge ran through my gut. He looked like his usual gruffly taciturn self, but I couldn't tell whether he was just a normal level of grouchy or "I'm peeved because I saw you making out with my buddies last night" grouchy. And if it was the latter, I wasn't sure what I could do to make it better.

"I think we'd better skip it," I said quickly. "Kai's at work; I don't want to distract him."

At least while he was at the Thrivewell building, he'd been able to confirm that the Gauntts had arrived on schedule and therefore were nowhere near my sister. Unless they had her stashed away in one of their offices, which seemed unlikely.

Ruin bobbed eagerly on his feet. "It doesn't matter where we start. Now your blood can lead us right to her! And then we'll show those assholes what's what."

I looked down at my arms, picturing the blood pulsing through my arteries and veins. "We don't know for sure that it'll work yet. It was just a theory."

"When Kai comes up with a theory, it's practically fact," Nox said. "Come on, let's give it a shot. You've got your inspiration?"

"Yeah." I pulled a T-shirt I'd taken from Marisol's suitcase out of my purse. When I held it to my face, a faint whiff of the sugary perfume she'd started wearing sometime in her teens filled my nose.

I closed my eyes and pictured her the last time I'd hugged her. The feel of her fragile body in my embrace. The joy that had shone in her face when I'd escorted her into the apartment. The awe that'd threaded through her voice when she'd taken in her room, visions of how she'd decorate it sparking in her eyes.

I thought of other things too: the farting unicorns and ditzy dragons she'd used to draw, the goofy games we used to play down by the marsh, picking bits of grass and reeds out of her hair afterward. And the last time I'd seen her, happily chowing down on pancakes and then hurling accusations at me.

All of those pieces formed my experience of my sister. I had to soak myself in the impressions of her like they were a salt bath, until all the essence of her I could collect had permeated my pores. Maybe it'd do my complexion some good too.

With each image, the hum of power inside me rose, wrapping

around a pang of loss and worry. What had happened to her after she'd run from the apartment? How was she now? Had the Gauntts hurt her —more than they already had when she was younger? Was she even still alive?

That last question heightened the hum into an outright roar. I focused on the energy resonating through my body and my sense of my little sister flowing alongside it, all tangled together by the pounding of my pulse.

Find her, I thought, not totally sure who I was aiming the command at. *Find the girl whose blood matches mine better than anyone else in the world. Feel all the little pieces of DNA that fit with hers racing through my veins and reach out until you touch their echo.*

It might have been a good theory, but Kai hadn't been totally sure how it would work in a concrete sense. He'd told me to try whatever occurred to me to get in touch with my awareness of my sister, to stir up the commonalities in my blood that I might be able to sense in hers as well using my weird watery powers. I'd never tried to find anyone or anything with my magic before. It wasn't like we needed a search party to locate the lake.

"Is it working?" Ruin asked in a hopeful hush.

I didn't open my eyes, but I could tell from the soft smack of sound that Nox had swatted him. "Let her concentrate."

I didn't have any sense of direction yet. I shifted my weight on my feet, groping for other ways I could shape the power inside me to my intention. I had to hone it to the qualities I shared with Marisol, the common elements that filled our blood… How the hell did I do that? I was a mailroom clerk, not a geneticist.

On an impulse, I started to move, my sneakers rasping against the sidewalk. I kept my eyes shut, but I trusted that the guys wouldn't let me walk into traffic. I swayed and spun and swept my arms through the air, mimicking the wild dances we'd played out as kids as I pictured them behind my eyelids.

I probably looked like some kind of manic mime to anyone passing by, but they could shove their judgments where the sun didn't shine. I just wanted to find my sister.

The rhythm of my strange dance brought the other melodies

flowing through me into tight focus. The rumble of passing cars and the hiss of the breeze over a nearby awning blended into it. A tingle filled my throat with the urge to put words to it, but an ache closed around the sensation an instant later.

No singing. Not while she was gone. I couldn't bring myself to do it.

I threw myself faster into the dance instead. The wind whirled around me. A quiver ran through the hum inside me—and latched on to my heart with a hint of a tug.

"That way," I murmured. With a leap of my pulse, I swiveled in the direction the tug seemed to be drawing me and pointed.

Nox didn't wait for further instructions. He plucked me off the ground and plopped me on the back of his motorcycle, hopping on in front of me. As he started the engine, I wrapped one hand around his chest and kept the other tracing memories in the air. With the thrum of the motor vibrating through the bike's frame, the tug inside me pulled harder.

Nox took off, not too fast, following my gesture. I kept my eyes closed, but I heard the other two guys set off alongside us. Marisol danced on inside my mind, and I set her movements to the tempo of my heartbeat.

So much of the same blood coursed through her body as it did mine. I needed to reach out to it. Needed to let it draw me to her. Please.

The tug yanked at me again. "There!" I said, jabbing my finger into the air again. I didn't dare look to see where we were going for fear I'd break the spell I'd conjured inside me.

Nox veered left, and my body swayed with his. The other bikes careened after us. The wind whipped over me, nipping at my clothes, but I didn't care. Joy was expanding inside me.

I was doing it. I was following the familial thread between me and my sister like it was a fishing line and I was reeling myself in to her.

The tug shifted. I switched arms, trailing the other through the air. Someone must have made a rude gesture in response, because Nox shouted out, "I bet your mom likes that!" My lips twitched with an unbidden smile.

The pull inside me was getting stronger, my pulse seeming to thump louder through my chest and skull with every passing second. We had to be getting closer. Where had the Gauntts hidden her away? What had they told her?

It didn't matter. I had to get her away from them, and then we could sort out the rest. As long as she was in their clutches, nothing else mattered.

A faint whine formed inside my ears, like the drone of a mosquito. I restrained myself from swatting at the non-existent insect and focused as well as I could on the image of my sister in my head. I poked my finger one way and another, tipping here and there with the swerve of the bike.

And then the tug started to fade. It dwindled in my grasp as if it were a candle on the verge of guttering. I clutched at it as well as I could with my mental faculties, but it kept waning, slipping through my fingers.

"Faster!" I called to Nox over the warble of the wind. "I think they're moving her. Maybe they noticed that we're getting close."

"Which way?" he shouted back to me, gunning the engine.

I felt for that place inside me that'd steered me right before, but I'd lost my sense of direction. The tug was so faint now it was only the vague impression that she was somewhere in the vicinity, not too close.

Alive. She was definitely alive. For a few minutes there, I'd almost tasted the rhythm of her own pulse thumping alongside mine.

"I don't know," I had to admit. "She's moving away too quickly."

Nox tore through the streets, chasing what amounted to a phantom. Although I guessed that was appropriate for a guy who'd been a ghost until about a month ago. My pulse raced on, and Marisol bobbed and dipped in her childhood prancing in my mind's eye, but I got nothing more than a chalky flavor seeping through my mouth.

Finally I shook my head against Nox's back. He eased the bike to a halt. I opened my eyes and found myself staring up at the garish window display for Kids Paradise Toy Superstore. The bug-eyed dolls and neon plushies staring out at us felt like an insult to our quest. What kind of kid actually wanted those nightmares in their house?

Better those than one of the Gauntts, I had to admit.

"What happened?" Ruin asked, hurrying over from his own bike.

I let him help me off of Nox's motorcycle and rubbed my forehead. The beat of my pulse had sharpened into a headache.

"I'm not sure," I said. "I thought I felt her—I thought we were going toward her. But then it all kind of washed away, like she was getting so far I couldn't reach her anymore. But maybe I imagined all of it. Stranger things have happened." The three guys standing around me were ample proof of that fact.

"The Gauntts could have eyes all over the city," Jett pointed out. "They don't want you finding her."

"They don't know about her secret powers yet," Ruin said.

"They don't," I agreed. "But they'd still be able to see if we're closing in on them one way or another." I leaned into him, exhaustion rolling over me that was even more difficult to fight off than the throbbing behind my temples.

Ruin pressed a gentle kiss to the back of my head. "Then we try again when they *can't* see us," he said.

Jett snorted at the simplistic-sounding suggestion, but as it sank into my weary brain, I had to say it made a certain kind of sense. If we went about our search in a stealthier way instead of charging around the city in broad daylight, we'd have a better chance of getting close enough to get to Marisol before the Gauntts' minions caught on.

I wrapped one hand around Ruin's arm and the other around Nox's. "Okay. Next time we'll try at night. And if any of the Gauntts are with her then… I have plenty of ways of dealing with them."

Nox smirked. "Now that's what I like to hear, Minnow. We're coming up behind them, and soon they'll have no idea what hit them."

Chapter Eleven

Jett

I SCRATCHED the pencil across the sketch pad propped on my lap, wincing at the hissing sound the tip made on the paper and the spidery lines left in its wake. I vastly preferred working my medium into my canvas directly with my fingers, but of course that didn't allow for the finer details I sometimes felt the need to accentuate.

I glanced up from the armchair toward the sofa, where Lily had curled up with a book, her legs tucked next to her on the cushions. Theoretically, she was unwinding from the stresses of the day by doing some reading. But while I wasn't as observant as our know-it-all Kai, even I couldn't help noticing she was only turning a page about once every five minutes. A couple of times she'd actually flipped backward, like she was reading in reverse.

I wasn't much of a book fanatic either, but that didn't seem to bode well.

She'd wanted to go out looking for her sister again tonight, but her earlier attempt at wrangling her blood had left her too wiped out. We'd gone outside, deciding to start from the apartment where she'd last seen her sister this time, but she hadn't been able to summon any of the connection she'd felt before. After a few tries, whirling and swaying on the sidewalk in increasingly frantic imitations of what she'd said were the childhood dances they played in, she'd crumpled like a marionette with its strings cut.

Thankfully, Nox had caught her before she'd smacked into anything. Then he'd ordered her to rest until tomorrow and carried her upstairs to the apartment before she could get out more than a few words in argument.

I didn't let myself look closely at the twinge that came into my chest at remembering her nestled in his arms. I had a whole lot of other twinges running through me every time I looked at her anyway. Some of them were acceptable.

We'd found new ways she could use her powers, new strategies for sticking it to the Gauntts, but how much more was this fight going to take out of her before we reached the end?

Were we even going to reach the end, or were we going to drag her down in our own war instead of raising her up the way we'd intended when we first barged back into town?

I didn't have the answers to either of those questions, so I drained the last of my cola, letting the sugar rush wash a little of my apprehension away, and added a few more lines to the page. When I'd captured the curve of her chin and the bend of her knee, I set the pencil aside and reached for my ink pad. It offered up enough colors to satisfy me without much mess, so it worked best for smaller portraits like this.

I could have used my supernatural powers on the paper and brought out colors that way, but somehow that seemed like cheating. Anyway, I shouldn't exhaust my own voodoo energies on something I could do just as well, if not better, through my regular methods.

As I finished adding the smudge of blue to her hair and started filling out her shirt, Lily shifted on the couch and lifted her arms over her head in a stretch. My gaze immediately shot to her, taking in the way her body filled out her shirt with its soft curves. Soft curves I could still remember pressing up against my chest.

Heat flooded me, condensing in my groin. In an instant, I was half-mast. My jaw clenched against the sensation, but my dick didn't really care how annoyed I was with it.

Drawing her had been a bad idea. At least right now when my control was still so frayed from that early-morning interlude. I *had* to be able to work with her image again sometime. What was the point in having a muse if I couldn't commit her own form to canvas?

Standing up abruptly, I closed the sketchpad and dropped it next to the inks on the side table I'd claimed as mine. Then I stalked into the bedroom that technically belonged to all four of us Skullbreakers.

Going in there might have been a bad idea. The Murphy bed where I'd lain next to Lily last week was raised, and we'd brought in a dresser and a chair and a stack of motorcycle parts Nox planned on beefing up his ride with, so it didn't look much like the room had that night. But the hazy glow of streetlamp light filtering past the window, which we still didn't have a curtain for, brought back the memories twice as clearly.

I turned away from the window and focused on the mural I'd been creating on the far wall—the only wall that didn't have any furniture against it at the moment. It contained the door to the closet, but I'd been incorporating that into my vague sense of the design. The paints I'd been using swerved and flowed across the surface in something that might have been a flash flood or a hurricane, blues and purples and oranges twining and colliding. But here and there, little pockets of calm had emerged. I was still figuring out what each would contain.

As I took the image in, a tingle of inspiration gripped me. I grabbed one of the little cans of paint off the top of the dresser, popped the lid, and dipped two fingers in.

With the stroke of my hand, the red flared like a beam of ruddy light out of the whorl I'd focused on. It was brighter than the reds I usually preferred, but that seemed to fit here. Maybe I'd add a little of my blood to the mix to shade it, if that felt right once I'd captured the shape tugging at my mind completely.

I'd finished streaking tendrils and dappling some of the surrounding area with faint dabs of the same red and was just wiping my fingers off on a rag when Lily slipped into the room.

She paused just inside the doorway when she saw me, a smile

lighting her face as she took in my work. Suddenly, I couldn't smell the tang of the paint anymore, only her sweetly aquatic scent. Every inch of my skin thrummed with awareness of how close she was standing, just a couple of feet away—and how much certain parts of me wanted to close that distance.

The other guys went to her so easily. But that was exactly why I shouldn't. I wasn't just one more jerk in the crowd.

And if I let myself get lost in Lily that way, I wasn't sure how much else I'd let slip from my grasp. What mistakes I might make. Being *that* close to her, absorbing her with my hands and mouth as well as my eyes, had brought out emotions far too close to the ones that'd overwhelmed me at the worst possible time before, only even more intense.

The draw I felt toward her was dangerous—for everyone around me more than for myself. I wasn't going to be selfish this time.

So I unfocused my eyes slightly, doing my best to transform the woman before me into a more abstract smattering of shapes like I viewed everyone outside my inner circle. I couldn't quite reduce her to mere blobs of color, but I let my vision of her melt and slide until I pictured her more like a Dali, warped features running amuck. There was nothing particularly appealing about that.

If my dick still twitched a little, I was just going to pretend it hadn't.

"Hey," Lily said, biting her lip, which I was currently imagining about half a foot to the right of her nose. "This is looking really amazing."

I jerked my gaze back to the mural. Next to her, even with the Dali treatment I'd given her, the sprawling landscape of paint looked flat and lifeless. But she saw something in it. I could tell from her tone that she wasn't just bullshitting the way most people did when they talked about art, complimenting the things they thought they should like and making awkward commentary on the rest.

"It isn't done," I felt the need to say. I wasn't sure how long it would take before I felt it'd gotten there. Maybe it never would. There were few pieces I'd actually felt fully satisfied with in my life… Possibly not any since I'd met Lily.

Not because she dragged me down. Oh, no, not at all. She'd given me a higher standard to aspire to, and every part of me ached with the desire to meet it. That was what a good muse brought you—ambition and vision.

I just had to prove myself worthy of those gifts.

"Well, hopefully we'll be here long enough for you to get it to a place where you're happy with it." Lily tilted her head to the side as her gaze traveled across the expanse of color. "I think it's spectacular already, so it's going to be absolutely breathtaking when you're finished with it."

"I'm glad you think so," I said gruffly, not having any words more adequate than those to express my appreciation.

Lily hesitated, ducking her head briefly. Then she said, "Can I talk to you a little? There's something I figure you'll understand better than the other guys, but if I'm interrupting you…"

Her uncertainty wrenched at me. That she thought she had to ask permission just to have a conversation with me—like I might shove her aside for daring to do more than praise my artwork—

But then, I *had* shoved her aside already. Well, really, I'd been shoving myself away from her, but it'd have amounted to the same thing from her perspective, wouldn't it?

"Of course," I said quickly, forcing myself to turn toward her and hold her gaze again, even though that was more difficult when I was imagining one of her eyes sliding down her cheek and the other up into her forehead. "What's up?"

"I just…" She leaned back against the side of the dresser, her lips twisting into a frown. "I don't know how you feel about your art, but I'm guessing it's at least kind of similar to how I feel about singing. Like there's something inside you that's just there, wanting to get out. Like you have things to say that just talking couldn't manage. If that makes any sense."

I couldn't stop warmth from blooming in my chest at how well she'd described the impulses that'd guided me since I was a kid. "It makes total sense. That's exactly what it's like."

"Okay. Then I don't sound crazy. At least in that one specific way." She let out a rough giggle and combed one hand through her hair, making the blue-dyed streaks tumble against her shoulder like a trickling tropical waterfall. Suddenly I was picturing pushing up against her under a waterfall like that, pinning her to a slick rock and kissing her with salt lacing our lips—

My dick started to rise again, and I jerked my mind back to the present. Giving myself a mental smack, I amped the Dali-ness up to 100. Now one of her eyes was stacked on top of the other, and her chin was halfway across the room.

She was still fucking gorgeous, damn it.

"I still have that feeling inside me," she was saying. "And I hear rhythms and melodies around me that I want to add a song to. But if I try to, the words just catch in my throat. I couldn't sing for ages after I got shipped off to the psych hospital, but it started to come back after you guys found me… Then I lost Marisol again, and it's like it's all locked up inside me. I can't find a way to let it out. I'm not sure… I'm not sure I even deserve to."

Her voice dropped to a whisper with those last words. My throat constricted. In spite of my intentions, I stepped toward her, letting myself touch her shoulder with a squeeze that was as gentle and reassuring as I could manage. "You deserve everything," I told her.

Lily gave me a smile I could tell was sad even though I'd distorted her face into a jumble in my head. "But if it's something I'm really meant to do, if singing *is* art for me and not just a silly thing I do, shouldn't it always come? You've never stopped making art. You were *dead* for two decades, and you started up as soon as you got back." She rubbed her temple. "That's not the point, though. Obviously you can't tell me what I'm meant to be doing. Mostly I'm just babbling. I thought you might have some idea how maybe I could let it out again, or you'd say I shouldn't even try, or—I don't know."

I was sharply aware of the heat of her body seeping into my palm through her shirt, but I didn't move my hand. I couldn't, not when she was making this appeal to me. To *me*, not Nox the boss or Ruin the comforter or Kai the genius.

And it could be that she'd been right to. There were things I could tell her, even if I wasn't sure how much they'd help.

I opened my mouth, and the words stuck in my own throat. I

didn't talk about this stuff. Some of it I didn't even like admitting to myself. But if Lily was my muse, I should be open with her. I should be able to tell her anything, at least when it came to that side of myself.

"I'm always making art," I said, "but that doesn't mean it always feels like I'm really getting what's inside me out onto the canvas—or wall or whatever. What you're talking about, I kind of feel that way all the time, no matter how much I smear paint around on paper."

Lily's brow knit. "What do you mean? You make fantastic stuff." She motioned to the wall.

"But it's not quite—" I paused, sorting through my thoughts to find the best way of explaining it.

"My parents were shit," I started again. "Like, I'm not even shocked by the crap we're finding out about the Gauntts and the kids they messed with, because as far as I'm concerned that's just what people are like. There wasn't a day when they didn't hurl insults at me and find some excuse to slap me across the head or kick the legs out from under me. That was life in our house. You never knew when the next blow would come. It didn't even need to have a reason."

I looked down at my other hand and curled my fingers into a fist. When I was big enough, I'd started giving them the same treatment in return. And not just them. There was a lot more in me than just art that sometimes screamed to be let out.

Lily reached up to set her hand over mine on her shoulder. "I'm so sorry, Jett."

I shrugged. "It's over now. I hadn't seen them in years even before I died. It's part of who I am. But that part..." I swallowed and met her eyes again. "I can let the art out, yeah. But it hardly ever feels totally right. Sometimes I think I'm just too messed up, too many broken pieces in there, for it to ever come together the way it should. I know where I want to get to, but I can't quite reach it, and maybe that's how it'll always be."

Unfairly, I expected her to murmur soothing words that I wouldn't believe about how that couldn't possibly be true. Instead, she pulled me into an unexpected hug. Suddenly her body was pressed against mine, her arms wrapped around me, and I could barely think at all.

"If there are parts of you that are messed up, then that's who you are too," she said. "And that's fine. Art can be messed up, right? It's not supposed to be neat and tidy. And whatever you make, it's still *yours*. Even if it isn't exactly perfect, I think that's still way better than someone who makes some painting that's practically a photocopy and gets every detail right, but their soul isn't in it at all."

I let my arms ease around her, my eyes sliding shut just for a moment. I didn't know if what she was saying was right, but I could tell her this much. "Maybe. But my point is that you don't think I'm not an artist just because I know I'm not doing everything I'd want to. So having trouble singing the way *you* want to doesn't mean you aren't one either. If there's something in you that's broken, we'll fix it as well as we can. We'll get your sister back. And if you need more than that, we'll figure it out too."

I heard the bob of her throat, drank in her scent, and then she was easing back from me—carefully, respectfully, like she didn't want to cross my boundaries. She had no idea that right now my body was clamoring to do nothing less than toss her up on top of that dresser and bury my face between her thighs until she was moaning my name.

"Thank you," she said. "I don't know how that's all going to work… but everything is definitely easier now that I'm not alone. We just need to make sure that Marisol isn't alone either."

"We'll find her," I said firmly. And if we couldn't, if the Gauntts had somehow torn her too far away from Lily for us to ever recover her, then those pricks would find themselves shredded like fucking coleslaw.

Lily gave me one last smile, a little brighter than before, and I couldn't look away as she drifted back out into the living room. Not until I noticed Nox standing by the windows, watching us.

His gaze caught mine, and his mouth curved into one of its knowing smirks, like he knew exactly what I'd been imagining. Like it mattered.

I scowled at him and shut the door.

Chapter Twelve

Lily

IT LOOKED like the guys had put enough of the fear of God—or at least the fear of the Skullbreakers—into the first Skeleton Corps group they'd tackled, because none of them had tattled on us. The man we were expecting showed up behind the convenience store promptly on schedule.

Too bad for him, the squad he was supposed to give orders to wasn't waiting for him, and the Skullbreakers were.

"Who the hell—" he snapped out as the four guys burst from the shadows, and that was all he managed to say before Kai had clocked him across the head with an order to "Shut up and stay where you are."

The man went rigid as a telephone pole. He appeared to be a bit older than the bunch we'd tackled before, no gray in his hair or anything like that, but his features were hardened beyond any hint of boyishness. I figured he was around thirty. That seemed to bode well for him having a little more authority than the others.

"What now?" Jett asked, stalking around the guy. "I'm guessing he's not going to cough up who *he* works under just like that."

The Corps guy just glared at him, looking like he was trying to spew all the threats he'd have liked to be making out of his eyes instead of his mouth.

Nox glanced the guy up and down and said with typical confidence, "I don't think beating him into submission will work any better than it did on the others. Ruin, how about an attitude adjustment?"

Ruin grinned and stepped forward with his fists raised. He paused for a moment as if deciding exactly what kind of attitude he'd like to convey and then pummeled our captive in the shoulder.

Apparently one burst of supernatural energy overrode the previous. The man stumbled to the side and moved to catch his balance, the motionless spell Kai had put him under broken. Then his eyes flashed. Before I could worry that Ruin had miscalculated and made the guy even more pissed off at us, he spun and started barreling out of the alley.

Nox charged after him. "Where the fuck are you going?"

"To teach those pricks who've been bossing me around a lesson," the guy snapped, and I understood. Ruin had made him furious—with his own colleagues. Furious enough to want to go confront them right now. And unlike the last guys, he seemed to know where they were.

Nox waved for us to follow, and we all hustled over to the motorcycles they'd parked nearby. The guy dove into his car like he was rushing off to carry out life-saving surgery instead of to yell at his fellow gangsters.

He zoomed off down the street, and we took off after him, following close behind. There was no need to keep a low profile when he didn't care about anything at the moment other than letting loose a few rants.

The guy didn't drive far, only to a pawn shop with a closed sign on the door. Driven by Ruin's inflicted fury, he ignored the sign, yanking at the knob so hard he managed to bust the lock.

"What the hell, man?" a voice hollered from inside.

The man burst into the shop. In the few seconds it took us to hurry in after him, he managed to shatter an entire tea set by hurling it at the guy who'd been cashing out behind the counter, slamming the pot into his head just as we got inside. It didn't look like the set had been anything all that nice anyway, so maybe that was the most appropriate use for it.

The guy he was attacking had cringed backward with his hands raised. "What the fuck's gotten into you, you lunatic?" he demanded.

"We have," Nox announced, and gestured to his men. Kai punched the first guy with the order to "Sit down and shut up," and Ruin smacked the guy behind the counter.

The new guy's expression flickered from angry bewilderment to worshipful awe. He bowed his head until his forehead touched the counter. "Oh, wow. It's an honor to be in your presence. I'm not worthy of witnessing your grand acts of vengeance."

Jett shot Ruin a baleful look. "Did you infect him with a Victorian sensibility along with the admiration?"

Ruin splayed his arms, laughing. "I don't know how it works."

"The important part works like this," Nox said, planting his hands on the other side of the counter. "You're going to prove how worthy you are by telling us everything you know about the people who run the Skeleton Corps."

The guy peeked up at him as well as he could while only raising his head an inch from the counter, still in full deference mode. "I'm so sorry. I have no idea who's at the top. I'm not worthy of *them* either. Not that they hold a candle to your greatness."

Nox puffed up his massive frame a little. I didn't think he minded the effusive compliments, overly formal or not. "Fine. Then tell us about the highest people you *do* know about. Who gives you your marching orders?"

The guy's mouth twisted. "I don't know her name, but I know the place she usually operates out of. I can bring you to her if that would satisfy your request."

"Sure, sure." Nox waved at him to get moving.

"It's like a fucking scavenger hunt," Kai muttered. "Collect all the pieces, and maybe we'll get a prize at the end."

"*Someone's* got to know what the hell is going on in this city," Nox said.

Presumably someone did, but it wasn't the woman the new guy led us to. She pulled a gun on us the second we sauntered into the back room of her laundromat. Thankfully, our guy was so concerned for the well-being of his honored brainwashers that he leapt between her and us, which gave Kai the opening to wallop her into dropping the gun and kicking it away. Then he sent the guy off to take a nap on top of the dryers while Ruin socked some terror into the woman.

She started trembling from head to foot so hard I thought she might jitter right into the wall. "Please don't hurt me," she mumbled. "Whatever you want—just leave me alone."

Nox folded his arms across his chest and spoke with a tone like he'd restrained a sigh. "We want to know who's in charge of the Skeleton Corps and where we can find them."

Although she didn't know either, she hastily babbled something about a construction site where some guys who might be able to tell us were working. "And off we go again!" Kai said in a singsong voice as we headed out to the bikes.

By the time we reached the construction site, it was late enough that all the regular workers had gone home. And dark enough that I couldn't make out much more than the vague shape of some steel girders and a very large, black pit. As far as I could tell, they were constructing either an immense swimming pool or a gateway to hell.

The lights were on in the small office trailer in the corner of the lot. We all tramped over there across the uneven dirt, picking up multiple voices carrying from inside. Jett, who couldn't do much to defend the group with his artistic talents, pulled the gun out of the back of his jeans and held it ready. I glanced around for anything liquid I could make use of. I didn't feel quite ready to start flinging people's blood around yet.

But it seemed the Skeleton Corps members weren't as distracted as they appeared. Before we'd quite made it to the trailer, the door flew open, and three men charged out at us, already firing their own guns.

Nox roared and swung his hand through the air, and as far as I could tell he used his ghostly energy to literally punch one of the bullets out of the way. Kai had ducked low at the first creak of the door's hinges, dodging another, and rammed into one of the men's legs, knocking him to the ground. "Shoot your colleagues where it'll hurt but not kill them," he ordered as they fell.

The guy gave it his best, well, shot, but his aim was shaky from the fall. His bullet went wide, and then Ruin collided with the third man, heedless of the bloody streak across his upper arm where the last of the initial shots had grazed him.

That guy immediately started whimpering and huddling in the dirt. The first guy swung around, pulling out yet another gun, but Jett fulfilled what Kai's dupe hadn't been able to and shot it right out of his hand, severing a few fingers in the process.

Nox hefted the one guy who wasn't under supernatural control up and hung him from the hook of a nearby crane truck. As the man dangled there, sputtering and cursing, a frog hopped up beside me and let out a curious croak.

"No swimming here yet," I told it. "But he sounds like he's practically speaking your language."

The second guy took aim again even though his services were no longer needed, so Kai gave him another wallop and ordered him to bring anything useful out of the office. Nox peered up at the guy he'd hooked.

"We don't really need all three, do we?" he said. "And this one's particularly annoying."

The memory of our other recent battle with a group of the Skeleton Corps guys came back to me with a prickling chill. "Wait. We should check them all for Gauntt marks."

"Right!" Ruin yanked up his victim's shirt sleeve, ignoring the dude's whimpers for mercy. "Nothing here," he announced.

Nox took a knife out of his pocket and simply sliced open the hooked guy's shirt from the collar to take a close look. He batted away the guy's flailing legs and frowned. "Damn it. This one's gotten the Gauntt treatment. I guess you'd better crack him open."

My heart sank as I stepped closer. The guy flailed harder, even though my version of cracking open was a heck of a lot less bloody than Nox's would have been.

"Let me guess," I said to the guy. "A long time ago when you were a kid, Nolan and maybe Marie Gauntt paid you a visit or two to talk about special school programs or some crap like that."

"What the fuck are you going on about, crazy bitch?" the guy sneered, like he wasn't essentially giant fish bait at this point.

Kai's man had just dumped a heap of papers on the ground outside the office. "Check him for a mark, and then get over here and shut this asshole up," Nox ordered Kai.

The office man didn't have a mark either, so Kai gave him another smack with the orders to climb up one of the girders as fast as he could go. He waited until the guy was so high he'd have trouble getting down without making like a lemming and going splat, and then swatted the jerk dangling in front of me. "Keep your mouth shut and stay still."

Nox lowered the hook so I could grasp the guy's shoulder. He stared at me, his eyes wild with panicked rage.

"I'm just helping you remember," I told him, a little tersely because, after all, he'd tried to shoot us. Then I focused my attention on the magic emanating from the mark.

This time I was surer of what I was doing. I called up the power inside me, which was already humming from the fight, and slammed it into the barrier that walled off the horrible moments from the man's past. Once, twice, three times, harder with each impact. With the last one, I gritted my teeth and let a flare of my frustration offer an extra burst of fuel.

The Gauntts' magic shattered. The man twitched, the fury fading from his eyes. It was replaced by a haunted expression.

Kai prodded him in the gut. "Stay still but talk."

"What the fuck did you do to me?" the guy demanded at once, wriggling on the hook. "I didn't—this can't be real—"

"I didn't do anything," I said. "*They* did it. The Gauntts. Tell us what they put you through, and we can make them pay."

He gulped air and shuddered. Kai's instructions must have forced him to say *something*, but it couldn't make him answer my question exactly. "No. Fuck no. I never wanted— I told them to go away— But they still— *No*. And then out there at the marsh—"

I perked up in an instant, my mind shooting to the marsh plants we'd found decorating the bedrooms in the Gauntts' home. "What about the marsh? Did the Gauntts take you out here?"

"I'm not telling you fucking anything," the guy snarled. "This is insane. I—"

Kai gave him one last smack. "Shut up and come with us. If you don't want to tell us, you can show us."

Chapter Thirteen

Lily

I COULDN'T SEE anything particularly special about the spot in the marsh that the Skeleton Corps guy had led us to last night. In the darkness, it'd had an unsettlingly creepy vibe, but all of the marsh did. It was hard for rattling reeds and groaning logs to give off a cheerful atmosphere even in full sunlight.

Which was how we were looking at them now, standing on the narrow spit where a sliver of solid ground jutted an extra twenty or so feet from the shore into the midst of the cattails, like a dock that'd sprouted out of the earth.

The rattling and the groaning blended with the softer whisper of the breeze and the gentle buzzing of nearby insect life into a song that rippled through me. My throat constricted, but I thought about what Jett had said the other night about making art around our brokenness. Maybe I couldn't be whole enough to bring music to life without being sure of Marisol's safety. That wasn't something wrong with my creative spirit. It just showed how important she was to me.

I wished I could give Jett as easy an answer to his own pain. The thought of what he'd been through with his parents—the strain that'd come into his voice when he'd admitted he wasn't sure he could ever create the art he wanted to—still brought an ache into my stomach when I remembered it.

He looked like his usual grimly obstinate self right now, no sign that he was fretting over those issues. I guessed he'd been living with them his whole life, so that made sense.

He slung his hands in his pockets and gazed along the length of the spit. "Where are we going to place these things? We really should have Kai along for this. He'll probably come and tell us we did it all wrong anyway."

Nox strode down the stretch of grassy earth, which was hardly wide enough for two people to stand next to each other—harder when one of those people was him with his increasingly brawny frame. "Kai's busy taking care of things on the *professional* end. Fucking suits." He paused, studying the tufts of reeds and the swaying cattails on either side of the spit. "The Skeleton Corps guy said the Gauntts took him out to the end here and dunked him in the water, right?"

I nodded, my gut clenching up even more at *that* memory. When we'd reached the spit with the guy in the middle of the night, a light smack from Ruin had broken his silence. He'd babbled about his trip to the marsh with the Gauntts while a squad of frogs had hopped over to join us, stopping around him in a semi-circle like they were enthralled by his performance.

Except it hadn't been just a performance. It'd obviously really happened. Nolan and Marie Gauntt had led him out here some twenty-five years ago when he'd been nine, made him strip, and soaked him in the marsh water until he'd been shaking so hard with the chills that he'd blacked out. Lord only knew what they'd done to him after that.

"None of the other people with marks we talked to mentioned coming out here," I said. "I wonder if that was some kind of special case."

But even as I said those words, I didn't really believe them. The Gauntts had brought pieces of the marsh into their home—slept next to them. Maybe they sometimes had the kids knocked out when they brought them here. Maybe not all of the kids qualified for whatever they'd been up to at the marsh. That guy had only remembered coming here once. And we'd only broken into a few other people's memories of their abuse.

Had Nolan dragged Marisol out here, years ago or recently?

The frogs that'd gathered around my feet today ribbeted but offered no insight. I frowned down at them. "It'd be really nice if you could figure out how to talk. I bet you've seen all kinds of things."

Ruin chuckled. "They probably don't pay attention to anything except the water and the flies they want to eat. Pretty nice life, being a frog." He loped over to join Nox by the end of the spit and swiveled to take in both sides of the marsh.

This spot was farther from the town than our previous haunt near my family's home, about two miles distant from where the guys' former bodies had been dumped. There was enough of a hill to the ground in between that I couldn't see the house from here.

"The marsh must be magic!" Ruin announced abruptly. "It kept us kind-of alive, and it gave Lily powers, and the Gauntts were doing something weird with it too."

"Lots of other people come out here," I said doubtfully. "I mean, not this exact spot." There wasn't even a proper road to this end of the marsh. We'd had to trek the last mile on foot. "But all around the lake. People go swimming out in the end by the marina or out of their boats. At least some of the tap water must be filtered from it. We don't *all* have special talents."

"It doesn't matter one way or another," Nox said. "We just want to catch the Gauntts if they come out here again and find out what the hell *they* use it for."

He pulled a small black device from his pocket and fixed it into the ground at the end of the spit so it pointed toward the foot. After folding several reeds over to disguise it without blocking the sensor area, he walked back to the foot of the spit and set up another device pointing across it, giving it the same treatment.

"Will the signal reach all the way to us even when we're in Mayfield?" I asked. Before he'd left for work, Kai had chatted up some techie contacts he'd made and procured these motion sensors for us.

But they didn't do us much good if we didn't know they were sensing motion.

Nox nodded. "As long as the batteries hold out—and they're supposed to be good for at least a week before we have to change them. There's some kind of a router or something they connect to that'll bounce the signal to us. I don't know. Kai talked about it like it made sense to him, but it's hard to tell with that guy. At least he thinks the woman who told *him* about it knew what she was talking about."

A couple of the frogs bounded past us, drawing my gaze. "And they won't be triggered by anything a lot smaller than a person?"

Nox's lips twitched. "I believe he asked about that factor specifically, considering your froggy fanbase."

I made a face at him, and he laughed, looping his arm around mine. "Good thing they're not your only fans, huh," he teased, leaning close enough that his breath tickled my ear.

A flush washed over me, and I swatted him. "They've been useful in their own ways."

Jett knelt down by the nearest motion detector and adjusted the angles of a few of the bent reeds. I couldn't tell whether he was simply enhancing their aesthetic appeal or improving on the camouflage.

I stepped close, and he pushed himself upright and away at the same moment, accidentally backing into me. I only stumbled for a second before he caught my arm. In that instant, we were so close that the flush I'd felt with Nox deepened into a flare of heat. When Jett was touching me, it was hard not to remember his hands on me that one early morning in bed, gripping my hair, squeezing my ass as he ground his groin against mine.

"Sorry," he muttered brusquely, and yanked himself away as if my heat had scalded him. I thought a visible shiver passed through his arm, and a lump rose in my throat.

I knew he wanted to protect me as much as the others did, but it was so hard to read where he stood other than that. Did I outright disgust some part of him? Maybe he thought it was obscene that I could want to get it on with all three of his friends and him too.

The other guys didn't seem to mind the sharing thing, but that didn't mean Jett had to agree.

I turned away and found Nox watching us with a pensive expression and a gleam flickering into his eyes. He jerked his chin toward the bikes. "Let's head out. Don't want there to be any chance of the Gauntts catching on that *we've* caught on to their special spot."

We tramped across the damp grass, the frogs following us in a hopping procession, until we reached the gravel-laced spot where the guys had parked their bikes. Nox studied his friends. "Ruin, why don't you go grab us some lunch? I'm craving the barbeque chicken from that place in Bedard."

"Perfect!" Ruin said, even though the trip would take him an hour out of his way. "They have the best spicy wings." He licked his lips, no doubt imagining sauce so hot it'd incinerate anyone else's tongue, and shot off on his bike.

Nox motioned to Jett next, unhooking the strap of the spare helmet from his handlebars and slinging it onto Jett's. "You take Lily. I have something quick to take care of that I don't want her along for."

"What?" Jett said, startled, but he didn't have time to argue about it. Nox swung his leg over his bike and was roaring off an instant later.

The artist glanced at me, swiping his hand across his mouth. "Well, I guess we'd better get going."

He climbed onto his motorcycle. I pulled on my helmet and positioned myself gingerly behind him. There wasn't much room on the seat for two, but the thought of pressing myself right against him like I would have with Nox, breasts to back and core to ass, made my nerves skitter. I didn't like the idea of Jett feeling awful the whole way back to the apartment.

"Get right on," he said gruffly, revving the engine. "I don't want you to fall off. That helmet won't do much for the rest of you."

At his insistence, I tucked myself a little closer, sliding my arms around his waist. Jett shifted on the seat as if to confirm I was secure and then took off down the potholed lane.

I kept my butt just a little farther back than I would have with Nox so there was a tiny gap between us in the most intimate region, but that meant I had to lean into Jett's back to keep my balance. I tipped my head to one side against the worn leather of his jacket and closed my eyes.

It was easier not to worry about anything when I was focusing on the fast yet steady thumping of his heart beneath my ear and the growl of the engine.

Through the smell of the leather, I could pick up whiffs that were distinctly Jett: a sharp note of paint, which he probably had a smudge of on him somewhere, and a hint of the cola he chugged so much of I wouldn't be surprised if it started coming out of his pores. The scent was so perfectly him that another pang shot through me, a mix of affection and regret.

He kept so much to himself that I wasn't sure I knew him anywhere near as well as I did the others, but I cared about him all the same. He'd been here for me, protected me when I needed it, talked me through my doubts even though talking didn't come naturally to him.

I wished I knew how to stop the uncomfortable vibe that developed between us so often.

It turned out that Nox had been thinking about that vibe too. We pulled up at the apartment next to his bike, which was already in the lot. It must have been a short errand—if he'd actually gone on one at all and not used that as an excuse to stick me with Jett. When we got upstairs, we found the Skullbreakers boss in the living room, anticipation radiating off him concretely enough that my skin quivered with it.

"All right," he said, all commanding authority. "Come with me."

He ushered us into the guys' bedroom. The Murphy bed was still lowered from the night before. A condom packet sat on the bedside table. Jett halted just over the threshold, stiffening a bit at the sight of it.

"What's going on?" he asked.

Nox set his hands on my shoulders from behind and then trailed them down to my waist, where he fingered the hem of my shirt. He gazed past me at Jett. "You want her. It's obvious to anyone who has freaking eyes. It's probably obvious to you too, so I don't know why you're insisting on holding yourself back."

A reddish tinge colored Jett's cheeks. "Just because I don't want to—"

"You fucking *do*," Nox interrupted, his tone getting firmer. "You practically fuck her with your eyes at least ten times a day. So I think it's about time you put yourself and her and all of us out of our misery and did the deed properly."

The heat that unfurled low in my belly wasn't entirely comfortable. "Nox," I started.

But Jett put to words my exact objection. "Are you seriously ordering me to have sex with Lily?"

"I'm ordering you to pull your head out of your ass and get out of your own way," Nox said. He grazed his fingertips over my waist beneath my shirt. "You want him too, don't you, Siren?"

My pulse stuttered. I wasn't going to lie. "I do," I said, a blush flaring in my cheeks. "But not if he isn't into it. I don't want Jett to force himself."

Nox snorted. "He's forcing himself *not* to touch you." He tugged at my shirt, and I raised my arms instinctively so he could peel it off. After dropping it on the floor, he brought his hands to my breasts, cupping them through my bra, and glanced at Jett again. "Tell me I'm wrong. Tell me it's not taking everything in you not to walk over here and worship our woman."

Jett's eyes blazed over my skin, and for a second I thought Nox was right. But he said in a taut voice, "Just because some part of me likes the idea doesn't mean it's a good one."

"What could possibly be wrong with it?" Nox demanded. "Give me one good reason why it's better for you to be driven to distraction by all the things you're not letting yourself have instead of just having them."

"She already has all of you," Jett shot back, more forcefully than he usually spoke. "Maybe I want something different with her. Does that bother *you* so much?"

Nox only raised his eyebrows. "Just because you get busy with her doesn't mean it'd be the same. Give us a little credit." He nuzzled the side of my face with a flick of his tongue along the back of my ear. His thumbs dipped inside my bra to roll my nipples, and the sparks of pleasure made me gasp even though I was trying to focus on Jett. "Is it the same with the three of us, Minnow? Do I fuck you like Ruin does? Or like Kai?"

The thought was so absurd I almost laughed. "No," I said. "You're all different. Very different." But still oh so good. Just remembering how they'd all worked me over together the other day in their various ways had me soaking my panties despite myself.

"That's right," Nox said in the same low tone he used when he called me "good girl." "You're not giving her something better by holding back, Jett. You're just denying her whatever it is that only you could give her. And denying yourself too."

Jett still just stood there, though he couldn't seem to tear his eyes away from Nox's hands on my chest. When he finally yanked his gaze back to my face and then to Nox, his voice came out ragged. "You don't know that."

"I do," Nox insisted. "That's why I call the shots. You don't feel right deciding to go for it? Fine. I'm taking that decision out of your hands. Fuck her in your own special Jett way. Make her scream until the people downstairs wonder why the hell they don't have it that good. You want it to be art? Make *her* art." Letting go of me, he grabbed a few of the paint cans off the dresser and set them on the bed.

Jett's gaze followed the movement, and his tongue darted out to wet his lips. A little of the tension in his expression faded, his eyes lighting up. A fresh quiver of heat raced through my veins.

Was that all there was to it? He needed to frame the act in the right way, to see it as more than just mindless hooking up? It would always have meant more than that to me, but maybe that hadn't been obvious.

He should know now that I was definitely a willing participant in Nox's suggestion. I reached behind me to unclasp my bra and let it fall to my feet. Then I shucked off shoes, pants, and panties, until I stood naked before the two of them. Ignoring the twinge of self-consciousness that tickled over my skin, I climbed onto the bed.

"It'd be an honor to be your canvas," I said softly.

Jett let out a low sound in his throat. He glanced at Nox as if he needed final confirmation that his boss really was not just approving this but urging him on. At Nox's motion, he moved to the edge of the bed. His gaze remained fixed on me now.

"Are you sure?" he said, the words coming out raw. "It'll probably be a mess."

I grinned wholeheartedly. "I've seen what you can do. Even if it is, it'll be a beautiful mess."

He eased over so he was sitting right next to me. His hand hovered over my shoulder, and for a second I thought he was going to kiss me. Then he grasped one of the paint cans instead. Once he'd opened it, he dipped his fingers inside. They came out dripping with a deep midnight blue.

Jett traced the first line along my jaw and down my throat. He flicked his thumb over my chin, and something in his eyes shifted. He tugged my face toward him and finally captured my mouth.

As our lips melded together, his fingers kept sweeping over my body, shadowing my collarbone and my sternum with blue, daring to dip under one breast. He broke from the kiss to grab another can, this one vibrant crimson, and streaked that over the curve of my shoulder and down my arm. Then he swiveled it around my breast, stopping just shy of the peak. A faint rasp had come into his breath as if he was having trouble keeping it stable.

My own breaths were quickening. I was dying to kiss him again, to lean into his touch, but I didn't want to take away the control he'd claimed over the situation, that had made this encounter feel right to him. So I kept my hands braced against the covers, even as I felt my arousal pooling between my legs.

Jett dabbed purple across my nipples, drawing a gasp from my throat at the contact. He paused, swirling the hue so it mingled with the red farther down, swiveling his thumb over the peaks again and again until they were harder than I'd ever thought was possible. A needy whimper tumbled from my lips.

Jett leaned in to kiss me again, a little harder and wilder this time. The fly of his jeans protruded with an unmistakable bulge. The urge to touch him swelled inside me sharper than before.

I let myself reach toward his shirt. "Can I—can I paint you too?"

Jett drew back and stared at me for a moment like it'd never occurred to him that I might ask that. He inhaled shakily, and his pupils dilated. "Yeah. Yes. Please."

I pulled off his shirt, doing my best not to let the sleeves get smeared with the paint on his multi-colored fingers. It was the first time I'd seen close up how much his spirit had filled out the once-scrawny body that used to belong to Vincent Barnes. He wasn't anywhere near as burly as Nox, but compact muscles lined his chest and abdomen. I swept my bare fingers over the taut ridges before remembering I was meant to be doing more than touching them.

I stretched my arm to find one of the pots of paint and caught some on my fingers. As I traced the blue lines down the front of Jett's chest, his breath hitched. For a minute, he didn't touch me other than resting his hands lightly on the sides of my waist, just watching me swirl and streak the colorful lines across his shoulders and neck, down to his abdomen, and back up to circle his nipples.

A faint groan reverberated through his chest. Then he was on me again, kissing me fiercely and trailing more paint across my torso.

He outlined my ribs with green and circled my belly button with purple. When he reached my hips, he dragged thick lines of red from my ass cheeks to the front of my thighs. I traced the same color across his cheeks and yanked him back in for another kiss.

I'd almost forgotten Nox was in the room. Possibly Jett had too. The Skullbreakers' leader cleared his throat softly where he was now leaning against the doorframe.

"Damn," he said. "That's fucking art all right." His hand splayed against the crotch of his jeans, where a bulge of his own was straining. "Do you mind if I fully enjoy the view, Jett?"

The implications of his question were clear, but there was so much respect in the fact that he'd asked permission at all after the orders he'd laid down earlier that I choked up a bit. The guys were devoted to me, but they had each others' backs just as much.

Jett didn't bother to drag his avid gaze away from me. "As long as Lil doesn't mind, it's fine by me. Art is meant to be appreciated."

The old nickname, soft with affection, made my heart swell with matching emotion. "I don't mind," I said, and pulled Jett back to me.

The whorls and lines that marked our bodies blurred together as we collided more eagerly. I tugged at Jett's jeans, and he peeled them off between increasingly urgent kisses. I caught the rasp of Nox's jeans unzipping and the rustling rhythm of him stroking himself as he watched, and that only made the fire of need inside me burn hotter.

Jett stroked swaths of blue down my thighs and buried his face between my legs. His tongue swiped over me like he was drawing me to life with that too, whirling over my clit and curling inside my opening, leaving me panting with the rush of bliss. My fingers dug into his hair, trailing streaks of red and blue amid the already unnaturally purple strands. As a moan slipped out of me, Nox echoed it with a groan from across the room.

Jett hummed against me almost desperately, having his way with my sex until I was trembling on the verge of release. Through the quivers of delight that shook my body, I managed to find my voice. "Please. Inside me."

Jett let out a groan of his own and surged up over me. He snatched the condom off the table and rolled it over himself in two seconds flat. But as he lowered his hips so his erection rubbed against my clit, he paused and peered down at us.

Paint was smeared over every inch of our chests in a jumble of colors that bled into each other. "It is a bit of a mess," I said, sliding my finger through the colors on his shoulder.

"Yeah." Jett caught my eyes. Some inner turmoil churned and then faded in his dark brown eyes. "But you were right. It's a beautiful mess. *My* beautiful mess."

I lifted my hand to his cheek. "*Ours*," I said.

A rough sound escaped him. He dove in to reclaim my lips as his shaft plunged inside me.

I gasped and moaned into Jett's mouth. He set a fast pace, bucking against me, and I was already so close from the magic his tongue had worked on me earlier. The slick slide of our paint-streaked bodies made our collision feel twice as intense.

I raised my legs on either side of his hips, urging him deeper. Jett groaned and plowed into me even faster than before. With each stroke, I careened higher and higher—until I burst like a firework, splintering into light and color at some distant peak that left me shaking and breathless.

My fingers dug into his back, and my thighs clamped around his hips. Jett dropped his head to nip the crook of my neck, heedless of the paint there. He dug his teeth in a little harder, and I came again, a fresh blaze of ecstasy right on the heels of the first. With a shudder and a hot wash of breath over my neck, Jett followed me.

He tumbled onto the covers next to me, keeping one arm around my waist. We gazed at each other, at the beautiful mess we'd made together, and a giggle bubbled out of me. Jett offered a rare smile.

"That was—" he started to say.

At the same moment, the door to the apartment crashed open.

Chapter Fourteen

Lily

Jett and I sprang off the bed as if we'd been zapped. Nox had already been tucking himself back inside his jeans. He whipped around as a horde of at least ten guys charged into the living room. They were all wearing ski masks printed to look like skeleton heads.

The intruders skidded to a halt at the sight of us, freezing up momentarily as they took in Jett and me in our naked, paint-drenched glory. It wasn't how I'd have wanted to make a first impression, but the shock our appearance provoked worked in our favor.

"What the *fuck*?" one of the intruders said, and in their momentary hesitation, Nox was already hurtling into the fray.

The leader of the Skullbreakers didn't have the same problem with only being able to target one or two people at a time like Kai's and Ruin's powers. The bursts of supernatural energy that flowed out from his body with each strike did their damage regardless of how many opponents he went on to pummel next.

He blasted through the onslaught with his fists, knees, and feet flying in one direction and another, even ramming his head toward a guy a few feet away who promptly crashed into the wall as if he'd been hit by a battering ram. The crackling sound of each strike electrified the air.

The Skeleton Corps men—because who else would be in that skeletal get-up?—careened this way and that, bruises and bloody noses appearing as if out of thin air. But there were too many of them for Nox to totally subdue more than a few of them. As more figures barged into the living room, the attackers swarmed in around him, only a couple of them knocked to the floor in a daze.

Jett leapt for his gun, which was lost somewhere in the tangle of his discarded jeans. Too panicked at the sight of all those skeleton faces converging on Nox to care that I was butt naked, I dashed into the room and reached the frantic hum reverberating through me toward the nearest sources of liquid.

Water gushed from the kitchen faucet and whipped through the doorway to smack this guy and that in the face. I couldn't hit them hard enough to knock them out, but from the grunts and pawing at their eyes, I'd hurt them, maybe even messed up their vision. I sent another flood gushing over the wooden floors, making them slip and stumble on the suddenly wet surface. It splashed against my legs, licking off streaks of paint to unfurl through the currents.

Jett charged out beside me, still just as naked but ferally terrifying with his purple hair spiking every which way, his eyes blazing with anger, and his body mottled with vibrant streaks and swirls that now passed for war paint. I sure as hell wouldn't have wanted to face off with him, no matter how well-clothed I was. He pointed his gun and picked off three of the attackers in quick succession, aiming at those closest to him and farthest from Nox.

Unfortunately, several of the attackers still managed to crash into the Skullbreakers' boss. As they tackled him to the floor, he lashed out with all his limbs, catching one in the gut, another in the jaw. They reeled backward, but those he hadn't managed to strike whipped out knives and guns of their own.

"You've got some explaining to do," one of them snarled, which gave me at least a little hope that they weren't looking to kill Nox *immediately*, although they definitely didn't appear to have any qualms about doing plenty of damage in the meantime. I'd prefer he kept all his body parts attached to said body.

With a yank of my powers, I managed to fling a few cans of pop across the room from the kitchen counter. They smacked into the skulls of a few of the guys hard enough for the thin metal to burst, showering them with sticky soda as well.

Jett got off a few more shots, but he had to be careful not to hit his friend. One bullet lodged in a guy's shoulder, another in one's ass. Then three of them threw themselves at Jett, smashing the pistol from his hand and tackling him to the ground too.

Right at that moment, Ruin walked in through the open door, laden with enough takeout to feed an army. Unfortunately, he hadn't brought an army with him.

"What's all the racket?" he asked cheerfully as he crossed the threshold. "Did you start a party without—"

To give him credit, he didn't stop to gape at the chaos he found himself staring at. He dropped the bags and launched himself right into the fray in mid-sentence.

For a minute, it seemed like Ruin's arrival might turn the tide in our favor. He walloped one guy and then another, tossing one off Nox and toppling one who was about to shoot Jett in the forehead. His emotional impact bounced through the crowd, the skeleton-masked opponents flying into sudden rages at their colleagues and then faltering when he'd punched too many other jerkwads. The chaos in the room took on an air of confusion.

Nox managed to heave himself back to his feet. Jett slapped his hand into one of his opponent's faces and proved that he could alter shape as well as color. The guy's nose bulged beneath his mask, so big it obscured his vision. Jett snickered and socked him in it hard enough to send a spurt of blood from the nostrils.

One of the Skeleton Corps dickheads must have decided I'd make a good hostage by virtue of being female—and maybe being naked had something to do with it too—because he lunged at me instead of the guys. I yanked up one of the pop cans and brained him across the head with it as hard as I could. He reeled to the side, and Jett recovered his gun soon enough to shoot the jackass in the heart.

But then five more masked men barreled into the room, and suddenly we were doubly outnumbered again even with the many enemies who'd fallen. Nox swore and whipped out his fists again. Jett pulled the trigger on his pistol—and it only let out a hollow clicking that spoke of an empty chamber. Ruin rammed into two of the newcomers only to be tripped by a third so he sprawled flat on his face.

As some of the men closed in around Jett and Nox, two fell on Ruin, one jabbing down with a knife. A shriek of protest left my lips, and I lashed out with my power before I'd totally thought through what I was doing.

I had to stop him. I had to stop him *fast,* or Ruin would die.

With that certainty, all of my attention condensed on the pumping of blood through the man's veins, clenching it with an iron fist of supernatural energy. The man stiffened and shuddered, his arm veering wide. I felt down to the core of my own being the way his heart strained and the rest of his body protested at the sudden obstruction.

My own heart thudded on in a rhythm suited for a funeral possession. I could ensure this man's imminent funeral right now. All I had to do was burst apart his heart like Kai had suggested.

A trickle of nausea wrapped around my stomach. I didn't *want* to be a killer. But if I didn't do this thing, then the asswipe would just go back to killing Ruin. For the second time.

If I was in this thing, if I was going to stand with my men, I had to go all in.

The decision darted through my mind in the space of a few heartbeats, and then I wrenched at the blood contained in the man's body like I was hauling on one end of a tug-of-war rope that would determine the fate of the universe.

Blood crashed into the man's heart in a violent punch. The impact of the shattering muscles echoed through my awareness. Then the douchebag was crumpling over, a streak of blood dribbling from the corner of his mouth.

I'd done it. I felt sick but also invincible. Ruin caught my gaze as he yanked himself out from beneath the guy and shot me a brilliant smile that made it all seem okay.

He whacked the calf of the other Corps man near him, who immediately barreled at his companions who were surrounding Nox. In the ensuing scuffle, Nox requisitioned one of the attacker's knives and did a little creative carving that left them all slumped in a pile. Ruin had rushed to help Jett next, and the two of them batted around the last few Skeleton Corps members like cats with wounded mice.

"Wait!" I said quickly before they could deal out the final fatal blows. "One of them might know something useful about the people in charge."

Jett grunted in approval and shoved one of the guys backward. Nox caught him, whirled him around, kicked his feet out from under him, and pinned him to the ground. Ruin rammed his hands out in a double punch, catching both of the other remaining dipshits in the stomach. They both crumpled, cringing with both pain and fear.

"No more," one of them started babbling. "You people are demons."

"Not quite," Nox said from his human perch, sounding amused.

"Now you tell us what you know about the people who told you to attack us," Ruin declared with apparent glee.

One of the men tipped over on his side and just rocked to and fro on the floor, sucking his thumb. The other trembled from head to toe.

"I can't," he whined. "If they find out—they'll hang my guts from a flagpole."

Nox cocked his head like he was thinking that might not be a bad tactic and then flashed his teeth. "What do you think *we're* going to do to you if you don't talk?"

The guy shuddered again. "You don't know what they're like. Please don't punish me. Just let me go. Or kill me. Whatever. I can't do this." His voice was rising into a wail.

Jett snorted. "I think you hit them a little too hard, Ruin."

Ruin looked down at his fists. "I don't know how to un-punch them."

An idea came to me, perfect and terrible at the same time. I raised my chin and forced the words from my mouth. "Maybe we need to show him just how bad things can get with us. We can do a lot more than just kill him. We can tear him apart from the inside out."

I raised my hand, and Nox's eyes gleamed with approval. He nodded and aimed another vicious look at our former attacker. "And Lily's the nicest out of all of us. Consider this a preview."

Somehow it was easier this time—maybe because I knew I might not have to kill him. Maybe because I *had* killed someone already, and the world hadn't fallen in on me. I summoned the hum inside me, tapping my fingers against my hip so the rhythm would give me better control, and reached toward the fluid flowing through the man's veins.

It wasn't hard at all. If anything, it was horrifyingly easy. I pushed and pulled at his bloodstream, making one vein swell and another deflate and battering his heart with little jabbing spurts. The man jerked with those assaults, his face going sallow, and guilt coiled around my stomach. But I didn't let myself stop.

He needed to tell us what he knew. We needed to end this war before the Skeleton Corps destroyed my men all over again.

"What are you doing?" he asked in a quavering voice, and gulped with an agonized sound when I prodded him again. His mouth twisted at a queasy angle. He pressed his hand to his chest.

"She can keep doing this to you, and she can do it to every one of your friends," Nox said darkly. "And this is her going easy. Do you want to find out just *how* bad it can get when someone's playing with your blood right inside your body?"

A sharper tremor ran through the man's frame, and his mouth burst open. "All right! All right! Please stop. No more. I—I'll tell you about my bosses."

Chapter Fifteen

Nox

I LOOKED across the street at the building and scoffed in disbelief. "*This* is what the big bad Skeleton Corps have been operating out of?"

"For the time being," Kai said, ever the pedant, with a nudge of his glasses up his nose. "The one guy before did tell us that they move their base of operations around a lot."

Ruin chuckled. "Hey, who doesn't like ice cream?"

He might have had a point there, but the ice cream parlor across from us still didn't have the imposing grandeur I'd been expecting from the home base of the Skeleton Corps's upper echelon. It was painted in pastel colors. The sign had a cute little kitten licking an ice cream cone. I'd be willing to bet a thousand dollars that the door let out a cheerful jingle when anyone opened it.

"Maybe the dope didn't know what he was taking about," Jett said with a similarly skeptical expression. "Or maybe he was still terrified enough of *them* to lie to us."

"Or maybe it'd make sense for them to use a place like this," Lily put in. "If no one would expect a gang to operate out of it, then no one's going to be coming around hassling them."

"And also," Ruin said, "free ice cream." From the gleam in his eyes, he was planning on scooping a bunch for himself once we got in there.

Lily rolled her eyes at him with obvious affection. "Yes, that is a benefit too."

I shifted my weight on my feet. I still didn't really *like* having her along for a confrontation like this. I'd have preferred for there to be several miles and multiple steel barriers between her and the menaces who'd slaughtered us two decades ago—and tried to murder us at least a few more times since I'd returned. But there was no denying that she'd held her own during the attack yesterday. The Skeleton Corps invaders might have *succeeded* in murdering us if she hadn't stepped in with the new bloody dimension to her powers.

And when I'd suggested that she let us handle this on our own, she'd refused before I'd even gotten all the words out. *Your fight with them is mine too, just like you wouldn't leave me alone to tackle the Gauntts. You said I'm part of the Skullbreakers now, didn't you?*

I couldn't argue with that. And it was her fight for all sorts of other reasons now too. Not least of which being the fact that it was her apartment we'd spent several hours cleaning bodies and blood out of last night.

There were still a few purple streaks in her hair by the nape of her neck, where she hadn't managed to wash out the final traces of paint from more enjoyable activities earlier that night. Even with the battle ahead of us, the sight made my cock twitch.

I'd never have said I was any kind of art aficionado, but the picture she and Jett had made yesterday? I'd call that a fucking masterpiece.

Jett cracked his knuckles. "So, strange place or not, are we sticking to the plan?"

I didn't figure we were in a good position to stand around here coming up with a new one, right across the street from our targets. I glanced at Kai, since the whole advance preparation thing was more his specialty anyway. He nodded.

"It may work even better in there than the kind of setting we'd have pictured. Less room for them to maneuver. We just need to make sure we keep our individual targets separate. If we double up, we'll only be half as effective."

I might have dropped out of high school, but I could follow that much math. I nodded and motioned to the others. "Let's teach them a thing or two about messing with the Skullbreakers."

"Don't break *all* of their skulls," Kai reminded us. "We don't know yet who offed us. It could be old-timers who aren't as active anymore. But someone in there should know."

He and Jett took out their guns. I left mine in the back of my jeans since my fists were better weapons with their new supernaturally enhanced punch, and we charged across the street toward the parlor.

It was technically open, but the Skeleton Corps didn't appear to have been doing much to drum up business in however long it'd been since they'd taken the shop over. When we burst inside, there was no one in the building but several men who looked to be coming up on middle-aged, sitting around two of the little formica tables pushed together into one long one. A dude in the middle of the bunch was eating a fucking sundae.

The lights gleamed down on them, the polished tabletops, and the glass display case on the left side that held the spread of ice cream tubs. A sweet, creamy smell hung in the air, making the violence we were about to commit feel momentarily absurd. But they'd chosen this venue, not us.

"Are you the Skeleton Corps?" I demanded as the men jumped up. I'd have preferred to skip the introductions, but we weren't sure exactly how accurate the squealer's information was. It wouldn't do us much good if we killed the wrong gang leaders and ended up with some other syndicate out for revenge on *us*.

The guy nearest us snarled and lunged, which was enough of an answer. If it'd been a simple misunderstanding, they could have just said so.

They *all* sprang up and rushed at us, guns and knives whipping out in a jumble of motion. We focused on the figures at the front of the pack.

Kai and Ruin leapt in first, as we'd planned. Kai socked the first guy in the jaw, ordering him to "Shield us from your friends and hit them back," at the same time. Ruin kneed another prick in the gut.

I hadn't been sure if he'd actually been able to follow through on the emotional programming we'd discussed, considering he didn't always seem fully in control of how it turned out, but the guy immediately spun around to face his colleagues with a yodeling sort of battle cry.

"Death to anyone who challenges the kings of the city," he bellowed.

The fact that he obviously meant us and not the men he'd been standing with seconds ago threw his friends for a loop. They wavered for a second in the middle of their charge. In that second, the first guy punched one hard enough to break his nose and the second headbutted another in the gut.

The other guys hollered for help, and a few underlings came hustling out of a door at the back of the room. But it was nothing like their attack on us last night. They must have felt pretty confident in their secrecy and their ability to defend themselves here. They'd been counting on the horde they'd sent after us to bring us down.

Tough luck.

The two men Ruin and Kai had supernaturally conscripted to our cause formed a buffer between us at the rest of the Skeleton dudes. They swung and slashed at anyone who tried to get by them. With so many still on the other side, a couple dodged past, but Ruin caught one of them with a jab that had him flailing and wailing like he'd been sent into a living nightmare.

Jett caught the other asshole and tossed him over the glass counter. I barged around it just as the jerk staggered to his feet and slammed his head into one of the ice-cream buckets. How was that for a brain freeze?

From the corner of my eye, I could see Lily working her own brand of magic. There'd been a bottle of vodka on the table, open for pouring into the scattered glasses, but she'd emptied it in an instant. The globs of alcohol soared through the air and seared into one guy's and another's eyes in quick succession. When she ran out of that, a spurt of blood spewed from the dude's broken nose and splashed another guy in the face, temporarily blinding him.

She could do way worse damage if she wanted to. The thought of how she'd conquered those imbeciles last night got me hard all over again. But it was only good if she was in the zone and loving it too. I didn't want her to push herself past the limits of her strength or her conscience.

Another guy came tearing around the display case toward me. Energy crackled through my arms, and I heaved him onto the tubs without even touching him. Now he was freezing his ass off.

I sure hoped whoever did the actual work around here knew better than to serve that stuff tomorrow.

The bosses of the Skeleton Corps were smart enough to know when they were beaten—and to realize that there wasn't any point in committing suicide via idiocy. The three of the seven still standing dashed for the back door. I motioned to Jett, and we sprinted after them. He shot at the escapees and caught one of them in the heel, sending him tumbling.

Just as the first of the bunch reached the doorway, still several feet ahead of us, his body jerked. His hand slammed into the doorframe, and he clutched at it as he pressed his other palm to his chest. Over his heart.

My gaze shot to Lily. She was staring at him from the other side of the room, one of her hands balled tight at her side, the other drumming some kind of rhythm on her thigh. Her hair lifted off her shoulders as if an electrical storm was whipping through it. A heady quiver raced over my skin.

She was some fucking woman, all right.

The guy she was targeting had blocked the doorway well enough that Jett caught up with the dude right behind him. He hurled that guy toward one of the tables, where Ruin fell on him like the Corps dude was some kind of banquet—except using his fists rather than his teeth, thank the Devil. With a one-two punch, Ruin had the prick curled up and whimpering for mercy.

The first guy Ruin had afflicted with his chosen emotions, the one who'd been battling valiantly for our side, snapped out of it. But his brother-at-arms under Kai's spell had been knocked out in the brawl, so Kai stepped up without hesitation and cracked the other jerk across the head with his knuckles. "Stand still and keep quiet."

The guy stiffened. The man in the doorway slowly turned, his hand still pressed to his chest, his face haggard. He swayed on his feet.

"What is this about?" he rasped. "Who the hell are you, and what the fuck do you want with us?"

Finally, someone was asking the important questions. I tipped my head to Lily, and her jaw worked as she must have eased off on the guy just a little. Jett dragged up the man whose foot he'd shot and smacked him down in one of the chairs, using his tie to attach him to the back of it like a noose. My artist friend held his gun at the ready in case he needed to blast the other foot to smithereens.

All of the underlings were lying dazed and useless. Of the seven top dogs we'd interrupted, one was gone from this world, one was temporarily dead to it, one was under Kai's control, and two were having nervous breakdowns thanks to Ruin. The heel-less prick and Mr. Heart Attack were the only ones in their right minds and conscious.

If I could add up those odds, I was pretty sure they could too. And you didn't get to the top by being willing to sacrifice yourself on principle. You got there by making whatever compromises you needed to in order to survive.

I stepped closer, folding my arms over my chest and staring down the bastard by the doorway. "You don't need to know anything about who we are except that we're no one you want to mess with. But hopefully our demonstration today has proven that well enough, since how we've dealt with your lowlifes didn't get through to you. We're not anything you're used to dealing with, and so you can either *make* a deal with us, or you can die too."

The Skeleton Corps guy wet his lips. "Then I'll ask again—what do you want?"

I raised my hand and popped up my forefinger. "First, no more attacks on me or anyone who stands with me. You back off on us, and we won't have to arrange another 'meeting' like this. We're not looking to take over your stomping grounds. All we ever wanted was some answers."

Well, and the appropriate compensation for those answers, but I wasn't going to mention that.

"Answers to what?" the guy snapped.

I tipped my head to Kai. It always looked better if it was clear more than one of you knew how to do more than swing your fists around.

The brainiac moved forward, his face flushed from the exertion of the fight. "Twenty-one years ago, a gang called the Skullbreakers was operating out of a hangout near Lovell Rise. A bunch of Skeleton Corps guys crashed the building and killed the leaders. Presumably at least one of you still knows who instigated that attack and who participated in it?"

"What does any of that matter to you?" the man demanded.

He was getting more spirit back than I liked. I motioned to Lily with an encouraging smile, and the drumming of her fingers sped up again. The man twitched, his hand slapping back against his chest.

"It's none of your business *why* we want to know," I informed him. "Cough up the answers, or we'll toss you aside and find someone else who's willing to give them."

The asshole's voice came out strangled. "I only know bits and pieces about it," he muttered. "I was new then, and no one talks about it much anymore. Branson was there." He nodded to the unconscious dude who'd previously been Kai's puppet. "I think McCallum and Perrucci gave the orders. McCallum's dead, and Perrucci is retired now."

An idea took root in my mind. We could have shot Branson right now and demanded to be directed to Perrucci… but that seemed like letting them off easy. I wanted all of them to face up to what they'd done with maximum torment. They had twenty-one years of payback coming to them.

"Sorry to hear about McCallum," I said casually. "But we'll have to get the rest of that bunch together. It was quite an event, and we'd like to celebrate it."

The man blinked, puzzlement crossing his face. "I guess that might be arranged."

Ruin let out a whoop. "Party time!"

I snapped my fingers. "There you go. That's our last condition—the condition of us not coming back and exploding your heart inside your chest or getting you to carve it out yourself because we said so. A reunion of the Skullbreakers' destroyers so we can properly repay them for all they've done."

Jett grinned, maybe a little too fiercely to pass as friendly. The man's eyes darted between us. But it must have been clear that saying "No" would be a death sentence.

He cleared his throat. "All right. It might take a little while to track down everyone involved, if you really want all of them."

"All of them still living," I said with a smile. "It wouldn't be fair to leave a single one of them out."

Chapter Sixteen

Lily

I LEANED my elbows onto the table and watched Nox as he paced by the apartment's living room windows, talking to Ruin with ample enthusiasm. They were working out the details of their big "party" where they'd "thank" the guys who'd had a hand in killing them for the blood they'd shed.

It was nice seeing them in such a good mood. They'd waited more than two decades for this revenge. But their good spirits only cast my own low ones into sharper relief.

"Do you think they'll recognize us?" Ruin asked, grinning at the thought.

Nox hummed to himself. "I doubt it. We don't look exactly like our old selves, and they haven't seen us in more than twenty years. Who knows how good a look they got at us when they were blasting us to bits anyway? We'd never dealt with the Skeleton Corps before. It sounds like they only came after us because of those Silver Scythe pricks talking shit."

"And they'd hardly be expecting to encounter the men they murdered twenty-one years ago to turn up both alive and unaged," Kai put in as he sat down next to me, bringing the laptop he'd bought—or, well, more likely stolen, knowing these guys—for himself. "The mind tends to reject evidence that contradicts what it believes to be possible. At best, they might wonder if we're direct descendants."

Ruin clapped his hands. "The sons of the fallen gangsters come back for revenge. I like that story too."

Nox snorted. "We'll try out both if we ever make it into a stage play. But we have to make sure we get all of the bastards who pitched in and are still around together. As soon as we take down some, anyone who isn't there will know to run."

Jett came over to make some suggestions of how he might use his powers to subtly manipulate the party décor in ways that would hinder any escape attempts—or provide additional avenues for torment—and Kai turned to me. "Your hashtag has accumulated quite a few submissions. I figured it was time we went through to check for the local videos and see if there's anyone around with marks we could break. Get a better idea of the Gauntts' preferred demographics too."

"Sure," I said, sitting up straighter in my chair. I was eager to get going with some kind of constructive planning myself. If I sat too long with my thoughts, the memories of wrenching at the Skeleton Corps guys' blood trickled up through my mind, especially the moment when I'd blasted apart the one man's heart. The echo of that sensation sent a clammy feeling over my skin even as my pulse thumped harder with a spurt of adrenaline.

I was powerful. I was a force to be reckoned with. But I couldn't say I loved the lengths I needed to go to with that power.

Kai tapped away on the keyboard. It was kind of amusing watching him glance at the letters, searching and pecking. He might be the brains of the Skullbreakers, but he obviously hadn't been any kind of computer expert way back when.

He frowned at the screen, jabbed at the touchpad, typed a little more, jabbed a little more. Then he sat back in his chair with his brow furrowed. "I don't like this."

My stomach twisted. "What?" I asked, leaning closer.

"They're just… gone." He clicked from one set of search results to another. When he copied a URL into the address bar, it came up with a Video Not Found page. "Computers," he muttered. "Someone broke the whole website."

My spirits were sinking fast. "I don't think so," I said. "The other videos are still working, aren't they? Search for something else."

Seemingly at random, he typed in "frog parade." Maybe he thought that wouldn't turn up much anyway. Instead, we got a long list of videos, everything from an actual parade of animated frogs to a singing Kermit to a statue of a frog at some shrine in Japan that was so big it'd have towered over me. I kind of wanted to bring my little amphibious friends across the ocean to see how well they were worshipped.

Unfortunately, as delightful as the results were, they appeared to confirm my suspicions. "The website isn't broken," I said. "Someone took down the video."

"*All* of them?" Kai said. "There were thousands yesterday. When I search for the hashtag or other keywords, nothing comes up. They were hardly salacious. Why would—" He stopped abruptly, not needing to finish the question to arrive at the answer. "The Gauntts."

Nox's head jerked toward us at the name. "What have they done now?" he growled.

"They had my sweater challenge video and all the videos responding deleted," I said. I had no trouble at all picturing Nolan and Marie coming up with some imaginary copyright infringement claim or similar to destroy the whole campaign with a snap of their fingers. "So we can't use them to look for other people they've marked."

"We don't need to," Ruin said. "We've already found a bunch—we found out about their special marsh place! We're still going to crush them."

But this was one more reminder of just how much power the Gauntts could wield—powers totally different from what we were working with, on a playing field we couldn't even reach.

I rubbed my forehead, and Jett came up behind me. His touch was still tentative, but there was a relief in seeing that he was comfortable resting his hand on my shoulder and offering a gentle squeeze at all, rather than keeping his distance. The understanding we'd found in each other the other night hadn't been temporary.

"We are," he said, expanding on Ruin's point. "We'll crush them into very small pieces, and then we'll piss on those."

As inspiring as that imagery was, it didn't do much to reassure me right now. I lifted my head. "We still haven't found anything that can lead us to Marisol. I want to try searching with that blood harmony strategy again. I should be rested enough. And going out at night means less chance of the Gauntts spotting me however they did before." I paused. "If one of you can drive me around on your bike, that'd be great, but if you all need to be focused on the Skeleton Corps situation, I could take my car—"

Kai was already shaking his head and standing up. "I'll take you. I've already given these numbskulls my opinions anyway." He flashed a smile at his friends to show the insult was meant affectionately. "It's my fault I didn't save the videos some way the Gauntts couldn't touch them."

"You're not exactly used to internet culture," I told him. "*I* should have thought of it."

"You shouldn't go on your own anyway," Nox said, shifting on his feet like he was preparing to insist he be the one to take me for that ride.

Kai obviously picked up on that intention too, because he motioned for his boss to stand down. "I can take care of Lily. Between my mind control and her blood magic, anyone who messes with us will regret it. We've got the truce with the Skeleton Corps now, so there shouldn't be much of anyone coming at us on the streets regardless. You three should keep planning. The sooner we pull this 'party' off, the less time anyone has to get really suspicious."

Nox let out a disgruntled sound, but he settled for planting a quick but demanding kiss on my mouth. "You'll find her," he said firmly as he drew back.

As Kai and I went down to the motorcycles, my nerves started to jitter. The cool night air did nothing to chill me out. I squashed down my doubts as well as I could. My powers worked better when I was confident and focused, and this particular approach needed all my concentration.

Once I was sitting astride Kai's bike with one arm looped around his waist and the other ready to direct him, I closed my eyes and tapped into the hum of power inside me. My body shifted against his as I moved with the memories of the childhood play Marisol and I had so often gotten wrapped up in. The hum expanded through me, and I waited for the tug to come.

There was a faint quiver, somewhere in the distance—so faint I couldn't tell for sure where it was coming from, like a sound you couldn't be sure you'd even heard at all.

I frowned and pushed the energies inside me harder, calling out to the harmony that linked my blood to Marisol's, all the common ties from our genetics. The sense of something in the distance wavered and pulsed, getting a little stronger just for a second and fading again. I still couldn't get a real lock on it.

"Start driving," I told Kai, swallowing my frustration. "Let's make a circuit of the outskirts of the city. I think they've taken her farther away—maybe I'll pick up her location better somewhere along the way."

Kai nodded without questioning me and took off down the street. For the first several minutes as we hurtled through the darkest side streets toward the edge of Mayfield, I let myself recover from my initial efforts, figuring there was no point in exhausting myself until I had a better chance.

When the shops and apartment buildings of the central city gave way to smaller apartment buildings mixed in with rows of crammed homes, and then those gave way to the more spread-out houses with lawns and driveways where city blended into suburb, Kai took a turn and started his circuit of the city. I dragged in a breath and summoned every shred of Marisol's essence in my mind again.

At first, I couldn't identify anything at all. I felt like a swimmer diving down meaning to tap the bottom of a pool, pulling and kicking and reaching and still only touching currents of water.

As Kai drove on, I finally caught the slightest tingling of an impression just beyond my mental fingertips. I groped at it, trying to cling on to it with everything I had. It expanded in my awareness, just a hint of a real tug now—

And then it dwindled away like a candle guttering out. What the hell?

I patted Kai's arm and called over the whir of the wind. "Turn around. Go back—go farther out from the city in the area we just passed through."

He veered around and shot down another street so fast my hair whipped out beneath the base of my helmet. I closed my eyes and stretched my senses again.

For the briefest instant, I thought I touched a tremor of *something*… and then it was gone again too.

My chest was starting to ache from how hard I was pushing myself, even though I hadn't done anything outwardly other than sit on the motorcycle seat. I gritted my teeth, but when I reached out again, I could feel all too clearly how my strength was flagging.

I motioned for Kai to stop. He parked by the corner of a quiet street, where a sprawling lawn stretched at least thirty feet before reaching a large house cast in thicker darkness by the shade of an oak tree. "Here?" he asked.

"No," I said, my throat constricting. "I still don't know. I couldn't get a good enough hold on her this time—not even as much as I got before."

He inclined his head thoughtfully. "They probably did take her out of the city, like you suspected. They could also be moving her around regularly to ensure she's difficult to track."

"But they can't be moving her around *constantly*," I protested, biting back a wail of frustration, and just then my phone rang in my pocket.

I yanked it out, and my heart stuttered. The caller ID said it was Marisol calling.

No one in the history of the universe has ever answered a phone faster. I flung the device to my ear, hitting the answer button at the same time. "Mare? Are you okay? Where are you?"

The voice that answered was definitely my sister's, but there was a hollow quality to her even tone that chilled me to the bone. "You need to leave me alone, Lily. I don't want to see you again. Stop trying to find me."

"What?" So many things I wanted to say jumbled together that it took me a second to fit my tongue around one. "You can't listen to them, Marisol. They're tricking you. I just want to—"

"Leave me *alone*!" Marisol snapped, and the phone line went dead.

I lowered my hand, my arm feeling abruptly feeble, like the muscles had turned to jelly. The Gauntts had put her up to placing that call, obviously. But they still had enough control over her to make her say those things, either because they were messing with her mind or because they'd threatened her into submission. My fingers squeezed around the phone so tightly I wouldn't have been surprised if I'd shattered the screen.

Kai was watching me. "They're keeping a very close eye on you," he said. "They must have known you'd left the apartment and at least suspected you were searching for her just now. The timing couldn't be a coincidence."

No, it probably couldn't. I glanced toward the star-flecked sky, my skin prickling with the sudden impression of being spied on from afar. "How would they do that?"

He shook his head. "There are lots of possibilities. We might be able to dodge them completely if we move you to a different location, get you a new phone, and keep you totally concealed… We'd have to get a new motorcycle or car to drive you around in, since they may have flagged the license plates. I'd have to talk to my tech guy about other options…"

All that, and it still might not work. The Gauntts had some idea what I was doing, and they'd already moved Marisol so far away that I'd barely picked up a trace of her location.

My head drooped. "If they're keeping tabs on me, there's no way we could be sure of them not following me. And you need to focus on dealing with the Skeleton Corps." My chest clenched tight, but I forced out the words. "We'll have to figure out another way. I don't think this strategy is going to get us anywhere. There's no point in trying just to fail all over again."

Chapter Seventeen

Kai

Lily stayed quiet for the whole drive back into the center of the city. There was a limpness to the pressure of her arms around my chest that had my mind spinning on high alert, barely paying attention to my darkened surroundings other than the basics of traffic lights and stop signs.

Her failure to use her new powers to find her sister and her decision that it was hopeless to try again had obviously knocked her down. We Skullbreakers had made progress with our own problems, but we still hadn't managed to help our woman the way we'd meant to. The fucking Gauntts kept out-maneuvering us at every turn.

I cycled through the possibilities at the same speed as the bike was whipping along the streets. The video had become a dead end. Lily's powers didn't extend far enough yet to make narrowing down her sister's location easy. Maybe we needed to work with her to exercise those powers and expand her abilities? But that could take quite a while.

Were there additional ways we could track down the Gauntts' other victims or learn more about what they did with them that could point us to Marisol's location? I might be able to weasel a little extra information out of the staff at Thrivewell who worked with the Gauntts most closely, although so far they hadn't provided much intel. I'd imagine a couple who'd been operating one of the biggest corporations in the country knew to keep their personal deviances separate from the workplace, or they wouldn't have made it this far without being exposed. You could only brainwash so many people at once.

Most of the information we'd gotten had come directly from their earlier victims. Fergus had revealed that Marie was involved too. That Skeleton Corps guy had led us to the spot along the marsh, which seemed important even if we didn't yet know why. The Gauntts' influence appeared to stretch far enough that a significant number of the Corps members had been affected. We'd found two already, after all. Who knew how many people in Mayfield carried their marks?

But we couldn't go around beating Corps guys into submission so we could check for marks and break them now that we were supposedly in a truce. That would set us right back to square one. I worked my jaw, adjusting my grip on the handlebars, and sucked in another breath laced with exhaust.

We *did* have a truce now. The Gauntts did appear to have affected several of their number. Maybe there were ways of using those facts that didn't require cracking open their memories one by one. After all, we didn't just need to know what the Gauntts were up to but also to have a way to beat *them* once we knew where to hit them.

I stewed on that line of thinking the rest of the way back to the apartment building. A giddy sense of anticipation, the high of a brilliant brainstorm, was tingling through me when I parked the bike. The second I helped Lily off, seeing the slump of her shoulders and her uncertain expression, my spirits deflated.

But this should brighten her up. I could offer her an alternate plan, one that would get us even farther toward destroying the couple who'd upended her and her sister's lives.

I grasped her hand and turned her all the way toward me. "It doesn't matter," I said. "We tried this one thing, and it didn't work out.

Not every experiment is successful—that's how you narrow down your strategies. I have another one that should be even better."

She did perk up a little, her chin lifting and curiosity sparking in her eyes. "What's that?"

"For the moment, we've got the cooperation of the Skeleton Corps," I said. "We can turn them into allies in our war against the Gauntts. Go from having two different enemies to only one, and gaining a huge hammer to smash them with."

Lily's forehead furrowed. "Why would the Skeleton Corps want to take on a corporate giant? You convinced them not to attack *you* anymore, but it seems like it'd be pretty difficult to force them to attack someone else—on a larger scale, not just one guy Kai's persuaded. Especially when it's someone as powerful as the Gauntts."

Our enemies' ability to stay one—or five—steps ahead of us was wearing down her confidence too, clearly.

I rubbed my hands together, eager to show her just how simple this could be. "I'd be willing to bet that at least one high ranking member of the Skeleton Corps has one of those Gauntt marks and was messed with by them in who knows how many ways as a kid. We just figure out who—it might even be more than one of them—and break the seal. When all the memories come flooding back, they'll have plenty of their own motivation to take them on."

Lily still looked doubtful. "The one who's been through it will. I don't think they're going to want to admit to their buddies what happened to them. Gangsters don't like to look weak, do they?" She arched an eyebrow at me.

"Well, it'll give us one or two votes on our side, and then we've got our powers and yours to shove the others over the edge. After they see how we deal with people who've crossed us and our former murderers are out of their number, they'll have even more motivation."

I glanced down at a flicker of movement and found that a frog had hopped out of nowhere to leap onto the motorcycle's seat. For a second, I was tempted to take a page out of Lily's book and ask *it* to convince her that this plan was solid.

We'd defeat the Gauntts and save her sister. There was no if about it. I wouldn't even say "or die trying," because we'd already been there, done that, and come back stronger.

Lily stroked a finger over the frog's back and sagged against the side of the apartment building. The breeze stirred her hair, tossing stray strands across her lowered face. "I'm not saying it isn't worth trying. It just seems like it would still be so many steps away from rescuing Marisol. We don't even know what they might be doing to her already. How scared she must be. What pain she might be in."

When she looked so dejected, every bone in my body ached to tell her she didn't need to worry. That her sister was fine and would still be fine when we found her. That the Gauntts couldn't possibly win.

But the truth was, I didn't have the evidence to say that with the certainty I'd need to convince her. The failing was mine, no one else's. There was too much I *didn't* know, too much that was still out of my hands…

I looked down at those hands and then back at Lily, and my mind went abruptly still.

Was it really facts or evidence she needed? In the past, I'd gotten caught up in my ideas of who she was and what was best for her, and those views had been too narrow. Just because I'd been around her for so much of her life, that didn't mean my instincts were automatically correct. I still had to really *see* her, recognize the cues she was giving off just as I would have with a stranger.

I couldn't let myself get so confident that I stopped taking her into account.

The frog croaked as if it'd picked up on my revelation and agreed with me. I studied Lily's posture and expression, taking in the details more thoroughly than I had before, the way I would have analyzed someone I needed to manipulate. In a sense, I wanted to manipulate Lily too, although not for ends of my own. Only to figure out what I could best offer that would bring her out of this despondent state.

What I saw hit me like a punch to the gut. She was withdrawing into herself, hugging herself, bracing herself against the wall—because she didn't feel she could lean on me that way?

Because facts and strategies weren't what she needed to hold her up right now, and that was all I was offering.

I wasn't Ruin, not by a long shot. PDAs had never come naturally to me. Getting turned on and acting on my desire was one thing. Figuring out how to show Lily I was here for her in every way she needed?

Why did that feel so hard when it should be so simple?

I had a perfect model for that kind of affection and support, though. What *would* Ruin have done if he'd seen Lily like this? What would he have said?

I wanted to be that for her too. I wanted her to know she could count on all of us when her hopes started to falter.

Stepping closer, I slipped my arms around her and drew her closer to me. My hand came up to stroke over her soft hair, and she tucked her head against my shoulder instinctively. She stayed a bit tensed, as if she was afraid I'd let her go if she pressed into the embrace too much, but gradually, as I hugged her tighter, her body relaxed against mine.

My throat had roughened for reasons I couldn't explain. I tried to clear it, but my voice still came out a bit ragged. "No matter what happens, I'll stand by you. We all will. We're in this however you need us, all the way to the end."

Lily made a slightly choked sound and dared to hug me harder. Some part of me wanted to stiffen up in turn, but I willed my stance to stay loose, my hold firm but tender. Maybe this sort of attitude didn't come naturally to me, but I meant it. I cared about her so much I wanted to storm over to the Gauntts' house right now and slice'n'dice the bunch of them just to relieve that worry hanging over her head. I *would* have, if I'd thought I could see a plan like that through.

When she mattered that much to me, offering a goddamn *hug* wasn't any kind of trial.

"I don't know how I'd have gotten through this if it wasn't for all of you," she mumbled against my shoulder.

I couldn't help chuckling. "I'd imagine *some* parts of your life would have been significantly simpler."

"Maybe. But there'd have been so much I didn't realize, so much still wrong that I didn't even know how to start tackling. I'm glad you guys came back into my life. I'm glad I have *you*, even if I argue sometimes."

I pressed a kiss to her temple. "Arguing is good. It keeps my mind sharp and makes sure I have all of my facts and explanations in order."

I felt her smile against my skin. "Well, I'm glad you see it that way. I guess we should go upstairs so you can go over the new plan with the other guys and get started on making it happen?"

"Is that what you want?" I asked, even though my first impulse was to do just what she'd said. "There's nothing wrong with needing a moment or two for yourself."

"I think I've gotten that." She eased away from me and then touched my cheek, bobbing up on her feet to press her mouth to mine. It was the sweetest kiss I'd ever exchanged with her, nothing like the urgent passion that'd flowed between us before—but right then, I wasn't sure I didn't like this one even better.

My decision to pause and really take in the situation carried with me as we headed up to the apartment. When we stepped inside, I found myself taking stock of my three colleagues in a way I might not have in quite some time.

Nox and Ruin were easy to read. They weren't really ones to keep their emotions close to their chests. Ruin bounded over to ask Lily how our search had gone and immediately enveloped her in a hug that was probably ten times more comforting than mine. I would just stick to believing that it was the thought that counted. Nox stalked around making growly remarks about all the things he intended to do to the Gauntts when he got his hands on them. Straightforward enough.

But Jett hung back from our group by a few steps, his eyes dark and a slight uncertainty to his posture. I wasn't seeing the same conflicted restraint in him as before Nox had somehow shaken him out of his resistance to getting physical with Lily, but he didn't look entirely at ease all the same. What was up with him?

Before, I might have dismissed it as his own problem to worry about. I'd been putting my brains toward tackling our enemies, not my friends. But it stood to reason that we'd make more headway with the former if the latter had less weighing on them.

From the little bit of distance he was keeping from us, I'd almost say he didn't think he belonged with us, not totally. Which seemed ridiculous, but my observations were rarely inaccurate.

I let Ruin and Nox continue heaping affection and promises of vengeance on Lily and went over to join the artist. Jett noticed me coming and ran a hand through his purple hair, straightening at the same time as if he'd pulled himself up by his scalp. He was trying to hide his discomfort from me, which was even more of a sign that he wasn't at ease with us.

Did he feel left out because his powers weren't as easily applicable in a fight as ours? Like he'd become the weakest link? That seemed like the most probable explanation.

I clapped a hand to his shoulder—tentatively, because one hug had hardly turned me into a master of physical demonstration. "You know, I should have said it earlier—that was some pretty amazing work you did against the Skeleton Corps dudes who stormed in here the other night—I saw the nose reshaping on that one guy while we were moving the bodies. Talk about rhinoplasty." I chuckled.

Jett looked at me as if he was wondering whether some totally new ghost had kicked the Kai he knew out of this body and taken it over for itself. "Thanks?" he said, like a question.

I groped for the right words to say. It was never hard to figure them out with people I didn't give a shit about. With the few who did, my tongue didn't seem to work quite right.

I gave him a little shake that should have conveyed manly affection. "We make an impressive team, all four of us. I'm going to incorporate your abilities more into our plans going forward. And I've always appreciated what you bring to the Skullbreakers. Just so you know."

Jett's puzzled expression didn't totally fade, but a hint of a smile crossed his lips. "All right," he said. "I guess that's a good thing to know." He cracked his knuckles. "And I'm ready to rearrange all the faces that need it, as literally as possible."

I laughed. "Sounds good to me." Now we just needed to rearrange our former enemies into our greatest weapon against the Gauntts.

Chapter Eighteen

Lily

"I STILL DON'T THINK they're going to jump for joy at the idea that we want to examine their armpits," I had to say as I tramped with the Skullbreakers over to the venue where we were meeting the Skeleton Corps leadership this time. This spot seemed a little more traditional than the ice cream parlor. The sign out front read *Crow's Feet Tattoos,* which didn't sound like the most stunning endorsement for the shop's services, but who knew what people were into these days?

"If they complain about it, I can work my way through them one by one," Kai pointed out without a hint of concern. I didn't know what'd gotten into him yesterday when he'd turned huggy all of a sudden—not that I'd minded—but he'd had a looser energy to him since then, like maybe he'd needed the hug as much as I had.

"They might complain even more about you going around hitting all of them when we're supposed to have a truce," I muttered.

"As soon as we find one of the big bosses who the Gauntts messed with and get him to remember what they did, it'll be a piece of cake," Nox said with his typically impervious air. He strode right up to the front of the tattoo shop and pushed the door wide, though I could see his muscles flex in preparation for an attack.

In theory, this meet-up was to discuss final preparations for the "party" the Skullbreakers were supposedly throwing to celebrate their murderers in a couple of days. I wasn't totally sure what all Nox and the others had told the Skeleton Corps leaders to convince them of their good intentions, but it appeared to have worked. We walked into the shop to find four of the men we'd confronted in the ice cream parlor as well as several underlings gathered in the far end of the room, beyond the tattoo chair.

They held no weapons, but seeing all those underlings sent an uneasy prickle over my skin. Were they here just for defense in case my guys got out of line, or were the Corps bosses less sure about this truce than they'd claimed to be?

The five of us stopped at the front of the store near the door and windows, both of which I supposed could make for a quick getaway if need be, although one significantly more painful than the other. Ruin gave the Skeleton Corps contingent a grin and a little wave, which was only met with glowers that didn't appear to faze him at all. Jett started shooting glances at the spread of designs tacked to the side wall, the twist of his mouth suggesting he'd have liked to revamp at least a few of them.

"Well, we're here," one of the Corps leaders said in an irritated voice. "What was so important?"

Nox drew himself up with a hint of swagger. "We'll get to the most important business in a second. I promise you that you'll be glad you stuck around for that. First, have you rounded up all your members for the bash this weekend? We want to make sure no one who helped end the Skullbreakers misses out on the celebration."

"It's pretty weird that you're so obsessed with a two-bit gang that bit the dust twenty years ago," another of the men snarked. I saw Kai bite his tongue against correcting him to twenty-*one* years.

Nox snorted as if the comment was ridiculous. "You don't know our history. Getting rid of those assholes had a *huge* impact on our lives. We'd be totally different people if it wasn't for your… help." He offered a broad smirk, clearly pleased with himself for the double meaning behind his words that they couldn't piece together.

The third man eyed us up and down. "What, did they steal your pacifier out of the cradle? You're still practically kids."

Ruin chuckled. "We're young at heart, but older than we look! The best way to be."

"It wasn't just us but people who came before us," Kai put in. "Like we've said, there's a lot of history we've only just finished dealing with."

"Anyway," Ruin added, "who doesn't like a party? You all get to come."

I felt like I should say something too, as the most normal member of the group, if only to show that we were all on board with this. I cleared my throat. "We're handling everything. All you need to do is show up and have a good time. It's kind of a celebration of the truce too, right?"

The Skeleton Corps guys shifted on their feet, looking like they weren't totally sure the truce was something worth celebrating and not cursing. But they didn't bother arguing anymore.

"We've gotten names and tapped people so they'll turn up," the first man said grudgingly. "There aren't a whole lot still with us, one way or another, but they'll be there."

"Perfect." Nox rubbed his hands together. "It'll be a spectacular time."

"What's this other important business you needed to bring up?" the second man demanded.

"Right." Nox fixed his gaze on each of them in turn. "We've found out that a whole bunch of your people, including at least one of you, has a common enemy that we share. Someone who messed with you without you even knowing it. We figured in the spirit of our truce, we should pass on that info and give you the chance to do something about it."

He was making a bit of a gamble. We couldn't be absolutely sure that one of the Skeleton Corps leaders had come under the Gauntts' sway as a kid. But it seemed like one out of every few guys we'd encountered in their lower levels had been marked, and the bosses were young enough—late thirties and forties, from the looks of them—that the Gauntts would have been adults when they were the right age. We didn't know when Nolan and Marie had gotten started on their bizarre game, but it'd obviously been going on for a while.

And if none of them had a mark, then there were plenty of underlings we could work with too.

The fourth man—the oldest of the Corps bosses, who'd been silent until now—folded his arms over his chest and scoffed. "You don't think we'd *notice* if someone had been messing with us? How the fuck could you know more about what's happening to us than we do?"

Nox shrugged. "How the fuck can we make you follow our orders or punch you from across a room? You're smart enough to be able to see that there are powers you didn't know existed until now, aren't you? We're not the only ones in town who have them—and the other people who do are a lot shittier than us."

"And they can get into your head so you can't remember," I said.

All four of the Corps leaders looked at us with uncertain skepticism. They couldn't deny what Nox had said about supernatural powers, but it didn't surprise me that they'd also be reluctant to accept that they needed us to give them an FYI about their own enemies.

"Well, spit it out," the first guy said eventually.

Nox tipped his head toward them. "Any of you remember getting visits from members of the Gauntt family back when you were a kid?"

Opening with that question got us exactly what we needed without any of them even answering it, at least with words. Most of the men standing across from us responded with expressions of varying degrees of confusion. But two of them—the third of the bosses and one of the underlings on the fringes of the group—tensed up. The boss recovered quickly, smoothing out his reaction as if nothing had happened, but if I'd caught the blip, he had no hope of Kai's sharp eyes missing it.

Kai pointed at him. "You did. They got to you—Nolan or Marie or both of them."

The other guys looked at him, a murmur of consternation moving through the bunch. The man's thin eyebrows drew together as he postured with apparent anger. "I don't know what the fuck you're talking about. No one's gotten one up on me. There's nothing wrong with my head."

"You have a mark," I said quietly, and the others fell silent so that my voice carried through the room. "Somewhere on your upper arm, probably the underside, about the size of a nickel, like a birthmark."

Again, there was a brief twitch of discomfort before he schooled his face into his preferred mask of indignance. "Get the fuck out of here. Now you're just making up bullshit."

Ruin's good cheer dropped away in an instant. "Lily doesn't *lie*," he said fiercely.

I waved for him to stand down and focused on the Corps guy. "I had one too," I said. "I managed to break through it so that I could remember what they blocked in my mind. I've done it for a couple of other Skeleton Corps men since then—lower-level guys. I can do it for you too. You *want* to know what they really did to you, don't you? How they might be controlling you even now? How can you run the Corps if someone else is running *you*?"

I'd used those words partly to convince his colleagues rather than him, so they'd turn on the pressure for him to comply. Weirdly, they all started to draw themselves up in a blustering show of authority, as if I'd somehow offended them.

"If he says there's nothing, then there's nothing," the fourth man said. "We didn't come here to listen to crazy stories."

"You don't know shit about any of us," the second agreed.

Nox let out a disdainful huff. "If you're not going to let us open your eyes willingly, then we'll just have to wrench them open. We can't have a truce with someone under the influence of the enemy."

Several of the Skeleton Corps guys moved their hands to guns partly concealed at their sides. "And how exactly do you think you're going to make us?" the third leader sneered.

Nox smirked at him. "Like this."

He whipped his hand out through the air and yanked it back in a fist so abruptly that a couple of the underlings flinched. It hadn't come within more than a few feet of the other men—but his talents were clearly expanding, and they hadn't been prepared that he could *pull* with his supernatural abilities as well as *punch*.

Electricity quivered through the air, and the third boss's shirt shot out from his body as if it'd been grabbed—because it had, by fingers of ghostly energy. He staggered forward across the space between us. The next second, Kai was smacking him in the head. "Stand still with Lily and keep your mouth shut."

That took care of our main target. But as he jerked to a halt next to me by the dingy shop window, the other Skeleton Corps members took aim as if we were kidnapping him rather than trying to break a magic spell on him. Which, to be fair, was probably a much more common occurrence in the criminal underworld.

Nox shoved me to the side so that the Corps guy would shield me from his colleagues' bullets if they started firing, and then all four of the Skullbreakers sprang into action.

Nox whipped out his fists, sending pistols jerking aside and in some cases clattering to the ground before their owners could get a shot off. Jett dashed in there fast enough to slap his hands against weapons still clutched in people's hands, altering the shapes of guns and knives alike. Suddenly the Skeleton Corps crew found themselves holding metal giraffes, wiener dogs, and butterflies as if a demented balloon-animal artist had swept through.

Ruin delivered a couple of blows that had two of the underlings lunging at their colleagues, snarling like feral wolves. Kai couldn't try to control anyone else while his power needed to work on my target, so he settled for landing a punch here and a kick there the old-fashioned way.

But it wasn't quite enough. Even with all the chaos careening through the room, the fourth of the Corps bosses kept his grip on his gun. He aimed it straight at Nox's head while Nox was grappling with a couple of underlings who'd tossed their gun-animals aside.

A cry ripped up my throat. "No!" And energy surged out of me alongside the protest, snatching around the blood flowing through the man's chest and squeezing it into his heart.

I hadn't meant to work the bloody part of my powers on anyone today. Seeing the guy seize up and sway, his skin graying, made me feel sick even though I'd watched this play out a few times already. Even though I knew I was saving Nox's life.

This wasn't how I wanted to save *anyone's* life—by holding someone else's in my hands, almost literally. But I didn't have much choice, did I?

"Stop," I said, my voice carrying over the clamor. "Stop fighting and tell the rest of your men to stop. I don't want to detonate your heart, but I will if I have to."

The Skeleton Corps guy turned his gaze on me, his eyes wide. He coughed and shook. "Enough," he said raggedly. "Fall back."

His submission gave me a queasy sense of satisfaction. The other two bosses stared at him for a second, but they must have been pretty rattled already. They hollered to the underlings, and as their people drew back, the Skullbreakers retreated to our side of the room too.

The Corps didn't know that I couldn't work my bloody magic when I was concentrating on breaking a mark, and hopefully they wouldn't get to find out that fact today. Without wasting any time, I jerked up the sleeve of the third boss, who was still standing rigidly by me. I raised his arm so the others could see the pink splotch right where I'd said it'd be on his upper arm.

"I'm going to break the supernatural power in this, and then he'll remember," I said. "That's *all* I'm going to do as long as the rest of you behave yourselves."

"And you should definitely listen to her," Ruin put in.

The Corps members stirred uneasily but stayed where they were. I closed my hands around the man's bicep and threw all the energy humming inside me at the mark.

Each time I did it, this procedure got easier in every way. I was starting to know how to hit the Gauntts' magical barrier at the angles that would crack it the fastest, to sense the weakening spots the second they started to give and focus more energy there. Closing my eyes, I rammed all the power I had at the wall they'd set up around those memories in the guy's mind.

I'd barely broken a sweat when the barrier shattered apart. The guy sucked a sharp breath through his nose, since Kai had told him to shut his mouth. He let out an anguished-sounding grunt.

Kai gave him a light swat. "You can talk but don't attack any of us."

The man's lips burst apart. "Those *fuckers*," he said, his voice raw with both anger and horror. He bobbed back and forth on his feet for a few seconds before focusing his eyes on his colleagues across from us. "These guys are telling the truth. The Gauntts— We've got to destroy those pricks. Burn them to the fucking ground."

Chapter Nineteen

Ruin

Lily put her hand over the mouthpiece part of the phone and let out a faint groan before she went back to the conversation. "Yes, I understand that the apartment was a little messy. That's why I'm giving up the damage deposit. But all the stuff you're talking about already wasn't working when I moved in. I can show you multiple emails where I pointed those problems out to you. I'm not paying any more money."

I stopped where I'd been wandering around the apartment, munching on my spicy beef jerky, and took in her tense expression. She'd been on the phone with her former landlord for several minutes now, fending off his attempts to suggest that the poor water pressure and leaky kitchen sink and who knew what else were somehow her fault.

"Do you want me to go deal with him?" I whispered with a lift of my eyebrows, drawing my finger across my throat to make my meaning clear. It would be my pleasure to end his harassment of our woman in the most final way possible.

To my disappointment, Lily shook her head. She rolled her eyes at whatever the landlord said next and slumped farther into the sofa cushions. "Yes, I understand, but that wasn't my responsibility."

I swallowed the last of the jerky, not enjoying its intense flavor as much as usual. I didn't like to see Lily stressed out at all, and in the past few days her spirits had seemed… darker than usual. Like there was a shadow over her. Something in her eyes when she stopped our enemies in their tracks by manipulating their blood, something in her expression and stance afterward that suggested she was hardening herself.

I liked her soft, sweet, and smiling. If she'd been happier taking on a harsh role, I'd have supported that all the way too. But the smiles had been coming few and far between.

Looking at her pose on the sofa, an idea sparked in my mind of one very simple strategy for bringing more light into her life. A fiery sort of light.

Unable to restrain a grin, I walked over to her and knelt by her feet. Lily jerked her gaze to me, knitting her brow. *What are you doing?* she mouthed silently.

"What does it look like?" I murmured back, and stroked my fingers over her knees. She was still wearing just her long sleep shirt that she'd spent the night in, which worked just fine for my purposes. "You need someone to counterbalance the awfulness you're having to listen to."

"Not like—" She cut herself off when she needed to respond to the landlord. "Of course. But my security deposit covers that. I looked at the lease."

While she spoke, I teased my fingers higher up her thighs and kissed the inside of her knee. Lily shifted her legs as if to close her thighs, but I nudged between them before she could and caught her eyes with a challenge in mine. "If you don't like me doing this while you're on the phone, tell him you're done and get off. *I'm* not done."

"Ruin," she muttered, but a huskier note crept into her voice alongside the irritation. When I flicked my tongue against her inner thigh, her breath caught with a restrained gasp. Whether consciously or not, she scooted just a little farther down on the sofa toward me.

I tugged her sleep shirt up to her waist and traced my fingers over the curves of her ass through her thin panties. The smell of her filled my nose, the perfect muskiness of her desire mixing with her usual wildflower scent. There wasn't any better snack than this.

I kissed a trail up her thigh, closer and closer to her pussy. Lily squirmed. When she spoke into the phone next, her voice quavered just slightly. "Right, but it was already like that. I keep telling you—"

Without warning her, I tugged the crotch of her panties aside and planted my mouth right on her cunt. Lily's voice cut off with the start of a whimper that she covered with a swift clap of her hand over her mouth. As I lapped at her from slit to clit, her legs started to tremble. Her chest hitched as she struggled to steady her breath.

"I'm fine," she managed to say. "I'm just"—a muffled gasp—"tired of listening to this bullshit. I've paid more than enough. Don't call me again."

Just as she hung up, I sucked on her clit with renewed force. Lily bucked against me with a moan she could now let out and slammed the phone down on the cushions next to her. Her fingers dug into my hair.

"You are the worst," she grumbled, and panted while I drank up the juices trickling out of her with another swipe of my tongue. "Don't stop."

I had no intention of even slowing down. I devoured her, grazing my teeth over her clit, curling my tongue right inside her opening, working my lips against her until she was outright writhing. The scratch of her fingernails against my scalp set off jolts of electricity that shot straight to my groin.

My cock throbbed for attention, but this moment was just for her. Just for my Lily. She needed to remember how precious she was.

A whine of need slipped from Lily's throat, I clamped down on her with even more vigor, and her thighs tightened around my head as she arched into her release.

She lay there, sagging against the sofa, for several seconds. Then, as I raised my head, she gave me a light swat. "Don't go around distracting me like that."

My mouth stretched into another grin. "I'll make sure to do it as often as possible."

"You…" she growled, and sat up straighter again, her sleep shirt falling back into place. Her eyes flashed, but there was as much passion as frustration there—an eager energy I hadn't seen in her in days.

I pushed myself back from the sofa and onto my feet. There were more games we could play. "What are you going to do about it? Teach me a lesson?"

More heat flared in Lily's gaze. She shoved herself upright with a predatory grace. "And would that work?"

"Oh, I think definitely so," I replied. "But you'll have to catch me first."

She took a grab at me, and I was off like a shot, dashing for her bedroom. Lily darted after me, her bare feet thumping across the floorboards. Abruptly, I was insanely grateful to be alone in the apartment with her just this once while the other guys finalized our party preparations. I didn't mind sharing our woman—I *loved* seeing her quake with the combined pleasure we could bring her to—but there was something to be said for the moments when I had her all to myself.

I spun around as I reached the foot of the bed, and Lily crashed into me. She pushed me backward without any real resistance and glowered down at me as she pinned me to the mattress, straddling my hips and bracing her hands against my shoulders.

I beamed up at her, knowing I could have displaced her in an instant if I'd wanted to, not having the slightest desire to do so. "Okay, you caught me. What will my punishment be?"

A mischievous smile crossed Lily's lips. She rocked her pussy against me, taking me from semi-rigid to stiff as steel with the torturous friction. "What if I don't want to punish you? What if I just want to make sure you finish what you started?"

My own breath was getting a bit rough now. "I think I could be on board with that," I teased.

"Hmph," she said, and trailed her fingers down my torso to the waist of my jeans. The heel of her hand skimmed over the button and swiveled against my already straining erection. "You think? I want you completely, one hundred percent, rock-solid on this."

A ragged laugh spilled out of me. "I'm definitely there."

"Good." She unzipped my fly and tugged down my pants and boxers to free me. As her hand rubbed up and down my cock, I tipped my head back with a groan. No other woman had ever touched me anywhere near as well as she did.

I wanted to be in her slickness right now, rocking her to another release, without any barriers between us. But I had Nox's voice in the back of my head reminding me to be careful.

Kai could probably have gotten away with it, at least if Lily had gotten on some kind of birth control. His host hadn't seemed to have much of a social life. But the popular guy I'd possessed had clearly gotten around. I couldn't trust whatever was left of him to be clean even if *I* hadn't been with another woman in two decades.

Lily wasn't one to throw caution totally to the wind anyway, no matter how much fun we were having. Without my having to say anything, she crawled over me up the bed, letting her breasts graze my chest through her sleep shirt, and grabbed a condom out of the bedside table. "Rock-hard and all wrapped up."

"And ready to be in you," I said, clutching her hips as she resumed her previous position.

She hummed to herself and stroked her fingers up and down my cock several more times, pausing only to tease them over my balls as well, until I felt like I was going to explode. Then, finally, she eased the condom over me and sank down to welcome me in.

Having the firm warmth of her channel close around me always felt like coming home. My breath stuttered as I bucked up to meet her halfway, and Lily let out a gasp she didn't have to hide this time.

She leaned forward, splaying her hands against my chest this time, and rode me at her own pace. The first slow, steady sways of her body had me groaning and my balls clenching already. But I held on, intending to be there with her until the end, no matter how deliciously torturous she made the journey there.

As she sped up, the ache expanded through my groin. Her breath started to fracture. I gazed up at her, my heart swelling with affection even as my cock did with lust. "That's right, Angelfish. Take everything you need. I'm right here with you."

She whimpered and bucked even faster. Her eyelids drooped as she chased her release. I brought my thumb to her clit, circling it against that nub as she bobbed up and down, and her fingers curled against my chest. With a cry and a shudder, her pussy clamped around me.

The second I felt her come, my dick flooded her. A torrent of heat surged through me and left me sprawling boneless on the bed. But I had enough strength left to tug her down into my embrace.

"Good enough revenge?" I asked.

Lily snorted. "You never get phone calls. I can't pay you back properly." She paused, tucking herself more closely against me with her head bent next to mine. Her fingers drifted along my arm. "You haven't talked to Ansel's family since the last time we went over there, have you?"

The memory of the confrontation with my host's mother made my stomach clench up. I wrapped my arm around Lily and breathed in her scent until my insides relaxed again. "No. Kai figured out how to block numbers on our phones and showed me. I don't want to talk to them ever again."

"You got really upset about them letting the Gauntts get at Ansel when he was a kid," Lily said hesitantly. "I've never seen you like that otherwise."

I could hear the implied question in that statement, but it took me a minute to figure out the best way to answer it. I rolled toward her and pulled her right against me, burying my face in her hair.

"I don't like getting upset that way," I said. "It doesn't do anyone any good, really. It's not like getting angry when someone hurts you, because then I'm defending you. Nothing I do changes anything that happened years ago."

"But you did get upset. And that's okay. You don't have to always be upbeat about everything. I was just surprised because it's not as if you *liked* Ansel."

"He was a jerk," I said automatically, and mulled a little more. The full story might make Lily sad—but on the other hand, it'd help her understand, which could make her feel better. And she was asking.

I wanted to make her happy, but I also wanted to be honest with her.

"I guess it reminded me too much of things about my own family,"

I said. "They weren't… They weren't *awful* like I think Nox's and Jett's were. They didn't hurt me. They just… didn't do anything for me at all. They'd tell me to go off and get into whatever made me happy, and then they'd get into whatever *they* wanted for themselves, even if they hadn't bothered to give me breakfast or make sure I had shoes that fit or whatever."

I heard Lily's frown in her voice. "I think that is hurting you. Kids need someone to take care of them. It's not exactly optional. Even my mom and Wade at least made sure that Marisol and I got regular meals and proper clothes."

I shrugged. "I got by. Sometimes I was hungry and sometimes I was cold—and a lot of the time I was lonely—but it could have been a lot worse. And the more I looked at the positive side, thinking about all the things I could do whenever I wanted since they weren't really paying attention, the less the bad stuff bothered me."

Lily pressed a kiss to my cheek. "So you got in the habit of always being positive about everything," she said softly.

"It's a lot easier to be happy that way," I told her. "Why should I let what someone else did get me down? I didn't need them in the end. I got through it, and here I am."

"But it must still bother you a little, or what Ansel's parents did wouldn't have upset you."

"Yeah." I cocked my head against the pillow. "Something about the thought of them just looking the other way, not caring what those assholes did to him right there in their own home… Even my parents didn't step *that* far back. They had things they'd rather do than take care of me, but they didn't offer me up for someone else's abuse. And it was hard enough, at least at first, to feel good about things even the way I had it. Ansel was a jerk when I took him over, but he must have been pretty miserable as a kid too. When he could still remember what happened to him."

"It would have been pretty hard to see a positive side to anything the Gauntts were doing," Lily agreed. "His mom deserved everything you said and everything you made her feel about herself. I was just worried about you. If being cheerful about everything is what feels best to you, then cheer away. Nobody can take that away from you."

I smiled and nuzzled her face. “They can’t take it away from you either, Waterlily. Don’t let anyone or anything bring you down.”

“How can I, when I’ve got you?” Lily said with a chuckle, but I couldn’t help suspecting I hadn’t so much cured her of the darkness that’d gripped her as only gotten it to lift for a little while.

Chapter Twenty

Lily

THE MEDIEVAL-THEMED RESTAURANT that the Skullbreakers had taken over as their new clubhouse had once been atmospherically dim. Now, there were lights everywhere I looked. Electric lanterns along the tables at the edges of the room. Flashing neon fixtures up by the ceiling. Even the throne where I'd had a very good time with Nox and Ruin what felt like a century ago was now smothered in strands of fairy lights.

Thankfully, there was also plenty of food, because the Skullbreaker guys could plow through an entire royal feast just on their own. So they'd had their associates bring in enough platters to count as approximately three feasts, one of which they'd already made short work of. I really hoped none of the Skeleton Corps members had particularly been looking forward to jalapeno poppers or spicy nachos.

The Corps members were trickling in, taking in the décor, the food, and the blaring disco music someone had thought it was a good idea to put on with expressions that ranged from skeptical to horrified. It might have been partly to do with the uninhibited dance Ruin was currently doing in the center of the cleared floor beyond the throne.

He was gyrating away like he'd now been possessed by the spirit of John Travolta, grinning the whole time.

I smoothed down the skirt of my dress, like I'd already done about a million times. I'd felt the need to dress up at least a little to match the supposed occasion, even though I didn't feel entirely comfortable in fancier clothes—although this was definitely a casual frock, not some ballgown—and it'd required I'd drive my car here rather than riding with one of the guys. Fred 2.0 had been getting neglected anyway.

Ruin boogeyed into another song. I elbowed Nox where he was standing next to me. "Shouldn't we, I don't know, put on some tunes from at least this *century*? Were *you* even born when this one came out?"

Nox scoffed. "My gram would have taken mortal offense to you criticizing the great Bee Gees. We couldn't figure how to download stuff onto our phones, and this was the only CD we could come up with that was reasonably party-like. It won't matter in a few minutes anyway."

Because in less than half an hour, he planned on the main musical accompaniment to the evening being gunshots.

He moved away from me to motion some of the Skullbreakers recruits onto the floor so Ruin didn't look quite so lonely. Jett immediately came up at my other side, a cola in one hand and a churro in the other. I raised an eyebrow at him. "Am I being babysat?"

He gave me a small smile that sent a tingle of warmth through my chest—just the fact that he would stand that close to me and smile with such open affection, even if it was still tempered by his usual taciturn reserve.

"You're the deadliest person in this room," he said. "You should be babysitting us."

That might be true, but it turned the tingle into a twitch of my nerves. I folded my arms over my chest, not wanting to stress about whether the guys could pull off their plan without a hitch while the targets of that plan were now spreading out through the restaurant. When hugging myself didn't dampen my restlessness, I gnawed on a slice of pizza instead, careful to avoid the pie Ruin had ordered smothered with hot peppers.

"I assume you're all sure who the guests of honor are?" I said in a low voice. They didn't want to slaughter *all* of the Skeleton Corps guys, only the few who'd been involved in their own murders.

Kai had just joined us at my other side, catching my question. He answered instead of Jett—he probably had an itemized list in his back pocket. "It seems there are five Corps members still in this world who were involved in the incident we're 'celebrating.' They're all supposed to be here tonight. We've arranged special seats for them with name tags and everything." He tipped his head toward the banquet table in front of the throne. "I've seen four out of those five so far."

"It looks like the leadership decided to come," I remarked. Three men I recognized from the ice cream parlor had already arrived, and one more was just strolling in. Of the missing two—not including the guy who'd died in the fighting, of course—one was probably in the hospital after the lessons in hospitality the Skullbreakers had given him, and the other…

The other was the one with the mark whose memories I'd unlocked a couple of days ago.

I frowned, scanning the crowd in case I'd simply failed to notice him. There were at least fifty people spread out through the restaurant now, eating and gabbing even if they weren't quite into the dancing yet—half of them Skullbreaker associates and half from the Skeleton Corps. After getting so up close and personal with the marked guy, I was sure I'd have recognized him.

A shiver ran through my stomach, but it was probably just nerves. There wasn't anything all that odd about him passing up the party. I was surprised by how many of the top brass *had* shown up. He might come later. Or he might be in a therapy session getting help for those years of suppressed trauma.

Probably better that he wasn't here to have tonight's events add to that load.

I gulped the last of the pizza slice and felt some regret about the lump it'd formed in my stomach. I didn't think my digestive system was going to be functioning properly again until this night was over.

Kai straightened up a bit, his gaze flicking to the front of the room. "There's the last of them. The pricks who mowed us down." More emotion than I usually heard from him wound through his voice. He might be treating this event as a mind game of sorts, but he was just as pissed off as the others about his untimely death twenty—excuse me, twenty-*one*—years ago.

I watched the latest arrival: a pudgy, balding man who looked like these days he must have conducted most of his gangster activities by yelling at people lower down the ladder to do his bidding. He walked tentatively along the table against the opposite wall, picking up a plate and helping himself to several mini spring rolls. His expression as he took in the space looked as skeptical as that on many of the others.

Kai clearly picked up on the same vibe. "I'm going to nudge Nox," he said, pushing away from the table. "We need to get this show on the road before any of them decide the party's not their jive and take off on us."

I glanced over at Jett, who took another gulp of his cola. "Do you need to help rounding everyone up?"

He shrugged and swiped his hair away from his eyes. "Nah. Nox and Kai can get everyone in place. My main contribution is going to be in the big reveal." A small, feral grin curled his lips. It was disturbingly sexy. Or at least, I had the sense that I should have been disturbed by how sexy I found it, even if I wasn't actually.

Ruin was still tearing up the dance floor, although at least he had some company now, awkwardly bobbing and swaying along without quite as much enthusiasm. Nox ushered the guests of honor past the dancers to their special table. They brought plates of food with them, and Kai hustled over with a few of the larger platters and then liquor bottles so they could help themselves without getting up. By all appearances, they were eager to pamper the five Skullbreakers murderers.

When the guests of honor were settled in and eating away, if still with somewhat puzzled faces, Nox made a brusque gesture. The music cut out. He clapped his hands, and Jett left my side to stand next to the others as they formed a line across from the banquet table.

Nox grinned broadly. "Gentlemen," he said, with the slightest of sarcastic sneers. "We're so glad that those of you who played a role in destroying the Skullbreakers two decades ago could join us today. We have an even more special surprise for you! If you'd just—"

He never got to say what he wanted them to do, because at that moment, the paneled ceiling broke open, and at least two dozen men in skeleton-print ski masks dropped down into the party with guns already firing. In an instant, it was literally raining men—and bullets.

The crowd broke apart with yells and brandishes of their own guns. As the shots thundered in my ears, I dove under one of the tables.

Peering out from beneath it, I couldn't help noticing that the Skeleton Corps men who'd already been part of the festivities didn't look particularly surprised. *They'd* all gathered at the front of the restaurant, other than the five at the head table, and they were yanking their own guns out now.

Ruin ducked under the table next to me, grabbing my arm. "Are you okay?"

"Yeah," I said. "But what the hell are we going to do?" It was utter chaos out there, bodies jerking and falling on both sides, people scrambling to find whatever cover they could. Several of the lights shattered in the hail of bullets, darkening the room and making it harder to follow the action.

"We've been double-double-crossed!" Ruin exclaimed. "Triple-crossed? Before we could even get to the double-crossing part!" His head jerked toward the table by the throne, and he must have noticed a couple of the men there bracing as if to make a dash for the doors. He bared his teeth fiercely. "We can't let *them* get away."

I was going to say that we really should focus on getting out of here alive ourselves and worry about the whole murderous revenge thing later, but Ruin had already scrambled out from under the table and dashed over to stop the guests of honor from making their escape.

The front doors burst open behind the main group of Corps members, and several of the Skullbreakers recruits pumped bullets into the mass of bodies. They'd been stationed outside to make sure the targets of our revenge didn't get away, but they'd obviously realized they were needed inside now.

A bunch of the Skeleton Corps members crumpled, but others flung themselves out of the way in time and shot back. Our own guys tumbled over with sprays of blood. I couldn't tell who was even winning.

Why had the Corps turned on us? Had they figured out what the Skullbreakers were up to? Maybe one of those recruits had decided it was worth the risk of tattling on us so they could get in good with the original higher power in the city.

There was no way to know right now. The hum of supernatural energy inside me prickled all the way to my skin, and I threw it toward all the liquid I could easily reach. I pelted liquor bottles and pop cans into every masked figure I could see still standing and anyone else I was sure was Skeleton Corps. It seemed like a faster way to deal with the horde of attackers than trying to explode their hearts one by one.

So then there were bottles and cans as well as bullets flying every which way and sometimes colliding, and more people ended up sheltering under the tables and behind the throne and pinball machine than out on the floor. A stray bullet shattered the glass top of the pinball machine, and I heard a groan of horror that was probably from Nox.

The gangsters were still shooting from beneath and around their hiding places. A guy lunged at me out of nowhere and immediately regretted it when I instinctively wrenched at his blood with all the power I had in me. His body seized up in mid-spring, streaks of crimson spurted out of his nose, and he sprawled on the floor next to me with his head lolling slackly to the side.

A nauseatingly meaty flavor filled my mouth as the jolt of sudden energy faded away. I was starting to rack up a body count.

The Skullbreakers were adding to theirs too. I peeked out and saw Kai descending on one of their murderers, who was trying to make a run for it. Kai shoved him down and stood over him, ramming his heel into the guy's back, his eyes blazing with fury. My guys hadn't been able to carry out their plan to their satisfaction, but he still wasn't going to make this an easy death.

"You tried to take us down, but we're back," he snapped, shooting the guy's calf and then his groin. The man beneath him flailed and groaned. "This is what you get for screwing over the Skullbreakers. We don't die!"

He unloaded the rest of his bullets into the increasingly desperate body one by one, finishing with a shot to the skull, appropriately enough.

Nox charged into view, pummeling another of the guests of honor with an onslaught of crackling punches. The guy swayed and staggered, only held up by the momentum of the Skullbreakers boss's swings. His chest had already started to cave in with broken ribs.

"You aren't getting off," he snarled. "Time to pay for the twenty years we lost."

He cracked the guy's head open against the seat of the throne and roared for his recruits to surround the other three before they could dash off too.

Ruin leapt into view, delivering a flying kick that knocked another guest of honor onto the floor. He plunged a spatula that must have been with one of the platters into the man's chest like it was a knife and laughed in delight.

Jett dashed in with a flurry of smacks that appeared to rearrange the fourth man's entire body in an impossible formation that was not conducive to life. He didn't stop until the dickwad was twisted up like a human pretzel—one made by a not-particularly-skilled baker.

As Nox strode up to the last of their murderers, the balding guy fumbled with a gun it appeared he'd already emptied. Nox wrenched the balding guy's gun out of his hand and rammed the muzzle straight through the murderer's eye socket into his skull. I winced at the gruesome sight, but I couldn't say it wasn't fitting.

I'd lost track of the other Skullbreakers. There were still guns firing and minor wrestling matches commencing all around the room, although the activity was starting to quiet down. Mostly because there were probably more bodies lying limp on the floor than standing on their feet at this point.

When the shots and the other sounds of the fighting faded away completely, I crept out from under the table and picked my way through the bodies toward the throne. It looked like the few Skeleton

Corps members who'd survived had decided they'd done enough damage and taken off.

Except for a greasy-haired man Ruin was looming over with a savage grin. The guy was hunched and shaking, clearly in the grips of supernaturally-inflicted terror.

"Please!" he was whimpering, clutching at Ruin's pantleg. "Don't hurt me. I swear I'll never do anything against you or your guys again. It wasn't even my idea. I just want to get out of here alive! Oh, God…"

I found it hard to have any sympathy. There was hardly anyone left *at all* in the Skeleton Corps's wake. It looked like my men had mostly survived because there'd been so many recruits who didn't have supernatural powers on their side taking bullets. A shudder ran through my body.

As we all gathered around Ruin, the man's gaze snagged on me. To my surprise, he lifted his hand to me next, his eyes widening with what looked like frantic hope. "The girl! You're with them—you can tell them to give me a break—I'll tell you where they have your sister."

I froze. "What?" I said, the bottom of my stomach dropping out.

"Your sister," the man babbled. "The kid. I—I can show you the last place they took her. I helped with the transport."

"How the fuck do you know anything about Lily's missing sister?" Nox growled, glaring down at the guy.

But he must be telling the truth, right? He shouldn't have known I had a sister or that she was missing unless he'd been involved.

The guy started trembling harder under Nox's glower. "I—I help out the bosses sometimes—they were doing it as a favor. Sometimes they do that. We do stuff for the big people in their tall towers, and they make sure the police stay off our backs and things like that. It wasn't *my* idea."

"Fuck!" Nox roared.

Kai's mouth had tensed into a pale line. He glanced at me. "The Gauntts have the Skeleton Corps in their pocket."

"Yeah," I said faintly. "I was putting those pieces together myself."

No wonder the Corps had ruled Mayfield so thoroughly until they'd been challenged by a bunch of guys with little sense of self-preservation, an intense need for revenge, and unexpected supernatural skills on their side. No wonder they'd attacked us tonight. The realization hit me with a jolt.

The words tumbled out. "They didn't double-double-cross you because they figured out your plan. They double-double-crossed you because you asked them to turn on the Gauntts." Which also explained why the marked boss hadn't shown up. Now that he'd wanted to go against their corporate benefactors, had his colleagues shut him up permanently so he couldn't make any waves?

That didn't matter right now. I yanked my mind back to the present. What mattered was all the deaths and the chaos had given both me and the guys what we'd wanted—their revenge, and my path to Marisol.

"Okay," I said to the Skeleton Corps guy. "You show us where my sister is, and we'll let you live. But if you're messing with us…"

"I'm not!" he insisted. "I swear. I'll take you there right now. We just need—"

A sudden shot blasted through the room. One of the men I'd assumed was dead had managed to lift his gun-hand to fire one last time. My heart lurched as my head whipped back toward the men gathered around me, afraid he'd shot our hostage before he could give me the answers I needed.

He hadn't. It was worse than that.

Ruin toppled back into the foot of the pinball machine, clutching his gut with blood bursting across his shirt like a miniature hurricane.

Chapter Twenty-One

Lily

"RUIN!" I cried, leaping to his side. Just in that instant, his shirt looked twice as bloody as before. He sagged further, sliding down the pinball machine.

My entire focus narrowed down to the man in front of me, and the hum of my magic expanded until it was roaring in my ears alongside my pulse. I felt *his* pulse, pumping more blood out through the severed vessels as if it couldn't drain him fast enough.

Clammy fingers of panic squeezed around my gut. I did the only thing I could think of and shoved all the blood I could fix my energies on back into Ruin's body.

He came to a stop sitting on the floor, still leaning against the machine. I thrust out my hands, hovering them in front of the wound. And the stain spreading through his shirt… withdrew. It contracted on itself like the coffee marks on the packages I'd had to de-saturate weeks ago, but I wasn't moving the blood anywhere else in the room. I was pushing it into his body. Into the veins and possibly arteries torn along the bullet's path.

I couldn't heal him like this. I knew I wasn't doing anything but staving off the inevitable. But as long as I was guiding his blood through his body rather than out of it, he couldn't bleed to death. So I'd keep fucking staving as long as I could.

What would I do without Ruin's joyful exuberance? What would any of us do? Watching his head sway, it struck me abruptly how much he held our group of five together, smoothing out all the rough edges that might have jarred against each other without his presence.

We couldn't lose him. We just *couldn't.*

Jett and Kai dropped down on either side of their friend. I was vaguely aware of Nox striding across the room to the gunman who'd crumpled again. The bang of a gun—once, twice, three times—made me flinch, but I knew the Skullbreakers boss was only making sure the asswipe couldn't hurt anyone else.

If Ruin's attacker survived three bullets in his brain, then we had bigger problems.

"Hey," Kai said, snapping his fingers in front of Ruin's face. "Stay with us. You're not allowed to go anywhere."

Ruin looked at him blearily and managed—even now—a smile, as wobbly as it was. "Always so bossy," he mumbled. Then his gaze slid to me. His eyes sharpened. "You need to go get your sister. Some of the Skeleton guys ran. Might tell the Gauntts we're on to them. Need to get her before they move again."

The knowledge that he was right wrenched at me. "We have to get help for you first," I said through the roar of my magic.

"*No,*" he insisted, waving a hand at me. "I've already died once. You need her."

"Ruin," Nox started.

The redhead swung his head to the side and narrowed his eyes at his boss. "Try to take me to a hospital instead of going for Lily's sister, and I'll tear the rest of my guts out myself."

I believed he'd make good on that threat. I bit my lip, and Kai pushed himself upright.

"Get him into Lily's car," he said, taking charge with his intellectual precision. "Between the three of us, we might be able to stabilize him *and* go after Marisol. Which is a better outcome than him committing seppuku by hand."

Nox muttered several swear words under his breath, but he motioned to Jett at the same time. He grabbed Ruin's shoulders as Jett hefted his feet. I kept all my attention trained on the flow of blood through Ruin's body—and making sure it stayed *in* that body.

"You too," Nox barked at the shivering Skeleton Corps guy, whose supernaturally-driven fearfulness hadn't faltered yet. "If *you* want to live, you'd better get us to her sister—fast."

The dope scrambled after us. We hustled out, me fumbling for the keys in my distraction, and piled into Fred 2.0 in a literal heap. Well, Nox snatched the keys when I tossed them to him and got into the front next to our guide, but Kai, Jett, and I squeezed into the back while laying Ruin across us on Kai's brisk instructions.

As Nox gunned the engine and the Corps guy started mumbling hasty directions, I stroked Ruin's bright hair, trying not to let the ache of worry in my stomach overwhelm my focus. He beamed up at me, but with a glazed quality to his eyes that only deepened the ache.

Kai nudged his glasses up his nose where he sat at the other end of the seat under Ruin's partly folded legs. "All right. I'm fairly familiar with the structures of the typical internal organs."

"Of course you are," Jett muttered.

Kai glowered at him. "Be thankful for it. *You* get to be the star of this show, though. You can change the shape of things—that means you should be able to adjust the shape of the pieces of Ruin that got broken so they're not so broken anymore."

Jett's jaw went slack. "You want me to—to perform *surgery* on him? With *magic*?"

"Do you have any better ideas?" Kai snapped. "Now let's get on with it before Lily bursts her own heart with all the effort she's putting into picking up our slack."

A dribble of moisture ran down my forehead and over my nose. I hadn't even noticed I was sweating before that moment. It wasn't just my stomach aching. A dull throbbing was creeping all through my nerves.

He was right. Maybe not about my heart specifically, but I was wearing myself out way faster than I liked.

I couldn't stop. Ruin needed me.

Kai leaned over and peeled up Ruin's shirt. "We have to see what we're dealing with. In that area, the bullet probably ruptured an intestine as well as a bunch of veins, maybe even an artery… Can you use your superpower to feel out what's already there just sticking your hand over it?"

"Yeah," Jett said, his voice a bit ragged and his face turning queasily green. He set his hand over the wound. "I think I can do that. But I don't want to piece the wrong parts together."

"Go in as far as you can reach into the flesh with your energy and see if you can sense a sort of bloody tube slanting on the diagonal downward. And if there are any breaks in it."

"There are," I said faintly. With Kai's description, my own awareness of the liquid I was manipulating—and the passages I was manipulating it through—got clearer. "There's one hole on the side where most of the blood is trying to escape. I think the bullet must have scraped across it on the way through."

"Fuck," Jett muttered, and closed his eyes. "Let me try. I don't know how well this will work."

"You can make a guy's nose grow to five times its normal size," Kai pointed out. "I think you can stretch a little arterial wall to fill in a bullet hole."

Jett bit his lip. His hand flexed against Ruin's broken flesh. And ever so slowly I felt the pressure of the blood that'd been pushing to get past my hold ebbing.

"You're doing it!" I said. "It's getting sealed up."

Jett drew in a shaky breath and continued his work, with Kai talking him through the levels of veins and intestines and muscles. Finally, the artist slumped back against the seat, all the color drained from his face, as if he was the one who'd been bleeding out. "I can't do any more. Not right now. I feel like *my* body's about to split apart."

Sometime during our efforts, Ruin had slipped into unconsciousness. Maybe that was for the best. I wasn't sure how much Jett's efforts might have hurt. He was breathing steadily. When I withdrew the energy I'd been sending into his body with a rush of relief, only a little more blood seeped out through the still-open bullet wound.

"That'll do for now," Kai said.

I swiped my sleeve across my forehead and glanced across the car at him. His expression was tight, his eyes gone hard, but I didn't think it was with lack of emotion. It was the opposite. He was shaken by Ruin's injury too.

"If it's not enough," I forced myself to ask, "if his body fails… could he find another one, like you all did the first time?"

Kai rubbed his mouth. "I don't know. I didn't even know we could definitely manage it the first time. I have no idea what the rules might be—whether our spirits might only be capable of it once, whether it makes a difference that theoretically we've avenged ourselves now so we don't have that factor holding us in the world of the living…" He exhaled with a rasp of frustration. "I'd rather not lose him and have to find out."

"Of course." I stroked Ruin's hair again, my gut twisting.

I'd been so fixated on him that I hadn't been paying attention to the guys up front. Abruptly, the Skeleton Corps dude stiffened in his seat. Then he lunged at Nox as if to grab the steering wheel.

Nox fended him off with a slap that sent the guy reeling in the opposite direction and hollered, "A little help here?"

Thankfully, Kai was right behind the dickhead. He leaned forward to swat him. "Keep quiet and point us the rest of the way to where Lily's sister is being held."

Ruin's emotional influence had obviously worn off. Kai couldn't force the guy to answer questions, but the command he had given clearly worked. Though the dipshit scowled the whole time, his hand jerked up whenever Nox needed to make a turn.

While we'd scrambled to help Ruin, Fred 2.0 had taken us most of the way out of the city. We passed the last of the tightly-packed buildings and rumbled on into the countryside, where the night swallowed most of our surroundings beyond the sporadic streetlamps along the highway.

I'd already guessed that the Gauntts had taken Marisol beyond the city limits, but a chill crept over me as we zoomed on through the darkness. Just how far away was she? And what were we going to face when we got there?

After a couple more turns, a dank odor crept through the car's ventilation that made my nose wrinkle. It smelled like… manure.

Most likely, it was manure. The Skeleton Corps dude pointed us down a bumpy dirt track that led to a spread of large farm buildings. There were several barns, two silos, and a big cement building I couldn't have labeled. A few lights were on around the outskirts of that building. From one of the barns, a disgruntled moo carried through the air.

As we parked near a couple of other vehicles already there, two men came out of the cement building to see what was up. A light over the door blinked on, illuminating them and making them squint at us through the dark.

Kai smacked our guide's shoulder. "Keep your mouth shut and don't do anything except bring the girl here."

The guy got out of the car. The men by the building clearly recognized him, because one of them nodded and called out a greeting. Following Kai's orders, the first guy said nothing and simply marched past them into the building. They shot puzzled looks at him and the car, and one of them headed in after him.

Raised voices carried from inside. Nox readied his gun and glanced back at the others. "We may need to do a little more laying down of the law. Get ready."

Even as he said the words, the guy strode back into view, tugging Marisol with him. My heart leapt to my throat. She was still wearing her pajamas, which were wrinkled and drooping now, although someone had given her a pair of grimy sneakers. Her head whipped to one side and the other, her eyes wide with confusion.

A few other men had gathered around our dope, demanding to know what was going on. One of them grasped his arm.

That seemed to be the Skullbreakers' cue. They shoved the car doors open. Nox sprang out, shooting two guys before his feet had even planted firmly on the ground. Kai and Jett squirmed out from under Ruin as gingerly as they could and dashed into the fray.

Murmuring a pained apology to Ruin, I laid his head down on the seat and heaved myself out too.

More men charged out of the concrete building, but not many. It wasn't anything like the crazed battle in the restaurant. The Skullbreakers picked them all off, charging around them so they could fire without risking Marisol.

That didn't mean my sister was having an easy time of it, though. She shrieked and ducked down, squeezing her arms around her knees. Her whole body shook as if she were in the grips of one of Ruin's supernaturally inflicted terrors.

The second the way was clear, I dashed over to her and knelt beside her, gripping her shoulder. "It's okay now, Mare. No one can hurt you now. I'm here. We're getting you home."

Her head jerked up, and I immediately knew it wasn't going to be that easy. Defiance flashed in her eyes.

"No!" she screamed, shoving away from me. "Get away from me!"

The Gauntts were still working their influence on her, making her terrified of *me*. She darted away across the farmyard, and I bolted after her.

I had to break the spell. That was the only way to bring her home properly. I couldn't stand to drive her all the way back to the apartment with her thinking she'd been captured by the enemy for some horrible doom.

I pelted across the hard-packed dirt as fast as I could go. Marisol wasn't any slouch, but she'd probably been sitting for most of the time she'd been in the Gauntts' custody. Her legs weren't up to a marathon. They wobbled under her as she veered toward one of the barns, and I caught her right by the door, wrapping my fingers around her upper arm.

"No, no!" she squealed, trying to slap me away. "I hate you."

I let the words bounce off me. They weren't her—they were only the garbage the Gauntts were pumping into her brain with their magic.

My nerves were frayed from helping Ruin, but from deep down inside me I hauled up one last surge of my marshy magic. With all my remaining strength, I threw it against the mark I could sense on her flesh.

I still had to batter it two times. But the second time, the crack of the mark shattering reverberated through my entire body.

Marisol gasped, and her arm went limp in my grasp. "Lily?" she said in a tiny voice. "I—oh my *God*."

The last word broke off with a sob. I gathered her in my arms and hugged her, and after a few seconds she squeezed me back even harder.

It would have been a perfect reunion if another car hadn't growled into view right then.

I lifted my head, eyeing the vehicle as it came to a stop off to the side of the lane. It didn't fit with the other cars already at the farm. Too big, too sleek, too posh. A tremor of apprehension ran through me.

"Come on, Mare," I murmured. "Let's get you out of here. You can even ride shotgun."

The guys had gathered around my car. They formed a human shield for me and Marisol as I hurried her over.

The posh car's doors opened, and four figures stepped out. Not just Nolan and Marie Gauntt, but Thomas and Olivia, their younger counterparts, too. My teeth clenched. So the younger generation was in on this psychotic scheme as well.

Nox didn't hesitate. He fired a shot at the Gauntts immediately, aiming at Marie's head over the top of her still open door. But her hand shot up and her mouth twitched, and energy quivered through the air. I watched in horror as the bullet pinged off some sort of invisible wall and plunked to the ground instead.

"Get in the car!" I shouted. I didn't want to wait around and see what other magic these monsters could throw at us. I had Marisol back, and I intended for us all to make it out of here alive, no matter what we had to deal with later.

Nox huffed but dropped into the driver's seat. He started the ignition while keeping his eyes and his pistol trained on the Gauntts. I pushed Marisol into the passenger seat, where she curled up with a shell-shocked expression, and darted around to the back with Nox covering me. Kai and Jett were squirming in beneath Ruin's prone body.

Nolan Gauntt stepped forward as I moved. He raised his hand too. "I'm afraid this ends here," he said, and started to twist his wrist.

Fear jolted through my chest, and the hum ripped through me from depths I hadn't even known I had in me.

"It ends for you!" I yelled, and whipped my power at him on instinct alone.

I felt the rush of blood through his bulky body and slammed it toward his heart in one urgent push. Nolan's arm faltered, and he staggered on his feet. The walls of his heart strained, the muscles fraying but not quite bursting.

The other Gauntts jostled around him, and more unnerving electricity laced the air. They were trying to fend off my attack. But I'd already gotten my grasp on him. I'd used up so much energy already, but if I could just hold on a little longer, wrench at him a little more...

Jett let out a yelp from the back seat. My gaze jerked over in time to see blood spurting from Ruin's wound. Our quick fix had been a little too temporary.

For a split-second, it felt as if the entire world hung in the balance. Nolan had fallen to his knees, wheezing. Marie had crouched to his side with a cry. Olivia and Thomas were marching toward me, a blast of energy hitting me across the head and making my mind spin. My thoughts narrowed down to one question.

Did I want this night to end in death or life?

It was only a question for another split-second after that. Then I was diving into the car, whipping my concentration back to saving one of the men I loved.

Nox hit the gas and tore backward over the dirt road so fast I was almost jostled back out the still-open door behind me. Ruin shuddered and gasped. Whatever the Gauntts threw at us as we fled, it made the engine groan and the metal frame shriek.

But they either weren't powerful enough to deal with us while we were speeding away from them, or they were too distracted by their fallen patriarch. Nox swung the car around, and we careened away into the night, leaving them far behind.

I leaned over and willed the blood back into Ruin's body while Kai and Jett spat hasty directions and observations back and forth. And somewhere in there, Ruin opened his eyes.

"Isn't anyone going to close that door?" he said, knitting his brow. "I like the breeze, but it seems kind of dangerous for Lily."

And that was when I knew for sure I'd chosen right.

Chapter Twenty-Two

Jett

RUIN WOULD NOT SHUT UP. That was nothing new, but you'd think a near-fatal gunshot wound would at least simmer the guy down a little.

"Oh, I love this show!" he exclaimed from where we'd set him up invalid-style on the apartment's sofa, sprawled out across the cushions with his head propped up and a blanket wrapped around him. Lily had even pushed the TV stand over so he could flip through the channels without having to crane his neck.

He was waving the remote at it now. "They *think* they're all in the afterlife, but really—"

"Hey!" Lily interrupted, hustling over. "Stay still. You don't want to burst your stitches."

He looked at her slightly mournfully before a renewed smile sprang across his face. "You're so good at taking care of me, Angelfish. I can't wait until I can take care of *you* again, too."

Lily sputtered a cough, her gaze darting to where her little sister was sitting at the dining table. Marisol's head was still drooped after the long talk, interspersed with many hugs and a few tears, that they'd had while the doctor Kai had tracked down had patched up my own attempt at bodily patchwork on Ruin. Or, the guy had seemed like some kind of medical person. From the amount of little hairs clinging to his lab coat, he might have actually been a veterinarian.

But then, Ruin could definitely be an animal. Hardy har har.

In any case, the guy had known enough about the human body to mutter several times that it was a shock Ruin was even still alive. We hadn't mentioned the magical component to that fact. There'd been a lot of slathering of antibiotic gels as well as plenty of stitching, to the point that I suspected even Ruin's stitches had stitches.

The doctor had left a bottle of foamy pink stuff that was supposed to sanitize Ruin from the inside out or something. Lily had stuck it in the fridge before Mr. Enthusiasm could down the whole thing in one go. Ruin was settling for gnawing on his favorite spicy jerky until it was time for his next dose. None of us were sure that eating anything, let alone the kind of stuff that'd burn your tongue off, was a good idea, but we were a little afraid of what he might try to do if we didn't at least allow him that small indulgence.

The guy annoyed me sometimes, but I couldn't imagine running with the Skullbreakers without him. We'd be a depressingly dour bunch, wouldn't we? I might value my grim moods for the creative flow they often got me into, but that didn't mean I wanted my surroundings to be equally somber 24-7.

Marisol didn't look fazed by Ruin's suggestive remark, if she'd even processed it. Lily bobbed down to give Ruin a quick peck on the cheek and then went back to her sister. "Do you want anything to eat?" I heard her murmuring. "Or you could get to bed. It is pretty late."

Marisol shuddered. "No," she said quickly. "When I close my eyes and let my mind drift, all that stuff comes back to me even more. I'll just—I'll watch some TV with Ruin."

She pulled her chair over to the living room area and shot our human-shaped beam of sunshine a cautious smile. Ruin, of course, grinned back at her. She'd only been introduced to us a couple of hours ago, but naturally he was already her favorite.

Kai was standing by the kitchen doorway, skimming through something on his phone. Nox took in the scene in the apartment and started stalking back and forth from one end of the main room to the other. The floor creaked faintly under his increasingly massive frame. It was hard to believe that body had once belonged to a professor with an entirely mediocre physique.

"It almost happened again," the boss growled abruptly, slamming his hand into his fist. He stopped by the dining room table, glancing at Ruin and then at the rest of us. "I fucked up and let you down again."

He spoke low enough not to disturb Ruin and Marisol on the other side of the room, but the frustration and anguish rippling through his voice was unmistakable.

Lily frowned and stepped closer to him. "What are you talking about? You didn't screw anything up."

"I did," he said, his hands now flexing at his sides like he needed something bigger to punch. "I fucked up twenty years ago by not cracking down on the fucking Silver Scythes hard enough, which meant they felt bold enough to go off inciting the Skeleton Corps pricks, and then I fucked up tonight not realizing the goddamned Corps was going to turn on us again. How many of our recruits kicked the bucket? *Ruin* almost kicked it!"

"We got our revenge," Kai pointed out, but with unusual hesitance.

Nox's eyes flashed. "Yes. We managed that one thing. But it would mean fuck-all if we died all over again in the process. And who the hell knows if we've finally put the fear of us into the Skeleton Corps or if they'll be after us again now that the truce is totally dead. They've got the Gauntts jerking their chains, so they probably won't back down. It's a fucking mess."

I couldn't dispute that. There was a hollow sensation in the pit of my stomach if I let myself try to think beyond the next hour or so, to contemplate what trials we'd have to get through next. But he was wrong in the other direction, about that first event. So fucking wrong.

The familiar guilt wound through my torso again, constricting around my guts and then my lungs. But how the hell could I just stand here while the best friend I'd ever had, the only boss I'd ever been happy to take orders from, beat himself up over *my* failings?

I opened my mouth and closed it again. I'd been holding the story in so long it felt like a bowling ball I was trying to shove up my throat.

"That's not your fault," Lily was saying. "None of us realized the Skeleton Corps were planning a double-double-cross or whatever you'd call it. Not even Kai, and he's supposed to know everything."

Seeing the compassion on her face just about killed me all over again. I wanted to grab her in my arms and drown myself in her scent like I hadn't let myself do until just a few nights ago, as if I could escape the sins of my past that way.

I'd only discovered just how good things could really be with her in every way, how coming together with her bodily woke up something *more* in me rather than making what we had between us less extraordinary. After she heard this, would I ever get the chance to touch her like that again?

Kai had made a face. "I'm not quite clairvoyant. But it's true that I should have been keeping a closer eye on activities outside the clubhouse."

"I ordered you to keep an eye on the assholes *in* the clubhouse," Nox retorted. "I'm the boss, it was my call, just like everything the first time around—"

My voice finally launched from my throat. "No, it wasn't."

All three of them jerked around to stare at me. An unwelcome warmth crept across my face, but I forced myself to keep talking, hoping the momentum would stop me from stalling out before I got to the important parts.

"I was the last one to get to our real clubhouse the night the Skeleton Corps came after us the first time," I said. "You remember? I was driving slow on my bike because the pattern of the stars was giving me an idea for a painting or something like that. I don't remember exactly. But there was this guy skulking around near the building, watching it and making notes on his phone."

Kai frowned. "You never mentioned that."

"I thought I'd dealt with it," I said. "And then I got distracted by whatever you all were talking about when I came in. It didn't seem like an emergency. I roared right over to the guy, and he pulled a gun on me. I was pissed off that he was spying on us and waving shit at me so

I ran the fucking bike right into him. Then I got off and fucked him up some more before tossing him in the ditch. It was already dark. I figured we'd get around to burying him sometime later that night."

"What does this have to do with the attack?" Nox demanded.

The intensity in his gaze made me want to shrink into myself, but I managed to keep going. "He wasn't dead when I left him. I was *sure* he was almost there, he had to be dy*ing*, but he still—the blood was trickling out of him into the puddles in the ditch, and his breath was leaving with this perfect rattle, and it was like a masterpiece, the way it all came together… and I couldn't bring myself to break it. It was too good. I wanted my last experience of the moment to be like that."

I glanced at the floor and swallowed hard. Even knowing what'd come after, even with Lily staring at me along with the others—Lily who got squeamish even killing a guy who was trying to do the same to her in that moment—the awe of the scene I'd created all those years ago still lit me up like a candle.

But it'd been garbage, not art. It'd been garbage, because—

"He mustn't have died," I said hoarsely. "At least not soon enough. He must have had enough life left to get in touch with the rest of his crew, and when they came racing over it wasn't a scouting anymore but retribution. If I'd finished the job properly instead of making something pretty, we wouldn't have been killed. It was *my* fuck-up, not yours."

I braced myself—I didn't know what for. I had no idea what to expect in response to my confession. I'd probably have deserved it if Nox had torn me apart, not just for my pretentious selfishness but for lying by omission all these years. Acting like I hadn't had any idea that anyone was gunning for us.

"If you knew it was the Skeleton Corps—" Kai started.

I shook my head with a snap. "I didn't. I had no clue who the dude was. He didn't have any insignia—I didn't even know he was part of a crew rather than some random asshole with a private agenda. But it was at least a fifty-fifty chance. I should have offed him before I walked away. I should have gotten us out there to take care of him the second I met up with you."

I couldn't remember what the other guys had been talking about, only that they'd been laughing and bouncing ideas back and forth with eager exhilaration. I'd been hyped up from making my bloody art, and in that moment, dealing with the body had felt like something that could wait. A chore I didn't want to bring us all down for until it was absolutely necessary.

So fucking stupid. I hadn't really known how much any of this mattered back then, had I?

Nox was still staring at me. "Fucking hell, Jett," he said finally. "Why didn't you say anything before?"

I shrugged. "You know how it was when we were dead—everything was so woozy, and then after… I didn't see how it'd do any good to bring it up, since it'd already happened, and I didn't know anything that could help with our revenge. We were finally *back*, and I didn't want to fuck that up by giving all of you a reason to hate my guts." So really, that decision had been utterly selfish too.

"Man," Nox said, exhaling in a ragged rush, and then he did the last thing I'd ever have expected. He walked over to me and yanked me into a one-armed hug.

He wasn't Ruin, so it remained just one arm, and it only lasted about two seconds, keeping his manly macho status intact. But I couldn't say Nox had *ever* hugged me before. I blinked at him as he drew back, totally bewildered. Had that been some kind of revenge hug where I would suddenly realize he'd stabbed a knife into my back in the process?

But all my internal organs felt to still be in working order, and Nox was cuffing my shoulder now, not quite hard enough to really hurt.

"That story is so fucking *you*," he said. "Making a masterpiece out of some jerk you ran over. We didn't even have anyone posted keeping watch to catch the pricks. We were all something back then, weren't we? Out of our fucking minds. Kings of Lovell Rise, but that wasn't hard to pull off. This time—this time we're doing it right. We know how to really rule."

It took me a second to reel in my jaw. "You're not pissed?"

"Of course I'm pissed," he said in his usual cocky tone. "But I also know that we've all been idiots plenty of times, and your fuck-up doesn't change the fact that I fucked up too, and—we're here now. We got our second chance. What's the point if we're going to sit around sulking about how we screwed up the first one? We have to make sure we keep *this* one."

I agreed with him, but I couldn't quite believe that I was getting off this easy. I glanced at Kai, whose mouth twisted into a thin smirk.

"I didn't fuck up to that extent," he said. "But I sure as hell wasn't keeping a close enough eye on things back then. And you know what? I like this second chance better than the first one anyway. We've got magic; we've got Lily. We got our revenge tonight. We're going to make this entire goddamn city our masterpiece."

Lily let out a soft laugh under her breath. "I'd like to see that."

So would I. A thrill tingled through me at his words, and suddenly I wanted to hug all of them, which was even more bizarre than Nox getting cuddly. "I guess I should tell Ruin too," I said awkwardly.

Nox waved the suggestion off. "He'll probably be overjoyed to hear it. Tell him whenever you feel like it, but I don't think you need to worry about *his* reaction."

I looked at the guy on the couch, chortling away at the actors on the screen as if his insides weren't currently held together with thread and shoddy surgical magic, and had to admit that our boss was right about that too.

Lily's sister let out a small laugh too, and a hint of a smile crossed Lily's weary face. "I think—" she started.

A frenetic beeping cut her off, emanating from Kai's laptop where he'd left it on the coffee table. He dashed over and snatched it up, flipping it open as he did. His face lit up with what I could only describe as maniacal enthusiasm.

"It's the motion sensors out by the Gauntts' favorite spot in the marsh," he announced, gazing around at the rest of us. "Someone's out there right now."

Chapter Twenty-Three

Lily

At Kai's declaration, my pulse stuttered. I reined myself in. "It could be anyone, couldn't it? A bunch of teenagers partying out by the water or some tramp wandering around."

Kai's eyes gleamed behind his glasses with manic intensity. "Possible, yes. Likely, no. There are a lot of stretches of the marsh that are closer to any given town if a bunch of punks wanted to splash around and throw beer bottles into the reeds. And it's not ideal stomping grounds for someone looking for shelter for the night. And you *did* just bring Nolan Gauntt to his knees."

"I didn't kill him," I said. "I *couldn't.*"

Nox had straightened up with renewed alertness. "You gave him a good punch in the heart, though, didn't you? That has to have left some damage. Maybe they're out there working some magic to heal him up like we did for Ruin."

"They won't do half as good a job as you all did," Ruin informed us with typical cheer, and then winced. He might have been pieced back together, but the pieces weren't exactly in prime condition.

Marisol had turned in her chair, her eyes wide. "If they're out at that spot you think is special, doing some ritual or whatever all they do —does that mean they could mess with my head again? Make me go back to them?"

The quaver that rippled through her voice and the way her knuckles whitened where she clutched the back of the chair brought a lump into my throat that almost choked me.

"No," I reassured her as emphatically as I could, going over to wrap my arm around her shoulder. "I took the mark off you. I broke their hold. They can't get at you again."

Not from afar, anyway. There were physical means a person could use to capture someone, and then who was to say they couldn't mark her all over again? I'd been thirteen when Nolan had done it to me. There might not be any age cut-off at all—they just happened to prefer groping and manipulating kids.

Which was why we couldn't ignore this.

"We should go out there," I said to Nox, my voice coming out quiet and strained. "If he's weak, we should take them down while we have the chance. Or at least we'd get the opportunity to figure out more about their magic so we can get the better of them when we're more equipped to do it." My gaze darted back to my sister. "But I can't leave Marisol."

"If we want a chance of destroying them tonight, we need you there, Siren," Nox said. "You're the one who nearly did him in to begin with. I can punch 'em around a little, but that won't do much if they can deflect actual bullets, and Kai and Jett have to touch 'em to work their powers."

"I'll be here with your sister," Ruin pointed out brightly, as if he was the more capable one between the two of them. If a bunch of bad guys came charging in here, Marisol would have to be the one defending *him*.

"No offense, friend, but I think she could use at least a little backup that can kick butt without tearing themselves open," Kai said matter-of-factly. He turned to Nox. "There were a few of the new recruits who held their own against the Skeleton Corps. We could ask them to play bodyguards. They've passed a bigger test than we could invent on our own."

"If they even want to side with us after that bloodbath," Jett muttered.

Nox huffed. "We did technically win. And there's no reason a sixteen-year-old can't learn how to defend herself damn well too." He nodded to Marisol. "I was fourteen when I first got my hands on a gun. You think you can handle one?"

"Um," I said, feeling like this conversation was spiraling out of control in a direction I'd never have intended, but the eager light that came into my sister's face stopped me. She raised her chin with a more determined expression than I'd ever seen from her.

"Hell, yes," she said. "I want to be able to blast those assholes away if they come after me again."

Well, in that case, who was I to argue? I opened and closed my mouth a few times as if that might jog loose a reasonable objection and settled on staying silent.

As Kai started making calls to the surviving Skullbreakers recruits, Nox strode into the guys' bedroom and came back with another pistol, a smaller one than his usual.

"Here," he said, motioning for Marisol to stand up. She lifted her hands, and he showed her how to grasp the grip.

"Keep your index finger off the trigger unless you're about to shoot," he told her. "It's too easy to squeeze instinctively if you get startled. Since you're a newbie, you'll want to steady it with your other hand. There'll still be pretty bad recoil when you fire it, since you're not used to that. If you need to shoot someone, aim for their chest. You're likely to hit something that'll at least slow them down, and it's harder to miss than trying for a head shot."

Marisol lifted the gun tentatively, pointing it at the bare wall, and practiced steadying it the way he'd shown her. Nox pointed to her feet. "If you have the chance to prepare yourself, it's better if you have one foot a little ahead of the other for balance. And keep your muscles as loose as possible, even if you're scared."

I'd never thought I'd want to see my sister learning how to use a gun. I still wasn't overjoyed that she needed to. But at the same time, watching the Skullbreakers boss coach her with so much confidence in her abilities sent a tingle through me.

I still wasn't totally sure how to explain to her about our odd relationship and how it'd come into being, but it already felt like we were all family.

"You good?" Nox asked, eyeing Marisol. "Ideally, we'd find a place to do some trial shots and all that, but we've got to head out. Tomorrow I can take you through more of the paces."

My sister's expression hardened with even more determination. "I'll do what I have to do. I hope I *do* get the chance to shoot him."

I didn't have to ask who she meant. My throat constricted. As she lowered the gun, I wrapped her in a tight hug. "If I have anything to say about it, no one's going to bother you at all. But don't be afraid to protect yourself if you need to."

She nodded. As I withdrew, Kai was just finishing up one last phone call. "I'm not having anyone come into the apartment," he said. "I'm sure you'd rather not have total strangers hovering around. We've got one guy outside the apartment door, two in the lobby, and two more outside the building, keeping watch. If they see any reason for concern, they'll let us know and take action."

I sucked in a breath. That was about as good as I could hope for. I bent down and gave Ruin a quick but emphatic kiss, trying not to let myself think about the fact that this could be the last time I got to do it. "We're going to give them hell for you."

He grinned back at me. "And plenty for you too. All the hell."

My lips twitched with bittersweet amusement. "All the hell."

There wasn't time for anything else, not if we wanted to have a chance to get to the marsh while the Gauntts were still present. We rushed out of the apartment, where a recruit fearsome-looking enough to reassure me a little was standing in the hall, and dashed down to my car.

Nox still had my keys, and I didn't argue when he got into the driver's seat. I'd imagine he had way more experience at high-speed driving than I did. Kai got into the passenger seat muttering instructions, so Jett and I ended up in the back again.

For all my efforts to keep Ruin's blood inside his body, there were still some damp streaks on the seat. I ended up sitting in the middle to avoid the worst of them, cringing inwardly and sending up another prayer to whatever powers might be that the sweetest of us would make it through tonight all right.

As the car took off down the street, my shoulder jostled against Jett's. I was so used to his previous aversion to physical contact that I tensed up, but a second later, his hand had wrapped around mine.

"We'll get through this," he said quietly, under Nox and Kai's hasty back-and-forth. "If for no other reason than because I had my head up my ass for too long and I haven't gotten anywhere near enough time to enjoy being with you."

The declaration from a guy who was usually so sparing with words made my heart ache in a way I didn't mind at all. My thoughts leapt back to his anguished confession, the guilt he'd obviously been holding on to for so long that explained so much about him I hadn't understood before.

The fact that he'd felt so guilty about it only proved how much he cared for the guys he'd thrown his lot in with. Maybe his brutally artistic outlook wasn't exactly typical or totally sane, but I knew he was there for them and for me in every way that mattered.

I tipped my head against Jett's, breathing in the tart scent of paint that clung to him even after everything we'd been through today, and squeezed his hand. "Good. Because I haven't gotten anywhere near enough of you either."

Of any of them, really. Wouldn't it be something if we could have a week or a month or, hell, a year of normal life as the family I'd gotten a glimpse of back in the apartment?

Relatively normal, of course. The guys were never going to be *normal* normal, and probably I wouldn't either. But something less chaotic and murder-y than this should definitely be possible.

We whipped through the city and out past Lovell Rise, so fast the tires felt as if they'd lifted right off the road at times. There wasn't much traffic this late at night, and once we were out of the city, Nox switched off the headlights to avoid drawing notice. We got out to the fields around the marsh in half the time it should have taken.

As we came closer to the spit where we'd set up the motion detectors, Nox slowed. Kai told him exactly where to stop, where he judged we were still far enough away that anyone at the edge of the water wouldn't be able to hear the engine yet. The road had just about ended anyway. Then we scrambled out and slunk across the fields, squinting through the darkness for any lights or signs of movement.

What if we'd missed them? What if they were already gone, and we'd come out here for nothing? Those questions gripped my chest as we treaded over the matted grass. My heart was thumping so loud I was a little afraid that our targets would hear *that* even if they hadn't picked up on the car.

We were just coming to a patch of trees that hid the last short stretch of dry land before the marsh began when hushed voices reached our ears from up ahead. We hadn't seen any other cars around, and no roads reached this far anyway. Had the Gauntts parked on one of the other lanes a mile or more away and walked the rest of the distance?

We eased to the side so the trees would cover our approach and crept closer. Once we reached the cluster of saplings, we peered between them toward the spit.

We hadn't missed the Gauntts at all. In fact, there were more of them here than I'd expected. Six figures stood out by the far end of the spit, vague in the moonlight. Two of them were clearly children, their frames gawky and their heads only coming up to the shoulders of the taller adults around them.

Whatever the family was up to, it looked like they'd brought Nolan and Marie Junior too.

We weren't close enough for me to make out any of the words they said, but a rapid chorus of murmurs was spilling out into the air with a dissonant rhythm that made the hairs on the back of my arms rise. The largest, broadest figure, whose face I briefly made out as the original Nolan's, had been held up between his wife and his son, his frame sagging. As we watched, they guided him forward… and lowered him down into the shallow water at the edge of the spit.

Chapter Twenty-Four

Lily

NOX GLANCED over at the rest of us, the slivers of moonlight that filtered through the saplings' scrawny branches catching on the whites of his eyes. He widened them as if to say, *What the fuck are they doing?*

Kai spread his hands in a gesture of confusion. I shook my head. Jett shrugged.

Nox frowned and then made a small motion with his hand for us to move closer.

The water lapped around Nolan's body, with a faint splash as he—or his family—pushed him farther into it. We bent down and crawled closer on our hands and knees. The guys might have felt like they were spies or super soldiers carrying out a dangerous mission. *I* felt like I'd been warped back into my childhood games of pretend. The pebbles lodged in the damp ground bit into my skin through my tights. I hiked my dress up so it wouldn't make any noise dragging across the grass.

I was definitely never wearing this outfit again.

We stopped by the cattails that choked the water at the foot of the spit. The Gauntts were still some twenty feet away by its tip, so focused on whatever they were doing with their murmuring and their impromptu bathing session that they hadn't noticed our arrival. We crouched there, peering through the swaying reeds and listening now that their voices had come into sharper focus.

At least they were giving Nolan Senior his bath on the side of the spit closer to us, where we could see reasonably well… even if we had no idea what we were really looking at.

At first, their words sounded as incomprehensible as they had when we'd been farther away. Maybe I hadn't been able to make anything out because they were using another language—or none at all—not because of the distance?

A soft thump near my foot made me flinch, but it was only a frog hopping over to join me. A few more amphibious friends plopped into place around us like some kind of squishy green bodyguards. Somehow I didn't think they'd be much help if the Gauntts discovered us here, but I appreciated the marsh's vote of support all the same.

I leaned closer, straining my ears. Most of the things the Gauntts were saying seemed to be nonsense words, but here and there I caught a few I recognized. Someone said something about "life and death," and someone else talked about "rejuvenating waters." The three adults still on the land started swinging their hands up and down like they were doing the wave at a ballgame.

The posturing looked ridiculous, but it was accomplishing something. A quiver of energy raced through the air, prickling over my skin. It intensified until I could feel it tingling through my body all the way down to my bones.

What the hell were they doing?

Something for Nolan's benefit, presumably. His breath rattled as he lay there, submerged in the murky water with only his face and a sliver of his chest showing. The gasps for air were coming farther apart than when we'd first arrived.

I'd really done a number on him. Unfortunately, it looked like they had some plan for reviving him.

I gritted my teeth and glanced toward my guys. Should we jump in and interrupt, to try to finish what I'd started? The supernatural power resonating through the air made me nervous. I didn't know how the Gauntts might have protected themselves already, how much they might be able to throw at us here.

This time, we didn't have a getaway method right next to us. If we showed our hand at the wrong moment, it could be a death sentence for both us and the people we'd left back home.

Nox caught my gaze and grimaced. He nudged Kai lightly with his shoulder. Kai studied the figures on the spit for several seconds longer and then shook his head.

"We wait," he said under his breath, so soft the words blended into the breeze. I could only hear him because I was so close. "Whatever they're doing, it appears to be taking a lot out of them. When they're leaving, they'll have exhausted all that energy, and we'll be more rested."

His reasoning made sense. Jett inclined his head in agreement, but he'd taken out his gun, resting it in his hand on the muddy ground in front of him. I reached into myself and focused on the hum of energy I could easily provoke with the Gauntts in my sights. I needed to be prepared to go on the attack—or the defensive—in an instant.

The Gauntts clustered closer around this side of the end of the spit. Well, most of them did. The girl stood rigidly in the same place she'd been all along, now a few feet away from the others. The boy, the grownups ushered to the edge of the solid ground and pushed into the water alongside his namesake.

He didn't look as if he went as willingly as his grandfather had. His limbs twitched as the water, which must have been uncomfortably chilly, washed over them, and his head jerked briefly to the side. But the adults kept up their bizarre murmuring, and Olivia—his mother—prodded him farther into the marsh. He bobbed among the reeds, looking as stiff as his sister, just horizontal rather than vertical.

The whole scene had already been creepy, but now a more potent tendril of apprehension coiled around my stomach. Abruptly I was sure that whatever they were going to do, it was going to be more horrible than anything I'd seen from them before.

The three adults still on the land knelt down along the bank of the spit. They lowered their hands into the water on either side of the Nolans' heads, Thomas in the middle between his father and his son,

Olivia at her father's—father in law's?—other side, Marie next to her grandson. A tremor ran through their hunched bodies.

They kept murmuring, scooping water with their hands and pouring it over the mostly-submerged figures. The vibration of ominous energy in the air thickened even more. I sucked my lower lip under my teeth and nearly bit right through it.

I wanted to reach out to the water of the marsh and tell it to stop this. To ignore whatever they were calling on it to do. But I knew how to bend it to my will, not how to convince it to shun anyone else. And the Gauntts knew about my watery powers. The second I tossed a wave or a torrent at them, they'd know I was here.

They were pouring marsh water over the Nolans' faces now. Nolan Senior made no sound other than a faint hitch of his ragged breath. Nolan Junior briefly sputtered and squirmed. My legs ached to run in there and drag him out of the marsh—but then I'd be trading his comfort for my life and my men's and even my sister's. I clenched my hands, my fingernails digging into my palms.

All at once, Thomas and Olivia shoved down on the older man. He plunged right under the water, probably all the way to the shallow bottom. As I clamped my mouth shut around a gasp, their voices rose louder, with more recognizable words tangled between the unfamiliar ones.

"Stream like a current… from one source to another… like silt and flesh… Rise up and take hold."

Thomas reached toward Nolan Junior at the same moment that Marie did. They yanked the boy's body overtop of his grandfather, who was still fully submerged. Bubbles of breath were popping on the surface of the water.

Were they going to *drown* Nolan Senior? What the fuck?

But something in me already knew it wasn't that simple. The supernatural power in the air surged over us, and my skin crawled with horror I couldn't totally explain. I braced myself, my nerves jangling with the sense that any second now I'd need to fight for my life.

It wasn't my life on the line, though. All three of the adult Gauntts gave another shove and pushed both Nolans beneath the surface. They held them there, their voices rising and falling in a high-pitched wail that had no words at all.

Jett shuddered next to me. Nox let out a near-silent curse. Then, just when I'd have imagined even the boy was turning blue and sucking water into his lungs, they tugged him up again.

They brought out only him, hauling him to his feet with much more gentleness than they'd displayed when sending him into the water, and helped him take wobbling steps onto the spit's higher ground. Nolan Senior didn't surface. As the other adults huddled around his grandson, it seemed as if they'd forgotten the patriarch altogether.

They'd stopped their wailing and their murmuring. There was a flurry of toweling off and the draping of a blanket I hadn't noticed they'd brought with them around the boy's shoulders. Marie touched the boy's cheek in an affectionate gesture that felt somehow not quite right from a woman to her grandson. But it was Thomas who spoke first.

"All okay in there, pops?" he said with a laugh as if he'd made a hilarious joke. Which he should have been making, talking like that to his own son.

But Nolan Junior tugged the blanket tighter around him and raised his chin at a haughty angle that looked far too familiar. Recognition clanged through me like an alarm bell before he even opened his mouth.

"It's unfortunate we had to make the transfer this early. It'll be half a decade before you can even justify having me in the office in any capacity." He shook his head with a tut of his tongue that sounded far too mature for his apparent age and glanced toward the water. "But good riddance to that failing body. You did well, getting me out here this quickly. I wouldn't have held out much longer. That witchy *bitch*."

The last words came out in a snarl. He was referring to me, I realized, and the attack I'd made on him, but that revelation was only a whisper beneath the deluge of horrified understanding washing over me.

Nolan Gauntt had been dying—because of me. So his family had brought him out here… to push his soul into his grandson's body, just as my guys had stolen new bodies of their own.

And not only that, they must have *always* been planning on using the boy that way. Nolan had said they'd made the transfer 'early,' as if it'd been scheduled for some later date. Holy fucking hell.

Shock rolled over me in waves. I was reeling so hard, the other possible implications rushing through my mind in a jumble, that I didn't notice that the Gauntts were now marching toward the foot of the spit until their feet rasped over the matted grass just a few paces away from us.

They might have walked right past us in the shadows, never knowing we were there. But we'd decided to wait until they left, not to back down completely. And the Skullbreakers must have been disturbed by what they'd seen too.

The guys leapt to their feet around me, their faces twisted with revulsion, and lunged at the Gauntts as one being.

Chapter Twenty-Five

Lily

A CRY STUCK in my throat. I sprang up in the wake of the guys' charge, not sure if they'd assumed I'd be right there with them, not even knowing who I'd want to aim my powers at now. Should I try to rip Nolan's new heart away from him in that child's body? But what if the child's soul hadn't quite been smothered, and there was still some way to bring Nolan Junior back? Who was the worst of the remaining adults—Marie or the parents who'd willingly sacrificed their son?

The frogs surged forward with me—dozens more than I'd realized had slipped out of the marsh to join us. The soft thunder of their hops bolstered my resolve. As the Gauntts spun around, I fixed my gaze on Marie. I knew for sure that she'd not only been instrumental in the spell tonight but also in molesting so many other kids. With a hiss through my teeth, I hurled all the energy I'd recovered since the last fight toward the thrum of her pulse.

But it didn't reach her. The Gauntts threw up their arms defensively with a crackle of energy whipping through the air. They must have conjured a broader, thicker wall of defense than they had against Nox's bullet before. The ones Jett fired now ricocheted off that section of air in rapid succession.

Kai and Nox slammed into the barrier and stumbled backward before their magic could affect our enemies. And all sense of Marie's blood snuffed out as my magic crashed into that wall and disintegrated.

The Gauntts drew closer together, backing away from us at the same time. The guys continued battering their magical shield every way they could, and I summoned a wave out of the lake to pummel them from above. At the sound of the roaring water, Thomas jerked his hands upward, and the wave splattered into another barrier above them.

The frogs flung themselves at the invisible wall too, with a chorus of hoarse croaks. Nolan—who had been Junior and now was Senior in essence?—eyed them and broke his taut expression just long enough to sputter a laugh.

"This is your army?" he sneered in a tone that sounded way too old for the childish voice that carried it. "Pathetic. We've been in charge here since before any of you were even *born*, and we'll still be long after you're dead."

"Fat chance," Nox snarled, and battered the transparent shield with his fists and the power he could drive from them. Dull thuds reverberated through the air.

We weren't going to break through it. I felt that in the weariness that gripped my lungs as I hurled as much of my own remaining power at the barrier as I could.

We'd already been weakened by two previous fights tonight. But the Gauntts were worn down from their soul transfer ritual too. With both of us exhausted, it didn't seem like either of us could overcome the other. They hadn't managed to do anything except fend us off.

Which meant that if we could catch them another time when they were weakened but we had our full strength, we should be able to crush them.

I clung on to that shred of hope and the thought of Marisol and Ruin back at the apartment, waiting for us. The longer the Gauntts kept us busy here, the more time there was for their lackeys to go after the most vulnerable members of our group.

"Let them go," I said to the guys with as much disdain as I could will into my voice. "We'll take care of them later." Maybe we'd even get a chance to do it right now after all if they let down their guards when we stopped our attacks.

Nox growled in defiance, but he stepped back half a pace, glaring at the Gauntts. Kai adjusted his glasses and nodded, easing farther back to flank me as Jett did the same. We watched the perverted supernatural family warily, braced to resume the fight at the first sign of trouble.

Nolan laughed again, and Marie squeezed his shoulder. A thread of nausea trickled through my stomach at a sudden thought. How many times had they done this before?

How many times had they shoved their souls into bodies that weren't theirs? How young had their previous hosts been? Melding their grown-up minds with the bodies of children… Was the blurring of the lines between child and adult what had warped their desires into something so disturbed when it came to other kids?

The possibility didn't make their behavior any less sickening. If anything, it was doubly horrifying that their awful ritual might have created something even more awful inside them, spreading the damage they did with their monstrous perversions all through the community around them.

I'd only had time to shudder at the thought when Nolan leapt forward with his arm stretching upward.

With a snapped word, he bounded off the ground and rammed his palm into Nox's face where the Skullbreakers boss was standing just a couple of steps ahead of the rest of us. We sprang at him, magic whining through the air, but Nolan already wrenched himself back to the safety of the shell that protected the entire family.

Nox fell. He crumpled like a rag doll, his legs giving out under him, his head lolling backward. He'd have smacked his skull on the muddy ground if Jett and I hadn't caught him.

His eyelids dropped shut. His mouth gaped open. And his skin shone deathly pale around a nickel-sized blotch like a birthmark that now stained the middle of his forehead.

No! Every particle in my body screamed in refusal. First Ruin and now him?

"What the fuck did you do?" I shrieked, launching myself at the Gauntts again with a rush of panicked fury. I propelled my magic at them, groping for even one thread of blood I could sense through the barrier and throttle someone's heart with.

I felt their shield waver and maybe even crack—but then they were chanting again, hustling away from us. Nolan's mouth set in a creepy childish smirk.

I hesitated between charging after them and trying to help Nox, but my own legs felt ready to give beneath me. I sank down next to the Skullbreakers boss, staring at Kai, who'd dropped to his knees too. He was patting the larger guy's face with increasing urgency. Nox's muscles didn't so much as twitch.

The question wrenched of me. "Is he *dead*?"

Kai looked up at me with haunted eyes. "I don't know."

Deathly Delinquency

GANG OF GHOULS #4

Chapter One

Lily

It took all three of us to haul Nox back to my car, and then only with the help of the emergency blanket I kept in Fred 2.0's trunk. After it'd become clear that no amount of hefting and hauling between Jett, Kai, and me could budge the Skullbreakers boss's massive frame more than a few inches across the matted grass by the marsh, I'd gone running back for it.

We'd shifted him onto the blanket with a lot of heaving and tugging. Now Kai and Jett were dragging him along by the upper corners, kicking rocks out of their way so he didn't have to jostle over them, while I held up the back end in an effort to stop him from sliding off.

A procession of frogs hopped along on either side of us, croaking like it was a funeral march. My stomach twisted tighter with every step. I wanted to tell the little creatures to scram, but they were here because of me. I was lucky the tension roiling through my body hadn't summoned half the lake to pour down on our heads.

Actually, it wasn't luck. It was the fact that I'd run the supernatural energies in me nearly dry in the past several hours. That was why we were moving Nox rather than seeing if there was anything we could do to help him where he'd fallen.

The Gauntts had fled, but that didn't mean they wouldn't send their lackeys to try to finish the job they'd started.

They *hadn't* finished. I had to take a little comfort in that fact. Nox looked dead to the world: his eyes shut, his jaw slack, and his face waxy pale other than the small blotch in the middle of his forehead where Nolan Gauntt had smacked him. But every now and then, his chest lifted with a breath. We'd been able to feel a sluggish but steady pulse when we'd checked his neck.

He was alive, on the most fundamental level. He just wasn't exactly *with* us. And we had no idea what precisely Nolan had done to him. The effects of this mark were clearly different from the ones that had blocked off memories in the heads of the young victims he and his wife—and possibly the younger generation of Gauntts as well—had used for their sick purposes.

It was a good thing we hadn't come on the guys' bikes. I wouldn't have had the blanket, and there'd have been no way to stick Nox on one of the motorcycles to drive him home. I pictured us struggling to get him balanced on the seat while he teetered this way and that, like a scene in a slapstick comedy, but couldn't summon any amusement at the idea.

It might have been easier if Ruin had been here. He knew how to put a positive spin on almost any situation. But he was back at the apartment healing from the brutal gunshot he'd taken earlier this evening. I didn't know when he'd even be able to walk around with full exuberance again.

That was two of my men down in different ways in the course of one night. How much longer would we have before the Gauntts came for the rest of us, especially now that we knew their darkest secret?

At least, I sure as hell hoped they didn't have any secrets darker than what we'd just discovered. Adopting kids so you could murder them and take over their bodies when you got old or ill was pitch-black already.

Once we made it to Fred 2.0, it took a lot of maneuvering to get Nox actually inside. We basically snake-slithered him onto the back seat, first sitting him against the car, then easing him up over the side of the seat. The whole time, his brawny body stayed slack. His breath didn't so much as stutter. His eyelids didn't give the slightest twitch.

Once he was inside, we stopped for a moment, staring at him and catching our breaths from the exertion of moving him there.

"We'll figure it out," Kai said, but his voice didn't hold half its usual know-it-all confidence.

"Let's get him home," Jett said gruffly.

Kai opted to drive, fishing the keys out of Nox's pocket, where the boss had stuck them after racing us out here. Since Nox had taken over the entire back, I sat on Jett's lap in the front passenger seat.

Another time, cozying up to him might have made for an enjoyable trip. After what we'd just experienced, I was simply glad that he'd gotten over his awkwardness around being physically close with me. That meant I could tuck my head against his neck and lean into the warmth of his embrace, and he hugged me to him without hesitation. Breathing in his familiar scent with its lingering tang of paint soothed my nerves just a little alongside the thrum of the engine.

When I closed my eyes, images from the bizarre watery ritual we'd witnessed rose up from the depths of my mind, like a body floating to the surface. Which seemed appropriate, given that those memories involved more than one body being shoved into the marsh's water. Only one had emerged.

Both Nolan Senior and his ten-year-old grandson, Nolan Junior, had gone into the water. In theory, it'd been Junior who'd come out. But his comments afterward had made it clear that the elder had possessed the younger.

The way Nolan talked about the ritual, his frustration that they'd had to conduct the transfer "early," held other implications. We'd forced his hand when I'd damaged his heart by using my watery magic to manipulate his blood, but they'd already been prepared. They'd already *had* a ritual.

"This wasn't the first time they've transferred a soul over like that," I said abruptly, opening my eyes to peer at the darkness beyond the windshield.

Kai nodded. "Definitely not. They gave every appearance of being fully comfortable with the proceedings and sure of the outcome."

The nausea that'd briefly eased off flooded my gut again. "How many times do you think they've done it?" How many bodies had the Gauntts taken over before?

He shrugged. "There's no way of knowing. At least a few times, I'd guess. I'll see what I can find out about the history of the family when I'm back at work on Monday."

Right. He'd have to return to the lion's den. The job he'd charmed his way into at Thrivewell Enterprises, the Gauntts' immense corporation, seemed like more of a liability than a benefit now.

"How can you go back?" I asked. "They saw you tonight."

"This is the first time they've ever seen me. It's not like they come down from the tip of their tower very often. The most they could know about their new employee is my name, which we didn't give them out at the marsh. Even if one of them happens to cross paths with me at the office, I doubt they'd connect me to a face they saw only in the darkness while emotions were running high."

I frowned at him. "You can't be sure of that."

"I'm sure enough to think it'd be silly not to take advantage of my position there while I still can," Kai said matter-of-factly.

Jett rubbed his hand up and down my arm before giving me a gentle squeeze. "We've got to get at them somehow. They'll be gunning for us even more now. And the girl…"

I tipped my head to glance up at him. "The girl? *Oh.*"

Nolan and Marie Senior had two grandchildren—the son Nolan had taken over, and the slightly younger daughter…

"She's meant for Marie," Jett filled in as the same conclusion hit me.

Kai clicked his tongue. "I think that goes without saying. They must have adopted the two kids for the primary purpose of having younger vehicles for the older generation as their bodies failed. It's a sound strategy… if you're looking at it from the perspective of a total sociopath who doesn't care about any life other than their own."

He and my other guys had come back to life in a similar way. But they'd stolen the bodies of four vindictive assholes at my college rather than kids, and they'd done it not for themselves but to protect me. Which I guessed made them partial sociopaths rather than total ones?

In any case, it seemed pretty obvious that Team Not Murdering Children had the moral high ground.

"We already knew that the Gauntts are deranged psychos," I muttered. They certainly didn't give a shit about *our* lives, or my sister's, or any of the kids they'd molested over the years.

We still didn't know for sure why they messed around with any of those kids in the first place. From the descriptions we'd gotten, it sounded like it was about more than perverted gratification. Their victims had mentioned times when they'd felt strange energy passing through them—or out of them. Was that how the Gauntts fueled their awful magic?

I pressed my hand to my forehead, but the contact didn't push my thoughts into any better order.

"There were a few things that went right tonight," Jett pointed out, the glass-half-full approach so unnatural on him that his voice came out stiff. He was trying his best to fill in for Ruin, I suspected mostly for my benefit. "We slaughtered a shitload of Skeleton Corps pricks, including the assholes who slaughtered *us*. Which also means fewer foot soldiers on the Gauntts' payroll. And we put the Gauntts themselves at a bit of a disadvantage."

Kai hummed to himself. "Yes, Nolan won't be able to command the same kind of authority while he has to pretend he's as young as his current body looks. The family will have trouble even bringing him into the office, since he's much too young to plausibly intern—or be taken out of school for that matter."

"That's why he was pissed off about the timing," I said. It was hard to feel like I'd scored much of a victory, though, when that victory had resulted in the death of a kid. I'd wanted to *save* any more kids from being tormented by the Gauntts, and instead my actions had led to one losing his life completely.

A particularly determined frog had hitched a ride with us. It chose that moment to hop up onto my knee. I gave its sleek back a careful pet, wondering if it wouldn't have been safer staying back at the marsh too.

When we reached my apartment building in Mayfield, I was relieved to see that the Skullbreakers recruits were still standing guard in the shadows off to the sides of the entrance. There hadn't been any attack on this place. Which made sense, considering that we had struck a major blow against the Skeleton Corps gang this evening.

They were probably still licking their wounds. It'd become clear tonight that for decades, the Gauntts had been paying off the gang with favors to do some of their dirty work. Maybe the Corps would reconsider their association with the family now.

A girl could dream.

After Kai parked Fred 2.0, we realized we now had the problem of getting Nox's substantial frame up two flights of stairs to the third floor. Since thumping him across the steps one at a time on the blanket didn't seem like a great strategy for his continuing health, whatever was left of it, we ended up calling over a couple of the recruits who'd been staked out inside the building. Between the five of us, we managed to cart the boss up the stairs holding the blanket like a makeshift stretcher, with a lot of huffing and puffing.

As we carried Nox into the apartment, Ruin sat up a little straighter where he'd been recovering on the couch. "Lie back down!" I hissed. The last thing I needed was to see him at death's door again too.

He sank down like I'd asked but craned his neck to continue peering at us. "What happened to Nox?" he asked, his brow furrowing. I guessed even he couldn't come up with a cheerful way of looking at this situation.

He kept his voice low like I had, and my sister's bedroom door was closed. I hoped Marisol had finally managed to get some sleep.

"The Gauntts happened," Jett said darkly.

"I'll fill you in on everything," Kai added. "It's been a wild night."

We lay Nox down on the floor between the dining table and the couch. His chest rose and fell at that moment, confirming that his body was still performing the basic tasks of life. Small wins.

As the recruits tramped back out again, I knelt by Nox's head. "I'll see if I can figure out what magic Nolan put on him—and if I can break it like the other marks."

Kai inclined his head, nudged his glasses up his nose, and went to give Ruin the full low-down. Jett grabbed a cola from the fridge and started chugging it.

I brushed aside Nox's red-tipped black hair where it'd drooped across his forehead and focused on the mark, tuning out Ruin's startled noises of excitement and consternation in response to Kai's story. The hum of my powers reverberated through my chest and out into my limbs. I rested my fingers over the mark and closed my eyes.

I *could* sense a barrier inside Nox's head, one that didn't feel terribly different from the kind that had locked away my and the other victims' memories of the ways the Gauntts had manipulated them. This one was larger, though, and… heavier somehow, as if a globe of thick glass had encased Nox's entire brain. My sense of it sent a shiver down my spine.

What would happen if I broke *this* spell? Shattering the others hadn't caused any ill effects other than the trauma that came from the recovered memories, so after a moment's debate, I decided I should at least try. It wasn't as if Nox could end up in a state much worse than the one he was currently in.

Drumming the fingers of my other hand on the wooden floorboards, I roused more of the energy inside me, as much as I'd recovered during the relative rest of our drive home. Picturing it condensing into a shape like an ice pick, I rammed the supernatural power at the wall around Nox's mind.

It ricocheted off, making the hum of energy inside me quiver erratically. My nerves jangled. I inhaled deeply and tried again.

I flung my magic at Nolan's spell over and over until sweat was trickling down my back and a headache expanding through my skill. Then I sat back on my heels. I had no impression of the barrier being affected, not the slightest crack. Was I just too weakened still, or was this spell that much more powerful?

I rubbed my forehead and realized Kai and Jett had come over to stand near me. I looked up at them, a lump clogging my throat.

"The spell's wrapped right around his whole mind," I said. "I can't make a dent in it. Maybe tomorrow after I've gotten more rest, I'll be able to shatter it."

Jett swiped his hand through his rumpled purple hair and grumbled a curse. Kai bent down next to Nox and studied his prone body. His mouth slanted into a deeper frown.

"Nolan knew what he was doing," he said. "If he'd killed this body, there'd be a decent chance Nox's spirit could have leapt free and we could have gotten him into another one. This is worse than death. He's trapped inside."

"Could *we* do the killing?" Ruin suggested in a tone that was weirdly hopeful considering he was suggesting murdering his best friend.

I hugged myself. "We don't know for sure that he *would* be able to possess anyone else the way he did before."

"And we don't know that even death would free his spirit now," Kai added. "This spell might seal his spirit inside no matter what happens to the body."

Just when I thought the outlook couldn't get worse. I swallowed hard. "All right. Then we've got two things to get to work on. One, figure out a way to break the spell. And two, destroy the Gauntts for good so they can never do anything like this again."

Too bad accomplishing either of those goals wasn't going to be anywhere near as easy as saying them.

Kai

BEHIND MY PLACIDLY FRIENDLY expression as I walked into the Thrivewell building, I stayed sharply alert to the reactions of every employee I passed. Even people talented at holding their cards close couldn't hide their emotions completely, and I highly doubted that the Gauntts had managed to staff their entire corporate headquarters with Oscar-caliber actors.

Nothing I saw gave me so much as a prickle of concern. Some people ambled by without more than a passing glance at me, not a hint of recognition crossing their faces. Others offered a casual tip of the head or a brief smile. The only employees who looked tense were those who were already hustling around when I walked by. They didn't seem to even notice my existence, they were so wrapped up in their own business.

By all available evidence, our stand-off with the Gauntts last night hadn't resulted in a bounty on my head. The family of psychotic pricks was probably too busy figuring out how to handle the fact that one half of their company's leadership now appeared to be elementary-school age to start speculating about mutinous sharks in their work pool.

By the time I'd reached my desk, I'd downgraded from high alert to understated wariness. I was going to continue keeping a close eye out for any signs of suspicion or concern, of course, but I had other goals to fulfill here that meant I needed to stick out my neck a little.

One of the guys who sat near me, Mike Philmore, had taken something of a liking to me ever since I'd shown mild support of his crush on Ms. Townsend, the secretary to the higher admin assistants. It made sense to start with him. After clattering away on my keyboard for a little while to give the impression of dutiful dedication to my work, I ambled over to the break room just as he happened to be grabbing a coffee.

"Mike," I said in a friendly tone, raising the empty cup I picked up toward him as if in a toast.

"Zach," he replied with a nod and a grin. I'd given the company the name of my host, since that was conveniently on my existing ID. It hadn't been hard to fudge the birthdate a little so I appeared to be the right age for my made-up employment experience.

As I filled my own cup, I kept my tone warmly conversational, as if I were just shooting the breeze but with a little more trust than I might have shown the average colleague. People liked feeling trusted. It made them want to prove how much they deserved it. "You've been at Thrivewell for a while, haven't you?"

Philmore cocked his head. "I'd say so. Coming up on five years now. Started out six floors down. We'll see if I ever make it any higher than this." He let out a self-deprecating chuckle that I could tell was designed to hide the fact that he really did hope to be making his way into the uppermost ranks eventually.

I chuckled back in solidarity. "Lots more years to accomplish that in. And when the company has been around so long, you know this place isn't going anywhere. More than a century since founding! Pretty impressive. Did you ever hear any interesting stories about the history? Hard to imagine what it takes to keep a business going this strong for all that time."

Philmore hummed to himself. "I know they had a big bash for the hundredth anniversary, but that was a little before my time. I get the impression a lot of their success comes from keeping it in the family. It's been Gauntts since the beginning as far as I know."

"Lucky for anyone born into the family, then," I said. "I wonder what the next generation has in store."

"Yeah." Philmore's brow creased momentarily. "I'm not even sure if there is a next generation yet. Guess that makes sense. The big bosses wouldn't have *that* much of their family time at the office."

Then one of our colleagues motioned him away to help with a file, but that was all right. It hadn't sounded like the guy knew much of anything about the Gauntts' personal history anyway.

Of course they wouldn't parade the kids around the office. If the plan was for Marie Senior to take over her granddaughter's body eventually, they'd probably want as few people as possible thinking about the fact that the power couple she and her supposed adoptive brother would make down the road had once been siblings. There was no blood relation, but it was still creepy as hell.

Could they even get legally married in their new personas? Maybe Thomas and Olivia would un-adopt one of them somehow to make that possible? Or it could be they'd never fully legally adopted one or both in the first place. You could get away with a lot of fudging of proper procedure when you had as much money and reach as the Gauntts did. One of them could be listed as a foster sibling or similar without the same permanent implications.

After puzzling over that conundrum for a few minutes, I decided I was spending too much time worrying about our enemies' marital prospects and went back to my desk. If we got our way, they'd be dead long before they had to worry about getting re-hitched.

Throughout the morning, I found opportunities to chat up a few other coworkers, but none of them were much more helpful than Philmore had been. No gossip about our head honchos' pasts or ancestry appeared to have circulated through the office in recent years, and no one could point me to anyone who might have some dirt, not even Molly from accounting, whose eyes lit up with a manic gleam at any mention of drama.

At the start of my lunch break, I meandered over to Ms.

Townsend's desk to approach my quest from a different angle. She was the most professionally in-the-know person out of all the colleagues I had access to, and I'd already established a good rapport with her. All it took was a couple of subtle compliments and expressing enthusiasm about growing my understanding of the company so I could serve it better, and she coughed up the location of an archives room in the basement where I could do a little digging into Thrivewell's history.

"Thanks," I said, flashing her a smile, and headed straight to the elevator.

My body still hadn't totally adjusted to the whole possession-by-ghostly-energies thing, so it was a good thing I'd stuffed a good assortment of snacks in my satchel. I chowed through them to stave off the grumbling of my stomach as I peered at faded labels and sorted through dusty boxes.

The dustiest ones, naturally, were from the longest ago. After a half hour's excavation, I unearthed a trove of newspaper clippings and press releases from the 1960s. Sitting down on the floor cross-legged, I pawed through them for any mention of the Gauntts.

There, in an article about a big donation the CEOs had made to a food bank organization. Partway down the page, I found a reference to "Nolan and Marie Gauntt, their son Thomas, and his wife Olivia." Just like that, as if it'd been written today.

But the Nolan and Marie Senior *we'd* tangled with couldn't have been more than young kids back in 1964. The Thomas and Olivia who were currently in their thirties would have barely been a figment of anyone's imagination. A sense of dread crept up through my chest. Just how far back did this go?

I dug farther, faster, knowing I was running down the clock. I could get away with failing to be seen at my desk for a little while after my break was technically over, but I didn't want to draw unnecessary attention. The archives room would still be here tomorrow… but now that the mystery was unraveling in my hands, I was chomping at the bit to chase it to its end.

There were a few more references to the Nolan and Marie of the 1960s in earlier files going back a couple of decades before then. Interestingly, the articles from longer ago didn't mention their supposed son and his wife at all, or any earlier generations either. It appeared that the Gauntts were very good at keeping the news focused on only one generation at a time, two at the most.

Which was presumably for strategic reasons, because when I got to the increasingly fragile papers left over from the 1930s, there were a few references to Nolan and Marie taking charge of the company… after the company's founders—Nolan's parents, Thomas and Olivia—had passed on, one within months of the other.

There wasn't much at all from farther back than that. I hauled out the last few boxes, sneezing at the copious clouds of dust, and found only sparse, scattered references to the company around its founding in 1912 by Thomas and Olivia Gauntt. So they'd been the first. It was all Thomases and Olivias, Nolans and Maries, back to the very first generation.

If I was adding things up correctly going by ages, that made for three of each. The current Thomas and Olivia and the current Nolan and Marie Junior were the third of their names in the family.

Were the current Thomas and Olivia the spirits of the very first of their namesakes, born well over a hundred years ago? Or had they initially only been passing on the names as part of a more typical family legacy, and the spooky supernatural aspect had only come into it later?

There'd definitely been something hinky going on by the 1960s, when the second Thomas Gauntt had ended up married to a woman who just happened to have the same name as his theoretical grandmother.

It would have been a little much to expect anything in the business archives to shed light on the paranormal aspects of the Gauntts' life. At least I'd come away with more information than I'd started with.

I snapped photos of all the key articles, making sure the sources were clear in case we wanted to track down other copies later, and put the boxes back in as close to the right order as I could remember. I couldn't replace the dust, so I took a rag I found in the corner and swiped it over a bunch of the lids so it wasn't obvious which ones I'd focused on if anyone came poking around not long after me. Then I headed back to my cubicle upstairs, my mind already spinning through the possibilities of how we could pry even deeper into the Gauntts' personal affairs.

We needed to know how they'd developed their spiritual powers and what those powers involved—the full extent, both so we could narrow down what might be afflicting Nox and be prepared for whatever they might throw at us next. Would the older generations have kept any sort of written record in case the transfers didn't leave all their memories intact? We hadn't found anything like that in their house, but with the amount of wealth the Gauntts had accumulated, they had to own multiple properties.

I was just stepping off the elevator on the fifteenth floor when a short, plump woman bustled over to me looking very stern.

"Mr. Oberly," she said. "Marie Gauntt would like a word with you. You're to proceed to her office on the top floor. Ms. Townsend is waiting to allow you elevator access."

As prepared as I liked to be for every eventuality, I hadn't been anticipating this request at all. My pulse hiccupped, but I had enough self-control to compose my expression into a mild smile. "Of course. Let me just collect the reports for that meeting from my desk and I'll be right up. Thank you."

My unfazed reaction seemed to reassure the messenger, as I'd intended. She swept off to see to some other business, and I wove through the cubicles toward mine—and then doubled back as soon as I was out of both her and Ms. Townsend's line of sight. I ducked into the stairwell and headed downstairs at a brisk but not panicked pace.

When you panicked, you made stupid mistakes.

Marie Gauntt wanted to see me—now, after I'd been working at Thrivewell for weeks without any interest from the top brass, only twelve hours after I'd witnessed some of her most questionable supernatural practices. The chances of the summons being a coincidence were nil. My best guess was that someone had made an offhand remark about my interest in company history that'd gotten back to her, she'd looked up my file, and somehow she'd put together the pieces.

Maybe she'd simply noticed that Lily and I had interviewed for our jobs there at the exact same time. She might not *know* anything, only want to verify her instincts. I'd rather not give her the opportunity to do it.

I'd milked my time at Thrivewell for everything it was worth anyway. If Marie wanted to stop me from uncovering the dirt buried here, she was too late.

In the front lobby, I sauntered toward the front of the building at a leisurely pace, peering through the broad windows. It only took a few seconds to pick out a couple of figures outside that I recognized from our recent dealings with the Skeleton Corps, loitering on the sidewalk. No doubt there were more gang members I couldn't see positioned farther from the entrance.

Yes, Marie had definitely caught on that *something* was rotten in the state of Thrivewell, and she was pulling out all the stops to contain the problem.

Too bad for her that this once I'd stayed one step ahead of her. I looped around through the main floor, slipped out through the rear delivery entrance, and hopped into the back of a mail truck while the delivery guy was carting a large package over to the building. I let the truck carry me several minutes away from Thrivewell, and then scrambled back out during another delivery stop, well away from any prying Corps eyes.

If they were after me at work, they'd come at us on our home turf soon enough. I flagged down a cab and sent the driver speeding toward Lily's apartment as fast as I could convince him to go.

Chapter Three

Lily

"Is he going to be okay?" Marisol asked, peering down at Nox with her forehead furrowing.

It was a fair question, considering I'd been asking the same thing since the Skullbreakers boss had fallen into his coma. And considering he looked half-dead already. And also considering that his condition had left him so continually immobile that we'd set him up on a bed made up of a couple of blankets and a pillow on top of a shipping trolley one of the recruits had brought around for us.

It looked odd, but it did make it easier to move Nox's brawny body around the apartment as need be without worrying about hurting him more with our efforts at dragging.

Fitting him onto the wheeled platform had required lying him on his side with his legs folded in and his head ducked down. His sneakered feet still dangled over the end of the trolley. Lying unconscious people on their side was a good thing, though, right? Or was that only in cases of inebriation?

Well, there was no way of knowing how Nolan's spell would affect

Nox in the long run. I'd count his pose as a better safe than sorry approach too.

"We don't know," I admitted to my sister, the knot in my stomach tightening with the words. "We're doing everything we can to snap him out of the spell, but we don't really understand what the Gauntts did to him."

Marisol rubbed her temples. "I wish I could remember more from when they called me away from you. It's all so blurry. I remember eating pancakes with you and then running with you to the car at that farm, but everything in between is just bits and pieces… It's like trying to sort out the details of a dream I had a month ago."

I gave her arm my best reassuring squeeze. "It's okay. It sounds like you weren't around the Gauntts much if at all anyway, only the gang they're paying off, so there probably isn't anything to remember that would make a difference."

"I just wish I could help him. I know you care about him. And he obviously cares about you. He helped *me* when I needed it." Her hand dropped to the small pistol she'd been carrying with her everywhere in the pocket of her hoodie. Nox had given it to her and taught her the basics of how to shoot it so that she could defend herself if trouble came when the rest of us weren't around.

Crazy as it might sound, that'd been the first time I'd really felt like we could all be a family together. A bizarre and chaotic family, but one I'd take over what Marisol and I'd had with Mom and Wade any day.

I didn't know if we could get back to that without Nox ruling over the Skullbreakers and offering his fiercely cocky version of protectiveness.

"I'm sure he'd appreciate that sentiment," I said. "But really, I don't want you going out of your way to get even more mixed up in all this —the Gauntts' powers and gang wars and everything else." I bit my lip. "I wish there was somewhere I knew was safe where you could hole up until we figure things out."

My sister shook her head vehemently before I could go on. "No. I don't want to hide. I just spent days forced into hiding away from you. There's got to be some way I can help in this whole situation. I want to be part of it. I want to hit back at those assholes."

A little shudder traveled through her body, but her eyes flared with determination as fierce as anything I'd seen from Nox. We hadn't talked in detail about the things she'd remembered about the more distant past, the ways the Gauntts had used her, but from talking to their other victims, I knew it couldn't be pleasant. I wasn't going to force her to dredge up those awful memories before she was ready.

I understood her vehemence—it resonated with my own resolve to take down the psychotic dickwads who'd gotten me consigned to the looney bin for seven years, molested and manipulated my little sister, nearly killed two of my guys, and wreaked who knew how much other havoc. But part of my own resolve was wanting to protect her.

I had to grapple with the words before I said, "I get that. And however you can be a part of it, I'll let you. Just… let me and the guys take the lead, okay?"

Marisol's mouth twisted, but she nodded. I was about to ask her if she wanted me to make her a late lunch from the limited supplies in the kitchen when Kai burst into the apartment with an unusual air of urgency whirling around him.

He flicked his dark brown hair away from his glasses and peered around the room with more typical analytical precision. I paused, my hand coming to rest on my sister's shoulder. "What's going on? Did something happen at work?" It must have, mustn't it, for him to be home this early?

Kai inclined his head with a jerk and motioned to Jett, who'd come out of the guys' bedroom at his arrival. "Pack up. I think we should get out of here, at least for now. The Gauntts know something is up with me, and they had Skeleton Corps guys staked out around the Thrivewell building. I'll be surprised if they don't come at us again here soon, especially when they know at least one of us is down for the count."

His gaze dropped to Nox, and his mouth tightened. Then he marched over to the dining table to grab the laptop he'd left there.

My heart started thumping faster. I hustled Marisol over to her bedroom, where she'd only just started unpacking the suitcase she'd brought from our childhood home. I hurried into my own bedroom to grab everything I couldn't bear to leave behind, leaving the door open so I could still talk to the others.

"Where are we going to go?" I asked.

Ruin's voice wavered up sleepily from where he'd been dozing on the sofa. "Go? Are we taking a trip?"

"Something like that," Kai said grimly. "You keep resting for now. I'll pack your stuff too—lots of snacks—and we'll help you down to the car. I don't think you should be trying to balance on a bike just yet."

Ruin let out a little huff. "It's my insides that fell apart. The rest of me is fine."

"Your outsides do affect the insides, you know," Jett muttered, emerging with a duffel bag slung over his shoulder. "We can't go to the clubhouse. They know about that place too."

"They do." Kai let out an exasperated sigh. "And Lily's car isn't really big enough for all six of us, especially with Nox in his current state. I suppose we could squeeze him into the trunk…"

I grimaced. "We're not making anyone ride in the trunk, regardless of level of consciousness. Don't you guys have your cars from your hosts?"

"I think they're all back in Lovell Rise since we switched to two-wheeled travel." Kai paused and hummed to himself as he grabbed Ruin's medicine and several packs of beef jerky from the kitchen. "Lily, Marisol, and our invalids can squeeze into the car. Jett and I will flank you on our bikes. That might be a better defensive position than all of us in enclosed vehicles anyway."

"We still haven't decided where we're going," I pointed out.

And we didn't get to decide even then, because a gunshot rang out from just beneath the window. My nerves jumped.

Jett rushed to the window. "Fuck," he snapped, which was all I needed to know about the situation.

I stuffed the sweater I'd been holding into my backpack and flung it over my shoulder. Marisol dashed out of her room with suitcase in tow as I rushed to get her. She yanked her pistol out of her pocket with her free hand, her face pale and her jaw clenched.

Footsteps thundered in the hall outside. More shots boomed

through the air. Kai loped to the front door, his own gun in his hand, the fingers of his other hand flexing. "I'll help clear the way."

Jett grabbed the handle of Nox's trolley, and I helped Ruin up off the sofa. He slung his arm over my shoulder, setting his feet carefully but steadily on the floor. His eyes darted from the window to the door nervously, but he still managed to smile as he tipped his head a little closer to mine. "At least I get a bonus hug out of this."

As fast as my pulse was racing now, I couldn't help snorting at that comment—and hugging him to me as tight as I dared in consideration of his still-healing injuries. As we all barreled toward the door as quickly as we could move without causing loss of life or limb, Kai stormed out. His supernatural energy was already so keyed up that a faint sizzle sang through the air with his movements.

We still had the few new recruits who'd survived the shoot-out at the clubhouse standing guard here. I caught sight of a couple of them in the hall, wrestling with the guys in skeleton masks who'd come for us. The Gauntts hadn't wasted any time siccing their gangster lackeys on us.

Kai charged right into the fray, smacking his free hand against the first masked head he could reach. "Take down as many of the Skeleton Corps people as you can," he ordered with a crackle of paranormal voodoo. Then he shot the next-nearest masked man, who'd just lunged at him.

The guy he'd worked his spell on whirled around and stabbed his knife straight into the belly of one of his colleagues. The opening gave the Skullbreakers recruits enough room to fire off more shots of their own. The rest of us pushed into the hallway.

More Skeleton Corps men were hurtling up the stairs. The tension inside me expanded into a frantic thrum. We had to get out of here before the hall turned into a death trap.

The bloody aspect to my magic couldn't hurt more than one person at a time, so instead of reaching toward our attackers, I threw the supernatural hum inside me back toward my apartment. At the tug of my attention, every faucet and fixture in the kitchen and bathroom groaned to life. With a swing of my arm, I propelled all that gushing water toward the stairwell.

It rushed past us in separate airborne currents like thick, watery snakes, only dappling my face with a faint sheen of droplets as they soared by. The torrents smashed together right as they crashed into the onslaught of masked men.

From the looks of it, I might have stolen all the water from the entire building. The tidal wave knocked all the men I could see off their feet and swept them down the stairs, limbs flailing. Jett let out a low whistle of approval.

Kai wheeled his arm. "Come on!"

We ran on across the now sopping carpet to the stairwell, the recruits and Kai's dupe charging ahead. As Ruin wobbled down the steps next to me, Jett eased the trolley along with a series of muted bumps. Nox's body jerked and swayed, but he was heavy enough that his center of gravity held him in place. Even that jostling didn't do a thing to wake him up.

We came around the second-floor landing and found a mass of dripping, pissed off dipshits waiting for us with guns raised. Jett looked down at his boss, mumbled an apology under his breath, and gave the trolley a shove.

At the sight of the cart with its massive cargo racing toward them, the Skeleton Corps guys took just a second to gape. A few of them scattered; others raised their guns. But the trolley, with Nox's weight adding to its heft, was already ramming right into their midst.

And so the Skullbreakers boss helped pummel our way out to safety without even being conscious.

The recruits and Jett fired off more shots. Kai's dupe lunged and thrust with his knife. And somehow we found ourselves barreling out the building's entrance amid scattered bodies.

The gang war had already made a mess of the building a couple of times before. This time we couldn't stick around to clean up. I was going to guess that today's evacuation might be permanent.

My heart sank, but I didn't have time to mourn the loss. When we hurried to the parking lot around the back of the building, Jett pushing Nox's trolley again, we found several more Skeleton Corps guys converging on us.

The recruits and Kai's dupe leapt forward. The masked guy

managed to take down a couple of his fellow Corps members before one of them realized he really wasn't a friend anymore and kicked him aside with a bullet in his chest. He slammed right into Nox's bike, sending it toppling.

Ruin let out a sound of consternation. "Look what they're doing to your ride!" he called to his prone boss. "You can't sleep through *this.*"

If there'd been any external circumstances that could have shaken Lennox Savage out of his coma, a threat to his bike did seem like the best bet. But Nox's expression stayed as slack as ever.

Ruin fired off a couple of shots, hitting one Skeleton Corps guy. Then I hauled him and Marisol over to Fred 2.0, thankfully undamaged. By the time I'd gotten my sister into the front seat with her suitcase and Ruin into the back, the guys had dealt with the remaining Skeleton Corps members—although for all we knew, there were more on the way.

We'd lost one of our recruits too. As far as I could tell, there were only three left from the motley crew of a couple dozen Nox had assembled a few weeks ago. Despite the fate all their comrades had met, these few stuck with us to the end, helping Kai, Jett, and I heave Nox off the trolley into the back seat. As the guys threw the trolley into the trunk and I rushed around the car to dive into the driver's seat, Ruin patted his boss's head when it came to rest on his lap.

"We'll fix it up," he promised, glancing at the fallen bike again. "Or get you an even better one." He glanced through the window at his own bike with its gleaming neon trim, momentarily puppy-eyed about abandoning his ride too. Then I was hitting the gas and spinning the steering wheel.

So long, dreams of a happy family home, I thought as we sped away from the apartment building. At least we were alive to make new dreams somewhere down the line.

Chapter Four

Lily

I LET Kai take the lead, roaring ahead of the car on his motorcycle and weaving through the city streets. He was the one most likely to have some idea where we should go from here. I sure as shit didn't have a clue.

Marisol peered out the passenger-side window with wide eyes and tensed shoulders, but a lot less shock than I might have expected from a sixteen-year-old who'd just witnessed a gunfight. Although I guessed it wasn't her *first* gunfight. There'd been a lot of guns blazing a couple of nights ago when we'd rescued her from the Gauntts.

It wrenched at me that she'd had to witness any gunfights at all. Why couldn't we have had normal lives that didn't include bullets and blood splatter?

Because of the Gauntts.

But the bullets and blood had come with a few things I appreciated. When I stopped at a red light, I glanced over my shoulder toward the back seat. "Are you doing okay back there?"

"Everything's good," Ruin replied, unfazed even by the loss of the sofa that'd been his main home for the last two days. "I don't think any stitches came open."

"Thank God for small mercies," I muttered.

Ruin chuckled. "I don't think God had very much to do with it. If he exists, he probably wouldn't approve of my career choice."

Fair.

I kept my mouth shut after that and focused on following Kai. He drove around downtown and into an industrial area with factories, warehouses, and way less traffic. Following some sense of direction I didn't share, he pulled off the road onto a lane that led around behind one of the factories. There, he parked in a lot that was empty other than an assortment of trash drifting in the breeze.

As Jett zoomed in after us, I parked and opened my door. "I'm guessing this isn't our new accommodations," I said to Kai.

"I'd prefer somewhere with more walls, as much as I enjoy the fresh air," Ruin piped up from behind me. The breeze washing over us past the open door was pretty cool.

Kai glowered at us. "Obviously not. I haven't exactly had time to reach out to my connections and figure out where we'd be safest laying low. It just seemed like a reasonable place to talk undisturbed." He drew in a breath. "And we do need to talk before we decide exactly how low we're laying."

Something about his tone made my gut clench. "What do you mean?"

He cocked his head in the direction we'd come from. "The situation has escalated. The Gauntts are on the warpath, and they're throwing all their resources at us now. If we're going to stay and fight, we have to be prepared for an even worse onslaught. Or we could take off for someplace out of their reach at least for long enough to regroup and recover on our own schedule."

"If we're beyond *their* reach, then they'll also be beyond ours," I said. "We can't—we still need to figure out how to help Nox. We don't know how long he can survive in this state. And the kids—their granddaughter—everything else they've done… We can't let them get away with it."

"I'm not saying we should," Kai said. "I just wanted to lay out the options. If we're sticking around, then in my opinion, we can't stay on the defensive. We need to strike back at them, hard, as soon as we can. Otherwise they'll keep battering us until we're beaten down."

I inhaled sharply and glanced at my sister. I'd just been regretting her exposure to gang warfare, and now we were talking about instigating even more of that war ourselves.

But what were our other options, really? If we fled completely, we might buy ourselves a little time to heal, but Nox could slip away from us in the meantime. And we'd be giving the Gauntts and the Skeleton Corps time to regather their forces as well.

Marisol met my gaze and folded her arms over her chest. "I say we destroy the motherfuckers."

Well, when she put it that way...

I turned back to Kai. "What she said. The sooner we crush them, the better. But how are we going to do the crushing?" The thought of the tall tower of Thrivewell Enterprises intimidated me more than I liked.

Kai gave us a crooked smile. "I'm not sure yet. We still don't know exactly what we're dealing with. But while I'm finding us new digs, I can think of at least one way you can work at uncovering their weaknesses."

Peering at ancient newspaper articles through a filmy screen wasn't quite what I'd have pictured as an act of war. Although it did seem to come with some possibility of physical injury. I'd been squinting at the display for so long that my eyes were starting to feel like they might melt into the backs of my eye sockets.

Ruin didn't look particularly impressed either. He spun on his stool next to me—not too fast, because I'd already given him a death glare when he'd risked toppling off it earlier—and chewed on a spicy gumball he'd brought along to keep him alert. At least, that was his official explanation.

He'd been assigned to keep me company mainly so we didn't end up leaving him undefended. Marisol had opted to cruise around with

Kai and Nox to pick out a place to crash for the night, and Jett was off on some errand he and Kai had murmured about in low voices before he'd taken off. That left me and my sunshine-y invalid at the county archives office.

"So where did the girls come from then?" Ruin said abruptly, apparently just finishing mulling over some of the information we'd uncovered about an hour ago. We'd been able to find adoption or, in the case of the first three generations, birth certificates for the men in the Gauntt family, but there was no sign of any of the women having officially existed other than the very first Olivia and Marie. Not as kids, anyway. The marriage records confirmed that women who currently went by Olivia and Marie had married each generation of Thomases and Nolans.

"Siblings can't legally get married, even if they're not blood relations," I reminded him. "I guess they couldn't officially adopt both kids when they wanted to resurrect their marriage after passing the buck down the line. Maybe they figured it was easier having the boys be the legit heirs since that kept the family name the same."

"But where did the girls come from? They didn't fall out of the sky."

"No, but I'm sure there are a lot of ways you can set up adoptions off the books if you have the money to back it up."

Maybe the Gauntts had gone overseas to poorer European countries. Maybe they'd preyed on struggling single parents here in the States. Kai had suggested it might have been a more temporary-sounding foster situation. Whatever the case had been, I had no doubt the Gauntts had orchestrated it with as much awfulness as they'd brought to everything else we knew they'd done.

A frog hopped by under my feet with a faint croak. "Keep a low profile, okay?" I murmured at it, shooting a glance toward the woman who oversaw this part of the office. Every now and then she glanced up from her metal desk on the other side of the room and narrowed her eyes at us like she was sure we had some nefarious purpose. I'd like to know exactly what sort of trouble a person could get up to with this kind of equipment.

I turned my attention back to the microfiche just in time to spot a mention of Marie Gauntt in a piece from the 1920s. Ah ha. I expanded the text on the screen, which made it a bit blurry but not unreadable. As my gaze skimmed over the article, my spirits leapt.

"Look at this," I hissed to Ruin, and immediately regretted my enthusiasm when he leaned over in his chair, probably stretching all kinds of patched up organs he shouldn't have been straining. I tugged at his chair so he'd scoot closer where he didn't need to bend over and motioned to the screen. "The first Marie was into spiritualism."

Ruin swallowed his gum, which probably wasn't any good for his internal situation either, and started gnawing on a piece of fiery jerky next. "She worshipped ghosts?"

"Not exactly." I skimmed over the piece, which didn't offer a whole lot of explanation because it assumed the reader knew the context, but I remembered reading a book that talked about the movement during my copious free time while under psychiatric observation at St. Elspeth's. "People got really into trying to communicate with the dead and wandering spirits. Receiving 'messages' from them, tapping into higher planes of existence and crap like that. It seems like Marie was gung-ho about that stuff. She hosted some big group séance at her house."

Ruin's eyebrows leapt up. "Then that's where they got the idea for shuffling spirits around, right? They figured out how to stop their souls from just wandering away."

"Something like that, I guess." I frowned at the screen. "Kai suspected they started with the possessions way back then. It seems like this confirms that they were in the right mindset. They must have found some practices and techniques that actually worked for manipulating the afterlife."

A shiver ran down my back. If the Gauntts had been studying the supernatural world for that long—if the four souls we were up against had more than a century of life experience under their belts—how much of a chance did we have of really challenging them? They had the advantage when it came to money, political power, and now paranormal clout too.

I knew life wasn't fair, but it did seem like the scales should have been tipped a *little* less in the asshats' favor.

As I started scrolling again, the woman at the desk stood up abruptly. I glanced down, prepared to defend my amphibious interlopers if need be, but it was Ruin she was staring daggers at.

"Are you *eating* while viewing the archives?" she demanded, in a tone that suggested that offense would be on the same level as ethnic genocide.

Ruin's head jerked up, his face forming an expression of apologetic guilt. The apology part was probably not helped by the fact that he was still chewing.

Before the office manager could turn any redder with indignation, I decided we were better off distracting her than attempting to suppress Ruin's appetite. He had internal organs to reconstruct, after all. So with a small twinge of guilt of my own, I tapped a soft rhythm on the table in front of me and focused my supernatural energy on the water cooler in the far corner near the woman's desk.

The jug started gurgling. A small spurt of water ejaculated from the faucet, followed by a more emphatic sploosh. The woman spun around with a yelp and ran over, groping around for something she could use to mop up the sudden puddle.

Ruin shot me a grin and popped the last of his current pack of jerky into his mouth. Then he composed his face into a model of perfect innocence for when the office manager happened to look our way again. I snatched the empty jerky packet from him and stuffed it into my bag where she wouldn't see it.

The rest of that microfiche didn't turn up anything else interesting about the Gauntts, and neither did the two I checked after that. I found a brief mention from some local paper so small it'd faded from existence over the past century, referencing Marie's "avid spiritual interests" as a passing remark, so at least that was independent confirmation of her supernatural dabbling. It didn't tell us anything about where that dabbling had led her, but maybe that was too much to expect.

Swallowing a sigh, I moved to one of the more modern computers. Ruin wheeled his stool after me, bobbing with the squeaking of the wheels. "What are we hunting for now?" he asked.

"I don't know," I said. "This is my last-ditch effort to get something more useful out of this place. Probably Kai and Jett will come up with more than we do, but Kai said I might as well look through *all* the different types of records they store here just in case."

Along with the birth and adoption records, I'd already checked death certificates and written down their sparse information about when each of the previous Gauntts had passed on. So far, there was nothing recorded for the Nolan Senior I'd met. I wondered how the family would handle his death. As far as I knew, they'd left his body in the marsh for the fish. Had they gone back and dredged it up later? Or maybe they simply had a doctor on their payroll who'd write up a certificate with no questions asked.

Now I entered the name Gauntt into every database the archives office contained. I got either nothing or boring business-y looking documents until I reached a list of property deeds.

The first few held no surprises. There was the mansion in the suburbs that we'd broken into a little while back, the immense tower of the Thrivewell head office, and a couple of satellite offices in the neighboring towns. But at the end of the list, after those, was a transfer agreement for a small plot of land not far outside Lovell Rise.

As I read through the details, understanding tingled through my mind. Ruin noticed my sharpened focus and tipped his head at the screen. "Is there something special about that one?"

"I think so," I said. "The Gauntts own about an acre of land along the lake—the description and the coordinates make it sound like it's right where we found them on the spit the other night. And they bought it back in 1937, just a month before the first Thomas died."

I looked over at Ruin, my chest constricting. "It's been all about the marsh all along."

Chapter Five

Lily

I PARKED at the end of the road that took us closest to the Gauntts' spit and got out with a full brigade of protectors around me. All of my guys who were currently conscious had insisted on accompanying me out to the marsh in case our enemies were hanging around. Nox had come along for the ride too, currently slumped in the back seat of Mr. Grimes's old car, which the other guys had picked up after we'd been ousted from my apartment. He hadn't had much choice in the matter.

I motioned for Marisol to stay in the car while I scanned the landscape ahead. I couldn't see the spit itself because of the cluster of scrawny trees between us and it, but I couldn't make out any other vehicles in the area or any signs of human presence. After several seconds, weighing the risks of leaving my sister here versus bringing her with us, I waved for her to come out.

"Things might… get a little weird," I warned her. My sister knew about my watery talents, but she hadn't witnessed them up close all that much. The last time I'd come out to the marsh for my own purposes, I'd practically drowned myself to tap into enough power to break the Gauntts' memory-blocking spell on me.

Marisol shrugged with typical teenage nonchalance. "I can handle it. I *want* to see your superpowers." She gave me a sly smile. "And if you can figure out a way to give me some, I'd be happy to put on a cape and tights."

Jett snorted with a rare outward show of amusement. I couldn't resist reaching over to ruffle my sister's hair. "I'm not sure how it works, and considering I had to almost die to get mine, I'd rather we didn't experiment. But if I come across some kind of magic potion, I'll be sure to grab a portion for you."

She gave a playful huff. "I guess I can live with that."

Speaking of conditions for life… I glanced at Nox's prone form. "Should someone stay behind with him?"

The other guys held each other's gazes, appearing to have a silent debate. Kai, who'd taken over as the highest authority figure in Nox's technical absence, nudged Ruin. "You shouldn't be walking around much anyway. Hang out in the car with him, and shoot anyone who looks like a problem."

Ruin waggled his gun. "I can do that. Just make sure you fill me in on the whole story when you get back."

Jett and Kai kept their guns out as we headed down to the water. We didn't encounter any people on the other side of the trees, though, only a small squad of frogs who'd hopped out of the marsh to meet us. They bobbed their heads to me as if kowtowing to their ruler.

"That's really not necessary," I told them. "You can go back to whatever you were doing." I hadn't meant to interrupt their froggy lives.

My assurances didn't persuade them. They bounded after me along the spit. I stopped by the spot where the Gauntts had conducted their ritual and peered down into the water, braced to see Nolan Senior's corpse staring up at me.

I couldn't make out anything through the murk and the tangled vegetation. Was he still there, just out of sight beneath the swirling silt and the reflections that played off the water? The cool breeze raised goosebumps on my arms even through my sweater.

The Gauntts had taken over this spot nearly a century ago, claiming it as their own in both a legal sense and, it seemed, by supernatural means as well. Had the marsh already contained paranormal energies, or had the Gauntts used it as a conduit for powers they'd developed elsewhere?

The frogs couldn't tell me, but maybe the water could, one way or another.

I knelt down at the end of the spit. Kai, Jett, and Marisol stayed at the foot, the guys surveying the area around us for trouble, Marisol focused on me. I tuned them all out, matching the rhythm of my breath to the whisper of the wind through the reeds.

These currents had seen so much. And there might be more than water out there. The Gauntts' spirits had passed on from body to body, but the kids those bodies had belonged to must have died for the transfer to happen. Had any of them lingered on like the Skullbreakers' souls had?

They'd certainly have plenty of unfinished business to hold them in this world.

I dipped my hands right into the water and reached my awareness out through it, searching for any sign that there was a presence that I could communicate with. Weeds tickled against my fingers. A few of the frogs croaked. The current twined around my hands, and I thought I felt the faintest tug.

"Who's there?" I murmured. "Talk to me. Let me see you. Reach out to me however you can."

A shiver of sensation traveled up my arms and through my skull. I propelled more of my magic into the water that'd granted it to me, letting the vague impression forming in the back of my mind take shape in front of me.

The surface of the water directly ahead of me bulged upward. It quivered and stretched toward the sky, smaller protrusions jutting out of it like it was some kind of aquatic gremlin, but gradually arranging into a more clearly humanoid form. A translucent face mottled with imprecise dips and peaks of eye sockets, nose, mouth, and ears gaped at me. Arms dangled at its sides. From the size of the figure, it was a kid—if I could expect this watery apparition to be to scale.

Even as I stared back at the liquid spirit, another tug came. I fed more of my energy into that sensation, and a second figure rose up from the water next to the first. Then a third and a fourth. They all stood around the same height. It was impossible to identify them with the vagueness of their features, though it wasn't hard to guess who they might be. More impressions nipped at my fingers, but I was already stretching myself thin just holding these four up. An ache was spreading down my spine.

Behind me, Marisol let out a little gasp. Jett muttered something inaudible to himself. I didn't dare glance back at them in case losing my attention would destroy the beings I'd conjured out of the water.

"You're here because of the Gauntts," I said. "They left you in the marsh." Whether they were the victims of past adoptees who'd been co-opted as hosts or victims of other sorts, I figured those two statements were almost definitely true.

The figures all nodded emphatically, though not in unison, with an erratic bobbing of their watery heads. One of them lifted an arm with a blob of a hand at the end and made some gesture I couldn't decipher.

"What?" I asked. "I don't understand. Is there something you can tell me that'll help us stop the Gauntts?"

That question spurred the figures to greater life. More energy rushed out of me with a greater strain on my nerves, as if the aquatic ghosts were dragging it out of me in their enthusiasm. They launched into a grand, watery pantomime, limbs whipping this way and that, the wells of their mouths opening and closing.

Unfortunately, I couldn't make much sense of any of it. They looked like they were performing a drunken interpretive dance that could only have been explained in the production's program, which no one had bothered to give me. Could beings made out of water get drunk?

Okay, that was probably the wrong question.

"Er..." I said, not sure how they'd respond to constructive criticism of their methods.

Finally, they acted out one scene I could easily recognize. One of them pushed another into the water just as we'd seen the Gauntts do to Nolan and his younger counterpart.

My stomach twisted. "Yes, we know about that. Is that what

happened to all of you? They drowned you and then used your bodies?"

Another chorus of nods, this one so eager a thin spray whipped off their heads and misted my face. It kind of felt like being spit on, even if I didn't think they'd meant it that way. I wanted to swipe the moisture off my skin, but I wasn't sure what would happen if I removed my hands from the marsh.

"Have you seen any of their other powers?" I asked, and immediately regretted it when I was treated to another extended drunken pantomime. Maybe they were saying that the Gauntts worked figure skating voodoo? Or that they regularly wrestled tigers? Somehow I didn't think I was interpreting this dance correctly.

When they slowed down, I broke in with the most important question I hadn't asked yet, even though my hopes had sunk as my energy dwindled. I didn't know how much longer I could keep giving them form.

"My boyfriend," I said. "Well, one of them. I don't know if you saw—when we were out here a few nights ago, Nolan smacked him on the forehead and left one of their marks, and now my boyfriend is unconscious and won't wake up. Do you have any idea how to snap him out of that spell?"

I braced myself for another bizarre dance show, but what I got was somehow worse. One by one, the watery figures shook their heads or splayed their hands in gestures of helplessness. My throat constricted.

What else could I ask them? I'd come out here, I'd managed to summon them out of the marsh, and I hadn't gotten a single useful thing from them. How could I give up now? A few of the frogs had plopped into the water next to my submerged fingers, but they didn't offer any insights.

Then Marisol's voice rang out from behind me, firm and full of teenage sass. "You've got to tell my sister something! Come on. Don't you *want* her to help you kick those pricks' asses?"

My mouth twitched into something somewhere between a smile and a grimace, but it was pride that swelled in my chest. Maybe she wasn't expressing her opinions in the politest way ever, but I loved that

Marisol was confident enough to speak up at all after everything she'd been through.

The translucent forms swayed back and forth for several seconds. I couldn't tell whether they were wavering indecisively or if they were reacting to my fraying control. The ache in my spine was stretching right through my back and along my ribs now.

They looked so mournful that I opened my mouth to tell them it was all right—it wasn't their fault we couldn't figure out how to communicate. Maybe we could teach them sign language like researchers did with gorillas in the jungle?

Before I could say anything, the nearest figure sped between the reeds toward me. My mouth snapped shut just in time, because the next thing I knew, the body of water was leaping out of the marsh and crashing down over me with a splash.

In the first instant, I thought it was some kind of attack, that the spirits were pissed off that *I* hadn't been more useful to them. But as the chilly water drenched me, soaking through my hair and trickling over my scalp, images washed through my mind.

I saw Nolan and Marie Senior barking orders at the kid whose memories I was receiving. A pinch of Marie's fingers around "my" arm, and a sense of panicked obedience rushing through me. Choking down gulps of food while the four adult Gauntts chattered around me as if I wasn't there, their voices warbled like I was hearing them through water. Staring up at the ceiling from "my" bed, unable to fall asleep. Then sinking down into the cold darkness of the marsh in the middle of the night while voices chanted over me.

The moment those images faded, the second figure threw itself over me. More water soaked me; more ghostly memories floated through my mind. Nolan and Marie looked decades younger, though still recognizable. An older man I didn't recognize—the previous Thomas?—chortled to himself as he prodded my sides. I was left alone in a kitchen for hours, unable to move, my fingers starting to itch to grab one of the knives and stab it into my own chest. Then another dunking into the frigid slurry of the marsh water.

The third and fourth figures cast themselves over me next, sending images full of the same desperation and anguish coursing through my mind. A sob congealed in my chest. I wanted to reach out through the filmy impressions and hug the children they belonged to close.

But they were already gone—at least all physical presence they'd had was. What remained was slipping away from me as water dribbling into the muddy ground beneath my feet.

Just as I thought it was over, a deeper, broader sensation swept up from my fingers where they were still submerged in the marsh. A cold, turgid wave of horror and revulsion rushed through my nerves and rippled through my chest.

I gasped, my hands clenching. The feeling fell away, leaving only my chilled, sodden body and an ache that now seemed to fill every part of me.

I stood up, and my legs wobbled under me as if I'd lived for over a century myself. I swiped my dripping hair away from my face and looked toward my sister and my guys.

"The spirits aren't happy," I said, "and I don't think the marsh is either. I don't think it likes what the Gauntts have put into it at all."

"Who would?" Jett muttered.

Kai studied me through his glasses. "What does that mean for us?"

"I'm not sure," I admitted. "But I think it means we've got all that water on our side… if we can figure out what we'd want it to do for us."

Chapter Six

Ruin

THE WINDOWS of the medieval restaurant that'd become our new clubhouse glinted with broken glass. I cocked my head at the sight, summoning the cheerful spin I knew I could bring to the situation if I just reached far enough. The painkillers I'd been taking helped, giving every sensation softly fuzzy edges.

"The police haven't messed with our stuff," I said. "No caution tape or chalk outlines. They must be scared of getting on our bad side."

"Or of getting on the Gauntts'," Kai said flatly, easing open the door on its battered hinges. "The Corps guy we talked to did say that they pay off the cops not to bother the gang."

Kai was not so great at looking on the bright side. But that didn't matter when I was so good at it, and he was brilliant at so many other things. I guessed that was why Nox had brought both of us onto the team.

Thinking of Nox brought up frustrations I couldn't put in any kind of positive light. I grimaced inwardly and stepped through the doorway into the mess of the restaurant, walking carefully so I didn't stir up any new pangs in my stitched-up insides.

The interior of the restaurant held the same autumn chill as outside, since the broken windows obviously weren't holding any heat in. In one particular way, the space was less messy than it'd been when we'd last occupied it. Blood stains marked the floor amid the toppled chairs and shards of glass, but someone had carried off all the bodies. And there'd been a *lot* of bodies.

"The Skeleton Corps—or maybe the Gauntts themselves—must have decided it was better for them not to leave a bunch of corpses around for anyone to see," Kai said, answering the question that'd only just begun to form in my mind in that eerie way of his. His ability to predict what you were thinking had been nearly supernatural even before the whole resurrection thing.

"Whoever came through, they were very enthusiastic," I said, taking in the newer parts of the mess. Someone had wrenched a bunch of the decorative weapons off the walls and tossed them around the place. The banquet table by the throne was cracked down the middle, and the throne itself had its seat caved in and the back snapped off halfway down. Spray paint streaked across the floors and walls with the Skeleton Corps's crossed bones symbol and a whole lot of obscenities aimed at us.

I was glad Lily didn't have to see them. Hopefully she and the others were staying safe in the foreclosed house we'd broken into as a place to crash for the night.

I wandered over to the area along the walls where the tables that'd held the platters of party food were now lying on their sides. Finger foods and dip scattered the floor, giving off an odor that was just crossing the line between greasy deliciousness and sour rot. I wrinkled my nose and dipped my head in a moment of silence. What a waste of tasty snacks.

Kai kicked aside an axe here and a platter there, the faint clangs echoing through the large room. We were supposed to be checking to see if the Skeleton Corps had left anything here that might be useful to an attack on them—and to make sure *we* weren't leaving anything they could use against us—but nothing jumped out at me in the mess. I supposed we could take some of those swords and run the assholes through, but guns worked faster.

Anyway, it seemed like we needed a more permanent solution than regular death when it came to the Gauntts. They kept resurrecting themselves like something out of a horror movie.

"Do you see anything?" I asked Kai, walking slowly around the throne. Remembering the fun I'd had with Lily on that seat—my first time with her—made me want to fix it, but I was afraid I'd bust something open inside me if I tried to wrangle the heavy pieces. She wouldn't be happy about that. It could wait until my organs had fused back into place a little better.

Kai blew out a breath and shook his head. "Not so far." He ducked into the room at the back, which had once been the kitchen area, and came back out frowning. "The guns and ammo we stashed here are all gone. No surprise there. I can always get more."

I glanced at the walls with their mottling of bullet holes and couldn't help chuckling. "It looks like we could load a lot of pistols with what's in the plaster."

Kai rolled his eyes at me and headed toward the front door. "Come on. We don't want to stick around any of our known haunts for longer than necessary."

I hummed to myself as I followed him. "I'd kind of like to run into a prick or two. Put some fear into them." I smacked my fist into my palm, and just then a guy appeared outside the shattered front windows.

He stopped when he saw us, and so did we. Kai's hand snapped to his gun, but before he'd even lifted it, the guy raised his hands in a gesture of surrender.

"I just wanted to talk to you," he said. "I promise, I'm not here to fight."

Kai narrowed his eyes at the guy. "I've seen you before. You're with the Skeleton Corps."

The dude didn't look particularly familiar to me, but I wasn't as keenly observant as Kai at the best of times, and the fuzziness of the medication was definitely making my memory more sluggish too. My friend was obviously right, because the guy nodded.

"I am, but I'm not here for them. They— I'm here for me." He moved one arm—slowly, as if he was worried we'd shoot him for any sudden movements—and touched his other bicep. "You asked before about the Gauntts and marks we might have on us. That girl did something to one of the bosses, made him remember something that got him angry at them… I've got one too."

"A reason to be angry?" Kai asked.

"A *mark*," the guy said. "I can show you—I want her to do whatever it is she does for me. I want to know what happened."

Kai and I exchanged a glance. The guy looked pretty harmless by our standards. I didn't see any weapons on him, and he was shorter and scrawnier than either of us alone, let alone both of us combined. I probably could have taken him even with my internal injuries and without my supernatural powers, if I didn't mind another trip to the doctor afterward.

And one of the enemy coming to us for help had to be more useful than anything else we'd found around here, right?

"Come inside," Kai said carefully. As the Skeleton Corps guy stepped through the empty window frame, Kai eased closer to the opposite window to peer down the street.

"I came alone," the Corps guy said. "Believe me, I don't *want* them knowing I'm here. What they did to the boss…"

Curiosity gripped me. "What did they do to him? He didn't come to the party!" Not that he'd missed anything other than a massacre. But it'd been a very impressive massacre.

The guy made a face. "I don't actually know. But after that meeting with the bunch of you, he was ranting about the Gauntts, and then the bosses all went off together… and I haven't seen him again since. The bosses get paid off by those rich pricks. They don't want to piss them off. So I've got to think they cleaned house."

Kai folded his arms over his chest. "Then you might not be able to go back after you've talked to us. What's so important about this that you're risking your life over it?"

"What do you think?" the guy said. "Obviously something fucked up is going on with these Gauntt people. I never liked that we let them jerk our chains in the first place. And there was…" His forehead furrowed. "I'm missing something. How the fuck am I supposed to know what to do about them if I don't know what *they* did?"

His words tugged at something deep inside me—not anything currently held together with staples and stitches, thankfully. I found myself thinking of the aimless days in my childhood home when it'd felt like I was just drifting on, barely even existing to anyone other than myself. Like nothing I said or did meant anything. Until I'd decided that I'd make it mean something. I'd find my own joys wherever I could, whether the people around me bothered to notice or not.

And then in a weird way I'd been free.

This guy wasn't free at all, in the opposite way. He had all kinds of assholes telling him his life was theirs, and he didn't even know all the shit they'd done to him. But he was trying to do something about that problem however he could. He was trying to make his life his, like I had. I could respect that.

Kai didn't look particularly impressed. I might not be a master at reading people, but his expression was all skepticism. "And you're coming to us about this *now*? Why?"

The guy spread his hands. "I was thinking about it. Like you said, it's a big risk. And then there was the epic fight and everything… People are saying crazy things… But I don't care about any of that. I decided I want to know, and you're the people who can make that happen. Simple as that. So are you going to do it or not?"

"Out of the goodness of our hearts?"

"No." The guy scowled at Kai. "If the Gauntts messed with me half as much as it sounds like they did the boss, then I'm on your side. I'll help you go after them—and the Skeleton Corps fuckers who let them get away with that shit—whatever way I can. There might even be more guys with the marks that I can bring on. But I can't promise anything until I know what's up."

Kai glowered back at him. "When you're asking for access to our woman after everything you pricks have done to us, that isn't going to cut it."

"Hey!" I said, holding up my hand. "We can make sure he's telling the truth. I'll just make him want to."

Kai's face brightened a little with approval. The Skeleton Corps guy looked significantly less enthusiastic. He backed up a step. "I'm not sticking around to let you beat me down."

I snorted. "That's not what I meant. All I've got to do is give you a little tap. Then you can be part of one of those crazy stories for a little while, and we can get our confirmation. Win-win!"

His eyes darted between the two of us. Kai was nodding. "I think that's fair. If you're not willing to trust Ruin that much, there's no reason we should trust you."

The guy's jaw clenched. For a second, I thought he was going to storm off on us. Then he propelled himself toward me. "Fine. Do it. Just get it over with."

That seemed like pretty good proof in itself, but when it came to Lily's safety, I didn't want to go just by my admittedly off-kilter instincts. I paused for a moment to think about the emotion I'd want to send into the guy and then gave him a light smack across the shoulder.

Energy crackled over my skin with the sense of awed respect I'd aimed at him, drawn from my own feelings for my friends and my love. The guy blinked at us, and something in his face relaxed. He sank down to his knees, staring up at us like we were a fountain he'd reached after a long trek across a brutal desert.

"I can't believe you're considering helping me," he said in a breathless rush. "You really are great. Amazing. Fantastic."

"And all the other adjectives," Kai said dryly, shooting an amused glance toward me. "Why do you really want our help? We expect full honesty if we're going to believe you're really committed."

"Of course! I'm putting myself in your hands. I'm sick of living under the Gauntts' thumb, and if they did something even worse to me that I can't remember…" He shuddered. "You're the only ones who can stop them. Who can get their mark off me, if they're the ones who put it there. There's no one else I can turn to. Please."

"And you aren't going to go running back to your buddies telling them what we're up to?" I asked.

He shook his head so emphatically it nearly popped off his neck. "No, I'd never do that to you. You deserve so much more loyalty than that. If you take me on, I'm with you until the end. Those fuckers who think they can cover up what the rich pricks are doing to the rest of us can suck my dick."

That sounded pretty similar to what he'd already been saying. I was ready to believe him, but Kai with his smarts made extra sure.

"Before my colleague here gave you a smack, did you have other plans?" he asked, taking on a smoothly reassuring tone. "Were you planning to betray us before you realized how fantastic we are? We won't punish you for it, of course. We just need to totally understand where you're coming from. Full honesty is key."

"I understand," the guy said, clasping his hands together. "But I'd already made up my mind before I came here. I mean, I was kind of concerned about how you'd all react, but I'm done with working for the Skeleton Corps. The assholes at the top showed that *they* don't care about loyalty."

A smile stretched across Kai's face, and I knew we were good. He motioned the guy onto his feet. "Come on then. It seems like we've got a lot of talking to do."

Chapter Seven

Lily

THE GUYS HAD PROPPED Nox up against the wall where we'd wedged his trolley into a corner of the empty dining room, under the theory that there was more chance he'd come back to life if he looked at least a little alive. I wasn't sure how much validity there was to that idea, but I had to admit it was a bit of a relief not to see him constantly sprawled on his side like he was already fully dead.

I sat next to his motionless form, watching the other Skullbreakers, who'd gathered around the Skeleton Corps guy they'd brought back with them. I'd broken the Gauntts' mark on his arm at his request, and he'd gone off into one of the house's other rooms for a while to stew with the memories I'd released. Now he was back, talking with the other men in low tones with a look on his face that was equal parts anguish and rage.

The Gauntts had hurt so many people in their ghastly quest for… for what? I wasn't even sure what their endgame was. Did they simply want to live forever? To use their accumulated wisdom and experience to make their corporation even more powerful? Or did they have even bigger, more disturbing plans?

I wasn't sure I could wrap my head around anything more horrendous.

"So now we've got a Skeleton Corps guy becoming an honorary Skullbreaker," I said to Nox quietly. "What do you think about that?"

He didn't answer, of course.

I cocked my head. "I guess you'd probably have gone by Kai's judgment anyway. He was convinced enough that the guy has the right intentions to bring him here. Ruin's always happy to make friends, so that wasn't a hard one. I don't think Jett's totally on board yet, though." The artist was hanging half a step back, his shoulders slightly hunched in a typical wary pose.

Nox continued to sit silently. Could he hear me from wherever his spirit was locked away inside his body? I reached over and squeezed his hand, which was at least still warm. Every time I moved to touch him, my pulse stuttered with the fear that I'd find his skin deathly cold.

The Skeleton Corps guy's gaze darted over to us and jerked away again, and I had to smile. "He's scared of you even while you're doing your best mannequin impersonation. You've definitely made an impact."

There were so many other things I wanted to say. *I'm sorry that I couldn't get any useful cure ideas out of those water-logged ghosts. I wish I'd realized what Nolan was doing and jumped in the way before he touched you.*

I miss you.

A couple of months ago, I hadn't had any of the guys in my life. I'd been overjoyed just to be leaving behind St. Elspeth's to begin the rest of my real life. But they'd wormed their way into every part of my existence both together and in their own separate ways.

No one had ever made me feel like Nox did, with the words so sweet and demanding at the same time rolling off his tongue. With the unshakeable confidence he brought to every problem the world threw at us.

We needed him. The longer he stayed under the Gauntts' spell, the farther away he seemed.

Kai ambled over, and I pushed myself to my feet to meet him. He glanced down at Nox with a discomforted twist of his mouth and then studied me, his eyes brightly alert behind the panes of his glasses.

"I think this development is going to be a real blessing in our favor," he said. "It's going to keep you busy. Our new friend Parker is planning to figure out who else in the Skeleton Corps has been marked and bring them back here so you can open their minds. We'll end up with our own little contingent of double-agents."

I studied the slim, scruffy-looking newcomer, who was ducking his head with a shy smile at Ruin's playful cuff of his shoulder. "Are you sure we won't end up double-double-crossed again?"

"He sounded genuinely pissed off at the way the Gauntts have been bossing around his gang before we even cracked open his head," Kai said. "And he definitely doesn't have any friendly feelings toward them now. Revenge is an excellent motivator, as we should know."

"True." I dragged in a breath. "That'll help us defend against any future attacks from the Corps. But what about getting at the Gauntts? It doesn't sound like the gang has any access to them beyond taking their orders or any idea about their supernatural abilities. They jump when they're called to and that's it."

Kai grimaced. "I'd agree with that assessment. It's one piece of the puzzle. The more we can take away from the bastards, the harder it'll be for them to hold us off."

One piece of the puzzle. His words made me think of our earlier gambit to figure out who else in the area had been abused and marked by the Gauntts. The viral video had failed because of their meddling, but there were others out there who might want the same revenge and were in a different position from Mayfield's gangsters.

I even knew who at least a few of them were.

My chest constricted around the suggestion for a few seconds before I forced it out. "Maybe we need to reach out to other unlikely allies. Other victims who'd want to tear the Gauntts down if they had the chance to."

Kai raised his eyebrows. "I take it you have someone specific in mind—ah. Of course." He paused. "Are you sure you want to go there? Dealing with that contingent would stir up plenty of uncomfortable memories for *you*."

I shouldn't be surprised that he'd followed my line of thinking before I'd said half of it out loud. I shrugged, bolstering my resolve on the inside. "If you guys can manage to forge an alliance with people from the gang that murdered you, then I think I can handle making nice with a few college bullies. We don't even know how much they actually wanted to harass me and how much it was Gauntt voodoo winding them up."

"True. Who do you want to start with?"

I knew the answer to that question, even if I didn't really want to say *that* either.

We only knew three of my former bullies at Lovell Rise who'd been marked by the Gauntts, and it made the most sense to start with one of them and work from there to figure out who else had been affected. One of them had been Ansel Hunter, whose body Ruin had taken over and therefore had nothing to say for himself anymore. Another had been a guy named Fergus who'd gone practically catatonic when I'd released his memories. I wasn't sure he'd be of much use for anything.

And then there was Peyton, the worst of the girls. I'd already appealed to her once a couple of weeks ago, and she'd told me off. But the conflict between us had still been fresh then, and she hadn't had much time to think about what I'd said or the crazy things she'd seen.

I didn't like her, but she was a heck of a lot stronger-willed than Fergus seemed to be. And I knew how fierce she could be when someone had threatened something important to her. If we *could* get her on our side, even as an enemy-of-our-enemies rather than anything resembling a friend, that should definitely work in our favor.

Especially when she'd mentioned that her mom worked for Thrivewell.

"I think I need to go pay another call on Ansel's groupie," I said. "Which means Ruin had better come along too."

It was actually the perfect day for approaching Peyton, because I'd shared a class with her on Tuesdays before I'd left the school. So I knew exactly what building she'd be walking out of at two o'clock this afternoon.

In total stalker style, Ruin and I lurked in the shadow of the neighboring building until I spotted Peyton's thick chestnut hair swishing as she exited the lecture hall. We hustled over, a little less hastily than I might have preferred since I was still worried about Ruin's insides becoming his outsides all over again.

We managed to catch up with Peyton before she reached her destination, which appeared to be the campus bar. I wasn't sure if she was looking to grab a snack or aiming to get started on some day drinking, but either way, she was temporarily out of luck.

"Peyton!" Ruin called in his bright voice when I motioned to him.

Peyton swung around, her eyes widening over her arched nose. When she saw the two of us, she stopped, but she folded her arms tightly over her willowy frame. "What do you want now?" she asked, not even trying to act friendly for the guy-formerly-known-as-Ansel's benefit.

I willed my hackles to stay down even though her mere presence made the hum wake up in my chest. Through force of will, I kept my voice even. "Just to talk. It's important. And it involves Ansel too."

Peyton's eyes flicked to Ruin again. It was even harder now for me to see his host in his gradually shifting appearance, but I'd gotten to know the guy he was now pretty well. Peyton must still have made out a lot of her former crush in him. She bit her lip and then nodded. "Okay. Fine. I'll give you a few minutes."

We stepped around the side of the building, out of the way of other early bar-goers. A chilly breeze wound around us, and I tucked my hands into the pockets of my jacket. The hiss of the wind over the grass and the rhythmic pulsing of bass emanating from a dorm-room window steadied me.

"I know a lot of what we said when we came by before must have sounded strange," I started.

Peyton snorted. "That's putting it mildly. It sounded fucking insane."

I resisted the urge to glower at her. "Well, it should be pretty obvious to you by now that a lot of strange things are actually going on. I mean, I'm assuming you've never been swarmed by frogs before. And then there's him." I jerked my thumb toward Ruin.

He nodded, holding Peyton's gaze with the kind of gentle smile only Ruin would be capable of. I doubted Ansel had ever produced an expression half that sweet.

"You know I'm not Ansel anymore, don't you?" he said, equally gently.

Peyton's face tightened. "I don't know how that's possible."

"It's… complicated," he said. "And I'm sorry that you lost someone you cared about. But I can tell from the way you reached out to him and tried to protect him when you thought he was in trouble that you *are* a caring person. Someone who wants to support other people. Right?"

That was probably the most generous spin any person could possibly put on Peyton's behavior, but hearing it put that way softened something in her too. She swallowed audibly, and her arms loosened over her chest. "I'd like to think so. When the people deserve it."

"Do you think *you* deserve it?" he asked.

Peyton blinked. "I—I don't know what you mean."

I held out my hand to Ruin, and he passed me Ansel's phone. We'd left the screen on the photo of Ansel in his bathing suit with the Gauntt mark clearly visible. I showed it to Peyton, pointing to the mark. "I tried to talk to you before about your mark. Ansel had one too. A lot of people do. Because someone with more strange powers has been messing with all of you. We want to stop them from doing more."

Peyton's eyes narrowed. "Is this that crazy talk about the Gauntts again?"

I gave the phone back to Ruin. "The point isn't who's doing it, not right now. The point is, do you really want to let someone else control you and manipulate what you do? Don't you want to know that your life is totally your own? Don't you want to hit back at the people who've hurt you before—who hurt Ansel?"

She shifted her weight on her feet, and it didn't surprise me at all that her hand rose to scratch at the spot on her upper arm where I knew her own mark was. A shiver ran through her. "I don't know anything about any of this."

"Exactly," Ruin said in his upbeat way. "But Lily can help you with that. Lily can break the memories open so you see everything they did."

Peyton backed up a step. "No. I don't trust her. She might do something even worse to me."

And she'd deserve it if I did lash out. But I kept that thought to myself. "If I just wanted to hurt you, I could have done that a dozen times. I never did anything to you at all until you came at me so much I had to make you back off. Don't make me out to be the villain here."

"It's your fault he's like this," she said, waving her hand toward Ruin. And the thing was, she wasn't wrong. Ruin had taken over Ansel's body to be with me.

I opened my mouth, still struggling to find the right words, and Peyton started to walk away. "Leave me alone. I'm done with all this crazy talk, and—"

Ruin leapt forward before I had to do anything at all. He clapped his hand to her arm, his expression almost apologetic.

Peyton halted and turned around. "I'm sorry," she said in a small voice. "I shouldn't have talked to you like that. Whatever you think you need to do, go ahead."

I shot Ruin a sharp look. "We were going to let her make the choice."

"She needs to know, doesn't she?" he said. "We *would* be villains if we let her go around without any clue what the Gauntts did to her. And we're not villains. So we're doing this for her own good. We *should* do it."

I didn't know how to argue with his optimistic logic. Maybe he did have a point. They were Peyton's memories. She couldn't know that she didn't want them when she had no idea what they even were. She didn't even believe me that she was missing anything.

"*I'm* sorry," I told her, and stepped up to grasp her arm. She stiffened just slightly and then relaxed. As the hum of my power rose up inside me, I sensed the barrier of magic inside her skin.

"This will only take a minute or two," I said. "Then whatever happens after is completely up to you."

I focused all my attention on the magic in the mark. My heart thumped in my chest, driving the supernatural energies inside me forward. Gathering them, I flung them at the wall of magic, again and again and—

The cracking sensation quivered through my nerves. I dropped Peyton's arm immediately and eased back to give her space.

Like it'd seemed to before when we'd gone through this process with Fergus, Ruin's influence faded as the unearthed memories rushed through Peyton's mind. She stared at us and then brought her hands to her face. Her arms trembled. "I— Oh my God."

"Yeah," I said quietly. "They did shit like that to Ansel too. And my little sister. And a ton of other people we've found. But we're going to make them pay. You don't have to like me or what's happened to Ansel to help us. Are you in?"

She took a few gulping breaths, seeming to be gathering herself. Then her hands balled into fists. "I can't believe… My *mom* knew, she let them…" She met my gaze, her eyes flashing. "What are you planning to do?"

I hadn't really thought that far. I hadn't known if we'd have anyone on our side to carry out a plan. Inhaling deeply, I found myself thinking of Nox in his silent vigil over the rest of us, locked away inside his body.

I knew what he would have said, and we were doing this for him too.

"I'm still working out the details," I said. "But one thing's for sure: we're going to go big. There's no way they're getting out of the mess they've made this time."

Chapter Eight

Lily

"ARE you sure you're okay with this?" I asked Ruin when we parked at the far end of the block from Ansel's family home. "I could go in alone. Or have Jett or Kai come with me later. We only need the keys."

"And I have them," he said cheerfully, holding up Ansel's keyring with a metallic jangle. "It shouldn't be a strain. All I've got to do is sit and type. My fingers don't have any stitches."

"Well, no." But I had other reasons to worry about his internal state. The memory of how furious he'd been the last time we'd come here, the way he'd stormed into the house and laid into Ansel's mother, remained stark in my mind. It was the only time I'd *ever* seen him really angry about anything other than someone trying to hurt me or his friends. "You just— Thinking about his parents seems to bring up a lot of unpleasant feelings for you."

Ruin cocked his head as if *he* had a little trouble remembering his last visit. Then he shrugged and beamed at me. "This will be more payback that they ought to make. Even if they won't be making it themselves. That's a good thing. And we're sure no one's home anyway, so we won't have to talk to them, right?"

"Yeah, Kai made a couple of calls to confirm they're at work." I dragged in a breath and smiled back at him. "Okay, let's do this."

I tucked my hand into his as we walked up the street and along the front walk to the porch. It took him a few tries to find the right key to open the door, but I didn't see anyone around who'd notice. When we stepped inside, he closed the door and immediately nudged me up against it, his head dipping close to mine. The warmth of his body and the familiar smell of him melted any desire I had to skip this mission.

"I like you looking after me, Waterlily," he murmured. "No one could be as sweet as you. If we didn't have some *very* important things to do, I'd show you just how happy you make me right now."

My voice came out a bit breathless. "I'm sure there'll be plenty of time later. Time that I'll be looking forward to a lot."

He grinned. "Good." Then, rather than totally leave me hanging, he pressed a kiss to my mouth that lit up my body from head to toe as if he'd channeled some of his supernatural electricity into my nerves.

We stalked through the house, quickly identifying a small room on the first floor as a home office. Ruin sat down in the chair in front of the computer, and I perched on the edge of the desk, watching the monitor blink on. Ansel's parents had enough faith in their home security that they hadn't bothered to put a password on it to wake it up.

"Check the email app," I said, swinging my legs where they dangled over the edge. "Hopefully they check their business accounts on this computer. But we can still use their personal contacts even if they don't."

It appeared that the computer belonged to Ansel's dad. There were two accounts, one a standard public one and another with the domain for the company he worked for, both in the name of Ronald Hunter. A wider smile stretched my mouth. "Jackpot."

Ruin tapped through to the contacts list for the business email, and his eyes brightened eagerly. "Look at all these people he talks to for work! Are we going to tell all of them?"

"Every one," I said with a rush of nervous adrenaline.

We weren't the only ones taking this step. Peyton and a few of the other local college students with marks we'd found and broken were taking similar action in their own homes. But it was the first attempt we'd made at bringing broader awareness to all the crap the Gauntts had been pulling instead of simply going at them directly.

This whole war was about to get so much bigger. I didn't totally know that it wouldn't blow up in our faces.

We had to try, though. They hadn't left us with many options. We were going to hurt them in every way we could until we found something that'd actually break them.

Ruin opened up a new email and gleefully tapped each of the contacts to add them to the CC list. "Important information about Thrivewell Enterprises and the Gauntt family," he said under his breath as he typed those words into the subject line. Then he tapped away at the keyboard some more to create the body of the email, pretending to take on Ansel's father's voice. Here and there, he was pleased enough with a line that he spoke it out loud too, putting on a falsely deep voice.

"I'm so incredibly ashamed that I let this go on for so long… My son deserved much better than this from me."

"And so do all the other children in Mayfield, Lovell Rise, and everywhere else the Gauntts have preyed on them," I suggested as an addition.

"Perfect!" Ruin typed that in too, wiggling in his seat with eager anticipation. Then he continued with his part of the message. "I looked the other way while they carried out their psychotic perversions because I'm a selfish bastard who—"

I touched his shoulder. "As true as that might be, it's probably laying it on a *bit* thick for being believable."

Ruin tsked at himself and deleted the last few words. "Because I saw an opportunity to advance my own career." He glanced at me for approval, and I nodded.

It only took about ten minutes to compose the entire email between us. By the end, "Ronald Hunter" had laid out the abuse against his son and his awareness that the Gauntts had pursued various other kids as well, and called for all the companies that associated with Thrivewell to demand just punishment. I didn't know how much any of those corporate goons would believe it or how much they'd be willing to do even if they believed, but it was something.

And when more and more stories started popping up pointing out the same crime, eventually the tide would shift and it'd be harder for people to ignore it than to react.

"Good to go?" Ruin asked me, hovering the mouse over the Send button.

"Let's blow this thing up," I said.

He chuckled to himself as he clicked. With a whooshing sound, the beginning of the Gauntts' public exposure flew off into cyberspace.

As Ruin wrote a slightly adjusted version of the email for all of Ronald's personal contacts, because who knew whether any of them might be in a position of influence that'd help us against the Gauntts, I texted Peyton to let her know we'd done our part. I wouldn't have blamed her or the other victims we'd located if they wanted to wait to make sure we stuck out our necks before they extended theirs.

But Peyton wrote back in a tone similar to the warily brisk one she used with me in person now. *Already sent mine too. Those assholes are going to pay. And I don't just mean the Gauntts.*

She'd been pretty furious with *her* parents when she'd realized how much she'd paid so that her mother could get her promotion.

After another whoosh, Ruin leapt up from the computer—so fast I grabbed his arm and frowned at him. "Careful."

"I feel fine!" he announced. "I feel fantastic. Stitches aren't going to slow me down. Can we go see the float now? I don't want to miss it."

I couldn't help grinning at his enthusiasm. And I had to admit I wanted to see all of the larger spectacle we'd arranged too, rather than only arriving in time to act as the getaway driver.

Checking the time on my phone, I nodded. "Kai was going to get it started right around the end of the workday when lots of people are leaving the buildings downtown. We've got half an hour before they'll launch it."

The second phase of our current plan had involved using our new allies' funds rather than their contacts. Or rather, their parents' funds. Peyton wasn't the only one who'd been happy to stick it to the people who'd stepped aside and benefitted from the perverted treatment the Gauntts had put them through.

It was horrifying but somehow not all that shocking how much people were willing to look the other way when a powerful figure wanted something. And I guessed looking the other way meant they had the plausibility of not *really* knowing what the Gauntts had done with their kids. Maybe some of those parents had been marked themselves decades ago, and Nolan and Marie had made use of that influence, but there wouldn't have been any need to reward them if the Gauntts had full control.

The result of our fundraising efforts was currently traveling down the street toward the Thrivewell headquarters. I caught a few glimpses of it as I maneuvered Fred 2.0 through the city traffic. We parked on the opposite side of the street a few buildings down from Thrivewell and watched it approach.

One of our few remaining Skullbreakers recruits was driving Professor Grimes's former car down the middle of the street. It was dragging a platform holding an immense parade float that loomed as high as the third-floor windows on either side of the road. The inflated figure was a massive child, a little boy in a school uniform with a jaunty sailor's cap on his head.

Okay, so it wasn't a super accurate representation of the Gauntts' recent victims, but we'd had to work with what we could get our hands on with short notice.

The chorus of honks from the cars annoyed at the traffic slowdown provided an urgent soundtrack to the float's gradual process. They were going to be even more pissed off when it outright stopped… like it was right now, directly across from the Thrivewell building.

Ruin bounced in his seat, his eyes alight as if he were a little kid in the biggest toy store he'd ever seen. I squeezed his knee to remind him that we needed to stay in the car. We didn't want to be spotted by Thrivewell people, and we needed to be ready to take off at a moment's notice.

There was a thin wall at the back of the float, which I knew was hiding two figures much smaller than the inflatable boy who were ready to give it a voice. A moment after the float lurched to a halt, Kai's even tone rang out with the thrum of a loudspeaker. It carried down the street and must have penetrated the windows of offices all around.

"The leaders of Thrivewell Enterprises have a dark secret that's been hidden for too long. They're sickos who like to feel up kids and make them prance around naked for them to ogle. We're not letting them get away with this any longer."

People had started to emerge from the office buildings along the street—including a security guard from the Thrivewell building. Our float driver moved to intercept them. We weren't done here yet.

Several of the other spectators had pulled out their phones to record the spectacle. Excellent. I'd like to see the Gauntts try to suppress all *those* videos.

Kai must have passed the megaphone over, because it was Marisol's voice that pealed out next. "Nolan Gauntt started coming to see me in my bedroom when I was just nine years old. He'd stare at me and touched me all over…" She faltered for a second, and my heart stuttered. But before the urge to race over there gripped me too strongly, she gathered her resolve again. "He'd kiss me sometimes, on my neck and shoulders and arms. And sometimes Marie Gauntt came too, just to watch."

My hands balled at my sides as I listened. She'd told us about what she'd say today, but it was different hearing her announcing it to the whole world now. I'd told her she didn't need to tell her story like this, that we didn't need her to, that it was okay if she sat this one out. But she'd been determined to give a first-hand account of her treatment, in case it'd make some small difference in taking down the Gauntts for good.

What she was talking about wasn't everything. She'd mentioned other things to me: that Nolan had often murmured words she didn't understand while he touched her, and she'd gotten a shivery electric shock feeling. Sometimes she thought he'd been taking energy or some other kind of power from her rather than predatory gratification. It'd have been hard to explain that part of the Gauntts' exploitation to anyone who hadn't experienced it, though, so we were sticking to the child molestation parts that everyone could understand.

Kai took the megaphone back. “If you need further proof, the evidence is all here. We’re exposing decades of lies and corruption. Don’t let innocent children suffer because you’re afraid of the power the Gauntt family holds. We have to stand up to them and show that we won’t let this kind of deviancy go unpunished.”

As his voice faded, a news van roared around the corner. Ruin let out a little whoop, and I smiled. That was exactly what we’d been waiting for.

A woman got out alongside a cameraman who looked like he was already filming. I spotted another crew hustling over at the other end of the street.

Kai must have noticed them too. He let out one more burst of accusations. “The Gauntts think they can get away with molesting kids all over the county because of their standing. I’ve heard more than a dozen stories from their victims. The family will try to explain it away, but we can’t let them drown out the voices that need to be heard. It’s time for justice!”

The news reporters were pushing closer to the float. I caught a flicker of motion as Kai and Marisol ducked out from behind the inflated boy. We’d set up the platform so they could stay out of view until they stepped onto the sidewalk between two of the cars, acting like they were just regular pedestrians who’d abruptly appeared to take in the show.

As they walked quickly toward us, one of the reporters clambered onto the platform. She prodded the float and picked up the object Kai had left behind—an unlocked phone with voice recordings from several of the other victims of the Gauntts.

That was all we’d wanted. Kai jerked open the back door of the car so he and Marisol could dive inside, I whipped Fred 2.0 around in a hasty U-turn, and we sped away from the scene of our anti-crime.

A giggle spilled out of Marisol’s mouth. She looked pale, her eyes overly bright as if slightly panicked, but the smirk she shot me in the rearview mirror was all triumph. “We really did it. They came to listen to us. Do you think they’ll believe it?”

"What's important is getting people talking," Kai said. "They'll definitely be doing that now. Even if we couldn't pull off anything else after today, those accusations are going to stick in people's minds no matter how the Gauntts try to brush them off. I doubt their magic can erase a story on this scale."

"But we're going to do even more," Marisol said. "This is only the beginning."

"That's right!" Ruin said. "Humiliation and then death to the Gauntts!"

"It's been a long time coming," I said darkly.

Marisol started to sway in her seat, humming a victorious tune. The melody wound its way into my bones and up my throat. I hesitated for a second, so out of practice that I automatically balked against putting words to the song.

But if there was ever a time to let my own voice out, wasn't it now? I'd always been able to sing for Marisol—*with* Marisol. I could reach for that dream alongside her. She'd already been so much braver than I needed to be.

I opened my mouth, and the lyrics that sprang into my mind tumbled out alongside her little dance. "We'll bring them down, one by one. They couldn't fall any farther. We'll tear them up, and when we're done, nothing will ever be harder."

A giddy laugh spilled out of my sister, nothing but joy and approval, and the same emotions swelled inside my chest. We were really going to do this, our strange little family, together. Right then, I believed we could conquer anything.

Chapter Nine

Jett

I FROZE at the base of the billboard as a lone car rumbled by on the street below. I was crouched in a thicker shadow amid the night's darkness, but I still waited until the headlights had swept by me before moving again.

Giving my spray can a quick shake, I finished the message I'd been adding to the Thrivewell advertisement: *CHILD GROPERS*. Normally I preferred to paint with my fingers, but the can got the job done much faster.

I was doing some work with my hands. After I'd sprayed the last letter onto the billboard, I pressed my palm to the part of the image that showed Nolan Gauntt's smiling face. With a jolt of my supernatural energy, I added demonic horns to his forehead and shaped his mouth into a leering grin.

Easing back, I considered my work in the dim light that glowed from the nearby streetlamps and nodded with a rush of satisfaction. People would notice that. And I'd given a makeover to billboards and other public advertisements for Thrivewell and its various subsidiaries all over town.

Talk about our stunt with the float was all over the news now, and tomorrow morning Mayfield's inhabitants would drive through the city with all kinds of visual reminders of what kind of people they'd let dominate so much of their city.

I rolled my shoulders, working out some of the strain that'd built up there over my hours of slinking through the night to do my guerilla artwork. Then I scrambled down the narrow ladder to where my bike was waiting.

Exhaustion was starting to creep up over me. I grabbed the bottle of Coke I'd been nursing and chugged the last of the cola, but the tart soda only gave me a faint boost with its lacing of caffeine. Definitely time to call it a night.

I revved the engine and took off toward the house where we were holed up for the night. There were enough foreclosed buildings in the shadier parts of Mayfield that we'd been able to hop from one house to another over the past few days, always parking at a distance and having a couple of recruits prowling the streets keeping watch in case the Gauntts or their Skeleton Corps minions tracked us down.

So far we'd gone unassaulted since the battle at Lily's apartment. Maybe the remainders of the Skeleton Corps were taking more time to regroup now that they'd seen we could still fight back just fine even without Nox's powerful fists in the mix. But I doubted we'd get a reprieve for long now that we'd gone so much more brutally on the attack ourselves.

Eventually, our efforts had to be enough. We'd beat the Gauntts down until they couldn't get back up. Maybe their defeat would break the spell on Nox. Maybe we'd be able to demand the cure in some kind of deal, exchanging it for a tiny particle of mercy, even if that was more than the pricks deserved.

I wasn't going to think about any scenario where we didn't get Nox back. He *was* the Skullbreakers, smack-dab in the middle of the picture. We didn't exist without him. So one way or other, we'd drag him out of the black hole he appeared to have fallen into.

I parked my bike out of sight down a secluded laneway and hurried the rest of the way to the house on foot. The recruit leaning against the house next door melded into the shadows enough that I only noticed him because I was looking for him. He gave me a small nod of acknowledgment.

This house had an enclosed front porch, no chillier than the rest of the house since the heat was off, so the whole place was pretty cold. The porch was our second line of defense, and both Kai and Ruin had hunkered down there in sleeping bags.

Kai let out a soft rasp with each perfectly even breath, like he was being strategic even in his slumber. Ruin hugged one end of the folded blanket he was using as a pillow, his mouth set in a dreamy grin. Of course that guy would be cheerful even when he was dead to the world.

Neither of my friends stirred as I slipped past them into the house. In the living room just beyond the front door, another bundle of blankets lay on top of an unfolded sleeping bag serving as a mattress. Lily was providing one final layer of defense for her sister and Nox, who we'd set up in the two bedrooms deeper into the bungalow.

My woman wasn't sleeping as soundly as the guys. Maybe she hadn't been sleeping at all. At the faint creak of the floorboards, she sat up, squinting through the darkness.

"It's just me," I said quietly, walking over to her. The sight of her, her hair and skin luminous in the pale haze that seeped through windows from the street, woke me up the way the caffeine boost hadn't.

She was my muse and my lover and everything else I could have wanted. It'd been more than worth dying the first time to come back to this.

"You didn't run into any trouble?" she whispered as I reached her.

I shook my head. "Got a couple dozen billboards and posters doctored, and no one seemed to notice me working. The real buzz will start in the morning when people can really see them."

"Thank you."

"Hey, they're our enemies too. I want them gone just as badly as you do." I hesitated, still a little awkward about my welcome after how long I'd shut down the lover side of our relationship. "Can I join you?"

"Of course," Lily said without any hesitation of her own, and scooted to the side under the blankets. I kicked off my shoes, shrugged off my jacket, and crawled in after her.

The unfolded sleeping bag made pretty poor padding against the scuffed-up floorboards. I set my hands against it with a surge of determination to make Lily's night a little more comfortable. Electricity crackled through my nerves, and the stuffing in the sleeping bag inflated to twice its previous thickness.

Lily let out a soft laugh. "So many uses for this talent of yours that we didn't realize at first."

"There's a reason I'm the creative one in the bunch," I said, and tucked my arm around her waist, tugging her close.

I'd only meant to cuddle with her. I might not have been huggy like Ruin, but with this woman… every inch of her body that deigned to rest against mine was a gift. But as her watery wildflower scent filled my nose and her hip brushed my groin, certain parts of me woke up *way* more than before. Suddenly I was thinking of the art we'd made with our bodies just days ago. The type of act I hadn't gotten to repeat in all the chaos afterward.

Since we'd first hooked up, I'd tried to show her in every way I knew how that I had no regrets. That I was totally here with her now. But maybe I should make a complete demonstration of it, just so there was no room left for doubt. Who knew when I'd get another chance?

When I trailed my hand up Lily's torso to her cheek, she automatically turned her face toward me. There was barely any distance to cross to bring my mouth to hers.

She let out a small sigh into the kiss, rolling her body to lean into me. I savored the heat of her mouth and the softness of her lips, intent on etching every sliver of sensation into my memory.

That first time, I hadn't really known what I was doing. I'd still been too stuck in my head to fully let go until we'd already been wrapped up in each other. Tonight, I wanted to do this properly from the start.

Lily kissed me back with increasing fervor. Her fingers traced over my face and into my hair, winding around the strands with a little tug that turned me on like she'd flicked a switch.

I teased my tongue across the seam of her lips, and she opened her mouth to me. Our tongues tangled together in a dance that felt as much like art as the shifting rhythm of her breaths.

One day, maybe I'd be a muse to her too. Spark a song inside her the same way she fueled my paintings. For now, giving her pleasure was a craft I could gladly immerse myself in.

And a craft I could bring my creative side to just as avidly as any other activity. Nox had talked about how we all offered Lily something different—that even if all four of us were hooking up with her, we still had something special. I intended to make my time with her as unforgettable as she was to me.

All kinds of ideas whirled through my mind, but I wanted her to be good and ready first. As I continued kissing her, I slid one hand up under her shirt. My fingers traced over the bare curves of her breasts. She'd taken off her bra to sleep—lucky me.

I swiveled my thumb over her nipple, gently and then with more force. Lily's hips canted toward me, a strained whimper seeping from her throat into our kiss. She bit her lip, her breath turning shakier. "We need to stay quiet. I don't want to wake Mare up."

True, having her little sister interrupt would definitely put an end to my plans. A sly smile curved my mouth. "Feel free to bite me as an alternative."

Heat flared in Lily's eyes. She kissed me again with even more passion, but when I pinched the peak of her breast, her head jerked down so she could take me up on my offer, clamping her teeth against the skin of my neck with a strangled growl. The little pricks of pain that came with the gesture turned my dick even harder.

"That's right, Lil," I murmured, easing my hand farther down. "Mark me up any way you like." I'd wear any nicks and bruises she gave me like badges of honor.

She exhaled with a stutter and buried her face in the crook of my neck. As I tucked my hand under the waist of her jeans and stroked her beneath her panties, she alternated between kissing and nipping my shoulder. Her slickness spread over my fingers, and the jerk of her hips became more urgent.

My own need was searing through me, my dick aching for release.

But I wasn't ready to bring this interlude to its finale yet. I intended to give my muse a masterpiece.

Beneath the blankets, I flicked open the fly of her jeans and tugged them down her legs. Lily squirmed the rest of the way out of them and reached for my pants. When her eager fingers curled around my rigid cock, I muffled a groan of my own against her hair. But before she could strip the pants right off me, I grabbed the large tube of paint I'd left in my back pocket in case I needed it for more subtle work.

It was acrylic, so basically plastic on the inside. With a flare of lust driving my supernatural energies, I willed the contents to meld with the casing into a solid mass. Then I extended and sculpted that mass into an arched shape with two prongs.

So many possible uses for my new tool. "I've got something even better for you," I said, and eased the toy between her legs. As one prong slipped easily into her slick channel, the other rubbed against her clit.

Lily let out a gasp she couldn't manage to suppress and gripped me tighter. She planted her mouth on the side of my neck with a pulsing pressure and a chorus of strangled sounds that vocalized her pleasure well enough. I worked the toy deeper into her, rocking it so it stimulated her clit the whole time, and she dug her fingernails into me alongside the edges of her teeth.

"Jett," she mumbled, so full of longing that her voice sent a bolt of bliss straight to my cock. I wanted to give her even more than this.

I eased my other hand over her smooth ass and stroked a finger over her puckered opening. Lily shivered and yanked my mouth back to hers. As our lips crashed together, I massaged her back entrance in time with the thrusts of my toy. Then I withdrew the pronged tool and adjusted its position, the closer end gliding against her slit, the slick end that'd been inside her prodding her other opening.

"Want them both?" I asked under my breath, my mouth brushing hers with the question.

"Fuck, yes," she muttered.

As I pressed both prongs into her, Lily's head tipped back. I took the opportunity to nibble *her* neck at the same time. She yanked forward, slamming her mouth against mine so hard her teeth nicked my lip, not that I minded. The kiss only partly muffled her moan.

Her legs trembled as I pulsed the toy in and out of her, both ends at once. The steady stream of noises she tried to swallow told me how much pleasure I was creating in her body.

I'd finally found the one art I could get totally right. Even if none of my paintings ever captured every impression I'd been trying to convey, there wasn't a single thing lacking in the opus of ecstasy I could bring to life in my woman.

Lily's tremors spread through her whole body. Her hips bucked to meet my thrusts. She muffled another moan with a bite of my shoulder and then reached back between us to grasp my straining erection.

"That feels so good," she whispered, "but now I want you. Just you. There's nothing better than that."

Something cracked in my chest, but in a good way, like I was splitting open to welcome a light that'd never touched me before. For a second, I couldn't find my words. All I could do was kiss her deeply as I withdrew my makeshift plaything.

I fumbled for my pockets to find the packet I'd made sure to have on me, and Lily ripped it open for me. As she rolled it over my throbbing shaft, I tipped my face as close to hers as I could get without continuing the kiss and let out the deeper ache inside me.

"I love you."

Lily's breath caught. I didn't give her a chance to answer, just reclaimed her mouth as I claimed her body by plunging into her. She gasped against my lips, rocking into my thrusts. I rolled us over so I was on top of her and tucked my hand under her ass to give me a better angle for delivering every possible pleasure I could on my own.

Even her face in the dim light, taut and glowing with bliss, was a work of art. I gazed down at her as I thrust deeper, shifting my position just slightly to follow the flutter of her eyelids, the parting of her lips. I'd never said those three words to anyone before, had never thought I would, but they couldn't have been truer. They were my signature on this masterpiece we made together.

Lily clamped her hand against her mouth, and I took that as my prompt to speed up my pace. As I slammed home, she whimpered against her palm, her eyes rolling back. Her pussy clenched around me, and the force of her coming propelled me over the edge with her. I hissed through my teeth, cutting off a groan as my cock erupted.

I sagged down next to her, the two of us a sweaty tangle of limbs and shaky breaths. Lily wrapped her arms around me and hugged me close, nuzzling my cheek. And possibly the most perfect piece of art was the way she drifted off to sleep within just a few minutes, nestled in my embrace.

I'd given her peace as well as passion. Here was hoping we could extend that peace into tomorrow.

Chapter Ten

Lily

It shouldn't have been remotely comfortable waking up in an unheated, abandoned house where I'd slept on the floor, but I wasn't going to complain about the sense of contentment that washed over me when my eyes eased open next to Jett's sleeping form. I tipped my head closer to his shoulder and got to enjoy the soothing warmth of his body for about five more minutes before Kai burst into the living room.

A couple of frogs hopped after him as if they were ready to join whatever urgent action he felt needed to be taken. I sat up, scrambling to pull my pants back on under the blankets.

Kai jarred to a stop. "I got a text from our inside agent. The Skeleton Corps are on their way here. Somehow they got wind of our location."

That didn't particularly surprise me. The Gauntts had been able to track us before, when I'd been looking for Marisol. And I'd bet the family had also gotten wind of our various additional attacks on them now that they didn't have a giant parade float in front of them capturing their attention.

"Is our guy on the inside going to help us against them?" I asked, pushing myself to my feet. At the movement, Jett grumbled and swiped at his eyes. He took in the scene and hastily started pulling together his clothes too.

Kai shook his head. "There isn't much he can do, and it's better if he doesn't break his cover so he can keep feeding us tips like this. He was going to bring around a couple of guys he figured out are marked today—I guess that'll have to be delayed. I need to work out a good place for us to move to." He whipped out his phone and frowned at his list of contacts.

Ruin's voice carried in from the enclosed porch. "They'll come and end up with nothing. Too bad for them! I say we go out to a restaurant to get some breakfast and chow down while they run around here looking like idiots."

Of course a trip for food would be his suggestion. A smile tugged at my lips despite myself, but as much as I liked the idea of walking away from the battle, my thoughts pulled me into a different direction.

"How long do we have?" I asked. "How close are they?"

"It sounds like they were just heading out when I got the text," Kai said. "We've got ten, maybe fifteen minutes. We'll need to get Nox to the car, and then we can just take off."

I inhaled deeply. "Yes to getting Nox in the car. We want to be ready to make a quick getaway if it comes to that. But I don't think we should leave."

All three of the guys paused to stare at me, even Ruin peeking in through the doorway. Kai's eyebrows drew together and then rose just as swiftly with a flash of understanding in his expression.

"You want to turn the ambush around on them."

He didn't sound like he thought the idea was totally insane. Of course, all of my guys were pretty insane in general, so maybe he wasn't the best judge of how crazy my plan was. But insane situations called for insane solutions anyway, didn't they?

"We have an advantage over the Skeleton Corps guys," I said. "We know they're coming, and they expect us to be unprepared. They're not going to stop attacking us until we convince them they're better off leaving us alone than getting whatever the Gauntts are offering them.

We might as well emphasize that point now while we have the chance, don't you think?"

Jett nodded. "Next time our guy might not warn us soon enough."

Ruin bobbed eagerly on his feet. "I'm ready to pummel a few pricks."

Kai inclined his head with a jerk. "Let's get everything prepared, then. Like you said, we need to be ready to make a getaway as need be."

At that moment, my little sister ambled out of the bedroom where she'd slept. She peered blearily at all of us, blinking hard. "What's going on?"

My pulse lurched. I was all for going into battle on our terms—but one of my terms was that I kept Marisol out of it if at all possible.

"The gang that's working for the Gauntts—the Skeleton Corps—is heading over here," I said quickly. "We're going to get you out of the way, and then we're going to take down as many of them as we can so that hopefully they'll rethink the whole 'blowing away the Skullbreakers' plan."

Marisol's shoulders stiffened. She reached to the pocket of her hoodie, where I could see the bulge of the small pistol Nox had given her. "I can fight too."

A lump rose in my throat. "I know you can, Mare. But you've never even fired that thing before. And—" A stroke of genius hit me with a rush of relief alongside it. "And we need someone watching over Nox in the car in case the Corps end up noticing him there despite our best efforts. You can shoot anyone who tries to get at him or you."

The prospect of having a useful role in the scenario seemed to bring down her hackles. "Okay," she said.

Kai snapped his fingers. "Come on, let's get moving. We don't have much time to get ready."

He and Jett hustled into the other bedroom and hauled out the trolley we'd thankfully left Nox lying on in his permanent doze. Kai barked an order at one of the recruits, who jogged with them away from the house down the sidewalk to where we'd stashed my car. Unfortunately we'd had to abandon Professor Grimes's car with the float, so we were down to just one multi-person vehicle again.

I nudged Marisol after the guys. My sister gave my arm a quick squeeze before hurrying along behind.

Standing in the enclosed porch, I focused on the hum of energy ringing through me and let it reach out into my surroundings. The two frogs who'd thrown in their lot with Kai hopped around my feet with determined croaks.

I could call more. They should have been too far away to make it to Mayfield from their marshy home, but I could sense my amphibious friends all over the city, lurking in sewers and backyard ponds and swimming pools. They'd already assembled to be close at hand for whatever I might need them for.

The light tugged at my heart, but I wasn't going to tell them they couldn't be of service. The Skeleton Corps hadn't needed to face my froggy army yet. That was one more way we could throw them off their game.

Come, I thought at all the sleek green forms I could feel around me. *Come and show these bastards they don't own the marsh. We do.*

As those impressions streamed toward me with an eager tickling of my magic, I extended my awareness in other directions. All the utilities in the foreclosed house were shut off, but that simply meant that turning on the taps or flushing the toilet the regular way wouldn't accomplish anything. The water was still running through the mains in the street. I could drag it out of the sewer grates or from the hoses of the neighboring houses.

And of course, if I needed to, I could make use of our attackers' own blood. I'd battered a few hearts from the inside out now.

The thought still made me a bit queasy, but I hardened myself against my instinctive hesitance. I was doing this to protect myself, my sister, my men, and possibly hundreds of children who might suffer if we didn't shut the Gauntts down. We'd reached out to the Skeleton Corps members who were marked. Most of them weren't under any supernatural influence, and they'd made their choice. They were still making that choice in light of the information that'd been spreading about the Gauntts' unsavory practices.

If they thought that family deserved loyalty, then they didn't deserve any sympathy.

A soft thumping reached my ears as a trickle of frogs leapt down the street toward the house. As I urged the new arrivals to nestle in the lawn's scruffy grass or around the sides of the house out of sight, the trickle expanded into a stream and then a torrent. By the time the guys came racing back to the house, I had a few hundred amphibious soldiers gathered around the place.

"I'm as prepared as I can be," I said to the guys. "How do you want to handle the rest?"

Kai glanced around the porch. "Open the windows just enough so you can shoot through the gaps," he ordered Jett and Ruin. "We'll pick as many of them off from here as we can, as soon as they arrive."

He frowned at the screen door we'd broken to gain entrance and slipped out of the house again. Seconds later, he returned lugging a huge garden gnome that he plunked down by the doorframe. "If they get close enough to try to get inside, that'll slow them down. When we need to take off, we'll run through the back. The fence there is low enough that we can hop it."

"*If* we need to run off," Ruin said with a fierce light in his bright eyes. He spun his pistol between his fingers and grinned with matching ferocity.

"Yes, if," Kai muttered. "Now get down or we'll lose all the surprise we're banking on."

We all crouched down below the level of the windows, which started at waist height. My pulse thudded in my chest. I rested a hand on the back of one of the frogs that'd come inside with me, feeling the bizarre urge to hold on to something, even though fighting with guns or other weapons had never been my style.

It was only a minute or two of tense silence before the growl of car engines reached our ears from down the street. Presumably not wanting to alert us, the noises cut out before they reached the front of the house. Brisk footsteps rasped along the sidewalk.

Kai eased up just enough to catch a glimpse through the windows. "Now!" he said in an emphatic whisper.

He sprang farther up as the other two guys did, opening fire on the figures converging on the house. I sent out a pulse of defensive energy toward the horde of frogs and then flung a surge of water from the nearest sewer drain.

There'd been maybe fifteen men hustling toward us outside. Several fell in the first hail of bullets, and the others leapt behind cars or hedges to take shelter. They were met by a torrent of frogs hurling themselves forward in a furor, and then a wave of sewer water that crashed down over them in a gray-brown deluge.

If I'd hoped that'd be enough to send the rest of the Skeleton Corps guys running, I was out of luck. Several more men rushed in from down the street, staying lower out of caution. The original shitheels who'd gone uninjured swatted away the frogs with expressions of horrified disgust, but they held their ground.

Then an SUV came roaring down the street and careened right up the front walk to crash into the steps.

We all fell back on our asses. The gnome shattered. Someone flung the porch door open—

And Jett whipped out his hands to snatch up the frogs that were sitting next to me. He hurled them at the men who were about to storm into the building.

At first, I thought he'd just been trying to distract our attackers. Then I noticed that the frogs looked about twice as big as I remembered them being.

And then they chomped fanged jaws they *definitely* hadn't had before into the flesh of the Skeleton Corps guy they'd landed on. He yelped, flailing to try to shake them off.

Kai and Ruin leapt forward together. "We can make a monster too," Kai said to Ruin in a rasp, who must have understood what he'd meant. They both tackled the second guy who'd been charging in at us.

"Fight off the rest of the Skeleton Corps people," Kai ordered him. At the same time, the emotion Ruin had propelled into the guy contorted his face into a mask of fury. The Corps guy turned with a bellow of rage and barreled back down the front walk, spewing bullets from his gun in one hand, swinging punches with the other. It was really something to see.

One of the fanged frogs had sunk its teeth into the first man's throat. He toppled over, still pawing at it with increasingly desperate whimpers. I whipped another tsunami of sewage at the asswipes still standing outside, knocked a heap more off their feet—and sent a whole bunch of them running.

We watched as the crazed man barged after his colleagues down the street. The swarm of frogs hopped after them, and the men closest by shoved themselves away with widened eyes. They'd obviously seen the treatment one of their companions had gotten and weren't taking any chances.

A quiet fell over the street, nothing disturbing it but the sight of the corpses sprawled on the road, the gurgle of the fanged frogs' victim, and now-distant booms of gunfire. Oh, and a faint peal of a siren that was no doubt coming our way.

Kai shot us all a sharp grin. "Excellent collaboration. Now let's get the fuck out of here before we end up in handcuffs."

Chapter Eleven

Lily

There was something to be said for central heating. And running water. And doors with working locks. Lucky us, the motel rooms we'd booked in a shabby joint an hour down the highway from Mayfield came with all three.

That was about as much as we got as far as amenities went, nothing fancier, but no one was complaining. Kai had decided we needed a break after all the running around we'd been doing. Just for tonight, we were leaving the city behind and hunkering down in *very* relative luxury.

We'd taken a couple of two-bed rooms with an adjoining door, one for me and Marisol and the other for the guys. I'd gotten to take a proper shower. Life was about as good as it could possibly be given our other circumstances.

I wasn't totally sure how Kai had paid for the rooms, but he'd assured me that the means couldn't be traced back to us, and he rarely said anything he wasn't sure about. I'd decided to take that one worry off my mind.

I let the shower water flow over me for the five minutes it took before it started to cool, reminding me just how low on the luxury scale this indulgence actually was, and then hastily dried off. When I came out into the main room, Marisol was perched on her bed, TV remote in hand, gazing wide-eyed at a news broadcast.

The image of our float graced the screen. For a second, I caught my sister's voice floating up from the speakers. Her mouth dropped open.

"It's all over the TV," she said. "This and the vandalized ads and something about certain business associates and key employees stepping back from Thrivewell. It's really working!"

I couldn't help smiling even as an ache came into my chest at the hint of disbelief in her voice. "Partly because of you. You gave them your story, and they had to listen."

"They didn't have to," Marisol replied. "But they did." She swiped her hand across her mouth, looking at least as anxious as she did awed.

"They never have to know it was you," I reminded her. "All they needed was a voice. You never have to talk about it with strangers ever again." Although I might encourage her toward therapy when all this was over. There had to be a way for her to talk through the gross-but-not-supernatural aspects, so some shrink wouldn't figure she was crazy over stuff that had actually happened, right?

I didn't think I was equipped to help her sort through all the trauma she must be carrying, and my guys… There was a lot to recommend about them, but more subtle shades of protectiveness weren't really their forte.

"I was going to go check on the guys," I said. "Do you want to come with, or are you good in here on your own?"

Mare cocked her head, considering, and flopped back on the bed. "I think I just want to chill. We're safe here, aren't we?"

"At least for tonight," I told her. And we did still have one of the recruits keeping an eye on things outside just in case.

I walked through the adjoining door into the guys' room and stopped in my tracks with a huff of amusement.

Jett had been redecorating. The pea-soup green walls were now a warm umber, the bedspreads a deep red to coordinate. He'd placed the room's single chair on top of the wobbly table for reasons I suspected

I'd never totally comprehend, and arranged a few tissues and the complimentary bible beneath it. The only thing that looked the same as our room was the TV, where Kai was flipping through the channels.

He stopped and switched the TV off at my entrance. All the guys turned toward me—well, all of them except Nox, who was lounging on his trolley like usual near the foot of one of the beds. Kai was perched at the foot of the other, with Ruin tucked into a sort of nest of pillows near the head of the same one, chewing on some snack from a plastic wrapper. Jett had been standing near the desk, but he swiveled and leaned against it, not seeming concerned about the way the chair swayed with its wobble behind him.

"You look like you've gotten cozy," I said.

"It's nice," Ruin said, waggling his feet amid the blankets. "I'm not that picky, but I do enjoy sleeping on an actual mattress."

"And lucky you, you get it all to yourself, since neither of us wants to put up with your squirming," Jett said dryly.

A mischievous gleam came into Ruin's eyes. "Maybe I'll convince Lily to share it, then."

I cocked an eyebrow at him. "Not overnight. I don't want to leave Marisol on her own for too long."

He lifted both of his eyebrows right back at me. "I'm sure we could find something to do that wouldn't take all night. Even if we let these spoilsports join in too."

The temperature in the room seemed to rise a few degrees just with that remark, as if I hadn't already had those sorts of needs satisfied very thoroughly by Jett just last night. A flush tickled up the back of my neck. But as I opened my mouth to respond, something in his words jarred loose a thought in a totally different direction.

"We did some other joining together today," I said. "You and Kai worked your powers together on the one guy, and Jett got creative with a couple of the frogs I summoned."

Ruin hummed to himself. "We did. It was good. There were only a couple of those guys close enough to touch, so we gave that one an extra whammy."

Kai nodded. "It generally seems like a waste to combine our

powers on the same target, but in certain cases, I can see it being quite useful."

Jett's lips curved into the faintest hint of a smirk. "I just believe in making use of whatever materials are close at hand."

"Yeah." But that approach was niggling at me in a way I didn't totally understand. I cast my gaze around the room, and my attention settled on Nox. A weird twinge, as wobbly as the hotel table, passed through my stomach.

The words tumbled out before I'd thought them through. "What if there are other things we could do by combining all our powers together. I tried breaking the spell on Nox on my own, and it wasn't enough. But if we all contributed somehow, maybe… Maybe that would do it."

The somehow was the sticking point. But Kai sat up straighter with a thoughtful expression, and an eager grin stretched across Ruin's face.

"Yes!" he said. "He's got to listen to all of us if we're trying to wake him up together."

Kai rubbed his mouth. "I don't know. I don't think it could be that simple."

"No," I said. "But if we were strategic about it—if we figured out the best way to bring each of our talents to the problem and worked on it together…"

He looked up and met my eyes again. "It's worth a try. I think… You're still going to be the key. You're the one who's cracked open all of the Gauntts' marks before. We should check if you can pass a little of your energies on to us, so we're all connected toward that common goal on the most fundamental level. Then let's see what comes to us."

My spirits lifted. We had a chance—a real chance.

Without really discussing it, we ended up kneeling on the floor around Nox's trolley. It was just small enough that we could manage to form a complete circle if we stretched out our arms and leaned forward to reduce the distance. You'd have thought we were going to carry out a séance, which I guessed wasn't that far from the truth. Although we wanted to wake up his body with the spirit we had to assume was still in it, not just commune with his ghostly self.

I gripped Kai's hand on one side and Ruin's on the other. "I'm not sure what to do," I admitted.

Kai gave my fingers a gentle squeeze. "Whatever power it is that you normally throw at the Gauntts' magic inside people, maybe do your best to send a little of that through the rest of us where we're touching? Not quite as forcefully as you'd generally go at the marks, of course."

"Of course," I said with a nervous laugh, and closed my eyes. The hum inside me felt more erratic than usual with the jangling in my nerves.

This was my idea. What if it didn't work?

Well, what *if*? Then we'd just be right back where we'd started. It wasn't as if this attempt should hurt anything.

I took a deep breath and pictured the wave of energy inside me that I normally hurled at the walls the Gauntts cast around their victims' memories. The wave I'd hurled at the wall around Nox's mind not that long ago.

Could I pass a little of that marshy power on to my men so that their talents might be even better at tackling the Gauntts' magic too?

Only one way to find out.

I urged just a thin stream of the energy down both my arms. It tingled as it passed into my hands where my fingers gripped the guys'. Kai twitched, and Ruin let out a soft chuckle. Then Jett grunted as the quiver of supernatural power must have reached him too.

Suddenly I could feel all of them like their bodies were mine too. The thump of their heartbeats, aligning with the rhythm of mine. The rise and fall of their breaths. The mild strain in their muscles holding this interlocked pose. An unnerving giddiness swept up through me.

When Kai spoke again, his voice was quiet. "I think this will make a difference. But not just to how we try to bring Nox back."

I opened my eyes and found him gazing at me through the panes of his glasses. "What do you mean?" I asked.

He wet his lips. "The way your energy tangles with mine… I'm getting a strong impression that if we work our powers in unison, our supernatural resonance will merge together in a way we might never be able to *un*tangle. Some part of you might end up tied to us in a way we won't know how to sever."

He didn't sound at all concerned about that fact. Ruin only looked curious, and Jett showed no reaction at all.

They were all watching to see *my* reaction, I realized. They'd already been bound together as friends, colleagues, practically family, before I'd come into the picture. I was the new element.

I was the only one who might feel I was losing something if a piece of my soul melded with theirs.

I didn't, though. The second that thought passed through my mind, the giddiness expanded through my ribcage, getting warmer and more mellow by the moment. I *liked* the idea of having a permanent connection to the men who'd done so much to prove they were mine.

If that connection made it harder for me to ever lose them, then I was all for it.

Another, starker revelation chased on the heels of that fact, but it was one I probably should have recognized earlier. The whole situation had just been so, well, crazy, and chaotic, and—

But I knew it now. I knew it with all the certainty that'd rippled through Jett's voice last night.

"It's okay," I said, and grimaced at myself. "No, it's *good.* I want to be tied to you. I want to be *with* you, now and wherever life takes us after this." I paused, swallowing thickly, and let my gaze travel around the trio. "I love you. All of you. And Nox too." My eyes dropped to his prone form with a twang of continuing grief.

When I glanced up again, Ruin was beaming so bright he outshone the light fixture overhead. "I've loved you since before we could even properly meet," he said. "If you want always, you'll get always."

Jett offered a smaller smile that provoked no less heat. "You know how I feel about you."

Kai's hand tightened around mine again, a little more forcefully this time. He blinked, looking momentarily, startlingly unprepared. Then a thin smile crossed his own face.

"I'm so used to focusing on reading what other people are feeling so I can use it to our advantage that I've gotten out of the habit of paying attention to my own emotions. But I don't have a sliver of a doubt that I love you with every bit of devotion I've got in me."

My throat constricted again, but I managed to smile back at them. "All right. Then let's bring Nox back to us, whatever it takes. I guess I'll just hit the barrier they put around his soul with everything I've got and hope whatever you all do gets us the rest of the way there."

Ruin shifted his position with eager vigor. "I'll send emotions into him to motivate him, get his spirit all riled up so he can fight hard from the inside."

A spark lit in Kai's eyes. "And I'll command him to do just that with everything he has in him."

Jett let go of Kai's hand to rest his fingers on Nox's forehead. "I'll feel for the structures inside him that aren't really him but the Gauntts' magic. If they've made a wall, then I'll reshape that wall until it can't hold up anymore, whether it's a thing we can actually see or not."

"All right." I squeezed Ruin's and Kai's hands and sent another pulse of my energy through them, knowing it would pass to Jett as well through Ruin's grasp. "Ready when you are."

And if it didn't work, then at least we'd know we'd given it our all.

Chapter Twelve

Nox

The worst thing about the overall shit sandwich I was currently stuck in was that the last image my eyes had taken in before I'd ended up here kept hanging at the edge of my awareness. It was like a fucking painting I could never quite turn far enough away from to escape. A painting of the twerp Nolan Gauntt had become when he'd made the leap into his adoptive grandson's body.

Just like any creepy painting, the impression of his gaze followed me no matter what I did too.

Not that I was doing a whole lot. Other than that image of kid-Nolan lingering in my mind, I wasn't aware of much other than a hazy grayness all around. Every now and then, I got a vague sensation of pressure or movement somewhere in my body, but not enough that I could have said which part or what might be going on. Faint murmurs of sound wisped by me, also too filmy to identify. And I couldn't see anything at all. I had no idea if that was because my eyes were closed or my brain wasn't connecting to them anymore.

I was pretty sure I *was* still in my head. When my spirit had been floating free after my first death, I'd been able to see and hear everything around me just fine, to move around through the world with more freedom than I'd ever had before, although significantly less ability to affect anything in that world. Unless I'd been trapped in a very boring version of hell, I didn't think I'd kicked the bucket again.

Kid-Nolan had done something to me. When he'd smacked his hand against my forehead, there'd been a sensation like a bear trap snapping shut around my skull. At least, what I imagined a bear trap might feel like, since I was lucky enough never to have actually experienced one. That was when everything else had fallen away into this grayness.

I turned in the amorphous space as well as I could, trying to grasp hold of something, anything, that I might be able to use to break out of this prison. Lily was out there somewhere. My friends were out there. Had the asshole given them the same treatment? Were *they* even still alive?

The uncertainty and my complete inability to do anything to combat it gnawed at me constantly.

How long had I been stuck in this state already? Time was moving in even more of a muddled blur than during my twenty-one-year limbo. It might have only been a few minutes. It might have been days. It *felt* like way longer than I'd have wanted to be out of commission, but I had no clue how accurate that impression was.

After a while, my thoughts started to drift more randomly. It was hard to stay focused on escape when every attempt slipped through my fingers. I found myself floating back, back, back to moments I hadn't thought about in ages.

There was the one time I'd seen my parents after Gram had taken me in. We'd been at the grocery store, and they'd slouched inside, looking hungover and crabby. Gram had been polite enough to nod. My heart had leapt, torn between the conflicting desires to run over and see if they'd offer any affection at all to my seven-year-old self and to hide behind Gram with the thought of all the not-so-affectionate responses I might get instead.

The latter had definitely been more common while I'd been living with them. But some little part of me couldn't help hoping. I'd been a kid, after all.

In the end I hadn't done either, just kept standing next to Gram while my dad averted his eyes and my mom grimaced before hustling into another aisle. Gram hadn't pushed the matter. She didn't want to risk them getting irritated and finding the energy to demand me back. But I'd heard her mutter under her breath as we'd gone to the checkout counter about how she didn't know where she'd lost her son.

Had she felt the same way about me once I'd started delving into my criminal activities? I'd never been like my dad—never thrown all ambition away to simply exist and take out my dissatisfaction with life on everything in my vicinity. I'd known from the start that I wanted to build something real with the Skullbreakers, even if it wasn't what most authority figures would have approved of as a goal.

I hadn't talked to Gram much about my activities, but she had to have figured. The money was coming from somewhere. She'd seen me come home worse for wear now and then in the early years when I'd been finding my footing. Her advice had always been more along the lines of *Don't bite off more than you can chew* than *Stick to the straight and narrow*, though.

I'd wanted to show her I was better than my dad. That I could look after her like she'd done for me. Damn it. The gloom of that thought made the fog in my head even grayer.

And now I might have lost the other people who'd stuck with me, the guys who'd made my ambitions seem possible. Ruin, who'd warmed up to me from the start for reasons I couldn't explain, other than maybe he recognized the batshit crazy that he kept under all that sunshine reflected in me. Full of boundless energy for any task I set him to, no matter how insane.

That could be it. He might have always sensed that I was going to give him an outlet for the relentless cheer that I had to think he might have eventually drowned in if he'd had nothing to aim it at.

And then I'd gone to Kai sometime during the last year I'd bothered to attend high school, hearing he was the guy to talk to if you needed something you weren't sure how to get. Despite the fact that his know-it-all attitude had gotten on my nerves even more then than it sometimes did now, I'd recognized him as a guy worth knowing. And the more I'd given him to figure out, the more people we'd needed to bring under our sway, the more he'd risen to the challenge.

I didn't know if anyone *had* really challenged him before. I'd seen him with his parents a few times, and they barely seemed to know what to make of him.

Jett had always been around on the fringes of high school life, keeping to himself. I hadn't even realized he was responsible for the little sketches and impromptu found-object sculptures that'd pop up around the building until later, after we were working together. But our paths had crossed when I'd come after some prick who'd owed me money while the douchebag was in the middle of hassling Jett, and I'd gotten to watch the artist let loose all the fury *he* kept inside.

But it'd been his smile that'd convinced me. That little satisfied smirk when he'd looked down at the dork he'd left crumpled and groaning on the ground. I wanted people backing me up who *liked* doing it. And Jett had always taken a certain pleasure in laying down the law for the Skullbreakers, whether he let it show all that often or not.

We'd really been going somewhere. And then the fucking Silver Scythes—and the Skeleton Corps—and now the Gauntts too… I had the urge to grit my teeth even though I had no sense of where my jaw even was.

How the fuck did I get out of this? I *had* to get out, because those fuckers needed to pay. We'd delivered our vengeance to our murderers, but so many people had so much more to answer for.

The sense of conviction held me through another muffled jostling. What the hell was going on out there? My thoughts scattered and wandered again, and I might have lost a few minutes or hours or days —I had no idea. The grayness wrapped around me tighter, until I was barely aware of even kid-Nolan's stupid face anymore. That realization didn't reassure me.

I was slipping through my fingers, and I had nothing to hold on to.

Then something pierced through the haze. A jolt of emotion from out of nowhere—a fiery bolt of lust and desire. My spirit stirred, aching even without a body for the woman I'd shared those sensations with to such amazing effect.

I needed her. I had to get to Lily and make every minute I'd been AWOL up to her. Nerves I hadn't even known were still working woke up with a fire to reach out to her, to worship her like she so often forgot she deserved.

A moment later, another sensation struck me. I needed to wake up in *every* way. Someone was calling on me—someone was commanding me to the surface of my consciousness. If I could just find the right approach…

I squirmed as well as I was able to within the dour gray space and got the faintest sense of a solid barrier around my consciousness. It was vibrating just slightly, enough to catch my attention. Ah ha.

Gathering all my mental energy and the fire of need searing through me, I hurled myself at that wall of magic. All I seemed to do was bounce off it, but the impulses urging me onward wouldn't let me stop, not that I wanted to.

I'd get through this. I'd get through to everyone who needed me. I had to give it everything in me.

I launched myself at the barrier again and again, more passion flaring through my awareness, more urgency yanking at my thoughts. The supernatural wall shifted a tad, and then a little more, as if it were made of overlapping plates that were sliding against each other into a new arrangement. Or was it simply cracking into pieces?

What did it matter? If there were seams, then there were gaps I should be able to break through.

Again. Again. My entire consciousness felt as if it were crackling with unfulfilled hunger. I caught a whiff of Lily's sweet scent, and it only spurred me onward. Faster. Harder. I would get *out*.

As I flung myself at the walls around me one last time, they splintered completely apart. The world spun. My eyes popped open, and I was abruptly aware of my mouth going slack, air rushing into my lungs, my limbs and back braced against some hard, flat surface.

And the faces. Not kid-Nolan, but all the people I'd actually wanted to see. Lily, Ruin, Kai, and Jett were leaning over me wearing matching expressions of strain, determination, and hesitant relief.

"Nox?" Lily said with a note of hope in her voice so fragile it nearly broke my heart. She must have been working even harder than the others, harder than I'd been. Strands of her hair clung to her sweat-damp forehead; the light in her eyes was almost feverish.

The lust that'd inflamed me while I'd been imprisoned had faded away like something out of a dream. But the woman in front of me was oh so real. A deeper need stirred inside me, rushing through every particle of my body.

I was back, and I was going to give her a fever that'd have her crying out with bliss instead of tensed up with anxiety.

I pushed myself off the thing I was sitting on and tugged her to me. "I'm never letting you go again."

Chapter Thirteen

Lily

THE SPARK in Nox's eyes and the passionate growl in his voice shattered the last of my fears. It was as if the spell had put him into a magical stasis, all bodily needs on pause, and now he'd snapped out of it like he'd only been knocked out for a matter of minutes.

There was no mistaking the crackle of life that was now coursing through his body like electricity. It electrified *me*, sending a tingle through my skin as he wrapped his arms around my torso. The only hunger he appeared to be feeling was for me. Heat was already pooling between my legs when he yanked my mouth to his.

His kiss took the vibe around us from steamy to molten in an instant. It'd been too long since I'd felt his demandingly passionate mouth against mine. The next thing I knew, he was hefting both of us off the trolley where he'd been sprawled and tossing me onto the nearest bed.

Nox's eyes gleamed darkly as he braced himself over me, gazing down. "What a good girl you are today. You broke that fucker's spell on me. I think you deserve *all* the rewards, Siren."

A giddy shiver ran through my nerves, but I wasn't going to take all the credit. "I couldn't do it on my own. The guys all pitched in. We managed it together."

Nox glanced over his shoulder to where his friends had stood up. The three guys were watching us, Ruin beaming, Jett's face briefly relaxed with relief, Kai's eyes alight with interest as he took in our pose. Just as Kai had suspected, the magic I'd shared with them had left a new connection between us. Only a tremor of an impression, but I could still hear the quickening of their hearts like a rhythmic whisper, taste the anticipation tickling through their nerves.

I didn't regret my choice one bit. It was exhilarating, knowing how closely I was joined with them.

Not just them but Nox too, the man we'd poured all our power into. As he smirked back at them, the vibrant pounding of his pulse echoed into me, the ripple of his desire passing into me turning me on even more.

"Then they'll get the reward of a show," he said, "and maybe the honor of taking care of you even more when I'm done. But for now"—his gaze snapped back to me—"you're all mine."

I had no interest in arguing, especially after he claimed my mouth again. Every heated press of his lips, every scorching touch as he trailed his hand down my body, proved just how much he'd truly returned to us.

If getting it on with me was the way he wanted to celebrate his comeback, I sure as hell wasn't going to deny either of us that pleasure.

Nox tugged my shirt off and opened the fly of my pants in a series of urgent movements, but for all his enthusiasm, he wasn't exactly rushing. He marked a path of searing kisses along my jaw and down the side of my neck. When I let out a little gasp, he lingered with a nip of his teeth at the crook. Holding up his substantial weight with one hand, he cupped the other around my breast. As he nibbled along my shoulder, he stroked and pinched the peak until my nipple was pebbled and aching and all sorts of other noises were working their way up my throat.

I yanked at his shirt, wanting to feel him against me skin-to-skin. Nox practically tore it off and tossed it aside. I was vaguely aware of the other guys still standing around us, taking in every beat of this dance with searing attention, and then I was drowning in the heat of Nox's touch again. But only in the best possible way.

He leaned down on his elbow, tucking his arm under me and letting his brawny chest brush my stomach as he brought his mouth to one breast and then the other. His tongue and teeth made short work of the rest of my breath. It was all I could do to keep my whimpers quiet enough that I wasn't worried Marisol would overhear from the adjoining room.

I curled my fingers into Nox's spiky hair, and he grinned up at me. "I love it when you let out the claws. You look so fucking beautiful when you're all flushed and wanting."

His words jarred loose an impulse inside me—the need to say to him what I'd said to the others now that he could hear it too. Now that it was impossibly clear to me how much I meant it.

"I love you," I said hoarsely, bringing my hand to his cheek.

Something flickered in Nox's eyes. For a second, he looked oddly solemn, and I wondered if I'd offended him somehow. Then he was rising up over me, his mouth crashing into mine all over again with enough force to set me on fire.

"I love you too," he muttered between kisses. "My Minnow. My Siren. My Lily. If I have my way, I'm never leaving you again, not for one fucking second."

A giddy giggle spilled out of me. "Well, I mean, you might need to take a shower now and then, or—"

"Not even then," he growled. "All showers come with Lily included from now on."

I didn't think he actually meant that, but I couldn't say I cared all that much in the moment anyway. He wrenched down my pants and kicked off his, and the hard length of his erection brushed my mound. I swallowed a moan of encouragement.

"Anyone around here have a fucking rubber?" he barked out. Kai was there in an instant, tossing over a foil packet.

Nox kept making his promises as he ripped open the packet and prepared himself. "I'm going to take you so high you'll forget what the ground is. Give you everything I know you can take and keep giving as long as you're with me. Just keep on making those perfect little noises and showing me how much you like it."

Fuck, I just about came from hearing him talk like that. He rubbed the head of his cock over my clit, and I gripped his shoulders with a growl of my own, all eager impatience now.

Nox didn't leave me wanting. He plunged into me, filling me with the heady burn of stretched muscles like he always did. I groaned and bucked to meet him, already trembling for my release.

But the Skullbreakers boss clearly intended to make good on his promises. He thrust into me with powerful but even strokes, a little deeper each time, grasping my hip and adjusting me as he felt me clench with the burst of pleasure when he hit that particularly special spot deep inside. My head tipped back against the pillow. I rocked with him, tracing my fingers over the bulging muscles of his chest and shoulders, a whole litany of needy sounds tumbling over my lips.

"Just like that, baby. I think you can take even more than this," Nox murmured, and called to the other men without breaking from my gaze. "Who's ready to help me send our woman right up to the stratosphere?"

He didn't need to ask twice. Kai was already close after bringing the condom. In no time at all, he was climbing onto the bed next to us, reaching to squeeze my breast as Nox continued plowing into me. As Kai flicked aside his glasses and leaned in to nip my earlobe, Ruin bounded onto the mattress on the other side. My fiery-haired sweetheart bowed his head to lap his tongue over my other nipple and then teased his hand between me and Nox to start fondling my clit.

I bit my lip against a louder moan, and then Jett was there by the head of the bed. He stroked his fingers over my hair and bent over me to claim my mouth upside down. The unfamiliar twist on the welcome sensation had me gasping, my lips parting to admit his tongue.

Nox kept his firm grasp on my hip, bucking into me even faster than before. His breath was getting ragged.

"Look at you," he said, with so much heated affection in his voice that it sent a tremor of delight through my chest. "Taking us all at once. You are a fucking wonder, Lily. Don't you ever forget that."

It was hard to remember anything at all amid the flood of pleasure

I'd been caught up in. I arched and squirmed into all the hands summoning bliss from my body, surging higher and higher on that wave just like Nox had promised.

Ruin pressed hard on my clit just as Nox slammed into me at just the right angle, and I careened over the edge. A little cry broke from my throat. My sex clamped around Nox with its ecstatic contraction, and he followed me with a stuttered groan.

But he wasn't done. He eased in and out of me a few more times, drawing out my release and his own satisfaction. As he withdrew, he studied me with eyes now heavy-lidded. "You took that so well. But I bet you could handle more still."

"Mmm," was all I managed to say in my hazy delirium.

A sly smile stretched across his lips. He motioned toward the other guys. "I want to see you try welcoming two at one time, Siren. Twice the joy? I know they'll make it good for you." He cut a glance toward his friends as if warning them of the consequences if they didn't.

I didn't fully understand what he meant, but the guys seemed to. Kai grinned and nudged Jett. "That was always one of your specialties, wasn't it?"

The artist licked his lips, the motion of his tongue inflaming me all over again whether I followed the conversation or not.

"Perfect," Nox said. "Then you can put yourself to good use too, Kai. Lie down—let her ride you."

Kai sprawled on the bed next to me without a moment's hesitation. As he undid his jeans, I sat up, my whole body feeling sensitized by the thorough fucking I'd already experienced.

"Strip him," Nox ordered, his voice like liquid fire.

I was happy to oblige. As I peeled off Kai's shirt, I ran my fingers over the footballer muscles he'd taken over with his host. He made a rough sound in his throat and tugged my mouth to his.

Through the kiss, I helped him disentangle his legs from his pants. "Get another one," I heard Nox command someone else, and then Ruin was pressing a packet into my hand. "Suit him up," the boss added.

He wasn't just aiming to get me off in as epic fashion as he could manage, I realized. He was also reinstating his authority after his relative absence—in the most enjoyable way possible. I didn't think any of us had complaints.

I slicked the condom over Kai's already rigid cock. His teeth nicked my lips, and then he pulled me into place, straddling him. I rocked against his erection and grinned at the groan he couldn't suppress. A whimper of need was building in my own throat despite the release I'd already gotten.

"You've got it," Nox said encouragingly. "Now ride him good."

I sank down, impaling myself on Kai's cock. We both exhaled in a rush. My sex throbbed around him, wanting to race with him to the next thrilling finale.

Before I could do more than bob up and down a few times, hands gripped my waist from behind. Jett tipped his head to kiss my shoulder and my neck, sweeping my hair to the side for better access. Then he teased his fingers down my spine all the way past my tailbone to my other opening.

My nerves jumped as he circled the rim, but with excitement as much as uncertainty. I glanced at Nox instinctively, and his warm grin steadied me.

"He knows what he's doing," the Skullbreakers boss said. "He'll fill you right up. Doesn't that sound good, Siren?"

A sound that wasn't much more than panting escaped me. Jett cursed under his breath and rubbed his fingers together, and a slickness spread over my skin. He'd created his own supernatural lubricant. Would wonders never cease.

A giggle fell from my lips, followed by a whimper as Jett worked his fingers over and then into my opening. He stretched the muscles there gently, sparking currents of bliss with each rotation. By the time he lined up his cock with my back entrance, I was almost dying to know how he'd feel there.

He took it slowly, easing me up and down over Kai and pressing a little deeper inside me himself with each motion. Kai squeezed my thigh with one hand and massaged my clit with the other, and I felt my own slickness gush over him as my arousal expanded beyond anything I'd ever felt before. The quivers of *their* bliss traveling through our magic-formed connection—ragged breaths I felt as well as heard, sparks racing through nerves—only further inflamed me.

I had just enough sense left to remember there was one other guy I didn't want to neglect. Ruin had stayed sitting on the bed near us, watching the proceedings with avid eyes. I beckoned him closer.

"I can take you too," I said in a husky voice that hardly sounded like my own.

Nox let out a low whistle. "That's our Siren," he said. "You are something else."

Ruin jerked down his pants, and I bent to the side as I started to rock more emphatically with the two guys who were penetrating me in unison. The first swipe of my tongue around Ruin's erection was shaky, but as the pleasure searing through me swelled, I managed to close my mouth right around him. He tangled his fingers in my hair, tickling the tips over my scalp, and arched toward me.

My awareness became a blur of heat and bliss and guttural sounds. I was filled in every way possible, joined both bodily and emotionally with these men, and it was the most incredible combination of sensations I'd ever experienced. I wanted it to last on and on and I also couldn't help chasing that peak that seemed to keep spiraling out of reach the faster I raced after it.

Jett and Kai surged into me. I sucked hard on Ruin's cock, and he exploded in my mouth with a gasped murmur that was both apology and praise. His flavor on my tongue and the force of his release tipped me over the edge.

I came and seemed to keep coming, over and over, wave rolling after wave, until I found myself sagged over Kai as if I'd washed up on a shoreline with him. Jett's sated sigh as he pulled back and a whisper of fulfillment tickling into me told me that he'd found his release just as the rest of us had.

"Now that," Nox said with a mix of pride and amusement, "is how we treat our woman right."

Chapter Fourteen

Lily

I WOKE up in my own bed next to Marisol's to the sound of crinkling cellophane.

"Rise and shine!" Ruin said. I rubbed my eyes and made out him standing by our room's table, laying out the most extravagant spread of vending machine food in the history of the universe. He set up the individual bags of chips and cheese puffs in rows bordered by chocolate bars, individually packaged brownies, and a few baggies of granola, the only breakfast-like food the motel's machine must have contained.

Jett, following behind him, tweaked a few of the items as if to arrange them into more artistic order.

Marisol sat up in her bed, blinking blearily. "Is that what we're having for breakfast?"

Ruin glanced at her uncertainly. "There weren't any restaurants nearby. But I could go looking if you want!"

"No, no, it's fine," my sister said, and shot a glance in my direction as if expecting me to protest the junk-food meal.

I laughed. "It's fine. I think we could all use a treat, huh?"

"I got the chocolate bars with nuts in them, so they're a little healthy!" Ruin announced, his smile coming back.

Nox came barging into the room through the adjoining door with an air of assurance like he'd never been laid low. Marisol's eyes nearly popped out of her head.

"You're okay!" she exclaimed.

In the middle of the chatter about breakfast, I'd forgotten that I hadn't been able to tell her about our success last night when I'd slipped back into this room—after Nox had, after all, let me step a few feet out of his sight. She'd still been fast asleep.

A grin sprang across my face. "Yep. We figured out how to beat the spell."

Nox flexed his arms, a fiercely pleased light gleaming in his eyes. "Good as new. They can't keep the boss down."

"But I'm going to kick you all out," I informed the guys, pushing off the covers. I didn't care about them seeing me in my sleep clothes, of course, but— "My sister needs a little privacy before we get down to breakfast."

Ruin's eyes widened, and Nox took on a look of consternation that he clearly aimed at himself. "Sorry, sorry," he said, holding up his hands in a more apologetic pose, and herded Ruin and Jett out.

I heard Kai's voice from their room just before the door swung shut. "Has anyone figured out how to get hot water out of this—" Then it was just me and my sister.

Marisol bounded off the bed as if she'd been infected with Ruin's typical energy and grabbed the one change of clothes she'd been able to pack out of her suitcase, which had thankfully survived all our hasty getaways. "I'm glad he's okay," she told me. "They're all— I'm glad you found guys who look out for you that much. And listen to you. They might be kind of crazy, but they're better than any of the boys I knew in school."

My mouth twitched, torn between amusement and regret. "We'll get you into that new school I found when all this is over. There'll be better guys there, or in college, or somewhere. You could probably skip the whole gangster part, since I've got that so well covered."

Marisol smothered a giggle. "I'll say. So, what are we doing now? How else are we going to hit back at the Gauntts?"

I sucked my lower lip under my teeth as I considered the question. "I guess we need to see how things are playing out with everything we've already done. Where's that remote?"

Marisol found it and switched on the TV, flipping to a news channel while I invited the guys back into our room. The table wasn't big enough for us all to sit around, so Ruin ended up tossing my and Marisol's selections to us on request and we snacked on our beds. The guys stood around the table, chowing down with their usual vigor and watching the newscast alongside us.

The first couple of stories didn't offer much enlightenment. It seemed that a truck transporting turkeys had broken down on a freeway, and now feathered menaces were gobble-gobbling and chasing cars all along the nearby exit ramp. According to the weather report, it was overcast with incoming rain, which was a little hard to buy into when the sun was beaming through the motel room window. But that was about as accurate as I found the forecast tended to be.

Then the newscast jumped to the "Top Story of the Hour." An image flew onto the screen of Marie Gauntt, flanked by Thomas and Olivia, speaking into a microphone while camera flashes went off around her.

"We have not and never will victimize any member of our community, let alone a child," she was saying. "These sick accusations must be the work of corporate opponents looking to undermine Thrivewell Enterprises for their own benefit."

"What!?" Marisol burst out. "That lying shit-cracker."

Apparently she'd picked up my tendency for creative insults. And I couldn't argue with her assessment of the situation.

"Of course they're going to put as positive a spin on it as they can," I said. "It doesn't matter what they say, only what other people believe."

But even as those words came out of my mouth, the feed switched to a couple of reporters in their studio. "What do you make of all this commotion, Ron?" the polished woman asked her colleague, sitting so stiffly straight in her chair she could have passed for a piece of furniture herself.

"They are incredibly disturbing allegations, Allison," the man said in one of those TV voices where every word is just a little over-emphasized. "It's hard to imagine that this kind of crime could have been going on for so long without being exposed before. From what I understand, there hasn't been any evidence or testimony offered by a named source. The so-called 'confessions' could be anyone, and they've left us with no way to verify their stories."

"I'm inclined to agree," the woman said. "The lengths these people have gone to in perpetuating their story seem more in line with the resources of a fellow corporate giant, not abuse victims seeking justice."

"Oh, for fuck's sake," Nox growled at the TV, the frustration in his tone echoing the matching emotion in me. "How the hell would you idiots know?" He jabbed the power button to switch it off.

Kai frowned. "Are they seriously saying that we went *too* far in establishing our case? They'd believe us more if we'd been quieter about it? They'd never have heard about it if we'd been any quieter—the Gauntts would have raced in to squash our attempt faster than a cat on fire."

Marisol had drawn her legs up to her chest, hugging her knees. The chocolate bar she'd been eating lay on the bed next to her, only half finished.

"I can do it," she said abruptly.

My head jerked toward her. "Do what? Mare, you've done plenty."

She raised her chin, but her voice came out strained. "They want someone who isn't anonymous to verify their story. I can come forward. They can't say *I'm* working for some corporate enemy or whatever."

Oh, no. No, no, no. My heart sank even more than it had listening to the newscast. "I'm not letting you put yourself in the line of fire like that."

"It's my decision, isn't it?"

Kai raised his hand before we could debate further. "It's your decision, but you should make it knowing all the facts. And the facts are that they *will* claim you're being paid off by some opponent to make your claims. They'll say it's still not enough. You don't have any concrete evidence or witnesses, right? Your parents never saw what went on."

"As if those deadbeats would testify anyway," Jett muttered, and he had a point.

Marisol deflated so fast that my throat choked up as I watched her. "I guess not," she said quietly. "Maybe… if we could convince some of the other people they messed with to speak up too…?"

"We can try," I said. "But I still don't want you being first. If you put yourself out there that obviously, who knows what the Gauntts will do to you now?"

She held my gaze, hers so haunted it nearly killed me. "Who knows what they're still doing to other kids? I don't want more people to go through that."

She had a point too. And she was sixteen—maybe not an adult, but old enough that she *should* be able to make her own decisions.

I sucked in a breath. "Look, we'll talk to the other marked people we found and see what strategy we can come up with that they'll get on board with." I had major doubts about whether any of them would want to step into the spotlight, though. The college kids hadn't minded sticking it to their parents from behind the scenes, but none of them wanted the entire world knowing about their painful history. They were barely comfortable with *me* knowing about it.

And the gang members we'd woken up… They'd be blowing their cover and risking wrath from both the Gauntts and their leadership. Plus I knew from personal experience that gangster men weren't super keen on openly sharing their vulnerabilities.

So I barreled onward, making up my plan as I spoke. "And I'll go back to the lake this morning. To the spot where the Gauntts do their rituals. I'll see if I can get any more information out of the spirits of the kids they left there. Maybe there's proof in the marsh."

Had they left *any* of the bodies of the older Gauntts behind? Or any other traces of their rituals? If they had, hopefully the lingering ghosts could point those out to me without too much additional pantomiming.

Marisol didn't look totally reassured, but she nodded and picked up the rest of her chocolate bar. "Okay. I want to come too, though."

"We should all go," Nox said firmly. "We stick together; we protect each other. That's why we're going to win this fight."

We finished the rest of our vending-machine breakfast with somewhat less enthusiasm than we'd started with, packed our remaining belongings in Fred 2.0's trunk, and explained to Nox why he no longer had a motorcycle. He growled so loud I was surprised the motel doors didn't shake off their hinges, but he got into the car with me, Marisol, and Ruin, taking the front seat for the first time since his bespelling.

It was definitely a relief having him sitting upright and fully conscious for once, even if his eyes were shooting murder daggers at everyone who crossed his path, like they were all complicit in the loss of his beloved ride.

"You can get a new one, right?" Marisol piped up from the back as I drove around the edge of Mayfield toward the lake.

Nox let out a harrumph. "It'll take a while to find another one that good. Fucking Skeleton Corps assholes have probably claimed her for their own." Then he shook himself and patted Fred's dashboard. "But we did a good job with this baby. I just don't like how long I had to be dependent on the rest of you lugging me around."

I shot him a bittersweet smile. "There was a lot of lugging, but we didn't mind it at all. I'm just glad you're back. We lost Professor Grimes's car, but we could swing back to Lovell Rise and pick up Ansel's old car so you have some kind of vehicle."

Nox grimaced. "Nah, I'm sure I can scrounge up a ride that's better than that today."

"If you get a new bike, I'm grabbing one too," Ruin said. "Even my insides barely hurt at all now. We need the whole brigade!"

"Let's see where we can fit that into our busy schedules," I said dryly.

I slowed as we came up on the end of the lane that took us closest to the Gauntts' marshland property. We hadn't passed any other vehicles in several minutes, and the stretch of scruffy grass where we'd stopped before was empty.

We parked there, Jett and Kai bringing their motorcycles to a halt on either side of the car, and peered apprehensively in the direction of the spit. No forms I could see moved along the nearby shoreline or between the trees that blocked our view of the spit itself.

"I'll stay here and stand guard," Jett said, pulling out his gun. "If I see anyone coming this way, I'll shout."

I wanted to suggest that Marisol stay with the car too, but one look at her told me that she wanted to be a full part of this expedition. Well, why shouldn't she? It wasn't as if the lake's spirits would hurt her, and if it'd make her feel more in control after the way the Gauntts had used her for so long, then she deserved to be included.

We tramped over the patchy fields toward the shore, giving the trees a wide berth so we could check out the spit from a distance before approaching it. The narrow strip of land jutting into the marsh was just as vacant as it'd been the last time we'd come out here.

A cool, damp wind licked over me, thick with the scent of algae. The thudding of our footsteps reverberated into my bones. I started to sing a soft, wordless melody under my breath alongside it, reaching for the inspiration to guide me in this quest. A sense of certainty settled over me.

When I'd broken through my own mark, I'd completely submerged myself in the marsh. Last time, I'd tried to commune with the spirits in the water from dry land. Maybe if I met them on their own turf, they'd be able to speak to me more clearly.

The guys had seen me go that far before, but my sister hadn't. I reached over to grasp her hand as we stopped at the foot of the spit. "This is probably going to look kind of strange. I'm just doing everything I can to get answers. Nothing I try will really hurt me. The spirits here want our help."

How much they could work through their communication issues to help us help them was a totally different story, of course.

Marisol nodded and squared her shoulders like she was bracing herself. Nox gave my arm a quick squeeze. "Do what you need to do, Minnow," he said.

I walked out to the end of the spit and peered down at the water rippling around the stalks of the reeds and cattails. *Were* there bodies down there, sunk out of sight like my guys' had been by their murderers? The thought sent a shudder through me, but I peeled off my shoes and socks and dipped my toes into the water.

It was as cold as I'd expected. Gritting my teeth, I sat down on the edge of the spit and hopped into the water right where we'd seen Nolan Senior's former body go under.

I cringed as I slid into the water, half-expecting my feet to smack into a water-logged corpse. But they hit the silty bottom, feeling nothing but the slick mud and a couple of small stones. The lake came up to my armpits there.

Ignoring the chill seeping through my skin, I waded around the end of the spit. As I pushed through the marsh vegetation, I prodded with my feet every which way, half hoping for and half dreading the moment when I might encounter the bulge of a bone. A couple of times, I even fished hard lumps out to study them in the air, only to find they were ordinary stones.

It wasn't really surprising that the Gauntts would have covered their tracks at least that well. They owned this land, whether they publicized the fact or not. They'd hardly want there to be any chance of someone uncovering bodily remains on their property.

A few feet beyond the end of the spit, the water lapped around my neck and tugged at my hair. I swished my hands through the lake in a rhythmic motion and closed my eyes. The hum in my chest reverberated through my limbs.

The spirits were still here. I needed them to come to me, to speak to me.

"I'm here," I said softly. "I want to know more of your stories. I want to know anything your killers did that would work as proof. Did they leave anything behind? Here, or in your old home, or anywhere else?"

The water shivered around me with a faint tug, like dozens of tiny fingers trying to catch hold of me. I balked instinctively for a second before following that tug and sinking all the way beneath the water.

As the cold liquid closed over my head, images rushed into my mind like the smack of a wave. It was like when the ghostly figures I'd summoned into watery form had splashed over me last time, only a longer and more intense deluge.

Impressions swam by of younger versions of the Nolan and Marie I knew as well as other adults I had to assume were the Gauntts' previous bodies—yanking the kids around, murmuring magical words to keep them still and compliant, alternating between cold aloofness, cutting anger, and brief moments of doting kindness. I got whiplash just watching it.

As far as I could tell, the Gauntts hadn't turned their perverted interests on their hosts-to-be. Maybe that had felt too close to incest, or maybe they'd been worried about somehow contaminating the bodies that would become theirs. I didn't have any faith at this point in them having the slightest moral compass. It was a small comfort anyway. Who'd want to choose between being molested and being murdered?

I didn't catch anything that looked like evidence we could turn against the Gauntts, though. Every action they took against their adoptive kids was either magical or designed to look like normal discipline. Nothing was done in public view where it might have been captured on camera, even accidentally. The spirits could hardly testify on their own behalf.

I opened my mouth, letting water stream in without fear. Moving my lips to form the question I wanted to ask. *Do you know where the bodies are?*

Visions swept over me of bloated corpses yanked out of the marsh and carted away with whispers through the dark of night. After that, the spirits didn't seem to have any clue what'd happened to the physical remains of the monsters who'd taken them over.

Damn it. Wasn't there anything I could use?

But another sensation was surging up through the fraught mix of fear and anger that resonated from the ghostly memories. I became aware of the entire marsh spread out around me, filled by the lake but a distinct part of that body of water. Water that'd been contaminated over and over by the Gauntts' dark rituals. They'd poured their influence into it, submerged bodies and then dredged them up, twisting sickening magic all through the currents.

Those impressions came with a rush of nausea. I'd sensed that the marsh wasn't entirely happy the last time I'd come out here, but if the water rushing into me now contained any emotion of its own, it was revulsion.

It longed to bring life, to shelter the plants and creatures that called it home, but the Gauntts were polluting those intentions with their own psychotic purposes. A dark energy radiated through the liquid around me, but from the marsh's reaction, it felt more like binding chains than liberating power.

What would happen to the Gauntts if this place could manage to shake off those chains?

It didn't do me any good wondering about that when I could taste the hopelessness of its situation in the desperate roar of the water through my awareness. Then I was thrashing up to the surface, the nausea making my stomach lurch so I spewed all the water I'd swallowed back into the marsh.

I stumbled over to the bank and simply leaned against the end of the spit for a moment, my breath coming raggedly, my head spinning. A frog swam up to me with a concerned croak, and I tipped my head to it. Through our new supernatural connection, faint but steady, I sensed my men shifting on their feet, wanting to rush to help but not knowing how to. And I still didn't know how either.

The only thing I was sure of after my commune with the marsh's spirits was that I never wanted my sister to feel as terrified or desperate as they did. I'd protect her from the powers looming over us, no matter what I had to do.

Chapter Fifteen

Lily

WHEN I FINALLY DRAGGED MYSELF OUT of the water onto the spit's solid ground, the three guys and my sister hustled to meet me.

Ever practical in ways I appreciated more by the day, Kai had grabbed the emergency blanket from Fred's trunk. He wrapped it around my sopping clothes, and for a minute I just clutched it around me, waiting for my shivers to subside as my body regained its warmth.

"Did you see anything?" Marisol asked, her eyes nearly round. "What happened?"

I hoped she hadn't been too disturbed by watching me all but drown. I gave her a small smile. "Not a whole lot. Really just more of what I saw last time. The Gauntts treated their adopted kids like shit and manipulated them with their magic so they wouldn't make trouble. They take the corpses of the older bodies away from the marsh—none of the spirits seemed to know where to. It seems like they've been pouring more and more magic into the water itself so that it can help them work their rituals, and the marsh isn't happy about that."

Ruin rocked eagerly on his feet. "So how does that help us take down the Gauntts?"

"It doesn't," I admitted reluctantly. "At least not in any way I can see right now." I paused. "I guess it's possible that if I damaged Marie's heart the way I did with Nolan, they'd be forced to come out here and do their ritual again, and maybe we could arrange for them to be caught in the act… But I'm not sure how easy it'll be for me to get close enough to her. The whole family must have a ton of protection around them now, and they've got every excuse to."

"We can't give up," my sister protested.

Nox drew himself up to the full extent of his substantial height. "Of course we're not giving up. This was just one strategy that didn't pan out. There's plenty more we can try." He tucked his arm around me and ushered me back toward the car. "You gave it your best shot, Minnow. Not your fault those water-logged spirits couldn't cough up anything useful."

His words didn't really reassure me. I knew what strategy Marisol was thinking of trying, and it was the last thing I wanted her to have to do. I twisted my hair in my hand to wring out some of the lingering moisture, straining my brain for something else we could try right now before she started talking about making public statements again.

Jett lifted his hand to us in greeting as we approached our parking spot. Then his head jerked around at the same time as an engine's rumble reached my ears.

Two engines rumbling, it turned out. A couple of police cars roared into view along the laneway we'd driven down. I stopped in my tracks at the sight of them and then hurried the rest of the way to Fred 2.0, my pulse lurching.

Whatever they wanted, I didn't think it could be good.

"Get in the car," I called to Marisol. The Skullbreakers guys braced themselves around me, tensed for battle. We could have all leapt into or onto our vehicles and made a run for it, but the cops were coming up on us fast and blocking the lane. I wasn't sure we'd actually be better off in flight.

Kai nudged his glasses up his nose, his other hand dipping toward the gun wedged in his jeans. "We should hear what they have to say. If this is something to do with the Gauntts, they might give away something about their plans. But stay where you've got shelter."

We opened the car's doors and positioned ourselves with those as shields. The guys kept their guns out of view—for now. As the police cars skidded to a halt across from us, my heart thudded hard.

We'd faced off with gangsters and other criminals before, as well as bullies who'd been on the attack. Fighting with law enforcement felt like an entirely different level of trouble.

If we crossed that line, could we *ever* come back, no matter what happened with the Gauntts?

Several of my froggy friends had bounded over to join us. I didn't take more comfort from their presence as they croaked at the cops stepping out onto the matted grass.

The officers didn't have any concerns about showing *their* weapons. Four cops emerged, two from each car, with pistols pointed in our direction. "Stay where you are," one bellowed. His dark hair was slicked back so solidly you'd have thought he was a plastic action figure come to life. "You're under arrest."

When he didn't follow that up with anything, we all just stared. Kai cocked his head. "Under arrest for *what*?"

"Don't ask questions," one of the other cops barked. "Put your hands up where we can see them and march on over here, buckaroos."

Oh-kay then. I'd never been taken into police custody before, but I was pretty sure this wasn't standard procedure. I frowned at them. "If we haven't committed any crimes, I don't think you can arrest us."

I mean, we had committed various crimes—well, mostly the guys had—but if the cops didn't *know* that…

Two of them shifted on their feet, looking impatient and maybe a little puzzled, as if they weren't totally sure what they were doing here either. Weird.

"We don't need any of your back-talk," the first cop said. "Are you going to come peacefully or not?"

"We have a right to know why we're being arrested," Kai spoke up. "It's part of state law. Which I'd expect you to know about."

The cops exchanged a glance. "You know what you've done," another said in a threatening tone.

Ruin beamed at them. "We took a walk along the marsh. Nothing wrong with that."

"That's not— You have been implicated in a *very* serious crime." The cop scowled at us as if her doom-and-gloom expression would make up for the fact that it was becoming increasingly clear she had no idea what that "very serious crime" was.

None of them did. What was going on here?

My nerves prickled with apprehension. I sucked in a breath, trying to think of something I could say that might diffuse the situation, and the cops started striding forward.

"If you won't come peacefully, then we'll need to use appropriate force," the first one said robotically. Now he sounded like an action figure too.

Nox made a gesture to Jett, who nodded and surreptitiously tucked his gun away. I guessed they didn't want to give the cops any current excuses to enforce this arrest if we didn't have to.

But that didn't mean the Skullbreakers were going to hand themselves over. As the cops got closer, the four guys stepped forward carefully to meet them, their hands partly raised.

"I'm sure we can clear up this misunderstanding," Nox said with a wry note in his voice.

One of the cops scoffed, and then the guys all moved at once.

Ruin and Kai lunged forward in unison, each swatting a different cop across the head like a momma cat cuffing a kitten. Kai's immediately swiveled and tackled the colleague next to him to the ground. Ruin's crumpled onto the grass too, raising his hands to his face as he turned into a blubbering mess.

Jett had snatched at the last cop's gun at the same time. The burly woman held on tight, but Jett wasn't looking to disarm her. Only to reshape the gun into a form that wasn't remotely threatening anymore.

The cop ended up holding a lump of metal in the vague shape of a leaping fish. She fumbled with it as if still trying to find the trigger. Then, with a savage snarl that seemed out of place with the professional uniform, she sprang at Jett.

Nox wasn't letting his guys fight this battle alone. He sprang in there as Jett raised his hands to defend himself and sent a wallop of crackling energy into the cop's midsection. The woman flew several feet back and fell on her ass. She sprang up again and launched herself at Nox.

Nox let her come and snatched at the woman's shirt at the last second, heaving the cop over his shoulders, spinning her around, and then sending her flying toward the lake. The sound of tearing fabric came with his heave. The woman whirled through the air like a maple key and thumped to the ground with the seam of her shirt sleeve gaping open.

And where it gaped open, a pinkish blotch about the size of a nickel showed against her bronze skin.

My pulse stuttered. "She's marked!" I said. "Maybe they all are."

Ruin leapt to check the sobbing guy, who was so distraught he didn't even bother trying to fend the gangster off. Ruin yanked at the guy's collar to reveal a matching blotch at the peak of his shoulder.

My stomach sank. Kai turned toward his dupe, who was still wrestling with his partner on the ground, and I caught his arm.

"I think we know what's going on well enough. Let's get out of here while we have the chance. I'd try to break the spell, but I don't know how much time we have. There could be more coming."

Nox clapped his hands. "You heard her. Move out!"

He dropped into the car, taking the driver's seat this time, and I jumped into the back with Marisol. As Ruin scrambled into the passenger seat, Jett and Kai mounted their motorcycles. In less than a minute, we were zooming across the bumpy field around the lane and back into the road as soon as we'd cleared the police cars.

"So… the Gauntts sent some cops to play with us?" Ruin said as we zoomed toward Mayfield, trying and failing to keep his tone lighthearted.

"It looks like it." I let out my breath in a huff of a sigh. "They used their supernatural control to convince the cops that they had to take us in, since apparently they don't have any evidence they could use to get us actually arrested."

"They're just as stuck as we are in that area," Nox said with a low chuckle.

"Except they *can* call on anyone who still has their mark," I said.

"If there are at least four county police officers they can manipulate… how many other people will they be able to send after us?"

"At least not all of the other people will have guns?" Marisol suggested in an attempt at optimism.

"There is that," I agreed. "Let's look on the bright side."

Ruin, naturally, was the expert at that approach. "Lily can break their marks, and then they'll be against the Gauntts!"

I grimaced. "Only if there isn't a bunch of them trying to attack us all at the same time. It does take a certain amount of concentration and time."

"You've got all of us working with you," Nox said. "Including me now, thank the Devil. We'll take whatever those pricks throw at us and send it right back at them."

It'd be nice to believe that it'd be that easy. But as we drove between Lovell Rise and the neighboring town, Mayfield's high rises looming in the distance, a deeper uneasiness gripped me. I couldn't help noticing that a couple of the cars cruising around on other country roads turned toward us after we'd come into their view.

By the time we were approaching the Mayfield city limits, we had three vehicles racing after us. Nox gunned the engine to stay ahead of them, his forehead furrowing.

"It'll be easier to lose them in the city," he said. "They look like regular people. I doubt they have a lot of experience with stunt driving."

He motioned to Kai and Jett through the windows, and they swerved off in different directions at the next intersection. The cars stayed on our tail. I guessed they were looking to maximize the number of targets they could tackle.

What did they think they were going to do if they "caught" us? *Were* they armed and planning to shoot on sight? Or were they just hoping to irritate the hell out of us?

They were definitely accomplishing that last part already.

As we passed into streets packed with buildings on either side, Nox pulled through a gas station's lot, tore down an alley, and doubled back on our previous course. We got a moment's relief of an empty rearview mirror before a car we drove by in the opposite lane pulled a sudden, screeching U-turn and barreled toward us.

Nox muttered a curse and whipped through another series of quick maneuvers that had us jerking in our seats. Every time we lost one follower, we seemed to pick up another before we'd driven more than a few blocks. The marked dupes appeared to be everywhere.

My pulse thumped on. I was starting to get dizzy with the adrenaline. "We're going to run out of gas eventually," I said. "Maybe we should leave the city."

"Then they'll have easy eyes on us for miles around," Nox said. "Fucking hell. If I could smack them around through the windows…"

"You'll only smash the glass if you try. Anyway, it isn't their fault, any more than it was Marisol's when she ran away."

He grumbled under his breath inarticulately, but he yanked and twisted the wheel until we'd shaken our current follower. Then he veered straight into an underground parking lot where we could stay out of view temporarily.

When we were sure no one had followed us in, he parked behind a column that hid us while still giving us lots of room to flee if we had to. Then he sank into the seat and reached for his phone. "I'll get Jett over here. He'll have to do a temporary makeover on your car. The Gauntts must be giving their marked people the impression of what it looks like so the idiots know what to go after. We've just got to make it look different."

As much as I loved Fred 2.0 as it was, I wasn't going to argue with his suggestion. We had to do what we had to do.

I squinted through the dim lot, my heart still racing. "That strategy will only protect us for as long as it takes before the Gauntts realize we've changed the vehicle… or until they find some other way for people to ID us."

Marisol rubbed her arms. "How are we supposed to figure out our next moves if we're being chased all over the place? We can't go back to the motel, can we?"

I shook my head. "I don't think that's safe. Too many people coming and going, too many who might have already seen us or the car there." Then I paused, an idea rising up that I examined reluctantly.

We'd already asked for a lot of help from people who hadn't been inclined to help us in the first place. But I wasn't sure we had a lot of choice. And keeping us in action against the Gauntts was for their benefit too.

"They're sending the marked people after us," I said. "So why don't we go to the people we've already unmarked?"

Chapter Sixteen

Ruin

WHEN WE PULLED up outside the little cottage, Nox muttered something about it being a "shack." I thought it was kind of cute. The clapboard exterior was all soft if faded pastels, with a narrow front porch where the inhabitants could sit and gaze out over the lawn to the rocky beach. The strip of sand and pebbles stretched about five feet before reaching the edge of the lake. It had a peaceful atmosphere—maybe the right word was "quaint."

Peyton didn't seem to think too much of it, though, even with it being a place she'd spent time at as a kid. She'd told us it belonged to friends of her family who lived out of town and didn't use the cottage in the fall. Her parents had a spare key, but there was no official connection between them and the property that the Gauntts could trace. She led us around the small building with a faint grimace that didn't budge.

"There are only two bedrooms," she said as she unlocked the front door. "But the couch in the living room is a pullout. And there should still be a couple of air mattresses stashed in the closet from when they'd have larger get-togethers here."

"That's plenty," Lily assured her. "We appreciate getting any kind of place to stay that's away from where the Gauntts' lackeys are looking for us."

Apparently Peyton had grown up near here in one of the towns a few over from Lovell Rise, farther along the edge of the large lake. We were almost directly opposite the marsh here—if I squinted, I could make out a greenish blur against the shoreline on the other side of the water.

That didn't mean the marked people the Gauntts had incited to hunt for us wouldn't come out this way, but hopefully even if they did, they'd have no idea that Lily's revamped car was the one they were supposed to be keeping an eye out for. It has a shiny new coat of gray paint thanks to Jett—"the color people are least likely to pay attention to," he'd said—and a slightly redesigned frame that had turned it more modern-looking than before.

Lily's lips pursed a little whenever she looked at it, as if it pained her seeing her car transformed into a different one, but Jett had assured her that he could change it back as soon as the Gauntts stopped being such dicks about everything.

He and Kai had shoved their motorcycles into the garden shed on the property, which had been just big enough to accommodate all of them except the back wheel. They'd closed the door as well as they could and draped a sheet of tarp over the bikes' rears so they wouldn't be identifiable.

Peyton hadn't said much during all that. She hadn't talked much in general since we'd come to her to make our appeal. With the door now open, she hesitated on the porch before offering the key to the cottage to Lily.

"I'll need it back afterward," she said. "And—if you could keep the cottage pretty clean… My parents' friends like to come out here with their family around Christmas, and I don't want them finding a mess."

"Of course." Lily offered her a smile that was only a bit tight around the edges. "You're doing us a huge favor. We don't want to make things any harder for you."

Peyton hugged herself even though the sunny day wasn't too chilly. "Well, we can't let those asshole Gauntts get away with how they've treated all of us. Come on, I'll show you around. Not that there's much to see."

Inside, she pointed out the doors to the two bedrooms, the bathroom, and the cramped kitchen that would have trouble holding more than one person at a time. Not that I figured we were going to be cooking any elaborate banquets while we were here, as unfortunate as that fact was.

I considered asking whether we could get delivery all the way out by the lake and decided it was better not to badger Peyton any more than we already had. Kai had managed to make a quick stop to grab a couple of bulging bags of premade grocery food, so we weren't going to starve, even if I was craving my spicy beef jerky. I'd finished my last package this morning.

Lily's sister didn't seem to have the same concerns about imposing on our obviously reluctant host. When we'd come to a stop in the middle of the living room, which held the pullout couch, a couple of armchairs, and a TV that looked old enough to have been in operation before our first deaths, Marisol prodded Peyton's arm.

"There are bigger ways you can help take down the Gauntts. If we all speak up together, show that we're not scared and we'll say what they did to us—"

Peyton jerked away from the other girl, her face blanching. "I'm not making any big speeches. To have everyone knowing what they did… what I went along with…"

"They were magically controlling us!" Marisol protested. "And we were kids. They were freaking intimidating even without the magic. No one's going to blame you for it."

"And if anyone does, they're a total asshat," Lily put in.

Peyton shook her head. "I just don't want that story tied to me wherever I go for the rest of my life. Which will totally happen."

"It's not just us," Marisol said. "If we could get the other marked people from the college on board—if all of us stood up together—the spotlight wouldn't be on just a couple of us."

"I don't think they're going to go for it either. And what if they back out at the last minute?" Peyton shuddered. Her gaze darted to me, as if she hoped I'd rescue her somehow.

She still did that here and there—look at me as if searching for Ansel, hoping he'd suddenly appear. Not that he'd seemed to be very protective of her even when he'd had control of this body. I wasn't sure why she would want that jerk back so much.

"I wish I could stand with you," I told Marisol. "But I don't know what exactly happened to Ansel. I guess I could make it up based on what we've heard from the other guys who were marked…"

Kai brushed past me with a bump of his elbow. "Bad idea, Ruin. The Gauntts switched things up a fair bit, it seems like. If you say one thing they can prove isn't true and they catch you in a lie, then you'd undermine the whole case."

My momentary hopes deflated. "Yeah. That makes sense. I definitely don't want that to happen."

Lily squeezed my arm. "You help in all kinds of other ways."

"If our *other* marked 'friends' would be a little more helpful, maybe we'd be getting somewhere without anyone needing to do a big public announcement," Nox said, glowering at his phone. He raised his head to glance at the rest of us. "Our man in the Skeleton Corps is having trouble bringing anyone else on board. The two other guys he found who have the marks have gotten skittish about letting us do anything about it since our last fight with the Corps. Worried they'll be punished for fraternizing with the enemy or something. It's like they *want* to be some rich prick's puppet." He snorted in disgust.

Jett waved toward me and Kai. "If we can at least bring them around, Kai and Ruin can force them to go along with Lily's cure."

Kai made a face at that suggestion too. "The first guy came to us willingly. I think we should uphold that pattern when it comes to anyone from the Skeleton Corps. We need these people to trust us, and they've got way more reason to be wary of us than the college kids did. We're better off if it's their idea. Otherwise they'll just see the Gauntts as *another* enemy while we're still one too."

Jett huffed, but he didn't appear to have any counter argument.

Nox glared at his phone again. "He's at least finally convinced them to meet with us so we can make a case. Not sure what we could say that he hasn't already, but we've got to take that shot." He ambled off into the corner, his fingers tapping away at the screen as he replied to the latest text.

Peyton watched him go, her posture somehow getting even stiffer. I couldn't be the guy she wanted, and I wasn't interested in being anyone's guy except Lily's, but she was doing a lot for us. I wished I could make her feel better about it. Say something that would cheer her up even if I couldn't make the guy she'd dreamed about suddenly appear. He hadn't really existed even when Ansel had been alive.

Sometimes I worked best when I just went with the moment and figured out what was right along the way. I moved to her side and motioned toward the door. "Take a little walk with me?"

Peyton blinked at me, her eyes going wide. She hesitated, but this time it didn't look like wariness, only surprise. Then she nodded emphatically.

I shot a quick glance over my shoulder at Lily to make sure she wasn't bothered, but she just gave me a fond smile. She knew how important it was to me to see the people around me happy—or at least as close to content as I could make them. The fact that she understood was one of the reasons I loved her so much.

And she loved me too. The memory of her saying those words hovered in my chest like a giddy bubble, one that'd never pop as long as I lived.

Peyton ambled with me down to the water. Little twinges of pain still ran through my abdomen with my steps, but between the doctor's work and Jett's, the discomfort wasn't too bad now. I'd been able to taper off the painkillers enough that my thoughts no longer felt like they were swathed in cotton balls.

Peyton kicked at the pebbles with the toe of her sneakers and peeked at me through her dark, wavy hair as it drifted across her face. "Did you want to talk to me about something?" she asked.

"Yeah," I said. "I know you're not really excited about all the ways we've intruded on your life."

Her cheeks flushed. "Well, I—I mean, it's been kind of crazy, and all the memories stirred up—and I still don't really understand what happened to Ansel." She gave me that hopeful look again.

I kept my tone gentle. "He's gone. But you're still here. And you're doing an amazing job fighting back against the Gauntts in the ways you can. I just thought you should know that."

Peyton's eyes narrowed abruptly. "Is this to try to get me to testify like Lily's sister keeps pushing for?"

I held up my hands. "No, not at all. That's got to be your decision. I just want you to feel okay, or even good, about everything you've already done."

"It's not so easy." Her gaze dropped to the rock-laced sand. "I barely know any of you. You've done some kind of shitty things too. Just not anywhere near as shitty as what the Gauntts are doing."

I found I couldn't argue with her point. But there were other things I could say. "That's fine. But, you know—you've probably noticed that I'm usually pretty upbeat about stuff. I like to find the positive in everything if I can. Yeah?"

A giggle slipped out of her. "It's kind of hard *not* to notice that, even not knowing you very well."

"Right. So, I first started being that way when I was a little kid. My parents wanted me to figure out how to keep myself happy, so I pretended I was happy all the time, hoping that when they saw I'd managed it, they'd care about me more. But it didn't work that way. And the happiness I made myself feel was kind of hollow for a long time… I think I only really started meaning it after I found people who did welcome me and support me the way they should have."

Peyton arched her eyebrows. "Those other guys you're hanging out with?"

"Exactly!" I said. "I've always belonged with them, and when I knew I could have their backs and they'd have mine, everything got so much brighter. And I think it can be the same for you too. Your parents let you down. They didn't protect you from the Gauntts. Some of your friends let you down too. But I'm sure you can find the right people who'll let you be happy too. Let you know you're making the right decisions about your life. It's not us, and that's okay. Now that you've figured out more about where you're coming from, it'll be easier to find them."

Peyton studied me for a long moment with the warm sun beaming over both of us. Then she offered me a small smile that looked more genuine than anything I'd seen from her earlier today.

"Thank you," she said. "In a weird way, that is kind of nice to hear. And I appreciate that you bothered to say anything at all. I know… you have a lot of reasons to be mad at me for how I treated Lily before."

"That wasn't totally your fault either," I reminded her. "You had the Gauntts egging you on. And everybody makes mistakes. You should probably apologize to her sometime if you haven't already, though."

She rubbed her hand across her mouth. "Yeah. Well. Like I said, thank you. I hope you guys come up with something even better to knock those pricks on their asses."

She went over to the car she'd driven here in, and I headed back to the cottage. Before I reached the porch, Nox stepped outside, rolling his shoulders.

"I'm going to see if I can talk some sense into those Skeleton Corps idiots," he said as Lily emerged behind him.

My success with Peyton had left me with more energy than usual zinging through my veins. Lily had told me before that my attitude was good for the group in ways I might not even be able to see, and maybe she'd been more right than she knew. Before I could second-guess the impulse, the words tumbled out.

"I'll come too. Maybe I can convince them the nonmagical way."

Nox gave me a slightly skeptical look, but he waved me along. "Let's go, then. We want to make this quick. They agreed to meet outside the city, but we're still going a little closer to Mayfield than I'd prefer. I don't want to stick around for long."

This time, since we weren't in the middle of a high-speed chase, he let Lily drive. It was her car, after all. He gave her directions until we ended up at a tourist shop standing alone along one of the country highways. The store clearly hadn't been open in quite a while. The grime on the windows looked almost as thick as the glass.

A few minutes later, another car pulled up. Three men got out—the one who'd come to us asking to have his mark broken and a couple of younger guys who I guessed were marked too. The first guy tipped his head to us, but the others just eyed us warily.

"Look," Nox said right off the bat, planting his hands on his hips, "you've got a bunch of rich bastards who've messed around with you, and they're stopping you from even knowing about it. What's the hold-up? You'd rather stay in the dark?"

One of the new guys narrowed his eyes at Nox. "Maybe we've seen too much of your craziness to think we should believe anything you say. *You* could be the ones who messed with us."

Parker groaned. "I've explained it to you guys. You saw what happened to Storek. Anything these guys have ever done wore off within half an hour. I've had these memories for days since they broke whatever was hiding them in my head."

"Who says we even need to know?"

I could answer that. Nox squared his shoulders, looking like he was about to try to berate them into submission, but I stepped forward first.

"I think we all want the same things," I said.

The second new guy scoffed. "How so?"

"None of us wants some assholes in a high rise controlling us and what we do, right? Trying to keep us down. They *want* us to fight with each other so we're not fighting them and getting back that control."

The first newbie glared at me. "No one jerks me around."

"But they can," I said. "They're already doing it all over the city. Any second now, they might tug on the invisible leash they've got on you and start calling the shots, and as long as you've got that mark, you can't do anything about it. But we can break the leash. We can bark right back in their faces and shove the collars they tried to put around our necks down their throats instead. Why should those pricks get to call the shots? Isn't Mayfield *your* city?"

Nox stirred discontentedly at that suggestion, but the Skeleton Corps guys all perked up a little.

"It is," one said. "I don't know why the guys in charge keep listening..."

"They get paid off," Parker said with a sneer. "That's all *they* care about. They're keeping us down too."

"It doesn't have to be that way," I added. "We're already fighting back, and we can hit them even harder if we're all together in this."

The other newbie eyed me with continued wariness. "You hit *us* before. Why don't you try to hit us now and make us do what you want?"

"Because we're not like them," I said automatically. "We hit you to protect ourselves and find out who screwed us over. Now we know the biggest screwers of them all are the Gauntts, so that's where we're going to aim our fists from now on."

"With or without you," Nox said, with an approving tip of his head when he caught my eye. "We're not going to force you. This *should* be your battle too, but we can't make you believe that."

"I've never wanted to hurt anyone," Lily said quietly. "I just don't want them to get away with all the damage they've done that so many people don't even know about."

There was a moment of silence. But something one of us had said must have gotten through, because the first guy sighed and turned toward Lily, shrugging off his jacket. He raised his chin. "No one controls me. But if *you* do anything that feels like you're fucking with my mind—"

Lily raised her hands. "I'm only going to take off the spell that's already there."

The second guy folded his arms over his chest. "I want to see this before I do anything."

He would see. He'd see that we could be on the same side. And maybe my appeal had made that happen.

Chapter Seventeen

Lily

I TUGGED the hood of my jacket lower over my forehead to shade my face and glanced across the street at Kai, who was similarly clothed and lurking in the alley opposite mine. We hadn't really wanted to come into the city while there were untold numbers of the Gauntts' marked dupes on the look-out for us, but one of the new Skeleton Corps guys had given us an opportunity we had to pursue. So we'd just taken every possible precaution to avoid being identified.

The young Corps member who was lurking farther down the street had undergone a much more extreme makeover. He'd been able to point out the usual driver who picked up the Gauntt grandchildren from school and brought them back to the house—the same man who'd picked up *him* a few times when the Gauntts had been "visiting" with him several years ago. Then Jett had used his magical powers of transformation to adjust the Skeleton Corps guy's features so they matched pretty closely.

We were counting on the Gauntts not scrutinizing the help in minute detail. And the Corps guy was counting on Jett being able to put his face back to normal after this little mission.

But before the mission could even get really started, we needed to create a distraction. Nox and Ruin were going to grab the actual driver before he could set off. Our guy was going to take the driver's place. We needed a bigger spectacle to divert people from the inevitable smaller commotion.

Kai signaled to me, and I raised the paintball gun he'd picked up somewhere or other with his usual resourcefulness. Not the Skullbreakers' typical weaponry, but one I felt a heck of a lot more at ease with. We weren't out to kill anyone today, only to do a little… rearranging and recording, and that was a relief.

Jett would have loved to play a part in this stage of the mission too, but we'd needed someone to stay with Marisol for her protection… and as Kai had pointed out with a snort when I'd commented to him about it, "Jett would have gotten too caught up in making it art instead of making them dance to our bidding."

Kai made the first shot, a blob of red paint splattering into the window of the limo company's building. I fired off a couple of rounds that smacked the dark compact limo just outside with splotches of bright yellow.

Ruin probably liked the makeover, but the company staff didn't seem too pleased. A couple of them hustled out just as Kai launched his next few shots.

Paint punched the man in the gut, the woman in the shoulder. I added a flare of magic to spray the paint even farther across them, gooping up their eyelashes and flecking their hair. It was makeovers all around today!

As they teetered and flailed, a couple more employees hustled out of the building to see what was going on. I fired between them, using my powers to improve my aim and making them jump apart as they dodged.

Just as planned, the driver we were targeting ended up a little farther down the street from the others. Kai and I alternated between shooting at the building, the other employees, and our target, aiming to compel him farther away. Soon that part of the street was looking like a kindergarten painting.

After the first few paintballs battered the sidewalk around his feet, our target hightailed it out of my view. I might have heard a muffled grunt.

The other employees were too busy squawking over their predicament and yelling at each other that someone should call the cops or a cleaning team or the boss—no one seemed to quite agree on who the proper authorities were. After several more explosions of color for good measure, we lowered our weapons.

A moment later, our replica driver strolled into view. He dashed past the others, motioning to them in a gesture designed to indicate that he had to hoof it to make it to his next job. His colleagues barely noticed him in their colorfully disturbed state.

Kai and I watched until another sleek black car with tinted windows purred out of the garage. When it'd disappeared down the street, we ducked down our respective alleys and met up a couple of blocks away where we'd parked Fred 2.0.

I dove into the driver's seat and started the engine. We wanted to be in place well ahead of time. As I pulled into the street, Kai flipped open his laptop. He still wasn't the most avid techie around, but his speed-reading skills and ability to quickly process information gave him a major leg up on his friends, who were just slowly creeping out of their twenty-years-delayed electronics knowledge.

"The camera is already on," he reported. "I'm getting the signal. Now we just need to record some usable footage."

That was the important part. And we needed to stay in range of the device for it to happen. I drew up a block away from Nolan and Marie Junior's school and turned off the gas. Kai studied his screen.

Was Nolan still going to school even though his body was now inhabited by a man who'd gone through more education than anyone in that building could have imagined? Or had the Gauntts come up with some excuse to disenroll him? I figured they'd probably set him up with some kind of home office or similar so he could keep contributing even in his child-like state. Remembering how pissed off he'd sounded that he was going to have to stay out of the public eye for years gave me a small twinge of satisfaction.

One tiny thing hadn't gone his way.

I squirmed uneasily in my seat, waiting for Kai's next update. It only took another few minutes. He sat up a little straighter, a smile crossing his lips. "Here we go. The kid's getting in—the granddaughter. Looks like she's alone. And our guy… he's attached the camera to her bag, just like we discussed. Perfect."

I got a glimpse of the camera's view on the screen, showing the girl perched in the limo's back seat, her legs swinging and her hands fidgeting with the plaid skirt of her uniform. She stared out the window with a dreamy expression and then leaned forward and asked for a specific radio station as the driver started the engine.

In that moment, she looked like a normal kid. We'd been hoping that'd be the case. The adult Gauntts obviously kept a tight rein on their adoptive children, but their supernatural control eased off over time just like Kai's and Ruin's did. After a full day at school, this was probably as close to being a typical kid as Marie Junior ever got.

Before Kai needed to prompt me, I pulled away from the curb and drove along a parallel route to the limo's, heading toward the Gauntts' mansion. Once, the feed jittered when I got stuck behind a teen doing a very slow parking job and the limo pulled too far ahead, but I hit the gas to close the distance as soon as I could.

The real success of this mission would depend on what happened once the limo got to the house.

I stopped at the side of the road just before the limo reached the mansion. As I yanked up the parking brake, Kai swiveled the laptop so we could both watch. I balled my hands on my lap and waited for the scene to unfold.

We might not get anything right away. We couldn't control what angle the camera ended up at when the bag was moved. But there should be a little something right off the bat.

The limo eased to a halt. The girl froze in her seat. Her head turned toward the window as she appeared to track someone coming over to collect her.

The door opened to reveal Thomas Gauntt. It'd been him and Olivia who'd carried out their perverted interests with our Skeleton Corps guy—our first confirmation that the two generations of Gauntts were equally predatory. I hoped he wouldn't feel too awful being that close to his molester right now.

Thomas didn't glance toward the driver. He grasped Marie Junior's shoulder with a clamp of his fingers that looked just shy of painful. "Come on then," he said in a flat voice that wasn't the slightest bit parental. "Quickly and quietly. And get your bag."

She unclasped her seatbelt and reached for the backpack. The camera's feed swam and rolled. She must have slung the bag over her shoulder, because we ended up with a view of the limo driving away from the front gate, which clanged shut afterward. The footage bobbed and swayed with the girl's footsteps all the way to the house. Her supposed father didn't say another word.

In the front hall, everything went still. All we could see was the door. Then Thomas said in the same firm voice, "Up to your room. We'll call you when it's dinner time."

Not a word of affection, not a single question about her day. But the girl followed his instructions mutely. We got the backward view of her tramping up the steps and into her bedroom—and then, miracle of all miracles, she set the bag down next to her desk with the camera facing her bed.

There wasn't much to see all the same. Marie Junior sank down on the edge of the bed, clearly visible on the feed, and just… sat there. And sat there. And sat some more, not moving other than periodic blinks and the slight rise and fall of her chest with her breath.

The longer I watched, the more my skin itched with discomfort. It wasn't any kind of in-your-face horror. The Gauntts weren't carving her into pieces or locking her in a cage. But there was something intensely awful about the sight all the same. A nine-year-old girl in a room full of books and toys doing absolutely *nothing* while she waited for her parents to tell her it was okay to take action again.

As if she only existed to carry out their will. Which wasn't far from the truth, was it?

After a while, Kai let out a low whistle. "You'd think they could let her at least *read* or something. How bored must she get?"

"Maybe she doesn't even notice much," I said. "Everything might be a fog in her head because of their magic—like it was for Marisol when they used their magic to make her run away and stay with their people. Which doesn't make it better. They're already stealing away the little bit of life she should be getting before they totally murder her." I grimaced.

We waited until the dinner call came. That was the first time Marie Junior stirred on the bed. She got up and walked out like a puppet on strings.

While the Gauntts presumably ate their dinner, Kai and I dug into ours of grocery store sandwiches and chips. Our enemies had also murdered my access to decent food. It took about an hour before Marie Junior walked back into her bedroom, with her namesake right behind her.

Marie Senior stopped her granddaughter with a hand on her shoulder and squeezed her like Thomas had. "You'll stay here all night and not make a mess, won't you?"

"Yes, Grandma," Marie Junior answered in a vacant tone that sent a chill down my spine. Then she sat down on the edge of the bed again. And sat. And sat.

After another hour of the girl staring motionless at the wall, I motioned to Kai. "I don't think we're getting anything else tonight. Do you think this is enough to make the news?"

"You can definitely tell something's really not right with how they're treating her," he said. "No healthy kid would act that catatonic. I think it'd work as proof that there's something wrong in paradise."

A deeper sense of relief washed over me as I turned the car in the opposite direction from the Gauntt mansion. I'd been braced for someone to notice us, to come at us somehow, but we'd escaped any consequences.

As I drove back toward the lake, Kai fiddled with the laptop until I heard the swoosh of a sent email. He folded his hands behind his head. "There we go. It's off to every major news outlet and a bunch of minor ones besides. Let's see how long it takes them to broadcast some clips."

He brought up several windows with various online newsfeeds to keep watch. I forced myself to keep my eyes on the road rather than the computer. Driving at legal speeds rather than Nox's preferred pace, it'd take us almost two hours to get to Peyton's cottage.

We were halfway there when Kai cleared his throat. He turned up the volume on the laptop. I didn't let myself look at the newscast he was streaming, but the reporter's voice pealed out loud and clear.

"We recently received footage from an anonymous source that appears to support the recent accusations that the Gauntt family is mistreating children. No one could see this video and not think that the youngest member of the family has had her spirit broken in some way."

Kai cackled. "We've got them now. I'd like to see them explain how this is all a lie. Oh, one of the other channels picked up the story too! Wanting to be at least second to the punch."

A thrill raced through me. We'd taken a risk, and it'd paid off. It couldn't be too much longer before the Gauntts' façade started to crumble.

Then my phone chimed in my purse. Probably one of the other guys checking in on us, not realizing I'd be driving right now. I tipped my head toward it. "Answer it and put it on speaker phone?"

Kai fished out the phone and tapped the button on autopilot. I don't think either of us was prepared for the voice that crackled from the speaker.

"This isn't a game, darling," a woman said, and my heart lurched. I knew that coolly firm tone. It was Marie Senior. "You strike at us, we strike back—at everyone. Their demises are going to be on your conscience."

"What—" I started, but she hung up with a click. Kai stared at the phone. With a jerk of his hand, he smashed it against the door handle. Then he rolled down the window to chuck it into the overgrown field we were just driving past.

"Had to make sure they can't track it," he said, sounding more unnerved than I was used to. "I don't know how they got your number in the first place."

"Magic," I muttered, but my own nerves were still jumping. "What did she mean about striking back at everyone—about 'demises'?"

"I'll see if I can find any info." He tapped at the keyboard, still in the hunt-and-peck stage of comfort. For the first several minutes, there was nothing but that sound and the thump of my pulse. Finally, he sucked in a sharp breath.

"*What?*" I demanded.

Kai wet his lips before they flattened into a grim line. His next exhale came out raggedly. "More kids. Not in any way we can prove is them. There are reports popping up of dozens of children across Mayfield and the surrounding towns suddenly being rushed to the hospital with some unknown illness. No, wait—" He tapped again. "Now they're saying it's a suspected poisoning. Oh, fuck."

"What?" I said again, but with less energy than before. My spirits had already plummeted before I braked so I could look at the screen.

"They're putting out a bulletin of the people they 'believe' might be responsible for the supposed poisoning," Kai said, swiveling the computer. "Thanks to an anonymous nudge from the Gauntts, no doubt."

Gazing back at me from the screen were five photographs—photos of me and the four lead Skullbreakers.

Chapter Eighteen

Lily

I STEPPED out of the hospital with a cloud of anguish hanging over me as dark as the deepening evening. The damp wind tugged at my hood, and I almost forgot to jerk it back down over my face. Cool drizzle started to speckle my cheeks as I hustled to the car where Kai and Ruin were waiting.

As soon as we'd heard the news about the Gauntts' latest act of war, I'd turned the car around and headed toward the nearest hospital. I had to assume that the Gauntts were causing the sickness in the kids—that these were kids they'd used for their supernatural and perverted purposes and left marks on that they were affecting them through. Marie was trying to punish us for our efforts by both hurting the most vulnerable people she could and setting us up for a fall at the same time.

I could easily picture her sitting in her office drumming her fingers together and cackling like a maniacal dictator.

Kai had told the others what was going on, and Ruin had insisted on zooming over here on his motorcycle for moral support, despite my protests. But honestly, it'd been a bit of a relief to have his strong arms wrap around me when I'd gotten out of the car. I knew Kai cared about me, but he wasn't exactly one for huge gestures of affection.

But even though I'd snuck into the hospital with slightly higher spirits than before, those hopes had been dashed to the floor, stomped all over, and kicked into the corner within a few minutes. I'd done a quick makeup job on my face with a few basics I'd had in the glove compartment, pulled back my hair, and even smudged brown eyeshadow on my hairline so if anyone caught a glimpse, I wouldn't look like the blond girl in the news reports, but I still had to avoid notice. And even if I hadn't been a wanted maybe-criminal, I couldn't have walked up to the front desk and said, "I want to see any poisoned kids you've got in here!"

We weren't completely sure there *were* any kids at this specific hospital, even though it'd sounded like enough children had gotten sick that any hospital in the county should have at least one. Because of privacy concerns for minors, the newscasts hadn't given any details about their specific locations. I'd hoped I'd overhear a comment or catch a glimpse of some clue that'd point me in the right direction.

And maybe I had. I'd caught a murmur along the lines of, "so young… no idea what's causing it…" and followed the nurse who'd said it down a hall. But the room she'd gone into had been guarded by a stern-looking police officer. I didn't think he'd let some random hoodie girl go wandering in—definitely not without a close enough look to give me away.

If the kids were getting sick through their marks, then I could cure them by breaking those marks. But I didn't know how to bring my magic to bear without touching them, or at least being close enough to see who I was working on. The Gauntts were exerting their influence from afar, and my range was so limited.

So when I trudged back to Fred 2.0, my hopes were as slumped as my shoulders. The drizzle felt like an appropriate accompaniment to my feelings.

Unfazed by the rain, Ruin sprang out before I reached the car. He gave me another hug and then checked my expression. "What happened?"

"I couldn't find any kids who're affected, if there are any in there,"

I said. "I came across one possibility, but there was a cop staked out by the room. Which I guess makes sense if they think the kids were purposefully poisoned instead of just getting sick."

Ruin gave me a reassuring smile. "Kai and I can take care of that. We'll walk right in and convince him you need to get inside."

"Ruin could probably get one of the doctors in a state where they'd point you to anyone else with the same condition who's in the place," Kai put in, leaning his elbow out the window he'd rolled down.

I shook my head. "There are too many people. You can't brainwash everyone in there simultaneously. And if you start pushing doctors and cops around in a crowded hospital, then they'll definitely believe the story about us being some kind of child-murderers."

"We could try to work our powers on all of them," Ruin offered with his dogged optimism.

Kai sighed. "No, Lily's right. Do you want to try another hospital?"

I glanced back at the gloomy gray building. "This is one of the smaller ones. The big ones in the city will probably have *more* security, not less." My hands balled at my side. "I need a better plan. Or better magic. Or… something."

As I growled that last word, a sliver of an idea occurred to me. It was a longshot, but that was more than the no-shot-at-all I had right now.

I went around to the driver's seat. "We're going out to the marsh again."

That declaration made even Ruin frown. "Those cops found us out there last time."

"We'll take a different route and walk the rest of the way—and keep a close eye out," I said. "If there's anyone nearby, we'll get out of there immediately. But… the Gauntts put a bunch of their magic into the marsh so they could build up their powers there and use it more effectively for their rituals. Maybe we can use that magic against them. And the spirits of those kids should be more upset about what those douche-canoes are doing now than anything before. If they can lend a hand, make some kind of a cure, help me extend my power with their energies… I need to ask."

The guys didn't debate my strategy. Kai kept watching the newscasts on his laptop as I drove toward the lake, but he didn't report any details that'd help us get to the kids to help them. The Gauntts hadn't inserted themselves directly into the conversation about the hospitalized kids either.

No one was talking about our video of Marie Junior anymore. Strict parenting was barely a blip on anyone's radar when children might literally be dying.

Would it occur to anyone to blame the Gauntts? They'd been accused of hurting kids multiple times in the past few days. But none of that hurt had been the type to send anyone to the hospital. There'd be no evidence of foul play when the sickness had been conjured by supernatural means none of the doctors would even believe in.

God, how many of the hospital staff might be marked too?

I shook off that thought as the stretch of water, currently slate-gray under the darkening clouds, came into view up ahead. I was abruptly self-conscious of the beams of the car's headlights streaking through the thickening night. But there weren't any streetlamps along these rough country lanes to guide my way otherwise. Ending up in a ditch wouldn't do us any good.

After a brief internal debate, I drove straight on toward the lake instead of veering down one of the side lanes that would have taken me closer to the spit. We were still a mile distant from that part of the marsh, and anyone keeping watch would *only* be able to see the lights. They had no reason to assume those lights belonged to a suspicious vehicle unless I headed toward the Gauntts' property.

I parked at a lookout spot at the end of the road just a short walk from the water's edge. During the summer, families would have come out here to have picnics and let their kids chase after frogs amid the reeds. The autumn days had gotten cool enough that I doubted there were many of those excursions happening now. Definitely not on a drizzly night.

Hugging myself, I stepped away from the car and peered through the dusk toward the spit. The last haze of the sun's light was fading along the horizon. Unless some vehicle over there flashed *its* lights, I had no way of telling how closely the spit might be monitored.

Both of the guys had followed me. "It's not worth the risk of going closer, is it?" I said to Kai, figuring he'd give me the unvarnished truth.

He frowned. "I don't like our odds. It'd be too easy for them to lie in wait and ambush us if there are minions over there keeping watch. But if you think it's worth it—"

"No." I paused, grappling with my sense of hopelessness. "The magic the Gauntts put into the marsh must stretch all through the marsh to some extent, not just around the spit. They haven't stopped the water currents from flowing around. The energies they've sent into it have got to be what I absorbed after I nearly drowned. Maybe they're what helped your spirits stick around for so long instead of fading away."

It was an unnerving thought that the very people we were desperate to destroy might have given us the powers we were depending on to do so—but also fitting in a way. I squared my shoulders. "I can call to the water. I should be able to reach out to the power in it from right here, and maybe the lingering spirits of their victims too."

"Anything you need from us, just say the word!" Ruin declared.

I walked down to the edge of the marsh, where a chorus of froggy croaks greeted me. It wasn't any hassle sitting on the damp ground when the drizzle had made me pretty damp already. I shucked off my shoes and socks, rolled up my pantlegs, and dipped my feet in the water up to my calves.

The now-familiar hum inside me expanded as if resonating with the lapping of the lake. I stretched my awareness out through the currents and eddies, a swampy flavor congealing in the back of my throat.

Could I feel a faint tremor from the direction of the spit? An answering energy that recognized me?

"I need your help," I called out to it. "You know all about the Gauntts' magic; you hold so much of it. They're using it to hurt people —kids—even worse than before. If you could lend me some of what they've given you so that I can really take them on, if you could give me the strength to break all the spells they're casting… Please."

I couldn't sense any kind of response. The cold water kept tickling over my feet. The cattails rustled around me. I might have tasted the faintest hint of resistance and fear.

"I'm not like them," I said. "I won't be like them. I won't use the power in you for awful things. I—"

I halted, memories surging up that made what I'd just said a lie. My throat closed up completely.

Kai's voice reached me from just behind. "What's the matter, Lily?"

I rubbed my hand over my face. "It's not totally true, is it? I've used the powers I already got from the marsh to *kill* people. I essentially killed Nolan and made the Gauntts come out here so they could murder their grandson. Why should the marsh or the spirits in it believe me?"

Ruin let out a dismissive sound. "You're nothing like them! You're the most wonderful person I've ever met."

My voice came out dry. "I think you might be a little biased."

"He's right, though," Kai said. "You're nothing like the Gauntts. Why did you strike out with your powers when you have? *Why* have you hurt people?"

I paused. "To stop them from hurting you, or Marisol, or me. But still—"

"No buts," he said. "As much as I enjoy yours. The Gauntts are totally selfish with their magic. They're hurting people who've never done anything to them so that they can have more life, more power, more everything than any human being is supposed to. They don't even care about the kids they're raising. But you—you're giving everything you have to protect people you've never even met. That's love and compassion the Gauntts would never comprehend."

"Yeah," Ruin put in. "They've got no idea how to be like you."

Kai nodded. "You stand for hope, for everyone getting to live a *real* life, not a few taking more than their fair share while the others suffer."

I swallowed hard, absorbing their words. Yes. I'd hurt and even killed people, but it was true that it'd never been because I'd wanted to. And never to get some special benefit for myself. I wished I never had to again. More than anything, I wanted the Gauntts stopped, unable to harm anyone ever again. Less pain, less suffering.

Love. Compassion. Hope. That *was* what I stood for. I had to hold on to that conviction. Right now, it resonated through my nerves with a glow that condensed at the base of my throat.

I opened my mouth, and a melody spilled out, as if maybe I could sing the marsh into trusting me, working with me. "Let them all rest and heal, let all the evil be sealed. We can do this together, we can stop them forever, if you'll only believe in me."

My voice fell away, but no response came. I couldn't tell if the marsh was even listening now. Sighing, I got up.

"Hey," Kai said, with unexpected gentleness in his tone. He hesitated for a split-second before slipping his arm around me. "We keep finding more ways to get at them. We aren't backing down." He stopped and shook his head at himself. "That's true, but that's not what I should be saying right now. Ruin's right. You're something special. No matter what the marsh or the spirits in it think. No matter what the Gauntts try to blame on you. You're something fucking precious, and I don't want you to ever forget that I think so too."

I peered at him through the darkness, his face all in shadows, his eyes barely visible behind the faint gleam of moonlight off his glasses. What I could see of his expression was solemn and intense.

Kai didn't normally talk like that. I wasn't sure how to take it. Or the way he carefully stroked his hand down the side of my face.

Maybe he thought I was breaking down like I'd started to when my searches for Marisol had failed, and he thought he had to force himself to act sweet to hold me together.

"I'll be okay," I felt the need to say. "I just—it's frustrating. I wish stopping the Gauntts wasn't so hard, but of course it is. You don't have to worry about me giving up."

Kai let out a hoarse chuckle. "I know that. That's not why— You know, I've always been the way I am, even when I was little. Wanting to learn everything I could, figuring things out quickly, seeing how to read people… It freaked my parents out, so they just kind of stopped dealing with me other than the necessities, and most of the other people I ran into didn't like how sharp I was either. I can't say I really had friends before the Skullbreakers."

An ache formed in my heart at the thought of the bright, brilliant, lonely boy he'd been. "I'm sorry."

"Don't be. That's not the point. They didn't matter anyway, not really. But you do. You're everything I could want, and I—I don't want to be sharp with you. Other than when it helps you. But the rest of the time… I'm trying to find the softer parts of me, even if they're smaller than what the rest of the guys can offer, so you can have that side of me too."

Sudden tears pricked at the backs of my eyes. Before I could figure out how to respond to his emotional confession, Kai tugged my face toward his. He caught my lips in a tender but passionate kiss that warmed me from my toes to the top of my head, chasing away the chill of the damp night.

Without breaking the kiss, he walked me over to a lone oak tree that stood several feet from the shoreline. The sweep of the branches, autumn leaves still clinging to them, gave us more shelter from the thin rain. Kai pulled me flush against him, one hand around my waist, the other lingering against my hair.

"You tried telling the marsh who you are and what you stand for," he murmured. "Maybe it'd be better if we showed it how much love you've got surrounding you." He glanced over his shoulder toward Ruin, who'd followed us over at a respectful distance. "Both of us, if Mr. Enthusiastic wants to join in as much as I suspect he does."

Ruin hummed and stepped around us to rest his hands on my waist from behind. "I'm always happy to give our woman a demonstration of just how much I adore her."

A giddy shiver ran through me. I wouldn't normally have gone for something like this, outside in a theoretically public place, but it was so dark I could barely see the car twenty feet away. We hadn't noticed any sign of anyone nearby.

Maybe Kai was right that making love would prove something. All the Gauntts seemed to do out here was inflict death. And even if he wasn't right, I wanted to show *him* how much his declaration meant to me.

"No arguments here," I said, and leaned in to kiss him again.

As my mouth melded with Kai's, he caressed my hip. Ruin pressed against me, pinning me between them. He swept my hair to the side and lowered his head to nibble the side of my neck.

More heat bloomed through my body everywhere the two of them touched. It might as well have been blazing summer around us with the way I was feeling now.

Kai stayed tender in his attentions, slipping his hand under my shirt and cupping my breast through my bra. He circled his thumb over the peak in increasingly tight circles until the quivers of pleasure had me whimpering against his mouth.

Ruin tucked his hand between Kai and me to massage my mound through my pants. I swayed with the motions of his fingers, a moan stuttering out of me. My ass brushed the bulge of his erection.

I rubbed back against him and teased my hand down to Kai's groin at the same time. The other guy was just as hard behind the fly of his jeans. I couldn't resist tugging down the zipper right then and gliding my fingers over the silky skin of his shaft. His groan made my heart leap.

I loved them too—so much. Maybe our relationship was crazy in all kinds of ways, but it was thanks to them that I'd found who I could really be, gained the confidence to stand up to Mom and Wade and now the Gauntts, become a force to be reckoned with while I stood between our enemies and my sister…

That was what real love was meant to be, wasn't it? Something that helped you grow into a better version of yourself.

Say what you want about my four ghostly gangsters—they'd supported me in spades.

Ruin tugged down my jeans and eased his hand right inside my panties. He made an approving sound, his breath spilling hot over my neck. "So wet for us. I love feeling how much you enjoy this. Nox is right—you're a *very* good girl."

Kai laughed as he squeezed my ass. "And a naughty one. Both at the same time. Aren't we lucky to have her?"

"Oh, yes. The luckiest." Ruin pecked kisses along my shoulder and dipped his fingers right inside me.

I couldn't contain my cry. As I rocked with Ruin's pulsing fingers, I fumbled to yank Kai's pants down far enough to fully free him. "I think I'm the lucky one. And I'd be even luckier with you inside me."

Kai let out a stuttered breath thick with longing, but the next second he was turning me between them. "My friend didn't get that honor last time. You should have all of us every which way." He lifted his chin toward Ruin. "Lean against the tree so you don't strain yourself."

Ruin followed his instructions with an avid grin. As he propped himself against the oak so it could take most of his weight, I unzipped his jeans too. His cock sprang into my hand, and he let out a groan of his own as he shoved his pants and boxers down farther. Then he slid his hand around me to pat my ass.

"Every which way," he said with undisguised fervor. "Are you going to take both of us, Angelfish?"

Kai had stayed with us, stroking his fingers up and down my sides. Now, they briefly stilled. My heart stuttered with a jolt of giddy nerves. "I— Do we have everything we need?"

Kai pressed a kiss to my shoulder and the nape of my neck, slipping his hand between me and Ruin at the same time to tease across my sex. "I think we can make sure it's nothing but enjoyable for you with what we have." He tugged my pants farther down and trailed the slickness from my sex to my back entrance.

As Kai started to massage me there, Ruin rocked against me, provoking my clit with his straining cock. Kai paused just long enough to retrieve a foil packet and hand it to the other guy. Ruin chuckled as he ripped it open. "It is good having friends who are always prepared for the important things."

A giggle tumbled out of me. I helped roll the thin material over his length, giving him an extra pump of my fingers so he groaned again.

"I want you to feel every bit as good as I can possibly make you," I said, my voice gone low and husky.

I felt Kai's smirk against the corner of my jaw before he nipped my earlobe. "And we both want the same for you. Isn't it perfect how that works out?"

He hefted me up so I could sink onto Ruin's shaft. Ruin grasped my ass, spreading my cheeks wider as if to offer Kai even easier access. We stayed there, me simply enjoying the sensation of being filled and held, as Kai worked more of my natural lubrication over my other opening. Then he nudged his own cock against it.

As he eased into me bit by careful bit, a thin whine escaped me, but it was nothing but ecstatic. I wasn't sure I'd ever stop being amazed by the delight of two of my guys taking me at once. The heady sensations rippled through my whole body, setting me alight even when we were barely moving.

And then we did start moving. Ruin stayed braced against the tree trunk and Kai leaned into us, and together they lifted me up and down, impaling me deeper on their cocks with each iteration. The rush of pleasure became a flood, all-consuming.

This was love too, wasn't it? Giving yourself over to the people you trusted most in the world. Honoring the joy you could create between your bodies because of that trust.

A soft, wordless song spilled over my lips and carried through the air. I shivered and quaked with the increasing pace, my breath quickening, but the melody only rising.

Kai thrust even faster and came with a groan and a tighter hug around my torso. "Fucking love you," he mumbled.

The sound of his release tipped me over the edge in turn. I clamped around Ruin, my head bowing as the final wave rolled over me and wrung me out to drift in the afterglow. Ruin kissed me hard on the mouth, his hips jerking as he followed me.

When we came to a stop, still clasped in our joint embrace, I couldn't tell if anything had changed in the marsh air. If any powers thrumming through the water had taken notice of our display or cared. But there was a new steadiness inside me.

I cared about so many people. I cared about getting to the truth and helping those harmed by it heal. And nothing the Gauntts did could stop me from pursuing that goal all the way to the end.

Chapter Nineteen

Jett

I'd saved the main Thrivewell building for last, for good reason. The other satellite companies in the county had security around them, but nothing on the same level as the Gauntts' home base. As I kept watch for the first several minutes from a shadowy alcove down the street, I started to feel more like a vigilante superhero than a rogue artist.

Well, maybe I was a little of both tonight. I'd certainly been taking to the air more than the average person did.

Two security officers were patrolling the outside of the building. At one point, the first stopped to talk to another guard just inside the lobby. I had no idea how many other officers might be staked out inside, but they weren't my concern.

I needed a chance to do my work on the outer walls without getting caught. And this wasn't a process I could rush if my magic was going to work right, especially when I was getting tired from the half a dozen spectacles I'd already designed tonight.

When I'd gotten a good sense of the security guards' rhythms, one of them pacing back and forth in front of the building while the other completed regular circuits of the full thing, I hustled farther down the street where I'd be out of view, crossed the road, and approached again by slinking through the dark patches between the glow of the streetlamps. I didn't walk right up to the Thrivewell building, of course. Instead, I darted around the side of the neighboring office building.

That one didn't have anywhere near the same kind of security. The squat concrete structure which only stood ten stories compared to Thrivewell's twenty housed a bunch of different companies on different floors, including an accounting firm and a recording studio, based on the sign out front. None of them were apparently inclined to put a big budget toward securing the building overnight, but then, unlike the Gauntts, they had no reason to anticipate an attack.

I gripped the handle and used a surge of my ghostly energy to shift the shape of the lock so it no longer held the door in place. As I eased the door open, the sound of footsteps made me freeze. I ducked down behind a large potted shrub in the side hall and watched as the sole security guard in this building ambled by, looking more interested in whatever he had playing on his phone than in his surroundings.

With a little luck, no one would ever realize the crime I was about to commit had taken advantage of his lax attitude. I had nothing against the guy. It had to be awfully boring walking around in dark halls for hours on end while shit-all happened.

Thankfully, I found a stairwell just a short distance down the hall. I hurried up the steps, less worried about noise now that I knew I'd left the security dude behind. The only time I paused was at the fourth floor, where the recording studio's vibrant red-and-yellow logo was emblazoned on a plaque next to the landing's door. I studied it for a second, committing the name to memory as I thought of the career aspirations Lily had talked about.

Wouldn't it be a punch in the Gauntts' teeth if she saw through that dream just one building over from where they'd tried to crush her?

I couldn't do anything more about that mission right now, though. I strode up the rest of the flights, cursing the lingering effects of my nerd host's lack of fitness as my breaths turned ragged, and pushed past the door on the top floor.

Now all I needed was a window on the side of the building facing

Thrivewell. Or at least a wall. I could make do with whatever, but it was helpful to be able to see what the hell I was doing.

To my satisfaction, I found a room toward the back of the building on the correct side with a spread of waist-height windows stretching the entire length of the space. I didn't need to reach Thrivewell in *exactly* the spot where my magic would take effect, only to make some kind of contact, and there'd be less light back there to expose my efforts.

Taking slow and even breaths to build up my focus, I marched over to the farthest end of the row of windows. There, I set my hands against the glass. Then I willed it and the concrete beneath it to stretch out like a diving board toward Thrivewell's glossy wall.

After my recent efforts, a prickle of exhaustion passed through my arms at the attempt. But the materials bent to my will, folding down and yawning across the ten or so feet between the buildings. To preserve energy, I only made the ramp a couple of feet wide. If I took an actual dive, it'd be my own clumsy fault.

The process was entirely silent, other than the wind that seeped through the now-open window pane and ruffled the papers on a few of the nearby desks. The patrolling guard walked by ten stories beneath me with a faint rasp of his shoes against the pavement. I peered down at him, waiting until the vague impression of his form in the darkness disappeared around the bend, and then crept out onto my enchanted ramp. Beat this, fairy godmothers.

To ensure my balance, I scooted along on my ass with my legs splayed and my knees gripping the edges of the ramp. It wasn't the most visually appealing display of coordination I'd ever put into the world, but I told myself that didn't matter when no one was supposed to see me anyway.

When I reached the far end, where I could brace my feet against Thrivewell's sleek siding, the plank was wobbling a little with my weight. I debated pulling more concrete along it to thicken it but decided it felt sturdy enough. I didn't have time or energy to waste. This was the keystone in my first real public show, the masterwork around which all the others were centered.

Leaning forward carefully, I rested my hands against the smooth surface just like I had with the window. But I didn't reshape the building in front of me. Instead, I closed my eyes and pictured the impressions I wanted to mark into the face of the structure.

Colors and forms and the lines of letters swept out from my imagination. I paused here and there to pay special attention to one detail or another, making sure every effect I created shared the same reflective quality. It wouldn't do if the curtains rose too soon and the Gauntts had a chance to cover up my show before the rest of the city got to see it.

Sweat trickled down my back and over my forehead. I didn't dare raise my hand to swipe it away. I just kept pushing the images in my mind into the surface in front of me, on and on, no matter how the mass of concrete and glass I was perched on bobbed with the rising of the wind.

A jab of fatigue shot through my mind. I shoved against it with one last burst of power, and then I sagged backward, dropping my hands to my sides to steady myself.

It was done. At least, as far as I could tell, I'd finished what I'd set out to do. I wouldn't know for sure how well it'd turned out for another few hours.

I scooted back to the other building looking just as dorky as I had on the way out, though considerably more relieved with each butt-length closer I got to solid ground. As soon as I'd scrambled through the opening, I turned to finish the last part of my task. With a yank of my supernatural voodoo, I pulled the glass and concrete back into place.

Okay, so maybe that window was now more of a parallelogram than a proper rectangle. And maybe the wall was slightly lumpier than it'd been before. Wiped-out artists did wiped-out work. If anything, I was shaking these office drones' lives up in some tiny way. They should thank me for the fresh perspective.

I snuck down through the stairwell and out the same door I'd entered through. When I reached Lily's car, several blocks away, she was still asleep in the backseat where I'd left her. A gun was tucked in her folded arms like a teddy bear.

She'd insisted that none of us should go into the city on our motorcycles, since the Gauntts' lackeys were probably keeping an especially close eye on our favorite type of vehicle. And after she, Kai, and Ruin had gotten back to the cottage to tell their story about the attack on the marked children and I'd declared that I had a mission of my own to see through, she'd insisted that I shouldn't go alone. That was okay with me. It was fitting that she'd be one of the first people, if not the very first, to witness the greatest work I'd made yet.

She only stirred briefly when I started the engine. I drove around to an underground parking lot where we could stay out of sight and tipped the driver's seat back as far as it would go. I needed to catch up on my sleep too. Before I closed my eyes, I set the alarm on my phone for just before dawn.

I woke up before the alarm at the rustle of Lily sitting up. "I'm sorry," she whispered when I glanced at her. "You can go back to sleep. I just needed to stretch a little."

I checked the time and shook my head. "No, I was going to need to be up soon anyway. We need to get into place to watch the sunrise. Then you can see what I made."

She clambered into the front passenger seat and watched me with open curiosity as I drove us back toward the center of the city. We walked the last few blocks, keeping our hoods up and heads low.

I'd picked out the perfect vantage point: a sixth-floor café in a shopping complex almost directly across from the Thrivewell building. It wasn't technically open yet, but I made quick work of the lock on the doors and led Lily over to the floor-to-ceiling windows at the front of the space.

It was still dark out, a faint glow just starting to touch the edges of the sky. Lily peered through the glass at the Thrivewell building. "What am I looking for?"

"Just wait," I said. "I made it so that it'll only show up when the sunlight hits it. We've got maybe another five minutes."

I tapped out a quick message to Kai telling him to alert whatever news contacts he'd picked up that there was something to see at the Thrivewell head office. I would let word about the other buildings I'd "painted" spread more organically. This one—this one needed to be blasted all over TVs and computer screens for the entire county to see.

The edges of the supernaturally painted shapes started to shimmer with the expanding light. Lily stepped closer to the glass, and I moved with her, tucking my arm around her waist. It still felt like some kind of miracle that I could simply be with her in every way I could possibly want, so easily. That I could offer something that would mean so much to her, even if it was hardly a romantic gift in the traditional sense.

Because the artwork I'd imprinted on the front of the Thrivewell building wasn't pretty by any stretch of the imagination. As the first news van rumbled into view on the street below us, the colors and lines came into clearer focus.

A quartet of monsters with the adult Gauntts' faces loomed over a crowd of children with sickly green skin. Thomas and Olivia dribbled toxic purple liquid over them. The beast that looked like Marie was wrenching one child's arm. He was wearing only an undershirt, and a blotch like the ones that marked so many other victims shone on his upper arm.

Words rippled around the image, framing it. *The Gauntts brought the poison. Check your children. See the marks they left.*

More vehicles were stopping outside the building. A yell carried faintly through the glass, too muted for me to make out the words. Lily pressed her hand over her mouth.

"It's horrible," she said. "And it's perfect. You pointed the finger right back at them and gave the parents and doctors the evidence to look for."

"They won't be able to prove that the marks came from the Gauntts or had anything to do with the kids getting sick," I admitted. "But all those parents *know* that they gave the Gauntts access to their kids at some point. I figured they could use a reminder."

"Yes," she said softly, and gave me a smile that was sad and grateful all at once. I wrapped my arms tighter around her and took one last look at my masterpiece. We needed to get going before the café workers came to prepare for the official opening.

The picture I'd painted wasn't the kind of subtle art that was usually my preference. It was so literal I'd normally have cringed. But right now, with what we were up against, it'd hit the exact note I was going for. It really was the most perfect piece I'd ever made.

And if I could create one piece of artwork that said exactly what I needed it to in every hue and stroke, who was to say I couldn't do that again in my usual style, sometime down the road. After all, I couldn't have asked for a better muse.

Chapter Twenty

Lily

When I woke up after a much-needed nap, the guys and Marisol were gathered around the little TV in the cottage's living room. Mid-day sunlight was streaming through the front windows. It'd have felt like a cozy little scene if not for the name "Gauntt" carrying from the speakers.

As I reached the couch, Nox grasped my hips and tugged me down onto his lap so I could join the three of them on the sofa. Ruin leaned forward in the armchair next to us and offered me a blueberry muffin. My stomach grumbled with the reminder that I hadn't eaten anything at all so far today. Despite the tightness in my gut, I took the muffin and dug in as I watched the news story play out.

"Repair crews have worked quickly to cover up the vandalism done to the Thrivewell buildings last night," the man on the TV was saying. "But images of the strange graffiti—if you can even call something so elaborate that—are circulating throughout social media. The Gauntt family has released a statement accusing their competitors and saying this is more corporate sabotage. And during all this, I'd have to say the children still fighting for their lives in hospitals throughout the county are the true victims here."

My throat constricted. I forced down the last bite of muffin. "No kidding," I muttered as the newscast moved to another story. "Is *anyone* actually investigating the Gauntts or considering that they could be lying?"

Kai rubbed his forehead. "The reporter mentioned that there've been some public petitions circulating, people calling for more transparency, whatever the fuck they think that means."

"The most important thing is the parents seeing that message, right?" Ruin said in his usual optimistic way. "Thinking that they made a mistake."

"If it actually bothers them to see their kids sick after what they already put them through," Marisol said with a grimness I didn't like. I reached over to squeeze her hand.

Nox took my other hand in his, stroking his thumb over my knuckles. "There's a lot of buzz around the images. We've got them talking even more than before. We're getting there. Now we just need to decide how to hit them next."

The words had only just left his mouth when a mechanical groaning sound emanated from outside. We all sprang up. Heart thudding, I raced to the window to peer across the terrain.

My car's hood had lifted open. I didn't see anyone around it. It looked like it'd just popped up of its own accord. Frowning, I eased out the front door.

As I walked over to take a closer look, all four of the guys flanked me with Marisol trailing close behind. But there was no one around at all. Just us and Fred 2.0… whose hood was now swaying up and down like it was doing an imitation of a shark's chomping mouth.

Static crackled from the car radio and formed into a voice. The hood kept swaying along with the words, giving the ridiculous impression that it was Fred talking to us.

"Lily Strom. This is a message for Lily Strom. Bring her here or repeat this message to her."

"What the fuck?" Jett said. He stepped closer to the car and leapt backward when the hood snapped momentarily shut like it'd hoped to devour a body part or two.

The next words weren't anything I'd have expected my loyal vehicle to ever say to me: "Lily Strom, this is your last chance to negotiate the return to health for all those children. If you care about seeing them live, you'll meet with a representative of the Gauntt family in the field east of the Strom family home. He will come alone. So must you. If you arrive with aggression, your chance and the children will be forfeit."

The hood crashed down once more with a resounding clang. Ruin sputtered a laugh. He ambled over and tapped at the metal frame as if trying to wake Fred up again.

Marisol folded her arms over her chest. "That's some crazy magic."

"They found your phone and then your car," Nox said with a growl. "Those fuckers had better learn to back off." He smacked his fist into his palm and glanced at his friends. "We should tear right over there to that field and show them—"

I held up my hand, even though my heart was still pounding painfully fast. "No. They said I should come alone."

Nox stared at me. "You can't go along with what those assholes want. They'll be looking to destroy *you*."

"Maybe," I said, "but it'd be hard for them to arrange an ambush in that spot. There's nothing around but grass." I could see the field in my mind's eye—it'd been my view from the front porch for most of my childhood. "It sounds like they might *kill* all those kids right away if I don't at least try to talk to them. I'm not going to go along with any crap they ask, but hearing what they say might tell us where they're vulnerable, right?"

Kai grimaced. "She does have a point." He gave me a firm look. "If you see *any* sign that there's more than their one representative in the area, you'll want to take off immediately. And keep a grip on his blood so you can take him down before he can try anything on you, if he decides to."

Nox let out another growl and shifted his weight on his feet. "I don't like this. They don't get to call the shots."

"They are, though," I said. "To some extent, we can't stop them until we figure out how to save those kids."

"I know." Scowling, he nodded to the car. "But you're not going anywhere in that. Now that they're turning your ride into their very own ventriloquist dummy, I think we've got to put it on ice until the Gauntts are out of the picture. Kai, do you think you can scrounge up another car quick?"

Kai clapped his hands together. "I'm sure I can take care of both problems at once."

I waved Fred 2.0 a fond farewell, hoping it wouldn't be for too long, and Kai zoomed off. He returned just half an hour later in a modest sedan that I couldn't imagine anyone glancing twice at, which I guessed was the point.

"No one will miss this for the time we'll be keeping it," he said as he got out. "Jett, you want to give the license plate a little makeover just in case?"

While Jett went around to the back to make a few adjustments, Kai tossed me the key. I got in, and Nox dropped into the passenger seat next to me.

"What are you doing?" I demanded.

The Skullbreakers boss gave me a look so fierce it'd have seared the flesh off my bones if it hadn't been mixed with protective devotion. "I'm not letting you really go out there on your own. You'll want to park far back from their guy anyway. I can keep out of sight. But this way, if you yell for help, there'll be someone to deliver it."

I couldn't bring myself to argue with him. I didn't want to face the Gauntts' representative and whatever else they might have in store for me alone. But I gave him a fierce look right back. "You need to make sure you're not seen and stay put unless it's *really* obvious that I'm in trouble that I can't take care of on my own. You know I can deal with a lot."

He huffed. "I do, Siren. I can keep my hands to myself. When I'm specifically asked to." A sly gleam lit in his dark eyes that set me on fire in all kinds of other ways.

"Fine," I said. "We'd better get going. They must have left some extra time in case I wasn't here to get the message right away, but I don't know how long they'll wait before they decide I'm not coming at all."

Jett walked around and pressed his hands to the windows one after another. "Adding a little tint so no one can see in," he told us. "Easier than having the boss squash down on the floor."

Nox grinned at him. "My ass thanks you."

I swatted him. "Once we get out by the field, you should stay low anyway, just to be safe."

In preparation, he pushed the passenger seat back as far as it would go while I drove. Then he stretched out his legs, which still reached almost all the way across the space.

"Is this how big you were in your original life?" I asked. "Or are you still filling out Mr. Grimes?"

Nox chuckled. "Worried I'll get too massive for you to handle? I think you'll do just fine, Siren."

I rolled my eyes, my lips twitching into a smile. "I'm only wondering."

He glanced down at himself. "I think this is about back to normal. It's hard to remember exactly after twenty-one years in limbo. It feels pretty right, anyway." He looked back at me. "Speaking of which—you know it's not right that the Gauntts are putting those kids' lives on your shoulders, right? *They're* the ones doing the killing. They're the ones who messed with them and marked them in the first place. They're just trying to get you to back down because of how hard you've been working to protect those kids from them."

I did know all of that, but hearing him say it so plainly released one or two of the many knots in my stomach. "I can't help thinking about how if I backed down, they might let the kids recover."

Nox shrugged. "And then they'd fuck up a whole bunch more kids because no one got in their way. You've seen how we work, Minnow. There's a lot of collateral damage in our chosen career. I know you're not used to that, but the way I see it, it's really just a reflection of how the whole world goes, just a little more in your face. There are always choices. Someone always loses. You just try to make sure it's mostly the people who deserve it, and that you make the choices that save as many of the people who matter as you can. But you have to realize you can never save everyone."

I swallowed hard. "Yeah." Then I didn't know what else to say. He was right. And the Gauntts *were* the ones forcing me to worry about saving anyone at all.

But all the same, if I saw an opening that'd let me save every one of those kids without losing even more, I'd take it.

Nox reached over and squeezed my knee. "That doesn't mean there's anything wrong with you wanting to protect everyone. That huge heart of yours is part of the reason I love you."

Those words still provoked a flutter through my chest. "Just part?" I teased.

He winked at me. "I do have a healthy appreciation for the rest of your body as well. And this brain that seems to be nearly as good at scheming as our know-it-all." He tapped the side of my head lightly.

The conversation hadn't changed anything in a concrete way, but the worst of my nerves had settled by the time we came into view of the field the Gauntts had directed us to. I spotted a figure standing in the middle of the grassy expanse, half a mile from the nearest building, which was my old house, standing on its lonesome in the distance. There was no one else around and nowhere for them to be hiding unless they'd shrunk to about six inches tall. Even if the Gauntts had staked out backup at the house, they wouldn't be able to reach me very quickly.

Nox sank low in his seat without prompting. I pulled onto the shoulder of the road at the edge of the field and parked. It was going to be a bit of a hike just for me to reach the messenger.

"If I need you, I'll shout really loud," I told Nox before I opened the door.

He saluted me. "And I'll run really fast."

I tramped across the field toward the waiting figure, a middle-aged man I'd never seen before. The familiar scent of the nearby marsh washed over me with the breeze. The Gauntts might have claimed part of the shoreline as their own, but this was my home turf. I wasn't going to let them intimidate me.

Remembering Kai's suggestion, I directed the hum of energy inside me at the Gauntts' man, getting a feel for the pulse of blood through his body. I could shove it all toward his heart in an instant if I needed to. I kept a close eye on his hands, watching for any attempt to reach for a weapon. He was holding a tablet, but that didn't mean he couldn't have a gun concealed.

I came to a stop about ten feet away from him. "I'm here. What did they want to say to me?"

The man didn't speak, simply tapped the tablet and held it up. The screen showed a video chat feed. Marie Gauntt peered at me from wherever she was conducting this virtual meeting. The new Nolan, the kid containing his old soul, came over to stand next to her chair.

"Miss Strom," she said in her usual cool voice. "I take it you're willing to consider a ceasefire."

I raised my chin. "I just want to hear what you have to say."

Marie gave a slight lift of her shoulders. "It's quite simple. You've seen how so many people are suffering because of your actions. You can end that all right now and have everything you ever wanted at the same time."

"And what exactly do you want from me for that to happen?"

Nolan piped up, his dry tone sounding odd in his newly youthful voice. "Give up your allies—this gang that's been causing havoc around the city. Come and work with us. We can set you up with whatever career you'd like, and you can keep it for as long as you want—just as we do. And all the animosity between us can end."

Every bone in my body balked at the suggestion of becoming like them in any way. I wanted to hear every detail they'd offer, though, in case we could use anything in the fight against them.

"What would you do to the Skullbreakers?" I asked.

"They seem to center their activities around you," Marie said. "I expect if you step aside, they'll be much easier to contain."

To kill, she meant. My jaw clenched. "And you're saying you'd make all those kids better again? They'd completely recover?"

"They were only ever ill because of your actions," Marie said. She was being very careful not to admit any of the Gauntts' involvement, I noticed. Probably worried I might be recording this conversation to use against her.

They could be doing the same with me. I crossed my arms. "I didn't do anything to the kids, and you know it. *You* made them sick to get back at me."

Nolan let out a huff. "See it however you like. Do you want to spare them or not? You know how far we can go and how much power we wield beyond anything you and your ruffians are capable of. You're never going to win. Why are you holding onto this grudge while so many children suffer by your hand?"

A prickle ran down my back. Did he really think that ending the supposed poisoning would end the suffering? What about all the other crap they'd put the kids through?

"Are you going to stop the rest of the stuff you're doing to kids like them?" I demanded. "You've been messing them up for longer than I've even been alive."

Marie tipped her head to one side, giving me a look so patronizing I wanted to punch her in the face. "I don't know what you're talking about. Any associations we've had with the people in those towns have solely been for drawing the necessary resources to keep our legacy going and satisfying what urges need addressing. The most vital energies come from youth, but we've never taken too much. We've never done any *harm*. We don't take things that far."

So that was why they targeted kids—because the energy the Gauntts could draw from their young bodies was the best for maintaining their magic? I guessed that made a sort of sense given that a lot of the family's magic went into keeping their spirits eternally alive from host to host.

Still, I had to snort in disbelief. Did she honestly buy her own story? I didn't know whether the energy they seemed to harvest from the kids hurt them any in the long run, but did she think somehow there were levels of molesting that were acceptable, just because they had some perversions to "address"?

Any amount was too far for the people they'd messed with. I'd witnessed the emotional harm done in my sister and in every other person I'd freed from the marks. If the Gauntts' repeated passage from adult bodies to juvenile ones had warped their proclivities toward "youth" in every area, then that was just one more sickening way their domination over this community had polluted it.

"Either you're lying or you're nowhere near as smart as you seem to think you are," I said. "I've seen the effects of your 'legacy' all over town. *I* felt it when you stole seven years of my life to cover up your dirty secret. And now you think I want to be a party to that sick behavior?"

Marie's face stiffened into a mask of disapproval. "We've made you a generous offer. You should think twice before throwing it back in our faces. Having observed you in action, we'd prefer to work with you to keep this all simpler. Having another ally who understands where we're coming from could benefit all of us. But if you insist, we'll have to enforce our authority the hard way."

The threat chilled me, but I couldn't see any way to get around it. I wasn't going to give the Gauntts control over my life, and I wasn't going to buy into their psychotic philosophy.

Nolan had said I was never going to win, but they wouldn't be making this offer in the first place if they weren't afraid that I could, would they? They were worried about how much *they* might lose if the battle continued. That meant even they believed that we had a chance of stopping them completely.

"Then make it hard," I said firmly. "Just know that you'll take the fall for every kid who dies under your spell. You have no idea how many cards we have left to play."

Both Nolan's and Marie's gazes hardened even more. "We'll see about that," Marie said tartly. "You've chosen your fate."

The video feed blinked off. The man tucked the tablet into his jacket and strode away without a word.

Chapter Twenty-One

Lily

My skin creeping with apprehension, I hurried back to the car. Nox didn't straighten up in his seat until I'd pulled the door closed. He took in my expression.

"They didn't dangle any bait you wanted to take?" he said.

I shook my head. "I mean, I didn't really think they would. But I didn't find out anything all that useful either. They were really cagey in what they actually admitted to, which isn't surprising. I did my best to persuade them that it'd be a bad idea if they make those kids even sicker, but I don't know if I was convincing enough."

Nox gave me one of his slow, broad smiles. "You can be plenty convincing." He paused, still studying me. "Is something else wrong?"

I swiped my hand across my mouth. "I don't know. They were talking about coming down on us 'the hard way,' as if they've been going easy on us before. I don't know what they meant by that. But they might have been bluffing just like I kind of was."

"Probably," Nox muttered. "Sounds like those fuckers' MO."

I started the car and swerved around to head back toward the cottage, scanning the landscape around us as I went. I couldn't see any sign that we were being watched, and the Gauntts' messenger hadn't come anywhere near Fred. That didn't mean they couldn't have some scheme to find out where we were hiding out now. I bit my lip.

But Kai, being the brainiac he was, had considered that concern before I needed to voice it. Nox had just texted the other guys, and at the ping of the responding message, he motioned to me. "Our know-it-all gave me the address for a parking garage we should stop at in Lovell Rise. He's arranging for us to swap cars there. When we come out, anyone keeping an eye on us won't know we're in the new one."

I exhaled in relief. "Perfect."

The garage Kai had directed us to was at the bottom of a large shopping plaza—at least, large by Lovell Rise standards. Cars were coming and going pretty regularly on this Saturday afternoon. One of our few remaining new Skullbreakers recruits waved to us and handed us the key to our new car. We drove out and zoomed off toward the cottage with the weight of that immediate threat lifted.

The cottage had just come into sight up ahead when my new burner phone rang. Nox fished it out of my purse for me and held it up on speaker phone. I didn't recognize the number.

"Hello?" I said.

An urgent voice spilled from the speaker. "Hey—it's Lily, right? I—I'm not sure what to do. It seems like they're coming for me. I don't think I can stay here any longer."

It took me a moment to place the guy with an image of him hunched at the base of a tree near the Lovell Rise College parking lot. "Fergus? What happened?" I'd broken the Gauntts' mark on him weeks ago, and he'd helped us with our plan to strike out at Thrivewell through their victims' parents. He hadn't sounded this distraught the last time I'd spoken to him, but then, we hadn't talked at length. The last contact I'd had was when I'd texted all our unmarked allies my new number in case anything important came up.

"I'm not sure," he said in the same rushed tone. "I can just tell—it's not safe here. They figured out I was trying to screw them over, and now they're trying to destroy me. I had to leave campus… I don't know how long it'll take them to find me…"

I had the sense of him pacing, his breath already ragged from an extended flight. My chest constricted. "You mean the Gauntts. They've come after you?"

"Yeah. Yeah. I didn't want to bother you, but—"

"No, it's okay," I said quickly. It was my fault he was becoming a target all over again—I'd drawn him into this fight. "Look, we've got a place where you can hide out safely. Can you borrow a car they wouldn't be able to trace to you? Or get a cab with cash?"

Relief rang through his voice. "I should be able to manage. Thank you."

"It's no problem at all. This is where you'll want to go."

I rattled off directions to the cottage as I parked next to it. Fergus offered many more effusive thank yous and hung up. I hurried over to the building, my stomach knotting all over again.

How long would it take before the Gauntts went after the other victims who'd helped hit back at them? Were any of them safe? Now I was doubly glad we'd taken so many precautions to make sure our enemies couldn't find our current hideout. It could be a safe haven for all of them if we needed it to be. We'd make do.

"Hey," I said as I came into the living room where the other guys were sitting around the table. Marisol appeared in the doorway of the second bedroom. "We're going to have company. The Gauntts have gone after Fergus, so I told him to come here. We can give him one of the spare air mattresses. I should probably check in with the other college kids who've been working with us."

Jett frowned, getting up from the table. "What are those pricks doing to the guy?"

"I don't know," I said. "He didn't get into the details. But he was obviously really upset. I think—"

Before I could finish that thought, my phone rang again. I snatched it up, thinking maybe Fergus needed more urgent assistance, but this time it was Peyton on the other end.

"Lily," she said without preamble. "Did you hear from Fergus today?"

I paused where I'd gone to the closet to pull out the air mattress. "I did. Has he talked to you too? Have you heard from anyone else at the college? It sounds like the Gauntts are starting to crack down."

Peyton exhaled audibly. "Yeah, I think they are, but maybe not in the way he might have made it sound. He called me up an hour ago and was asking some kind of weird questions about you guys—if I knew where you were or what your plans were. Trying to make it sound like he just wanted to pitch in, but something about it… The more I think it over, the more I'm convinced he wasn't asking for himself."

A chill washed over me. "What do you mean?"

"I mean I think maybe the Gauntts have already gotten to him. And convinced him to throw the rest of us under the bus to save his skin or get some kind of benefit. I don't know him that well, but I wouldn't say he's super strong in the spine department."

"Shit." I had to agree with her assessment. I stared blankly at the closet door as her suggestion sank in. "I told him about the cottage—how to get here. I thought he was in trouble."

Peyton echoed my curse. "You'd better get out of there then. Find someplace else to hide out at least until we can be sure. I could be wrong. But—"

The growl of an engine cut through her voice. "Wait," I said, and hustled to the window.

Not one but three cars were approaching along the lane that led to the cottage. And it was way too soon for Fergus to have gotten here from Lovell Rise. My stomach sank. "I think we're already out of luck. *Someone*'s coming, and it's not Fergus. I've got to go."

"What's going on?" Ruin asked, breezing over to the window as I hung up.

I motioned to the cars. "Peyton thinks Fergus caved to threats from the Gauntts and double-crossed us. It looks like she was right."

"He's a fucking nitwit," Nox growled, and started waving to the room around us. "We don't have time to make a run for it. It's better if we have walls around us for a standoff. Grab your guns and anything else you can use as a weapon. We've beaten them down before; we'll do it again."

In the time it took for the cars to reach the cottage, we'd pillaged the building for all other possible weapons. I held a butcher knife in one hand. Marisol had grabbed a heavy bronze bust from the dresser in her bedroom that she could use as a bludgeon, clutching her little gun as well. The guys each had their pistols in one hand and the other free for inflicting their powers, but they'd gathered a heap of knives, frying pans, glass bottles, and even the ceramic logs from the decorative fireplace near the door in case they needed to switch weapons.

We watched from the windows as men burst out of the cars. Unlike our last stand-off, they didn't make any attempt at caution. I guessed it must have been pretty obvious that we'd see them coming. They opened fire from the moment they were clear of their cars.

The front windows shattered in on us. We'd all ducked down at the boom of gunfire. I yanked my arms over my head to shield my face and tugged at Marisol to do the same.

As the shards rained down on us, more bullets whizzed by over our heads. They weren't giving us the chance to bob up and get a single shot in ourselves.

My awareness raced over to the nearby lake, the hum from within my chest reverberating through the water's currents. With a heave of concentration, I brought an epic wave soaring up over the lawn and crashing down on where I thought our attackers were still standing.

The water pounded against the grass—and several bodies thumped onto their backsides with the liquid pummeling. The gunfire briefly cut off. The Skullbreakers sprang up and pulled their own triggers, sending a hail of bullets to follow the deluge of lake water.

Unfortunately, most of our attackers had stayed close to the cars, and even with those who didn't have shelter, it was hard to land an effective shot from a distance on someone sprawled on the ground. The men behind the cars started shooting over the trunks and around the windshields, and for several seconds there were so many bullets flying back and forth it was a wonder the air itself didn't crack up.

Of course, when you're firing a million bullets a minute, you tend to run out pretty quick. It was only a matter of time before the clicks of empty chambers carried from all around me, both on our side and our attackers', after multiple re-loadings. The guys tossed their guns aside and snatched up whatever they could set their hands on from the heap.

Our attackers had other plans for us. One of them hurled something that looked like a pop can through the smashed window, and it thudded to the ground in the middle of the living room, streaming smoke. In an instant, we were coughing, my eyes burning at the noxious gas billowing from the canister.

We had no choice but to flee. As we burst out onto the lawn in front of the cottage, I summoned another wave from the lake with a roar of rushing water. The Gauntts' people—it looked like a mix of Skeleton Corps guys and a few more official bodyguards, based on the suits three of them were sporting—scattered in an attempt to dodge. All the same, I managed to smack several of them onto their asses again. A couple I even swept with the flow of the water all the way back into the lake, where they splashed around like half-beached whales.

Ruin swung a cast iron pan at one guy's head, braining him with a cracking sound like his skull was an egg. That was one way to make an omelet.

"Skewer your colleagues!" Kai ordered another with a whack of his fist, and shoved a meat thermometer into the guy's hand. The Skeleton Corps dude spun around and plunged the makeshift weapon into the chest of the man next to him. The thermometer made a whining sound as if to indicate its target needed more cooking.

Another car roared toward us, and I tensed, catching my balance on the sopping and therefore slippery ground. But I recognized this car—it was Peyton's. From the way she tore down the lane, she'd raced straight here as fast as the vehicle could go after I'd hung up.

Some of our attackers spun around to respond to the new threat. And she proved to be a threat indeed. Peyton parked on the other side of our enemy's cars with her window already rolled down and immediately started hurling objects at the nearest men. A full water bottle clocked one guy across the temple. Her ice scraper battered another square in the face.

A third guy lunged at her door, and she whipped out a little cannister of pepper spray. At its hiss, he started to do an impromptu jig of pain, clawing at his eyes.

One man grabbed something out of his trunk and leapt toward us, a fresh gun in his hands. Marisol yelped in warning and jerked her gun hand up, and my pulse lurched.

Maybe she could have gotten off the shot. Maybe it'd have made more sense to let her go for it. But I knew what it was like to carry lives ended on your conscience, even of people you had no reason to mourn. I didn't want that for my little sister.

I was supposed to be protecting her.

I flung my powers at our attacker first, pummeling his heart with his own blood like fists converging on every chamber through the arteries and veins. The guy stiffened and keeled backward, hitting the ground before Marisol had quite gotten her finger around the trigger.

I glanced at her to check her reaction, and in my distraction, one of the other men snatched the gun from his colleague's hand. As my head jerked back toward him, he fired.

Kai's body wrenched to one side. The blare of pain echoed faintly but unmistakably through our supernatural connection. He crumpled, his hand pressing against his chest.

A cry burst from my throat. The rest of my guys gaped at Kai for a split-second, horror flashing across their faces. Then their expressions flashed to pure, scorching rage that radiated into me alongside my own inner turmoil.

True chaos erupted across the lawn. Nox barreled forward, sending out punches of supernatural energy in every direction he could reach. Ruin gave a vibrant battle cry of his own and whirled around our attackers with his frying pan thudding into flesh and bone on one side and his fist sending the men into fits of terror or dismay everywhere he could reach. Jett raced to Kai, pressing his hand to his friend's shirt just below the wound, his face tensing with concentration.

It should have been enough. We'd already almost won. But in the bedlam around me, I didn't see the dickwad charging straight at Marisol until it was almost too late.

He had a knife in his hand. Possibly he'd planned on taking her hostage rather than killing her, not that I'd have been super pleased with that outcome either. As he grasped her wrist and wrenched her arm behind her back, I flung my powers at him.

His heart burst. His body seized as a metallic flavor filled the back of my throat. The knife fell from his hand, glancing off my sister's shoulder with a nick of blood—but his fingers momentarily clenched around her wrist as he fell. There was a snap of breaking bone, and she sobbed, groping at her arm that now hung limply at her side.

A surge of my own fury loomed inside me. I dashed to her and spun around, ready to smash anyone who was still standing to smithereens.

There was no one. Just us and a whole lot of corpses—and Kai slumped against the side of the cottage, looking like he might soon add to that number.

Chapter Twenty-Two

Kai

I'D NEVER FELT pain like this. Or maybe I had, in the fleeting seconds when the bullets had hit me just before I'd died the first time. That memory had gotten hazy over the years in limbo. I wasn't sure how much I'd absorbed the sensation before I'd kicked the bucket anyway.

This agony I was fully aware of. It blazed through all my other senses, making it hard to even focus my eyes or process the shouts and bangs around me. Every thump of my pulse sent the pain spiking harder through my chest.

At least the fact that my heart was still pumping meant the bullet hadn't hit me there. I hurt because I was still alive. See, I could look on the bright side just like Ruin did.

Through the throbbing, I registered someone's hand on me. A gruff voice giving curt instructions. That was definitely Jett, even if I couldn't focus enough to distinguish the words. Something was shifting, stretching, melding against my ribs… The pain dulled just slightly. I blinked and managed to fix my attention on his face.

"I don't know how long that'll hold," he was saying, his normally sullen voice laced with unusual urgency. "I don't know how much got damaged in there. We should bring the guy who patched Ruin up."

I attempted to agree and only managed to let out a vague "mmm" sound. When I inhaled, my lungs burned but held the air. Had they been leaking before? I couldn't remember how much I'd been breathing during the worst of the agony. It was the sort of thing I usually took for granted.

Couldn't take anything for granted anymore. Fucking corporate pricks with their attack dog gangs and crazy voodoo.

I coughed with a bit of a sputter and managed to croak, "My phone. Dr. Morton. Tell him… we'll pay double last time."

Jett had no idea how much I'd paid him the first time, so he took that in stride. Our funds weren't in the best state since we'd been spending more time waging war than conducting business after we'd made our grand return, but we could manage it.

The sounds all around me had fallen away. I squinted past Jett and noted that the only people still standing were the ones I wanted to see—well, and the college girl who had the crush on Ruin's host, but as far as I could tell, she was on our side at the moment.

They'd all turned to stare at me. Jett rattled off what I'd said about the doctor—well, he was a vet. That was a kind of doctor. He knew how all the parts were supposed to be attached, which was what mattered. Nox stepped toward me and then hesitated.

"I don't know if we should move him." He peered at me. "Do *you* think we can move you?"

I should know that, shouldn't I? I was the know-it-all. I opened my mouth and closed it again, tasting the dryness that'd crept through it. The image of Ruin in the back seat of Lily's car, blood spurting from a wound we'd thought we'd closed, flashed through my mind.

But it wasn't good for us to stay here, either. The Gauntts knew our location now.

Of course, it looked like all their remaining goons were now lying dead on the lawn. Could we hope we'd finally run them dry?

"I'm not sure," I said finally.

Nox's mouth twisted. He might not ever have heard me say those words before. Possibly they disturbed him. They kind of disturbed me.

"I'll bring him here," he said abruptly. "Let him decide. The Gauntts have never sent two onslaughts right after each other—and if anyone else *does* show up, the rest of you know how to deal with them."

Jett handed him my phone with the contact. Nox jammed it to his ear as he hustled to the car, and the artist moved to Marisol. For the first time, I noticed that her arm was hanging limply, her wrist twisted to the side in a way that didn't look right at all. Lily was hugging her gently as her sister blinked back tears.

I wasn't the only one those pricks had injured. The urge shot through me to push to my feet and apply whatever medical knowledge I'd accumulated across my life so far to the problem, but just a tiny shift of my body sent the pain inside me from aching to stabbing again. I gritted my teeth and resigned myself to staying where I was, leaning against the side of the building.

Peyton raked her fingers into her hair and stared at the scene around us. "Oh my God. Fucking hell. We can't leave this place like this! How in the world could I ever explain— If they find out I let a shoot-out go down on their property—"

She sounded like she was starting to hyperventilate. Ruin shot a concerned look at Marisol but seemed to think his skills could be put to better use with the other girl. He gave her a light pat on her arm which calmed her down in an instant.

"We'll clean things up," he promised with a smile. "I'll help you."

"We'll need a truck," I rasped. "Get all the bodies together and then… hose the rest of the grass down. Call Lamont. He'll get something together."

I wasn't sure my instructions had been coherent, but Nox paused where he'd been about to get into the car. "You shouldn't be hauling corpses in your condition," he told Ruin. "Or we'll need the doc for you too. We're lucky you didn't already bust your guts out all over again in that fight." He let out a growl of frustration before stalking over to our man of sunshine and shoving my phone with the vet's address into his hand. "*You* go get the doc. Then you can mostly be sitting, and you can make sure he understands the importance of getting here quickly."

Ruin nodded with a swift bob of his head and jumped into the car. As he tore off, Nox pulled out his own phone, presumably to call Lamont. He grumbled a few orders into the phone and then got to work dragging bodies off to the side of the property near Peyton's car. The college girl shuddered but moved to help him, her lips curling with disdain.

Jett was murmuring to Marisol in a low voice as he worked over her arm with obvious care. Her jaw was still clenched with pain, but her expression looked more hopeful now. We'd have the good doctor take a look at her too after he got here.

Maybe only her. I couldn't tell whether I'd actually make it that long. The pain kept zapping through me at odd intervals alongside my breaths and any twitch of my body. There were plenty of vital organs that might have been scraped, nicked, or outright punctured.

If I went now, at least I'd protected everyone who mattered in the meantime. I'd showered Lily with all the adoration I was capable of. I'd leave her knowing just how much she'd meant to me. That was the best I could ask for.

And hey, maybe I'd get to return all over again. I'd be a little more thoughtful in picking my next host, that was for sure. No pushy family members or asshole friends.

I swallowed and coughed. I hadn't realized she'd gone inside, but Lily emerged from the cottage a moment later and carried a glass of water over to me. She held the glass to my lips for me.

The cool liquid slid down my throat like some kind of paradise. I knew the bullet had hit significantly higher than my stomach, so at least I didn't have to worry about whether quenching my thirst was a fatal move.

Lily let me drink my fill. Then she set the glass down and touched my cheek. For a few seconds, she just gazed at me. Her face was etched with tension.

"I'm sorry," she said abruptly.

I managed to raise an eyebrow. My voice came steadier now. "Pardon? I'm pretty sure *you* weren't the one who shot me. Difficult to accomplish when you're not even holding a gun."

Lily gave me a baleful look and glanced over her shoulder at her sister. When she met my eyes again, hers were even stormier.

"I got distracted," she said. "If I'd been paying enough attention to everything, I'd have seen that guy in time. I was trying to keep Marisol safe. Maybe I went a little overboard. I just don't want… I don't want her to have to deal with even more crap than she's already had heaped on her. But I don't want to see you get hurt because I freaked out either."

The anguish in her voice made my heart ache in a very different way. I leaned my face into her touch. "You didn't bring the danger into our lives—or your sister's life—any more than you called it into your own." I halted to catch my strained breath before going on, stating what to me was utterly obvious. "This is all on the Gauntts. And you can't protect her from everything, you know. There'll be times when you can't be there. It's better if she learns how to defend herself, isn't it?"

Lily grimaced. "Just because I was okay with Nox teaching her *how* to shoot doesn't mean I want her to have to put those lessons to use."

"You might not get the choice," I had to point out with as much gentleness as I could offer. "That won't be your fault either. I don't think she's going to blame you."

"No." Lily let out a laugh that sounded almost startled. "She might even blame me for interfering. But she's only sixteen."

I couldn't quite shrug. "We were already building up the Skullbreakers when *we* were sixteen. What do they say—age is nothing but a number."

Lily narrowed her eyes at me again, but she didn't argue. She sank down on the grass next to me and swiped her hand over her face. "We're going to have to go on the run again—as soon as we can safely move you. I don't know what to do next. How are we going to beat them? The longer this fight goes on, the worse it gets."

"We're running out of options," I agreed. "And they've upped the stakes. But we still… we have a chance. We can defeat them. We hit them back one last time with everything we have, do whatever it takes…"

I just couldn't see how. My thoughts wouldn't arrange themselves into a coherent strategy. Too much pain was prickling through them, nudging them in odd directions instead of their usual orderly flow.

The Gauntts' minions hadn't just taken me physically out of the picture. They'd messed with my ability to contribute my brains to our operations as well.

A rare flicker of panic shot through me, but I clamped down on it and turned all my focus on the woman next to me. The sweet yet fierce woman who'd stayed strong through so much.

"You'll figure it out," I told her. "You're smart, and you've got something even more important than that."

She cocked her head. "Which is what?"

"You understand. You know what the Gauntts' victims have been through, what it's like to have your life controlled by outside forces. You know how to find the strength to rise up and fight against someone who's so much bigger than you." I coughed but managed to regain my voice. "We have an army of people out there. We just need to figure out the most effective way and time for them to strike… we have to make them totally committed… You can do that."

Her head drooped. "I don't know. You're the one who can always see how to nudge people in the right directions, how to use all the information you have as leverage."

"This isn't about leverage," I told her. "It's about… connection. You've got this. I don't know if I'm going to be alive to see it, but I'm absolutely certain you'll pull it off."

I couldn't tell if those words were enough, but Lily tipped her head in acknowledgment. She squeezed my hand, searching my face as if I might still have the answers to our predicament there even if I couldn't find them myself. "Thank you," she said.

When she got up to check on her sister, I watched her walk away, hoping against hope that I'd given her all the push she needed to do what I couldn't.

Chapter Twenty-Three

Lily

"How does it feel?" I asked Marisol, studying her arm.

She held it gingerly in the makeshift cast Jett had conjured for her using dirt he'd scooped off the ground. "I think it's okay. Jett said it felt like only one of the bigger bones was fractured, so he sealed that up. It doesn't hurt badly anymore, just kind of aches, so I think he must have been right. If we need to, we can crack the cast open so the doctor can take a look."

I wasn't sure the doctor we were relying on had enough experience with human bone structure to identify any more subtle problems, but I knew how adept Jett had become at using his powers. If she wasn't in major pain, we could wait until I could safely bring her to a proper hospital.

She was taking this whole situation in stride so easily. Somehow that made me feel almost as bad as when I'd heard the bone crack. She shouldn't have needed to live a life where facing off against gangsters and having her arm fractured was a normal occurrence.

But like Kai had said, it hadn't been my choice. The Gauntts were forcing us into this situation, and blaming myself wasn't going to fix anything.

The other things he'd said were still running through my mind. I understood what it was like to have my life torn apart by the Gauntts better than any of the Skullbreakers did. I knew how it felt to lose time and memories you should have had, even if it wasn't quite the same as what the other victims had experienced. I'd gone through the same frustration of having someone else calling the shots, taking over control.

We needed to rally our allies and end this war as soon as possible, before the Gauntts destroyed even more. Before they decided I couldn't make good on my threat and murdered all those kids as their psychotic version of punishment for my disobedience. And maybe there *wasn't* anyone better to figure out how to stop them than me.

I'd let the guys take the lead so often in this conflict, figuring it was their world more than mine. I hadn't minded serving mainly as backup. But the conflict with the Gauntts actually belonged to me more than them. It was my life and my sister's that family of asswipes had purposefully ruined. I didn't think they'd even known about the murders of the Skullbreakers—that'd just been the Skeleton Corps handling their own sorts of business.

And it might not be a matter of figuring out the right plan, only of finally stepping up and saying what we needed to say to carry out the most obvious one.

Nox was still busy hauling bodies into the growing corpse mountain he was building with Peyton, and Kai had closed his eyes while he rested. Ruin had taken his phone anyway. I went over to Jett, who was temporarily unoccupied as he recovered from the energy he'd expended with his attempts at healing.

"You've got Parker's phone number, don't you?" I asked.

He studied me as he pulled out his phone. "I do. Why?"

"I don't think we can let this go on any longer. And if we're going to tackle the Gauntts, we need to take away their soldiers first. I'll just have to see if I can talk our guys on the inside into taking that final step."

Jett nodded and brought up the number to show me. He didn't

argue or suggest that he or one of the others should handle it instead. I still had an anxious twinge in my gut, but his lack of concern settled my nerves a little.

I tapped in the number on my own phone and raised it to my ear. I wasn't sure I'd get an answer, since Parker might be in dangerous company, but he picked up on the second ring. "Hello?"

"Hey," I said. "It's Lily. From—you know."

Before I could go on, he groaned. "I'm so sorry—I only just heard about the guys that got sent after you. It was people I'm not very connected with. Is everyone okay?"

I wasn't surprised that he wouldn't know everything immediately. He worked under one of the Skeleton Corps's head guys, but they segmented their operations without a ton of communication between the different squads to make it harder for anyone to damage them. It was kind of a relief hearing Parker sound so concerned about us.

But then, he'd already been rebelling against his bosses when he'd first come to the Skullbreakers. Knowing what his bosses were supporting had only strengthened his resolve.

Would it be enough for him to strike against them in a much more overt way?

I glanced toward Kai, debating how to answer Parker's question, and just then our new car pulled up with Ruin behind the wheel. He ushered out the man who'd stitched him up before. Another waft of relief swept through me.

"They hit us pretty hard, but we all made it through," I said, praying silently that my statement remained true. "The Gauntts have made even more threats, though. I don't think we have much time left unless we want to see kids dying all across the city—and it's getting almost impossible for us to stay out of their reach. We need to pull out all the stops to take them down first."

Parker's voice turned more cautious. "What did you have in mind?"

I sucked in a breath. "You and your friends are our secret weapon. The Gauntts have mostly been able to threaten us and keep us on the run with all the Skeleton Corps guys they keep sending after us. I think we have to topple the Corps leadership completely, end the gang's ties to the Gauntts, and then we can go right at them. Maybe we can even convince some of the other members lower down the ladder to join in the revolt."

There was a moment of silence and a rustle of fabric as Parker shifted his position. "I don't know… You haven't had to work with these guys. If we make one wrong move…"

I gathered my own resolve. "Then what? They'll hit you back? What could really be worse than having them make you do the dirty work of the family that messed you up for all these years? Don't you want to start living your *own* life finally?"

"Of course I do," he said. "I just… It's not that simple."

"I know it isn't." I closed my eyes, gathering my thoughts. "Look—the Gauntts had me shut away in a psych ward for seven years. I lost a third of my childhood—completely gone. They took away your sense of security and your ability to make decisions for your own life. They've done it to hundreds of other people. And that means we're not alone. We're in this together. There are a hell of a lot more of us than them. We don't have to let them terrorize us into being victims all over again. We can take back the control they stole from us."

I hadn't been sure exactly what I'd say until the words spilled out, but they felt perfectly right. They resonated through my chest and over my tongue, and something about them must have hit Parker in just the right way too.

He sighed. "I don't want those kids getting even more hurt. I don't want to keep being bossed around by people who'd support those sickos. If you're in this with us—"

"We are," I said, and a lightbulb lit in my head. "And *you* get to take control right now. You call the shots. Figure out with the other guys when the best time to strike would be, tell us when and where, and we'll race right over to back you up. We know you want to win this war just as much as we do. We'll put our lives in your hands."

A note of awe came into Parker's voice. "Okay. All right. I think we can pull together something pretty quick. With everything that's going on, I can probably plant the idea with the bosses that they need to have a meeting today. I'll be in touch soon."

He hung up, and I hurried over to see what the doctor—animal or otherwise—had to say about Kai's current state of being.

The man was crouched down across from Kai, who'd opened his eyes and was nodding in response to something the doctor had said. His eyes looked bleary, but he was at least conscious enough to carry on some kind of conversation. My heart thudded faster as the doctor peeled back Kai's shirt to examine the wound Jett had sealed.

He tutted to himself and shook his head. "I don't know what strange voodoo you all can work. Never seen anything like this." He pulled out a stethoscope, which he pressed to Kai's chest and then his back, instructing him to breathe deeply. Then he tutted some more, as if he thought he could heal wounds with his disapproval.

"There doesn't appear to be anything urgently wrong, but he needs his fluids replenished and plenty of rest. And it'd be good to keep him monitored somewhere with proper equipment in case he takes a turn for the worse. If I could give him an X-ray, that'd cover even more bases."

"Well, we need to get out of this place anyway," Nox said, and lifted his head. A small delivery truck was just rumbling toward us along the lane. "And there's our clean-up crew. Perfect."

It seemed like a little bit of an overstatement to call the one recruit who was driving the truck a "crew," but he did dive right in with Nox, Jett, and Peyton carting the bodies from their heap on the grass into a new heap in the back of the truck. The doctor looked the other way and started tutting more quietly. If he regularly took gangsters as clients, I supposed he'd seen plenty of bodies he couldn't stitch back together in his time.

I grabbed the cottage's hose and washed the blood down to the lake, sending silent apologies through my humming energies for adding to the violence it'd been roped into. I didn't know what we were going to do about the smashed windows on the cottage, but that problem seemed much farther off than the others staring us down.

As the last corpse thumped into the truck, my phone's ringtone chimed. It was Parker. I whipped the phone to my ear. "Hey. Any news?"

"Yeah," he said, a little breathless but with undisguised eagerness. "We've set things in motion. There's a meeting happening, and we'll all be there—if we move on the inside and you guys charge in from the outside at the same time, I think we can topple them. There aren't many people left for guards. Just be at the Castle Top Bakery at five o'clock. Wait until the icing hits the window."

"We can do that," I said, wondering what to make of his last strange instruction, but he dropped the call before I could clarify.

Nox was watching me from where he was standing by the truck. "What's going on?" he asked.

"We're going to take down the rest of the Skeleton Corps bosses," I announced, "and then we're going to go straight at the Gauntts."

In a hasty back and forth, I explained what I'd told Parker and the instructions he'd given us. Nox rocked back on his heels as he took it in.

Ruin was bobbing on his feet with typical enthusiasm. "We're going to go crush them, right?"

"We can't leave them hanging," I said. "I told them we were coming."

Nox rubbed his jaw. "Are you sure we can trust them, Minnow?"

That was the big question, wasn't it? But I already knew the answer. I wouldn't have reached out to Parker if I hadn't.

I nodded. "He came to us from the start. He put his life in our hands, going against his bosses back then, trusting *us* that we'd do the right thing and give him his memories back. That we wouldn't backstab him. He and the other guys he brought to us know how awful the Gauntts are. We've got to stand with them now. It's our best chance of breaking the Gauntts' hold and weakening them enough to stop them for good."

"All right then," Nox said, so easily my heart swelled with love. He really meant it when he called me one of the Skullbreakers—he trusted *my* word that much.

He motioned to the recruit. "The doctor and Kai will ride with you. Drop them off where he tells you, ditch the truck where we discussed, and meet up with us at this bakery." He turned to Peyton. "I'm guessing our college friends won't be up for much of a fight, if we can even trust *them* now."

She hugged herself. "I came to help because I set you up here, but

I'm not rushing into another gang battle, thank you. I don't know where the others are at, but I wouldn't be surprised if the Gauntts have put pressure on more than just Fergus."

"We appreciate that you came out here at all," I felt the need to say.

She caught my eye and tipped her head in what felt like the first really respectful acknowledgment she'd given me since all the insanity had started. Maybe it was even friendly.

"That's fine," Nox said, and pointed to Marisol. "Can you bring the kid with you just for—"

"Hold on." My sister stepped forward, interrupting him. "I'm not just a kid, and I don't want to be left behind. *I* can fight."

My stomach lurched. "Mare—"

She shook her head and met my gaze. "I've still got my good arm. I can still shoot a gun. It's my fight too—maybe more than any of yours."

Every particle in my body clanged with the desire to refuse her, to force her to stay away. But I didn't know if I even could. And should I?

The Skullbreakers had wanted to protect me every way they could, but I'd insisted on fighting alongside them for the exact same reasons Marisol had said. Because I could, and it was my battle too.

I'd tried to protect her from so much. I'd stood in her way when she'd wanted to go public with her story of abuse, I'd intervened when she might have shot that guy—and she'd gotten hurt anyway.

I couldn't defend her from every possible threat, and I did have to let her grow up sometime. She'd already had to grow up faster than any sixteen-year-old should in the worse sorts of ways. Didn't she deserve to reclaim more control over her life too?

I wavered and swallowed hard. "Okay. You can come with us. But you're injured and you don't have powers, so you stay at the back where we can give you a little extra protection, all right?"

She grinned at me like I'd approved an epic sweet sixteen bash. "Deal."

"Then we're set," Nox declared. "Everyone move out! Let's take these fuckers so far down they'll find themselves having dinner with the Devil himself."

Chapter Twenty-Four

Lily

I WAS GOING to guess that at least one member of the Skeleton Corps leadership had a sweet tooth, given their habit of holding meetings in places like ice cream parlors and bakeries. Castle Top looked like a pretty tasty venue, with a castle-shaped chocolate cake on its sign and fanciful pastries etched on the front window. Definitely not a gangster vibe.

A CLOSED sign hung on the door, and the window itself was dim. It had a pinkish tint that made it doubly reflective, showing more of the street outside than what was going on within. I just hoped we'd be able to identify Parker's signal when he gave it.

We were poised in our car just a couple of buildings down the street on the opposite side, all of our gazes trained on the broad pane of glass. Tension coiled through my chest, vibrating with the hum of my supernatural energy. My thoughts kept tripping back to images from our standoff at the cottage—Kai crumpling, Marisol's arm cracking.

Was Kai definitely secure wherever the doctor had taken him to give him more thorough treatment? I guessed he was safer than he'd have been here, anyway.

My sister shifted in her seat in the back where she was poised between Ruin and Jett. She had the gun Nox had given her in her hand, ready to go, like they did. Glancing at her in the rearview mirror, I felt my stomach twist.

This time, I wouldn't leap in when she was about to defend herself. I didn't know what worse outcomes I might fail to prevent if I tried to save her even from the discomforts she was willing to face. But that didn't mean I liked being in this position.

Nox stared through the windshield with an air like the calm before the storm, silently ominous. "They'd better not screw us over like the whole Skeleton Corps did last time."

"We know *why* the bosses double-crossed us," I reminded him. "They found out we were after the Gauntts, and they didn't want to lose their corporate backing. They even double-crossed one of the other bosses. These guys haven't got any reason to."

"Other than not wanting to risk dying," Jett put in.

"Pretty sure they're risking that just by being part of a gang in the first place," Marisol said with typical teenage snarkiness. I did appreciate hearing her show her spirit—and anyway, she had a point.

"We mow them all down, right?" Ruin said, rubbing his hands together. "All the bosses. Can't trust any of them after last time."

I nodded. "They're the ones who made the deal with the Gauntts—the ones who take their orders. With the bosses gone, maybe the Skeleton Corps will fall apart, or maybe Parker and his friends will step up and change their direction… Maybe the Gauntts will be able to find new leadership to work with them again, but not fast. It's going to be chaos for at least a little while."

A savage smile crossed Nox's face. "And while that's happening, we cut them off at the knees—and then slice and dice them into as many pieces as we feel like."

Jett grunted. "Let's not get ahead of ourselves. We haven't even gone at the Skeleton Corps yet."

A crash sounded from inside the bakery, loud enough that it

filtered through the windows. We all stiffened in our seats. My hand shot to the door handle.

Then, with a creamy squelch, a blob of icing as big as a fist smacked into the window just beneath the etching of a churro, making it look like the balls on a pastry dick.

"That's our cue," I shouted, shoving open the door.

We hurtled across the street as more thumps and bangs emanated from inside the bakery. Nox slammed right into the locked door. An electric crackle vibrated through the frame as he smashed the lock open with a combination of physical and magical strength, both of which he had no shortage of.

We charged inside, skidding on the goopy mixture of icing and mashed dough that coated the floor. Our three allies were guarding the back of the building as promised, preventing the three remaining Skeleton Corps leaders and their handful of lackeys from leaving. A couple of those lackeys and one of the bosses already lay face down on the floor. From the looks of them, with bits of cake and pastry splattered all over them, you'd have thought they'd died by over-gorging on desserts if it weren't for the pools of blood spreading into the sugary mess.

The other Skeleton Corps members had thrown themselves behind the large display case that stretched the length of the room. Most of the cakes, tarts, and other sweet delicacies behind the glass had been the other casualties of the battle so far. The display window had been shattered and several confections blasted apart as if someone with a grudge against gluten had stormed through.

The final two bosses and their lackeys had been scuttling toward the front door in the hopes of escaping, crouched down below the level of the display. Glass shards and shiny sprinkles dappled their hair as if it were post-modern cupcake frosting.

Our arrival cut off their escape route, and they didn't take very kindly to the affront. I'd barely had a chance to suck in a breath of the sugary air before they were raising their guns in the hopes of blasting us away.

The energy inside me instinctively reached for the most liquid objects in the room. Pies full of jellied filling that'd escaped the initial massacre flipped off their stands and smacked into faces, throwing off the men's aim—and leaving their faces drenched in a gelatinous mess. As they swiped at their faces to clear their eyes, we closed in on them.

With a surge of energy, Nox punched the cash register next to the display case and sent it flinging into the nearest dude's head. Ruin purposefully slid on his feet across the slick floor toward our allies, spraying bullets as he went. A few more pastries bit the dust. The Skeleton Corps dudes sank even lower in their dwindling shelter.

"Truce!" one of the bosses yelled. "Ceasefire! We don't have to do things like this."

"Oh, yeah?" Nox snarled. "How do you suggest we do them, then?"

"We came to an agreement once. We could join forces again."

The Skullbreakers leader snorted. "The only thing you joined forces in was trying to send us to an early grave all over again. We know who's holding your leashes. We don't make deals with lapdogs."

"There's no point in sticking with them if they don't have our backs," the other boss said. "Aren't you better off with us on your side than having us dead?"

"Why should we trust *you* to have *our* backs?" I demanded, stepping forward. I could sense the racing of the man's pulse through his veins from here. He was legitimately terrified, but that didn't guarantee anything more than the most temporary loyalty.

I fixed my glare in his direction. "You've only ever served the Gauntts. You didn't even look after your own people! You turned on one of your own when he realized the people you've obeyed are sickos. You didn't give a shit what they might have done to any of the men working under you. Why do you think those men are turning on you now?"

I swept my hand toward our three inside guys, who nodded.

"You sold us out too many fucking times and in too many ways for us to believe a single word out of your mouths now," Parker snapped.

I focused on the lackeys hunched around their bosses. "The people in charge are the ones who made the really shitty decisions. The rest of you can make better choices. We're happy to have any of you step away from them and join us now. It's just the two who were at the top who're going to have to pay for how they helped the Gauntts terrorize this city."

There were five lackeys still surrounding the bosses. They glanced at each other and at their employers with queasy expressions.

"Don't you fucking dare," one of the bosses growled, but if anything, his attempt at a threat had the opposite effect to what he'd intended. Faces hardened. All five of the men started to scramble away.

"You goddamn traitors!" the other boss shouted, and opened fire at the men leaping over the glass-scattered countertop. The lackeys dove out of range, and our guys let loose a hail of bullets that had the bosses diving into the compartments right under the counter.

They had nowhere left to run, but they were the ones who'd backed themselves into this corner. Imagine how differently it might have gone if they'd listened to their colleague about how toxic the Gauntts were and supported us in our campaign against them weeks ago.

We might have taken the family down so much sooner. Those kids might never have gotten sick. Nolan Junior might not have lost his life to contain his adoptive grandfather. We'd dealt out a lot of violence, but the worst of it was on their consciences, not ours.

My men and our allies marched closer to deliver the final judgment—and one of the lackeys who'd abandoned ship staged a reverse mutiny. Maybe he thought there was still a chance of his bosses coming out on top and that if he orchestrated it, he might nab one of the vacant spots alongside them. Maybe he was simply incredibly offended by the blatant destruction of cake. For whatever reason, he launched himself at Nox, whipping out his gun.

Before I could yank my supernatural energies toward him, Marisol yelped, the sound merging with a thunderous bang. A bullet blasted into the side of the guy's skull, toppling him before he could get in his own shot.

My sister sucked in a breath, staring at the slumped man and then at the gun braced between her two trembling hands. Her eyes darted to me. Her face was pale but firm.

"He was one of the guys who helped the Gauntts keep me away from you," she said in a rough voice. "I remember him from the bits of memories. He laughed at me, thought it was hilarious that he could spit on me or push me around and I couldn't fight back…" Her gaze settled on the dead man again. "He deserved it."

A lump rose in my throat, but I smiled in spite of it. "I'm sure he did."

Nox swiveled to take in the other lackeys who'd joined us. "Anyone else want to take a pointless stand for assholes who didn't give a fuck about you? No? Good."

As the lackeys backed away, a couple of them even tossing aside their weapons to make a more emphatic show of good faith, Nox motioned to the other Skullbreakers and our allies. They circled the ends of the counter, positioning themselves just out of view so the bosses couldn't shoot at them. Then Nox barreled toward the counter on the shop side, swinging both fists at the same time.

The energy he propelled with his strikes smashed right through the wood and sent the men in hiding tumbling out of their shelter across the floor. At the same moment, the rest of our men sprang into action. Bullets tore up the floor and into the two stunned figures from both sides. In a matter of seconds, the last of the Skeleton Corps bosses were as holey as a box of donuts.

Ruin raised his gun and let out a whoop of victory. A startled laugh of what sounded like relief spilled from Parker's lips. We looked around at each other, a sense of finality sinking over us—and then the walls of the bakery shuddered.

We spun around. "What the fuck?" Jett demanded.

My first thought was that we'd been struck by a very coincidental earthquake. But as the building around us continued to creak and rattle, I made out a familiar posh sedan that'd pulled up across the street. The windows were tinted, the figures inside hidden, but I was gripped by total certainty of who they were.

The words creaked from my abruptly constricted throat. "The Gauntts have come for us."

Chapter Twenty-Five

Lily

RUIN BOUNDED over to get a closer look out the bakery window. "This is a good thing, right? We wanted to blast them apart too, and now we can."

I wished I could share his sense of optimism, but in this particular case, the groaning of the building's foundation and the cracks I spotted spreading through the ceiling were putting a damper on my sense of victory.

"We've exhausted some of our powers, and they're probably fresh," I said. "And if we're not careful, they're going to use *their* powers to bring the whole building down on our heads."

I tried to reach my awareness across the street and through the car, but with the distraction of the quaking building and no visual to latch on to, I couldn't focus in on a single pulse. The cracks overhead were widening. I didn't have time to get my act together.

"Let's get out of here before we're buried!" I hollered, and tugged Marisol toward the back door.

The men all ran with us: the Skullbreakers, our original Skeleton Corps allies, and the four lackeys who'd thrown their lot in with us when they'd realized their bosses were about to go down. We'd been on opposing sides in the past, but now we were united in one common goal: survival. There was a kind of harmony to the thudding of our racing feet and the rasps of our urgent breaths as one guy yanked open the door for the rest of us, another waved us along while he braced against a trembling wall, and a third yanked us faster out into the alley behind.

It wasn't just survival, was it? It was freedom. Freedom from the asshats and shitheels who'd tried to keep *us* down, who'd used us for their own ends, who'd demanded our obedience without offering any loyalty in return.

And I'd helped bring about this harmony. I'd woken up the marked guys—I'd said enough to get through to them and the other lackeys, to give them the conviction to step away from their bosses.

As we hustled down the alley, hearing the first screeching thuds of the bakery's framework collapsing, an idea bloomed in my head like a blossom unfurling.

We had to stop the Gauntts, but we couldn't do it alone any more than we could have tackled the Skeleton Corps leadership with just the six of us. And I knew exactly the allies we needed now. If I could empower gang members who'd once wanted to shoot us down, then I had to be able to do the same for the people I wanted to turn to next.

I stopped at the end of the alley, watching the street beyond in case the Gauntts pulled around to launch another attack.

"We've got them scared and desperate," I said between ragged breaths. "They risked coming out here to take us on themselves. I don't like our chances if we go head-to-head with them right here, but I think we can lead them into a different kind of trap."

Ruin grinned and gave the air a couple of eager punches. "All right. We'll show them who's boss."

I hoped I could follow through. I grabbed my phone and dialed Peyton's number.

"What now?" she said when she answered, but her mildly irritated tone was offset by the concerned question she couldn't help following with. "Are you all okay?"

My lips twitched with wry amusement, but I got straight to the point. "For now. I need you to pass on a message—tell all the marked people from college whose memories I cracked. At least one of them should report back to the Gauntts."

Peyton audibly perked up. "What's the message?"

"Tell them we figured out a way to destroy the Gauntts' source of power. We're going down to the marsh to do it now, so no one who's been hurt will have to worry for much longer."

She inhaled sharply. "Are you serious? Then why—"

"It's complicated," I said. "But it'll work if the Gauntts come chasing after us. Can you pass the message on?"

"Yes. Just the first part and not the chasing bit." A brief, raw laugh spilled out of her. "I hope you give them all the hell they deserve."

Nox drew his impressive frame up even taller and motioned to the people around us, assuming he knew my plan. "All right, we're taking this to the marsh. Head out, grab the nearest vehicle you can, and converge for an ambush near the entrance to the lane off—"

"Hold on," I interrupted. We didn't have much time to get this right now that word might be passed on to the Gauntts at any moment. Sirens were wailing in the distance, speaking of more complications we needed to avoid. "I don't want everyone there, and we're not going to ambush the Gauntts. I've got another idea, but I don't think anyone should come except those of us who have… extra ways of protecting ourselves."

"And me," Marisol insisted. I squeezed her hand, knowing there was no point in arguing.

Nox frowned, authoritative menace radiating off him. I knew how badly he wanted to crush the Gauntts on my behalf, and the best way he knew how was to blast them hard with everything we had. "We can do this," he insisted. "But we need all the manpower we can get."

I held his gaze with a pointed look. "We have other allies down at the marsh."

He made a scoffing sound. "They haven't managed to do anything other than drench you."

"I don't think I encouraged them the right way. They either weren't able or willing to help me, so this time *I'm* going to offer my help to them. I'm sure it's our best chance of destroying the Gauntts. Please, trust me."

Nox stared back at me, and something in his expression softened just a little. He did trust me, or we wouldn't be here to begin with.

"All right," he said. "I haven't got any feet to stand on arguing against crazy tactics. You just tell us everything you need." He waved at the Skeleton Corps guys, unable to resist aiming a little more of his commanding attitude toward the people he could order around. "Get going. Lay low, keep quiet, and we'll call on you if we need you. Just steer clear of the Gauntts and the other pricks you worked with."

Parker nodded and ushered the other guys away with an unexpected air of authority of his own. Maybe the Skeleton Corps would still have a future—a better one—once the dust had cleared.

The rest of us slipped out of the alley in the other direction. Nox ran for the car and brought it swerving around to collect the rest of us. Then we raced off toward the marsh with the Skullbreakers boss's usual disregard for all speed limits.

"Are you going to tell me exactly what the hell you're going to do out there?" he asked me.

I swallowed against the sudden dryness in my throat. "I think it's more of a 'I'll know what to do once I'm actually doing it' kind of a situation."

He let out a discomforted sound but left it at that.

Not long after we'd zoomed past the city limits and were roaring along the country highways between the smaller towns, Marisol twisted around in the back seat. Her voice came out wobbly, and not just because of the vibrations emanating from the straining engine. "I think they're behind us."

I swiveled to check. In the distance, I made out a darkly shiny car that did look suspiciously like the Gauntts' sedan. My pulse thumped faster. But—

"That's good," I said. "We want them to come. We need them out here if we're going to take them out."

As long as this gambit worked the way I thought it should. As long as we got to the marsh far enough ahead of them for me to make the necessary preparations.

This *was* the right way, wasn't it? What if I was going too far off the deep end?

I closed my eyes and gathered my faith in myself. Letting out my inner crazy was what had allowed me to do so much—to fend off my bullies, to break open my memories, to save Marisol. This strategy felt *right.*

If the battle against the Gauntts was mine more than the Skullbreakers, and Marisol's more than mine, then it belonged to the spirits and the marsh where they'd been abandoned more than anyone. Sometimes you just needed someone to show you the way.

The Skullbreakers hadn't pulled me from the marsh all those years ago, after all. They'd simply urged me to find the strength to save myself. That was when I'd gotten these powers, and now I could pass on the same favor.

Nox maneuvered the borrowed car with far less care than he'd shown for Fred. He drove it right past the end of the final lane, as far as he could get the wheels to keep turning over the uneven field beyond. That left us with just a short dash down to the spit.

"Stay close to the water," I yelled to the others as I darted down the narrow strip of land to its tip, where the Gauntts cast their magic. "Shield Marisol as much as you can. I'll try to be ready before they get here."

But the dark car was closing the distance by the second, growing larger against the horizon. I didn't hesitate. As the guys spread themselves out in a human wall near the foot of the spit, keeping my sister behind them, I plunged right into the water.

The cold water closed around me up to my shoulders, soaking my clothes in an instant. I reached out through the rippling currents for the energies I'd felt before and the spirits still lingering alongside them.

"Please," I said, or thought, or maybe both. With all my concentration fixed on the hum inside me and the contrasting resonance in the water, it was hard to pay attention to anything else. "Bring out all the power they've poured into you. I want *you* to use it, and I'll be right here backing you up with everything I have in me. We can do something better with it. We can break the hold they have over you, to save lives instead of taking them. *Please*. This is what I want to do for you."

I brought up an image in my mind of how I pictured this showdown playing out if the lake would cooperate, how I'd lend my powers to the anger and horror I'd sensed here before. Shivers of energy tickled over my skin through the water, as if the spirits were prodding me with giddy fingers. At least, I hoped that was giddiness and not fear. I needed them to be on my side too.

"They stole your lives," I urged them. "Both when you were living those lives and after. You can make sure they never do that to anyone else again. This is your war, and now's your chance to really fight it."

Deeper quivers reverberated through my flesh. I gathered the hum inside me and urged it out toward those spirits, toward the water that had held them for decades. An answering thrum flowed back into me, intensifying the energies inside me.

Was the marsh answering? Would it come through as much as we needed it to?

I was about to find out. The growl of a nearby engine penetrated my water-logged daze. I tuned into the shore enough to see the dark sedan bumping to a halt near where we'd parked our car on the grass. The doors flew open, and a sizzling wave of energy whipped through the air.

Nox struck out with both his fists, and Jett and Ruin fired their guns, unable to do more across the distance. They only got out a couple of shots before the Gauntts' powers slammed them and Marisol back on the bank.

My heart flipped over. We had no time left at all. The next second might mean a fatal blow.

"*Now!*" I screamed, inside and out, and raised my arms.

The marsh water rose with me as if I were summoning it upward like a conductor for some grand aquatic orchestra. It surged higher and higher into one, two, three, four—then more forms than I could make out around me. They loomed over me and the spit like liquid giants, towering fifteen, maybe twenty feet off the ground. Gleaming arms lifted from their watery sides; massive translucent heads turned toward the Gauntts' car.

With the marsh's power combined with my own, I'd given the spirits of the murdered grandchildren the only kind of life I could offer them. Massive, vengeful life.

More energy wrenched in and out of me as I swept my arms toward the shore. The gigantic figures rushed forward, sloshing water around them as they went. They charged right up onto the shore, splattering the grass but holding their humongous forms.

Someone in the Gauntts' car tried to strike out at them. Magic warbled through the air; the watery legs wobbled. But their forms held, powered as much by the fury I could sense shrieking through their makeshift bodies as by my own magic now.

I couldn't tell how much of that rage belonged to the marsh or the spirits when both of them hand been equally used by the villains they were bearing down on. Either way, they intended to have their revenge.

"Stop!" a voice I thought was Marie's cried out, while those around her chanted in the strange language I'd heard during their ritual. "You're *ours*. You do as we say. We—"

The person behind the wheel must have realized they weren't taking back control right now. The engine gunned abruptly, the doors slammed shut in anticipation of a hasty escape—but the marshy giants were already on them.

The spirits plowed their immense fists into the windows, smashing the glass. The water that gushed into the body of the car flipped the Gauntts out through the holes of the front and back windshields and tossed them onto the open ground. It was just the four of them: Marie Senior, Thomas, Olivia, and Nolan in his new younger body, squirming and sputtering on the soggy terrain like fish that'd leapt out of their tank.

The spirits poured more water down on them, and more, and more, saturating them from the inside out. The Gauntts cried out words of power, erected a transparent shield over them, but the forms that now contained so much of their magic cracked straight through those with a few thunderous punches. They poured their water down the Gauntts' throats and up their noses until their frantic panting turned to gurgles and their chests swelled.

And on and on and on, until all four bodies finally lay still. It was done. All of them were dead, and no one was left to carry their spirits over into a new victim. Their reign of horror was finished.

A headache was spreading through the back of my head, every nerve felt like it was on fire, but I was gripped by a dazed sense of release.

The Gauntts had infected the marsh with their sick intentions, and those intentions had come back to claim them. All I'd done was provide a conduit to make that vengeance possible.

And now I was utterly exhausted.

I teetered and toppled backward into the marsh, the water closing over me as if it meant to reclaim *me* after my narrow escape fourteen years ago.

Chapter Twenty-Six

Nox

Before I'd even managed to shove myself back to my feet, I was drenched. I grabbed Ruin's hand to help him up and then all we could do was gape at the lumbering masses of water as they pummeled the Gauntts into total submission. They beat those bastards with their watery fists until they were bloated and broken, and then they crashed down on them in what felt like a final "Fuck you," vomiting their watery selves over their murderers.

As the flood of water swept back toward the marsh, I spun around —just in time to see Lily sink beneath the surface, looking close to lifeless herself.

"No!" I hollered, defiance roaring through me. I'd let Lily take charge against all my instincts because she'd connected with the spirits here in ways the rest of us hadn't, but I wasn't letting the marsh take her away from me, no matter what it'd done for us. No fucking way.

"Look," Marisol gasped, pointing in the other direction. My head whipped around, and I realized that not all of the marsh monsters had flowed back to where they'd come from.

One of the colossal heaps of water was still poised over the farthest body. The body that'd once been Nolan Junior before the Senior had taken over residence inside a couple of weeks ago. A jolt of understanding shot through me.

It *had* only been a couple of weeks. The body had been kept living all that time—and it couldn't have changed much. There was a chance, wasn't there?

Every bone in my body ached to race to Lily's rescue, but I knew what she'd want me to do more.

That didn't mean I was abandoning her, of course.

"Jett," I said, jabbing my hand toward the spit. "Get Lily. Make sure she's okay." Then I hurtled toward the boy's corpse.

Images raced through my head alongside my pounding feet across the squishy ground. Fragments of my childhood rose out of nowhere into my mind.

I was wincing away from the swing of my father's fist. I was huddled in the closet to avoid another of his and Mom's drunken screeching arguments. Shivering under my thin blanket in three layers of clothes because they'd forgotten to pay the heating bill.

It'd been a shitty childhood until Gram had pulled me out of it. How had I repaid her, really?

But I could do this. I could pay it forward instead. I could do my very fucking best to give *this* kid another chance at an actual life.

The boy looked just as swollen and vacant as the others. His skin was already turning blue from the chill of the water. But unlike the adults, he wasn't quite as battered—his limbs lay at regular angles instead of unnatural ones, and I couldn't see any sign of broken ribs in his bloated chest.

I dropped down next to him. Rolling him onto his side, I thumped him between his shoulder blades, and the water gushed from his mouth and nose. Then I pushed him onto his back again.

The human-shaped heap of water was still crouched next to us. I glared up at it. "You've got to do some of the work here. Leave the marsh behind and jump on into him. Slam your heart—get it started again. I'll do my best, but if you're not in there, your jackass of a grandfather might try to yank it back."

The liquid mass shuddered. Then the water started to slough off it like it was shedding its skin, shrinking by the second.

I sucked in a breath and placed the heels of my hands on the boy's chest, dredging up every memory I could from the CPR course I'd taken years and years ago in case I ever needed it to save Gram.

I hadn't been there when she might have needed me, but I was here now. I was saving someone. And I liked to think if she was watching, she'd have given me one of her toothy grins with a double thumbs-up.

How many compressions was it? Ten? Twenty? Thirty? I just keep going—*pump, pump, pump, why won't you start, you fucker?*—as an ache spread through my arms. Maybe the spirits had drowned him too much. Maybe his soul didn't have the energy left to dive back in after all. Maybe—

I jammed my hands down one more time, and a bolt of energy zapped past them into the boy's chest. I slapped at my fingers, my skin searing, and then stared at the body in front of me.

The chest rose and fell. I pressed my palm to it again, and the erratic thump of a heart echoed against my hand, growing steadier by the moment.

Had the kid made it, or had I inadvertently brought that asshole Nolan back to life all over again? I hovered over the body, my fists ready to give him a pummeling of my own as need be.

The boy's eyes blinked. He peered up at me. Then he flipped over and coughed and gagged as a whole bunch more water heaved out of him. Apparently I hadn't done the most thorough job.

As he lay there, panting, he managed to find his voice. "Thank you," he said raggedly, sounding only like a kid, not like a corporate megalomaniac pretending to be one. "I—he—thank you." Then he started to cry.

I might be okay with doing a little heroic life-saving, but I had no clue at all what to do with a sobbing child. To my relief, Ruin and Marisol had followed me sometime during my grand effort. They sank down on either side of the restored boy, who I was going to guess would like to pick a name other than Nolan Junior now that he had the choice. Ruin tapped his shoulder, and the kid automatically relaxed.

"It's going to be okay," Marisol said in a soothing voice, patting his damp hair with her good hand. "You're going to be all right now."

I spun around with a stutter of my pulse, my gaze darting to the end of the spit as I thought of the other soul I wasn't sure we'd saved.

But there was Jett helping Lily walk with swaying steps along the spit, both of them soaked through, his arm around her back and hers slung across his shoulders. She caught my eyes with a shaky smile that grew when she noticed the boy beyond me. Tugging at Jett, she urged her feet faster across the muddy ground.

I hurried over to meet her and caught her in a hug that could have rivaled any of Ruin's, not caring that my drying clothes were getting soppy all over again.

"You did it," she said, breathless with disbelief. "You—you brought him back? Nolan Junior, not the old Nolan?"

"I think he did the hardest part," I allowed generously, and hugged her even tighter. "And *you* did it. You let them unleash holy terror on those menaces. They're gone. It's all done—it's over."

She pulled back with a sudden look of concern. "Do you think all their magic is gone with them?"

I didn't need to be Kai to figure out what she was talking about, and neither did her sister. Marisol had already pulled out her phone and started tapping away at it.

"It's so soon," she said. "I'm not sure how long it'd take before—oh! Here, one of the kids who was in the hospital, her brother is posting about how she's just snapped out of her coma. She seems totally fine now." She glanced up at us, her eyes shining. "If one of them recovered when the Gauntts died, then they all must have, right?"

Ruin cocked his head. "I wonder if all the marks will fade too. Will all those people remember what the Gauntts did to them?"

Lily's smile turned crooked. "That won't be all happy for everyone. But at least they'll know. And if there's enough of them willing to speak up after we've already put the story out there, maybe they can make sure the Gauntts get the right legacy *after* their death."

"They fucking well better," I declared. "But right now, we deserve to celebrate ourselves. We'd better make sure Kai's insides held together too. And…" I looked back at the boy, who was sitting up, staring at his hands while he turned them frontward and backward like he couldn't quite believe they were his again. "What are we going to do with him? With all of them?" My gaze traveled to the water-logged bodies.

Lily went silent with thought, exuding the calm confidence that was starting to come more naturally to her. I loved seeing it so much that I had to restrain myself from kissing her—which I'd definitely do later, but distracting her in the middle of a brainstorm seemed counter-productive.

"We leave them here," she said after a minute. "*We* didn't touch them. It was their own magic that killed them. There'll be an investigation, and probably the police will be confused about how they died, but it shouldn't come back on us. And him…"

She eased out of my arms and walked over to the boy. When she reached him, she crouched down next to him. He raised his head, his eyes still gleaming with pooled tears.

"Where would you like to go?" she asked. "We could take you to the house that was your home. I think… Now that the people who hurt you are gone, it's technically yours. There'll be lawyers who can figure out all the details. But if you don't want to go there again, that'd be okay too. It must have a lot of awful memories for you."

The boy cleared his throat, but his voice still came out rough. "I—Marie will still be there, right?"

It took me a second to realize he meant Marie Junior, his sister. Lily rested her hand on his shoulder. "As far as I know. She might be in a tricky situation—it doesn't look like they officially adopted her."

The boy raised his chin. "I'll make sure she's okay. I can look after her now. That's the way it *should* have been."

Lily beamed at him, and right then I really hoped that our ghostly swimmers still had some juice, because damn, would she make an amazing mom one day.

"All right," she said. "We'll make sure you get home. Come with us for now." She caught my eyes. "Do you think our false limo driver would be up for making a repeat performance in his role?"

I grinned back at her. "I bet he would. You drive, and I'll tell him where to meet us."

And then everything and everyone would be where it should be, possibly for the first time in my entire life. Or should I say, lives.

Chapter Twenty-Seven

One year later

Lily

"AND THAT'S A WRAP," the producer said over the intercom, giving me a thumbs up and a broad grin through the sound booth's window. "That last take was fantastic, Lily. I think we've nailed this track."

I pulled off my headphones, a laugh that was both relief and exhilaration tumbling out of me. "Just three more to go, then."

As I headed out of the recording studio for the day, I had to resist the urge to pinch myself and make sure I wasn't dreaming. After months of writing songs, making contacts with musicians, and putting together a demo tape, I'd somehow managed to land a record deal. I'd been in and out of the studio working on my debut album for weeks now, but it still didn't feel quite real. How could this be my life?

Whenever I mentioned any thoughts along those lines to my guys, they scoffed and said things like, "How could it not be?" After we'd settled into a new, much more peaceful status quo with the Gauntts gone, they'd all encouraged me to pursue what really was a dream, even if I'd made it come true. Jett was the one who'd pointed me to this studio, just next door to the Thrivewell building, saying he had a good feeling about it.

We all liked to think the Gauntts were rolling over in their long-delayed graves, hearing the joy in my voice that they hadn't been able to extinguish.

Kai was waiting in the reception area, tapping away on his phone. I walked over and nudged him. "You're becoming a regular internet addict after all."

He snorted. "It's still full of garbage. But if you know the right way to look for things, there *is* plenty of information there too—stuff you can't get anywhere else." His eyes gleamed at me from behind his glasses. "Uncle Stu sent me a link to a blog on investment strategies. I think I can double the amount of money we're making without anyone having to get their asses kicked, just like you prefer."

"You're going to put the gang out of a job," I teased as we took the elevator down to street level.

A couple of months after the Gauntts' fall, another of Kai's host's relatives had reached out to him, and Kai had discovered a kindred spirit. Apparently Zach's mom's brother wasn't from the same all-American jock mold as the football player's immediate family, and he'd been off pursuing his intellectual pursuits all on his lonesome. Kai had been ready to send him packing before they'd started talking and immediately hit it off by showing off how much they both knew about pretty much everything. Now they kept in touch with regular emails and texts.

It was amazing seeing how delighted their conversations made Kai. He was still the same know-it-all he'd always been, but he'd loosened up even more from the efficient and practical guy he'd been when I first met him. From what he'd said, no one in his own birth family had ever understood his quick mind or love of learning. It might have come decades late, but I was glad he'd found that kind of connection now.

I often drove to the studio on my own in Fred 2.0. The car was purring along good as new despite the Gauntts' temporary possession.

But when the guys were available, I still got a thrill out of riding with them on the back of one of their motorcycles. Kai led me over to where he'd parked his, and I hopped on easily, wrapping my arms around his waist.

"Nox headed over to the graveyard a little while back to check up on things," he said. "Should we swing by and remind him he's got another engagement tonight?"

I leaned into his solid frame. "Sure. I'd like to see the final result anyway."

We roared through the streets toward the cemetery where Nox's grandmother was buried. It wasn't hard to spot her section of the graveyard now. Nox had put a bunch of his recent earnings into designing and building a monument to replace her previously spartan gravestone. Sunlight gleamed off the pale gray marble slab that stood a couple of feet taller than the massive man gazing up at it.

I hurried up the hill to join Nox, slipping my arm around his when I reached him. He tugged me closer and nodded to the slab, which held a life-sized etching of a broad-shouldered woman with a steely gaze but a warm smile, her arms crossed over her bosom and her chin held high. She looked like she was about to demand to know what exactly we'd been up to—and to praise us for a job well done, as long as we'd committed to it fully regardless of exactly how legal it was.

"It's lovely," I said.

"She wasn't any angel, and she'd have laughed if anyone suggested she was," Nox said. "I figured she'd like this a lot better than some cheesy statue with wings. The stoneworker Jett found did a great job from the photographs I managed to scrounge up. It's almost like she's right there."

Jett had offered to imprint an image on the marble with his supernatural powers, but Nox had refused, saying his Gram would have seen that as cheating. *I'm going to pay for it to be done the usual way,* he'd insisted. And he looked nothing but satisfied with the outcome.

"It's not the home I wanted to give her while she was alive, but at least she's got a real presence in the afterlife," he said as we headed back down the hill.

"Granite would have been more durable," Kai couldn't help piping up.

Nox shot him a narrow look. "As you mentioned before. But she deserves something that's pretty too. If that one gets messed up, I'll just buy her a new one." He guided me toward his own bike. "You ride with me the rest of the way."

Despite the way he said it, I knew it was a request, not a command. But I didn't mind following through anyway, and Kai certainly wasn't offended. I squeezed onto the seat behind the larger man and let him carry us home.

As much as I'd loved our first apartment in Mayfield, it'd gotten awfully tainted by unpleasant memories during our few weeks there. And it hadn't really been big enough for all of us. After the Skullbreakers had gotten some time to revitalize their, er, business interests, we'd paid a generous fee to break the lease early and found a couple of three-bedroom condos in the same neighborhood up for sale that we'd been able to renovate into a larger two-story home.

The upper floor was technically mine and Marisol's, although the guys hung out up there with us plenty. It included a terrace where we'd been able to set up a little artificial pond for the various amphibious friends who still liked to stop by now and then. The lower floor was where the Skullbreakers hosted their new recruits and business partners as need be. Only for non-criminal activities, of course, but Kai wasn't the only one who'd branched out from that area.

When we came into the lower level, a waft of spice hit me in the face, making my eyes water.

"Sorry!" Ruin called cheerfully from the kitchen over the whir of the fans that were displacing the worst of the airborne burn. "Just finishing up a new batch. My ghost pepper blend!"

"It'll burn your tongue off," my sister informed us, appearing in the doorway with safety goggles, an amused expression, and several orange smears on her apron.

Ruin had discovered that he enjoyed creating hot sauce as much as he did eating it—possibly even more, since that way he could customize it exactly to his tastes. After he'd shared a little of his personal blend with a man the Skullbreakers had been negotiating with who worked in food processing… among other things… our spice addict had found himself with a production deal.

Ruin cooked the stuff here in the apartment, various workers came to collect it, and the manufacturing company bottled it, labeled it, and distributed it to select high-end grocery stores. The manufacturing guy had been bugging him about handing over his recipes for mass production, but Ruin wasn't interested in that. Especially since his favorite part was experimenting with new flavors, not making money.

Marisol had taken to helping him out in the kitchen if he was at work there when she got home from school. Her smile as she peeled off her apron gave me a much deeper rush of relief than anything I'd felt earlier.

"Your history test went okay?" I asked.

"Yeah," she said brightly. I was starting to think Ruin's high spirits were rubbing off on her. "I aced all the questions except one I wasn't totally sure about, but I checked the textbook afterward, and I'm pretty sure I covered that completely too."

I studied her face, taking in the faint blush that'd come into her cheeks which I didn't think had anything to do with her studies. "Did something else good happen?" I asked with a gentle poke of her shoulder.

Her smile turned both shy and sly. "That guy I think is pretty cool, Jason—he asked me to go see a movie this weekend."

"Hmm," I said, as if I were debating whether to approve the date, but I couldn't stop a grin from springing to my own face. "That's awesome. Just make sure he stays cool."

"Or we'll cool his heels in all kinds of ways he won't like," Nox piped up from behind me.

Marisol rolled her eyes, but her expression of teenage rebellion only made me happier. We'd arranged for her to talk to a counselor about all the crap she'd been through with both the Gauntts and Mom and Wade, but I was pretty sure her own innate resilience deserved a lot of the credit for how well she'd bounced back. She was stronger than she maybe even realized.

I hoped that was true for all the formerly marked victims. The Gauntts' magic had clearly departed along with their long-overdue souls as I'd expected, cracking open sealed memories all across the county. A couple dozen people had come forward to speak up about their treatment at the family's hands shortly afterward, and we had no idea how many more were dealing with the lingering trauma more privately. I suspected local therapists had experienced quite the boom in business.

There hadn't been much we could do about it directly, but I'd insisted that we donate a healthy portion of the Skullbreakers' early business profits to Mayfield's pro bono mental health initiatives.

"Okay!" I said. "Everyone grab something to eat, preferably something that will leave your tongue intact. We've got to be out of here in half an hour. We don't want Jett thinking we've forgotten."

Kai chuckled. "The way he was talking this morning, I'm not sure if he'd rather everyone in town showed up or no one at all."

Nox cuffed the other guy in the shoulder. "You know how he is. No heckling him at the show."

Kai arched his eyebrows at his boss. "I would never."

Ruin emerged from the kitchen with another whiff of spice and pulled me into one of his exuberant embraces before planting a kiss on my lips. "We fried up some burgers while we were at it. I don't think *too* much pepper got onto them."

"They're safe," Marisol confirmed.

We chowed down on the burgers, and I changed from my studio-comfortable tee and yoga pants into a silky knee-length dress that had all three of the guys eyeing me appreciatively when I came back downstairs. I swatted Nox's hand away when he reached to squeeze my ass and wagged a finger at him. "Practice your self-control."

He smirked at me. "Oh, I'll be practicing it all night, but it'll be worth the wait."

I glowered at him, but thankfully Marisol was upstairs getting herself ready, so she didn't need to hear the suggestive remark. When she reappeared, we all headed out together, the guys coming in the car with us for once since they didn't want to mess up the more dapper clothing they'd put on for the occasion.

Jett was having his first ever public show for his art at a small but hip gallery in downtown Mayfield. Like Ruin's new business endeavor, it'd kind of happened by accident. He'd been tossing some of his old canvases in the dumpster behind our building, and the wind had caught on a sheet of paper and tossed it over to the sidewalk, where the gallery owner had just happened to be walking by. When Jett had gone running to retrieve the piece, the gallery guy had struck up a conversation, and three months later, here we were.

Sometimes I wondered if there weren't some other spirits watching out for us that we didn't even know about. Maybe Nox's Gram had stuck around after all. Maybe the ghosts we'd helped get their vengeance against the Gauntts sometimes took a trip up from the marsh to lend us a hand.

Or maybe fate simply figured that my guys had been through enough bad times during their first lives that it was time to heap on some good luck to balance the scales.

I was happy to see we weren't the first to arrive, even though we'd shown up right at the show's start time. A few browsers were already circulating through the white-walled space, peering at the paintings and mixed-media compositions. I saw one woman knit her brow as she eyed a streak of reddish brown that I was pretty sure Jett had pulled from his veins rather than any paint tube. There might have been some hot sauce mixed into a few of the pieces too.

He did like to make use of whatever materials were available to him—and to literally bleed on the canvas.

Jett hustled over us with uncharacteristic energy, his posture stiff but nervous excitement vibrating off him through the supernatural connection that still tied me and all the guys together. "There might be a reviewer from an art magazine coming," he said. "And someone already asked about buying one of the paintings. Someone actually wants to hang my work in their house." He looked dumbfounded.

I elbowed him. "Hey, *we* hang your art all over our house."

He made a face at me. "You have to."

"I want to. And it's great that this critic is coming, but it doesn't matter what some magazine dude thinks anyway, right?" I glanced around at the array of pieces, each of them provoking little jolts of emotion in me as if I could re-experience what Jett had been feeling when he'd applied himself to them. "How do you think it turned out?"

He rubbed his mouth, his gaze darting around the room. "I mean, there are always things that aren't quite what I was going for, no matter how I try… but I think this came together pretty well. It's got the vibe I wanted. That's what matters the most."

Several more people meandered in, including a few familiar figures. "Hey!" I said to Peyton, giving her an awkward little wave. She waved back with a lopsided smile.

We'd been on friendlier terms since we'd faced off against a murderous gang together, but we definitely weren't besties. I was never sure exactly how warm to be with her. But we'd at least established some kind of consistent dynamic of tolerant respect, which was more comfortable than the animosity between us before.

I did see her more often than I'd expected to, because somehow she'd ended up clicking with Parker, who I greeted next. He and a couple of the Skeleton Corps guys who'd continued their alliance with the Skullbreakers had turned up to see Jett's other kind of work.

Peyton stuck close to Parker as they moved through the room, tucking her hand into his. I didn't totally get their relationship, but then, stranger things had definitely happened. Who would have thought *I'd* end up dating not one but four gangsters—and resurrected ones, no less?

"Whoa," I heard one of the Skeleton Corps guys say under his breath as he stared up at a painting that stretched wider than he could have spread his arms, streaked with violent reds and violets like a fiery thunderstorm. Jett's lips quirked into a grin of pride.

The next patrons I recognized arrived an hour into the show. I turned around after grabbing a glass of wine just as Nolan and Marie Junior walked through the door, a man who must have been one of their guardians behind them.

Two kids, who were now ten and eleven years old, should have looked out of place in an indie art gallery, but the Gauntts' adopted grandchildren had picked up a few useful skills from their departed family members. They held themselves with the poise of CEOs—which they would be, once they hit eighteen. The Skullbreakers and I had worked as hard as we could behind the scenes to make sure the kids the Gauntts had meant to exploit came out of the situation as well as possible. We hadn't seen them in person in ages, though.

Nox sauntered over as they eased into the room. "Are you sure you should have come around for this?" he said in a wry tone. "It seems like associating with people like us could be bad for your reputation."

Nolan Junior, who like his sister had opted to keep his name for now in the hopes of writing a new legacy to go with the overused moniker, gave the gang boss a smooth little smile with a twinkle in his eyes. "We're expanding our cultural horizons," he informed us with his childish bravado. "It's very important to be well-rounded. Our teachers tell us that *all* the time."

A burly guy in an expensive suit brushed past us, clearly not recognizing the Gauntt children from the past news stories. "Kids in a gallery," he muttered in a disdainful voice, and proceeded to down two glasses of wine back to back before shooting the server an equally disdainful glance. "This is garbage. You really should provide better for an event like this."

"Prick at two o'clock," Nox murmured under his breath, sizing the guy up from the corner of his eye. He exchanged a look with Kai, who started tapping on his phone. Ruin rubbed his hands together.

Seeing how the Gauntts had exploited so *many* people had left the Skullbreakers with a slightly revised perspective on how they wanted to carry out their own domination of the city. These days, they mostly stuck to jobs that involved ripping off or intimidating whatever jerks they happened to run into. "Asshole tax," Nox liked to call it.

There seemed to be plenty of ideal targets around here, thankfully none of them as powerful as the Gauntts had been. We'd been keeping a close eye out for any signs that those psychos' souls had stuck around and managed to make a grab at new bodies, but so far, so good.

I liked to think that their victims in the marsh had not just destroyed their bodies but swept their spirits all the way out of our world into the next, from which there was no returning.

"No 'taxing' until *after* the show," I ordered Nox now.

"Don't worry," he said, grasping my waist from behind and giving me a quick peck behind my ear. "We're not going to ruin Jett's big moment."

The show lasted until midnight. At ten-thirty, I sent Marisol home in an Uber with instructions to get some sleep before school tomorrow. By the time the gallery was closing up, Jett had sold nine pieces—two of them to the young Gauntts—and looked so pleased I half wondered if Ruin had swatted some joy into him.

Kai, who'd had the least to drink, volunteered to drive Fred. I ended up in the back seat with Nox and Jett.

Nox walked his fingers up from my knee, displacing the skirt of my dress. "I don't think the night's over for us yet. We've got a mark to chase down. But I could use a little inspiration first."

I cocked my head. "Oh, yeah? Are you turning into an artist now?"

He guffawed. "Just a simple man who needs your lovely moans and whimpers to keep me going, Siren." He glanced across at Jett. "Although I'm sure the actual artist here would love to celebrate his muse too."

Jett traced his fingers up my other thigh. "I'll definitely never say no to a chance to expand my creative vision."

"I think we *all* need to celebrate," Ruin declared. "Find a good place to park, Kai!"

A giggle spilled out of me, turning into a gasp as Nox's thumb grazed my already dampening panties. I gave myself over to their collective embrace.

A little more than a year ago, I hadn't been able to focus on anything except surviving—and on making sure my sister did too. The journey toward really living had come with a lot of hitches along the way. But we'd found our place in this mad world, and it seemed like we'd even made it a little better with our own special brand of insanity.

I couldn't wait to see where that craziness would take us next.

Their Kind of Family

A GANG OF GHOULS BONUS EPILOGUE

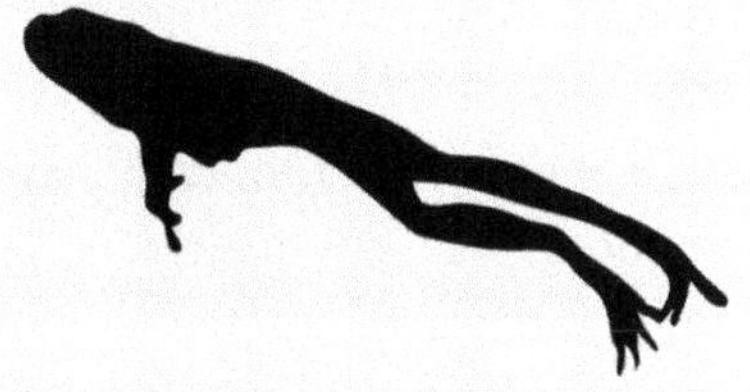

Lily

EVEN WHEN I wasn't using my watery powers, music felt like magic. My voice pealed from my throat in time with the harmony of guitar, piano, and drums swelling around me. The stadium lights washed over me in an array of colors, like a rainbow pouring down from the ceiling.

But the most thrilling part was the silence that gripped the audience as they swayed with the melody, hanging off my every lilting word.

I strode across the stage, letting the sound carry me like a wave, and raised my free hand into the air with the final lyrics. As my voice rang out across the vast stands, I lifted the microphone too.

A roar of applause surged up to meet me, whoops and cheers mingling with the avid clapping. I couldn't restrain the grin that sprang to my lips—but then, why would I want to?

These were my fans. Five years into my music career, I was headlining a worldwide stadium tour for my third album. I'd have pinched myself to confirm the moment was real and not a dream if that wouldn't have looked awfully strange to the on-lookers.

"Yeah, Waterlily!" a voice called out from the side of the stage.

My gaze darted to Ruin where he was standing just out of view from the audience, his bright red hair stark against the black curtains, pumping his fist in eager approval. Next to him, Jett was clapping in a more subdued fashion, but the sear of his deep brown eyes showed how affected he was.

I shot them a smile and turned back to the crowd. As I dipped into a bow, several flowers, an assortment of cards and notes, and a few more… unusual items that security would need to deal with pattered onto the stage, hurled by the particularly eager spectators.

"Thank you, Paris!" I shouted into the mic. "You've been amazing! I hope I'll be back here soon."

I gave one last bow and waved to the now-milling crowd as I headed off stage, my final encore complete.

The second I'd stepped out of sight, Ruin caught me in one of his epic hugs. He whirled me around. "That was the best one yet, Angelfish."

I laughed. "You always say that."

Jett tugged me to him for a quick kiss, his eyes glinting brighter now beneath the dark purple tufts of his hair. "I think he might be right this time. Even I got swept away."

My cheeks flushed. "It felt really good."

A couple of the stadium techs gave me thumbs ups, and my manager bustled over with a wide smile. She flicked her fingers through her rumpled auburn pixie cut. "That was great, Lily. Take a few minutes to catch your breath, and then we've got the backstage-pass people to meet with."

I nodded. "I'll be there in five."

It only took a couple more steps before I spotted my other two men. Nox and Kai were standing on either side of Marisol in an out-of-the-way corner, Kai studying a phone I knew was my sister's from the glittery turquoise case and Nox's brawny frame looming over her in what I recognized as his over-protective mode.

As I headed over to join them, Ruin and Jett trailing behind me, the gang leader's forceful baritone reached my ears. "—might not know much about these meet-up sites, but you've always got to keep an eye out for warning signs. Who knows what this guy really wants? Don't get too close to him, make sure you can grab your pepper spray fast out of your purse—maybe I should give you one of my guns…"

I cleared my throat. "Um, what's with the arming my little sister now?"

Nox jerked around with a vaguely guilty expression, but Marisol just snorted. "Oh, I'm going to get a late dinner with this local guy I started talking to online. I'm not going to do anything stupid. But you know how these guys are."

As if to prove her point, Kai nudged his glasses up his nose and handed the phone back to my sister. "I don't see any obvious signs of catfishing or other deceptions. But you can never be totally sure. If you give me half an hour to run some proper searches…"

Marisol let out a huff of refusal. I shook my head at both Kai and Nox, but my smile lingered on my lips.

The Skullbreakers had treated Marisol like she was their little sister too from the moment she'd come to live with us, and after what she'd been through, I'd rather they looked out for her too much than not enough.

But at twenty-two, Mare was more than old enough to make her own decisions about who she hung out with. And she did have pepper spray in her purse that she wouldn't hesitate to use. She'd tagged along for the European leg of my tour as her college graduation celebration, and I wasn't going to stop her from celebrating in every way she felt like.

"Text me the info you have on this guy and where you're meeting him," I told her. "Just in case. And do be careful. But I don't think firearms will be necessary."

Nox muttered something under his breath while Marisol gave me a quick hug. "Believe me, I don't trust anyone on first sight. I'll see you tomorrow, sis!"

As she darted off, I tapped Nox's muscular arm teasingly with my elbow. "I do appreciate the sentiment, if not all of your tactics."

He gave a humph, but a smirk tugged at his lips. "There are very few problems a pistol can't solve."

"Maybe true, but most of the time you end up with a whole bunch of new problems afterward." I reached for my carefully styled blond waves and pulled them back into a casual loose bun. "I've got to go do the after-show meet and greet. You can come protect me from my adoring fans, if you need more to do."

All four of the guys followed me down the hall to the lounge room set up for the backstage-pass holders. My agent ushered us inside, and the men drifted to the far end beyond the sofa, simply lurking around keeping an eye on things. They'd become accepted by the tour staff as my unofficial bodyguards.

The twenty backstage-pass holders filed into the room a moment later. A few teenaged girls who reminded me achingly of a younger Marisol squealed and dashed over to gush about how excited they were to meet me. Their parental figures hovered farther back, looking affectionately exasperated.

When I'd finished chatting with the teens, a gay couple came over with several bits of tour memorabilia for me to sign, letting me know with thick accents that they'd made it to my first two European tour stops as well. I thanked them effusively as I scrawled my signature on each item with my now-trademark metallic markers.

I turned from the two men to find myself staring at a woman around my age with a baby strapped into a carrier on her chest, her husband squeezing her shoulder from behind. She beamed at me and clasped her hands in front of the bulge of the carrier. "I'm so glad you could all the way across the ocean to France! I've loved your music since the first album." She patted the baby's head. "I bet Milo is your youngest fan."

The baby cooed, twisting his head to peer over at me with huge blue eyes. A deeper ache formed around my heart.

"He's adorable," I said. "And so little! You must be exhausted."

"Oh, yeah," the woman said, and nuzzled his downy hair. "But it's totally worth it. And I knew if I was going to do one not-motherly thing this year, it had to be this concert. Can we get a picture with you?"

"Of course!"

She turned and slung her arm around my waist while her husband aimed his phone's camera, grinning at her enthusiasm. The sweet baby smell wafted into my nose. Milo burbled happily as if he really did appreciate the chance to meet me as much as his mom did.

After, the woman stroked his cheek and shot me another smile. "Isn't he a darling? So calm after the big crowd. You'd never know he'll also wake me up wailing in the middle of the night because his blanket isn't tucked just so."

There was nothing but affection in her tone and her eyes when she gazed down at the baby. The ache spread right up to my throat.

That was one lucky kid. I'd never gotten to experience that kind of devotion when I was growing up—and there was no chance of finding it from my parents now.

And offering it in the other direction… It was easier not to think about that possibility.

But I mustn't have hidden my reaction as well as I meant to. After the group of fans had been directed out again and I'd gathered with my guys in my dressing room to change out of my final stage outfit, Ruin tipped his head close to mine. "You *really* liked meeting that baby."

I reached up to muss his hair. "He was the only person there who didn't ask for anything from me."

Jett shook his head. "No," he said with his usual brevity. "It was more than that."

Delight lit Nox's dark blue eyes. "You know if you want to try—"

I held up my hand to cut him off. "We've talked about this. My career is really taking off—I've gotten a chance an awful lot of people don't. I've dreamed of opportunities like this for years. I can't risk putting it all on hold. And I'm only twenty-six. There'll be lots of time to fit kids in later."

Kai cocked his head, his gray-green gaze thoughtful behind his glasses. "We are in a bit of a unique situation. You've got four dads to pitch in and make sure parenthood doesn't interrupt your other activities too much."

Ruin clapped his hands together. "Yes, we could do all of the work! We'd be the best dads, and all you'd have to do are the fun parts."

I raised my eyebrows at him. "I'm pretty sure none of you can *gestate* the baby, so I'm going to have to handle a few bits that aren't so fun. And do you have any idea how much work children actually are? Even that lady who thinks her kid is the best baby ever was talking about how he wakes her up in the middle of the night crying."

"We could manage it," Ruin insisted.

Nox folded his arms over his broad chest. "Sure, we could. One little infant? Piece of cake."

I snorted. "Yeah, that's exactly the kind of attitude that tells me you'd be in totally over your heads. We'll talk about it again in another few years, after I've seen how far I can ride this wave of success."

I tugged them close to offer each of them a kiss to show them I appreciated their offer all the same.

In each new city, my manager hooked us up with a pair of adjoining hotel rooms, because the Skullbreakers needed space to spread out in. But it was pretty unusual for the guys to leave me completely alone on my side of the makeshift suite.

When I woke up late on our third morning in London to find the rest of the bed empty , I peered around the room in confusion for a few moments before deciding it might actually be nice to have a shower all to myself for once.

By the time I'd scrubbed myself clean and dressed, my men still had yet to make an appearance. With more than a little apprehension, I opened the adjoining door.

A thin wail reached my ears, followed by Ruin's cajoling voice. "There, there."

My pulse hiccupped. I hustled all the way into the room and found all four men clustered around something between the two queen-sized beds. Something that was letting out another quavering cry.

My stomach dropped right through the floor. "What the hell is going on?"

They all spun around—including Nox, who had a bundle topped by a peach-toned head cradled in his arms.

As my jaw dropped, Kai hastily stepped forward to explain. "It's not real! We wouldn't practice with someone else's *actual* baby."

"That wouldn't give us an accurate example anyway," Ruin piped up. "If we kidnapped a kid, they'd be more upset than a usual one."

When my gaze caught Nox's, his mouth twisted in a slight grimace, but he tucked the baby even closer against his chest. "It's a doll."

"An 'infant simulator,'" Kai corrected, always keen on accurate terminology.

Jett eyed me warily, as if worried about my response. "We bought it online. It got here this morning."

Ruin patted the doll's head, showing no concern of his own. "You weren't sure if we could really handle a baby. So we're going to prove that we can! It's supposed to do all the normal baby things for as long as it's on. And we're not allowed to turn it off for two whole weeks. We agreed. Right?"

He shot a fierce look around at his friends. They all nodded emphatically.

I had to open and close my mouth a few times before I could get my voice working again. "You really think this is a good test? It's made out of plastic."

Kai gave me his usual matter-of-fact tone. "We'll get a report after we're finished to show whether we met all of its needs properly. And the company we bought it from offered custom programming so the simulator would arrive ready to go. We asked for the hardest setting."

To be fair, the fake baby was still wailing away, no sign of letting up even as Nox rocked it in his arms. He glanced down at a bottle that I also assumed was fake on the bedside table. "It wasn't hungry. Changing didn't help. What else could be the problem?"

Jett frowned. "Did anyone burb it after we fed it that first time?"

"I don't think so." With unexpected care for a guy who mostly got his way by barging and bashing through situations, Nox eased the doll onto his shoulder and gave its back several firm but careful pats.

The electronic crying stopped. The leader of the Skullbreakers beamed like he'd just inherited the world's biggest weapons locker.

Ruin grinned his approval. "There—we're already getting the hang of it. Between the four of us, we've got to be able to handle everything."

My gaze slid between all four of the guys, my mind whirling. This seemed like an insane reaction to our conversation earlier this week… but then, my resurrected gangster boyfriends weren't known for being particularly sane at the best of times.

They'd only had the thing for an hour or two. If they got frustrated and called it quits before the two weeks were up, then we'd all know where they stood as far as managing parental responsibilities.

And if the tour staff noticed and found it odd, well, they'd already accepted an awful lot of other oddness from the guys. Two weeks with a little extra strangeness wasn't going to end the world.

Jett was watching me in my silence. "We're going to make sure you don't need to pitch in at all. No crying disturbing your sleep or anything. You didn't hear it until you opened the door, right?"

"I didn't," I admitted, and let out a disbelieving laugh. "Does it really mean that much to you to see whether you can handle fatherhood?"

Kai had taken the doll from Nox and peered down at it now as he swayed it in his arms. "It'll be an interesting experiment. Parenting seems like an awfully complex life change to enter into without thorough preparation."

Ruin moved to my side and slung his arm around my shoulders. "We want to be a family in every way we can be, if we can."

Nox stepped forward too so that he could tuck his fingers under my chin. "From what I've seen, it means a lot to you too, Siren. Don't you want to know for sure whether we're up to the task?"

Something about the question sent a quiver through my insides that was both eager and unsettling. "I—I guess so. I wouldn't have asked you to prove it this way, though."

"You didn't have to ask," Ruin said cheerfully. "We've got it covered all by ourselves."

The doll chose that moment to start up a digitized whimpering. Kai studied it, tsking his tongue. "Maybe it's not warm enough…"

"You and Ruin handle this crying fit," Nox announced. "Jett and I figured out the last one. Our woman needs our attention too." He turned his gaze to me with a smirk. "We'll just have to give that attention in shifts for the next two weeks. How does a room-service breakfast sound?"

As he ushered me back toward the quieter room, a laugh tumbled out of me. "I could go for that."

And we'd see how long my four former ghosts could tolerate parental duty.

Parenting even a fake baby definitely wasn't easy, especially on the extreme setting the guys had asked for. Over the next week, I got used to one or another of them ducking out of the room to switch off dad duties with one of the others. It didn't seem like there was ever a moment one of them wasn't within arm's reach of the simulator doll, which might actually have been more doting than was totally necessary.

I kept waiting for the other shoe to drop. There were plenty of moments that looked like they could push the guys over the edge. While my men kept their promise not to rope me into any of the work, they couldn't completely hide the effort it was taking.

There was the car seat that Kai and Nox spent an hour and several Youtube videos on before they finally figured out how to attach it to the back seat of our rental car in Glasgow. After which they realized that they'd looped the straps for the baby out of reach, so they had to uninstall it and start over again.

There was the evening when three of my men joined me in my room for some more intimate recreational activities, with Jett gamely agreeing to stay with the baby. We hadn't gotten much past kissing when all three of the other guys' phones buzzed with an alert I'd never heard before.

"We'll be right back, Angelfish!" Ruin promised with a hasty apology smooch before they raced back to the adjoining room.

Ten minutes later, I peeked past the door to see how they were getting on. They were clustered around the folding travel crib, taking turns crooning lullabies to the doll while it emitted a high-pitched shriek. Sweat shone on Nox's forehead, and even Ruin's smile had faltered.

I leaned against the doorframe, my mouth twisting at a crooked angle. "If it was a real baby, Kai could just tap it and tell it to be quiet and still. Or Ruin could pass on some happiness to it."

My men jerked around to look at me with matching expressions of surprise—and horror.

"We wouldn't use our powers on a *baby*," Nox growled.

Kai, who was currently rocking the doll, cuddled it closer to his chest with an unusually tender air. "If it's upset, that means there's something wrong that it's trying to tell us. Pretending the problem away would be dangerous, even if we could."

I blinked at them, startled to find a lump of guilt forming in my gut over the fact that I'd suggested the possibility even flippantly.

A couple of days later, there was the time I came backstage after a soundcheck and found Jett and Kai racing around searching for the bottle one of the stagehands had moved when they weren't looking. Ruin dappled the doll's head with soothing kisses as it fussed in its digitized way.

But they didn't let out a single curse, creative or otherwise, while they checked every nook and cranny until Jett snatched up the missing bottle and raced over to deliver the needed "meal" at lightning speed.

Nox crossed his arms and laid down the law. "We need to get a proper diaper bag."

And by the time the concert was over, they had one—black leather with a large patch sewn on the flap that said, *Property of Lily's Men. Touch It and Die.*

I hoped the venue staff didn't take the message *too* literally.

When we got together for brunch the next morning, Marisol eyed the bag and the doll with her eyebrows slightly raised before turning to me. Amusement gleamed in her eyes. "Is there some important news you need to tell me?"

My cheeks flushed. "They're just… seeing what it's like. For *way* in the future."

"Mmhm," Marisol said, as if she didn't totally believe me, but she let it drop to dig into her omelet.

And finally, there was the night more than a week in when I got up in the wee hours to use the bathroom and noticed that while Ruin was still lying in my bed snoring, a streak of light glowed under the adjoining door.

I eased it open just a crack. Nox was pacing the room with the baby in his arms, Jett and Kai flanking him, all looking equally weary.

"We've tried everything she could want," Kai said. "Food, burping, diaper, clothing change, blankets, rocking…"

Jett groaned. "Maybe she wants Ruin?"

Nox let out a huff. "I'd rather let him catch up on some sleep. Come on, we should be able to figure this out. She *needs* us." He paused and gazed down at the plastic form. "Sometimes babies cry just because they need to let it out, right? So we keep showing that we're here until she's sure she's safe."

Watching their unshakable dedication even through their fatigue, hearing them talk about the baby as if it—*she*, now—were an actual living being depending on them, I had to press my hand against my chest. The pang of affection that resonated through me was forceful enough to be almost painful.

They… They actually were really good at this.

But under that swell of love, I still felt something deep inside me balk.

"Fourteen days," Ruin declared as I stepped between the adjoining rooms on our first morning in Amsterdam. He spun around with the doll tucked tight in his arms, like he did with me sometimes. "We made it!"

Kai pinched the bridge of his nose where he was sitting at the small table by the window that overlooked the big canal outside. He'd started developing dark circles in the tan skin under his eyes, but he managed to restrain a yawn as he consulted his phone. "We passed. More than passed. That was an A grade with a little room for improvement."

"If those stage guys hadn't wandered off with the bottle that time," Nox muttered, but his face had brightened all the same.

Jett let out a rare laugh from where he was slumped in the armchair across from the beds. "With a real baby, we can have a dozen bottles ready to go that'll all work fine. No special tech necessary."

I looked around at them, the strange mix of elation and uneasiness I'd felt before twisting around my gut. "Wow. I lost track of the days. You really survived."

Ruin raised his hand in a victory gesture. "We *triumphed*!" He gazed down at the doll. "It feels wrong to turn it off. But I guess the programming has all run out anyway. It's not going to do anything except lie there."

Nox chuckled. "We'll keep it around in case we need more practice later. There'll be ways to set a new program."

A lump clogged in my throat. I couldn't think of anything to say.

Instead, I walked over to the window to gaze out over the dark water flowing past the line of hotels ours stood in the midst of. A soft breeze warbled past the window, but it didn't ease the tension inside me.

I forced myself to turn and face my men again. "You know, even if this was the hardest setting, a real baby would be even harder. You'd have to prep real milk; the kid would squirm when you're putting clothes on or swaddling it; we'd be dealing with diapers that actually stink; and—"

Jett stepped toward me and rested his hand on my arm, holding my gaze. "We know that, Lil. It wouldn't be only two weeks either. But being able to trade off the work and share the stress is something we have that most relationships don't."

Ruin's forehead had furrowed. "We don't need to try anytime soon. But you said—is there some other reason you're worried about us having a kid?"

My throat constricted even more. The answer popped into my head without my even having to think about it.

Maybe I'd always known, I'd just been able to avoid thinking through that question while I could blame my hesitations on concerns about my guys.

But the four of them had proven beyond any reasonable doubt what doting, devoted fathers they could be. I couldn't possibly claim they were the problem.

Which only left… me.

Unexpected tears pricked at the backs of my eyes before I even tried to speak. I drew in a shaky breath. "What if… what if *I* screw things up?"

Nox's eyebrows drew together. "What are you talking about?"

I waved vaguely toward the doll. "Even if the four of you are doing most of the heavy lifting, I'll still be her—or his—mother. I'll have to be in there helping raise the kid too. I'll *want* to be a major part of its life." I'd want it so much more than I could even put into words. "But I—hell, even with barely being involved at all, I talked about using your powers on her."

Kai studied me. "It was only a joking remark. I know you, Lily. You might be a barracuda when you need to be, but you'd never want us to do that for real."

I hugged myself. "We don't know, though. I've never been put in a situation like that. Dealing with those first few years puts so much stress on any relationship. I've heard tons of horror stories. I've *been* the kid in one of those horror stories. How am I supposed to act like a good mom when I've never had one to show me how it's done?"

That was the crux of the problem right there. The words left an ache inside me as they fell from my mouth, and then I couldn't take them back.

Ruin set down the doll and hustled over to me as Jett ducked his head to kiss my cheek. The redhead slipped his arm around me from the other side and wrapped me up in his warmth. Kai got up from his chair, and both he and Nox joined the circle around me.

"No one knows for sure what kind of parent they're going to be," the Skullbreakers' leader said with all the fierce authority he could bring to bear. "Lots of people with shitty parents do a lot better with their own kids. Lots of people with great parents turn out shitty."

I swiped at my eyes. "Sure. But plenty of people who had shitty parents just pass on the shittiness."

Nox shook his head vehemently. "That might be true, but we do already know that you're a hell of a lot better than your parents were. Look at how great your sister is doing. You only raised Marisol for the last couple of years that she was anything like a kid, and you managed to undo the sixteen years of crap she went through before that."

Ruin nodded and pointed to the desk that held a few pieces of paper marked with dark lines of ink. "Last night she gave me a whole comic strip she drew about us finding frogs in the canals. She's got amazing skills now that she's letting herself get into it. Jett's lucky she likes cartoons more than artsy fartsy stuff, or he'd have some real competition."

Jett made a dismissive sound. "She's been having the time of her life traveling around. But she's still there for every concert cheering you on, because she loves seeing how well you're doing too."

Kai fixed me with his best assured stare. "Every piece of evidence makes it pretty undeniable that you've been an amazing guardian to her."

When they pointed all that out, it was hard to argue. Marisol *had* come out of her shell quickly after I'd taken her in. Observing her confidence in going out and exploring each new city on the tour without shrinking from the challenge had brought so many smiles to my face.

Knowing I'd done all right by her didn't unravel the knot of tension in my belly, though.

"I see your point," I said. "But it still makes me nervous. I mean, I screwed up with her at least a little. I lost control of my powers and ended up getting taken away from her when she needed me the most."

Nox snorted derisively. "You didn't even know you *had* powers then. You can control them perfectly now."

"But when I'm sleep-deprived and frustrated because it's the third crying fit that night, and nothing seems to be calming the baby down…"

Ruin nuzzled my hair. "Then we'll be there. At least one of us will always be around to step in and give you a break before you're ever that on edge. But I don't think you'd ever cross that line anyway, no matter what happened. You've controlled yourself around some pretty awful people lots of times before."

Jett cleared his throat. "You don't have to do anything, no matter what we say. You know that, right? We'll be happiest with whatever makes you the happiest."

"Right," Nox said, his voice lowering. "We just want you to be able to have all the happiness that's out there, if you do want it."

A soft smile curved Kai's lips. "No reason to limit yourself."

My love for them swept through my entire body. I tugged them all closer in our joint embrace. "Thank you. You have no idea how much it means to me that you're trying. I guess it's kind of silly for me to worry so much about it anyway when we don't even know if you *can* have kids in your situation."

Nox chuckled. "If ghostly swimmers can't get the job done, there are other options. I'm not against adoption. We could definitely do a better job than the Gauntts did."

"Fair point." I shook my head with a small smile of my own. "I'll keep the offer in mind."

As the waitress set down our desserts with a waft of buttery scent reaching my nose, Nox raised his mug of beer over the restaurant table.

"No," he said, continuing the playful argument he'd gotten into with the other men. "The best moment was that group of friends who convinced everyone in their row to hold up neon letters spelling out *LILY STROM ROCKS OUR WORLD*."

Ruin shook his head. "*I* think the most impressive show of dedication to our Angelfish was the group who arranged to throw, like, a hundred waterlily blooms on the stage all at once."

Marisol laughed and took a swig from her own beer. "My favorite was when we found out someone had handed out lighters for everyone to use that gave off blue and green flames to match the streaks in Lily's hair. I still don't know how they made those."

I sank back in my chair and sipped my rum and coke, the mix of sour and sweet flooding my tongue. The friendly voices carrying from all around us seemed to wrap our table in our own private space. "I'm just glad I get a couple weeks for a break before we move on to Asia and Australia."

We were celebrating the end of the European leg of the tour in Stockholm with a late-night dinner and drinks, just me, my sister, and my men. I'd loved every chance I got to perform, but I could admit that being on night after night got a little exhausting. Plus, my mind was bubbling with ideas for new songs I wanted to start laying down the base melodies for.

Marisol stretched out her legs beneath the table and grinned at me. "It's so amazing that you have fans all over the world like this. I wish I could keep tagging along, but I've got that graphic novel script coming in next week, and there's no way I'm going to be able to concentrate on working while we're on the road."

"Next time," Kai suggested. "The average musician of Lily's popularity goes on worldwide tour once every two years. You should have lots of chances."

Jett shot me one of his quiet smiles. "By the next album, I bet we'll see even more spectacular displays of fandom."

"I'm always happy to have you hanging out with us whenever you can make it," I told Marisol. "But I'm excited to see how your first major project turns out."

Ruin beamed at my sister. "Right! Soon you're going to be a star too."

Nox shifted restlessly in his seat as if he wasn't totally happy about that idea, but it wasn't for any nefarious reason. His voice came out in a protective growl. "And we'll make sure none of the *bad* fanatics who come out of the woodwork ever get close to you."

Marisol giggled. "Somehow, I don't think 'comic artist' is going to attract quite the same level of adoration as 'blockbuster pop star.' And that's okay."

Looking around the table at her and them, absorbing the comfortable flow of our conversation, I realized it really was okay. *We* were okay. The six of us here in our makeshift family, closer knit than plenty of the regular families around the world.

We'd made something pretty amazing together out of the crap hand we were all dealt to start.

Marisol was good. Marisol was building a life I could already see was going to take her so much farther than we could have imagined back when we were living like ghosts ourselves in Mom's house. And I'd helped her get there.

Hell, I'd also helped my men figure out how to integrate back into the society that'd moved on for two decades without them. This family wouldn't exist without each and every one of them, but I was the person who'd brought us all together.

A glow lit in my chest, expanding through my veins until I felt as if my whole body was shining beneath my skin. No fears rose up to try to claw back that happiness.

I'd gone for what I wanted when it came for my music. Hoping for a career like this, for any career at all, had been a gamble, but I'd given the dream my all.

Why shouldn't I do the same with every other part of my life?

I knew what I wanted when I set the worries aside. All I had to do was start walking toward my goals.

The glow stayed with me through the rest of dinner and back to our hotel, where we parted ways with Marisol in the hallway. The men followed me into to my room. As I closed the door, Nox trailed his finger down my back. "Is our siren up for a little *more* celebrating tonight?"

There was no mistaking the suggestive note that'd entered his voice. It sent a quiver of anticipation down my spine alongside the heat of his touch.

I wanted them—around me, over me, in me. I always did. And tonight, the thought was even sweeter.

Tonight, I could take that first step. No more waiting. No more holding myself back out of fear.

I knew who I was. Lily Strom didn't back down.

I wet my lips and cast my gaze around at each of the men, the hunger smoldering in their gazes setting off sparks through my nerves. "A private celebration sounds perfect."

With typical efficiency, Kai moved to the suitcase where we'd stashed the condoms. I cleared my throat before he'd reached it. "We, ah— We can do without those for now. I'd like to see what happens." I swallowed thickly, but this time, it was hope bringing a lump into my throat rather than terror. "Whether what we all want could happen."

Ruin's eyes widened. Jett sucked in a startled but heated breath.

And Nox swept his hands down my body to sear against my thighs. His voice came out equally scorching. "Now that's the woman I love. You've worked awfully hard pleasing all those audiences in the last few weeks. You deserve all the rewards we're going to give you. This night should be about reminding you what a good girl you are."

A giddy shiver shot through me at his words. Then Ruin was scooping me right out of Nox's grasp and carrying me to the bed.

He lay me down in the middle of it and leaned over me, trailing kisses along my jaw. "Less talking, more rewarding."

Kai set aside his glasses with a flick of his tongue over his lips and climbed after us. "You know," he couldn't seem to resist saying, "based on where you're at in your cycle, in just a few days it should be the perfect timing—"

Jett swatted at his friend. "We aren't going to schedule a seduction. If something that miraculous is going to happen, it should come naturally."

"Right," Nox rumbled. "Priority number one is making our woman feel every bit of how spectacular she is."

He bent by my legs and lifted one foot so he could start charting a path with his mouth from ankle to knee. As Ruin nibbled at my ear and Kai jerked down the side zipper on my dress, a hint of a smirk curled Jett's lips.

The artist dug into his shoulder bag and pulled out what might have been the last microphone I'd sung into. He twirled it between his fingers. "I figured they have enough of these that no one would miss it. And I'd like to see what kind of exciting memento I could turn it into."

The mic shifted in his grasp, melding and morphing into a shape Jett was no doubt already imagining all kinds of *very* fun uses for.

I laughed and tipped my head back into the pillow. With the stroke of Kai's deft fingers over my breast and the delicious heat of Nox's and Ruin's kisses enflaming my skin, I gave myself over to wherever our incredible lives would lead us now.

About the Author

Eva Chase lives in Canada with her family. She loves stories both swoony and supernatural, and strong women and the men who appreciate them. Along with the Gang of Ghouls series, she is the author of the Shadowblood Souls series, the Heart of a Monster series, the Bound to the Fae series, the Flirting with Monsters series, the Cursed Studies trilogy, the Royals of Villain Academy series, the Moriarty's Men series, the Looking Glass Curse trilogy, the Their Dark Valkyrie series, the Witch's Consorts series, the Dragon Shifter's Mates series, the Demons of Fame Romance series, the Legends Reborn trilogy, and the Alpha Project Psychic Romance series.

Connect with Eva online:
www.evachase.com
eva@evachase.com

Milton Keynes UK
Ingram Content Group UK Ltd.
UKHW050804071123
432058UK00005BA/88